Look What Happened While You Were Sleeping™

by

A FRIEND OF MEDJUGORJE

Look What Happened While You Were Sleeping™

by

A FRIEND OF MEDJUGORJE

CARITAS OF BIRMINGHAM
STERRETT, ALABAMA 35147 USA

ISBN: 978-1-878909-09-1

Printed and bound in the United States of America

For additional copies contact your local bookstore or call Caritas of Birmingham at 205-672-2000, ext. 315 — twenty-four hours a day.

Foreward

Many who will read this book have been following the writings of A Friend of Medjugorje for over twenty years. His original and unique insights into the important events of our day have won credence in hundreds of thousands of hearts around the world. His moral courage in the face of so many leaders caving in to the pressures of a politically correct world is not only refreshing, but according to thousands of written testimonies, has helped to deeply strengthen those who desire to live the fullness of Christianity. His insights, that are often prophetic, have their source in the apparitions of the Virgin Mary in Medjugorje. Deeply and personally influenced by the events surrounding Medjugorje, he gave himself to the prayerful study and application into his life of the words that the Virgin Mary has been speaking of over the past quarter of a century. He discovered that She has come to speak to mankind in this time because the dangers we face are on a scale unlike any the world has ever known. Millions have been deeply affected by his writings.

For those who approach this writing with skepticism concerning the apparitions of the Virgin Mary, whether you are of a faith that is inclined to reject such apparitions or a nonbeliever, we suggest that you not let that deter you from reading this book, but simply read the messages of the Virgin Mary as comments such as a pastor would make. We say this because there are a great many things that are threatening our nation's future and that knowledge is important for all men to understand, especially Americans because of the position God has placed us in the world. The truths contained within this writing have an important contribution to make in the ongoing national dialogue that will determine whether America will continue on the path of destruction it has been on for the past several decades or will find the will to return to the ideals and the vision of their founding fathers. Look What Happened While You Were Sleeping™ places in the hands of the reader the answer to which all our woes can be corrected, when each Christian accepts to change his life and live according to all the precepts given to us by God. In doing so we will be contributing more to the future peace and security of the United States of America than any government or military agency or program. For as the author often writes, "a people are not so much protected by their armaments as they are by their way of life." In the United

States of America, the way of life of *"we the people"* has always been based in the living of Christian principles. If we wish to have the protection of God that we have always enjoyed in this nation, if we wish America to be saved from all of the impending evils that are surrounding us, then America must return to living Christianity in its fullness. By doing so, we will become God's children of light again, and He will reach down from the Heavens and save us. We thank God for allowing Our Lady, the Queen of Peace, to be with us in these trying times, as His ambassador from Heaven. May we heed Her words to return to the Father, who is waiting for us that He may once again bestow His blessings upon us.

—The Publisher

Medjugorje

The Story in Brief

THE VILLAGE SEES THE LIGHT is the title of a story which "Reader's Digest" published in February 1986. It was the first major news on a mass public scale that told of the Virgin Mary visiting the tiny village of Medjugorje, Bosnia-Hercegovina. At that time this village was populated by 400 families.

It was June 24, 1981, the Feast of John the Baptist, the proclaimer of the coming Messiah. In the evening, around 5:00 p.m., the Virgin Mary appeared to two young people, Mirjana Dragicevic* and Ivanka Ivankovic*. A little later, around 6:40 p.m. the same day, four more young people, Milka Pavlovic*, the little sister of Marija, Ivan Ivankovic, Vicka Ivankovic*, and Ivan Dragicevic saw the Virgin Mary. June 25, 1981, was the first day the six visionaries, Ivanka Ivankovic,*, Mirjana Dragicevic*, Vicka Ivankovic,* Marija Pavlovic*, Ivan Dragicevic and Jakov Colo saw Our Lady, or the "Gospa," on the hill. These six have become known as and remain "the visionaries." These visionaries are not related to one another. Three of the six visionaries no longer see Our Lady on a daily basis. As of March 2009, the Virgin is still appearing

* Names at the time of the apparitions, the women are now married with last names changed.

everyday to the remaining three visionaries. The supernatural event survived all efforts of the Communists to put a stop to it, many scientific studies, and even the condemnation by the local bishop; yet, the apparitions have survived, giving strong evidence that this is from God because nothing and no one has been able to stop it. For over twenty-seven years, the apparitions have proved themselves over and over and now credibility is so favorable around the world that the burden of proof of their authenticity has shifted from those who believe to the burden of proof that it is not happening by those opposed to it. Those against the apparitions are being crushed by the fruits of Medjugorje — millions and millions of conversions which are so powerful that they are changing and will continue to change the whole face of the earth. The purpose of the apparitions is the interception of the world's destructive path; to warn, correct, and show man the path to inner peace and civil peace.

See **mej.com** for more information.

* In the last ten years, scores of Protestants are changing their view of Mary as a "Catholic thing." They are beginning to accept Her role as the Mother of Christ, and He being God, makes Her "Mother of God." Christ, our Brother, makes Mary our Mother.

ACKNOWLEDGEMENT

God alone deserves the credit for the publication of this book. It is from Him that the messages are allowed to be given through Our Lady to all of mankind. He alone deserves the praise and honor.

TABLE OF CONTENTS

CHAPTER SEVEN

CHAPTER EIGHT

CHAPTER NINE

CHAPTER TEN

CHAPTER ELEVEN

CHAPTER TWELVE

CHAPTER THIRTEEN

INTRODUCTION

The following is an important and major writing. What is meant by "major?" It means that contained in these pages are words that will educate you of things that before reading you were not aware. It means that you will be placed in a position of acting on these words, and it means you will receive guidance concerning what path to follow.

THE BELOVED HOME

Dear Friends,

Liberty: the state of being free; freedom or release from bondage or slavery; freedom from arbitrary or despotic government, or, often, from other rule or law other than that of a self-governing community; freedom from external or foreign rule; freedom from control, interference, obligation, restriction, hampering conditions; [1] Natural liberty consists in the power of acting as one thinks fit without any restraints or controls except from the laws of nature. Natural liberty is only (lessened) and restrained as is necessary and expedient for the safety and interest of the society, government or nation. A restraint of natural liberty not necessary or expedient for the public is tyranny or opression.[2]

* * * * * * * * * * * *

No nation is great because it has grand buildings and cathedrals, or great cities, or mighty armies and navies. These are beautiful and impressive, and often necessary, but a nation with all these still may not be a great nation. A nation can be great only when the hearts of its people are good, and noble, and home-loving, and fair and just to others.

The *home* is the basis of a nation. A man who loves his home, no matter how humble it is, will fight to protect it and his loved ones. The reason why the English-speaking people who came to America succeeded, and why the other colonizing nations failed, was because the Englishman, when he came to America in early colonial times, brought with him his wife and children. For them, he built a cabin home, and cultivated and learned to love, a patch of ground. The French and Spaniards did not do this, and so they failed. And that is why we speak the English language in America, because the English-speaking colonists made *homes* here.

'*The homes of the people,*' and not its grand cities and buildings and its armies and navies, are the safety of a nation. If the homes be right, the nation will be right; and if the homes be right, the great cities and the cathedrals, and the armies and the navies will be right; for with the homes right, the armies and the navies will never wrong other nations—they will protect not only the homes of their owners but also homes in other lands.

The little, beloved *home* is the *real* basis of every nation that is great and good. [3]

"I went to Washington the other day, and I stood on the Capital Hill; my heart beat quick as I looked at the towering marble of my country's Capitol, and a mist gathered in my eyes as I thought of its tremendous significance; the armies and the treasury; the judges and the President; the Congress and the courts, and all that was gathered there. And I felt that the sun in all its course could not look down on a better sight than that majestic home of a republic, which had taught the world its **best lessons of liberty.** And I felt that if honor and wisdom and justice abided therein, the world would at last owe that great house in which the ark of the covenant of our country is lodged, its final uplifting and its regeneration.

"But a few days later, I visited a quiet country home. It was just a simple, modest house, sheltered by big trees and encircled by meadow and field, rich with the promise of harvest. The fragrance of the pink and of the hollyhock in the front yard was mingled with the aroma of the orchard and of the garden, and resonant with the cluck of poultry and the hum of bees.

"Inside the house were thrift, comfort, and that cleanliness which is next to godliness. There was the old clock that had held its steadfast pace amid the frolic of weddings, that had welcomed in steady measure every newcomer to the family, that had kept company with the watches at the bedside, and that had ticked the solemn "requiem" of the dead. There were the big, restful beds and the open fireplace, and the old family Bible, thumbed with the fingers of hands long since still, and blurred with the tears of eyes long since closed, holding the simple annals of the family and the heart and the conscience of the home.

"Outside the house stood the master, a simple, upright man, with 'no mortgage' on his roof, and 'no lien' on his growing crops; master of his lands and master of himself. Near by stood his aged father, happy in the heart and home of his son. And as they started to the house, the old man's hand rested on the young man's shoulder, laying there the unspeakable blessing of the honored and grateful father and ennobling it with the knighthood of the Fourth Commandment.

"And as they reached the door, the old mother came with the sunset falling fair on her face, and lighting up her deep, patient eyes, while her lips, trembling with the rich music of her heart, bade her husband and her son welcome to their home. Beyond was the good wife, happy amid her household cares, clean of heart and conscience, the buckler and the helpmate of her husband. Down the lane came the children, trooping home after the cows, seeking as truant birds do, the quiet of their home nest.

"And I saw the night descend on that home, falling gently as from the wings of the unseen dove. And the old man, while a startled bird called from the forest and the trees thrilled with the cricket's cry, and the stars were swarming in the bending sky, called the family around him and took the Bible from the table and read the old, old story of love and faith. He then called them to their knees in prayer, and the little baby hid in the folds of its mother's dress while he closed the record of that simple day by calling down God's blessing on their simple home.

"And while I gazed, the vision of the great marble Capital faded from my brain. Forgotten were its treasure and its splendor. And I said, 'Oh, surely here in the homes of the people are lodged at last the strength and the responsibility of this government, the hope and the promise of this Republic.'"[4]

Henry Woodfin Grady

What you have just read is sweet to read and reflect upon, as much today as it was 120 years ago. Sadly, what was just described is no longer the norm for the majority of American homes. And because it is not, our society, **the way of life** that Americans have always been blessed with and enjoyed, is rapidly vanishing. It is time we "awake" to the fact that the "war on terror" is not only beyond America's borders in places like Iraq or Afghanistan, but that there are active plans to destroy the very soul of America from the inside out. And these plans are succeeding, much to the dismay of the majority of Americans who see, or at least sense, it happening, but do not know how to stop it.

With our society so ingrained in error, it often takes years of prayer to receive a grace to even gain the knowledge that a particular action or way of doing something is not correct or according to God's Commandments. Prayer leads to change, as well as coming to the recognition that God must give the grace to make the change. This writing is the result of following Our Lady* for over two decades through Her messages of Medjugorje, and in

* The term "Our Lady" is a term of fondness, referring to the Virgin Mary, Mother of Christ. This writing refers to words She has spoken through the world-wide occurring apparitions to six visionaries in a village called Medjugorje. The apparitions have foretold many things about the future, including chastisements or purifications which will affect the whole world, soon to come to the earth. More is explained on page vi at the beginning of this book. It is recommended to read this page, "Story in Brief," to grasp more fully all that is written in this book.

this one writing, you benefit by advancing quickly, even immediately, in what took years of prayer to discern. Pray to the Holy Spirit, on your knees, before reading. Open your heart. Ask for wisdom of all things written and left unwritten, that the Holy Spirit may fill you with grace, enlightenment and action.

Beginning in 1992, for the past fifteen years, literally millions of prayers have been prayed per year through "The Seven Novenas for the Reconciliation of Ourselves, Our Families and Our Nation Back to God," inspired by the apparitions that took place at Caritas in the Bedroom and Field,* and spread through Caritas of Birmingham. This year, and the coming years, are more crucial than ever to be praying for our nation. For the thoughtful, for the prayerful, for discerning hearts, it is very obvious that not only our nation, but also many nations are at a crossroads. Decide for God, and He will decide for you. Decide against God, and He will decide against you. Our Lady said:

* At these two sites, over the past nearly 20 years, there have been more than 141 apparitions of the Virgin Mary to Medjugorje visionary Marija Lunetti. The primary site of the apparitions has been in the Bedroom of a "beloved home" with over 111 apparitions in this room, which is the heart of a group called the Caritas Community, similar to the first Christian communities 2000 years ago. The Field was consecrated to Our Lady for the conversion of our nation. The two sites are connected in that the Bedroom represents the family, "the home", and the Field, our nation. We cannot hope to heal our nation without first healing the family home. Our Lady has come to convert and heal individuals. Individuals make up families. In turn, converted and healed families bring peace to nations, thereby bringing peace to the world.

March 18, 1996

"...Do not reject from yourself the name of God, that you may not be rejected..."

It is clear that Heaven is placing the earth under a mandate, through the apparitions of Our Lady, Queen of Peace, in Medjugorje. It is a full confrontation and accounting to God before Whom we stand. Everyone must answer, no matter what religion, culture or nation they are from. We must make a choice for God or against Him, not with our words but with our very lives. How we live out the Christian life determines if we have truly decided for God or not. Living for God, we are accepted. Those nations following God's precepts preserve themselves. Those who do not, destroy themselves and God withdraws, giving them over to themselves. It is not God's desire, but rather man himself who repeatedly banishes God until God gives in, regretfully, and says, *"As you wish."* Without recognition of God's sovereignty over homes, nations and all society, man then begins to destroy all future security for himself. In essence, he tears himself apart without realizing how it came to be.

This writing was begun during Holy Week of 2006. On Good Friday, just as the above paragraph was finished, a fax came in of the words the Holy Father, Pope Benedict XVI, spoke during the Good Friday Stations of the Cross at the Coliseum in Rome. The spiritual subject of this writing was already determined and begun. The Pope's words echoed what had just been written above. As the Good Friday Stations began with Pope Benedict, Archbishop Angelo Comastri, who accompanied him, said:

> *"'Sin' is self punishment; it carries its own retribution. A few texts of Jeremiah clearly make this point:* ***'They went after worthlessness, and became worthless themselves...your wickedness will punish you, and your apostasies will convict you; know and see that it is evil and bitter for you to forsake the Lord, your God; the fear of me is not in you.'"*** Jeremiah 2–5, 19 [5]

The Archbishop read on, clearly applying this Scripture to the present time in which we are living.

> *"Isaiah,"* he said, *"is equally insistent."* **"(Your)** ***iniquity shall become for you like a break in a high wall, bulging out, and about to collapse; its crash comes suddenly, in an instant; its breaking is like that of a potter's vessel that is smashed so ruthlessly that among its fragments not a sherd* is found..."*** Isaiah 30:12–14 [6]

* Sherd is a variation of the word shard which is a fragment of a pottery vessel found on sites where pottery-making people have lived.

The Archbishop continued:

> *"Let us listen again to Jeremiah…"* ***"They acted shamelessly, they committed abominations, yet they were not ashamed, they did not know how to blush."*** Jeremiah 6:15 [7]

If you are tempted to think this doesn't reflect the Pontiff's view of society today, it was the Pope, himself, who took what the Archbishop read at the beginning of the Stations and applied it to today, clearly stating that we are living in a satanic society. At the third station, Pope Benedict said:

> *"We have lost our sense of sin! Today a slick campaign of propaganda is spreading an inane (empty; void) defense of evil, a senseless cult of satan, a mindless desire for transgression, a dishonest and frivolous freedom, exalting impulsiveness, immorality and selfishness as if they were new heights of sophistication."* [8]

If you are in agreement with Pope Benedict and your thought is that many people are wicked, dishonest, impulsive, and selfish but, as Pope Benedict stated, "they" can't see it because society is so sophisticated, then you must also accept what the Holy Father stated at the beginning. "'**WE**' have lost our sense of sin!" We, you, are a part of it. Is your thought, "Not me"? Are you honest in all things? In your work, you never lie? You never set unclean things before your eyes? You are never frivolous in your freedom? You never allow filth in your homes? (The more your sensitivity of sin grows, the more you will recognize that newspapers in your homes are filled with filth.) Do you work on Sundays? Do you go to restaurants, service stations, grocery stores, paying your money to others to work for you on Sundays? Do you think it is no big deal when in the Book of James, God's Word says when you break one commandment, you transgress all of them?

You don't kill, but if you are angry with your brother or do not forgive someone, then you kill. Christians no longer are startled by filth because they rationalize away their own "little" sins. They have become desensitized to grave sin.

Remember, human nature tells us that when ancient Israel was first attacked by the Assyrians, they blamed and faulted the Assyrian's wickedness and schemes. In time, though, they realized it was their own transgressions against God's laws that led God to allow the Assyrians to attack. Parallel this Biblical example to what happened on 9/11. Everyone blamed the terrorists, and on a human level, rightly so…but who is asking the question, why did it happen? Why did so many factors work to the favor of the enemies to our nation? Are our lives distinctly pleasing to God? We are blind if we believe that all the wickedness befalling our nation has nothing to do with us. Do we not believe we violate the Sabbath by going out to eat on Sundays, or filling stadiums for sports events on Sundays? Is it only a minor violation? If, at least, we admitted it, *"I'm doing wrong. I'll confess this sin,"* then perhaps we could spare ourselves many of the woes we now suffer from. But instead virtually everyone, all Christian, Catholic, Baptist, Methodist, Assembly of God...all denominations, including pastors, priests and bishops, are in denial that what we are doing is wrong, carrying on as if to say, *"It's nothing. So what!"* By Christians not acknowledging these violations, it is the very **denial** that is the major sin. It is why our society has grown insensitive to sin and will continue more so until we admit sin for what it is. Be true before God. Our Lady said:

July 25, 1996

> **"...decide for conversion, that your life may be true before God, so that in the truth of your life you witness the beauty God gave you..."**

Where is the beauty of today's society? Of the beloved home? The greatest crimes taking place today are from Christians who deny sin! This Sunday, count how many people stay in their pews at Communion time.* How many are staying in their pews with a sensitivity of sin and will not bring damnation upon themselves by receiving the Eucharist unworthily? Then look around the Church and count how many go to receive the Eucharist, nearly 100%. Include yourself in that number. How can that be when on any given Saturday only a handful of people show up for Confession? Or in regard to Protestants, those who have not repented of their sin? No one sins anymore? No, it's rather that few Christians actually recognize sin any more.

> ***"Therefore, whosoever, shall eat this bread, or drink the chalice of the Lord unworthily, shall be guilty of the body and of the blood of the Lord...For he that eats and drinks unworthily, eats and drinks judgement to himself."*** 1 Corinthians 11:27–29

We have become blind to our own transgressions against God and no longer recognize the *filth* in our midst. Blind hearts and blind intellect blinds all wisdom. There must be a sweeping revolution, in fact, *two*

* Several denominations, such as Catholics, Lutherans, Episcopalians, Orthodox, and Eastern Rite Christians, and even a growing number of Protestant congregations abide by Scripture, ***"Whoever eats My body and drinks My blood unworthily, eats and drinks damnation upon themselves."*** — meaning when one receives Holy Communion, one must be in a state of grace.

revolutions. This word, "revolution," is not just something being stated flippantly as one may hear on a TV or radio talk show, but rather, if we and our posterity are to have a future, it cannot be unless we undergo, *literally*, two revolutions in our near future.

CHAPTER TWO

THE FIRST REVOLUTION: THE CHURCH

Why were the Assyrians allowed to attack and destroy ancient Israel? Sin is the reason. Why have unbelievers, today, been allowed to get in positions to turn our laws upside down, destroying our nation? Sin is the reason. The unbelievers are in offensive positions. We, Christians, find ourselves in defensive positions. It is ludicrous that individual States have to pass amendments to defend marriage! We are fighting from a defensive position! The fact that we are having to pass amendments testifies against *us*, not the unbelievers. They, like the Assyrians, are being allowed in such positions. All authority is from God, and we have lost authority over wickedness. We do not have the power to do as an exorcist does, ordering the demon to leave the body. We try and instead, the demon recognizes our powerlessness, and simply says, *"No,"* convulsively laughing at our weakness, weakness that has manifested because of our weak living of God's Commandments. The godless proudly parade their unmentionable and illicit lifestyles that cannot even be described in these writings, their abortions, their decadence, all the while imposing them forcibly upon society as the norm, flaunting in our faces that *"You cannot stop us!"* Many have answers as to what needs to be done to cure our nation but are at a loss as to why we cannot bring these changes about. It is as if an invisible wall is stopping us. Yes, prayer, as Our Lady tells us, is the way that leads to change, but that will not work while we continue in our own sin and its denial. The history of the Israelites proved that. Our Lady also said in regard to making prayer effective, that **"...you must change the direction of your life..."** March 25, 1990. Not acknowledging sin and denying sin leads us in the wrong direction. Living the Commandments is not simply stating, *"I keep them."* Living the Commandments is recognizing that often we don't keep them, that we have broken them in our lives, and that we acknowledge that we have sinned against them. That is the road to waking up, which will lead to God rescuing our nation from its present course of suicide. The recognition of what sin is and being sensitive enough to repent and confess our weaknesses will lead us towards the right direction. That is what it means to keep the Commandments. Wisdom can then be obtained of how to gain authority over wickedness. The Book of John says:

"My children, I am writing this to you so that

> ***you may not commit sin. But if anyone does sin, we have an Advocate with the Father, Jesus Christ the righteous one. He is expiation for our sins, and not for our sins only but for those of the whole world. The way we may be sure that we know Him is to keep His Commandments. Whoever says, 'I know Him,' but does not keep His Commandments is a liar, and the truth is not in him. But whoever keeps His Word, the love of God is truly perfected in him."*** 1 John 2:1–5

As the above Scripture shows, sin can be forgiven, but must be acknowledged. The first step to keeping the Commandments is to acknowledge the fact when we violate one. The obligation to keep the Ten Commandments did not end with the Old Testament, but in New Testament times it is still obligatory to obey the Laws of God. Our Lady said:

October 25, 1993

> **"...I love you and wish to protect you from every evil, but you do not desire it. Dear children, I cannot help you if you do not live God's Commandments..."**

There are not nine, but rather Ten Commandments. O Christian, acknowledge, repent, and start living the

Commandment of the Sabbath: ***"Remember to keep holy the Sabbath Day,"*** or we, by our own accord, will doom ourselves. Our nation's future depends upon our recognition and acceptance of the following:

> ***"Here, then," said the Lord, "is the covenant I will make. Before the eyes of all your people I will work such marvels as have never been wrought in any nation anywhere on earth, so that this people among whom you live may see how awe-inspiring are the deeds which I, the Lord, will do at your side. But you, on your part, must keep the Commandments I am giving you today*** Ex 34:10–11***...For six days you may work, but on the seventh day you shall rest; on that day you must rest even during the seasons of plowing and harvesting*** Ex 34:21***...Take care to keep My sabbaths, for that is to be the token between you and Me throughout the generations to show that it is I, the Lord, who make you holy. Therefore, you must keep the sabbath as something sacred. Whoever desecrates it shall be put to death."*** Ex 34:12–14 *(In New Testament times, violations calculate out in destruction of the family, divorce, the destruction of the home, the deterioration of society, oppression, the loss of peace, the taking of our private property, loss of other*

freedoms that are leading us to become more and more enslaved, and a state of overall restlessness amongst nations and peoples with non-ending problems. In essence—death. Read again the last line of the above Scripture: "Whoever desecrates it shall be put to death." We must realize by the positive or negative actions of the laws of consequences, violations of God's law results in adverse consequences, and continued violations result in destructive adverse consequences. The blatant denial of violating the Commandment of the Sabbath is the "root" reason for the desecration of our nation.) ***"If anyone does work on that day, he must be rooted out of his people. Six days there are for doing work, but the seventh day is the sabbath of complete rest, sacred to the Lord. Anyone who does work on the sabbath day shall be put to death. So shall (you) observe the sabbath, keeping it throughout their generations as a perpetual covenant. Between Me and (my people) it is to be an everlasting token; for in six days the Lord made the heavens and the earth, but on the seventh day He rested at His ease*** Ex 31:14–17***....Thus, then, shall it be: if you continue to heed the voice of the Lord, your God, and are careful to observe all His Com-***

> ***mandments which I enjoin on you today, the Lord, your God, will raise you high above all the nations of the earth. When you hearken to the voice of the Lord, your God, all these blessings will come upon you and overwhelm you."*** Dt 28:1-2

America once lived and accepted this Commandment and the following was our lot.

> (By living the Commandments) ***"May you be blessed in the city, and blessed in the country! Blessed be the fruit of your womb, the produce of your soil and the offspring of your livestock, the issue of your herds and the young of your flocks! Blessed be your grain bin and your kneading bowl! May you be blessed in your coming in, and blessed in your going out!"***

> ***"The Lord will beat down before you the enemies that rise up against you; though they come out against you from but one direction, they will flee before you in seven. The Lord will affirm His blessing upon you, on your barns and on all your undertakings, blessing you in the land that the Lord, your God, gives you. Provided that you keep the Commandments of the Lord, your God, and walk in His ways, He will establish***

you as a people sacred to Himself, as He swore to you; so that, when all the nations of the earth see you bearing the name of the Lord, they will stand in awe of you. The Lord will increase in more than goodly measure the fruit of your womb, the offspring of your livestock, and the produce of your soil, in the land which He swore to your fathers He would give you. The Lord will open up for you his rich treasure house of the heavens, to give your land rain in due season, blessing all your undertakings, so that you will lend to many nations and borrow from none. The Lord will make you the head, not the tail, and you will always mount higher and not decline, as long as you obey the commandments of the Lord, your God, which I order you today to observe carefully; not turning aside to the right or to the left from any of the commandments which I now give you, in order to follow other gods and serve them." Dt 29:3-14

Our nation cannot recover if Christians do not acknowledge the Commandment of the Sabbath and live it. The following is offered as solid spiritual direction of how to "live Sunday" as a Christian, because those who call themselves by that name no longer even know how. How do you live and keep holy and sacred the

Lord's Day in a secular world that has deeply infected and changed the Church of Jesus Christ? We are in a serious crisis and are enduring great sufferings due to this infection, which Our Lady has been trying to reveal to us over these past 27 years. What follows has never been published and is one of the rules of the life of the Community of Caritas. It is how we came to live Sunday as a sacred day and the rich blessings that came upon us once we did. It is not called a "rule," rather it is called "a way," reflecting the way of life Our Lady has given to us since She asked for the community to be established in 1988.* She is, therefore, viewed as the Foundress of the Community of Caritas. "A Way" came to be written down in compliance with a request from the Bishop of the Diocese of Birmingham, Alabama. As the rule was written directly to the Bishop, the manner of speaking, in what follows, is expressed in a more personal nature, from myself to the Bishop.

From "A Way in a New Time"

The "Way" of the Community of Caritas

("A Way" Rule #22)

Date Written: September 19, 2001

Step by step, Our Lady has led us to a new way of life. Our

* After an apparition in the Bedroom in December 1988, visionary Marija said that Our Lady desired to see a community created here in Alabama. Since then a community has developed based on the living of Scripture and its understanding for today's man through Our Lady's messages.

Lady said in a public message* through Marija on January 25, 1987:

> **"...behold, also today I want to call you to start living a new life as of today..."**

This message surprised me, for I had watched villagers praying for three hours a day, going to daily Mass, fasting, going to the mountains, praying in the middle of the night, offering novenas, and special penances. What could Our Lady mean by telling the villagers, *"Now, today, begin living a new life as of today?"* Had they not already been doing that? But in time, I began to understand that Our Lady had just gotten the village at a point where they were praying and sacrificing enough just to get them where they would now have the strength to realize what She wanted conveyed from God. Our Lady said in a public message on January 25, 1995:

> **"...pray to have strength to realize what I am telling you..."**

This message shows Our Lady wanted something more than just an addition of prayers and sacrifices in their lives. Our Lady said in a public message on March 25, 1990:

> **"...you must change the direction of your life..."**

* "Public" message here refers to the messages of Our Lady, Queen of Peace, to the visionaries of Medjugorje who receive the message to be passed on to everyone in the world.

For us in community, we realized that it wasn't sufficient just to pray and sacrifice, we must live differently, not swept into the patterns of present society, but to seek God's will whatever the cost. Today, to be truly Christian is difficult. We began to realize Our Lady was saying something else to us—that our lives must be true before God. Our Lady said publicly on July 25, 1996:

> **"...be true before God..."**

We must live His Commandments if our lives were going to be true before God. Our Lady said in a public message on September 25, 1992:

> **"...In a special way he** [satan*] **wishes to destroy your souls. He wishes to guide you as far away as possible from Christian life as well as from the Commandments, to which the Church is calling you so you may live them..."**

I began to realize that our life was not true before God; that as Christians, as community, we did not respect all the

* satan does not deserve respect or honor when references are made to him. Most of you have probably noticed for years we have not capitalized his name because we refuse to give him this honor or recognition. Why should the application of grammar rules apply to him who has an insatiable desire to be exalted, even above God? We refrain in our references and writings from giving him the same stature afforded even a dog's name. We are not radical in that we don't tell others they must do the same. It's up to each individual to decide for themselves. For the harm he has done to man, whom he despises, we will not grant him that which is even reserved for man.

Commandments of God. We thought we were, but four hours of prayer a day began to show me we were not true in our Christian walk. We began to realize to wear the title "Christian" meant something, "a way" of life different from the wave sweeping through all society, even all of Christendom. Yes, it was easy, very easy to rationalize away what crept up in my conscience, but four hours of prayer kept it there. It nagged and gnawed at me. My conscience bit me. My life in community wasn't true before God. Our Lady said in a public message in 1985:

> **"....it is necessary to respect the Commandments of God in following one's conscience..."**

Our Lady made it clear. Our conscience must be formed on God's Commandments. Then the properly formed conscience should be followed as God whispers to it. I would go to Mass on Sundays, then go to the service station to fill up my car. Sometimes we would go out to eat at a restaurant. I wasn't going to work on Sundays, but didn't mind paying someone else to work for me. When traveling, I began to notice that the airports were full on Sundays, as just any other day—but didn't people have to eat? Did they not have to fly? The three prophets in the book of Daniel—Shadrach, Meshach and Abednego—willingly walked into the fire rather than bow down to an idol. The mother and her seven sons in the book of Maccabees* gave their life rather than eat pork. My conscience was challenging me. Was I so weak in my walk that I couldn't rearrange my life, my schedules, my itineraries, fill up gas on Saturday, to honor and respect God's Commandment? I wasn't even being asked to offer my life. I was only being asked to inconvenience myself. I dared not reveal this to the community; surely they would choke as I was. We loved going to get ice cream on Sundays. We worked hard all week for God! He understands. But my conscience rose up, incited by prayer, as well as the words Our Lady was saying in Her messages, and I could not loose myself from it. My conscience repeated... **"Live my Commandments. Let your life be true before Me."** I couldn't hide the truth, but it seemed such a small violation, and yet, the mother and sons in Maccabees gave their lives over such a trifle as simply not eating pork. Our Lady's words rang:

> **"...behold, also today I want to call you to start living a new life as of today..."**

Her message kept ringing in my heart:

> **"...pray to have the strength to realize what I am telling you..."**

* The book of Maccabees is found in Sacred Scripture and was part of all Bibles since the New Testament origins. During the Reformation, the momentum went on to reject these two sacred books of Maccabees, among others, from Scripture. Nevertheless, they still are to be held "sacred" and holy writings by all Christians and are an aide in the Christian walk.

I wasn't, as a Christian, true before God. I wasn't, as a Christian, being true to myself. Our Lady said on August 25, 2001, in a public message:

"...Be real with yourselves..."

If this caused agony in my conscience, what did the mother of Maccabees go through? I revealed to the community my conscience, which Our Lady was prodding through Her messages. We didn't even know how to accomplish it. I had no spiritual philosophy. I prayed. Neither the community nor I wanted to become like Pharisees, but we knew most members of the Church were nowhere near fulfilling this Commandment, not even close, and we were riding the same wave. Everybody is breaking it or offering tokens in respecting Holy Sundays.

My first attempt of rationalization was "everyone's doing it." I found myself in the state of New Hampshire at 6:30 a.m. on a Sunday morning at an airline counter. I had given a talk the night before. The woman behind the counter was wearing a wedding ring. I could tell by her actions, having come into work so early, that she was still in the rush mode. I asked her if she had any kids. She said yes. I asked her how many, and she told me two young ones. I said nothing more and walked away. Strolling through the airport, everything was open. I said to myself that if I stopped doing this on Sundays, the woman would still be behind the counter, the shops and restaurants would still be open, the planes would still fly. So what is the difference whether I travel on Sundays or not? The voice of my conscious said, ***"You will have to stand in judgment before Me by contributing to it."*** I was shaken, not so much by this voice in my heart, but by the realization that I had no more excuses to rationalize my actions, and it was at this point I committed to living this precept of God despite the cost.

I began to earnestly pray, slowly realizing that although some things we couldn't change immediately, there were other things we could. Some outside the community made sport of us in justifying themselves in continuing their way. We stopped visiting stores on Sundays. If we needed something, we would wait until Monday. It trained us to get what we needed on Saturday. No cappuccinos from Texaco and no filling up the gas tank after Sunday Mass. Buy ice cream on Saturday and have it at home. What to do about traveling? We immediately rearranged all flights. Our next year's pilgrimage dates were re-adjusted. No flying on Sundays was to become "a way." Traveling by auto on a Sunday would be as far as we could go on a tank of gas that we filled up before midnight Saturday night. I was stumped about hotels on Sundays and really prayed what to do when we had to be somewhere over the weekend. After earnestly seeking, the answer came in prayer. *Mary and Joseph traveled. They stayed in inns. Do not place anyone in a position of having to work for us on Sunday. The room exists. It is there. There were certainly rooms at the inn on the Sabbath.* We learned to tell employees of hotels on Saturday not to clean our room on Sunday. We arranged not to check in or out on Sundays. If we had to leave on a Sunday night to drive to our next destination or home, we pre-checked out on Saturday night. On Saturday, we got extra towels. We fast on Fridays; it was, therefore, no big deal to fast on Sunday. Or we could buy what was needed beforehand and at most we ate a simple meal.

As soon as we began to "live Sunday," some extraordinary things began to happen. My wife and I were in Jerusalem. On Saturday we went to Tiberius. On Sunday we were scheduled to take a bus to the dock to board boats on the Sea of Galilee, which would take us to Capernaum. How difficult it was and how badly we wanted to see Jesus' hometown, but how could we violate what God had made so clear? We couldn't. We decided to buy bread, olives, water, and cheese on Saturday. At Sunday dawn, we decided to walk. We saw the bus pass coming to pick up our group. We later walked by the dock as our group boarded the boat. We didn't view them with any fault, for they had not been shown what God had shown us, so they could not understand any more than we ourselves did before our prayer life and Our Lady's messages led us to this understanding. We could not pretend away what had been revealed to us, that God expected us to live this Commandment, as well as all the other Commandments.

While walking, we cut down to the shore of the sea. We walked and walked. We hopped rocks, passed streams flowing into the Sea of Galilee, got cut by grass weeds, passed grapefruit orchards, ate some off the ground. We remembered Jesus and His apostles doing the same, through reading Scripture and stories of the saints—the flowers, the smells, everything just as in Jesus' days. We trailed hour after hour. We saw the town of Magdala off in the distance. Tiberius became hazier in the background. Our Lady was gracing us. We felt a strange peace. We saw and were seeing the real Israel. We were off the beaten path, on the shore. We passed Magdala and had walked ¼ to ⅓ of the way around the Sea of Galilee. We wanted to make Capernaum, but began to realize that we would not be able to cover that distance in a day. We were tired and hungry, so we backtracked a little and climbed a mountainside above Magdala. There were flowers everywhere. We climbed into a cave to rest. We ate our humble meal. My wife fell asleep. The view to our right in the distance was Tiberius, off to our left was Capernaum. At our height, the view and experience was worth more than words. I opened the Bible to read. The page fell randomly to the book of John when Jesus was feeding the people near Tiberius. Afterwards, He retired to the mountain and told His apostles to wait for Him by the shore. They evidently became impatient, and took off and left. As they neared Capernaum, Jesus came walking on the water toward them. They thought He was a ghost. I looked up and could see Tiberius to our right then Capernaum to our left and the straight line Peter's boat must have traveled. I imagined Jesus coming back down the mountain to meet His apostles only to realize these characters actually left Him! Seeing the actual visual geography was a great grace. Jesus must have thought, "*What am I going to do with these guys?*" He must have been so tired that he used a little supernatural liberty and decided to walk in a straight line on the water rather than go around the sea to Capernaum. I didn't blame Him. We had just walked it in the daytime, and if we could have walked on water, we surely would have done the same. It all seemed so humorous. It was an insight that we would never have understood from the Bible had we not walked, not lived our Sunday; an insight we would never have received from a boat or a bus. We left the leper's cave and made it back just after dark, having walked around 24 miles, receiving a memory of grace that we will never forget. Somehow, we knew if we had been on the bus and boat, we would have remembered little and we would have missed an experience of a lifetime.

I know not everyone could walk as we did, but that is what we chose to do. We could have just as easily stayed around the hotel, as anyone could have, to avoid placing others in a position of working for them on a Sunday. One might also think that walking 24 miles distance was work. It was not. It was prayer and grace-filled. My conscience was in peace.

A few have been agitated by our living this Commandment and often try to rationalize it away. We do not sit in judgment of anyone else. After all, it took years of prayer for God to open our hearts to this. But it was in our heart to be held bound to that which God showed us in order for our lives to be true before God. Our eyes are not on anyone else, but on ourselves. We have to live it. It is our conviction that grace is increasing in the hearts of Christians, and that we must recognize that we are remiss in regards to living this Commandment. We, therefore, as a community, are to witness on behalf of this Commandment to all Christendom. The membership of Christianity must reconcile back to this Commandment.

Meanwhile, something extraordinary began to happen in the community once "living Sundays" began to root itself into our lives. The more we desired to fulfill the command of God by love, the more our experiences were touched by grace. Being raised Catholic, I can say I had never before in my life experienced the grace associated with living this Commandment. Why should I? I had never lived it. I didn't even know a grace was available. In doing it as "a way" of life, it was within six months that Sunday became an extraordinary day, filled with graces. One Sunday, when I first experienced this grace, I felt as though Sunday lasted for two days. Monday morning, as the community met, we all shared the same experience, "a day that seemed not to end." One could easily believe this to be exaggerated, at least stretching it. But it is easy to unveil this truth by simply living this Commandment—not to test God to see if He gives the grace, but with a real commitment to live the Commandment. We certainly, on some Sundays, find that we have an "ox in our ditch" that must be rescued, but this reason is often used by Christians as a basis to unnecessarily "break" and "violate" this Commandment of God. There are life-sustaining necessities that still must be performed on Sundays, but buying food at the store or attending sporting events, along with 99.9% of all other activities where it is necessary to spend money or to work, are not life-sustaining necessities.

My son once went to apply for a job, and I told him to put on the application that he would not work on Sunday. He knew it might cost him the job, but he wrote it anyway. He was hired, even though Sunday was their biggest day. He was eventually made manager, and I was told by the owners that they had never had an employee to match him. He worked there six years and never worked a Sunday. We strongly believe that, again, if a family is martyred for eating pork, we must then be willing to lose our jobs and be thankful that we still have our lives. The dollar, food, or pleasures cannot be put in front of God.

Our Lady has taught us that infractions of this Commandment by Christians have allowed much of the great sins of our society. Can God answer our prayers to end abortion, ***"Thou shall not kill,"*** when we ourselves are breaking a Commandment? Is it not a wonder, after 35 years of praying for an end to abortion that we haven't been granted an answer to our prayers? It is because of our sins. The Israelites, after being defeated by the Philistines, decided to take the Ark of the Covenant out with them for the next battle, and they were defeated worse than the first time. A prophet among them revealed that they made the Ark weak by their sins. If one holy man, Elijah, closed the Heavens for three years and then opened them again by his prayers, why cannot hundreds of millions of people worldwide close off the womb to abortion and open it only to birth? Is not a baby worth more than rain? Are not hundreds of millions of people praying worldwide worth more than one man's prayer? God does not say he "might" answer prayer. God says, ***"Knock and it shall be opened unto you."*** Thirty-five years of prayer and no answer? ***"I say verily he who shall ask in my name, it shall be given unto him."*** As the Israelites were in sin and were no longer holy and were defeated, we also have been defeated repeatedly in rolling back abortions. But Christians respond, *"At least I am not committing abortion."* The fact is Christians are praying to end something that they are contributing to. We learned by Our Lady that we have been praying to end something that in front of God is contradictory. We stand before God saying, *"O God, O God, please bring an end to abortion,"* when all the time, we are in violation and guilty of breaking the law ourselves. James 2:10 states:

> ***"Whoever falls into sin on one point of the law, even though he keeps the entire remainder, has become guilty on all counts."***

Verse 11 clearly shows James is speaking of the Ten Commandments—not eight of them or nine of them, but ten of them.

> ***"For he who said, "You shall not commit adultery," also said, "You shall not kill." If, therefore, you do not commit adultery but do commit murder, you have become a transgressor of the law."***

It took Our Lady leading us to four hours of prayer a day to understand this. T. Manton was quoted saying, *"It is satan's custom by small sins to draw us to greater, as the little stick sets the great ones on fire, and a wisp of straw enkindles a block of wood."* For abortion to end, there must first be a purification of God's people, a return to honoring all the Commandments of God, before there can be a purification of abortion and other major sins. This is the reason, among other reasons, why Our Lady says, **"...pray to have the strength to realize what I am telling you..."**

We, who live Christianity today, are no longer a holy people. Our Lady wants you to be holy, to live holy, to change the direction of your life, to change and convict society. We are to be salt. Salt preserves that which is prone to decay. The meat (society) decays because the salt (Christians) has gone flat. We no longer have the convicting power of light. We do not live light, and darkness prevails. We must become children of light for the children in darkness. You must kill small sin in your life to kill big sin in the lives of others.

Two New York criminologists were studying how to reduce crime in New York. Down the street from their precinct, two warehouses closed down. One was kept up, maintained, grass mowed, fence maintained. If a window was broken, it was immediately fixed. The second warehouse got a broken window and was not fixed. Soon five windows were broken, then ten. Soon the whole place was trashed, and a graffiti fence was torn down. The first warehouse needed only a broken window fixed every now and then, and then little work by comparison. The two policemen questioned and reasoned through what would happen if the police force became very strict on misdemeanors, fixing the small broken windows, placing severe fines on jaywalking and other minor violations? They convinced New York City to try, and when they put their theory into action, strongly penalizing misdemeanors, murder and other major crimes plummeted down 30%! If you cannot get away with jaywalking, you will never get away with murder. Paralleling this to our situation today, the second warehouse represents Christians who are not walking the Christian walk. If we, as Christians, did the same in living out our Christianity, just as the first warehouse was maintained, then many of the problems of society would go away. Regular maintenance of an empty warehouse kept serious destruction from occurring. The same can be applied to living Christianity. We, the believers in Christianity, need to fix our broken windows. We will never do away with the murder of abortion until we ourselves do away with the widespread violations of keeping the Lord's Day sacred and holy. We have learned in community from Our Lady that our broken window not being fixed, in regard to Sundays, has allowed all the other windows of God's Commandments to be broken. When we fix it, we can expect all the windows to be fixed, including abortion and other plagues of society. In our community, in living "a way" with Sundays, it has become by far the most favorable day of the week. We can say that all of us have experienced abundant graces that we did not even know were available to us. ("A Way" #22)

CHAPTER THREE

SOCIETY SUFFERS BY NOT KEEPING THE LORD'S DAY HOLY, BUT HOW DO WE KEEP IT?

What you fix on Sunday, breaks on Monday, Tuesday, Wednesday, Thursday, Friday and Saturday. We cannot renew our nation *until there is a revolution in Christendom to go back to living the Commandment of the Sabbath*, one of the founding principles of our faith. Only when this is achieved, will God reverse the woes sinking our nation. Society must be restructured by a Christian worldview to regain the favors of God. To help achieve the above in your own lives, we give some simple steps, added to those already mentioned. The following may sound simplistic because it is. Our Lady said:

March 25, 1997

> **"...you, too, can become true apostles of faith; when, in simplicity and prayer, you live faith ..."**

Violating the Sabbath Commandment has complicated your life. Living it will result in simplifying your life. You may be only one person and may think, "What difference will it make?" First, you won't have to stand in judgement for contributing to the Lord's Day being profaned. Secondly, you, as an individual, will make a difference as the numbers of Christians increase in honoring the Commandment of the Sabbath. Airports, stores, restaurants, etc., will decrease working on Sundays, as they need numbers to stay open to do business. As numbers dwindle, of those wanting service on Sundays, it will become less and less profitable for businesses to stay open.

Forming the Biblical Worldview to Restructure Society in Order To Live the Sabbath Commandment and Restore Society

1. Hospitals, doctors, nurses and other medical personnel can greatly reduce having to work on Sundays:

   First, schedule serious surgeries with the longest recovery time on Mondays. The next most serious surgeries should be scheduled on Tuesdays, progressing through the week to the least serious and least recovery time needed scheduled on Thursdays and Fridays. Today, even some patients with brain operations are released from the hospital in two, three, or four days. This would greatly reduce the number of Sunday medical staff and begin a cycle of grace that we, in our Christian village here at Caritas, have already experienced by our living Sunday. It is, without a doubt, that we say God will collaborate with your efforts. He will restore people's health more quickly through grace. He will decrease the amount of emergencies on Sundays, which will happen simply because there will be less injuries caused by less traveling, sports activities, etc. There, of course, will continue to be emergency medical surgeries, but these situations are the "ox in the ditch," the exception, not the rule to follow. But, in general, a grace will prevail, that if you become serious in aligning your thoughts to live the Sabbath Commandment with action in structuring your life as best as you can, God will return a blessing upon you and your efforts, and keep many oxen out of the ditch for you.

2. As already stated, the more Christians live Sundays, the more traveling will diminish, which will diminish the need for emergency personnel, the service of the police, the need for service stations to be open, etc.

3. In service work, such as hotels, restaurants, construction, travel, wholesale/retail stores, manufac-

turers and other similar non-life necessity types of work, flatly, adamantly, unequivocally refuse to work on Sunday in your heart, but nicely inform your employer that you can no longer, as a matter of conscience, work on Sundays. As a matter of conscience, they will have a hard time firing you. But, if you lose your job for keeping God's commands, by the positive action of the laws of consequences, something better will happen or be given to you. Sir William Blackstone, a professor of law in England within the same time period as America's Revolutionary War, called this "interposition." You do not give up something to stay loyal to God without something higher and greater replacing what you sacrificed. We've termed it "the positive or negative action of the laws of consequences," which means because you lose your job for God's law, something of a higher plan will play out to your good, always! At the same time, there are also negative actions of the "laws of consequences." For example, if you willingly keep your job, now with full knowledge that you are in violation of God's law, a negative consequence will result from your decision, no doubt, worse than when you did not realize the violation and addressed the situation in the first place. To whom much is known, much more is expected. Whether knowing or not knowing – the first results in negative consequences; the latter in more grave negative consequences. Presently, all of Christendom is suffering negative results from the violation of the Lord's Day.

4. When you fill out an application for employment, write in extra remarks (if there is no space, add a sheet for writing) that you, as a matter of conscience, cannot work on Sundays. Remember, parallel this action in the other areas of your life. You must align your "matter of conscience" with actual corresponding "actions." That means you do not shop on Sundays, or eat in restaurants or commit any other violation on Sundays, no matter how inconvenient it may be. What kind of witness would you be if your employer caught you out shopping on Sunday, while on your application you said you would not work?

5. What about farming? Our community has an extensive agrarian operation that includes beef and dairy cattle, chickens, hogs, horses and sheep. Some of these are divided into other segments, such as steers being fed-out, bulls being raised for breeding, and cows raised for calving. To

avoid work on Sundays, we feed double on Saturdays and arrange to do everything we can on Saturday to do the least on Sunday. Some of the animals, like horses, do not get fed grain on Sunday, but with extra hay or when on pasture they are not in want. With pure intentions almost all work can be cut out, even in agriculture.

If we've had several days of rain and then Sunday is the first dry day, dry enough to plow or harvest and rain is coming on Monday, we still do not work. As a result, we have experienced repeatedly positive actions of the laws of consequences with blessings in abundance.

Remember Exodus 34:21

> ***"...but on the seventh day you shall rest: on that day you must rest even during the seasons of plowing and harvesting."***

Once we had hay in several fields. It was our lush, late spring cut; the best cut of the year. Saturday, the hay was not quite ready to bale. Sunday would be the perfect day to bale, but we knew we were not to work on Sunday, so we had to plan to bale Monday. By Saturday evening a strong chance of rain was forecasted beginning

Monday morning. We thought we couldn't afford to lose this much hay. Surely, God would not be offended if we went ahead and baled Sunday. Would God not see our ox was in the ditch? We needed every bale we could harvest to put us through the next winter. If we did not bale it Sunday, we might lose the crop. We had enough sound rationalization to say our ox was in the ditch, so that we could bale the hay, but in our hearts we said, "No, we must trust God." If we honor Him on Sunday, keeping the day holy, He will honor our Monday and preserve the hay. We placed our trust in Our Lady's intercession and did not even pray that it wouldn't rain, but only that God would take care of us because we honored His command.

We went through a beautiful Sunday and Monday came with a beautiful morning. Our hope in trusting God was invigorated, but within two hours after sunrise the storm moved in and it poured and poured and poured. Thinking that God was testing our faith, we thought, "OK, we will just bale a lower quality hay Tuesday or Wednesday." Tuesday it poured and poured and poured. Wednesday the same. We lost the whole crop. So much for positive action of the laws of consequences. But we kept good attitudes and said, "God giveth and God taketh away." And did He ever taketh! Our best crop! Yet, we did not regret keeping the Commandment because Scripture stated clearly do not work on the Sabbath, ***'not even to plow or harvest.'***

With the rest of the cutting that summer something amazing began to happen. We normally get three cuttings. That summer we got five! Every crop was more than normal. We filled our hay barn with a harvest so full that we've never had so much hay since that year! We were faithful to God, and through the positive action of the laws of consequences, God was faithful to us! We were so happy. We are convinced had we baled that crop that Sunday, we would have had far less hay in our barn from the rest of the cuttings, maybe even losing more to rain. We could have never imagined losing so much hay, only to end up with so much more than our need, ending up with a large surplus.

6. If you own a store, a shop, a restaurant, etc., you cannot be blessed when you require your employees to work for you on Sunday, and you

entice your customers to sin against the Sabbath Commandment by patronizing your business. Chick-Fil-A is a fast food restaurant. They generally charge more than any other fast food restaurant. They have from the beginning closed on Sunday for the purpose of honoring the Lord's Day. At lunchtime, on the other six days of the week, the majority of their restaurants are always packed. Some stores even cause traffic congestion at lunchtime because they are so packed. Without question, they are blessed.

What if you were the owner of a company that takes in $100 million a year on Sundays alone. Imagine also that you owe several bankers a lot of money. Then imagine that you began realizing that as long as your stores were open on Sundays, you were not honoring God, and you were preventing your employees from being able to worship on the Lord's Day. How would you feel? Afraid? That's how David Green, a devout Christian, felt when placed in that exact situation, as the founder and CEO of the retail chain, Hobby Lobby, Inc. [9] Hobby Lobby is the largest privately owned arts-and-crafts retailer in the world. It operates more than 300 stores in 27 American states. It opens a new store about every two weeks. There were many challenges God placed before Green to measure his business practices according to the ways of God instead of the ways of the world. However, closing his stores on Sundays would take more faith than he had ever had to muster up before. He states:

> *"I didn't have the courage—or faith—to shut down on Sunday all at once, so I took a baby step instead. 'Let's try this out in one state—say, Nebraska,' I told our team. Of course, we had only three stores in Nebraska!"* [10]

He contacted the three managers and had them place a sign in their store windows:

> ***"Closed Sundays to Allow Employees Time for Family & Worship"*** [11]

Sales immediately began to drop, and the decision attracted the attention of the local newspaper. A reporter called their corporate headquarters and was told by the advertising director of Hobby Lobby that *"...if everything works out, we're going to close all the stores, not just Nebraska."* [12] When

David Green read that article about his decision he was ashamed of his actions.

> *"...something nudged me on the inside. It was as if God was saying to my spirit, Oh... so if you're blessed, you're going to be obedient? But if the numbers don't work out for you, then maybe not?"* [13]

Green knew he had been testing God and he knew that wasn't right. From that moment, the decision was made to close all Hobby Lobby stores on Sundays. In horror, Green watched sales drop but he made a decision, even if it went against him. But, by the laws of consequences, soon after, the volume of sales began to climb and then surpass their previous levels! Once the switch was entirely made nationwide, the following year they:

> *"...showed the highest percentage of profit in our history. Once we did what we knew we were supposed to do, profits took off."* [14]

A positive action of the laws of consequences. If God can grow extra hay for honoring His Commandments, why would God not bless more abundantly a business which honors His Commandments? Before Green had made the decision to close on Sundays, he had taken a step in this direction with another decision he had made contrary to normal business practices. He decided to begin closing earlier for their employees so that they could be home with family. [15] The same thing had happened concerning profits. They had a fearful drop in profit. Gradually the profits climbed back to their previous level and then surpassed it! A positive action of the laws of consequences. On the other hand, how many stores are now open on Sundays and while satan insures Sunday is their busiest and most profitable day of the week, it is a deception. Their overall profits are lower than if they closed on Sunday. A negative action of the laws of consequences. Hobby Lobby's CEO stated:

> *"...in response to our window sign,* (Closed on Sundays to Allow Employees Time for Family and Worship), *our main competitor in the home-and-craft industry put up a sign for a while that said, 'Open on Sundays for the Convenience of Our Customers.' That's all right; they certainly have a right to run their business as they choose. I*

> *just continue to believe that if God is able to make 90 percent of a tithing person's salary go further than 100 percent, he is able to make six days better than seven."* [16]

Hobby Lobby's hometown newspaper, *The Daily Oklahoman,* wrote in an editorial:

> *"In an age of elastic morals and 'no controlling legal authority,' holding to one's beliefs stands out. Retailers voluntarily closing on the Sabbath will probably remain as rare as ham on a Passover plate, but we commend those who make the sacrifice."* [17]

Whether it be that you are an employer, an employee, a factory owner, etc., it is God's intention that, as Christians, it must no longer be the rarity but must become the norm to close on Sundays. You must revolt against society's course of dishonoring the Lord's Day, but instead, as business owners shut down your businesses on Sunday, as employees refuse to work on Sunday, and as customers refuse to patronize businesses open on Sunday. All these things must happen if you want the blessing of Almighty God.

Michael Medved* is an author, film critic, and has his own nationally syndicated talk radio show. He is also an Orthodox Jew. Though a Jew his whole life, it wasn't until his adulthood that he came to a full realization of what his faith meant to him. At a time when Medved was building his career, having several successful books that he had authored, he was given an invitation to appear on Johnny Carson's Tonight Show.[18] The date they gave him fell on the second night of Passover. Medved was extremely disappointed when he realized he would have to turn the invitation down, as he couldn't break his Jewish commitment to Passover, though he hoped they would give him another date. The producer was a little surprised at Medved's commitment, but agreed to find another date. The second one he offered landed at the end of Passover, which was also considered a full religious holiday in which practicing Jews could not work. Medved couldn't believe his bad luck, but he still said "no." The producer couldn't imagine anyone passing up the Tonight Show for such "religious scruples." Medved's hope had died that he would get another offer. He said, *"Considering the horrific martyrdom (death, dismemberment, disposses-*

sion) my ancestors experienced for the sake of their faith, this small sacrifice seemed utterly insignificant, but it still left me feeling sour." [19] To his surprise and delight, two days later, a third time the producer called back with yet another date, one that he was free to accept. By "coincidence," it just so happened, for the first time in a year, a certain TV producer, while watching at home, tuned into the Carson show that one night. He was the producer for the TV show, "Sneak Previews." He was so impressed with Medved's performance, he called to invite him for an interview that resulted in Medved becoming a co-host for the show, "Sneak Previews." This would be one of the turning points in Michael Medved's career. What, at first, seemed a coincidence, turned out to be a "Divine Coincidence" by God's hand. Reflecting on this turn of events, Medved wrote:

> *"While I thought that my inconvenient religious commitment might cause me to sacrifice an important opportunity, by following that traditional path, I ended up as a guest on the show on the night—the only possible night—when my appearance led me to an even greater opportunity that opened a whole new direction in my career."* [20]

This is just another example of seeing God's positive actions replacing whatever it was that you sacrificed, for something greater, through the laws of consequences. No one gave up more than Our Lady when She gave up Her Son to the Cross and no one has received more than She for doing so.

7. What about catastrophes hitting and people having to call for help? Again, there is the provision in God's command that if your ox is in the ditch to pull it out. However, Scripture says pray that tribulation does not come in the winter.

Matthew 24:20

> ***"Pray that your flight may not be in winter or on a Sabbath. For then there will be great tribulation..."***

Do you not think if you are living the Sabbath Commandment that God, being mindful enough not to let a sparrow fall from the sky without His knowledge, will not let anything but His Will happen to you? Be mindful of God and He will remember you in loving care.

8. It is important not to put anyone in a position of having to work on Sunday for you unless for seri-

ous life necessity. For instance, we wrestled with what happens if our power goes out on a Sunday.* We wrestled with it until we realized we were trying to rationalize what God had put into our hearts about honoring Sundays. We knew that if we kept holy the Lord's day, He would bless us and look out for us. In making the decision for God, we also remembered that some of the best times our children have had was when the power was off. The answer to the dilemma was to wait to call the power company until Monday morning.

9. Many ministries have TV and radio shows where people are working cameras, employees working equipment every Sunday, but because it's for religion it's OK. This is baloney! The world will not end if these religious broadcasts do not require work of their employees. Pre-produced programs and automation can factor in on broadcasting. If it goes down…it simply goes down. If it can't be done, it can't be done. Prayer will

* Wouldn't you just know it that right after these words were penned that our power went out the following Sunday morning. Anyone's first thought would be to call the power company but for us there was no question that we would not do so until Monday. When the power company came out, they reported that though it was unusual, it was only Caritas' power that was out. It was the only time in Caritas history that only *our* power went off (other than in a major storm). The main feed fuse to Caritas had worn out and blew.

help navigate a way to comply with God's laws. There may often be difficulties you encounter before the way is made clear, but the process will be grace-filled if you seek to comply with all your heart, rather than trying to navigate a way around it through rationalization. It may seem an insurmountable problem to convert to no Sunday workdays for company employees who work a 24/7 schedule, but with computers and automation, more efforts by companies should be made in letting employees be on call, rather than having them automatically go in on Sundays. Even if it means installing more sophisticated and specialized equipment for automation, such as power plants do, the responsibility of corporate heads who call themselves Christians is to explore every avenue to let plants and various work places run without human involvement on Sundays or just shut down. God will bless these efforts because in Exodus it says, ***"I will work such marvels as have never been wrought in any nations anywhere on earth, so that this people among whom you live may see how awe-inspiring are the deeds which I, the Lord, will do at your side. But you, on your part, must keep the Commandments I am giving you today.***"

In the aftermath of Hurricane Katrina, when most of the men at Caritas, with a great deal of heavy equipment, went to Mississippi to help in the emergency work, we worked nearly around the clock. But on Sundays, even in the midst of the disaster, we stopped. And yet, we were repeatedly told that we accomplished more than any other group up and down the Gulf Coast and were among the fastest cleanup, though others worked on Sundays.

10. Because Sunday is to be a day set apart from the six days of work, household duties should be kept to a minimum, and the week should be organized so that as little work as possible is done on Sunday. In the Caritas Community, it has always been important to allow the mothers of the household to enjoy Sunday along with everyone else. For that reason, the Sunday meal is always pasta because it is a simple and easy meal to prepare and not time consuming. It creates tradition which strengthens the bonds of family. Dinner is served around 1:00 p.m., so mom can get out of the kitchen early in the day and have a day of rest as well. There is no evening meal, but rather the family may eat leftovers or have some other snack.

It is an easy habit to use Sunday to "catch-up" on household duties that you didn't accomplish in the week, but in order to live Sunday as a day for God, family and rest, a strong decision and discipline must be applied not to do so. One man wrote that when he first began to live Sundays, his wife always found the need to continue to do the laundry until one Sunday, she found a note on the laundry room door.

We are tired.
We wash and dry all week.
We no longer will work on Sundays!

Sincerely,

The Washer and Dryer

Again, rearrangement of what can be done during the week, will leave only minimal basic duties of life's necessities to be performed on Sundays.

All the above and more was arrived at with serious prayer pleading with God to show us, as a community, how to live the Sabbath Commandment in a religion whose membership, from top to bottom, no longer lives it. What is not written here for you who may find yourselves in unique situations, God will reveal to you how to achieve compliance through prayer. If you think it cannot be because your situation cannot be changed, will the One who created the universe in six days and rested on the seventh not reveal to you a way out? We must ask ourselves is God so limited that He is not able to help us comply with His commands if we have the will? The only caution to you is do not justify your error or rationalize away your violations of this very important Commandment because it seems you cannot do anything about it. It is up to you to act. Through grace, the laws of consequences will find you with their negative or positive actions.

The Sabbath is the one Commandment Christians do not take seriously, thinking it is such a minor violation, if even a violation at all. Yet, you will find in Scripture this one Commandment is the most written about in why it is so vital to keep. Christians have lived so long with the fruit of so many negative problems, resulting from breaking the Sabbath Commandment, that negative consequences have become the norm and not identified as tangible evidence to the violation of the Sabbath. The loss of sensitivity to this sin keeps us from identifying our problems in our family and nation.

CHAPTER FOUR

A BIBLICAL WORLDVIEW
VS
A SECULAR WORLDVIEW

WHICH ONE DO YOU HAVE? ARE YOU SURE?

Christians are being conditioned by the *"...slick campaign of propaganda that is spreading an empty defense of evil,"* [21] conditioned to falsehood and to reject truth. This conditioning affects every class of people. Everyone has been touched in some way with a lost sense of sin, violating especially the Sabbath Commandment, which has resulted in **a lost sense of correct judgement.** Just as what happened to God's people in Scripture who became confused because of their sins, Christians have become confused because they have formed much of their opinions from the media, the world's propaganda, from those supposedly "in the know." As a result, Christians have become dull-minded, without correct judgment, and have become useless in convicting the world. Just one example of the loss of correct judgment follows: Iraq had a ruthless dictator, a minor antichrist figure compared to the one who will come, but wickedly evil in the same characteristics. He killed, gassed, tortured and imprisoned hundreds of thousands of his own people. He massacred and buried in mass graves tens of thousands of others. This is just to name a few of his crimes. Scripture states that a glass of cold water given to a stranger will not go without its reward. How much more would be given for removing a monster that stood against all human dignity? It's that simple. Case closed. We did the Godly thing. All other voices and arguments against what we did and are doing are designed to create diversion issues to draw our attention away from the Godly virtue of rescuing a people from a great evil and the good that will result from this in the future, even if by appearance in the present, the "issue" of Iraq seems disheartening.

Christians are not reading the Bible. They are reading the newspapers and listening to the news, which is not only devoid of wisdom, but glories in vice, lewdness and scandal, the opposite of Godly virtue. It is the godless media that have convinced Christians that we had no business going to Iraq! **The Gospel of Jesus Christ is flowing into Iraq!** Can no one gather enough wisdom to see God's plan! satan vehemently hates that we are in that nation. Why?

The prince of darkness, satan, knows a domino effect of spreading Christianity in the Middle East is in the equation of probabilities. Darkness senses a quake and is in fear at what is unfolding. The many voices under his influence that deny God's actions are continuing to try and make America give up her resolve. Some may question that if the Crusades couldn't bring conversion to that area of the world, why do we think it can happen now? It is for this reason Our Lady is coming to the earth daily to give the world an impulse to live fully the religion Her Son founded as the Christ. Any other religion vs truly lived Christianity decreases when matched up to Christianity. All religions have some aspect of truth, but Christianity is the fullness of truth among all religions of the earth. Christianity is the most pluralistic and tolerant of all religions. Most religions focus on stopping the act of murder. Christianity focuses on stopping the anger and hate which causes the murder. Likewise, most religions focus on stopping adultery, whereas Christianity focuses on attacking the internal lust, which manifests in the act. Christianity grows, flourishes and has the power to convert when its members live the Christian tenets in fullness, with passion and determination, instead of living mediocre Christianity.

With that said, a very important clarification must be made. It is not with force that Christianity is to spread, but rather through living the witness of Jesus Christ. Our Lady in Medjugorje has never come with a forceful or heavy hand, but always invites us towards living our Christianity with greater fidelity, commitment, boldness and love. Christians are to be salt. Christians are to be light. And by this witness, they attract and draw men to them. Muslims have nothing to fear from Christians who live their faith in fullness. In fact, the majority of moderate Muslims would only be too happy to see the faith of Christians making an impact on the rampant immorality that is being spread throughout our nation. Many moderate Muslims do not agree with the violence and the terrorist schemes of radical Muslims, but seeing their own traditional cultures threatened by the illicit, decadent, and godless culture that America's media glorifies, actually is forcing these moderate Muslims into the camps of the radical Muslims as they see it as the only hope of stemming the flow of decadence into their own homes through the media. They know if they do not stop it, it will destroy their families and their culture just as America's culture is being destroyed by it. The Muslim way of life has a lot of shared values in common with Christianity. What many moderate Muslims would like to preserve in their own cultures, Christian America would like to re-establish in ours. And so, we need to realize that we have a lot more in common with moderate Muslims than we have with those who call themselves American, but who espouse and spread the liberal, godless ideologies that are bringing our nation to ruin.

Christians, for too long, have accepted secular worldviews in their outlook on events and no longer know how to look at the world, or world events, with a Biblical worldview. One example: Those darkened souls, who in the name of Christianity, protest at the funerals of soldiers who were killed in Iraq; they are a disgrace to the faith. The protesters say that God is punishing American troops for doing what we did in Iraq, among other reasons. Aside from desecrating the memory of the fallen soldier, they lack wisdom, standing in conflict with facts. The book Saddam's Secrets, [22] was written by General Georges Sada, one of the chief generals in Saddam Hussein's army. He is a Christian who knew Hussein before his rise into power and remained in his ranks for his country's sake until Saddam's fall from power. This general gives a firsthand account of events, a direct witness. By reading Saddam's Secrets, one can directly learn what was going on in Iraq and what is now going on at this moment. General Sada's personal account is not filtered through the media. Sada's firsthand testimony contradicts virtually everything the media has stated concerning the events surrounding the war in Iraq. If one searches, you will find many other sources giving firsthand accounts, which do the same. These contradictions clearly display the manipulation of the media to lead the thoughts of the people. Opinions vs facts, viewed with simple logic and reason, show which is the superior conclusion. Who would want opinions over facts?

Another source among many for those of you who would really like to understand a true picture of the events of the war in Iraq, seen through a Christian worldview, is the book, A Table in the Presence, which gives a firsthand written account of the invasion of Iraq, not a third party media report. In other words, just as in General Sada's book, Saddam's Secrets, the information in A Table in the Presence, flows from the writer, who is one who actually experienced the events himself, to the one who reads his account—two parties—minusing out the third voice, the media. One, the witness and two, you, the reader are the two parties. The media's information, to say it again, is a regurgitation of the event, that ranges from giving false information to biased facts purposely slanted in order to alter, change or condition your view. Why is one man's firsthand witness to an event less credible than the second man's (a reporter) who reports about what the first man did? Both are individuals, but one man is the event participant and the other man relays the event through the media. Who do you want to hear from?

"The media," is usually one individual, representing a media conglomerate. Often an individual from another media conglomerate picks up the story from the first media source. They come together with other conglomerates to form their own god-like authority that gives biased, exaggerated, sensational, false reporting of events, creating a tainted picture of what is really going on. When, in fact, the originator of the event or participant of the event is hardly heard from as to what really happened. So you receive, by a shuffling of information from the second-handers, so called facts to base your views on. In a court of law, this is called "hearsay" and not admissible as evidence! Of the 100 percent news a Christian or anyone for that matter takes in, 5 percent or less comes from the actual participant's account of an event. Search out and read the original speeches or interviews, etc., given by individuals. You will often find that 95 percent or more of the information given in an article about the speech or event comes from the media machine that is always paraphrasing for you what the participant actually said.

As already stated, the source or event maker is the first party. You, the recipient, are the second party. The inserted voice between the first two is the third party. All efforts should be made to hear directly from what the source/event maker says, unedited, and not what others say they said. In some cases, third party information will be the only news you will find. If it's not a trusted source, given from a Christian worldview, then how can a Christian form a correct view from the third party? It would be better not to listen at all than to subject oneself to secular worldview reporting.

In A Table in the Presence,[23] a United States Chaplain, a direct Christian source by the name of Lt. Carey Cash, writes of his experience when he accompanied a marine battalion in the invasion of Iraq. These marines turned out to be the 1000 man battalion who were given orders to take Saddam's palace in Baghdad. They, with thousands of other troops, had already witnessed the fiercest sandstorm in decades, which stopped them dead in their tracks for over a day.[24] This storm called to mind another sandstorm that had taken place during the first Gulf War. In the first war in 1991, as soldiers were making their way through the desert, a sandstorm descended upon them and uncovered a minefield that would have cost many soldier's lives had the storm not come. Many viewed it as the hand of God. This was widely reported at the time. The story held particular interest to those who follow Medjugorje because of a message Our Lady once gave in Medjugorje. She said:

February 15, 1984

> **"The wind is my sign. I will come in the wind. When the wind blows, know that I am with you… I am with you in the wind. Do not be afraid."**

Twelve years later, another sandstorm descended upon American troops, and though there were no reports of mines being exposed, reviewing the situation from a Biblical worldview gives confidence that there was a purpose for such a storm to brew up at that time, though we do not know the reason. Knowing the message above, also helps us to look to the Divine in our troops being stopped—that all works towards the good for those with good intentions.

The chaplain, Lt. Cash, relayed that their battalion waited for 40 days in Kuwait before receiving their orders to cross into Iraq…40 days in the wilderness, a Biblical number that was not lost on them. [25] In those 40 days, there was a great deal of soul searching in the hearts of soldiers who faced a very dangerous mission. Many of them were afraid. Many of them wanted to make peace with their God. Many wanted assurance that there was a God who truly existed, who could forgive them their past sins, and who was bigger than this conflict that awaited them. The day the sandstorm hit, fell on the day Our Lady gave one of Her monthly messages to the world. It was **March 25, 2003**. When reading the chaplain's account of this day, to read of the turmoil and fear in many of the hearts of the soldiers, to read the actual prayers the soldiers were praying with every part of their being, we wanted to see what words Our Lady ***gave this day***.

March 25, 2003

> **"Dear children! Also today I call you to pray for peace. Pray with the heart, little children, and do not lose hope because God loves His creatures. He desires to save you, one by one, through my coming here. I call you to the way of holiness. Pray, and in prayer you are open to God's Will; in this way, in everything you do, you realize God's plan in you and through you..."**

A few days after the raging sandstorm on March 25, the soldiers received orders to attack Saddam's palace, where the fiercest battle of the war would take place. Upon entering the city of Baghdad, on April 10, soldiers said it was like Star Wars; tracer bullets filled the air only inches apart from each other. So thick were the bullets that it seemed no one would be able to survive. Buildings surrounding the palace had missiles, barrages of gunfire, and other ballistics hailing down on the exposed soldiers who were on top of armored and unarmored vehicles manning machine guns. The chaplain, for months, had prepared these men for this moment by having services each night. Up to 200 soldiers at a time would come. He baptized 49 of them,[26] gave communion, and at every chance, led them in small groups to encourage constant prayer for God's protection. Our Lady's March 25 words, given just days after American troops entered into Iraq and began heading towards Baghdad, are interspersed throughout the description of the battle.

> **"...Dear children! Also today I call you to pray for peace..."**

When American soldiers entered Baghdad to attack Saddam's palace, they found it was a trap. They had fallen into an ambush. Saddam and his men had planned their own "shock and awe" throughout the buildings leading to the palace, and they unleashed it on our men. Many of the U.S. troops with their armaments got disoriented, turning down the wrong streets, passing each other, causing others to turn to follow after them, only to arrive back to the same intersection and head down yet another wrong street. It was total confusion in the midst of being trapped in an ambush with the hail of firepower descending upon them from every direction.[27]

> **"...Pray with the heart, little children, and do not lose hope..."**

Then the miracles began to happen. One marine was shot in the head only to find that even though the bullet had penetrated his helmet, instead of going through his head, went up and around his head, lodging on the other side of his helmet.[28] Another who was at his machine gun on top of his Amphibious Assault Vehicle (AAV) and completely exposed to the gunfire, was hit full force in the side of the head with a rocket. The rocket didn't explode, but the impact of it threw his body back *"like a rag doll."*[29] It was easy to conclude that the soldier was not only dead but that his head had been decapitated. The ten other marines standing next to him were shocked, not only to see he was alive, but without any serious injury!

> **"...do not lose hope because God loves His creatures..."**

The miracles kept coming. The 1,000 soldier battalion needed reinforcements but then realized the confusion of being lost, going aimlessly up and down streets, was God's providence because it gave the appearance that their numbers were much bigger than what they really were, both in the number of vehicles and troops they had. This put fear in the enemy, as so often happens in Scripture, when Israel was out manned. [30]

> **"...Pray, and in prayer you are open to God's Will; in this way, in everything you do, you realize God's plan in you and through you..."**

More super miracles occurred throughout the battle. Believers believed more and non-believers came to believe in the Divine protection of God. Some American troops, being attacked ferociously, were able to stop at an angle, to block the firepower shooting at them, by an overpass on the way to the palace. The leading officer noticed the overpass was filled bumper to bumper with American AAV's, (Amphibious Assault Vehicles) forming, with the overpass, a shield of protection for them, like *"a steel wall."* [31] But then, he realized that none of them had the "bold white letters and numbers," markings that identify to whom the trucks belong. He couldn't figure out where they came from, but at that moment it didn't matter. It was saving their lives. When the battle was over, at his first opportunity, he went to see the convoy of trucks to find out who had helped to save their lives that day. He found no trucks and was in disbelief that there also was no overpass. He searched all the streets, all areas around where they were and it did not exist. [32]

"...He desires to save you, one by one..."

In another armored vehicle were two Christians and a "self-proclaimed atheist." As they were moving into the heat of the battle, the atheist's roof-mounted gun jammed. Right as he was able to get it unjammed, he looked to his right and saw the silhouette of an enemy soldier no more than 25 feet away. He was kneeling with an RPG rocket pointed right at him. But instead of firing the rocket, which would have instantly killed all three of them, the gunman suddenly *"...stood up as if he'd seen a ghost. He looked at another gunman standing close-by, waved his arms frantically, and together the two ran full-speed into a darkened alleyway. They never once looked back..."* [33] It happened so fast that the atheist didn't have time to think about what happened. But the next day, while speaking to the chaplain, this man, *"...who had doubted all his life, who had searched for answers, who had demanded evidence..."* [34] got the answers that brought him to the faith. The Iraqi apparently saw something Divine which caused him not to fire and instead flee away.

"...He desires to save you, one by one..."

Another incredible incident happened when a Humvee, with four marines, was hit by a missile that came "into" the vehicle and then exploded. A flash of flames engulfed the vehicle with the four men, two in the back and two in the front. The two in the front, who were professed Christians, were amazed to find themselves alive. The one next to the driver began to feel the driver's arms and legs to see what was blown off because the driver was sitting exactly where the blast occurred, but he was completely uninjured. Knowing the other two behind him were dead, as there was no way they could have survived such an explosion, they didn't bother looking back at them. But finally, when they did look back, they saw them very much alive and uninjured; a miracle witnessed by four men; an inexplicable phenomenon.[35]

"...He desires to save you, one by one..."

Who would not have marveled at such a news worthy event? The witness of these four soldiers offered enough credibility to be all over the world news but not one word from the secular worldviewists. With journalists imbedded with the troops, it is impossible that they did not hear of these miracles, or see them, themselves. But secular does not accept the Divine. For secular to do so would give evidence of the Divine. The Divine and the secular cannot co-exist equally. One must dominate. As marines talked to marines, thousands of miracles had occurred. All knew that the hand of God protected them. While several soldiers were injured, *only one was killed* during this ferocious 12-hour battle, yet so many were exposed to the fiercest gunfire and should have been killed. Two days after the battle, while sitting in the courtyard of Saddam's palace, the chaplain noticed another marine who had been questioning God's existence. The chaplain could see the soldier was very troubled and went to him. The marine was realizing that he had lived a bad life. He hadn't believed in God and yet he made it through the battle alive and completely uninjured. He began to weep. Why would a God save him? But he now knew there was a God. As 10–15 soldiers watched this whole scene unfold, all were deeply moved, as the young man asked Jesus Christ into his life. The next day, this marine became the first man to be baptized a Christian in Saddam Hussein's palace, right in the middle of Baghdad! This took place on Palm Sunday, with Easter just a week away. That same month, less than two weeks later, it was time for Our Lady's next monthly message. On April 25, 2003, Our Lady spoke of the trial by fire the soldiers went through, not only physically, but also spiritually, and about the joy they experienced in knowing they should have died, but were protected.[36]

April 25, 2003

> **"...In the 'foregone' time of Lent, you have realized how small you are and how small your faith is. Little children, decide also today for God, that in you and through you He may change the hearts of people, and also your hearts. Be joyful carriers of the risen Jesus in this peaceless world, which yearns for God and for everything that is from God. I am with you, little children, and I love you with a special love..."**

For days and weeks after, the soldiers who were participants in this battle retold their stories to each other and anyone who would listen, many were moved to tears of deep joy in seeing no other explanation of how they could have survived this battle except that God's hand was their shield. Two weeks after the battle, having had time to reflect, they lived Easter in a particularly profound way.

Remarkably, Our Lady's words on March and April 25, 2003, also could be applied to the Iraqi people. Two days before the marines marched into Baghdad, they passed through a city named "Saddam's City." [37] Two officers were patrolling the streets when a commotion broke out amongst the Iraqi civilians. Dozens of men and women began approaching the marine officers' vehicle, frantically waving their arms. The closer they came to the officers, the more frantic they became. *"Pree-zun, pree-zun, pree-zun,"* [38] they began shouting, while at the same time *"clasping their hands tightly around their wrists. They were indicating handcuffs or shackles or some other form of bondage."* [39] At the same time, others *"held out their hands at knee level, palms facing down."* [40] Gradually the two officers began to understand what they were saying. *"A sickening thought ran through (one of the officer's mind): Are they trying to tell us there is a prison full of children?"* [41]

> *"The more he watched them gesture, the more convinced he was that this wasn't a wild mob. These were parents, pointing in the direction of a building where they believed their children were being held...The edifice definitely looked prison-like in its austere construction...Already a few of the men and women had begun to grasp and shake the gates with both their hands, peering down a darkened hallway, shouting and raving at the top of their lungs. Suddenly there was the sound of screaming—not the screaming of*

adults or women, but of children. Then, like a river bursting through a weakened bank, as the iron gates swung open a mass of frail children came pouring out onto the stone terrace and into the arms of their waiting parents. They were malnourished and filthy, many of them wearing nothing more than rags for clothing. There were dozens at first; and then there were hundreds, mostly males between the ages of eight and fifteen. They flooded the lot in front of the building and soon were grabbing the necks of (the two officers), crying, kissing them on each cheek, then jumping back into the arms of mothers, fathers, sisters and brothers…Little boys, many of whom were no older than seven or eight, were sobbing and clinging to their parents." [42]

The marines came to discover that these boys were the sons of parents who had refused to support Saddam's regime. Many of them had been in this "children's prison" for more than five years. Once they turned 15 or 16, they were forced into the Iraqi army, often put into positions on the front line, meaning certain death. As the story began to spread throughout the troops, the soldiers were shocked. *"What kind of place is this?"* they asked, *"A children's prison?"* [43] Though the soldiers did not need reasons to confirm their belief in the mission they were undertaking in defending the United States of America, this event was the first of many in witnessing the liberation of the Iraqi people, which made them all the more determined to confront the evil regime that would do this to children. What a beautiful and awe-inspiring story of liberation.* Yet, incredibly and shamefully, this story too, never made it into your homes, "your" newspapers or "your" TV's.

Though we hear in the media, in great detail, whenever an American soldier has even *allegedly* fallen in disgrace, we *never* are told of the thousands of good works our soldiers have been doing in Iraq since Saddam Hussein's evil regime was destroyed. Such as the immediate assistance they gave the people of Iraq with food and medical help, that has continued day after day; also the rebuilding of their schools, buildings, and bridges. And most importantly, their commitment in teaching a people, who have lived all their lives under intense oppression, how to be a free people, and how to govern themselves. All of this is done under the threat of losing their own lives. They have lived and are living everyday the words of Our Lady on April 25, 2003:

* Go back and read again Our Lady's words from March 25 and April 25, 2003. But instead of reading them from the perspective of the soldiers, read them from the suffering endured by the parents and children of these Iraqi people and see that Our Lady was speaking, also to them, as their Mother.

> **"...decide also today for God, that in you and through you He may change the hearts of people...Be joyful carriers of the risen Jesus in this peaceless world, which yearns for God and for everything that is from God..."**

Former Secretary of Defense, Caspar Weinberger, co-authored a book entitled, Home of the Brave: Honoring the Unsung Heroes in the War on Terror.[44] These heroes are "unsung" because the media refuses to talk about them, their sacrifices, and the good they are doing in the war on terror. Quoted in the book was U.S. Marine Captain Brian Chontosh, who won the Navy Cross, the second highest medal one can be honored with, for his courage and bravery in the early days of the war. Captain Chontosh *"believes the mainstream media continue to give Americans a stunningly distorted and negative view that stands in sharp contrast to the countless positive developments he has seen firsthand."*[45] He said:

> *"Absolutely there's a difference! (The media is) so focused on the negative things. I've seen the great, beautiful things. I look at the Iraqi children. They're fabulous...The elderly people, when you sit and talk to them, you find that they're good, decent, people who want us there...There are a lot of great things going on there. We talked about the elec-*

> *tions, but even in the area I was in, Ad Diwunijah, alone, we built 134 schools! Where is that in the news? We refitted two hospitals; clean water is in greater supply than prewar levels; sewage disposal; waste management is getting taken care of properly. There are a lot of things going on that people (in the media) don't see and don't want to concentrate on. It's not interesting. It's not (lewd)."* [46]

> *"I'm very optimistic...It's awesome. It's beautiful. We're watching what America looked like right from the get-go that we weren't around to see over two hundred years ago. All the challenges and everything—they're not going to be perfect in a day. It took us two hundred years to get it halfway right, because we're only halfway right as it is. But it is beautiful to sit and watch it…All I know is that there is a lot of good that we're doing over there that you don't see. The children—we're doing good things."* [47]

U.S. Marine Corporal Armand McCormick, a recipient of the Silver Star Medal for his bravery in Iraq, spoke of his own experience with the Iraqi people. He said that at least 80 percent of the Iraqi people love them. *"They want (us) to be here. They're real thankful for (us)."* [48]

David McCullough, a Pulitzer Prize winning historian, with multiple bestsellers including his most recent book, 1776, said that if today's media had covered the Revolutionary War, George Washington and the Patriot's Army would not have been successful in winning America's independence.

> *"I have to say too if that war had been covered...by the media, and the country had seen how terrible the conditions were, how badly things were being run by the officers, and what a very serious soup we were in, I think that would have been it."* [49]

The United States of America would never have existed. This continent would have been split and divided as much as Europe, and the principles and philosophies that created our government, a government that has lasted longer than any existing government in the world today, would have gone up in a puff of smoke.

To read the above makes one angry at the propaganda machines of the newspapers and network news around our nation. They do not report "the news." They report "propaganda" that is leading and conditioning our nation to darker days. Literally thousands of conversions happened through the miraculous events of the invasion and battles in Iraq, as well as throughout all the days of the ground war and beyond. These are the testimonies of those who both experienced and witnessed the events. Facts, not opinions, are what views must be based upon. It is disturbing to see conditioning by *a slick propaganda campaign* of opinions put forth to herd, like cattle, Christians' thoughts away from recognizing God's ways and plans. The godless media has done much to undermine our leaders and the security of our nation. We must attain wisdom through prayer and learn how to recognize truth. We must guard our information intake; look for direct sources from the event makers to make accurate judgments of events that take place in the world around us. Then we must shape our thinking and reasoning upon a Christian worldview.

Did God send Christopher Columbus to bring Christianity to an uncivilized people who knew not of our Divine Redeemer, or was it only a human motivation that led Christopher Columbus to discover this unknown land? Were events Divinely calculated for the fulfillment of Scripture when, *"Tonight a Savior is born in Bethlehem"?* Or was it just happen chance that Scripture was fulfilled by shear luck when, through human motivation, Caesar Augustus ordered a census to take place and so *"Joseph went…to register with Mary (to Bethlehem)"?* What were the real reasons? The answers are different according to a Christian or secular worldview. Man has his reasons, but we must rise above human issues, attaining wisdom to see that often there is a higher plan at play. Instead, Christians often allow human issues, falsely and biasly given, to lead them down a path where they may find themselves actually opposing God's plans without even realizing it.

Again, so that it is clearly understood, we must shape our thinking and reasoning on a Christian worldview instead of a secular worldview. Virtually everything we read, see, and hear is indoctrinating us with a secular worldview. If the Biblical view, the Christian worldview, is given by secular voices of information, it is to ridicule or to twist what is presented or to reinterpret the Christian worldview. Those with a secular worldview are incapable of presenting the Christian worldview, therefore, they should never be trusted. Many Christians, as well as people in general, are often weakened by the information if they are not strong in their understanding of Biblical teaching and keen in their perceptions. The well-publicized book, The Da Vinci Code, is a heretical writing made into a movie that claims many terrible things about Christ. Weak Christians and non-believers, knowing little or nothing about the faith, will be influenced by these false teachings. St. Paul writes in the book of Timothy:

"For the time will come when people will not tolerate sound doctrine but, following their own desires, will surround themselves with teachers who tickle their ears. They will stop listening to the truth and will wander off to fables." 2 Timothy 4: 3–4

The following is a typical example of the secular voice presenting the Christian view. *National Geographic Society* published an article describing the translation of an ancient writing titled "Gospel of Judas." The writing was found in the 1970s in the Egyptian desert. St. Irenaeus, a Church Father in Lyons, denounced the writing in 180 AD as fictional/heretical. As often happens, articles are written under the pretext of being objective but, in actuality, the motivation is to discredit and ridicule the Christian faith. *National Geographic* explored the meaning of the "Gospel of Judas," for the benefit of its audience, giving this false "gospel" the same weight as Holy Scripture, the inspired Word of God. This, in turn, opened the floodgates for all other media sources to jump on the bandwagon. *Newsweek* magazine promoted the story in its April 17, 2006, issue, even using a portion of their front cover to advertise it. It is evident in the following excerpts from the *Newsweek* article that not only did they report on the *Nation-*

al Geographic's story, but they patterned their own bias from the same slant.

As discussed earlier, this is a good example of a story by one individual reporter and his conglomerate *(National Geographic),* picked-up by another individual reporter and his conglomerate *(Newsweek),* passing along the various distortions at each step. In essence, this shows, by example, the collaboration of secular worldviewists bunching together, echoing each other, to ridicule Christianity. *Newsweek* states:

> *"This gospel tells us that Judas was Jesus' only true disciple to whom he imparted secret mystic knowledge and whom he* ***asked*** (Judas) *to turn him* (Jesus) *in to the Romans..."* [50]

The reporter conveys that Jesus and Judas were actually in it together, that they planned everything together, and that Jesus told Judas to turn Him in to the Romans. Even this was a distortion because Jesus was not turned in to the Romans by Judas, but the Sanhedrin. We know the above false "gospel" is not true because the real Gospel, John 13, says that at the Last Supper, after Judas took the morsel that Jesus gave to him, ***"satan entered him"*** and he left. The ridiculing of Holy Scripture by *Newsweek* is evident as one continues the article.

> *"He says in Luke 22,* **'But woe unto that man by whom he is betrayed!'** *In other words, Judas is damned for helping bring about the salvation of mankind.*
>
> *"* ***'...That thou doest, do quickly'—and Judas 'went immediately out...'*** *Newsweek* then stated, *"...But it sounds almost as if he were obeying an order that both of them understood. The secret wisdom Jesus confides (to Judas)—when he's (Jesus) not laying out a hierarchy of angels, gods and more gods that makes Hinduism sound minimalist..."* [51]

Newsweek finishes speaking of how the book *about* the Judas gospel, as well as other books about the book on the Judas gospel, will report on the original report and will go on and on from there.

> *"But right now, people are loving the idea that Jesus and Judas were dear friends who were in it together—it's such a downer to think the guy* **sinned** *and* ***felt bad****—and the hoopla machine is grinding away. The book. The book about the book. The National Geographic TV Show about the book and the book about the book. The audio book..."* [52]

Newsweek goes on and ends the article with more than just a sacrilegious statement, but a total blasphemous statement not mentionable in this writing.

Michael Medved, who was mentioned earlier in this writing, has had a long career in the public eye. Through his appearance that one night on the Johnny Carson Show, he ended up 12 years a film critic on the TV show, *Sneak Previews*. He wrote an autobiography, entitled Right Turns,[53] explaining his step-by-step conversion from a very liberal-minded individual who believed 100 percent in their ideologies, to a very conservative Jew, becoming one of the most outspoken critics of Hollywood.

Medved began to observe that film companies were actually taking financial losses on R-rated films, rather than produce more G-rated (family friendly) films that consistently grossed twice as much as R-rated films. Why? It made no sense. What company or business is satisfied with making less money than they could if they changed their business practices? When Medved pointed this out, he wasn't thanked by Hollywood, but brutally slandered in the liberal press. Medved wrote in Right Turns:

"Many critics of the popular culture have attacked the members of that establishment (movie industry) *as bad citizens; I became notorious for attacking them as bad businessmen. As I researched* Hollywood vs. America (a book Medved authored), *it became increasingly obvious to me that the sleaze and cynicism that offended tens of millions of Americans helped to keep those potential patrons away from the multiplex—and crippled the industry's all-important bottom line. This proposition seemed so self-evident, so inarguable, that it amazed me that pop culture apologists still resorted to the line that insisted, 'the show business moguls just give the public what it wants.' Does the public demand harsh language in its entertainment?…In panel discussions and on television showdowns, I've frequently asked my opponents to cite one scrap of empirical evidence—or a single survey, marketing study, or commercial analysis—that suggests that foul language enhances a film's appeal. They have never responded because they can't: all data suggest that at least 75 percent of the public regularly expresses displeasure at the crude language in movies of all types (with PG apparently now standing for 'Profanity Guaranteed') and, increasingly, on TV...*

"As a critic who paid close attention to the financial fate of the movies under review, I recalled too many instances when shock value fell far short of delivering decent box office returns, while gentler offerings aimed at families fared far better with the public…a comprehensive database was used to analyze all 1,010 domestic releases between 1983 and 1989. During this period, all G films achieved a median box office gross of $17.3 million, PG titles did almost as well at $13.0 million, while R pictures languished with $8.3 million, ...even though R films accounted for more than 60 percent of all titles released in this period.[54]

"In response to such figures, featured prominently in my book, defenders of the status quo offered irrelevant excuses to justify the industry's dark obsessions…Of course, I never suggested that an R-rating ruled out a film's success; I simply argued that this designation made profitability less likely and that Hollywood 's continual determination to saturate the market with adult R-rated material made no practical sense…To this day, I refuse to accept the premise that there's even the slightest contradiction in asking Hollywood to offer more wholesome, Middle American alternatives

in entertainment while also pointing out that the industry could serve its own financial interests by doing so.” [55]

The obvious question is why does the film industry willingly and with purpose choose to make the majority of their films with a rating that they know will not bring in the highest profits possible? It makes absolutely no sense, unless there is something more important to them than money. Influencing the culture towards their ideologies, their secular worldview, is more important, and all of us can judge how successful Hollywood has been in furthering their destructive causes within our culture.

Medved’s testimony confirms how the medium is used to condition people to a secular worldview, even at the loss of profit. These people are dedicated, active and will even sacrifice millions of dollars in order to push their own secular worldview.

During Ronald Reagan’s Hollywood days, he became president of the Screen Actor’s Guild and spent a great deal of his time and effort fighting communists who were doing all they could to bring their influence into the film industry. The following comment is attributed to a screenwriter by the name of John Howard Lawson, one of the most influential communist in Hollywood who Reagan was fighting. In a book Lawson wrote, entitled Film in the Battle of Ideas, printed by a communist publisher, he wrote:

> *"As a writer do not try to write an entire Communist picture, but try to get five minutes of Communist doctrine, five minutes of the party line in every script that you write."* [56]

Lawson despised religion and used his influence to unite the efforts of Marxists in the film industry in order to wage a *"campaign against religion, where the minister will be shown as the tool of his richest parishioner."* [57]

Reagan's efforts did much to defeat the efforts of the communists in the 1940s but sadly, satan found ways to infiltrate the industry and make it what it is today—his voice to lead today's culture towards godlessness. Though Hollywood continues to wield immense influence over the culture, more and more conservative voices are rising up in protest. Michael Medved is one of many. Though Medved is not a Christian, he believes strongly in the need for this nation to maintain its Christian heritage, which he acknowledges as an Orthodox practicing Jew.

> *"Whenever my fellow Jews question my long-standing and collaborative association with the*

> *so-called Christian Right, I try to explain to them the many ways that committed Catholics, Protestants, and Mormons actually help to ensure a vital Jewish future in this country. Most importantly, Christian revival in the United States is 'good for the Jews' because it's good for America. On every significant challenge—whether it's crime or poverty or family breakdown or drug addiction or educational inadequacy—serious Christianity represents part of the solution, not part of the problem...The generous heart of Christian America is so striking, and so strikingly obvious, that the fears of so many American Jews seem perplexing if not inexplicable."* [58]

As a Jew, Medved is a strong advocate in working together with Christians to fight against the destructive ideologies that are destroying our nation.

> *"A more Christian America need not menace Judaism (or any other minority religion), but it does threaten secularism—and despite confusion on the part of left-leaning agencies in the Jewish community, the interests of secularism and Judaism do not count as identical* [59]*...Christian revival doesn't endanger Jewish endurance, but secularism most certainly does. According to the American Jew-*

ish Committee, more than a million Jews—nearly 20 percent of the Jewish community in the United States—identify themselves as religiously unaffiliated...As my friend Rabbi Dov Fischer pointedly observed more than twenty years ago, the real problem for the future of the Jewish community isn't 'Jews for Jesus,' it's 'Jews for Nothing.' My children and grandchildren will live better and more secure lives as both Americans and Jews in a more conscientiously Christian United States." [60]

Following a Biblical worldview, although Medved's work involves the film and television industries, and he even hosted his own television show, he never allowed a television in his own home. His children grew up in a TV-free home.[61] He and his wife wanted to be the ones to shape and form their children's minds and, as a result, their destinies. The result of their efforts was demonstrated in a striking way at their oldest child's Jewish high school graduation, in which she was valedictorian. She refused her father's help in writing her speech, wanting to express in her own words what she had learned so far in the youth of her life.

"The most important thing that I learned...is the courage to be different...Abraham, the first Jew, had the courage to recognize that his society was

incorrect, and to follow what he knew to be right, despite the great risk it posed to himself. Our mission as well is to live our lives differently, and to be willing to stand alone. The idea of conformity—of going along with the crowd and following the path of least resistance—is the opposite of the eternal mission of the Jewish people. We are expected to be separate...to disregard what others may think of us, and to take a stand for what is right." [62]

The DaVinci Code, *Newsweek's* article on *The Book of Judas*, the film industry's refusal to listen to the majority of Americans who want more family oriented movies... how many other countless assaults could we find of our faith being denounced, ridiculed, and marginalized?

CHAPTER FIVE

WHAT ABOUT CHRISTIAN NEWS SERVICES? ARE THEY ANY BETTER THAN SECULAR NEWS SOURCES?

Christians have vacated positions of influence to non-believers as well as to Christians whose philosophies are no different than that of pagans.

Our Lady says:

1984–1985:

> **"...There are many Christians who live like pagans..."**

The medium or the 'communication' line feeding news and educational information reflects a live current going through society and the Church of cultural corruption and the erosion of truth. It is up to each of us to stop the medium that gives us information that communicates a secular worldview. The great Christian author, C.S. Lewis, wrote:

> *"We must attack the enemy's line of communication. What we want is not more little books about Christianity but more little books by Christians on*

> *other subjects, with their Christianity latent.* You can see this most easily if you look at it the other way round. Our faith is not likely to be shaken by any book on Hinduism. But if whenever we read an elementary book on geology, botany, politics or astronomy, we found that its 'implications' was Hindu, that would shake us* (our belief). *It is not the books written in direct defense of materialism that make modern man a materialist; it is the materialistic assumptions in all the other books. In the same way, it is not books on Christianity that will really trouble him* (induce him to believe). *But he would be troubled* (induced to believe) *if, whenever he wanted a cheap popular introduction to some science, the best work on the market was always by a Christian. The first step to the reconversion of a country is books produced by Christians."* [63]

C.S. Lewis believed that Christians should not confine themselves to writing only about Christianity, but that it was vital they write on all other topics, presenting the Christian worldview within those topics. Christians must open their minds and hearts only to the Biblical worldview. Everything should be studied, taught, and

* Latent means: hidden, concealed, secret, "latent motives." Secular worldviewists are very active, often hiding their motives in their information.

understood through the Biblical/Christian worldview. Apply the Scriptures to everything. Apply Christianity to everything. All modern dictionaries reflect and parallel our present society's corruption. The godless philosophies of our day have influenced and changed even our vocabulary, introducing slang, "politically correct" terminology and even altering the meanings of words so to be able to interpret the culture with a secular worldview. Some say, don't mix religion with sports, religion with government, religion with politics, etc. In essence, "Don't apply Godly influences to all matters of the earth," and yet, all that matters *is* God and what *He* thinks, not man.

Noah Webster understood as well as our country's Forefathers that a dictionary was crucial. He and they believed that the dictionary was so important that it was second in the home only to the Bible.* That it was to reinforce the Bible and that the words in it should define and form a Christian worldview. Noah Webster learned 24 languages, working for over 20 years, to put together the "gold standard" of the English language. To define a word, he studied that word in each of the 24 languages, talked to people across the land, formulating, from his study, the truest and fullest meaning. [64]

* Page 505 contains information on how to obtain Noah Webster's *An American Dictionary of the English Language* (1828)

Adam was told by God to name all animals and plant life. Adam didn't name things "ugh, thug, grunt, etc..." Adam spoke words, which he did not learn from an earthly father because he was not "born of man." So we must assume that Adam received the gift of language from his Heavenly Father. Therefore, language is from God Whose very Son, the Second Person of the Trinity, was named The Word. Language was given to man as the means to conceptualize who God is within our own mind and soul. It is a gift God gave to us that we could speak to Him directly, as well as communicate knowledge of God with each other, a gift of words that other creatures do not have. The truth in language can only be discovered through a Biblical and Christian worldview. We can, therefore, assume that satan hates language and will always work to not only degrade it, through slang, filth, etc., but as he is the master deceiver, he uses this gift God gave to man to deceive man. Whereas God presents the truth to man through The Word (Jesus Christ and the Bible), satan presents the anti-word and thus language becomes the primary tool in satan's hands to destroy faith and morals.

As one can observe, today's battles are primarily battles over words, over interpretations and meanings of words. The battle is over the minds of the people.

Just as satan did to Eve in the garden, he works to convince man through clever arguments, that God's Word is oppressive, unjust, untrue and that if we reject God's Word, we will find true freedom. Language is targeted by satan to degrade and bring down the human race because if we follow his advice, it will lead us not to freedom, but to slavery and oppression. By this means, satan uses the language of man to declare the opposite of what he intends. "Happy hours" are filled with many "unhappy" people. "Pro-Choice" speaks of liberty and freedom but leads to enslavement by satan. And where is the "choice" of the child? "Inclusive language" infers that no one is excluded but in actuality it is divisive and separates. For example, the phrase "All men are created equal," is truly inclusive. In today's culture, supposedly, to be inclusive we should say "All men, all women are created equal," but then little boys and little girls are not men and women, so we now have to say, "All men, all women, all little boys, and all little girls are created equal." Then what of poor teenagers, they are neither little or adults? All this segregates and excludes different groups when "all men" is truly inclusive of everybody.[65]

Noah Webster recognized that every age is subject to the demoralization of its language. If the demoralization of language is not checked and controlled, it becomes the principle instrument of destruction.[66] How is language used to demoralize society and culture? Through allowing change for the sake of change, through vulgarity and slang, through changing the meanings of words, through introducing new words created not to elevate but to lower the moral standards by which man lives, through allowing other languages to compete and dominate over our own, and through allowing the influence of godless, virtueless cultures to compete, dominate and prevail over our own Christian culture and way of life. In other words, how and what we speak is what we become. Demoralize the English language or the languages of other countries, if you are from another country, and, you demoralize the cultures of those lands.

One of Webster's expectations for his English dictionary was to forge the United States into a single body of citizens through the one language of English. He knew that the unity of the country would depend on the English language as the language of America and he fully expected that this one book would unify America, making it forever inseparable from one side of its boundaries to the other. Webster's work of over two decades was a major factor in making our nation strong and undivided. He had a keen vision of the importance language would play in our nation's continuance and he believed this principle of being a nation of one language would apply to the nation's future security.

The meaning of the words were vitally important to defining the new nation, and the fundamental beliefs that laid its foundation, and for this reason, Webster was meticulous in studying each word in many languages. Webster, therefore, understood, as we also need to understand for our day, that Biblical Christian understanding of constitutional word meanings (words used in our nation's founding documents) was primary to our nation's continuance. If those meanings were to change, the life of Americans in the United States would also change. This is why it has always been seen as a primary importance to Americans' future security to educate our youth as to the history of the United States (without revisionist* input) so that young Americans would be enlightened to the "dreams of their Forefathers" and would see that those dreams be carried into the next generations. Noah Webster believed that the young must be embodied with "a love of virtue, patriotism and

* Revisionists are those who change or distort history in order to redirect events of the present or future. More will be defined in regard to the meaning and the actions of revisionists which is of epidemic portions in the educational systems of our day.

religion" that must be taught. In the preface of Webster's History of the United States, he wrote:

> *"Republican government loses half its value, where the moral and social duties are imperfectly understood, or negligently practiced."* [67]

In short, through the ruination of our language by the means discussed earlier, we are now assailed with information and word meanings that are forming our thoughts contrary to a Biblical worldview, especially in regard to understanding our nation's founding and its founding documents: the Declaration of Independence and the U.S. Constitution. The information many Americans are receiving is corrupt, and is leading our nation towards embracing a secular worldview. *Secular means without God.* To insure that this doesn't happen, Christians need to *decrease their intake of society's "normal" avenues of information*, by-pass third party media with their *"slick campaigns of propaganda in defense of evil,"* and *increase their intake of information from direct sources*, prayerfully reading and studying their content. The conditioning of thought, more and more, to a secular worldview is hitting not only outside, but also inside the Church, and from every angle possible. You cannot even trust Christian sources such as **C**atholic **N**ews **S**ervice (CNS) to give you the real picture as they too work to invoke in you a desired outcome by conditioning you. SRN News Service of Focus on the Family, primarily made up of those from Protestant faiths, gives much better, more direct, and stronger quotes from Pope Benedict than the Catholic News Service. Catholic News Service feeds news to all Catholic diocesan newspapers in America, as well as other nations. In an article concerning the events that took place during Holy Week of 2006, CNS ignored the profound statements made by Pope Benedict that you are reading in this book. Of the 966 words written by the Catholic News Service, only 16 words were even quoted directly from Pope Benedict in regard to the powerful Stations of the Cross. Those 16 words came *after* the stations had ended.[68] Through careful observation of CNS's reporting, an agenda begins to manifest for society's change, as they are always referencing social justice statements while ignoring powerful references that they reject, such as the following strong and alarming words the Pope spoke concerning the diabolical forces altering society:

> *"...love is fading away, and our world is becoming cold, inhospitable, intolerable...our affluence is making us less human, our entertainment has become a drug, a source of alienation, and our society's incessant, tedious message is an invita-*

> *tion to die of selfishness* [69]*...Today we seem to be witnessing a kind of anti-Genesis, a counter-plan, a diabolical pride aimed at eliminating the family. There is a move to reinvent mankind, to modify the very grammar of life as planned and willed by God. But, to take God's place, without being God, is insane arrogance, a risky and dangerous venture."* [70]

After years of observations, it is clear that CNS does not have a Catholic interest at its base. Catholic News Service purposely chose not to give you any of the profound words the Holy Father spoke that night. Instead they gave 16 words that were the most neutral and generic statements the Pope made, not even taken from the Good Friday meditations, but after the event was over. The words CNS decided to publish of what the Holy Father said follows:

> *"We cannot be just spectators in the Way of the Cross..."* [71]

They complete the Pope's sentence with their own words "about" what the Pope said. The above statement included 11 of the 16 words quoted directly from the Pope. The other five come at the end of a sentence that CNS begins:

"The Way of the Cross reflects '*all of humanity's sufferings today*...'" [72]

This sentence, written by the CNS reporter, continues in a diatribe of nothing-talk, that brings up real Church concerns, but not in light of what the Holy Father very clearly communicated that night. Instead, what we received was CNS' own "latent" "social justice" reporting that is common for their news reports. Compare the 16 words printed above to the other quotes of the Holy Father during the Good Friday's Stations of the Cross that are placed throughout this writing, and ask yourself if you were given the truth of what the Holy Father wanted to express to the Church.

That is what most Catholics receive of what the Holy Father is saying. Over the years, there has been an identifiable socialist slant, with a detectable anti-American sentiment, within these Catholic news sources. The technical director of the Holy See's internet office, Sr. Judith Zoebelein, in a 2004 interview with *Inside the Vatican* magazine had this to say concerning *why* the Holy See created their own internet site, starting back in 1995:

"What most people knew about what the Church was saying today was encapsulated in two lines

and a paragraph in their local newspaper. Often in the case of the United States, it was not very positive. The distribution (through the internet) *of the Church's teaching is enormous now. Everyone says that the site has really helped...Now people will go and they have the easy access to download a document and read it. And it's been a* ***revolution*** *in that manner. People have been able to judge exactly what the Church is saying."* [73]

Whether you are reading religious or secular news sources, most often you will not read the quotes of Pope Benedict in their writings, rather you will read, "here is what the Pope meant." We must keep asking ourselves, why feed on what someone else said about what the Pope said, or any news report for that matter, that is filtered through the media? Decrease your information intake from the slanted media and increase direct source information to find exactly what the Pope or other world leaders said—from them to you. There are sources that provide such information, some of which are listed at the end of this book.

Our Lady has repeated many points in Her messages over the past 25 years. She wants them to become part of us, part of our thinking. Education requires learning by repeating lessons, repetition. So another final point to make is that you not just read these points in this writing, but that you really learn them. There were just over 1,000 words the Pope said in his meditations and prayer at the Stations of the Cross. One thousand words which would strike the most spiritually lax Christian to pause and say a prayer or at least to spiritually be provoked to think. The Catholic News Service gave almost 1,000 words of garbled nothing that would not even motivate the most spiritually inclined soul to say one prayer. The Pope's actual words, satan silenced through a system of information which tells you "about" what he said, not what he "really" said. Remember and learn not to allow yourself to be conditioned any more by third party information. The Pope's ingredients of words spoke profoundly and powerfully, feeding the listeners, whereas the Catholic News Service, in their ingredients, gave *nothing talk*, empty of nourishment, throwing in a strong dash of latent "social*ist* justice."

The implanted information system, between you and the source, must be by-passed and replaced with other direct sources. Imagine what would happen if thousands of Christians began canceling their newspaper and cable subscriptions to revolt against the anti-god propaganda that everyone knows is present in these news sources, and with their cancelled subscription, enclose a letter of why they are canceling. The fact that Christians won't do this, only encourages the news media to continue their own agendas. This is a shame upon Christians. We do not accept that we are to be in the world, but not of the world, and so satan continues as the Pied Piper, while Christians blindly follow after him. You must act by disconnecting from these sources. If you do, newspapers will decline and fold as some are now doing. They depend on us, so quit depending upon them as your information source.

CHAPTER SIX

OPEN YOUR EYES! RECOGNIZE SIN!

Pope Benedict shocked the media by his Good Friday statements describing what amounts to as a "satanic society," which the media immediately began squelching by focusing in on mundane things surrounding the Pope. The Pope, at the 3rd Station, added:

> *"Lord Jesus, open our eyes: Let us see the filth around us and recognize it for what it is so that a* ***'single'*** *tear of sorrow can restore us to purity of heart and the breath of true freedom.* ***OPEN OUR EYES!"*** [74]

A single tear of sorrow! That's all. Recognize sin. Don't rationalize it away. As already stated, our nation is in decay, not so much because of our sins, but because of our denial of them. One tear of remorse will cure the sin. We must say, *"Yes, my Lord, we are angry with those who are wicked and what they are doing to our nation, but we too, are guilty. We violate the Sabbath and we are your children and yet, we deny we are doing anything wrong."* The primary religious figure of the world telling us that "one tear" offered to God can restore us, should shake us into recognition of why our nation is falling. We must confess and say, *"It's because of me."* Your Mother tells *you*:

March 25, 1987

> **"...I do not want you, dear children, to live the message and be committing sin which is displeasing to me..."**

During the last decades we have become blind, which has allowed those in darkness to hijack our nation, and now we seem helpless to stop them. We have let ungodly rulers rule us into godlessness as the following letter shows.

> *Dear Caritas,*
>
> *"Many years ago, at a dinner party my cousin was hosting at her house, a discussion came up concerning the governor of our state who had recently been caught in an adulterous affair. It made national news. The question discussed that night was whether a government leader's moral behavior necessarily made him a better or worse leader in terms of his government responsibilities. All those gathered at my cousin's house were church-going Catholics, and I was shocked to hear the unani-*

mous opinion that despite the governor's infidelity to his wife, he had done well with the economy and was overall a good leader. His 'indiscretion' was 'unfortunate' but apparently not the cause of alarm. It was just 'one of those things.'

"My thoughts ran contrary to these. If a man can betray his wife, the closest relationship two humans can have with each other, how confident can anyone be that he will not betray those of his state and country if temptations came along to do so? If there is no disciplinary action taken, what message is being sent to the youth of our nation concerning 'cheating' in marriage? But mostly, I thought, what the governor was involved in was 'sin.' Sin separates us from God. God is the source of all knowledge and wisdom. You can never commit sin and 'get away with it.' What results from sin is a loss of grace and wisdom. We, as citizens, have the responsibility of keeping our leaders accountable. Yet, it seems that the citizenry of our nation is always willing to turn a blind eye upon every immoral action our government leaders commit, as long as the economy is good—as long as it doesn't affect our own pocketbooks. That is also 'sin.'

> *"It has been almost twenty years since that dinner party. Now it is commonplace to hear of 'scandals' in the personal lives of government leaders, and at most they are met with a shrug of the shoulders. We have entered a time in which little trust is held by the American public in either the Democratic or the Republican parties. Time has proven that if a government leader can commit adultery against his wife, he is also likely to sell out his nation for money and power. What makes Christians any different? As long as our personal finances aren't threatened, we are silent in the face of public immorality—unwilling to rock the boat. Can we feign shock and surprise then, to find our freedoms eroding away and an economy that, at best, is built on shifting sands?*
>
> *Saint Louis, Missouri*

President Garfield said:

> *"Now, more than ever before, the people are responsible for the character of their Congress. If that body be ignorant, reckless, and corrupt, it is because the people tolerate ignorance, recklessness, and corruption. If it be intelligent, brave, and pure it is because the people demand these high*

qualities to represent them in the national legislature." [75]

We have received what we have tolerated. As a result, our sins have made us as powerless as the Israelites were helpless against the Assyrians. Only when they cried their tears of sorrow did suffering reverse for them and they began to see. But for now, we do not see nor understand why we are being prevented from anchoring our nation's direction upon its founding, upon the Declaration of Independence and the U.S. Constitution. Nor do we see or understand that we are failing and falling into an abyss of such a satanic recipe that once baked will lead to the end of our nation. When the Declaration and U.S. Constitution were upheld, respected, and followed, we were protected from such threats. It is amazing how clueless so many of the masses are. Most all do not realize the magnitude of the battle in our midst over America, nor how great is the risk of our nation coming to an end. The Republic of the United States is at a crossroads. The sun is setting on this nation unless we reverse the bad path that is leading us into the twilight. We still have an opportunity before us that can lead to a new dawn, a resurrection of the most open and Christian nation the world has ever known. But if this opportunity is not taken, we are doomed as Isaiah stated, when his words were read by Archbishop Comastri on Good Friday, and we will be:

> ***"…smashed so ruthlessly that among its fragments not a sherd is found…"*** [76]

We cannot allow the godless to interpret the Constitution. How can one who is not rooted in God interpret correctly something that is rooted in God? Some judges may object, saying they do believe in God. If they go to church but rule secularly, they are godless, regardless of whether they say they are believers. The actions of a judge, more than his words, reveal his true nature. The power to rise up to stop those who are godless will come if we recognize our sinfulness and repent. Just a tear amongst us as a people.

> ***"And if my people, upon whom My Name has been pronounced, humble themselves and pray, and seek My presence and turn from their evil ways, I will hear them from Heaven and pardon their sins and revive their land. Now My <u>eyes shall be open</u> and My ears attentive to the prayer of this place. And now I have chosen and consecrated this house that My name may be there forever; My eyes and My heart also shall be there always."*** 2 Chronicles 7:14 – 16

Our Lady said:

March 18, 1996

> **"...Hear my call and my supplication which I direct to you. Consecrate your heart and make in it the home of the Lord. May He dwell in it forever. My eyes and my heart will be here, even when I will no longer appear..."**

CHAPTER SEVEN

THE SECOND REVOLUTION: OUR NATION

Our Forefathers, <u>all</u> 250 identified Forefathers who founded this nation, unanimously intended the Declaration of Independence and the United States Constitution to be interpreted by people of the Christian faith.

> *"...The Christian religion is the most important and one of the first things in which all children, under a free government, ought to be instructed... No truth is more evident to my mind than that the Christian religion must be the basis of any government intended to secure the rights and privileges of a free people..."* [77]
>
> *Noah Webster*

We are in a great struggle...a real live fight...a conflict that will not end in a treaty or negotiated settlement. The stakes for our nation's survival are greater than the threats when our nation almost did not come into being at the time of the Revolutionary War, or later during the crisis of the Civil War. In past struggles for our nation, men were dealing *with men* and thankfully our Forefathers understood, acknowledged, and accepted God's precepts. God, therefore, assisted them. In this present war for our nation, we are dealing directly *with God* as men (us) who accept in words but do not accept all of God's precepts in our Christian walk. We are ignorant of our hypocrisy in our demanding "Thou shall not kill" in the womb while we do not demand of ourselves adherence to the Commandment, "Thou shall keep the Sabbath holy." We talk the talk but do not walk the walk. We will not win this battle if God is against us, and if God is with us we cannot lose, once our pulpits begin to ring out across our land in a revolution in the Church, calling all back to this Commandment. What we need, then, is a revolution in our nation to parallel the revolution in the Church; but first the Church, and then the nation.

Once we are living the fullness of this precept of God, how then do we change back to a Christian nation so to have God bless and favor our nation once again? By returning to the ways, wisdom, and <u>thinking</u> of our Forefathers. Ponder these words of the Holy Virgin Mary. Ponder these words of Hers as the Mother of God. Did She actually mean them? Did Our Lady really want the following to be acted upon? What was Our

Lady's intent by mentioning the words **"in your home country"** just before the words that follow?

August 25, 1994

> **"...I pray and intercede before my Son, Jesus, so that the dream that your father's' had may be fulfilled..."**

Had? What was "had" in "your home country" that you now need to fulfill? Who are these fathers? What did they dream? How can we know what they dreamt? We can know their dream by studying what they wrote, what they said, what they lived, not through third parties, but going directly to their writings. Then we will have a map back to the Godly, happy, and richly blessed nation we once were. Our Lady wants this for all nations, but in a particular way She wants this for the United States as She was consecrated the official Patroness of our nation. This consecration was led by the first U.S. bishop, Bishop John Carroll, a friend of George Washington and brother of the signer of the Declaration of Independence, Charles Carroll, who also was Washington's business partner. The U.S. again was consecrated to Our Lady in 1846 by all the U.S. Bishops. *[78] This message, of Our Lady, to return to our Fathers' dream, therefore, first applies to the United States of America. Yes, this is a bold statement to say that this first applies to the United States, and some may even judge it to be an arrogant one. But all who truly understand the founding of this nation, would agree with this statement, for they know that the conception of America was through a Divine plan. Included within the Virgin Mary's title, as Patroness of the United States, were the words "conceived without sin."

> **"With unanimous approval and consent, the Fathers have chosen the Blessed Virgin Mary, conceived without sin, as the Patroness of the United States of America."** [79]

The bishops purposely placed these words in Our Lady's title long before this recognition was even given to

* On May 13, 1846, during the Sixth Provincial Council of Baltimore, Archbishop Samuel Eccleston and 22 bishops of the United States were gathered in the city of Baltimore, at the Cathedral of the Assumption of Our Lady. On this day, they adopted a decree by which they chose the Blessed Virgin Mary, conceived without sin, as Patroness of the United States. The decree is as follows: **"With enthusiastic acclaim and with unanimous approval and consent, the Fathers [of the Council] have chosen the Blessed Virgin Mary, conceived without sin, as the Patroness of the United States of America."** This is quite amazing in the fact that the Church had still not declared the dogma of the Immaculate Conception, nor had the apparitions in Lourdes, France, taken place in which Our Lady revealed to St. Bernadette that "I am the Immaculate Conception." It was eight years after the U.S. Bishops gave Mary this title as Patroness of the United States that Pope Pius IX pronounced the dogma (1854), and 12 years later that Our Lady appeared to Bernadette in Lourdes (1858).

Her by the Church. It, therefore, is true that this message applies to the United States of America as to no other nation. No nation in the history of the world was conceived by a group of men who sat down to create a government based on the Christian principles of Our Lady's Son, Jesus Christ. We can learn this from our Fathers. John Adams declared:

> *"The general principles on which the Fathers achieved independence were…the general principles of Christianity…I will avow that I then believed, and now believe, that those general principles of Christianity are as eternal and immutable as the existence and attributes of God; and that those principles of Liberty are as unalterable as human nature."* [80]

Adams' own words, along with literally **thousands** of other statements in the writings of the Fathers of our nation rejected any notion that the United States would be anything less than a Christian nation. From America's conception and founding, throughout its history and throughout all future ages, the principles of Liberty, which are rooted in the principles of Christianity, are "*unalterable as human nature.*"

All these things are important to study and to educate ourselves so as to realize what choice we must make to get out of the mess we have made of society. We must give sovereignty of ourselves to our one true God, not to material things or money. It starts with you as an individual. We must realize Medjugorje is the school of Our Lady. She says that She has come to teach us and to show us…

> **"…the way out of every situation that has no exit…"** March 28, 1985

Therefore, we must be enlightened daily by Our Lady's messages and what our Fathers' dreams were to understand the call to live God's Commandments in order to make the right choices. Do not restrict Our Lady's messages to subjects solely about Church and praying the Rosary so to give the appearance that "I am living the messages." We need less self-righteous "holy do-gooders" and more courageous, active "sinners" who have learned to acknowledge their sin and are willing to jump into the trenches of this war and make a difference. Our Lady said:

December 25, 1989

> **"…read everyday the messages I gave you and transform them into life…"**

Our Lady's messages are all encompassing, touching

every single aspect of our lives and our future, to lead us to peace. The plan of satan is to control every single aspect of life. Peace with God is the only way to happiness. Our Lady is educating us and is bearing down on us to make choices. Mirjana, one of the six visionaries of Medjugorje, once had an apparition with Our Lady where she was awestruck by Our Lady's majestic appearance as well as what and how She spoke. Perhaps she was given a tiny preview of the radiance and majesty of Christ when He comes back in Glory. Mirjana said she has seen every emotion of Our Lady throughout the years but never did she see Her so strong, so stern as She did March 18, 2003: [81]

> **"...I call you to make a choice. God gave you free will to choose life or death. Listen to my messages with the heart that you may become cognizant of what you are to do and how you will find the way to life...without God you can do nothing; do not forget this even for a single moment...Do not anger God..."**

"Become cognizant of what you are to do." Choices must be made with wisdom. Wisdom is obtained from God. God gives wisdom to those who follow His law. The violation of the Law of the Sabbath throughout Christendom has struck dumb the membership of Christianity. We are continuously silenced by wicked actions of people who, at every level, promote the destruction of our nation, schools, institutions, government, down to the human body itself. Pope Benedict said at the 10th Station on Good Friday:

> *"Today bodies are constantly bought and sold on the streets of our cities, on the streets of our televisions, in homes that have become like streets... When will we realize that, without purity, the body can neither be alive nor life giving…purity has everywhere fallen victim to a calculated conspiracy of silence: an impure silence! People have even come to believe a complete lie: that purity is somehow the enemy of love."* [82]

We must live purity—purity of intention, purity in obeying God's Commandments, purity of heart—then we will see, then we will change our nation. Cities, right now, <u>today</u>, can stop abortion! If city governments can find ways to steal land with improper use of eminent domain, they can find ways to close down abortion clinics in a day. They do not have to wait on a court to say so. Why have the cities not done so? Abortion is the purest form of a body's desecration! Why the silence? Because our city councils are no different than infidels in their behavior and rulings, even though many wear the title "Christian." They pass ordinances controlling noise, litter, speeding, zoning and on and on. And they can't stop abortion? That's a lie! They can regulate abortion clinics out of business. City councils and county boards can pass many different ordinances against abortion clinics. If the clinics take them to court, and the city loses, they can immediately file a new ordinance with a requirement of a $200,000 license fee for every abortion clinic. If that gets struck down, they can require medical inspection ordinances for abortion clinics, just like the Health Department requires of restaurants, and through imposing many and various other rigid methods to comply with these ordinances, abortion clinics can be shut down. They can be regulated to death. This is not about fairness. This is about declaring war. Environmentalists have done this to many industries, shutting them down to save a frog, an insect, or the air, but somehow we cannot stop abortion and save the children? But why is this not happening? Because Christians do not have the power to convict even with God's convicting authority, when they are not living God's Commandments themselves. If Christians were, they could, with great confidence, take over city councils and demand with authority to close the abortion clinics. Pope John Paul II said in his exhortation *The Church in America:*

> *"America needs lay Christians able to assume roles of leadership in society. It is urgent to train men who….can influence public life….(through) a deeper knowledge of Christian ethical principles and moral values (that) will enable them to be (champions or advocates)…proclaiming (moral values and Christian ethical principles)…to the* ***so called neutrality of the state.****"* [83]

"It is urgent," the Holy Father said, that we influence public life. From our city councils all the way to the positions in Washington, Christians have abdicated the leadership of our nation to men who are not mindful of God's ways. One woman, Julie Watts of Sioux Falls, South Dakota, said in a May 2006 issue of *Citizen Magazine*:

> *"If someone had told me two years ago that I would be active in politics and lobbying, I would have said, 'Whatever!' Little did I realize at the time that when God moves, you follow. It all started when I tuned into Focus on the Family... about the need for Christians to become involved and active…(Later) (Reading an article) I was shocked to read that abortion clinics in almost all states are not regulated and inspected… I could not seem to shake the feeling that South Dakota*

should regulate and inspect abortion clinics. I began with complete ignorance of how to get a law enacted…I immediately called state legislators and lobbyists…gathering as much information as I could. Copies of abortion regulation bills from other states arrived in my mail, and with those materials in hand I found a sponsor for a bill here." [84]

One woman with no experience successfully led a battle which ended in a bill that passed and was signed by the Governor of South Dakota. It would have taken affect in July 2006, basically shutting down abortion in South Dakota. However, the bill was challenged, and was left in the voters' hands to decide whether or not it would become law. Planned Parenthood is reported to have spent over $17 million on a mass media campaign encouraging voters to overturn the ban. [85]

South Dakota has a pro-life legislature, a pro-life Governor, is a state where only 800 abortions were reported in 2005 (one of the lowest in the country), has only one abortion clinic in the whole state.[86] Yet, there was such an incredible amount of out of state effort before the election that was held November 7, 2006 to have the new anti-abortion law repealed. And what happened? What happened in the November 7th election proves the points being made and proves what these writings are saying. The South Dakota's Ban of Abortion Law was defeated! How could that be? Convents were praying. Christians were praying. Sixty-five percent of South Dakota citizens are against abortion. The Governor, both Houses, were for the new anti-abortion law, and they all lost! Why did God not answer? Why were their efforts and prayers petitioning to end abortion not granted? We must ask ourselves, why? There is no other explanation than that Christians are standing before God, guilty of breaking His Commandments, with unrepentant hearts, an unwillingness to change and, therefore, their prayers of 35 years to end abortion go unanswered by God. Christians will not see wide scale victories until we begin living the Sabbath Commandment. And once all Christians do, you will witness a tsunami of victories, sweep over our land. We will look in awe upon God's grace poured forth upon this nation. Our Lady once said that She doesn't need one-hundred Our Father's said, but rather only one, if that one is prayed from the heart.

March 9, 1985

> **"You can receive a grace immediately, or in a month, or in ten years. I do not need The Lord's Prayer said a hundred or two hundred times. It**

is better to pray only one, but with a desire to encounter God...

In order to answer a righteous prayer, God doesn't need us to bend over backwards to get His attention. He just needs a pure heart. We, therefore, cannot point our finger at Planned Parenthood for what they are doing, without finding three fingers pointing back at ourselves.

A few may say this is mixing religion with politics. If that is your thought, you've just proven the whole premise of this writing. You are thinking with a secular worldview. It's time you re-educate yourself to the dreams of your Fathers.

CHAPTER EIGHT

THE SILENT MAJORITY HAS BEEN SILENT TOO LONG

Our nation has not lost the Christian faith, but our nation has lost the "Christian principles" which have always governed everything in our nation. We cannot, however, lose Christian principles without eventually losing the faith. Therefore, it is clear that we have an uphill battle, but a battle easily won if we return to God just as when the Israelites repented and the Spirit of God always then led them to victory. Everyone has to get involved. First, it must be understood that the present political system is corrupt. Christians must rise above it and demand a certain response just as Julie, from South Dakota, did. The intent here is not a call to run for political positions, for again, the *system is in a great moral crisis of corruption* and, therefore, weak. Thomas Jefferson said:

> *"When once a republic is corrupted, there is no possibility of remedying any of the growing evils but by removing the corruption and RESTORING ITS LOST PRINCIPLES; every other correction is either useless or a new evil."* [87]

It is obvious that our republic is corrupt, so the lost principles that Jefferson spoke of are Christian principles that every citizen in society were formally bound by, no matter their belief. So what do we do to remove what is corrupt in our republic? First, we can have more power by influencing and holding accountable those who are in positions of authority, rather than becoming part of a political system that is bankrupt on principles, honesty, and integrity. We know of Christians who have gone the political route, with good and pure intentions, but were taken in by the system rather than changing the system towards Godly virtues and principles. *You cannot sanctify corruption. Purification is the only answer.*

Secondly, the American Revolution depended heavily upon the churches of the land. The pulpits rang out and were not silent. Reread what John Paul II said about the urgency to proclaim moral values and Christian principles. *"America needs lay Christians able to assume roles of leadership in society. It is urgent to train men who...can influence public life...(through) a deeper knowledge of Christian ethical principles and moral values (that) will enable them to be (champions or advocates)...proclaiming (moral values and Christian ethical principles)...to the so called neutrality of the state."* [88]

Pray for your pastors, priests, and bishops. Encourage them and educate them just as you are being educated to what is confronting us as a nation. If they are disinterested or even hostile to your entreaties, do not become discouraged yourself. The action of God, if you are good-willed, will open other doors for you to spread and educate as many as possible.

Thirdly, there is *a great need* for Americans to educate themselves to the thinking and reasoning of their Forefathers, especially in some specific areas, which are detailed in this chapter. Without this clear knowledge and understanding, we will fall far short in the actions that we, as a people, must begin taking if our nation has a hope of surviving. Education must come first in order to understand what we can do to reverse the tide that is leading us toward destruction.

From our nation's founding up until the late 50s, churches were allowed the constitutional right of free speech. It was Lyndon B. Johnson who in congress had legislation passed to silence the constitutional right of free speech of 501(c)(3) organizations, which are churches and non-profit organizations. This caused, for the first time in the history of our nation, a great vacuum, a spiritual void in the political arena. The accountability held above the government by the churches was erased and the Christian worldview that had been foundationed in our nation from its creation was easily replaced by a secular worldview.

Many Christians today are conditioned to believe that God/Prayer and the State are to be separated. This is absurd and is a new thought that has taken hold in recent decades. There is no wall of separation. It does not appear in the Declaration nor the Constitution. Jefferson's writings, along with the writings of our Forefathers, were clear that the Christian faith, principles, and beliefs not only could, but should be influential throughout government. The government could not, however, establish or endorse one Christian denomination over another. That was the original intent and that original intent threaded through all laws and institutions of our nation up until 1947. It is perfectly legal for the United States government, for public schools, etc., to state that we are a Christian nation. It is explicitly and undeniably clear our Forefathers founded and intended this nation to be a Christian nation, to behave as a Christian nation, and to make and interpret laws through the guiding principles of Christianity, but *only* that the government could not endorse or name an official Christian denomination over another.

Muslims, Hindus, and those of other faiths have a protected right in our nation to practice their beliefs. Our Forefathers also clearly acknowledged that. Not only does our government defend that right, but Christianity does as well. The tolerant principles accepted and lived by Christians demands such, but tolerance does not, in any way, mean Christianity is the same to our nation as other faiths or beliefs are to our nation.

In looking back at the original intent of our Forefathers when they created this new nation, it is clear that other religions do not have the same level "rights" as Christianity in becoming a guiding force over our nation or its general population. The Christian faith is embedded everywhere throughout our nation and for nearly 200 years its principles formed our common laws that all Americans lived by. These principles were considered Judeo/Christian ethics by our nation's Forefathers. Christian prayer has always been a part of our civil and public assemblies. They are in the oaths we make, *"So help me God,"* on our currency, "*In God we Trust,"* in our pledges, "*One Nation Under God,"* and inscribed on our government buildings from Washington D.C. to every state in the Union. By virtue of the fact that this *is* a Christian nation, other beliefs have no claim of equal time when prayers are said in public, whether it be before public functions or required meetings of government, before military gatherings, before public school events and graduations, and so forth. Our Forefathers even acknowledged that atheists were to be schooled by the "principles of Christianity," as they believed that an atheist who is held to Christian principles in his behavior would not be harmed by these standards. John Adams wrote to Thomas Jefferson about the army.

> *"Who composed that army of fine young fellows that was then before my eyes? There were among them Roman Catholics, English Episcopalians, Scotch and American Presbyterians, Methodists, Moravians, Anabaptists, German Lutherans, German Calvinists, Universalists, Arians, Priestleyans, Socinians, Independents, Congregationalists, Horse Protestants and House Protestants, Deists and* ***Atheists****, and Protestants 'qui ne croyent rein.'... **All** educated in the general principles of Christianity... The general principles on which the fathers achieved independence were...the general principles of Christianity..."* [89]

It is our right as Christians to honor the God of our nation, the God of our Forefathers, who placed Christ's principles in the primary position of our public institutions, who foundationed our very government upon His Creed.

This writing is not calling for or promoting a theocracy,* for Christianity's principles do not compel one's conscience by force. Rather, it is a call to return to that which was built, from the beginning, into our basic code of law, which are the Christian principles, for the standard of society. Every individual benefits from that basic code, be he a believer or non-believer. An individual is free to choose his faith, but the standard for all in American society are the *principles* of Christianity.

In Saudi Arabia, Iran, and every other Muslim nation, their prayer to Allah is held by their society as primary both by government and religious leaders. Israel, likewise, is a Jewish land, recognized as a nation where Judaism is primary. The United States is not like the European Union who refused to put God in their constitution because, as they said, they are no longer Christian nations.

The United States of America is a Christian nation who has been bullied into silence by a minority who wants God and His Son, the Christ, taken out of this country so to move forward their own godless, secularist agendas, who want us to adopt a more European mentality of denying our Christian roots. England, France, Germany, and other countries are now being dominated

* Government of a state by the immediate direction of God.

by Muslims who are taking over all of Europe. Having abdicated their Christian heritage, God gave into their wish and is withdrawing. Now they are losing the very souls of their nations. America, wake up and look at your own future—which is peering at us from across the ocean. We too will lose the soul of our nation if we refuse to stand up and fight for the recognition of our founding and roots as a Christian people. This Christian nation must stand upon our Fathers' dreams and *never concede,* to any other religion, the position Christianity holds in this nation. It begins by prayerful study of what and why our nation was founded. We *cannot* vacate the rightful and God-given position Christianity holds as the guiding force of this nation. If we hold the line, there is the hope that through our example, other nations will find the strength to place their own foundations back on God, and reclaim their Christian roots.

To reiterate, our nation guarantees others' right of worship (of legitimate religions; this does not include witchcraft, wicca, etc., as legitimate religions which will be discussed later in this writing). But we do not have to compromise, practice quietism, nor apologize that our nation is Christian. On one of his radio broadcasts, Paul Harvey read the following commentary by Nick Gholson:

"I don't believe in Santa Claus, but I'm not going to sue somebody for singing a Ho-Ho-Ho song in December. I don't agree with Darwin, but I didn't go out and hire a lawyer when my high school teacher taught his theory of evolution. Life, liberty, or your pursuit of happiness will not be endangered because someone says a 30-second prayer before a football game. So what's the big deal? It's not like somebody is up there reading the entire book of Acts. They're just talking to a God they believe in and asking him to grant safety to the players on the field and the fans going home from the game.

"'But it's a Christian prayer,' some will argue. Yes, and this is the United States of America, a country founded on Christian principles. According to our very own phone book, Christian churches out number all others better than 200-to-1. So what would you expect—somebody chanting Hare Krishna? If I went to a football game in Jerusalem, I would expect to hear a Jewish prayer. If I went to a soccer game in Baghdad, I would expect to hear a Muslim prayer. If I went to a ping-pong match in China, I would expect to hear someone pray to Buddha. And I wouldn't be offended. It

wouldn't bother me one bit. When in Rome...(do as the Romans do.)

"'But what about the atheists?' is another argument. What about them? Nobody is asking them to be baptized. We're not going to pass the collection plate. Just humor us for 30 seconds. If that's asking too much, bring a walkman or a pair of ear plugs. Go to the bathroom. Visit the concession stand. Call your lawyer! Unfortunately, one or two will make that call. One or two will tell thousands what they can and cannot do. I don't think a short prayer at a football game is going to shake the world's foundations.

"Christians are just sick and tired of turning the other cheek while our courts strip us of all our rights. Our parents and grandparents taught us to pray before eating, to pray before we go to sleep. Our Bible tells us to pray without ceasing. Now a handful of people and their lawyers are telling us to cease praying. God, help us. And if that last sentence offends you, well...just sue me. ***The silent majority has been silent too long****...it's time we let the one or two who scream loud enough to be heard, that the vast majority don't care what they want. It is time the majority rules! It's time*

we tell them, you don't have to pray. You don't have to say the Pledge of Allegiance, you don't have to believe in God or attend services that honor Him. That is your right, and we will honor your right. But, by golly, you are no longer going to take our rights away. We are fighting back and we WILL WIN! God bless us one and all, especially those who denounce Him. God bless America, despite all her faults, she is still the greatest nation of all. God bless our service men who are fighting to protect our right to pray and worship God. May (this year) be the year the silent majority is heard and we put God back as the foundation of our families and institutions."

If you are at a restaurant that serves good food, but you do not care for the music, you are still inclined to stay for the good food. If a non-Christian is at an assembly where Christ's name is mentioned in prayer, is he still not inclined to enjoy the fruit of what the cause of the assembly was held for? So just tune out the prayer to Jesus if you wish, just as you tune out the music you do not like at the eating establishment, to enjoy what is offered — whether you are attending a rodeo for entertainment, or a required military function that begins with a prayer to Christ. You can do what non-Christians did for 200 years. Respect this nation's roots.

We are a nation in which 84.2% of the citizenry holds to Christian beliefs. Many who are of the Jewish faith have recognized and respect the Forefathers' original intent of being Christian and as Judaism and Christianity share the same roots, we also share a system of values in our Judeo/Christian beliefs. But as a nation, there can be no argument that we are a Christian nation. Presently, our nation's government, by satan's design, has a strangle hold upon all voices which could redeem it. Christians are mainly to blame for this, first and foremost, because of not living the Sabbath. This has led to the loss of wisdom which results in our succumbing to the conditioning of secular worldview educational and media systems which propagate an anti-christian bias; systems that never miss an opportunity to blame Christians for offending others whenever we are "caught" exercising our faith. But in truth, we *are* at fault, not because of what the anti-christian bias accuses us of, but because of our failure to live fully the principles of our Christian faith.

How is it that the same darkness we see today in general society was not able to cast its darkness over the light of Christians of bygone days? And yet today, the Christian light *is* overshadowed by darkness. By their very nature, when Christian principles are lived, it is an impossibility for the light of Christ not to shine and overpower darkness. A contradiction then exists because if we are truly the light, we would be lighting up the darkness. So the truth is that the prevailing darkness is a testimony against **US**, not against darkness. We are now disabled, paralyzed, and unable to act. Thankfully, there is an uprising among people of the Judeo/Christian faiths who are discontented with the godlessness of our nation and its present political system. We, therefore, must put our own house in order and be active and ready *to seize the moment* that God gives us to **take back America** and place it back on the foundation of our Fathers' dreams, our Fathers who first gave us this "homeland."

Americans are no longer schooled in the fact that the Founders did not like government, and that the Constitution's purpose was to chain the government, not the people. We have lost our understanding that government must always be checked and kept small by the people, lest the people become oppressed and enslaved by it. Whether they be at the local, state, or national level, governments always tend to be against the people. Thomas Jefferson said:

> *"The two enemies of the people are criminals and government. So let us tie the second down with*

the chains of the Constitution so the second will not become the legalized version of the first." [90]

Abortion is just one of many items that the time has come to clean house. "Seizing the moment" must be first manifested in our own cities. Cities and county commissions are the power kingdoms of today. They exercise far too much control over the citizenry who are suppose to be living in a republic. Yet they suddenly become weak and even unwilling to use their power to confront the wickedness in society, and instead, often end up protecting it. Most people blame federal and state government for the godlessness and lack of morality in society, but the truth is that this mostly comes through local city councils who comply with the oppressive federal measures. Why? It comes down to money and power. They won't get their piece of the pie of state and federal funds unless they comply. And so they sell out their neighbors in order to keep the cash flow going into their local systems that are just as corrupt as the state and federal levels. Most problems of godlessness are implemented through the cities. It was the city police who stopped the priest from bringing

Terri Schiavo* her final Communion. [91] It's the city and county officials, who regulate to death the community's citizens with godless ordinances, yet do not do the same for undesirable establishments such as abortion clinics or sleaze places. It's the cities and counties who are taking land. It's the cities and counties whose school systems allow curriculums that promote a secular, anti-god, socialist worldview, and on and on. If you look at the cases put before the U.S. Supreme Court, most originate within a city. Thoughtfully observe where much of the godlessness in our society is coming through and being exercised from. Who is allowing it? Who is ignoring it? City and county officials derive their power from the people. However, today city and county officials are exercising powers not for the people, but against the people. In the Declaration of Independence it says:

> *"...equal station to which the laws of Nature and of Nature's God entitle them,... (men) are endowed by their Creator with certain unalienable*

* The fierce, public battle over the life of Terri Schiavo in the Spring of 2005 divided not only Terri's family but the entire nation, as the Florida courts made a decision to take Terri off of her feeding tube, allowing her to slowly starve to death. Her parents, brother and sister were devastated by the court's decision and there was a national outcry against the court decision, with even Florida Governor Jeb Bush strongly denouncing it along with his brother, the President of the United States, George W. Bush. The judge declared that Terri was to receive no food or drink of any kind, and though she was Catholic, not even Holy Communion could be given to her on her deathbed. City police officers were positioned outside her door to carry out the judge's orders.

> *Rights, that among these are Life, Liberty and the Pursuit of Happiness—That to secure these Rights, Governments are instituted among Men, deriving their just Powers from the Consent of the Governed, that whenever any Form of Government becomes destructive of these Ends,* ***it is the Right of the People to alter or to abolish it, and to institute new Government…when a long train of abuses…it is their right, it is their duty to throw off such Government and to provide new Guards for their future Security….”***

In the case of Terri Schiavo, what if the city's mayor and police chief refused to follow an order from a judge that was illegal because it violated her unalienable right to receive Holy Communion? How do you view it?

We are empowered, by the Declaration of Independence, to rise up against all those elements destroying our nation, which contradict and oppress natural law and the unalienable rights that every man is born with. Any objections made that *“we do not adhere to the Declaration but to the Constitution”* are thoughts conditioned through our present systems of education, the media, and by history revisionists who want you to think that so there will not be a rising of the sentiment of *“we the people.”* If *“we the people”* rise up, the revisionists know that we can alter the present godlessness in the political process that keeps us in the bondage of decadent laws. A plan was made and an agenda was followed by revisionists who resented the position God was given in our nation by its citizens. They made it their aim to isolate and separate "religion" so that it could not have any influence over public life whatsoever. God was to be replaced with *"a religion of humanity, guided by reason, to provide an organizational home for those who regarded themselves as too enlightened to remain within the confines of splintered sectarian Christianity."* [92] They called it the *Religion of Liberalism*. An organization by the name of "The Free Religious Association" made nine demands in the name of their "religion." As you read the items listed, reflect upon how successful they have been in achieving several of their demands.

1. *We demand that churches and other ecclesiastical property shall no longer be exempt from just taxation.*

2. *We demand that the employment of chaplains in Congress, in state legislatures, in the navy and militia, and in prisons, asylums, and all other institutions supported by public money shall be discontinued.*

3. *We demand that all public appropriations for sectarian educational and charitable institutions shall cease.*

4. *We demand that all religious services now sustained by the government shall be abolished; and especially that the use of the Bible in the public schools, whether ostensibly as a textbook or avowedly as a book of religious worship, shall be prohibited.*

5. *We demand that the appointment by the President of the United States or by the governors of the various states of all religious festivals and fasts shall wholly cease.*

6. *We demand that the judicial oath in the courts and in all other departments of the government shall be abolished, and that simple affirmation under the pains and penalties of perjury shall be established in its stead.*

7. *We demand that all laws directly or indirectly enforcing* ***the observance of Sunday as the Sabbath shall be repealed.***

8. *We demand that all laws looking to the enforcement of "Christian" morality shall be abrogated,*

and that all laws shall be conformed to the requirements of natural morality, equal rights, and impartial liberty.

9. *We demand that, not only in the constitutions of the United States and of the several states but also in the practical administration of the same, no privilege or advantage shall be conceded to Christianity or any other special religion; that our entire political system shall be founded and administered on a purely secular basis; and that whatever changes shall prove necessary to this end shall be consistently, unflinchingly, and promptly made.* [93]

What is most surprising is not the demands themselves, but that they were written in the year 1873! Look at what their constancy of effort has accomplished in a little over 100 years. Having achieved several of the demands, they continue towards achieving the remainder.

Ponder the following thought and reason it out. Demand number 7 is proof of the laws that existed for most of our nation's history and reminds us today of what "we the people" used to know: that our institutions, our court systems and all society accepted the laws of the observance of thc Sabbath for nearly 200 years because we knew it was crucial to do so for the continuance of our nation. The existence of the Sabbath laws that liberalism demanded to be repealed in 1873, also proves that before that time, some did not want the Sabbath observed. Hence, laws were passed to close establishments on Sundays. But think, when the Sabbath observance was first established in our nation, the minority of those who did not want to observe it were not a consideration. It was not considered that by observing the Sabbath, Christians were offending this minority. Rather, the greater society boldly proclaimed that the Sabbath will be observed by the government, by institutions, by businesses, etc., to the point of passing laws to enforce the observance because "we the people" of by-gone days knew that not to observe it as a society would be the destruction of society. Think and reason it out. Even liberalism knew the first place to weaken and crumble Christianity was to get us to ignore and forget the sacredness of the Sabbath. Think and Reason! They wrote it, and we conceded to it.

Today, this nation finds itself at war, largely over the various points listed in the nine demands of liberalism. The war is waged between two ideologies; the above humanist, secular ideological worldview vs the Biblical/Christian worldview. Much of the headway that was made from these secular humanists came from their *"demanding"* the changes, and their hard work, diligence, persistence, commitment and determination in not giving up over the long haul, generation after generation. And the churches, filled with Christians, largely sat by and let them do it without a fight. To reverse the damage that has been done and to reclaim our nation back to God, we must do the same as they did. We must make our own demands—saying "NO MORE!" And then we must have every bit as much commitment, determination, hard work, diligence, persistence and resilience to win the victories for our nation's survival.

And what is the Christian response to the nine demands that obviously seek Christianity's destruction in our nation? In answer to the question, two things must be understood. *First*, all must take seriously and learn that no where in the Declaration of Independence, the Constitution, or any of the writings of our Forefathers was the separation of Church and State called for, or as it is interpreted today. To understand why courts now use the phrase "separation of Church and State," we must look at references by the Forefathers when they used the word "religion." When they used the word religion, they were referring to the various Christian denominations. It was never the intent of our Forefathers that our nation's government be influenced by any religion, except Christianity. To know what our Forefathers wrote and thought, believed and intended, one must know the word meanings of the time, and use them as the basis to interpret all present law by those meanings. It is not only in our present times that justices over-stepped their bounds. There were recorded cases, even at the dawn of our nation of some justices trying to do what liberal justices are now doing today. Thomas Jefferson admonished Supreme Court Justice William Johnson for this very violation.

> *"On every question of construction, carry ourselves back to the time when the Constitution was adopted, recollect the spirit manifested in the debates, and instead of trying what meaning may be squeezed out of the text, or invented against it, conform to the probable one in which it was passed."* [94]

James Madison also declared:

> *"I entirely concur in the propriety of resorting to the sense in which the Constitution was accepted and ratified by the nation. In that sense* ***alone*** *it is the* ***legitimate*** *Constitution. And if that be not the guide in expounding it, there can be no security for a consistent and stable, more than for a faith-*

> *ful, exercise of its powers...What a metamorphosis would be produced in the code of law if all its ancient phraseology were to be taken in its modern sense."* [95]

All law must be interpreted in light of their original meanings as understood and defined by our Forefathers. The modern meaning of what religion means today, for example, cannot be factored in to interpret laws that were foundationed upon what the word "religion" meant over 200 years ago. To do so would change the constitutionality of the law. The original intent of our Forefathers is shown by a 1853–54 report of the House and Senate Judiciary Committee:

> *"...In this age there can be no substitute for Christianity; that, in its general principles, is the great conservative element on which we must rely for the purity and permanence of free institutions. That was the religion of the Founders of the republic, and they expected it to remain the religion of their descendents."* [96]

Of all the Founding Fathers, only Jefferson wrote the words "separation of Church and State" and he did so only once, in a private letter. But he did not mean separation as it has been interpreted today, divorcing Christianity, its principles and moralities out of government.

This false notion of separation came from revisionists' reinterpretations, partly based on Jefferson's letter and partly through their separating the First Amendment from Article VI, Section III of the Constitution. The First Amendment states:

> *"Congress shall make no law respecting an establishment of religion or prohibiting the free exercise thereof..."*

Article VI of the United States Constitution states:

> *"... no religious test shall ever be required as a qualification to any office or public trust..."*

By separating the two through the 1947 court case Emerson vs Board of Education, the U.S. Supreme Court pronounced the modern concept of "separation of Church and State," thereby erecting for the first time in our nation's history a wall between the two.

The newly conceived "wall" was a result of divorcing the First Amendment from its original purpose, thereby inventing this new concept, not only devoid of past historical court precedence, but one that was clearly in denial of our Forefathers intended meanings. For this one obscure line in a single private letter that Thomas Jefferson wrote, there are hundreds of others he wrote or quoted to show their interpretation to be completely unfounded. Just as one Bible verse cannot be interpreted without the light of the rest of Scripture, Jefferson's quotes, the First Amendment and Article VI of the Constitution gives meaning to the others. For 170 years, all these formed the basis for the decisions of the courts.

The First Amendment's "no establishment of religion" clause was for a very narrow purpose and stated very specifically the violations of establishing one national Christian denomination over another. It was never the intent of the Founding Fathers nor in any of their writings to lay aside Christianity or to allow other faiths an equal footing with Christianity but rather, as explained by Justice Story's *Commentaries:*

> *"The real object of the First Amendment was not to countenance, much less to advance, Mahommetanism, or Judaism, or infidelity, by prostrating Christianity; but to exclude all rivalry among Christian sects."* [97]

It is easily understood by the careful study of the thoughts of those who founded our nation, that they laid a foundation which they desired to see held throughout the ages to this generation and beyond, which was to prevent the Federal government's establishment of a singular national Christian denomination. The amendments and articles of the Constitution were intended as a one way street, not only to advantage Christianity's principles, but to protect the freedom of Christian principles to guide and influence government. The Constitution restricts government, but does not restrict Christianity. Another way to view it is that religion is free; the government is shackled.

It is a great paradox that the U.S. Supreme Court, one of the three separate powers of government, in pronouncing judgment after judgment, supposedly stating that government cannot have anything to do with religion, has actually made so many religious judgments that no other governing body, including the Church itself, has had so much to do with guiding religion in this nation. The courts have influenced, directed, impacted, turned upside down Christianity in America. The Supreme Court has become the great *"National Theology Board,"* placing itself above the Bible on moral issues of abortion, illicit behavior, when or where one can pray, place a nativity, etc., etc. If enemies to Judeo/Christian principles want to claim a "wall", then let it be understood that it is a one way street, grounded into law, containing many gates to which all Christian denominations were given keys to pass freely through. The purpose of this was to hold accountable and keep in check our government by demanding adherence to straight moral codes, to Judeo/Christian principles, along with the principles of self-government. The government has no key. The Constitution shackles the government and by valid law makes it powerless in regard to restraining religion — that word religion meaning specifically Christianity. Christians, not only have every right constitutionally to thread Christianity's principles throughout government, but they also have the right and responsibility to hold accountable every aspect of government, even in requiring that office holders believe in God. Our Founders believed that any oath or affirmation, including that of elected officials, to uphold the Constitution *presupposes a belief in God.* George Washington and the Founders believed that belief in God was a requirement to holding office, so to fulfill their oaths of office. Washington states:

> *"Where is the security for property, for reputation, for life, if the sense of* ***religious*** *obligation desert the oaths…?"* [98]

They saw this as fundamental and never considered in their wisdom that this was any sort of religious test. Rather, it was for them common logic that if you did not believe in God, you could not be trusted to give a sincere and honest oath, testimony, or, once in office, make just decisions. They held it as constitutional that an atheist could not hold office or give testimony since these things required a belief in a higher power. What inclination does an atheist have to keep the oath or give honest testimony or just judgements and decisions, if he has no fear of negative consequences in breaking an oath, giving false testimony, or making evil judgements? There is no fear because there is no belief in a higher power that avenges the violation, the lie, or the evil judgement in this life or much less in the next. Washington's words, referring to the reasons why atheists could not take office, argued that the consequences of deserting the religious obligation of the oath would "fruit" into the loss of the security of private property and of life. Washington's wisdom is proven in our midst by the decisions of non-believing office holders of today who do not believe in God's laws and statutes. It is proven by their decisions to rampantly take away life through abortion, as well as the taking of private property.

Many office holders today publicly profess belief in Christianity, but their actions are atheistic, thereby proving what they truly profess in their heart. In essence, an atheist would not have a proper conscience to be credible in upholding the oaths, testimonies, decisions, and judgements rendered. This shows us that no one needs to be sensitive to an atheist's belief or accommodate them on a level constitutional playing field. This statement of not accommodating atheists on a "level constitutional playing field" may stun many mentalities. If it does, you must change your mentality, adapting back to the old mentalities that guided this nation right up to a few decades ago. God is God. He exists, and for a professed atheist to believe that He does not exist, does not cause God's existence to cease. So who do we honor? The atheist or God? Who do we respect? The atheist's belief that God doesn't exist or those who believe He does exist? Both cannot be accommodated equally. One will offend; one will be offended. It is one way or the other. So whose way is to win out? Throughout the last decades, it has been the atheist's mentality. However, it is time to make all things right. An atheist does not have an equal right to prevail in his views or to be accommodated in law. He has the right to excuse himself, nothing more. The Christian attitude toward the atheist or non-believer is to be one of love and respect. The atheist has a free will to choose not to believe. He does not have a right to impose his belief and mentality into our laws or institutions.

On the other hand, as a Christian nation, we have a right to impose Christian principles into our laws and institutions and to expect behavior based on them. It is to the advantage of the atheist, pagan, Christian and those of all other faiths to be governed in all of society by the *"principles of Christianity."* It is to the disadvantage of atheists, pagans, Christians, and those of other faiths to be governed in all society by atheistic and pagan beliefs. There is no need for studies and research to examine this truth. In former times, all abided by Christian principles, even those who did not believe or practice a belief, and society was generally safe, wholesome, and righteous. Now many abide by secular atheistic principles and society is unsafe, loathsome, and unrighteous. The situation is now rapidly digressing into a grave crisis for our nation, endangering our continuance.

Yes, a Muslim in this country is to be respected, but he is to be taught and must learn what our Founders placed into law and the way we are supposed to be governed, and he is to abide in society by these laws, mutually respecting that this is a Christian nation. This includes that any oaths taken must be taken upon a Bible.

John Quincy Adams on July 4, 1837, stated that the American Revolution:

> *"connected in one* ***indissoluble*** *bond,* ***principles*** *of civil government to the* ***principles*** *of Christianity."* [99]

In the quote above, what was indissoluble? The principles of civil government and the *"bond"* relating to and uniting them to the principles of Christianity! What are the efforts of darkness in our nation presently doing, except moving to dissolve this bond? Reread John Quincy Adams' very important quote about this 'welded bond' and then you will understand the mentalities of our Founders and what foundation our nation rests upon. It is a *case closed* quote. Think about it. Reason it out.

As late as 1952, it was still ingrained and known through law that this nation was a Christian nation. An exhaustive study by the U.S. Supreme Court themselves declared it so.

> *"In 1892 the United States Supreme Court made an exhaustive study of the supposed connection between Christianity and the government of the United States. After researching hundreds of volumes of historical documents, the Court asserted 'these references add a volume of unofficial declarations to the mass of organic utterances that this is a religious people...a Christian nation.' Likewise in 1931, Supreme Court Justice George Sutherland reviewed the 1892 decision in relation to another case and reiterated that Americans are*

> *a 'Christian people' and in 1952 Justice William O. Douglas affirmed 'we are a religious people and our institutions presuppose a Supreme Being.'"* [100]

From the original writings of our Forefathers, a perverse twisting has taken place by the same mind-set held by those of the "Religion of Liberalism," who made the nine demands. This mind-set has led citizens to falsely believe that there is to be no Christian direction or influence in government and/or public life. It was never the intent, never even a remote thought in any of the minds of our Forefathers that Christianity, which was foundationed and threaded throughout our nation's founding and 170 years of its operation, was ever suppose to be segregated from the State. It is a shame against our Christ that many Christians have prayed so little, studied history so little, discerned so little, as to result in such widespread acceptance among Christians to have allowed the denial of Christ throughout our government, our institutions and all bodies across America. This acceptance among Christians is equivalent to some of those early Christians who committed apostasy by denying Christ when their lives were threatened, the latter being only a few degrees lower in graveness.

In regard to what the Christian response should be to the nine demands of the Religion of Liberalism, as was written earlier, two things must first be addressed and understood. The first is to educate ourselves concerning what is truly behind the separation of Church and State and our Forefathers' vision for our nation, which was just covered. The *second* is that we, as Christians, do not have to make demands to counter the demands of "Liberalism," as we have the authority of truth in achieving our aims. Therefore, we can make *a declaration* of our aims. These aims, however, do not exclude Christians themselves, who must be the first to be convicted to adopt them.

The intent of the nine demands made by the "Religion of Liberalism" was to wrestle away something they did not have at the time the demands were made – that being the power to achieve the demands. Each point started with 1. "We demand… 2. We demand… 3. We demand…," etc. Because Christians were so strong, all those who promoted the anti-god Religion of Liberalism could do was demand and wait...while snaking their way through our educational, political, and religious systems, which eventually led to political and judicial success in the courts. They were content to weaken Christians and Christian principles step-by-step, to achieve results over the long-term. They understood as well that education was necessary before they could expect successful results. To cancel the Religion of Liberalism's inroads, all we have to do is strengthen the people to live more fully the Christian life. The following are Nine Declarations for Restoration of Christian Principles. We must hereby institute these declarations throughout our nation to re-Christianize society by returning to the Christian principles which will secure our children's future and our nation's continuance.

1. To our God and to our non-believing brothers, we hereby seek forgiveness for our bad witness in failing to live the Sabbath. Even though some non-believers are not wanting the Sabbath lived in society, we have hurt the possibility of convicting them by our not doing so. With sincerity, we Christians seek and ask forgiveness for our hypocrisy.

   We hereby insist, holding each other accountable, that we as Christians honor the Natural Laws of God and keep holy the Sabbath. Christian numbers throughout our nation, comprising over 84 percent of the population, must begin to reflect this in general society in order to restore laws which keep businesses, government, and non-life threatening bodies closed on the Sabbath. Christians are to be mindful that both the Old and New Testaments show that a nation is not so much protected by its armaments, as by its way of life. The call to return to the Sabbath must be understood as the security for our nation, through which abundant blessings will pour forth upon the land and its people. Without compromise, we must return to the former Sabbath observance and fully restore God's law and Natural Law, as "the law" of our land.

2. We hereby insist that the Freedom of Speech that was enjoyed by all churches and non-profit institutions for the first 170 years of this nation's existence, be reinstated as a guaranteed right of the Declaration of Independence and the U.S. Constitution as is granted by the First Amendment, and that the 1950 Act of Congress that unlawfully took this right of freedom of speech away, be hereby repealed.

3. We hereby insist that the harassment and court marshalling of paid military chaplains who are being punished for speaking Christ's name publicly at various military and public functions, cease and desist, and new military regulations be established to return to their original roots of honoring and proclaiming the Lord's name, with-

out embarrassment. In the military, it is considered more important to avoid offending Muslims or those of other faiths who may be offended by the "Word" Jesus, than offending and rejecting Jesus Christ, Himself, by forbidding His name to be mentioned in prayer. This is a gravely serious offense. In recognition that the United States of America is a Christian Nation, all other restrictions must cease against Christian chaplains and those designated to speak for the faith, be they employed by Congress, the State, the Military, or any other public institution. We insist on protection for this freedom of Christian prayer, as well as full restoration of our nation's Christian Heritage in government, military, civil, and private bodies throughout our nation.

4. We hereby insist that our Christian heritage be acknowledged and honored throughout our government, especially in regard to Christian religious services. That religious services continue to be allowed by the government in all areas where they are still performed and where any of these services were abolished, they be restored. We hereby intensely insist on the right of the use of the Bible in all school systems, which was a constitutional

principle, as well as common law for 170 years, until the 1947 Emerson vs Board of Education case. The Bible is to be allowed without prohibition or harassment by teachers, professors, or other school/government/court officials, or any of those of the minority opinion who object. Also teachers, school officials, parents, etc., will be freely, without restriction, able to participate with the students. Teachers must unite, discarding the NEA, forming new organizations to rebel against the state school system and the anti-god spirit. They should defy any and all rules that try to stop them. God is removed out of school, so there is no protection and there will not be until He is reintroduced. Many Christian schools, because they have so many secular aspects within them as to be more secular than Christian, are not excluded. There are no students or teachers safe in a system which has denied the Judeo/Christian ethic principles and the Christian faith. It is a reality of our time that it is a matter of life or death. God is protection. Where God is not, there is loss of protection and death.

5. We hereby insist the official designated government-honored religious days of Christmas, Eas-

ter and Thanksgiving be renewed and restored to their full meaning and all redefining by revisionist policies concerning and referring to these days as nonsectarian* cease throughout local, state, and federal agencies, as well as all bodies of our nation. Also rejected is the secularization of these days to de-emphasize their religious significance. Be it known that Christmas, Easter and Thanksgiving are to be recognized in their origins by all government, civil, and educational bodies, as in former days, as holy days, rather than "pleasurable holidays" as progressive revisionist mentalities are conditioning the nation's people to accept.

That Fourth of July, Memorial Day, Veteran's Day, Patriot's Day, etc. be held as sacred days of reflection upon our nation that was destined to become "One nation, under God," and that recognition be given of God's repeated actions of protection over our nation throughout our history on these days.

With equal insistence, we call for the absolute removal of the revisionist scheme, known as

* Nonsectarian means not affiliated with or restricted to a particular religious group. In this case, denying these days as Christian.

"President's Day" and the return to honoring the Father of our Nation, known as George Washington, on his own birthday of February 22nd. This day will be proclaimed throughout all government, civil, institutional and educational bodies so to encourage the study of his life and the principles by which he lived. The same adherence is insisted upon in honoring Abraham Lincoln on his own birthday of February 12th by the Nation's governing bodies so to reflect upon his life and the direct example he gave in restoring our nation to the morals and principles of its Declaration of Independence. On both of these days, the nation's governing bodies be closed so to honor, respect and reflect upon the lives of these great Fathers of our nation. In addition, the celebration of these days may not be moved for the convenience of making a three day weekend, which results in a loss of reverence and loss of reflection for the actual birth dates and their significance.

6. We hereby insist that all oaths and the swearing in of all individuals for office holders, as well as for testimony for all government, civil, education-

al and public organizations be affirmed with the physical use of the right hand placed upon the Holy Bible and the words, "So help me God," as has been the accepted procedure in the founding of our nation by our Forefathers and carried on through common law. Wherever this has been removed, a full restoration is insisted upon.

7. We insist, with the Founding Fathers of this nation, that no Christian denomination be recognized over and above another by the federal government. We, however, insist as did our Forefathers, that the whole of the Christian faith, encompassing all denominations, be advantaged in law, as was common law for nearly 200 years, and be free from harassment and persecution for its teachings. We insist that states take back constitutionally given rights to encourage Christianity, its principles, and its morals throughout its governing bodies. Further insistence that no privilege or advantage is given to secular worldviews over and above Christian worldviews. Where any and all governing bodies have advantaged secular worldviews while disadvantaging the Judeo/Christian Biblical worldview, they hereby cease and desist. We insist that Christians

be protected in all work places and public and private institutions from harassment and threats when they voice Judeo/Christian Biblical worldviews in response to or in opposition to secular worldviews.

8. We hereby insist that Christian principles and morality be returned as the standard for all laws and as the guiding rule for interpreting of all laws in our nation. We hereby obstinately declare and insist that all law be based upon unbroken and unconstrued precedence. In the establishment of our nation, precedents were set, and as law rulings progressed from one to another, it must be understood that we strayed from those beginning original precedents, which led to the present degradation of society, therefore, all laws, based on broken precedents, generationed down from the ***"points of breakage"*** of precedence or construed precedence must be recognized and taught by all government, civil, and educational bodies of our land as invalid laws. Be it known that all laws, no matter how many, back to the *"point of breakage"* from precedence, must be struck down by all judges, all enforcement bodies, and by "we the people." These laws are not constitutional

because they are not based in the morality and principles set forth by the Declaration of Independence. The Declaration sets forth the original precedents of laws for our nation from Natural Law. It is especially noted that Christian judges are to take courage to rectify false precedented law such as the 1947 Supreme Court ruling of Emerson vs the Board of Education which led to the 1963 ruling against school prayer. As this ruling had no valid precedence, it must be ignored as an invalid law. We insist upon the righting of what was both common and written law for almost 200 years, whereby students, teachers, and officials, etc., were free to pray Christian prayers, unrestricted, throughout all government, military, civil and educational bodies of our nation.

Roe vs Wade is another example of a law that is invalid as it broke from precedence of all preceding laws of its kind since our nation's inception. Instead of doing as Thomas Jefferson said, of "conforming to the probable meaning" of past laws, the decision from Roe vs Wade resulted in the Supreme Court construing from past laws what the desired, not probable, outcome should be, which was to legalize abortion. Decades of laws are now invalid as they have been based on the invalid law of Roe vs Wade, which created a false bridge of precedence. As these laws are invalid, city councils are to deny building permits and business licenses to abortion clinics. Health departments must close down these clinics which operate under the ruling of the invalid law of Roe vs Wade. All judges are to base all future decisions back to the "points of breakage" and of valid precedents, made valid not by man's opinions, but because they were connected and continuously "generationed" back to Natural Law, which was the valid basis for the Declaration of Independence and upon which the Declaration was foundationed.

Reason with truth: If a judgement was made that broke from historical precedence and this "point of breakage" was construed 'valid' in order to erroneously give rulings legitimacy, it certainly should be insisted that to by-pass laws "backwards," or in other words, previous to the "points of breakage" to reset law upon that true original precedence, also is valid. Judges must take courage to make the same bold moves legally that those who ruled in favor of the "point of breakage" did illegally. The judges, who broke from precedence, did not consider the havoc that would be caused to society by their decisions. Neither should judges who reverse these decisions consider the havoc that will be caused in returning society back to the good. There can be no fear of negative consequences of this action, even if the system is turned upside down, since it is a return to truth and the abandoning of the deviation from truth which can only result in long-term, positive consequences for good, the same consequences which our nation thrived under for 200 years previously.

9. We hereby insist that creation by a Creator be taught in all public institutions of learning in equity to Darwinism. That modern science's *objections* disproving Darwin's theory of Evolution, be taught side by side with the theory of evolution. Christian teachers both in public and private schools should immediately educate themselves and initiate these teachings in their classrooms. Defy the regulations and restrictions that are aimed at preventing criticism of Darwin's theory, just as Christ did to the learned scribes of His day. Challenge the educational establishments as to

why school textbooks aren't being updated with the modern scientific data that casts the shadow of falsehood over how Darwin's theory is being promoted and taught to promote atheism. All Christian teachers seeking truth should hold their ground in allegiance to God against the harassments and threats for challenging the god of Darwinism, just as the revisionists did in bringing about the "Darwinist teaching denial" of creation. These atheistic teachings cannot be supported by science, where as known realities of creation makes known an existence of a Creator. Just as science has never proven a black hole, but accepts its existence because of the evidence of stars being drawn into it, a Creator teaching of creation can more than prove itself with known realities that logically and intelligently shed light on the mystery of the earth, nature, and the universe when broken down and studied. In addition, many phenomenon defy science through suspending the laws of nature or reversal of physical laws which can only point back as a common denominator to a Superior Being over the actions of the universe.

CHAPTER NINE

THE DECLARATION OF INDEPENDENCE GAVE THE LEGAL BASIS FOR THE LEGAL AMERICAN REVOLUTION IN 1776

THE DECLARATION OF INDEPENDENCE GIVES THE LEGAL BASIS FOR A LEGAL REVOLUTION NOW

To institute these Nine Declarations for the Restoration of Christian Principles, we must start by going back to America's very beginnings and seek the wisdom of our Fathers who will speak to us from generations long past. We must then foundation our lives, our families and our institutions upon this wisdom so to rekindle and reawaken the dreams of our Fathers throughout this great land. We must all "go back to self school" and re-educate, reform and reacquaint ourselves with the truths of who we are as a people. When was the last time you sat down and read The Declaration of Independence? The Declaration is not just a historical document, it's a locked and unevolving permanent document that holds the key to freedom, giving continued life to every generation unto today. To lose sight of this document is to put our precious freedoms into precarious hands.

The following should be read slowly and carefully and not only understood but learned.

Every corporation in America has a charter or articles of incorporation, which brings the entity into existence. Caritas of Birmingham has one. I.B.M. has one. They also have what are called by-laws for the governance of the corporation.

The articles of incorporation brings the corporation into existence and identifies the corporation's purpose and intent. The by-laws establish its governance. In the case of America's foundation, the Declaration of Independence is the "articles of incorporation" that brought our nation into existence. The U.S. Constitution provides the "by-laws" of our nation and explains how it will be governed. The Declaration of Independence (the articles) cannot be superseded or done away with by the Constitution (the by-laws). There are no clear moral values of right and wrong within the U.S. Constitution because the Founding Fathers had already placed the moral value *in* the Declaration of Independence. The Constitution is not the foundational document of the United States, rather the Declaration of Independence is the foundational document of our Constitution's form of government. In Article VII, the Constitution attaches itself to the Declaration of Independence.[101] It's very important to understand that the Constitution **cannot be** interpreted independently of the

Declaration of Independence, as the Declaration sets forth the "principles" of how the American government would operate. The two documents are not independent but interdependent on each other. The Declaration of Independence had such a continued importance that all the Founding Fathers dated their government acts from the signing of the Declaration of Independence, July 4, 1776, not by the date of the signing of the Constitution.[102]

John Quincy Adams said that the virtues which were "infused into the Constitution" were the principles "proclaimed in the Declaration of Independence," further stating that the Constitution's platform of virtue, its republic character, are from the principles within the Declaration of Independence. [103] Nearly 100 years later, Abraham Lincoln said:

> *"(Our fathers) established these great self-evident truths that ...their posterity might look up again to the Declaration of Independence and take courage to renew that battle which their FATHERS began, so that truth...and Christian virtues might not be extinguished from the land...Now, my countrymen, if you have been taught doctrines conflicting with the great landmarks of the Declaration of Independence...let me entreat you to come back...*

come back to the truths that are in the Declaration of Independence." [104]

What was in Lincoln's thinking, by the above statement? Why does he say to look again upon the Declaration of Independence and to take courage? What was he contemplating in his office when he wrote the above? Study the words carefully and you will understand what he was saying. Abraham Lincoln was accused of violating the Constitution, he was never accused of violating the Declaration. He admitted that to save the Constitution, he had to violate it. He did so by the principles rooted in the Declaration. Because the Declaration cannot be superseded, Lincoln actually forced the Constitution into an inferior position to the Declaration, using the principles of the Declaration to do it. On one occasion, Abraham Lincoln was confronted by his Secretary of Treasury, Salmon P. Chase, who was objecting to Lincoln and actions he was taking, saying they were in violation of the Constitution. 's response follows:

" (told Chase) *...the story of an Italian captain who ran his vessel on a rock and knocked a hole in her bottom. He set his men to pumping, and he went to pray before a figure of the Virgin Mary in the bow of the ship. The leak gained on them. It looked at last as if the vessel would go down with*

> *all on board. The captain, at length, in a fit of rage at not having his prayers answered, seized the figure of the Virgin and threw it overboard. Suddenly the leak stopped, the water was pumped out, and the vessel got safely to port. When docked for repairs the statue of the Virgin Mary was found stuck, head foremost, in the hole.*
>
> Lincoln (then said), *'I don't intend precisely to throw the Virgin Mary overboard, and by that I mean the Constitution, but I will stick it in the hole if I can. These rebels are violating the Constitution in order to destroy the Union; I will violate the Constitution, if necessary, to save the Union; and I suspect, Chase, that our Constitution is going to have a rough time of it before we get done with this row.'"* [105]

Rebels today are violating the Constitution in order to destroy our nation. We allow it because by stopping the rebels, we think we infringe upon their constitutional rights. Our nation is being destroyed by foundationless "constitutional rights."—rights which do not exist. In our time, as in Lincoln's, it is necessary to reestablish the Declaration of Independence and its principles, which supersedes the Constitution, in order to reestablish and save the Constitution. Look at the dates. The Declaration was adopted on July 4, 1776. The Constitution was signed on September 17, 1787, and not ratified until 1789. Over 11 years later! The Declaration, which most everyone ignores and does not understand what it declares, pre-dates our Constitution by 11 years, 2 months, and 14 days! Yes, our country used the Articles of Confederation in part of the interim but they did not go into effect until March 1, 1781. Look again at the dates. That is still 4 years, 7 months and 26 days behind the Declaration of Independence. Our Constitution cannot exist without the Declaration, but our Declaration did exist for some time without the Constitution. Therefore, we must always first look to the first document. The reason our nation has gone astray, is because we began operating solely on the Constitution, without referencing the Declaration. To renew our nation, the Declaration, applying it to today, must be carefully studied for the legal basis of restoring our nation and a basis for a legal revolution. Look to the Declaration, not to the corrupt political processes, for the basis of renewal. The Declaration of Independence, carefully studied, gives a legal basis for a revolution to restore America. Even Thomas Jefferson said:

> *"The tree of liberty must be refreshed from time to time with blood of patriots and tyrants...God forbid we should ever be twenty years without such a*

> *rebellion. What country can preserve its liberty if their rulers are not warned from time to time that their people preserve the spirit of resistance? Let them take arms."* [106]

Abraham Lincoln told his fellow countrymen to come back to the Declaration. Lincoln did not say, come back to the Constitution. If it was necessary to do so 100 years after the Constitution was ratified, then why would it be different for us in our present crisis? It is by the craft of satan, with his master intellect, that the courts, over the last 50 years, divorced the Constitution from the Declaration of Independence. The Declaration is the conscience for the Constitution. The Constitution will not hold the course as a stand alone document as the Declaration did. By standing alone as a document, divorced from the Declaration, judges become the conscience of the Constitution, with the Declaration no longer fulfilling that role. This is illegal. The Founding Fathers foresaw the possibility of this happening and were gravely concerned because even with all the checks and balances they instituted, if judges began overstepping their bounds, it would mean death to the republic. It is in this way that satan is attempting to steal our nation from the Divine Creator who was given sovereignty over the United States of America from its inception. The more Christians will educate themselves and teach their children, their families and their friends these truths, the sooner our nation will be healed.

The prince of darkness, satan, hates a document which first declared independence from an earthly kingdom, England, and then secondly, declared dependence upon God. In this way, the Declaration of Independence was a dual declaration. A primary reason of importance for minusing out the Declaration when interpreting the Constitution is to get away from the words *"the Laws of Nature and of Nature's God."* In this phrase, the Fathers of our nation found the legal basis for separation from England. But what do these words mean? To find their true meaning, we must look past the degradation of present word definitions to the original definitions as understood by our Founding Fathers. These are the only valid meanings, which can be applied to today.

Again, do not only read but learn the following three pages. It is the result of much prayer to explain in a brief, simple way what many do not fully grasp or realize.

The Fathers of our nation were greatly influenced by the writings of Englishman, Sir William Blackstone, who was mentioned earlier in this book. From Blackstone, the Fathers of our nation fashioned the ideas of liberty and placed them in the language we are familiar with in the Declaration of Independence. However, truth always trails back to the source of truth, which is public revelation, known as the Holy Scripture. Therefore, Blackstone was hardly the originator of such ideas, as these concepts were being defined within the Church even before the Magna Carta came into being in the early part of the 13th century. By the 16th century, two centuries before the Declaration of Independence was written, a Jesuit priest by the name of Fr. Francisco Suarez was "the chief champion of the rights of the people" who fought against the doctrine that kings were kings by "divine rights." Prominent Church leaders also echoed these doctrines in the same century.

It is from Blackstone's writings that the words and understanding of the *laws of nature and of nature's God,* written in our Declaration, were taken. *Laws of Nature* (or Nature's Laws) are laws God made which apply to Creation. Laws of gravity, for example, cannot be changed. God created matter and marked it with certain principles that it can never deviate from. Vegetation and animal life are governed by the same laws and they must follow these laws involuntarily to exist. And so, the first part of that phrase as written in the Declaration, *"the laws of nature,"* are laws that are characterized by a rule of action dictated by some Superior Being. Blackstone called them involuntary laws of governance. The second part of the phrase as written in the Declaration, *"laws of nature's God,"* pertain to God's Holy Word, the Sacred Scriptures. Blackstone said:

> *"The doctrine thus delivered* (by God) *we call the revealed or Divine law, and they are to be found only in the Holy Scripture. These precepts, when revealed...*(when compared to nature are) *a part of the original Law of Nature."* [107]

From the Laws of Nature and the Laws of Nature's God, we arrive at what is the revealed Natural Law. Natural law is law that man declares in submission to *"the laws of nature and of nature's God."* Laws of creation (*Nature's Law*) and God's revealed law, the Scriptures (*of Nature's God*) are superior to natural law because they are declared by God, Himself, while man's law (natural law) is only the human reasoning of what we imagine the Divine Law to be. Nature's Law, together with God's Law of Revelation, Holy Scripture, are the foundations by which Blackstone said, "depends all human law," which is Natural Law. [108] This might sound confusing but it is important to fully grasp the previous statement before reading further so reread if necessary beginning at "The Fathers of our nation were greatly influenced ..." Reread until you understand. This will enable you to understand what follows.

Nature's Law + God's Revealed Law = Natural Law. Natural law applies equally (equal station) to everyone upon the face of the earth. The Declaration of Independence states: **"(the) equal station to which the Laws of Nature and of Nature's God entitle them..."** Therefore, there can be no law made upon the earth by anyone or any nation that any man anywhere is bound to obey when the law is against natural law. To obey laws against natural law puts us in transgression against Divine Law and, therefore, the law is invalid and is to be defied as if it doesn't exist because there is no basis for it to be. All law is to be based on God's law or it is invalid.* Therefore, the "authority" for human law is derived from nature's laws and nature's God, from which, Blackstone said, "depends all human law." By this authority, Pope Benedict communicated to citizens of Spain who work in adoption agencies, that they are to defy Spain's new laws of illicit marriages and adoptions and refuse to fill out any paperwork or grant adoption of children to illicit and unnatural

* God, of course, grants liberty to man to make civil law that is left up to man's reason, such as how much to import, limits of speed when driving, etc. These are defined rules of conduct that we are obligated to obey. But even these laws are derived from the authority of the Laws of Nature and of Nature's God.

marriage unions. [109] Spain's new laws are against nature and nature's God, and therefore, against natural law and have no authority. Therefore, Spain's citizens are *obliged* to defy them. They would not be disobeying, since the law disobeys natural law. No human law against natural law is valid. The Catechism of the Catholic Church confirms this:

> *"The natural law is written and engraved in the soul of each and every man, because it is human reason ordaining him to do good and forbidding him to sin...But this command of human reason would not have the force of law if it were not the voice and interpreter of a higher reason to which our spirit and our freedom must be submitted."* [110]

> *"The natural law is immutable and permanent throughout the variations of history; it subsists under the flux of ideas and customs and supports their progress...Even when it is rejected in its very principles, it cannot be destroyed or removed from the heart of man. It always rises again in the life of individuals and societies."* [111]

Once the preceding is grasped, it can be understood that we have a duty to do what the Declaration states. Read slowly, comprehending and absorbing each word and its meaning.

"(The People) are endowed by their Creator with certain unalienable Rights, that among these are Life, Liberty and the Pursuit of Happiness—that to secure these Rights, Governments are instituted among Men, deriving their just Powers from the Consent of the Governed, that whenever any Form of Government becomes destructive of these Ends, it is the Right of the People to alter or to abolish it...But when a long Train of Abuses and Usurpations, pursuing invariably the same Object, evinces a Design to reduce them under absolute Despotism, it is their Right, it is their Duty, to throw off such Government, and to provide new Guards for their future Security... "

Go back to our beginning—to the first document of which the establishment of our nation was founded, instituted over 11 years before our present Constitution was drafted and ratified. Lincoln understood that in order to save the nation, we must return to what declared it into being. We must act upon our Declaration to save our Republic. These writings are not about endorsing anyone or any party. As already stated, the present political party system is corrupt, incapable of being renewed. It is so far from operating within the framework of Godly principles that it is as Thomas Jefferson said:

> *"When once a republic is corrupted, there is no possibility of remedying any of the growing evils but by removing the corruption and restoring its* ***lost principles****; every other correction is either useless or a new evil."* [112]

It, therefore, is without the integrity necessary to be reformed. Those lost principles are Christian principles that are found threaded throughout our Declaration. Christians must realize it is impossible for our current government to be renewed from within. Our nation and its Declaration of Independence and Constitution have been betrayed and a surrogate system, a third party, has placed itself between "we the people" and the Declaration and Constitution. The surrogate system must be cast out. Something new must rise up by the hand of God, just as Christ rose from the tomb. As Pope Benedict said at the 14th Station:

> *"Faith is truly a little lamp, yet it is the only lamp that can light up the night of the world: and its lowly light blends with the light of a new day... so the story does not end with the tomb, instead it bursts forth from the tomb...it happened and it will happen again!"* [113]

We must pray, change our lives and be ready to seize the moment when God grants us the opportunity to complete-

ly restore our nation back to its foundation. Signer of the Declaration of Independence, Benjamin Rush, sat next to John Adams in Congress when the Declaration was read. Rush whispered to him if he thought they would succeed in their struggle with England. Adams answered, "Yes— if we fear God and repent of our sins." [114]

Our Lady once said:

November 21, 1983

> **"...It is necessary to make them come back to their promises, which were made at the beginning, and to pray."**

June 23, 2002

> **"My children, I am calling you back to the beginning..."**

To know what to go back to, you must learn what happened in the beginning of our nation. What did the Declaration do? What rights does it give us today? If we do not educate ourselves and our children to the dreams *our Fathers had* in the beginning of our nation's founding, they will slip away from us and we will lose the way. Deuteronomy 4:9 says:

> ***"...take care and be earnestly on your guard not to forget the things which your own eyes have***

seen, nor let them slip from your memory as long as you live, but teach them to your children and to your children's children."

On the other hand, Hosea 4:6, states:

"My people perish for want of knowledge."

John Adams said:

Liberty cannot be preserved without a general knowledge among the people. We must know our beginnings to determine our future. If we do not, others will determine it." [115]

The school at Caritas, *Our Lady of Victory School*, usually has a theme that becomes the foundation for each school year. The community teachers request something to be written each September, reflecting that theme and how it connects to the way of life of the Community of Caritas. The following was written for Caritas' 2003–2004 school year.

The Sacred Bond

HE FOUND A SECLUDED SPOT AND PLACED THE DIRT. He wanted to make a strong foundation. He put water on both sides. He wanted it to be hidden, for it was a gift to his mother.

On two occasions, it would be found,*a but he managed to keep it secret until he was ready to give it to Her and then it happened. It was found. And soon after he gave it to her who by then was QUEEN with many titles.
He called it...AMERICA.

The upper part He peopled from all over the earth and then did the impossible, by miraculously uniting these people of different backgrounds.
He put in their hearts an illumination,
to build a nation as the world had never seen.
Never in the history of the world had such a diverse group of people come together for such a common cause, and though the divine was involved,
only the prayerful understood it.

So vivid was this vision that the original Founders
recognized clearly all was orchestrated
by the hand of Providence.
And now the veil lifts further, to reveal that
this nation's existence from the beginning,
was to be used by the QUEEN
for Her purposes of Peace, consecrated to Her
as Her instrument, Her tool,
to bring stability to all other lands.*b

A foundation to build upon, a land to bring freedom

such as the world has never known before,
to all people of the earth.
For the prayerful, discerning heart, this is easy to see. For the one without prayer,
it is impossible to understand.

The UNITED STATES OF AMERICA, being consecrated to its patroness, the VIRGIN MARY, is united to Her in a SACRED BOND to be used for peace, as no other land
or nation has ever been throughout all of history.

Her enemy, trying to take it away from Her,
divided it from within,*c but She Herself
came back to reclaim it as QUEEN OF THE SOUTH.*d
As gold, She now purifies it to make it one,*e
united, strong, shimmering from sea to sea;
America the Beautiful, the QUEEN's necklace,
Her Son's rod...for peace.

AMERICA...
MAY GOD THY GOLD REFINE.
TILL ALL SUCCESS BE NOBLENESS, AND EV'RY GAIN DIVINE.

*A Friend of Medjugorje**f
September 11, 2003

*a, *b, *c, *d, *e, *f The description of each of these are found on page 481–482.

Deuteronomy's words ***"...teach your children and your children's children..."*** now haunt us because we have forgotten what we have seen, kept it not in our hearts, have let it slip away, nor have we taught our children. We have lost who we are. By not knowing who we are, we do not realize the authority we have and, therefore, do not know how to object and denounce the ungodly when they claim rights, which they do not have nor are entitled because they oppose Natural Law.

A few years ago, at our U.S. Military base in Ramstein, Germany, the Catholics were preparing to celebrate the Easter Vigil on a Saturday evening, in which several new members would be entering the Catholic faith. All other Christian denominations and those of the Jewish faith on the military base share the same chapel. In a spirit of cooperation, each group signs up for the time they want to reserve the room each week. The night of the Easter Vigil, however, everyone was dismayed. In the room right next door to the Mass, another group was holding its services. This group had recently petitioned the United States Military to be recognized as a "religious" group so as to have the same rights and protection as all religions. They were granted recognition as a "religion," and so were given the same rights to a place of worship as the Christians and the Jews. They reserved a room the same night as the Easter Vigil, from 9:00 p.m. to midnight. Who was this group that would be holding their worship service right next door to the Catholics celebrating the death and Resurrection of their Lord, Jesus Christ? They were a group of witches called wiccans, and they had gathered for the practice of witchcraft. Every one of the various faiths were astounded that the military would allow this. They also learned that as every religion of the military is assigned a chaplain's assistant from the military, that the wiccans now had that right to claim as well. They were assigned a Catholic chaplain as their advisor. The military's decision was supposedly based from the rule that the "law is blind" in regard to expression of religion as a constitutional right. However, if decision makers in the military were educated to our nation's founding and to our Forefather's views, and what paganism and devil worship vs religion is, they would have known that no such right exists for the practice of witchcraft under the U.S. Constitution and adamantly refused to acknowledge the wiccan's request.

It was never the intention of our Forefathers that the Constitution would be used to give the practice of witchcraft a constitutional right under freedom of expression of religion. This false right is a clear example showing how word meanings have been changed over time by pagan revisionists. "Revisionist" is a nice name for nasty actions of people whose agenda is to rewrite history, so that they can force the nation's acceptance of countless immoral, anti-god behavior which otherwise would never be accepted or allowed. These various groups have reshaped American culture through education and the courts. By changing and reinterpreting history, they are able to promote their message, thereby, changing also the present and even the future of our nation. Present-day decisions, when deciding which course to take for the future, are normally influenced by past experiences, either our own or others, existing documents, common law, the heritage and customs of a people, etc. If existing documents, common law, past and/or historical experiences can be changed, manipulated, altered, and/or ignored altogether, one can then reshape the future course of decisions. How is this achieved? By creating a vacuum for 'impulsive' decision-making, grounded on nothing more solid than whims and feelings.

The course that was originally set for our nation by existing documents, past experiences, etc... has been redirected. These revisionists have contradicted Our Lady's words to "fulfill the dream your fathers '*had*'" and Her message to "*go back as it was in the beginning.*" satan's minions, with the help of some humans, are very active in revising history. Through not living God's commands, Christians lack wisdom and knowledge of standing against these tactics and, therefore, many are deceived into believing that it is a constitutional right to let wicca services have equal access to a chapel as Easter Mass services. Even though those in the military who made the decision may disagree with wicca services, they give way to it, conditioned in their thinking that they have to do so, because some falsely class wicca under religion. If instead Christians were honoring the Commandments and had wisdom and integrity, they would have known they had every legal right to revolt, as Jesus did, with a whip in the Temple. Driving them out physically is clearly within the options of our Christian walk. To allow idolatry in a sacred place reserved for worship is just as serious, if not more so, as selling doves and pigeons in the Temple, "*Turning my Father's house into a den of thieves.*" Turning my Father's house into a den of witchcraft. Our Lady said on April 25, 1988:

> **"...Understand that the Church is God's palace... Churches deserve respect and are set apart as holy because God, Who became Man, dwells in them day and night..."**

The love Our Lady teaches is love God before anything else—love to God being more important and over love to a person. Love to a person being more important and over love to a right. What do you love more? A so-called "right" to perform witchcraft, desecrating a place where God is worshipped—or do you love God above such a claimed right?

Our Lady said:

October 2, 1986

> **"...nothing else is important to me, now not one person is important to me but God..."**

Following Jesus' example, the Catholic, Protestant and Jewish position had and has every moral right to remove idolatry from their place of worship, and yes to react strongly, even physically removing it as Jesus did. Jesus did not sin and neither would they have sinned by doing so, even if using whips. Jesus was not a wimp, but many Christians have turned into such spineless cowards. Judas Maccabees knew the Israelites had no future if he did not first purify the Israelites themselves and then second, purify the nation Israel of idol worship. Neither do we have a future, until we, with conviction and courage, say enough and draw the line in the sand that ungodly public actions will no longer be tolerated.

The real question must be asked, did these Christians, by tolerating the wiccans, sin by not acting? We've lost honor by not honoring God. Without honor, we have no integrity. A signer of the Declaration of Independence, Benjamin Rush, said:

> *"By integrity I mean…a strict coincidence between thoughts, words and actions."* [116]

Or in other words, according to David Barton in his book, Original Intent:

> *"Integrity is an alignment between words and actions regardless of whether in public or private matters."* [117]

Many Catholics and Protestants were upset about this wicca service. They spoke words about this all over the military base, but where were the words aligned with action? To stand by and let this wickedness take place is perverted tolerance and is clearly a sign of our weakness because of our own failure of not honoring God's precepts, particularly of the Sabbath—all of which, through our fault, now allows others to violate the First Commandment, 'Thou shall not have other gods before Me.' All of this has been achieved by revisionism through education, the media, etc.

Barton's Original Intent explains:

"Historical revisionism—a process by which historical fact is intentionally ignored, distorted, or misportrayed in order to maneuver public opinion toward a specific political agenda of philosophy. Historical revisionists accomplish their goals by:

1. *Ignoring those aspects of American heritage, which they deem to be politically incorrect and overemphasizes those portions which they find acceptable;*

2. *Vilifying* (to defame; slander) *the historical figures who embraced a position they reject; or*

3. *Concocting* (lying) *the appearance of widespread historical approval for a generally unpopular social policy."* [118]

So, how does a wicca service end up right next door to Easter Mass on an American military base? Through ignoring and changing the original meanings of words in the founding documents of our nation. The Declaration of Independence and the Constitution can only be understood by studying what the words that were placed in these documents meant at the time they were used by our Forefathers. If you rely on current dictionaries to understand the meaning of religion to interpret the First Amendment of the U.S. Constitution, you will find the following definition:

> *Religion: a set of beliefs concerning the cause, nature and purpose of the Universe.*[119]

This definition is all encompassing of any group to define anything. If you look up the word "religion" as our Founders understood it, in Webster's Dictionary of 1828, you will find:

> *Religion: includes a belief in the being and perfection of God, in the Revelation of His will to man, in man's obligation to obey His commands, in a state of reward and punishments and in man's accountableness to God; and also true Godliness or piety of life, with the practice of all moral duties.*[120]

A distance in meaning between the two definitions as wide as a galaxy.

The revisionist's modern definition of religion, illegally and falsely changed the meaning of the religion clause in the Constitution to now include non-religious groups. The Founders of the United States of America never intended, or for the intent of this writing, could *never have even 'dreamed'* that Christian worship would one day be held as equal to wicca, devil worship, idolatry, etc. So, we must interpret the Founders' "intent" by their beliefs based on their public and personal writings. There was no "intent" for these groups to have any rights under the religion protection clause of the Constitution, and they should have no power over Judeo/ Christian worship. Yet again, this is another example of what we have allowed through our loss of wisdom as a result of our denial of sin, which has resulted in the wicked man gaining more strength than we as Christians possess.

Noah Webster is considered one of the 250 Founding Fathers. We can look to his thoughts, his *dreams*, his understanding to see what Our Lady interceded before Jesus to have fulfilled, through Her words, "the dream your Fathers had." Barton writes:

> *"Noah Webster, while fitting into no specific group, was among the first to call for the Constitutional Convention...the man to whom many delegates, in the Constitutional Convention, turned to help lead the ratification efforts for the Constitution..."* [121]

His leadership, unquestionably, contributed much to the success of the American Revolution. A quote by Noah Webster, stated earlier in this writing, clearly shows the belief the Founders held, that for the United States Constitution and government to be preserved, it would depend upon the education of our children to the fact that Christianity is the basis of our government. Webster said:

> *"The Christian religion is the most important and one of the first things in which all children, under a free government, ought to be instructed…No truth is more evident to my mind than the Christian religion must be the basis of any government intended to secure the rights and privileges of a free people."* [122]

This is what Noah Webster thought. This was the *dream he had.* This is the man who put definitions to words, words used and written into the Declaration of Independence and U.S. Constitution by others who looked to Webster for leadership. The meanings and ideas he derived from words threaded through the thoughts of other Forefathers, from one to the other, which influenced what they wrote into the nation's founding. Yes, they struggled to form their opinions together, but they had clear and unified meanings of the words that were put into the documents of the Declaration and the Constitution. Yet, few today know or understand the essence of what these men painstakingly wrote, in order that all future generations would know the dreams they had. Revisionists have successfully distorted history.

In our day, not only are children not being educated about our nation's founding and of its laws based in Christian principles, but Christian adults are nearly as illiterate, if not entirely so. Our nation prospered and flourished for nearly two centuries since its founding because its vision was clearly defined in what America stood for. Now, however, America is floundering and has been for the last 50 years. Its future security hinges on realizing, once more, who we are and what we stand for. These writings have nothing to do with politics but simply that God founded this nation in a profound, marvelous, miraculous way, that we understand our Fathers' dreams and want to help Our Lady fulfill them. Founding Father Benjamin Rush said, in regards to our nation's divine origins:

> *"I am as perfectly satisfied that the Union of the States in its form and adoption is as much the work of a Divine Providence as any of the miracles recorded in the Old and New Testament."* [123]

A profound thought when you contemplate the miracle of God leading the Israelites out of Egypt through Moses and the Pharaoh, among countless other events, in the Old Testament, as well as the New.

The history changers do not want you to be educated about our nation's founding. In that way, God can be removed. Revisionists have touched and left their mark on every educational system, every textbook and even our Christian thought to bury who we are, in order to bury our nation. A prominent national figure said:

> *"I spent three years on my law degree at Yale Law School…I was assigned huge, leather-bound editions of legal cases to study and discuss. I read what lawyers and judges, professors and historians said **about** the Constitution. But never once was I assigned the task of reading the Constitution itself…(Afterwards) I have become a student of the Constitution, searching each line for its meaning and intent. It is amazing how much more you will learn when you quit studying about it and pick it up to read it for yourself."* [124]

Rather than go to direct sources, we are conditioned to go to indirect sources. Why was this student not told in school to simply read the Constitution? It requires more intellectual effort to read volumes rather than just reading the original documents, such as the U.S. Constitution or, as stated earlier, the Holy Father's comments, the President's speeches, or testimonies of actual witnesses of events. It is important to focus your information intake to what actually was written, what actually was said, what actually was carried out. The present day distortions through an outside party between the source and you for information is an insult to even the most minimally intelligent person. This is why Our Lady pointed to our "Fathers'" thoughts, their "dreams," so that you would learn by them directly. Our Lady excites our hearts to search the thoughts, ways, and lives of our Fathers so to know their dreams, in order that they may be fulfilled, so that Christ's presence may dwell in our hearts and our land; that Jesus Christ will manifest Himself in our land.

August 25, 1994

> **"...I am...praying for the gift of the presence of my beloved Son in your home country..."**

CHAPTER TEN

WE ARE AT WAR. HOW DO WE FIGHT?

It was necessary to walk you through the previous nine chapters to understand the following. After 27 years of apparitions, we now know through Our Lady's messages that we must *first* change the direction of our lives before we can expect change anywhere else. That to be holy is to fully embrace God's Ten Commandments. That love is best displayed by obedience. That Our Lady's call to peace is a call to peace with God. That once we reconcile with God through humble repentance, acknowledging and <u>recognizing</u> we are a weak, sinful people, then we can become the salt of the earth and can be strong in convicting. We then will have authority over wickedness, just as Judas Maccabees* did with the sword in purifying Israel. Except our "sword" will be with our thoughts, words, and actions, aligned with Scripture, enlightened by Our Lady's messages. This is the sword that will purify our nation and restore it to its former glory as we become a people who, with one heart, with Christ, across the land, will glorify God.

* Refer back to the footnote found on page 26.

Who are we in the heart of Our Lady? America is the freest nation on earth. Its ideals and principles of freedom are programmed in its founding document. Though to a much lower degree, it parallels and images the gift given to man by God, *free will.* But through sin, we have continued to lose freedom. More and more controls are being placed on us such as the widespread taking of lands through wrongful use of eminent domain. The freedom to even guide our families, even to raise our own food, is all being threatened, as well as so many other freedoms that are man's unalienable rights, given to him from God. Widespread taking of land? Socialist regulations? Cannot raise your own food? Are these just bloated statements?

Control Over Your Private Property

FIRST, THE TAKING OF YOUR LAND. Unalienable rights are certain natural rights which cannot be taken away because they are rights given to man by God. To work and to own private property is an unalienable right. Thirty years ago a plan began to develop to take lands from private citizens across the United States. We are now seeing this plan manifesting, under the name of Sustainable Development and Smart Growth. Sustainable Development cannot be defined in one or two sentences. Your understanding will become clearer as you read further through this book. Sustainable Development and Smart Growth root back to documents that reveal a grand plan to remove not only individual rights to own private property, but entails controlling virtually every aspect of individuals lives. "The Report of Habitat: The United Nations Conference on Human Settlements" held in Vancouver, May 31 – June 11, 1976, stated:

> *"Land...cannot be treated as an ordinary asset, controlled by individuals and subject to the pressures and inefficiencies of the market. Private land ownership is also a principal instrument of the accumulation and concentration of wealth, and therefore, contributes to social injustice; if unchecked, it may become a major obstacle in the planning and implementation of development schemes. The provision of decent dwelling and healthy conditions for people, can only be achieved if land is used in the interest of society as a whole. Public control** (government control) *of land use is, therefore, indispensable."* [125]

* When private land is handed over to the public, the public is never in control. A small select segment of the government or even private groups is the structure that controls.

This plan for the "greater good" is typical of the plans and schemes of a socialistic society. If the greater good of "society as a whole" benefits, does the greater good get to decide? No. Decisions will be made by a small, select group who decides to take away your "want" of private property for the good of all. Once you are conditioned that your "want" for a little or large piece of land is unjust, then you, along with everyone else, can accept that private ownership is social injustice and contributes to the sin of accumulation of wealth which is an obstacle to the leftist socialist mentality that runs it. Your "want," therefore, must be conditioned away, which is happening already, through the educational systems and information mediums. The United Nation's statement used the word **"schemes"** for their plans. Under the definition of "scheme" in Noah Webster's 1828 Dictionary, providentially and amazingly, it gives an example for scheme, making a point about removing your want as mentioned above. The following sentence was used to illustrate the meaning of the word:

> *"The stoical "scheme" of supplying our wants by lopping off our desires is like cutting off our feet when we want shoes."* [126]

This fits the definition of the U.N.'s "schemes" from their, quote, *"the planning and implementation of de-*

velopment schemes." The individual's right to own land and his desire for land is slowly being taken away through elaborate plans to burden him so much by means of adding costs to the purchase of the land he desires to own. Environmental impact fees, cost assessment fees, permit fees, along with many other fees and crippling regulations, eventually causes the "want" for his own piece of property to go away because of the burden of these costs and regulations, just as his desire for shoes goes away once his feet are cut off. How is this being achieved? You are told that you are free to live or to operate your business wherever you want to, but you won't "want" to when "identifiable costs and regulations" are placed upon you. You may be surprised to learn that the U.N. plans are being implemented all across our nation in small communities and neighborhoods such as where you, yourself, live. One adoption of the U.N. plans in the local community of Homewood, Alabama, demonstrates the control that is making its way through every community across America. The following statement was taken from the city's plan for development.

> *"People should be able to choose where they live and do business, as long as they pay the identifiable costs of those choices and do not impose*

unaccounted-for costs on other people or nature, now or in the future." [127]

Upon researching what this means, you will discover that you *will not* have a choice "where you live and do business" in that fees, permits, licenses, regulations, etc., will so exhaust your financial means that you will not be able to afford to choose except where the Sustainable Plans, implemented through Smart Growth, say you can live or do business, and that includes many having to move from areas you presently own. Even if you can afford to pay out "identifiable" costs, it is designed not to be economically feasible to do so. Take, for example, the story of David Bischoff.

> *"Three years ago the Orford, New Hampshire resident built a one-room cabin with no utilities in a pasture. What this simple shack lacked in amenities it made up for with its panoramic view of nearby hills and distant mountains. But Bischoff recently learned his room with a view comes with a steep price—seven times more valuable than if it had no view, to be exact—according to his property assessment. Bischoff and other rural residents in the region call this a "view tax." They're angry because they expect their property taxes to skyrocket...State officials deny there is a view tax.*

Instead, they call it a view factor...For Bischoff, his views added $140,000 to his property's underlying value of about $23,000. That could raise his property taxes from nearly $500 last year to more than $3,000." [128]

This is part of Sustainable Development and Smart Growth; to force people off their property and into "in-fill zones" of tightly packed, populated areas. If David Bischoff can't afford to pay several thousand dollars in a "view tax" each year, then what choice will he have except to give up his property? That is the basis of the U.N.'s Sustainable Plans: to open up large portions of land, free from human habitation, and crowd people into dense, highly populated areas. Henry Lamb, expert on Sustainable Development, wrote in an article entitled, "International Influence on Domestic Policy":

"The ultimate goal is...to convert at least half the land area of the United States into wilderness areas, off limits to humans, and to manage most of the rest of the land for conservation objectives, forcing humans to live in islands of human habitat, surrounded by wilderness, euphemistically called, 'sustainable communities.'" [129]

Through your own research and being attentive, you will discover that David Bischoff's experience is just one of thousands of stories you will hear and read about that have already been taking place all across the United States, especially over the last two years. People are outraged. Most have not realized what is happening and when it happens to them, they don't understand how something like this is possible in America.

Sustainable Development and Global Governance

UP TO THE 1990S, LITTLE SUCCESS was made by the U.N. to implement their schemes in the United States, of what they termed "Sustainable Development." Therefore, in the 90s the move was to go to local city councils and county commissioners to implement U.N. land policy, namely in regard to what you have already read but which is repeated to emphasize the seriousness of what is happening in your own backyard:

> *"...private land ownership is a principal instrument of the accumulation and concentration of wealth and therefore, contributes to social injustice. If unchecked, it may become a major obstacle in the planning and implementation of development schemes... Public control of land use is therefore indispensable."* [130]

Every county and city across our nation is presently

"under siege" to adopt the United Nation's plan called Agenda 21.* [131] Agenda 21 is the godfather document of which Sustainable Development, Smart Growth, eminent domain, wrongful use of environmental concerns, etc. fall under. It is not a secret, nor a conspiracy. It is easily discovered through little and simple research by examining the U.N.'s Human Settlement information such as the above statement: ***"Land...cannot be treated as an ordinary asset."*** And then connecting the dots from your own city and county commissioner's Sustainable Development plans to the U.N. documents. The present out-of-control use of eminent domain is connected to the U.N. schemes of Sustainable Development under the title of "Redevelopment," a nice word for wrongful use of eminent domain.

Through the false use of environmental issues, the U.N.'s plan is global governance. Henry Lamb, already quoted, writing about the United Nation's Agenda 21 plan, says:

> *"There can no longer be any question about the U.N.'s quest to establish global governance, nor can there be any question about the nature of the governance that is being imposed. Global governance*

* Agenda 21 was adopted in 1992 at the Rio de Janeiro U.N. Conference on Environment and Development. This document defines Sustainable Development and sets forth policy for its implementation.

is grounded in socialist philosophy: government is omnipotent, and is responsible for meeting the need of people on an equitable basis; all resources are owned collectively by the people and government is responsible for assuring that the earth's resources are shared efficiently, and equitably, by the current, and subsequent generations. This philosophy is the essence of 'sustainable development.'" [132]

Much of the world accepts these policies of global governance without alarm, just as when Communism and Nazism grew, without resistance, until everyone realized the real face of the monster that they were, but by then, it was too late. The U.N. global governance policy has one obstacle and that is the United States of America. The political philosophy in the United States is that 'government' is not omnipotent (God). Henry Lamb states:

"(The U.S. Government)...*is limited, empowered only by the consent of the governed. This philosophy* (the dream your fathers had) *has been eroded rather substantially in recent years, not only to meet international obligation, but also because of the U.N.'s influence over education* (public & Christian schools and universities) *has produced a growing percentage of the population who pre-*

> *fer the U.N.'s goals and methods, over the value of limited government and national sovereignty."* [133]

Henry Lamb continues:

> *"The U.S. Constitution provides no authority for the federal government to regulate the use of private property."* [134]

It's not uncommon to find U.N. Clubs in public high schools and universities, even elementary schools, where young students join to learn about different countries, but are actually being manipulated and indoctrinated in the U.N.'s Agenda 21 schemes. One of the U.N.'s Millennium Development Goals is by the year 2015 all 191 United Nations member states have pledged to *"integrate the principles of sustainable development into country policies and programmes..."* [135] Schools, both public and private, are targeted as part of their main objective to see this happen. AMUN, which stands for **A**merican **M**odel **U**nited **N**ations, Inc., is *"a non-profit, educational organization founded in 1989 to provide students with the highest quality, most professionally run simulation of the United Nations available. AMUN strives to combine educational quality with highly realistic simulations of the United Nations to give students an unparalleled Model UN learning experience."* [136] Simply explained, students are assigned certain nations to study throughout their year. They study the culture, the economics, the unique problems and crisis that the country faces, as well as the U.N.'s regulations, forms and protocols. The assigned nation becomes the country the student will represent in the U.N. The students strive to learn how to implement policies that will bring solutions to their countries' problems. On the AMUN's website, model statement policies written by past students, who have gone through this program, are available to review. The following statement is from a student who was assigned the Roman Catholic country of Sub Saharan Africa. The following is the student's policy report:

> *"Related to the world HIV/AIDS crisis, we recognize the issue of education in the prevention of the disease. As a Roman Catholic country, we find that some of our long-standing cultural traditions and religious beliefs are being called into question upon this issue. Our stance, therefore, is twofold. While we do not want to actively encourage our youth to engage in* (illicit behavior) *through the early exposure to them, we feel that it would be wrong for us to passively stand by and watch individuals suffer and die from this horrendous disease."* [137]

Obviously many of the students participating in these U.N. clubs are Christian. Re-read the text from the students report.

Are our Christian students being taught that if the youth in Sub Saharan Africa behave illicitly, to solve the problem, it must be realized that viable solutions will not be found within the teachings and traditions of the Roman Catholic faith? That they, therefore, must look elsewhere to find other means to prevent disease brought on by the illicit behavior? Yes! That is exactly what our young students are being conditioned to accept and believe. There is no discussion of maintaining moral standards that the Christian faith teaches as a way to prevent HIV/AIDS. In fact, it is these "long-standing cultural traditions and religious beliefs that are being called into question." That since these youth are behaving illicitly, they at least must learn how to protect themselves in the course of illicit behavior.

The essay above was written by high school students. In order to come up with a solution to the above "problem," they would have to discuss the problem, be exposed to it, which they themselves recognize that exposure helps to lead youth toward active participation. Isn't it a bit ironic that these "youth" are concerned about not wanting to "actively encourage our youth to engage in (illicit behavior) through the early exposure to them," yet in order to come up with a solution to this problem, that problem has to be "exposed" and discussed, how it came about, what spreads the problem, what helps and what doesn't help, etc. We can only imagine what those discussions might sound like in today's educational, anti-god environment. Certainly, as mentioned above, the Christian religious views, such as teaching and encouraging morality, would be considered too out-of-date in finding a solution to the problem, even though it offers the only sure proof solution to protect the children, for if you don't behave illicitly, you don't get the disease. But even that is beside the point. The topic is not appropriate for children, even those who are in high school, to be discussing.

Who is shaping the child's view of all the issues that are integrated in this subject: marriage, pre-marital relationships, lifestyles not sanctioned by the Church, the roles of women and men, child upbringing, birth control, abortion, etc. It should be alarming how easily we give our children over, without reflection, to those who would teach and form them through godless ideologies on subjects of such vital importance, not only for the life of the family on earth, but also, and more importantly, for their eternal life. On September 5, 1994, a delegation from the Vatican was participating in the working sessions of the U.N.'s International Conference on Population and Development in Cairo, Egypt. Hearing of the U.N.'s agenda for their family planning project (population control), Pope John Paul II, who had stayed in Rome, did something he rarely ever did. He really lost his temper and retorted:

> *"Tell them no! They must reconsider the project. Let them convert! The family is not an institution to be changed around at will…It is part of the most sacred heritage of mankind."* [138]

And yet parents, most of whom are Christian, unsuspectingly place their children in the hands of those who, without apology, work to discredit the Church and the faith in the lives of countless children across this nation, moving them step by step towards a secular worldview and tolerance. The above is just one small example. We could walk you through a variety of issues, from abortion to gun control and tell equally disturbing scenarios. Students involved in these programs are not being taught traditional American ideals, but rather are manipulated and encouraged to learn and accept an anti-American bias with a secular worldview, regardless of the topic. We are not only talking about public schools here. In May, 2006, a top Catholic Boys High School from Philadelphia won the debate competition that had gathered together students from U.N. clubs, not only from high schools across the country but from students around the world.[139] This award is a tragedy for those who understand that the U.N. is conditioning the brightest students to their plans and agendas. At what cost do you become a school "on top of the world"? No parent should allow their children in any such program. If they are already part of this club, parents strongly should insist they quit to save their children from being brainwashed.

It is not just in U.N. clubs that you have to be concerned. Back in 1949 when the United Nations Education, Scientific, and Cultural Organization (UNESCO) met for their first major project, they created a series of training sessions that they entitled: "Toward World Understanding." The contents would teach teachers how and what to teach concerning the U.N's objectives towards conditioning "world-mindedness." [140] In training session V, the following was the advice given to teachers:

> *"...it is sufficient to note that it is most frequently in the family that the children are infected with nationalism...this may be more ridiculous than dangerous, but it must, none the less, be regarded as the complete negation of world-mindedness.*

We shall presently recognize, in nationalism, the major obstacle to the development of world-mindedness. As long as the child breathes the poisoned air of nationalism, education in world-mindedness can produce only rather precarious results." [141]

The word nationalism was obviously penned very "schemingly" to confuse the reader—that to be patriotic and have love for one's country is the same as being for something like Hitler's Nazism or is an error equivalent to being for slavery. Therefore, "nationalism" must be removed from the people. They purposely, though latently, equate nationalism to patriotism and love of country, then clearly indicate that it is a sin against world-mindedness. World-mindedness is necessary to establish world governing. Socialistic ideology is being promoted in preschool, grade school, high school, and college classrooms throughout every state in our country. As is already happening, these students, your children, will grow older, fill jobs, and adapt positions to world-mindedness.

Nationalism means:

"The sense of national consciousness exalting one nation above all others and placing primary emphasis on promotion of its culture and interests

as opposed to those of other nations or supra-national groups." [142]

Notice the above definition from a modern dictionary states the word *"supra-national groups."* This clearly refers to the ultimate supra-national group, the United Nations. In turn, patriotism, as defined in Webster's 1828 Dictionary, means:

"Love of one's country; the passion which aims to serve one's country, either in defending it from invasion, or protecting its rights and maintaining its laws and institutions in vigor and purity. Patriotism is the characteristic of a good citizen, the noblest passion that animates a man in the character of citizen." [143]

Nationalism was not even a word in the 1828 American Dictionary of the English Language. Its meaning as a word today had to be conceived as a negative'ism' to usher in the new *positive* word, *world-mindedness*. Nationalism/patriotism is out and world-mindedness is in. Again, change or invent words and their meanings and then change society. The nationalism definition makes patriotism negative because it makes victims of other nations or of supra-national groups. This is clear evidence of how we are being conditioned to accept that the United States should not be positioned above the

United Nations in our loyalty, defense or protection of our laws. This is not a gray area or interpretive. Plans are clear to erase not only America's sovereignty, but the sovereignty of other nations as well. These plans were implemented beginning with the U.N. 1949 objectives for the training of teachers to turn young hearts away from the love of their nation through UNESCO's program, "Toward World Understanding."

Detailed documents exist showing the close collaboration the **N**ational **E**ducation **A**ssociation, the NEA, and the U.S. Department of Education had in those early years with the U.N.'s educational plans, and that collaboration has continued over the years. Henry Lamb states that:

> *"The curriculum for social studies, math, and environmental education — at every level — is replete with the principles advanced by the United Nations...Familiar programs, such as* ***'Outcome Based Education, Goals 2000, School to Work, and No Child Left Behind,'*** *are all constructed on the U.N.'s principles of developing 'world-mindedness' —* ***at the expense of accurate American history, the supremacy of national sovereignty, and the benefits and responsibilities of individual freedom.****"* [144]

These types of programs and others, such as what is called "Governor's School" are **very dangerous** to your children. These specialized schools hurt not only a student's faith and values, but there is documentation of the mental and physical well-being of students also being damaged. At the very least, children come out of these sessions with radically changed views, further away from the Christian worldview many of them once held. While there are good, even positive things that can be said about these schools, they are mixed with poison that corrupts and destroys the values of your children. Some have committed suicide, lost their faith, become depressed, or rebelled against their parents after attending. One report shows that at least several Governor's schools prey on parents by the flattery of the invitation for their child's participation. Being the brightest and most gifted gets them recognized in the local paper. They then are sent to spend six weeks at the Arkansas' Governor's School, or the North Carolina's Governor's School, and so forth. Shelvie Cole, mother of Brandon Cole, who was a student who attended Arkansas Governor's School,[145] in concluding her testimony given before the joint interim Education Committee, with other concerned parents, stated:

"I would like to close by reading you the first entry into Brandon's log (when he first arrived at the Arkansas Governor's School) and then I will read one that was written three weeks later."

"Moms are the best people around and my mom is the best mom on earth..."

Three weeks later Brandon wrote:

"My mom is so closed-minded. I feel like we will have a stand off soon..." [146]

Brandon, who was a well-balanced and outgoing youth, later committed suicide less than a month after attending these sessions. He was one of four students who committed suicide after attending Arkansas' Governor's School. Brandon's mother also stated that he suffered no depression nor had such tendencies before attending the Governor's School.[147] The details of what students are subjected to are horrifying and all the while connected to our federally controlled educational system.

Don't buy into it when your child is chosen to attend such similar types of special schools or sessions because of being at the top of their studies, or having a high IQ. Brandon was chosen because of his gifts and talents in the area of music. His mother assumed because of this that Brandon would be learning about this area of interest, meeting composers of music, etc.

Though he attended a few classes on music, the vast majority of his time was spent in the indoctrination programs designed by the Governor's School's curriculum. If a fisherman knows how to use the best lure to catch the prize fish, satan, who is not dumb, but rather has a superior intellect, will "lure" the best minds with attractive tactics to capture and transform the minds of our youth. These groups have an agenda, and they are purposely picking the top creme of our youth to indoctrinate and change their thinking. They are very clever and mostly successful in doing so. In September, 2006, a mother and father from out of town decided to visit our mission at Caritas, spending some time before picking up their daughter from the National Young Leaders State Conference held at the Hilton Hotel in Birmingham, Alabama. They told us it was sponsored by the Congressional Youth Leadership Conference. They, of course, were honored that their daughter was invited. All that faded when they picked her up. She was confused in what once was her firm beliefs, formed by strong Christian teachings. In the next days the parents found out the three topics of discussion were:

1. Cloning
2. Abortion
3. The Right to Die

To reiterate, these sessions are blanket brainwashing and indoctrination and will, to varying degrees, confuse the most value-based student. Parents must beware of these facades to get to your children's minds. It is blatantly clear that your children are targeted. Home schoolers are no exception. In September of 2006, German police arrested Katharina Plett for her resistance to obey a *"Nazi-era law banning home schooling. The next day, her husband and children fled across the border to Austria."* [148] The European Court has now upheld Germany's right to prosecute home schoolers. The reason:

> *"The United Nations Convention on the Rights of the Child, an international treaty signed by Belgium now imposes restrictions on parental rights in educational matters."* [149]

The United States did not sign this treaty but as you will read, non-binding treaties are a threat to United States sovereignty and many are concerned that United States courts may import European and United Nation's laws, taking the child's education out of the hands of the parents.

Control Through Non-Binding Treaties

So, ALONG WITH SUBVERTING YOUR YOUTH and adolescents in America's schools, how is the U.N. succeeding in bringing the United States in line with its plans? Through our Constitution! Article VI of the U.S. Constitution states that "Treaties are the supreme law of the land." The U.N. passes non-binding treaties to get policy in place and then immediately begins to work on making them tighter and legally binding. Hence, by graduating slowly by degrees, most enactments of treaties are imposed with negative consequences against the United States. Several tactical plans of the U.N. have been to move forward in the implementation of policies and treaties from the 1970s, one little step at a time, building on each accomplishment. Like the frog thrown into boiling water, it immediately jumps out. But a frog placed in cool water that is slowly heated, is boiled to death.

Through treaties, the United States has begun to lose sovereignty over itself. Sovereignty is possession of supreme power. Some of the members of the Supreme Court, as well as judges across our country, have considered the laws of other nations and international law in deciding our law in United States courtrooms. It is unheard of in the history of the United States that U.S. judges allow themselves to be influenced by the laws of other nations, thereby rejecting the sovereignty and supremacy of the U.S. Constitution and the Declaration of Independence as our guiding rule of law and principles. Americans must clearly, plainly, and very seriously understand and state to each other and their children that the Declaration of Independence and the U.S. Constitution are not to become co-equal, submissive, or influenced by any other nation's law, including international law, if those laws violate our foundation documents. These two documents have total supremacy and sovereignty over our nation. No other nation's laws are to ever alter even a part of our law. To do so is an act toward the death of our nation. In our founding, we are a stand alone nation in the concept we hold of our republic. We are the oldest government on earth. As a nation, we are the most prosperous, most generous, and the most successful, but the moment we look to other governments and laws, we will die as a nation. Italy, itself, in the last several decades, has had more than 35 different governments.

The sovereignty of the oceans now belongs, for the most part, to the U.N. The U.N. is not a government, but is striving to have the power of global supremacy and governance. The U.N. has not made quick moves toward global governance because it does not "yet" have authority to tax. But because we must submit to treaties, the United States is now bound to pay taxes labeled as "permit fees" to explore the seabed. Anything we extract from the ocean requires us to make "royalty payments." So far, the United States has been able to block over a dozen attempts of the U.N. to impose a world tax. If that were to happen, the U.N. could then build its own enforcement body of order (police or mercenaries) to which all nations would be subject to its power, by treaties and international law.[150]

Control Over the Information

One obstruction to U.N. schemes is the internet because it is a free source of information and is the major tool in empowering the individual to find out for himself what is going on, such as with the Agenda 21 scheme of the United Nations. For this reason, the internet is being targeted by the U.N. to be brought "under control," *their* control. The schemes of the U.N. and revisionists cannot succeed as long as any person can go and look up instantly what "dream our Fathers' had," and compare it to the dreams of the U.N. They are threatened when we can read, right at our own fingertips through the internet, our Forefathers' own words, their documents, their letters, their intentions and compare them to the U.N.'s words, documents, letters, and intentions. If enough Americans do this, it would be enough to block the U.N.'s agendas. That is why it is of the U.N.'s vital interest to have control of information, so to be able to condition us towards a secular, socialist worldview. So, in December of 2003, the U.N. convened a "World Summit on the Information Society" in Geneva in which delegates agreed to create a U.N.-sanctioned "**W**orking **G**roup on **I**nternet **G**overnance." The **"WGIG"** met four more times in preparation for the second "World Summit on the Information Society," in Tunis, in 2005. The agenda is to continue to meet, planning strategies to *"wrest control of the internet from the United States,"* [151] to give control of information to the United Nations and regulate it with their governance, philosophies and laws.[152] Certainly to come will be strong efforts to tax it, both for control and a revenue source. This is another primary example of your freedoms being taken away: freedom to get information. Restricting and distorting information is oppression. Think about this one example of the U.N.'s efforts to take your freedom, and Patrick Henry's words can be grasped more in understanding what it would be like to live in such a system presently being built. Think about the U.N. statements already mentioned, and then Patrick Henry's words, ***"Give me Liberty or give me Death."*** Why did he say that? Why would he rather die than live under control and loss of property, and then realize that in this age efforts are being made to control even our thinking. With the failure of socialism in the

20th century, it is a wonder that as we begin the 21st century, socialism has cast its shadow upon every facet of our lives. Its growing world-wide structure makes 20th century socialism and its controls mere minor infractions. Jacqueline Kasun, in her book The War Against Population, stated:

> *"These controls are to be imposed not through the electoral process but by 'consensus', ostensibly at local levels, but in fact through the concerted action of a mammoth international network of 'independent, voluntary' organizations and national and supra-national agencies. Ironically, this century (the 20th), which has illustrated so vividly the failure of government controls, is ending with a massive drive toward the most comprehensive controls ever imagined by man."* [153]

The above are only a few tidbits to begin educating you about the **"signs of the times"** Our Lady keeps mentioning. The more you study and research Agenda 21, Sustainable Development and Smart Growth, the more you will see that it's not about the environment, though that is what the powers behind it want everyone to believe. Many of the "workers" of the eco-movement are sincere and believe what they are doing is good. What they do not realize is they are being used. The eco-issues are the veils being used by a higher level group of people who want to alter society through their socialist ideas of cultural engineering and population controls. In the past, those of this mind-set failed to move forward their agenda. But in our time, they have banded together and have achieved great success in pushing forward a super, secular worldview, in total contradiction to the Biblical worldview, to achieve their goals to control every aspect of life. This group unites proponents to animal rights, population control, radical feminists and environmentalists, left wing radicals and other groups under the same banner of Agenda 21. It is a growing monster manifesting itself everywhere, just as dark agendas of the past, in other times, covered mankind with the philosophies of Socialism, Communism, Nazism, etc.

It is imperative for Christians to learn of these things, to be educated so as to contradict these views through a Christian worldview. You will find, doing your own research, things that will alarm you of the real assault of darkness to take away the sovereignty of the United States in order to destroy this nation whose light Our Lady is calling to shine. For example, plans are in action through The **S**ecurity and **P**rosperity **P**artnership of North America (SPP) for the United States, Canada, and Mexico to join together to form a similar union as the European

Union. Talk is already spreading about the "Ameros" (the new currency for the United States, Mexico and Canada) replacing the U.S. dollar as "Euros" replaced various European currencies.[154] We suppose that because so many of their other agendas are passing through without America's notice, that the U.N. and the various interest groups who are working to destroy our nation believe Americans are too stupid to question their argument that by getting rid of the borders between Mexico and Canada, that America will somehow become more secure. So instead of having to watch the border "lines" between our nations, the United States will now have to worry about the giant horseshoes that will have to be guarded, thousands upon thousands of miles, to secure the entire continent of North America.

We'll go no further with this particular issue, other than making the point that U.S. sovereignty over itself is being assaulted on all fronts. America, with our Judeo-Christian principles and values foundationed and rooted to our very existence, has been the light of Freedom for the world. Italy, the home of the Catholic Church, is part of the European Union. Pope John Paul II repeatedly chastised the leaders of the Union for denying Europe's Christian roots. The Pope insisted they place language in the constitution recognizing these roots.

The then acting president of the new European Union refused to place it in the constitution arrogantly answering the Pope that Europe is no longer Christian but a secular state. Robert Royal, author of the book The God That Did Not Fail in which he demonstrates how religion built and sustains the West, said this concerning Europe's denial of its Christian past:

> *"Perhaps the most naked manifestation of the impulse to deny Christianity's role in forming the West came during the debates over the European Constitution in 2003 and 2004. In early drafts of that document, a brief survey of the history of Europe jumped from the classical age to the Enlightenment, as if the entire continent were suffering from a collective and willful amnesia about its strongly Christian past."* [155]

The same agenda that brought Europe to this sad state of affairs is assaulting our nation as well. The joining of North America through Sustainable Development will erode America's sovereignty and, in turn, we will follow suit in denying our Christian roots, just as the European Union denied theirs. To preserve our Christian heritage, we must convert and wake up to the grievous threats that are poised to destroy our nation and enslave us.

Why is all this happening? The United States is the only nation on earth whose value system and philosophies within its foundation can act as a roadblock to stop Agenda 21. Agenda 21 is about control, control that the U.N. wants. If the U.N. achieves their goals, we will no longer enjoy the freedoms we have always taken for granted in being Americans. As they move closer to implementing their plans, they can't help but expose their intentions. The more the plans are implemented, the more naked they must become and the more they will be brought into the light, exposing the evil agendas. But to stop them while there is still time, an uprising among ordinary Christians must take place. Christians must begin educating as many people as possible, as quickly as possible. Ordinary citizens must begin to hold their city and county commissioners accountable. They must learn where their elected officials stand on Sustainable Development and Smart Growth. State and nationally elected officials must be held accountable as well. It starts from the bottom up—first making our local officials accountable, second our state leaders and third our national leaders.

What God Wants, satan Wants

THE SUSTAINABLE DEVELOPMENT, AGENDA 21, U.N. plans have several documents and treaties that must be exposed to understand the grave threat they present to Christianity and our nation. The United Nation's Biological Diversity Treaty Instruction Manual for the implementation of the Global Biodiversity Assessment, under Agenda 21, gives specific details about how society should be organized, how land will be used and regulated, and how resources will be regulated and controlled.[156] The plan especially targets the United States because if the United States can be brought to compliance, it will be easier to bring the rest of the world to compliance as well. The instruction book has devised policy where animals can travel from state to state, from the East Coast all the way to the West Coast, on a continuous stretch of vast amounts of land, without ever seeing a human being. The policy's goal states:

> *"Eventually, a wilderness network would dominate a region...with human habitation being islands. The native ecosystem and the collective needs of non-human species* ***must take precedence*** *over the needs and desires of humans."* [157]

Yes, you read that correctly. The "collective needs" of "non-humans" will take precedence over the needs and desires of humans. Humans in submission to insects! Vegetation! Animals! Water! Larva! Whatever the native ecosystem may be. Man will be contained to islands or "land zones," known as "in-fills" to "fill-in" taking up every available space where humans live, while animals roam free. Go back and re-read the above-italicized statement. Again, one may think that no one will accept these statements as being possible to implement, but think…no one would have believed 50 years ago that abortion would be commonplace or that marriage would be threatened by revisionists and others redefining it, or that so many other errors would become so ingrained into today's society, as to threaten our very future. Remember, the nine demands that were made in 1873 and are largely manifesting today. These writings expose and connect the dots of what is coming to the age of tomorrow; humans submitting to the environment, to the animal kingdom and to societal control. These policies are already being introduced and implemented in several areas today. Agenda 21 Sustainable Development plans have volumes of references that confirm that this statement (humans in submission to native eco systems) means what it says. And again this policy does not contradict a secular worldview. But it clearly contradicts a Biblical worldview. It is opposed to what God, Himself, wants and states in Genesis 2:15, 1:27–30:

> ***"The Lord God then took the man and settled in the Garden of Eden, to cultivate and care for it. God created man in His image in the Divine***

image He created him. Male and female He created them. God blessed them, saying: "Be fertile and multiply; fill the earth and subdue it. Have dominion over the fish of the sea, the birds of the air, and all the living things that move on the earth..." "See I give you every seed-bearing plant all over the earth and every tree that has seed-bearing fruit on it to be your food; and to all the animals of the land, all the birds of the air, and all the living creatures that crawl on the ground, I give all the green plants for food."

This above Biblical doctrine is called anthropocentrism, that man was given dominion over creation, and it is clearly targeted by Agenda 21 to be changed.

What the U.N. Wants vs What God Wants

UN's Plan	God's Plan
Animals and all the earth "take precedence" and dominion over man, or at the very least, are to be equal with man.	Man has dominion over animals and all the earth.

UN's Plan	God's Plan
Man to fill up in cloistered land islands.	Man to fill the earth.
Animals, plants, and "collective needs" take precedence over "needs" of humans.	Man is given all animals, birds, and seed bearing vegetation to be used for food, clothing, medicine and every other need to help him.
Unalienable rights to creatures, vegetation, subspecies and even water and matter.	Unalienable natural rights to man.

The above statements may be hard to believe or take seriously. After all, most people would reason that there is no one who would 'want' or expect that man's worth and his needs are to be equal to animals or even to physical matter. But that thought changes when you review the following. First, understand satan's "wants." In Isaiah 14:13–14, satan made known five of his "wants:"

"I will ascend into Heaven."
"I will exalt my throne above the stars of God."
"I will sit upon the mount of assembly."

"I will ascend above the heights."
"I will be like the Most High."

We can see five times satan wants those things which are God's. Understand by this that whenever, wherever God acts, satan parallels a plan of likeness, often so similar that many become confused and, therefore, deceived. God sends Our Lady for a plan. Our Lady says:

January 28, 1987

> **"...Whenever I come to you my Son comes with me, but so does satan..."**

satan is there always, duplicating and mimicking the same plans of what God first initiates. Dr. S. M. Davis, in a talk entitled "Why satan Wants Your Firstborn and What to Do About It," shows this quite clearly. Following are excerpts from this teaching.

> *"satan was fighting for the first position in the universe...Ever since then, satan has been saying he wants every other first thing he can get his hands on because he knows that's what God wants. satan is saying,* ***'I want to be the top one. I don't want people to be giving God the first part of their lives, I want them to give that to me. I don't want them to be giving Him the first***

part of the day, I want them to give that to me. I don't want them to be giving God the first part of every dollar, I want them to keep that for me.'

"satan hates the entire Bible. He fights against all of God's truths but there is one verse, I believe, that has been and continues to be more attacked than any other verse in the Bible. If satan can make people believe the first verse of the Bible is a mistake in any way, then he can make them believe that the rest of the Bible is a lie as well. If satan can destroy the truth of **creation**, *it won't be long before he destroys the truth of* **salvation**. *With no hesitation at all, I say that every detail of Genesis 1:1 is true:*

'In the beginning when God created the heavens and the earth…'

"God wants all the first things and satan wants what God wants. That's why it's so hard to crawl out of bed in the morning and give God the first part of the day…satan wants what God wants. That's why the Super Bowl is on Sunday. That's why the Indianapolis 500 and golf tournaments and baseball games and all kinds of other sports

and entertainments take place on the Lord's Day. You say, 'Oh well, the reason that they do that is because people have the day off.' No, it's not the reason why. They do that because it's the Lord's Day and satan wants to mess up the Lord's Day…

"That's why motorcycle races and soccer games are on Sunday…I want to tell you whatever you got that is a priority over the Lord's Day—you need to do something about it. W.E. Gladstone, an English statesman once said:

'Tell me what the young men of England are doing on Sunday, I'll tell you what the future of England will be.'

"Look at England today. Why has England gotten so far from God? Because, one of the reasons is they totally have forgotten the Lord's Day. The atheist Voltaire said:

'I can never hope to destroy Christianity until I first destroy the Christian Sabbath,'

"referring to Sunday. Consider this statement. This is a powerful thought:

'Our great-grandfathers called it the Lord's Day. Our grandfathers called it the Holy Sab-

bath. Our fathers called it Sunday and today we just call it the weekend.'

"satan wants what God wants." [158]

The point being made is that whenever God wants to introduce something, satan immediately schemes to hi-jack it. While God's plan is to give us freedom by what He initiates, satan's plan is to enslave us using the same plan. *"I will ascend into Heaven."* This is very important to understanding what motivates the Sustainable Development movement. If you look at Our Lady's messages, you will find a parallel of what God wants and, therefore, what satan wants. Our Lady speaks strongly for Creation and finding God in Creation. She wants us to have an encounter with God through nature. satan is now paralleling this call, except his call is to block this encounter with nature/creation, by making nature itself, god, and, thereby, man is nothing but one of its animals. The organization, People for the Ethical Treatment of Animals, stated:

"Mankind is the biggest blight on the face of the earth." [159]

This contradicts the Judeo-Christian teaching that man is made in the image and likeness of God. But there is a dangerous mentality growing in the world of promoting the opposite of Judeo-Christian teachings. More and more, we are discovering that people with this mentality are in decision-making positions and have tremendous influence on education of all ages and levels, corporations, and local and national governments. Michael W. Fox, Vice President of the Humane Society in the United States, stated:

> *"The life of an ant and the life of my child should be granted equal consideration."* [160]

These are not isolated thoughts. We have an army of people moving into decision-making positions, which have been conditioned, through our public and private educational systems, against Judeo-Christian beliefs and values and see the United States as an obstacle to their many agendas. Peter Singer, known as the "Father of Animal Rights," states:

> *"Christianity is our foe. If animal rights is to succeed, we must destroy the Judeo-Christian religious tradition."* [161]

Our Lady's message of October 25, 1995, said:

> **"...In thanking Him you will discover the Most High and all the goods that surround you..."**

God provides for man, goods of the earth, both animals and plants, so to feed, clothe and shelter him. The Judeo-Christian belief is that the earth daily produces fruits for man. But the foundation document of the U.N., known as Agenda 21, states that this is endangering the earth. Because "fruits of the earth" is a Judeo-Christian teaching, our tradition "must be destroyed" and give way to the next step that Jerry Ulasak, spokesman for Physicians Committee for Responsible Medicine, states:

> *"If someone is killing, on a regular basis, thousands of animals* (for food) *and if that person can only be stopped in a way by the use of violence, then it is certainly a morally justified solution."* [162]

We could say these people are just way off base, just pray for them, and then write the whole thing off…except that there are *so many* who have been conditioned to accept, adopt and promote these mentalities, and they are positioning themselves over general society. While we are busy with all of life's necessities, they have been busy devising plans for "controlling" all of life's necessities, including food, shelter and life itself. It is pervasive in the U.N.'s biodiversity documents that man is no different than animals in his rights. Therefore, man should be on equal ground with animals. Steven Wise, Harvard University lecturer states:

> *"If a human 4-year-old has what it takes for legal personhood, then a chimpanzee should be able to be a legal person, in terms of legal rights."* [163]

Those who hold these mentalities know they must prevail to destroy Judeo-Christian traditions. Ask yourself, why did Our Lady say so strongly:

May 25, 2006

> **"...think of Heaven. Only in this way, will you have peace in your heart that no one will be able to destroy..."**

Our Lady's words tell us there are plans "to destroy," and that conditions of the earth are becoming so grave as to lose peace in the heart.

Animals are not equal to man. Man was the climax of God's creative activity, because man was made in the image and likeness of God, and it was God's desire to give man dominion over all creation. Creation was created first to glorify God and then for man's sake. This is what God wants for you and it's what satan, under a veil of ecological and earth concerns, wants to take away from you. Using ecological concerns, satan's plans are to condition man towards making earth, god, or actually a goddess, in which man then commits sins against god the earth. This is the problem with those of Our Lady who are bringing about what God wants and those of darkness bringing about what satan wants. This all sounds absurd and because you may reject it, why go into the subject deeper? Because after you read and become knowledgeable you will realize that not only do we have a dangerous situation, but it's in your children and loved ones' present and immediate future. We need to understand that there are serious reasons for over 25 years of daily apparitions.

The Cultural & Spiritual Values of Biodiversity

THE BIBLE FOR THE GLOBAL BIODIVERSITY ASSESSMENT, or rather the 'conscience' of the U.N.'s Agenda 21, Sustainable, Smart Growth, Environmental program is entitled: **"The Cultural and Spiritual Values of Biodiversity."** [164] We will, for the sake of this writing, give it the name, "The Biobible."

Even at the beginning of the Biobible, it makes a bible-like statement of its text. It states that the Biobible is to:

"...be treated with respect." [165]

Radical environmentalists had failed to push forth their agenda for 20 years until they paralleled what the radical feminist movement did when they finally were having to face throwing in the towel due to their own failures to bring transformation to society. So to better understand how the U.N.'s agenda, through environmentalism, was able to advance so rapidly, it will be helpful to reflect on the advancement of the feminist's agenda. Catholic author, Donna Steichen, infiltrated the feminist movement and documented their meetings and plans in her book, Ungodly Rage. In the aftermath of the 1970s, after failing to get an Equal Rights Amendment written into the Constitution, radical feminists realized it was over for them. In her book, Steichen writes:

> *"...only veterans of the failed Equal Rights Amendment drive talked about 'women's liberation' anymore. Disillusionment and resurgent normalcy had deprived militant feminism of its charm for the general public. Geraldine Ferraro had proved to be a political disaster; witty liberal essayist Nora Ephron had ruefully admitted that women got nothing from the women's movement but the Dutch lunch; young couples had started having babies again; Ms Magazine was lurching toward bankruptcy. When asked what the feminist movement could hope to accomplish in the future,*

> *Betty Friedan told reporters, 'I can't tell you that now. You wouldn't believe it anyway. It's theological.'"* [166]

To simply explain a complex scenario, what happened was when the feminist movement failed, they realized they did not have the grass roots support to spread their agenda, but *the Catholic Church did* and that was what was "theological." The feminists did not believe in the Catholic Church but many retained "membership as a camouflage while revolutionizing from within." [167] Feminism swept into the Church causing many orders of nuns to drastically decline. In 1955, there were 180,000 religious sisters in the United States. Today there are 75,000 of which half are over 70 years of age.[168] What kind of teachings led to such a decline in vocations? Sr. Dorothy Olinger, from the School Sisters of Notre Dame, reflected in a statement what many "nuns" (and we use that term loosely here) were saying:

> *"We **are** part of the earth, and we must work out our evolution into the beings we must become, in harmony with the earth."* [169]

There flowed into the Church, women who were radical feminists. They joined, among others, many ex-nuns who had renounced their vows and loyalty to the Church, but remained in the Church to spread the feminist agenda. Steichen explained that they mixed:

> *"…'ancient wisdom' of Eastern monism, 'goddess' paganism…dubious 'Native American traditions,' voodoo, witchcraft…(and) 'spirits' of newly invented earth religions…"* [170]

These influences in the Church did great harm and led to ever-greater apostasies.

Through the radical feminist agenda and other influences, an even more dangerous movement has evolved as satan's next step. The Biobible for the Agenda 21, Sustainable Development and Smart Growth plans, revealed that the same tactics and schemes that led to the success in the advancement of the feminist agenda, are being used by the Green movement for their own advancement. The key to their success was in becoming a parasite within the Church, they were able to infiltrate the Church with their ideologies. Not surprisingly, it is found within the Biobible a strong emphasis on what they term as "Ecofeminism." [171] And so goes the evolution of radical feminism "hitching a ride" with the eco-agenda, to move their own further ahead. And just like a chameleon,* they change their appearance to whatever will help achieve their own

* A chameleon is a type of lizard that is capable of changing their color.

goals. Though they deny God, they parallel His religion by creating their own "ecofeminist" faith. The earth goddess' name is "gaia." Its prayer in the Biobible is, "All that Is—Is a Web of Being,"[172] denying God's great word, "I AM WHO AM." The prayer also condemns the Biblical truth that the earth is for man, stating rather, "We belong to gaia." From Ecofeminism, the Biobible then arrives at the "sin of ecocide."[173] The "Biobible" states:

> "*...processes* (i.e. such as raising cattle, cutting trees, building your home) *and the ensuing loss of control over native lands* (resulting from these processes) *are among the main cause of disintegration of indigenous communities, a phenomenon that has been termed ecocide.*"[174]

And again it states:

> "*...the sheer brutality of genocide or ecocide, both being manifestations of religious and political persecution...*"[175]

Which means that Christopher Columbus committed the sin of ecocide, by means of converting those who lived an uncivilized way of life, leading them towards Christianity. Ecocide is a term that criminalizes, among other things, those who change the lives of native people through the conversion that happens when the Christian Gospel is shared. Jesus' last words given to men before He ascended into Heaven were, according to the Gospel of Mark:

> ***"Go into all the world and preach the gospel to the whole creation. He who believes and is baptized will be saved; but he who does not believe will be condemned."*** Mark 16:15–16

According to the Gospel of Matthew, Jesus said:

> ***"All authority in Heaven and on earth has been given to me. Go therefore, and make disciples of all nations, baptizing them in the name of the Father, and of the Son, and of the Holy Spirit, teaching them to observe all that I have commanded you..."*** Matthew 28:18–20

In fact, Jesus' entire three year ministry was a training school for apostleship—to go out and spread the Good News. He was not making a suggestion to His disciples to spread His Gospel, He was *commanding* them to do so. That call to evangelize has been passed down to every generation of Christians since Jesus' death and Resurrection. To do so today, however, is to commit "ecocide" and Christian missionaries are being told they can no longer "interfere" in the lives of indigenous peoples from the powers that be, within the U.N. itself, because Christianity is an enemy to the way of life of indigenous people. One example they gave in the Biobible was from an Indian tribe in Indonesia.

> *"...Under the direction of European missionaries and colonial administrators, head-hunting and traditional religious ceremonies were forbidden..."* [176]

The message being delivered in the Biobible is that Christians should leave well enough alone; live and let live. If it is a people's custom to be headhunters, so be it. What right do Christians have to interfere with the lifestyle of another people? That's all fine and good for the head-*hunter*, but what about the head-*huntee*. Unless, of course, humans are no more than a herd of deer, and the survival of the fittest should win out in our tribes and communities, as much as any other species of animals. All this, of course, is in direct opposition to Jesus' command to ***"make disciples of all nations...(and) teach them to observe all the commands I have given you...,"*** which includes, thou shalt not kill.

But all of this is not really the point. When you begin to study and research the philosophies behind Agenda 21, when you begin to observe what happens in your own communities that are implementing Sustainable Development and Smart Growth, then you know that all the pretty language and descriptions in their 700+page Biobible is veiling their true intentions, or in other words, is a bunch of biobabble. They don't care about the indigenous peoples around the world, any more than they care about the American farmer trying to put food on the table to feed his family. What they do care about, however, is that Christianity not spread because the philosophies of freedom and liberty come from the teachings of Jesus Christ, and the U.N. socialist agenda to control every aspect of people's lives around the world cannot succeed unless they bring down Christianity. They slam Christians who want to bring Christ's light into the head of a headhunter, not because, as they say, he has a right to his own culture, but rather because they are mortally afraid of those head-hunters being turned on to Jesus. Once that happens, they will become far less manageable to accept controls under the veil of the "sustainable" agenda, being enlightened to its unbiblical agenda. Where will it stop? Do you think the U.N.'s World Court, already built in Hague, will want to bring to trial anyone from any nation committing crimes of ecocide? Raising cattle where they designate you cannot, or spreading the teachings of Christianity to indigenous people, civilizing and changing their culture?

Both are crimes of ecocide in the Biobible.[177]

Unfortunately, there's more. We will go to your backyard to show that this will personally affect you. The Biobible indicates that ecocide is destroying the Integrity of Creation. A review of Sustainable Development and Smart Growth will reveal regulations that to even build a deck onto your house destroys the integrity of the ground you cover. Within local governments, these violations are being tallied up with a new environmental accounting system ascribing costs for hurting the integrity of the ground you cover by penalizing you through having to pay for costly permits. Others are having to give over large areas of their lots or land to compensate for what they took from the ecosystem. As a consequence, they cannot in the future, alter their property, but must leave it in the untouched natural state. On a global scale, destroying the Integrity of Creation is defined not by Christians, but by the eco-movement, as committing a mortal sin. [178] The Biobible states:

> *"The Christian Mass, Eucharist, Communion, has been celebrated and reinterpreted to stress that the doctrines of Incarnation and final Resurrection relate to more than the human being; namely, the sanctification of the whole of creation and the resurrection of the cosmos. Conversely, to destroy*

the Integrity of Creation becomes equivalent to committing a sin for which you have to repent before you can participate in communion." [179]

The Biobible is 731 pages long. It mentions Christianity 88 times, most often in a negative light and blames most of the earth/world's problems on the teachings of Christians and Muslims. Of these two groups, it is apparent that Christians are the most responsible. From within this group, the next level of "who is to blame" is the Christians of western civilization. The next level of blame goes to the Christian male of western civilization, and the highest level of blame falls to the white male Christian of western civilization, the Christians who are the most responsible for committing ecocide throughout the ages by Christianizing native people and civilizing them.[180]

The Catholic Church Is Targeted to Spread Agenda 21 Throughout Christendom

The Biobible is not a comparable error put forth like The DaVinci Code or the *Judas Gospel* that is here today, making a fuss, damaging weak Christians and non-believers, but for the most part, gone tomorrow. It is an agenda. It is a Marxist/Stalin/Lenin type writing and philosophy with its impact on man's thinking and thought processes, reshaping views and understandings to a secular worldview. Remember, in order for their plans to succeed, they must destroy Christianity and their means to do so is not through bloodshed (yet), but through destroying Christianity in the minds of believers and unbelievers, alike. This document is a danger to society and especially to your children. The "spiritual values" of the U.N.'s biodiversity agenda are latently planted within school curriculums across our nation (and other nations as well), in both public and private schools, including Christian/Catholic schools. Its teachings are flowing worldwide to the Judeo-Christian and Muslim people.

Are we saying there is nothing of value, nothing we would agree with as Christians in the U.N. Agenda 21 documents? No, but it's not the truths that we should be concerned with in the glass of water. It's the drops of arsenic that poison the whole glass. Therefore, it's not a question of finding common ground to work towards reform because there are too many drops of arsenic in this document. It condemns Christianity many times, distorting its teachings, while all praises go to native people's faiths entrenched in idolism and the gods of Hinduism, Buddhism, and radical feminism. Their plans must be rejected. Besides, the teachings of Christianity already encompasses care for creation. We do not need godless, secular world-viewists preaching to Christians what sin is and when we should and should not be going to Communion. All this exists within the Catholic Church and other Christian denominations.

As was mentioned previously, at the failure of the feminist movement to achieve their goal of the **E**qual **R**ights **A**mendment, known as the ERA, they aimed their sites on using the Catholic Church to "parasite" their objectives. For 20 years, the environmental issues not only lost ground, but the movement, itself, weakened until five of the world's major faiths, initiated by the ecoists, were invited to Assisi, Italy,[181] a politically correct move choosing St. Francis' hometown, with the plan to get the religious active in ecological work. Targeting the world's religions to parasite their objectives, the Biobible shows their intent to take the lead, through the efforts of secular eco-influences, by the title they used in describing the gathering in Assisi: ***The Greening of the World Religions.***[182]

The religious groups gathered in Assisi met with the environmental groups who orchestrated and put forth an eco-agenda. The aim of this religious/eco summit was to influence the major religions to come to terms with the fact that the environmental groups were the good guys and victims of western, Christian worldviews and that their secular worldviews must be respected to counter the dominant thinking of the western Christian worldview. The Biobible states as an objective for the Assisi gathering:

> "*...that alternative world-views and ethics must be respected to counter current dominant* (Biblical) *thinking...*" [183]

Those gathered from the different faiths were put on a guilt trip from the beginning of the meeting, by being blocked at the entrance of St. Francis Basilica in Assisi by a 'Maori Warrior," dressed in all his battle array.[184] Before any participants of this U.N. gathering were allowed to enter, formal apologies had to be made by all the faiths for the crimes that were said to have been committed that brought the destruction of indigenous people of the 3rd World! The psychological moves continued once inside, in which they went through more repentance and elaborate ceremonies and made a "New Alliance" all to the favor of the eco-agenda. In a grand scheme to hi-jack the faiths to "please let us, as victims, use you as our megaphone," the Biobible reported that the initiative helped reach untold millions worldwide with a conservation message through religious channels.[185]

Just as the feminist movement experienced a rebirth once they became a "parasite" within influential areas of the Church, the U.N. religious summit achieved a major breakthrough for the eco-movement by the same means. How did they achieve this so easily? Because Christians no longer honor God on Sundays, because they are not living the Commandments, because they are forming their opinions and beliefs on daily doses of information from secular worldview sources, the ecoists were able to "song and dance" their way to their predetermined outcome and gain a consensus from the five major faiths.

It takes prayer and reasoning to realize that satan has a master intelligence, far superior to man. He creates ways to manipulate and move the masses in the direction he wants them to go, much like the Pied Piper did in the well-known fable. You may have heard of the term, *The Delphi/Alinsky Process* and/or *Consensus Building.* These are highly manipulative processes, which are employed in order to lead a group of people to a conclusion that they normally would not choose or agree with. The people walk away, often times not happy with the conclusion, but believing they at least were given an opportunity to influence the outcome, and though the decision did not go their way, they believed they were treated fairly and democratically. The reality, however, was that the "conclusion" was already "predetermined" from the beginning. With skillful manipulation by the facilitator of the group, decisions are made without the people realizing they are being misled.

Whether or not you have heard of the Delphi/Alinsky Process and Consensus Building, these processes are well known by these groups. They are being used everywhere, even in our churches, to lead groups of people towards predetermined decisions that are not in the best interest of the people, but for those who want to deceptively get you to approve of their plans or decisions, so as to overcome any objections which would stop the agenda. In other words, instead of waiting to present a plan that will get resistance and be possibly stopped, the schemers set up a system to manage the people who have issues or a stake in the decision, so to lead them to the decision the schemers want. Even though one may not like the final decision, you are deceived into accepting it because they gave the appearance that you were part of the decision-making process. Consensus building is for one purpose: to eliminate dissent. It is important for you, as Christians, to educate, research, and familiarize yourselves with this process because often Christians are the ones who are being manipulated through these means. Following is one example of how the process works within a facilitated meeting to cultivate a desired conclusion.

> *"Basically the idea goes something like this: An organization or group (such as a school, planning commissioners, developers, etc.) has already decided what it is going to do, but it wants to avoid the appearance that it has acted without public approval. So it schedules a public meeting which is advertised as being held for the purpose of soliciting community input. In fact the organization has no desire to solicit opinions; rather the real intent of the meeting is to give the community the impression that input was solicited.*
>
> *"The meeting goes like this: Everyone arrives and sits down. After an introductory talk, audience members are told that they are going to be divided into numbered groups. So everyone is asked to count off from 1,2,3…6,7,etc., going up and down the seated rows. They start over after the capacity number is called. Each person is then directed into a group whose name is the same as the number that they counted off. So for example, if you counted "2" when the count came around to you, then you go to Group 2. There are, of course, (a certain number of) group leaders who then care-*

fully direct the discussion of each group. Each group leader controls the format and, to a great degree, the content of each group's discussion.

"Toward the end, group members are asked for inputs, which are then listed on a big sheet of paper by the group leader. At the end of the meeting, everyone reassembles. The sheets from all the groups are posted around the room and each group leader reads the list of suggestions that are on his list. Unpopular or unusual inputs are glossed over and downplayed, while the majority of attention is focused on those ideas that are generic enough that almost everyone would agree to them. At the end a summary is delivered and everyone goes home.

"The purpose of the count off is to split up anyone who came in together, so that each of the numbered groups will most likely consist entirely of people who have never met, and almost certainly will not contain any two or more like-minded individuals who may have come in together. Once everyone is split up in this manner, the group leaders can then easily control the group conversations because dissenting or outspoken individuals are generally alone in each group, and such people quickly discover that they have little or no support from other group members.

"The purpose of the sheets of paper is to graphically display to everyone, at the end, that everyone's opinion has indeed been registered. And finally the whole meeting format is designed specifically to avoid community input; obviously a bunch of strangers divided up into groups and chatting for two hours are not going to accomplish anything of importance." [186]

As mentioned, this is one example of how the Delphi/Alinsky process is practiced. It may not always have this exact appearance as the above example. They may not have people count off to put them in groups. They may not divide the large gathering into groups at all. But once you become educated to the manipulation, it becomes obvious that this is what is taking place. If you then make an attempt to upset the facilitator's "apple cart," by voicing an opinion or suggestions that go contrary to their agenda, it becomes very apparent that your input is no longer wanted or appreciated. The process is used extensively in the Agenda 21 plans from those in the higher positions down to local city councils, schools, and even in churches.

Hence, we have the Assisi Declaration that the religious groups think they came up with when, in fact, the whole meeting had a pre-determined outcome before it even started. It's a dishonest action in violation of the Commandments and is used extensively by many interest groups, including eco-interest groups, which is why you, as Christians, need to educate yourselves so as to recognize when this process and other propaganda is being used against you in your communities or town councils, etc. to make or accept a decision that is not right or even a lie.

CHAPTER ELEVEN

FACT VS FICTION

The wheels of propaganda are constantly turning these days. Many examples of such propaganda exist and cover every topic under the sun: threatened species, endangered species, wet lands, the death penalty, global warming, illegal immigration, the bird flu, recycling, public schooling, mass transit, and a hundred more subjects that you may or may not be in favor of, but if you educated yourself, you would rethink your worldview. To show and then prove to you how you are "conditioned" to accept something that is true as false, or false as true, we picked one subject among many: Global Warming. Global warming is the large atmospheric increase in temperature caused by the increase of greenhouse gases. With the advent of the Industrial Revolution, man has and continues to release so much gas into the atmosphere, as to raise the earth's temperature, causing the greenhouse effect. Evidence is given that there are too many automobiles on the road and too much consumption of oil, coal, etc., which is causing the temperature increase. As a result of these temperatures increasing, we are and will continue to experience horrendous flooding, increases in storm activity, and catastrophic worldwide climate changes. Global warming is said to be so dangerous that it is necessary for an immediate and dramatic reduction in the world's energy use of coal, oil, etc., and a severe program of international rationing of technology.[187]

Students in universities down to kindergarten classes are being taught the threats from global warming. Everyday, somewhere in the media, you will find articles warning of imminent dangers to our future from global warming. Those who hold political offices often speak of the global warming threat and our need to reduce carbon dioxide from the atmosphere to stop temperatures from rising because of the dangers mentioned above. Special interest groups are calling for an increase in mass transit systems in order to keep cars off the road to stop the oceans from flooding, ice caps from melting, forests from burning up, the living earth from being severely damage-stricken, all of which threaten man's very survival.

The media often speaks in unison with political sources and everyday they echo each other in heralding the coming disasters due to global warming. *USA Today*, on three consecutive days, May 30, 31, and June

1, 2006, ran a whole series of articles, reporting on the danger to the world because of global warming. In only three days coverage, these articles contained 17,000 words! *TIME* magazine printed a pictorial report called "Nature's Extremes" which states:

> *"Man's continued reliance on fossil fuels that emit carbon dioxide is extremely harmful to the planet's climate. The search for alternative fuel will be a dominant theme of 21st century science."* [188]

Anyone who has maintained a clear, Biblical worldview would have an aversion to all the above. You may not know the facts, you may not understand why you don't buy into global warming as a threat, but you know God is in control, and He will sustain and balance out the earth, if need be. But is there a need to do something about global warming?

Tied to Agenda 21 and Sustainable Development, the United Nations passed the Kyoto (Japan) Global Warming Agreement, in December 1997, along with other proposals. It urged for all nations to work to limit greenhouse gases. All countries, except the United States and Australia ratified the proposal.[189] The U.S. is scorned for not doing so and efforts are now being made to make the Kyoto treaty binding, forcing the U.S.

to comply through international law. Meanwhile, Canada, who had signed the agreement, failed to meet Kyoto's reduction emission, rating 35% over compliance. Environmental Minister, Ronda Ambrose, announced the week of May 11, 2006, that to comply with the Kyoto protocol targets, "we would have to take every train, plane, and automobile off the streets of Canada." She said, "That is not realistic." Canada is making plans to abandon Kyoto global warming plans.[190] But what about the danger of global warming if Canada does this? Consider the following: Thirty-one thousand seventy-two… that's 31,072 scientists signed a petition stating:

Global Warming Petition

> *We urge the United States government to reject the global warming agreement that was written in Kyoto, Japan in December 1997 and other similar proposals. The (U.N's) proposed limits on greenhouse gases would harm the environment, hinder the advancement of science and technology and damage the health and welfare of mankind."* [191]

What? You've never heard that in the media, or from the political green voices, or within the educational system. The U.N's Kyoto Agreement of limiting greenhouse gases to stop the danger of global warming will actually harm the environment?! Harm health?! Harm the welfare of mankind?! That's what *satan* wants. To harm the environment, health, and man's welfare. But the global warming alarmists are supposed to be the good guys, helping man and the earth!!

Consider this: 31,072 physicists, geophysicists, climatologists, meteorologists, oceanographers, environmentalists, and other specialists of chemistry, biochemistry, biology, and of life sciences, who have signed the above declaration, also stated the following:

> *"There is no convincing scientific evidence that human release of carbon dioxide, methane, or other greenhouse gases is causing or will in the foreseeable future, cause catastrophic heating of the earth's atmosphere and disruption of the earth's climate. Moreover, there is substantial scientific evidence that increases in atmospheric carbon dioxide produces many beneficial effects upon the natural plant and animal environments of the earth."* [192]

What? The more carbon dioxide produced actually *benefits* nature, animals, and the environment?! God wants to benefit nature, animals and the environment. satan wants to take away those benefits. satan always wants to harm man. The program, through the Kyoto Accords, is to reduce oil consumption, the use of coal, etc., and to reduce carbons released into the atmosphere caused by the Industrial Revolution unto industry today! This will disrupt the balance of population in relation with the production of nature. Confusing?

A prevailing number of scientists, by an overwhelmingly large margin, concur that just 300 years ago, an unusually cold period known as the "Little Ice Age" [193] brought one of the lowest sea surface and atmospheric temperatures over a 3,000 year span. We now are in a natural warming trend, recovering temperatures from those cool temperatures, a warming period that scientific facts show is not caused by man. We do have a carbon dioxide increase, an increase scientists say is safe to assume man is causing. But temperatures rising are not due to carbon dioxide or other gases being released into the atmosphere...yet this is being promoted religiously as fact by global warming alarmists. The "danger" of global warming was a theory, never fact; a theory that has been easily disproved by scientific data and a theory that is no longer valid. Again, global warming is happening, but it is not a threat nor is it caused by man. The global warming alarmists know these facts as well. But they also know they have an agenda to achieve. There is also billions of dollars to be had in promoting the false *threat* of global warming. Global warming puts fear into the masses in order to get the masses to concede to an agenda involving multiple dishonorable interests from several groups who have come together to share the spoils of both money and power, gained through the increase of controls. These controls involve locking away wilderness areas from man, but also involves birth control, population control and a host of other controls that are slowly being placed upon American citizens through propagandist conditioning.

Not just man, but all animals, and the ocean itself, among many other things, release carbon dioxide. Man and his activities release the least. The promotion that the release of carbon dioxide by man is raising the earth's temperature is in clear contradiction to what scientific facts show. Yes, man has caused greater release of gases, which is a benefit, scientists say. But man is not causing the earth's temperature to rise. Who is behind the slick campaign of global warming propaganda? The media, environmentalists and politicians. They stand together on one side and on the other side stand the scientists. The overwhelming majority of scientists support the opposite claim of global warming, including 83 percent of climatologists. [194] The global warming propaganda machines promote that carbons (dioxide, etc), being released because of 'pollutant' man, is resulting in temperatures rising, which is causing a dangerous greenhouse effect. The scientists say the opposite is happening:

> *"Indeed, recent carbon dioxide rises have shown a tendency to follow rather than lead global temperature increases."* [195]

Consider this: Do people build cold frames in their backyards, and nursery plant growers build greenhouses in their nurseries to make their home gardens and businesses more prosperous? Yes! You guessed it! Plant life flourishes because the greenhouse effect is a good environment for growth. Why would you know the answer is "yes" and the global warm-ists not know this? Unless, of course, they do know. The release of carbons that causes the greenhouse effect is a positive good for man. And yes, this good can be attributed to man because of man's use of oil, natural gases, etc., brought on by the Industrial Revolution. In addition, data from scientists released by the Oregon Institute of Science and Medicine (OISM) and the George C. Marshall Institute stated that:

> *"...data show that present day temperatures are*

not at all unusual compared with natural variability, nor are they changing in any unusual way." [196]

The year 1996 was the 38th coolest year of the 20th century and 1997 was the 56th! [197] Studying layers of sediment on the ocean floor show there are no "global warming" catastrophes recorded in human history during the last 3,000 years, even though temperatures have been far higher most of that time than our present temperature.[198] About 1,000 years ago, the earth reached one of the highest temperatures of the 3,000 year span. In that time period, scientists discovered that everything in nature was ordered for the best. There was a flourishing of nature. All creation adapted to the temperature changes and produced the "most good," or as Webster's dictionary would define the word ***"optimum****, the greatest degree attained or attainable under specified conditions."* That period is known in science as the "Medieval Climate *Optimum*." [199]

Wouldn't it be just like God to have a trigger mechanism in the earth that as man populates and develops the earth, he helps contribute to its health by releasing more carbons in the air, triggering more plant growth, feeding more animals to feed more people! Talk about balance! Apparently, the media, ecoists and politicians haven't figured it out that God has it all figured out. Or maybe it's because they don't want to. When we bring coal, oil and the like out from underneath the earth's surface and use it, we add enriching CO_2 to the atmosphere, helping all living creatures as well as benefiting man. God's mechanism, triggered by the 'use' of resources that God made for us, along with the increase of man's activity, unlock the earth's ability to expand its capability to feed, clothe and shelter the increasing population; the two work together in proportion to each other's growth. To more plainly state this: God's marvelous, abundant creation grows as man grows and decreases as man decreases by the monitoring system built into nature by its Creator, to gauge man's activity and respond to it. The genius and greatness of God displayed! On September 2, 2006, Our Lady said to Mirjana:

> **"...My children, God is Great. Great are His works..."**

The marvelous works of creation are confirmed by the scientists of OISM and the George C. Marshall Institute who stated:

> *"Greenhouse gases cause plant life, and animal life that depends upon it, to thrive. What mankind is doing is liberating carbon beneath the Earth's*

> *surface* (mining, coal, oil, etc.) *and putting it into the atmosphere where it is available for conversion into living organisms."* [200]

What scientists are telling us will help lift man out of poverty. And yet, the media, environmentalists and politicians are telling us in order to save plant life, animal life and the earth, we must greatly reduce, even stop the use of these resources which will hurt those most impoverished. This is the opposite of what the scientists are saying. Hence, why the scientists' declaration, that includes 31,072 scientists' signatures, states:

> *"...limits on greenhouse gases would harm the environment, hinder the advance of science and technology and damage the health and welfare of mankind."* [201]

What God wants, satan wants so that he can fruit it into the opposite. And his mimic pretends to save the earth by restricting resources but will actually put the earth out of balance, resulting in just the opposite of God's abundance and will bring about the decline of man. In clear terms, the plans of darkness, restricting resources from the present population in relation to its present numbers, will cause an overrun of the necessities of life by leaving less carbon dioxide, resulting in less plants and animals being fed in relation to the population. This will bring about an imbalance of creation, resulting in the impoverishment of man. With higher concentration of carbon dioxide in the atmosphere, we can expect a greening of agriculture. Carbon dioxide added to crops show flourishing growth as these gases are like fertilizer. Even in dry conditions, the greenhouse gases will benefit areas such as Africa, portions of western United States, and other dry regions of the earth. The report, *Environmental Effects of Increased Atmospheric Carbon Dioxide* states:

> *"As atmospheric CO_2 increases, plant growth rates increase. Also, leaves lose less water as CO_2 increases, so that plants are able to grow under drier conditions. Animal life, which depends upon plant life for food, increases proportionally."* [202]

Our Lady says She leads us into a new time where we will get to know God more.

January 25, 1993

> **"...I guide you into a new time, a time which God gives you as grace, so that you may get to know Him more..."**

Our Lady says we will know God and encounter Him in nature.

October 25, 1995

"...I invite you to go into nature because there you will meet God the Creator..."

Our Lady's messages point us to nature and confirms for man the wondrous work of our creation. But satan is pointing man, with all his might, away from creation and its use. The scientists of OISM state that CO_2 fertilization has greatly benefited agriculture and:

"...benefits in the future will likely be spectacular."[203]

satan doesn't want us to know that. Nor does he want us to know that animal life will increase proportionally to the increase of CO_2. The scientists state:

"(In) a study of 94 terrestrial ecosystems on all continents except Antarctica, species richness (biodiversity)" is tied more to *"the total 'quantity' of plant life per acre than with anything else."* [204]

The four scientists who wrote the scientific research report on global warming, Arthur Robinson, Sallie Baliunas, Willie Soon and Zachary Robinson, concluded their findings with these words:

"Human use of coal, oil, and natural gas has not measurably warmed the atmosphere, and the

extrapolation of current trends shows that it will not significantly do so in the foreseeable future. It does, however, release CO_2*, which accelerates the growth rates of plants and also permits plants to grow in drier regions. Animal life, which depends upon plants, also flourishes.*

"As coal, oil, and natural gas are used to feed and lift from poverty vast numbers of people across the globe, more CO_2 *will be released into the atmosphere. This will help to maintain and improve the health, longevity, prosperity, and productivity of all people.*

"Human activities are believed to be responsible for the rise in CO_2 *level of the atmosphere. Mankind is moving the carbon in coal, oil, and natural gas from below ground to the atmosphere and surface, where it is available for conversion into living things. We are living in an increasingly lush environment of plants and animals as a result of the* CO_2 *increase. Our children will enjoy an earth with far more plant and animal life as that with which we now are blessed. This is a wonderful and unexpected gift from the Industrial Revolution."* [205]

Now isn't that just like God to want that? And isn't that just like satan to stop that?

The threat of global warming is a lie. It is satan's lie to strike out at God, the Creator, to condition people toward shortage ecology in order to harm man. Shortage ecology is a mind-set of a fear that we will run out of resources. Therefore, it is necessary to severely restrict or entirely stop the use of these resources. This is an atheistic mind-set, one that believes that there is no God who has programmed provisions into creation to provide for man in his needs. We've lost our ability, through a lack of wisdom, to see with clarity what is truth. If you felt an aversion to the lie of global warming, your soul is on the right track. Change your life further, accepting and living fully the Sabbath Command, and you will see these traits of darkness and why they are occurring. Ask yourself why the same person who would not stand outside an abortion clinic to pray to end abortion will stand outside a prison for a candlelight vigil to stop the death penalty. Why is that? Some are for life. Some pretend to be for life. They fight for a cause to stop, for instance, the death penalty, which advances their agenda for a more tolerant society, tolerant towards sin. Many issues today are for the destruction of society. Those who believe strongest in Biblical teaching would subscribe to abundance ecology and those not believing in Biblical teaching subscribe to shortage ecology. It all comes down to a prevailing atheistic mentality. We are allowing atheistic mentalities to condition us through media, political, and environmental sources who are without the Triune God, and who are impressing upon our thinking secular worldviews which are leading man away from God. The more we hear Christians using the word "ecology," the more we know that success is being made in changing the Christian worldview to a secular worldview. *Ecology* is the secular terminology for what Christians should know and refer to as *Creation*. Again, the language game plays in conditioning your worldview.

A Different Perspective on Pollution

SOCIETY IS CONTINUALLY BEING CONDITIONED to adopt a mentality that says the taking of goods from the earth wounds the earth, even to the point of damaging it irreparably. This is resulting in another mentality: Ban man. Lock away land from him. Man is the great polluter simply by virtue of being human. Pollution is all his fault. Man is the disgrace of all species. Review the many voices: educational, political, environmental, the media, and you will see this mentality ranging from the subliminal to blatant, exaggerated, and false indictments of man. Yet this mentality that is growing is contradicted by a report of the Geophysicists Institute in Fairbanks, Alaska. Larry Gedney, seismologist of the Institute writes:

> "*...it's not human habitation that most often causes stream and well water pollution. It's Nature herself.*" [206]

If you place ⅓ cup of sugar in ⅓ cup of water some of the sugar will not dissolve. The water, holding the maximum amount of dissolved particles of sugar, leave no room for the rest of the solid sugar to melt. Add ⅔ more water, giving more space to each dissolved particle and all the sugar will melt. Seismologist Larry Gedney writes:

> (In Alaska)"*...it is often a shock to first-time kayakers, rafters, or river boat travelers to find that these pristine waterways sometimes have the appearance of something they wouldn't want to stick a finger into...Glacial streams and almost all the large rivers which they feed, are carrying the maximum amount of glacial silt that they can transport. This causes a hissing which can easily be heard when tiny particles brush beneath a canoe or raft.*" [207]

After the water's capacity is maxed-out with dissolved silt, like the sugar, particles of silt that do not dissolve must go somewhere which end up on the banks and at the bottom of rivers. A large ship churning by turns water to a milky color from these deposits. In the second week of March 2003, winds in Alaska picked up enormous amounts of dry silt from the banks of Alaska streams and rivers making massive streamers of pollution that streaked over the Gulf of Alaska, closing Anchorage airport, and causing injuries and damages across the region.[208] On top of that, add active volcanoes and their pollution. Add to that the silt produced by over 100,000 glaciers clogging up the waterways. From that you can form a mental picture of the Valdez oil spill, in comparison to the massive amounts of pollution created by Alaska's own ecosystem. It would be like placing a flea next to an elephant. And yet, so much was made over the "catastrophe" of the Valdez oil spill by the media, environmentalists and politicians. The ecological facts of Alaska's enormous daily, nature-producing pollution, side-by-side with the oil spill, makes the oil spill miniscule and insignificant, whether speaking of the amount of pollution it caused, the loss of animal life, the air quality, etc.

Nobody wants an oil spill. However, the media pushed the story of dead birds to an extreme and grandstanded events to condition the public about the Valdez incident. Anyone with common sense, who understands the dynamics of wild Alaska, couldn't help but be amused, if not suspect of the intentions behind the environmentalists' "concern and created fears." For all those who saw through the propagandist's motives, there was one memorable moment that brought the "incident" full circle, which took place during a media/environmentalist grandstanding event. Members of the Green movement had raised $225,000 to purchase and transport a seal to the waters of the oil spill after the clean up was complete. There they planned to release it amidst the celebration of the clean-up in the presence of distinguished guests of the Green movement who had come to witness this great event. Proud of their achievement, patting each other on the back with smiles, they jubilantly released their seal, watched it as it entered the water, saw it swim a short distance away and then get gobbled up by a killer whale.

It's O.K. Nobody's watching if you laugh. Mind you, seals flourished in the surrounding areas and even after the clean-up, the seals quickly repopulated. The point being made is when you cut your finger or scrape your knee, it heals.

Most people have noticed this.

Think of the 100,000 glaciers pouring unimaginable tons of polluting silt into waterways, or account for acid volcanoes filling the air, and dust storms filling the skies. It is conceivable that Alaska creates more silt pollution than the construction industry combined produces in the lower 48. Yet when you go a few miles from any of the 100,000 glaciers, you will find pristine clear waterways by actions of gravity pulling the silt downward and depositing it on the bottom and banks of rivers. You'll find enriched soils due to the deposits from volcanoes. You'll find rain-washed beautiful skies formerly filthy with pollution.

Most people have noticed this.

Not being naive, we know that pollution does exist. Anyone living in places like Los Angeles, California will tell you that one can see, almost any time of the day, an orange haze surrounding this city, caused by thousands of vehicles on the road, and pollution of other kinds. Los Angeles gets very little rain. But even if you go to another big city, such as New York City that does frequently receive rain, the pollution is no where near as bad because of the frequent rainfalls. You can see and experience a great difference in the air that you breathe in New York compared to L.A. caused by cleansing rains. Yet, even as we speak of this comparison, Our

Lady has come to reveal certain truths to man during this age, one of which is that God does not intend man to be so crammed together in large cities. This is man's design, not God's. Our Lady said:

October, 1981

> **"...the West has made civilization progress, but without God, as if they were their own creators."**

The earth is quite capable of balancing out and neutralizing the pollution caused by man when man is spread out throughout the land. In the name of progress, man eliminated God from the equation. He did not seek His wisdom as the modern world developed and now suffers from a civilization that harms not only his soul, but also his body by being separated from the land, from the earth, from His creation. And so man is no longer able to enjoy the fruits of God's creation which were made for him and for his good. Most Americans eat processed foods instead of fresh produce grown in their own gardens, fresh meat provided by grass and natural grain raised animals, fresh milk from their dairy cows. Processed foods are known to be bad for the human body. Today's man **is not** succumbing to cancer and diseases because the earth cannot handle the pollution caused by too many men on the planet, he is succumbing to these things because today's man is living contrary to the way God intended man to live. Man inherited a world of self-made problems and diseases through removing God. Again, Our Lady explains the errors of our ways.

April 10, 1986

> **"...A flower is not able to grow normally without water. So also you, dear children, are not able to grow without God's blessing. From day to day you need to seek His blessing so you will grow normally and perform all your actions in union with God..."**

Even in this example, Our Lady uses creation to explain that without God's blessing we cannot grow normally. A flower without water wilts; it is more susceptible to diseases; it has little resistance to heat, cold, frost, and wind. It becomes brittle, parched, and falls more and more into a weakened state, disease ridden. It does not grow to its full potential. Our Lady says of our growth, not to even take a step without God.

September 2, 2006

> **"...Do not deceive yourselves that you can do anything without Him, not even to take a single step..."**

Change your life, live God's commandments, adopt a strong Biblical Christian worldview and notice how your finger, knee and the earth heal and recover. You'll then have insight in recognizing agendas that wish to squash God out of everything so to build a world without God. You will no longer be blind to the elements that have conditioned you to build a world without God. We repeat Our Lady's words:

October, 1981

> **"...the West has made civilization progress, but without God, as if they were their own creators."**

You Must Change Your Mentality

CONSIDER ALL THAT YOU HAVE JUST READ about global warming and pollution. How many other issues do you not have the facts about? And if you did, how would you rethink your position? Do you think, *"O.K. I've learned truths about global warming but on other subjects I have a good perspective."*?

Darwin referred to the cell as the simple base element. Do you realize that there are two trillion chemical actions in a single cell in one second? Did you know that man has not even the capability to build a computer that could equal to one cell? Do you know man cannot even *imagine* a computer that could equal to the workings of a single cell? Do you know that the respected Professor of molecular biophysics and biochemistry who is one of the country's foremost biophysicists, Harold Morowitz, came to the conclusion that for man to come up with a chemically evolving cell, as described by evolutionists, it would take 10 to the 340 millionth power of years to evolve this simple, base element?[209] Did you know that electrons, and not grains of sand or dust, are the most plentiful element throughout the earth, our galaxy and the one billion other galaxies that exist? Did you know that science calculates that there are 10 to the 80th power of electrons throughout the entire universe, throughout all of creation? That number will give you a new perspective for how long it would take to evolve a single cell, through time, according to Professor Morowitz's 10 to the 340 millionth power of years calculation! An unimaginable number of years.

Evolutionists say that human life evolved through just over four billion years of the earth's existence. So let's say 4½ billion years. Yet, according to Professor Morowitz, four and a half billion years is not enough time for a human life to have evolved. Forty billion years is not enough time. Forty thousand billion years is not enough time. Forty million billion years is not enough time. And forty billion, billion years is not enough time, not even close to evolving just one single cell in the way evolutionists claim we evolved. Dr. Emile Borel, who discovered the laws of probability, said:

> *"The occurrence of any event where the chances are beyond one in ten followed by 50 zeros is an event which we can state with certainty will never happen, no matter how much time is allotted and no matter how many conceivable opportunities could exist for the event to take place."* [210]

Evolution, as taught, is false, though it is promoted by curriculums in all levels of education as worthy of belief so to deny God, His immensity and His sovereignty. Do your own research. You will find these atheistic teachings are being taught, without being challenged by you, to your children, deforming their outlook on God, which is leading to a more atheistic society.

Atheism needs to believe in an atheistic evolution in order to disprove God, such as life evolved over a period of a few hundred million years from a pond of green slime, mixed with sunshine. The evolutionists have their own mantra: evolution is the sole origin of creation. That's why you will find no debate by academics around the world because they know evolution is easily challenged and torn apart. Simple disapproval of evolution as taught is evolution itself. Where is the evolving ¾ ape and ¼ man, ½ ape and ½ man, ¼ ape and ¾ man? Did we evolve from ape to man on an involuntary path of evolution, and suddenly, the involuntary law of evolution decided to voluntarily stop evolving? Pause and ponder the stupidity to believe what we have been indoctrinated with. The same case is made for millions of other species. There is not one identified "part something" and "part something else." Scour the earth. Nothing exists that is in transition. Is that not an assault against logic? Then what is evolution, as taught, but a lie? If you ever enter a dark cave and find pools of water, you will find fish, such as Brim, without eyes. They've adapted to their environment. It is the same today with some primitive people who live high in the mountains and walk barefoot in the snow because of *adaptation*. Over generations, their feet grew shorter and veins increased for more blood flow which gave greater warmth. Their feet also thickened, enabling them to tolerate ice and snow without a problem. So it's not to say some things do not change, but is it evolution?

A brand new, idiotic evolutionary idea was released recently. The following was given credibility by being published in the science section of an international news magazine. It shows how the media honors evolution, and because it is from anthropologists of the University of California, it is elevated as sound theory.

> *"Humans developed into intelligent, observant creatures with color vision and depth perception for one main reason — to avoid snakes. So says anthropologist Lynne Isbell of the University of California, who has proposed a radical new theory about human evolution. She says the development of primates was driven by an evolutionary arms race with snakes. For early primates, snakes were among the most dangerous and ubiquitous predators. It was to detect snakes at close distance, Isbell proposes, that early primates developed color vision, three-dimensional sight, and bigger brains. About 60 million years ago, snakes developed a new weapon: venom. 'The snakes upped the ante,' says Isbell, 'and then the primates had to respond by developing even* <u>*better*</u> *vision.' The theory is more than an interesting way to view our evolution, Cornell evolutionary biologist Harry Greene tells Live Science. It also could explain why the fear of snakes is so deeply imbedded in human psychology and legend. 'We have such*

extreme attitudes towards snakes, varying from deification to ophidiphobia,' or the irrational fear of snakes." [211]

This theory and view of a California University anthropologist, a Cornell University biologist, and an international magazine, in its science section, are three absurdities mixed together in the "green pond of slime," which will incubate for a year or two while circulating in the intellectual circle. By then, it will have *'evolved'* enough credibility for schools to present the new theory to young minds in schools to condition and direct them.

Though this "theory" may have amused you, it should have made you angry. Any whisper of the origins of Creation, by a Creator, from anyone, teacher or student, challenging an atheistic evolution, even as theory, within the walls of a public school or university, and a lynch mob is sent out to silence you. Yet it would take far greater faith to believe in the above stupid, hair-brained theory that humans today see in color because of evolutionary reactions to avoid snakes.

Your so-called schools, institutions of learning, and governments are teaching a falsehood; the creation and evolution of the humanistic man is the truth that is evolving, associated with evolution, as it is taught. But one may say things evolve! True, as with a fish in the blackness of a cave, if you want to call that "evolution." These *adaptations to conditions* is not what is being taught by atheistic evolution. Evolution, as taught today, is for the evolution of the humanistic man, growing an atheistic world society, which denies God, the Creator who can instantaneously create a cell, a cell that would take 10 to the 340 millionth power of years to evolve by the Theory of Evolution! As stated earlier, *"Forty billion, billion years is not enough time, not even close to evolving just one single cell."* Forty quintillion as it would be called, or forty billion, billion years is 4 followed by 19 zeros. Get a stack of paper out. Write the number 1 and then write 340 million zeros behind it and you'll begin to get the picture of 10 to the 340th millionth power. Yet a fish, which is much more complicated than a single cell, in a few generations loses its eyes through "adaptation," obviously programmed into its makeup by the Creator. Evolution, as taught, is another round of lies used to kill belief in the Creator in order to place man at the source and center of all things. Our Lady's words:

October 1981

> **"...progress, but without God, as if they were their own creators."**

Writing about the documentary *"Darwin's Deadly Legacy,"* Gary Schneeberger of *Citizen Magazine*, writes how Darwinism has inspired Planned Parenthood founder, Margaret Sanger, Hitler, and Columbine High School killer Eric Harris. He writes that the documentary:

> *"In relatively short order....makes sure viewers understand that Darwinism not only has been responsible for hundreds of millions of deaths historically, but also that it's based on slipshod science that continues to be passed off in public schools as gospel."* [212]

So does it seem reasonable as a parent or teacher to revolt as stated in #9 of the Nine Declarations, now knowing the facts? If you still do not think strongly challenging these teachings and institutions are justified, then think of the Darwin Theory which inspired the elimination of the "undesirable" members of the human "species" – Hundreds of millions of people in just one century! Then think of the cute little diagrams of chimpanzees, with each stage slowly turning into modern man, drawing upon Darwin's Theory that inspired Planned Parenthood founder, Margaret Sanger, Carl Marx, Lenin (who didn't believe the theory but found it useful), Adolf Hitler, and Eric Harris. All of them adopting "natural selection," the survival of the fittest—which translated into actions in one form or another that all undesirables must be eliminated. While "natural selection" as defined "as survival of the fittest" is true in nature, Darwin's theory of man evolving from organisms and then from animals, classes man in the same lot as all other animals in the animal kingdom through which "natural selection" can then be applied. This is why Lenin, Hitler, and their company liked Darwin's theory that man is just one of the animals of the earth. It gave them the "theological" means to achieve their aims. Eric Harris wrote on his web site the day of the Columbine High School killings in Colorado, in which 13 people were killed and 24 injured:

> *"You know what I love? Natural Selection... The best thing that ever happened on the earth. Getting rid of all the stupid and ignorant organisms."*[213]

That fateful day Eric Harris wore on his T-shirt his motto from Darwin's Theory, the words *"Natural Selection."* In essence meaning, "man was not made in God's image, but is just a by-product of biological happenstance."[214] Think now, are you not justified to strongly and steadfastly challenge the educational system, turning it upside down as happened with the money changers in the temple?

Yet, if you still do not think justification exists, pause and think about it, as society continues in this atheistic direction, you as Christians are already being considered by many as an unnecessary organism. First steps of this mentality are showing up in Europe by referring to Christians as the *"Christian race."* These signs mirror what took place in the 1930s — a time when those who could have done something did not. We know what resulted and if we do nothing now, the mirror will continue to reflect the same results for us.

So see, in a few pages, you gain a new mentality about the godless evolution theory that has been drilled into you and into your children by an education curriculum bent on denying God, the Creator. Once you take charge of what you allow to condition you, there will be literally hundreds of false "facts" and ideas that you will have to "re-think," changing your thoughts, positions, and mentalities to a Biblical worldview. That is what Our Lady wants.

> *"Metanoia. A Greek word meaning a change of mind. A radical revision and transformation of our whole mental process…whereby God takes*

center place in our consciousness, in our awareness, and in our minds." [215]

Metanoia is the process of conversion. It's the process of convincing our thinking to think through everything, apply everything with God being the central thought that connects-the-dots. Metanoia is a new-minded way of looking at life.

"...it's an idea of stretching or pushing beyond the boundaries with which we normally think and feel...a complete change of perspective... Metanoia, often translated 'repentance,' but it's not a backward-looking glance of regret, it's a forward-looking vision of hope. Metonoia is a new openness to what is truly objective, beyond ourselves, our view of life, how we put the data together." [216]

Even as Christians, how we put data together determines a Biblical or secular worldview. It's why Our Lady has said:

1984–85

"...There are many Christians who live like pagans..."

What will determine society's future, is what prevailing worldview is held by its citizens. Christians must put the Bible into life. Our Lady's words provide for us today, the impulse to adapt Scripture that is 2,000 years old to our modern times. Her words are the bridge that connects a time when man traveled by foot, camel and donkey to a time when man now flies on silver wings. But we have grown dumb, speechless in our inability to convict because of our inability to understand the significance of breaking the Commandment of the Sabbath, all the while condemning a non-believer for breaking the Commandment of killing (abortion.) How does God view a pagan, who is without knowledge of His ways, in comparison to one who has knowledge of His ways, but who lives as a pagan? What is pagan in your life? What do you need to change? By sincerely identifying and changing these things in your life, wisdom will flood in and all things will become clear. You will not learn these things or accomplish them through the state schools and university systems nor through the media, but rather through Scripture and Our Lady's messages, through prayer and the Spirit of God. The Holy Spirit will guide you from there. You will know how to compute the world's data into a Biblical worldview that will result into solid life direction. In this way society will change and by no other means.

By not looking at all things Biblically, we are easily overcome by darkness and begin to lose our freedoms, not so much through the deceptive powers of darkness, but by our loss of power to convict. When one can no longer convict, one grows tired and then complacent, knowing nothing can change. It is why we are in constant need of conversion, a process which Our Lady said never ends until we die:

July 17, 1989

> **"...Conversion is a process which goes on through your entire life."**

News investigators, newspapers, reporters, etc., are suppose to investigate events. How is it that these writings can easily reveal the lie behind global warming— and anyone can do the same if they seek it. How is it that a host of news conglomerates, massive news organizations, TV and newspaper investigators have not uncovered this scandalous lie of our times about the fallacy of the "threat" of global warming? One can easily conclude that the media is filled with liars and cheaters driven by agendas incapable of giving honest information. They are no different than news agencies such as 'TASS', Russia's former communist news organization, whose soul purpose was to make, protect and support the state god through controlling the free thought of those living under the socialist system of that day. TASS news served propaganda then, as the Associated Press feeds newspapers across the world today. It is dangerous to watch or read the news, to be educated by a public school system which denies God, or to listen to any of the voices of the world. You must form and build a solid Biblical/Christian worldview, and you cannot do that through the present media, educational, and political systems.

Very few are pausing to think: "I'm sending my children, or grandchildren, to a public school which denies God!" Think for a moment how incredulous it is to send your children to such a system, a school of the state in which to learn, you must open your mind and heart to a system which prohibits God. It does not matter if a teacher "sneaks" in God. The curriculum promotes secular humanism; a godless system producing a godless society. Save the children. Get them out! School them at home. You must change the direction of your life, pray, live the Commandments, read the Bible and Our Lady's messages everyday and then all things trying to guide your thoughts will emit, either light or darkness, and you will be able to navigate towards the direction you must walk. As a prophet of old, you will have knowledge of what is unseen by the world and will know God exists in all matters because you will know truth.

June 16, 1983

> **"I have come to tell the world that God is truth; He exists..."**

CHAPTER TWELVE

"I INVITE YOU TO GO INTO NATURE"....... OH, NO YOU DON'T!

The monkey of God, satan, wants to injure God by taking away what He wants. God wants your soul. satan wants to take it away from Him. Our Lady wants nature to display the glory of God to man. Our Lady's words confirm that this is Her desire. satan, therefore, creates and institutes a plan closely paralleling God's plan — but for the purpose to keep man *from nature*, so that he can have what God wants.

October 25, 1995

> **"...I invite you to go into nature because there you will meet God the Creator. Today I invite you, little children, to thank God for all that He gives you. In thanking Him you will discover the Most High and all the 'goods' that surround you..."**

There was an incident with a group who was traveling through Georgia. They said upon stopping to attend church, they noticed signs posted next to the church grounds: "No Human Trespassing. Wet Lands. You Will Be Prosecuted." All the land that could be seen was dry land. Agenda 21 plans, such as this one, are cropping up everywhere, and you will see more and more that **"I invite you to go into nature..."** will become more and more difficult and unlawful. Federal and State Parks have for decades been good sources to "go into nature." So it came as a shock when, recently, a couple visiting a glacier park in Alaska was stopped from going to see a mammoth waterfall because a bird laid an egg in the area where one would have to walk to get to the waterfall. The bird was not an endangered or threatened species. It was one of among tens of thousands flying through the 17 million acre park. The couple, along with many other visitors to the falls, would most likely never have another opportunity to come back again to encounter this beautiful part of nature, as Our Lady invites. But a new mentality is emerging that the needs of non-human species take precedence over human needs. It was evident to them that the bird was far enough to the side that it would not have even been bothered by those walking the path to the falls, which was a distance away. But even if it was, animal space now is not only equal but superior to man's space and his right to go into nature. Our Lady clearly echoes the Scriptures that good's' of the land belong to man, not man to the goods.

May 25, 1989

> **"...You see, little children, how nature is opening herself and is giving life and fruits..."**

Giving life and fruits for man in his needs.

August 25, 1999

> **"...Also today I call you to give glory to God the Creator in the colors of nature. He speaks to you also through the smallest flower about His beauty and the depth of love with which He has created you. Little children, may prayer flow from your hearts like fresh water from a spring. May the wheat fields speak to you about the mercy of God towards every creature. That is why, renew prayer of thanksgiving for everything He gives you..."**

While these messages would seem to be the goal of what Sustainable Development is, Agenda 21's goal is rather the opposite. Sustainable Development is the closing off of nature. It is a plan of packing people in tight living zones while creating "human-free" zones in nature, vast areas where humans are not able to live, even if they own the land. Again, it is encouraged to do your own research. You will find innumerable numbers of laws, treaties, regulations, government partnerships with private organizations called N.G.O.'s (Non-Government Organizations) which continue to rapidly move towards ultimately controlling or denying every unalienable right given to man. This contradiction between man's enjoyment, use, and stewardship of creation vs the sustainablists' agenda shows a clear conflict. But it confirms and also displays what God wants vs what satan wants. Viewing one vs the other, they almost appear to be the same. But again, it's a mimic, not quite but almost the same, giving a very close appearance of a clone, as satan orchestrates to redirect God's movement of man, through Our Lady's call, toward creation. A view of the application of Christian use and stewardship of creation, appears in Maria Valtorta's Poem of the Man-God.* Valtorta recorded Jesus' explanation of the use of creation:

> *"... when God created woman, Adam's helpmate, like him made in the image and likeness of God... God said to man and woman: 'Be fruitful, multiply, fill the Earth and conquer it, and be masters of the fish of the sea, of the birds of heaven and of*

* Maria Valtorta, an Italian mystic from the 1940s authored the writing The Poem of the Man-God, on the life of Jesus and the Virgin Mary. The work became popular when the Virgin Mary in Medjugorje was asked if these books could be read by the faithful. Our Lady responded by strongly encouraging the reading of these books.

all living animals on the Earth,' and He also said: 'See, I give you all the seed-bearing plants that are on the Earth, and all the trees with seed-bearing fruit, that they may serve as food for you and for all the animals of the Earth and for the birds of heaven and for everything that moves on the Earth and has in itself a living soul, that they may live.'

"The animals and plants, and everything the Creator made to be useful to man, are a gift of love and a patrimony committed to the care of His children by the Father, so that they may use it with profit and gratitude to the Giver of all providence. Therefore, they are to be loved and treated with proper care... Man must take care of what God with providential love has placed at his disposal. Care does not mean idolatry or immoderate affection for animals or plants, or anything else. Care means feeling of compassion and gratitude for the minor things that serve us and have a life of their own, that is their sensitivity.

"The living soul of inferior creatures mentioned by Genesis, is not the same as the soul of man. It is life, simply life, that is, being sensitive to real things, both material and emotional. When an

animal dies it becomes insensitive because death is its real end. There is no future for it. But while it lives it suffers cold, hunger, fatigue, it is subject to injuries, to pain, to joy, to love, to hatred, to diseases and to death. And man, in remembrance of God, Who gave him such means to make his exile on the Earth less difficult, must be humane towards animals, his inferior servants....

"I solemnly tell you that the works of the Creator are to be contemplated with justice. If one looks at them with justice, one sees that they are 'good.' And good things are to be always loved. We see that they are given for a good purpose and out of an impulse of love, and as such we can and must love them, seeing beyond the finite being, the Infinite Being, Who created them for us... God made everything with a good aim and with love for man. Man must use everything with upright purpose and with love for God, Who gave him everything on the Earth, that it may be subject to the king of Creation (man)." [217]

So similar are God's plans and Agenda 21's plans for creation's use that it's easy to be deceived. It is for the very purpose of deceiving that satan closely parallels and mimics the plans of God. While very close in appearance, the difference of the two is shown clearly by the statement Maria Valtorta says that Jesus said.

> *"Care does not mean idolatry or immoderate affection for animals or plants, or anything else."*[218]

The eco-movement is in clear contradiction of this statement. Of the two views between what God wants vs what satan wants, one view only will win out and, as of right now, the Biblical view of creation is losing.

In the U.N. document "Sustainable Communities Report of the Sustainable Communities Task Force," there is much about making communities sustainable. It sounds like the supreme answer to all the world's problems. But upon looking into their detailed documentation, which the news information sources ignore and do not report, with the help of the influence of revisionists, you will begin discovering the inroads and controls being made in your own hometown "places" and cities where you live. If there is not yet a plan for your area (often called "comprehensive zoning plans"), be on the lookout because these plans are presently hitting like a tsunami. A few Christians are slowly becoming aware of how these plans have and continue to develop, especially with private property and not being able to use their's for life, liberty, and the pursuit of happiness.

What About Food? Controlling the Growing of Your Own Food

AT A U.N. CONFERENCE ON HUMAN SETTLEMENTS, IN ISTANBUL, June 1996, the Department of Housing and Urban Development turned in a 25-page report. It declared:

> "*...we will be growing foods, dietary supplements, and herbs that make up* (for our) *unsustainable reliance upon foods...*(which they claim damage the soil and environment, like sheep, cattle, etc.) *Less and less land will go for animal husbandry and more for* ***grains, tubers and legumes.***" [219]

This is the King's Crown of genius ideas. We'll be able to eat plenty of leftover "**grains**" because cattle will diminish and "**legumes**" will allow us to eat like a bird because we'll have plenty of seeds, and **"tubers,"** such as carrots and potatoes, will be your determined range of food, so you can eat until you turn orange. Notice the human settlement "mentality" of telling you what you will do, *"we will be growing food..."* and "*less and less land will go for animal husbandry.*" Where's your decision if you want meat or other foods? While this may seem ridiculous to you, remember you are being educated to these agendas while most of the population is being conditioned into accepting them as necessary for the future. More and more graduates from our universities are indoctrinated and programmed with these concepts and have been taught that taking these steps is the answer to a host of problems the world is facing. They are conditioned to believe that unless we take these steps, "we are all going to die and the earth's light is going to burn out." As mentioned earlier, it's an atheistic philosophy called ***"shortage ecology."*** Create a shortage and people will accept anything, even the loss of freedom.

It's simple reasoning that it's not up to man to make the world sustainable. It already is! In case some have not noticed, God designed the earth to be sustainable and though this may come as a shock to the U.N.'s Agenda 21 plans, the earth actually heals, replenishes, and expands itself through the direct laws of nature. It's called ***"abundance ecology."***

The shortage ecology mind-set would say we are overpopulated and that the current levels of population are life threatening and a danger to the world's future. Man must do something. The abundance ecology mind-set would say that nature provides for whatever population increases we have. It is God who is trusted to watch over the earth. Our Lady's message clearly reflects abundance ecology.

July 25, 1992

> **"...everyday I bless you with my Motherly Blessing, so that the Lord may bestow you with the abundance of His grace '<u>for</u>' your daily life..."**

Foods are "goods" from the earth that are a grace of "His abundance." "Give us this day, our daily bread." Our daily bread God will provide. All we have to do is obey God's commands and to bless creation as Our Lady says:

December 25, 1988

> **"...Today I give you my Special Blessing. Bring it to all creation, so that all creation will know peace..."**

Christian precepts contain everything necessary to bless the earth in our responsibility for its care. We do not need secular humanists telling the Church what to believe. We are to use creation, use animals, use plants, subdue and have dominion over them. We will not run out as we have been conditioned to believe. Jacqueline Kason's book, <u>The War Against Population</u> states:

> *"No more than 3% of the earth's ice-free land area is occupied by human beings, less than one-ninth is used for agriculture purposes. Eight times,*

and perhaps as much as 22 times, the world's population (5 billion as of 1988) *could support itself at the present standard of living, using present technology; and this* (will still) *leave(s) half the earth's surface open to wild life and conservation areas."* [220]

"Shortage Ecology Doomsdayers" say we are going to run out of everything. Space! Food! Water! Alarmists know it's not true, but if it's reported long enough, they will achieve their agenda. The earth is abundant! The water Jesus washed His hands with still circulates upon the earth. It evaporates, comes back in rain, and cycles again. The earth is not fragile. It is a very strong, tough, healthy, vibrant planet, which has in-house recovery methods designed into it by its Creator who is ever watchful over it. Abandon a large city and in 30 years time it will become a green, animal-filled jungle, displaying a remarkable recovery system that most people are fighting constantly around the globe in their own yards to keep limbs off their roofs, leaves out of their yards, weeds from their flowerbeds, squirrels out of their attics and rats out of their houses. Zillions upon zillions of actions of creation per second across all the earth disprove man's arrogance that the earth's survival depends upon him. No to you, O man of humanistic mind-set. No to you, egotistical man. You are not so important. It is God who is important and your plans only uncover the lie that control is your goal. Our Lady says:

July 25, 2000

> **"...Do not forget that you are here on earth on the way to eternity and that your home is in Heaven. That is why, little children, be open to God's love and leave egoism and sin..."**

Sin will destroy the earth and that is what Our Lady has come to teach us. Our Lady said satan wants:

> **"...not only to destroy human life but also nature and the planet on which you live..."** January 25, 1991

That would be accomplished only through sin, not by using goods of the earth that God has given us.

But even sin will not be allowed to destroy the earth until God's time is ready for it to happen. It is true that Ivan, one of the six Medjugorje visionaries, said that had Our Lady not come to call us to leave sin, the world would have destroyed itself, and it is true that Our Lady has intervened several times to stop nuclear war.* [221] But the fact is, the world did not destroy itself, even though it was going to happen, because Our Lady intercepted the disaster. The world will not end until God is ready for it to end. To take away freedom is satan's goal, because it would lead a multitude to perdition. Our Lady entreats us to be with the land. Being with nature is key to Our Lady's message. The right to have and own property and decide for its use is an unalienable right given to man by God. George Washington said:

"Private property and freedom are inseparable."[222]

Michael Shaw of "Freedom 21 Santa Cruz" states that:

"Sustainable Development has three components.

1. *Global land use*
2. *Global education*
3. *Global population control and reduction.*

The international focus for Sustainable Development is the United States. This is because America

* See the booklet *"Twenty Years of Apparitions"* by A Friend of Medjugorje. It was written in the year 2001 for the 20th Anniversary of Our Lady's apparitions in Medjugorje. It describes many world events that coincide with important Marian dates, especially revealing Our Lady's involvement throughout history when Christian civilization has been greatly at risk. Most impressive is the presence of Our Lady in the events involving the destruction of nuclear arms this past century. See www.mej.com to download.

is the only country in the world based on the ideals of private property. Private property is incompatible with the collectivist premise of Sustainable Development." [223]

You might think, "O.K., with the points made, no one is going to go for the U.N.'s scheme, Agenda 21, Sustainable and Smart Growth Plans." That may be a true assessment. But you came to this assessment only after you read about these plans of darkness and it enlightened you. That's the point! Inform and educate yourself and everyone else. Chapter 8 of Proverbs relays that the highest wisdom becomes identified with the spirit of God through whom the world was created, preserved, and through whom enlightenment is brought to mankind.

"The Lord created me at the beginning of his work, the first of his acts of old. Ages ago I was set up, at the first, before the beginning of the earth. When there were no depths I was brought forth, when there were no springs abounding with water. Before the mountains had been shaped, before the hills, I was brought forth; before he had made the earth with its fields, or the first of the dust of the world. When he established the heavens, I was there, when he drew a

circle on the face of the deep, when he made firm the skies above, when he established the fountains of the deep, when he assigned to the sea its limit, so that the waters might not transgress his command, when he marked out the foundations of the earth, then I was beside him, like a master workman; and I was daily his delight, rejoicing before him always, rejoicing in his inhabited world and delighting in the sons of men."
Proverbs 8:22–31

Wisdom! Our Lady is wisdom. We should strive to deposit in our hearts each word of each of Her messages. Open your heart to receive the spirit of wisdom. The spirit of God is with the man who commits to accepting God's Commandments and living them. In doing so, man receives that common wisdom that brings enlightenment just as can be felt in your heart as you read through this writing, and to a higher degree **if** you made a commitment to change your life to live the Sabbath. The masses are not so enlightened. It is Our Lady who says:

March 18, 2006

"...recognize God's love and the signs of the times in which you live..."

God is freedom. The loss of God is the loss of freedom. In these times, there are so many signs that show this. As we get further down the godless road our nation is traveling, the more these losses of personal liberty and freedom will manifest. We, therefore, must not negate how powerful the conditioning is through the common information sources of our day. Our Lady's words on the previous page begin with the word, **"recognize."** It means to recollect or recover the knowledge of. We recognize a person at a distance when we "recollect" to ourselves that we have seen him before or that we formerly knew him. We recognize his voice or his features. "Recognize God's love…recognize the signs…" Not recognizing the signs or ignoring the signs will lead to the same result as those societies where Communism and Nazism were given freedom to rise. Man gave up control, not recognizing the signs, and eventually became irrevocably tied to the errors that destroyed everything he held dear…family, homeland, and freedom.

CHAPTER THIRTEEN

CONTROL OVER EDUCATION

Though we have covered education in other sections of this writing, this chapter explores how successful the U.N. has been in forming the minds of our youth towards their agendas. After global land use, the second component of the U.N.'s agenda to implement Agenda 21, Sustainable Development, Smart Growth, etc., is through education, which Michael Shaw listed as Global Education.

Dr. George Barna is the head of Barna Research Group, specializing in cultural trends of Christianity. He was astounded at what he discovered through national surveys and up-close interviews. He described:

> *"..the younger generation as being comprised as* ***non-linear*** *thinkers, who cut and paste their beliefs and values from a variety of sources and are* ***comfortable with contradictions!*** *'Almost half don't know and don't care about moral absolutes. To them, it's just a nonissue not worth arguing about...When we try to show them logically that*

two things really don't work together—that one is right and the other is wrong—you will get a giggle and then the response, 'Yeah, how about that?' There's no ***right*** *decision that they're trying to make. All they're trying to do is to please themselves, to gain fulfillment and satisfaction in life. So they arrange all the information in their minds in whatever way that* ***feels*** *best, or* ***seems*** *right, or what they've seen other people do. And then they make decisions that linear thinkers would consider to be illogical, and didn't make sense.'"*

In the course of Barna's research into people's worldviews, they made some amazing—and disturbing—discoveries about the younger generation. Their surveys showed that:

- *9 percent of all teenagers in the U.S. are certain that there is such a thing as absolute moral truth;*
- *6 percent say absolute truth probably exists, although they could be persuaded otherwise;*
- *8 percent are certain there is not and cannot be such a thing as moral truth;*
- *21 percent say there probably is no moral truth, although it's possible; and,*

- *55 percent really don't know what to think on this whole issue.* [224]

Barna discovered that today's parents do not see it as their role to influence and form the moral truth and views of their children. Barna stated:

> *"This is one of the scariest things to come out of our research in a long time. I'm not saying the parents don't love their kids. They love their kids and want to be with their kids. But in terms of shaping those core fundamental truth views and moral views...that's not something that's part of their agenda."* [225]

The diminishing and rapid destruction of Christian influence in our culture is due to the failure of parents and the Church to indoctrinate their child with the Christian faith and moral values. The late Marlin Maddox, host of the Christian radio program, "Point of View" had a regularly scheduled guest, Dr. Robert Simonds, who often disagreed with Maddox over whether parents should work with the public school system to change it. Maddox advocated for students to leave public schools for home schooling, or, as a second choice, private schools. Simonds believed change could come about in public schools with committed parents working towards it. Eventually, Simonds changed his position and agreed with Maddox. Maddox wrote:

> *"I often disagreed with him* (Simonds) *about leaving Christian children in the public schools, but I have watched his efforts and must admit he gave his best in trying to work with the system. But after a fifteen-year effort, he finally concluded, 'Christians must exit the public schools as soon as possible.'"* [226]

Simonds states of the public school system,

> *"It is a deteriorating, crumbling system. It is much like communism—it is a failing system with leaders shouting its success from the rooftops, even while it self-destructs. It is definitely self-destructing—and Christians can no longer afford to wait before rescuing their own children."* [227]

He goes on to relay he does not blame teachers and administrators, though they must bear some responsibility, when they see things that are clearly wrong yet do not rock the boat in regards to the anti-christian, anti-moral view promoted.

Dr. James Dobson, from the organization Focus on the Family, stated on his July 8–9, 2002 national broadcast:

> *"What I was saying was that this godless and immoral curriculum and influence in the public schools is gaining momentum across the nation in ways that were unheard of just one year ago. It's as though the dam has now broken and activists representing various causes…are rushing through the breach in ways that are shocking."* [228]

He also stated on his March 28, 2002 Focus on the Family national broadcast:

> *…I've been very careful not to be negative to the public schools because there are many Christian teachers that are struggling mightily to do what's right there, and I haven't wanted to put pressure on them…but I think it's time to get our kids out."*[229]

The heart of the problem of the public school system is the curriculum and indoctrination your child and others are receiving despite how nice the teachers are. The battle is for the minds and souls of your children. In order to protect your children you must become aware and educate yourself, which is the purpose of this writing, to bring you enough insight to incite you to get involved with strong formation of your child's mind with a Biblical worldview or you are in danger of losing your child. One mother told us that her daughter, in her first year of college, spent much of her time defending her Christian faith. Her second year in college, she became silent concerning her faith. In her third year of college, she lost her faith. She graduated, "educated and degreed" as an excellent, but now godless student.

This is the reason that Michael Shaw listed "Global Education" as one of the U.N.'s top three goals to accomplish under the Agenda 21, Sustainable Development's Smart Growth plans. The elements who want to make America godless and without morals understand that education is their primary tool, making no American child safe in public schools. "No child left behind." These teachings have been spilling over into the curriculums in private schools as well. A study, in fact, put private schools only four years behind public schools in students abolishing basic Christian tenets. Dr. Dan Smithwick, head of the Nehemiah Institute in South Dakota tested 20,000 students in over 1,000 high schools in four worldviews; Christian theism, moderate Christian, secular humanism, and socialism. The results alarmingly show that a plunge downward toward, hard-core, secular humanism and socialism is taking place in Christian schools, as well as public schools. The downward plunge just moves a little slower for Christian schools. He says the Christian student in the public school system in the United States of America will fall to socialism in 2014 while modern day Christian school students will land there four years later, in 2018. Smithwick explains:

> *"The test measures understanding in five categories: Politics, Economics, Education, Religion and Social Issues. Consisting of a series of statements carefully structured to identify a person's worldview in those five categories, each statement is framed to either agree or disagree with a biblical principle."* [230]

Dr. Smithwick said the testing showed:

> *"...in Christian schools...for the last fifteen years...we're seeing the trend become worse and worse. The students are becoming more secular humanistic in their thinking. But parents don't seem to be bothered enough to remove their kids from an environment where they're absorbing and embracing socialistic philosophies of life."* [231]

This decline is from a baseline from the mid 1980s where most students in Christian and public schools still held a:

> *"...moderate Christian worldview classification... But with each subsequent year of testing, they*

> *found the students' understanding of the Christian worldview to be lower than the year before."* [232]

Smithwick concluded:

> *"The results of several dozen Christian schools tested in the fall of 2001 continued to show the downward trend in Biblical worldview understanding by Christian youth. Results are approximately 16% lower than last year, an ominous sign for Christian America…that trend is still fading... and may occur before the 2014 benchmark."* [233]

This calculates out as students move into business, government, education, and other occupations. Their thinking as humanists and socialists will erode our freedoms, leading society towards what they have been conditioned to themselves. As stated before, Europe has fallen so much towards this way, that it is influencing our nation toward the same. Europe presently has no hope but that the United States reverse this direction. As the past often repeats itself, just as Europe's hope rested on the United States during WWII, it is the same today in the spiritual war we are waging worldwide. If we follow Europe, we will decline as they have, and be lost. If we break loose from the shackles that are attempting to be placed on us, then Europe has hope for themselves.

CHAPTER FOURTEEN

FACTS ARE FACTS
LOGIC IS LOGIC

If the following does not set your blood pumping then you do not understand the crisis we face now, Our Lady's reasons for coming, the signs of the times, nor are you reading your Bible of which Our Lady says:

January 25, 2006

> **"...I call you to be carriers of the Gospel in your families. Do not forget, little children, to read Sacred Scripture. Put it in a visible place and witness with your life that you believe and live the Word of God..."**

January 25, 1999

> **"...Put Holy Scripture in a visible place in your families, read it, reflect on it, and learn how God loves His people. His love shows itself also in present times because He sends me to call you upon the path of salvation..."**

August 25, 1996

> **"...Little children, place the Sacred Scripture in a visible place in your family, and read and live it. Teach your children, because if you are not an example to them, children depart into godlessness..."**

An excellent example of how good Christian people are being educationally conditioned across the nation is the use of Mad Cow disease to move people to accept restraints and loss of freedom that they otherwise would never accept. Mad Cow disease is known as **B**ovine **S**pongiform **E**ncephalopathy or B.S.E. B.S.E. is not contagious. It cannot be spread to other animals or to humans. There is no need to quarantine or evacuate an area when Mad Cow disease is found. A cow can only get the disease if it eats the brains or spinal cord of a diseased cow. The only way a human can contract the disease is if he eats the brain or spinal cord of an infected animal. How cows got the disease in the first place was by being fed infected cow feed that contained the brains and spinal cords of other cows. Today, no cow under 30 months of age can contract the disease because it is now against the law to feed cattle the brains and/or spinal cords of other cows (as of January 2004)[234] It was against natural law to start with and as the positive or negative actions of the laws of consequences occur when natural law is violated, Mad Cow disease became a world threat. Cows eat grass and grain.

Through the spirit of consumerism and maximizing profits, producers began feeding ground up cow brains and spinal cords to herbivorous animals, to give them a cheaper source of protein, thereby making more profit. Little wisdom is needed to realize when you violate God's "nature" (natural) law and feed cows something other than what He made them to forage on, then, "naturally," there will be negative consequences. It is natural law. When man passed a law not to feed cows the brains and spinal cords of other cows, cattle health came in harmony with natural law, which is all that was necessary for the disease to go away. Everything is that simple. Follow God. Be in union with Him and everything corrects itself. Remember, that it is not up to man to make the world sustainable; the world was made sustainable by natural law. However, these facts about Mad Cow disease are told to show you how manipulative are those who want to control every aspect of our lives and that the sins society repeatedly breaks by going against natural law, are resulting in these controls, through the laws of consequences.

Society is being manipulated, through a constant bombardment from the media, that emphasizes fears and concerns of "what if this happens, and what if that happens." States across the land are running to ID animals, using the issue of Mad Cow disease, riding on the fear wave of the people. Officials are getting their initiatives passed with ease. What does it mean to ID an animal? It means having a computer chip placed in or on the animal so that the animal can be tracked and identified through a national animal identification system. The manipulation is uncovered with a simple question. Why ID animals if, when natural law is obeyed, the disease is cured by dying out? B.S.E. actually is no longer a threat.

But Mad Cow disease is used for the reason to put forth to the public that "we must track diseases." Alabama had the third cow in the United States found with Mad Cow disease. The diseased cow was tracked by conventional methods. But the USDA, influenced by global governance, is pushing animal ID.[235] It starts off voluntary and then becomes obligatory, using the same tactics as the passing of non-binding treaties. Once the treaty is passed and put into place, the treaties are changed to binding and enforcement begins. The state of Wisconsin was attempted to comply during 2006 and many states are following. Here in Alabama, all owners of animals are now being strongly encouraged to voluntarily register (non-binding treaty tactics), all places where animals are kept, under "Premise ID Registration." If you are a responsible citizen, or so you are told, you need to voluntarily register your premise, every single place where animals are located on your property. By the year 2008, USDA plans this registration to be mandatory, conditioning citizens through non-binding ID programs and then once generally accepted, binding everyone. Without being passed by law nor voted on by the people, by 2009, all animals will be tagged or injected with a computer chip,[236] all under the hysteria of "what if" an emergency situation occurs. No one is asking thoughtful questions like, *"Haven't cattle some how survived since the day Noah let them out of the Ark? And what about chickens? They've been around at least since Peter heard the cock crow!"* These issues are being used to put fear in people in order to lead them to accept such enslaving and oppressive constraints, that they otherwise would never have consented to. Our Lady does not want us to be in fear, and one reason is so that we will not succumb to manipulation aimed at taking away our freedoms by the use of fear.

January 25, 2001

"...Little children, the one who prays is not afraid of the future and the one who fasts is not afraid of evil. Once again, I repeat to you: only through prayer and fasting also wars can be stopped—wars of your unbelief and fear for the future. I am with you and am teaching you little children: your peace and hope are in God..."

All across the nation, in all states, all animals, be they cats, dogs, horses, goats and yes, even every chicken, down to a parakeet, is to be stamped with a chip according to the goal of the USDA, by 2009. Even in homes where only one animal exists, like your cat or dog. All states have similar schedules. This may not alarm you if you have only a cat or dog in your apartment or home somewhere in town. You may like the idea that if your pet gets lost, he can be located through an ID chip. But where does it stop? All things heading in a direction, do not suddenly stop and stand still. They continue progressing toward more of the same direction. Obviously, someone is going to have to pay for the immense cost of instituting a national animal ID program. Already popping up in discussions at city and county councils is the subject of pet taxes. Let's say they settle on $1.00 per pound per year. Your dog weighs 40 lbs, so you pay

$40.00 tax a year. You can afford it, so it is no big deal. But what if you don't pay it? Global Positioning System is a satellite tracking system that can identify the chips' locations within a few feet. Today it is used extensively, everywhere. Will they locate your pet through its G.P.S. chip? What happens then? Confiscation? Fines?

Over the road diesel trucks must pay taxes for fuel stickers in each state they travel through or they must buy fuel in each state. If you take your pet across state lines to visit Dad and Mom for a few months or to spend time in a vacation home, will you have to purchase a permit? Will you owe that state or city a tax? Yes, this is ridiculous, but clowns hold many offices in our government and bureaucracy, **and if they are not resisted, there is no limit to how far they will push their agendas.**

Thomas Jefferson said:

"The spirit of resistance to government is so valuable on certain occasions that I wish it to be always kept alive." [237]

We have lost this resistance programed in our republic. The government is supposed to be in fear of "we the people." We have accepted regulations and controls that the government has no right to burden us with.

And today, from abortion to the taking of private land, many fear the government and what they might do next.

Thomas Jefferson also said of government:

> *"Does the government fear us? Or do we fear the government? When the people fear the government, tyranny has found victory. The federal government is our servant, not our master!"* [238]

So even if you only have one pet, if you are thoughtful, you would be alarmed. No one should give such control to municipal, county, state, or federal agencies and governments. Our nation is not founded on such false premises of holding such powers—maybe in other countries but not in America.

In regard to the cost of the computer chip implants, they say it will be passed to the owner of the animals. Since there will be a cost per animal, many small farmers will not be able to stay in business. For instance, if a farmer owns 300 chickens, he would have to cover the cost of the chip implant on all 300 chickens.

Much is revealed when one contemplates that the only exemption of individual animals being ID'd will be the mega operations housing tens of thousands of animals. That means it will be the small farming operations that will be restricted, even though they care much more about the care, feeding, and health of their animals as opposed to corporations whose sole motivation is the dollar. It is the small agrarian communities, as Medjugorje once was, that Our Lady is showing us to go back to and which satan now wants crushed. It is the large operations where most animal health risks come from who will be exempted. This reveals something in and of itself of what is behind animal ID-ing. And all this supposedly for the *possibility*, just *in case* there is an emergency situation!....and people are buying into it out of fear, being conditioned to a "what if" or a "maybe" disease outbreak. We already have a system called **C.O.L.** – **C**ountry of **O**rigin **L**abeling,[239] that can track diseases. It has worked successfully for years. So, if tracking diseases is the motivation behind instituting animal ID-ing, then there is no valid reason for such a system to be put into place, being that we have one that has already proven to be successful. So then, what is the true motivation? Already, in Alabama, 2,000 premises have been ID'd voluntarily.[240] But that's not where it stops. According to USDA's information, you will not be able to move your animals without a permit. You cannot load up a horse and go trail riding 10 miles down the road without first calling to get a permit. And if you don't call...the GPS, known as Global Positioning

System, will show your animal is off its "premises ID location," through its chip. Will you be fined? USDA enforcement policy has yet to be determined but it's probable that a fine and/or seizure of animals will be its policy.[241] Animals confiscated? Do not think that it will never happen when we have a government that allows a full-term baby to be stabbed in the back of the neck and killed through partial birth abortion. In Europe, where ID-ing has been in place for five years, stories are surfacing of what happened after it was instituted. One small farmer of 12 cows, who refused to ID, was visited by government officials. They were accompanied by sharp shooters who killed his 12 cows on the spot.[242] Local county committees, to city counsels, to state legislators think nothing of taking private property, and they will think nothing of taking anything else. We are headed for serious tribulation and suffering. Our Lady said:

March 25, 2006

> **"Courage, little children! I decided to lead you on the way of holiness. Renounce sin and set out on the way of salvation, the way which my Son has chosen. Through each of your tribulations and sufferings God will find the way of joy for you..."**

Sin and not acknowledging or keeping the Sabbath Commandment is leading us to tribulation. Our Lady wants us to renounce disobedience and sin so She can lead us to joy, not sadness; freedom, not oppression. Have Christians lost so much wisdom as to not be able to stop, reason, and think! Why is Our Lady so strongly telling us, **"Read your Bibles."** Think what St. John, Christ's apostle, wrote in the book of Revelation, 13:16–18.

> [The antichrist system] ***"It forced all men, small and great, rich and poor, slave and free, to accept a stamped image on their right hand or their forehead. Moreover it did not allow a man to buy or sell anything unless he was first marked with the name of the beast or with the number that stood for its name...six hundred, sixty-six."***

Our Lady wants you to recognize the signs of the times by reading your Bible everyday. We, in community, have learned what is being revealed to you on these pages you are now reading by reading the Bible and reading Our Lady's messages everyday. It is where we get our "take," our understanding, our view of all our "information intake" that we hear or read. It's how we form our Christian worldview on every issue, and why the above

Scripture description of an antichrist system greatly troubles us when a system wants to ID premises, and place a chip in every animal. A system that makes progress one step at a time. Non-binding to binding. What next? Who's next?

In 1971, George J. Laurer invented the bar code, a system where a computer scans all merchandise with a line code for a price. The bar code system that Laurer invented ended up with three bars protruding from beginning, middle and end which resembles the meaning of the number six. While it is said the computer does not read the first and middle number that way, the inventor Laurer says the code for six is there. The barcode inventor states when asked about the 6-6-6:

> *"Yes, they do resemble the code for a six,"* but he added, *"there is nothing sinister about this nor does it have anything to do with the Bible's mark of the beast."* [243]

He stated it's purely coincidental. But why wasn't it any other number? Why does it end up resembling 666? While Laurer refers to the 666 as coincidence and even hogwash in connection to Revelation, it still is a fact that it's there. Laurer says even though it coincides with the Bible, there is no significance. The fact is, however, it has to do with buying and selling, with commerce. Should his opinion that there is no connection to the mark of the beast be accepted because Laurer, himself, did not intend it? Laurer did not have to deliberately put the 666 there for it to be tied to Revelation 13. When Laurer asked how the 666 got there, he relayed that was how it worked out on its own logic. He stated of the 666 pattern:

> *"The assignment of digits to specific patterns was arbitrary."* [244]

Webster's 1828 dictionary defined **arbitrary** "*as having no external control over: (not) depending upon will or discretion; not governed by any fixed rules.*" [245] A modern dictionary defines it as "*a decision made on a whim or impulse.*" [246]

And so, in the end, it was not up to Laurer. John, in Revelation, said:

> ***"Moreover, it did not allow a man to buy or sell anything unless he was first marked with the name of the beast..."***

If you take John's description of what he saw, translating it into Greek, the word "mark" becomes "charagma" which comes from the word "charax." Another word for "charax" is "palisade." "Palisade" means: like a picket fence. Look at a bar code. It certainly looks like a picket fence.[247] John saw this mark 1900 years ago, and today the bar code with 666, marks the buying and selling of everything. Maybe it is all by coincidence in its conception, but it is what it is. Scripture states that unseen principalities are at work. While on a human level, looking from a secular worldview, it's coincidental. But looking from a Biblical, spiritual worldview, there is a match that can't be ignored. Yet still, a bar code is not marked on the person. True, and therefore, the present barcode cannot be a blanket match for the mark of the beast. But clearly and factually it can be stated that it is a forerunner, or a **"sign of the times,"** as Our Lady keeps saying, that is leading us to it.

On March 2, 1999, Thomas W. Hecter, an inventor from Houston was issued a patent. The summary review of the patent read:

> *"A method is presented for facilitating sales transactions by electronic media. A bar code or a design is tattooed on an individual. Before the sales transaction can be* ***consummated****, the tattoo is scanned with a scanner. Characteristics about the scanned tattoo are compared to characteristics about the other tattoos stored on a computer da-*

> *tabase in order to verify the identity of the buyer. Once verified, the seller may be authorized to debit the buyer's electronic bank account in order to* ***consummate*** *the transaction.* (Patent # 5,878,155) [248]

It is extremely interesting that Thomas Hecter's summary, of the patent he invented, twice used the word "consummate." It doesn't matter if the word appears purely by coincidence or if it appears with real purpose behind it, for again, unseen principalities are at work. The word "consummate" according to Webster's 1828 Dictionary, means:

> **Consummate:** complete; perfect carried to the utmost extent or degree; perfection of a work, process or scheme, the end or completion of the present system of things, the end of the world. Death, the end of life.[249]

Does this not stun you from a Biblical worldview, while a secular worldviewist would yawn at the tattooed barcode patent and definition. This definition should quake our hearts, make it beat fast with awe of what is in our midst. Amazingly, this antichrist system is clearly defined by means of this word "consummate/consummated," which shows up in the U.S. patent 5.878.155 for a system that, without a doubt, would be a perfect match of John's Revelation 13 prophecy and vision of the picket fence mark. The argument made against all the above is that this is "hysteria," the making of 15 out of 1, nonsense, hype, and as the barcode inventor, Laurer said, *hogwash*. But facts are facts. Logic is logic. And John writes in Revelation 13:18:

> ***"A certain wisdom is needed here with a little ingenuity anyone can calculate the number..."***

Perhaps John knew wisdom was necessary and foresaw the ridicule and mocking by those, even Christians, who would say when the time comes, "Come on, don't be ridiculous. It's just a mark." If this does not fit the description, what does? If not now, when?

Terry Watkins of Truth Ministries writes:

> *"Is the barcode paving the road to 666: the Mark of the Beast? Yes. The barcode undoubtedly is paving the road for 666: the Mark of the Beast. The barcode did something very important to help bring in 666: the mark of the Beast. The barcode opened the door (in fact, it not only opened it, it kicked the door down) to the 'digital world.' Everything is now a number. Everything gets a barcode. As someone truly said, 'If it exists, barcode it.' I remember when barcodes first*

started appearing. I began telling people back then, the barcode was preparing the world for 666: the Mark of the Beast. Was I ever laughed at… even by the Christians. I can still remember their laughing and ridicule, 'You mean to tell me, everything is getting one of those 'marks.' You mean, I'll go even to the local '7-Eleven' and they'll have laser scanners and they'll scan these 'marks.' No way. It would be too obvious what was happening. Everybody would know the mark of the beast is coming.' But isn't it amazing 25 years later…and nobody gives the 'mysterious' barcodes even a 'second thought.'" [250]

Do Christians not understand the reason for Our Lady's coming? If a Christian is not alarmed by these things, his spirit of understanding is nil. In *Paragon Magazine,* an article was printed about computer chipping animals. Within the article, an Amish farmer was quoted:

"The Amish farmers say any computer-based tagging will cost people their salvation and refer to the Book of Revelation. If you attend a livestock auction you will not be able to buy or sell without a premise ID and your livestock will not be allowed to sell without an animal ID. Rev. 13:17, "And that no man might buy or sell, save he that

had the mark, or the name of the beast, or the number of his name." [251]

The article continued, stating:

"Is this the forerunner of population control? Could this be a global program to upgrade and fine tune the technical skills needed in this gigantic operation of identifying millions of animals and birds? Once in place the system can very easily be adapted to the human population. The American people are already being desensitized to accept this technology.

"In the 1970s Sweden began implanting microchips into hospital patients without their knowledge as part of a mind control experiment. In 1999 the August edition of Time Magazine carried a story about how the University of Virginia Hospital planned to begin micro-chipping all newborns in the belly buttons to prevent baby snatching. The Weekly Reader that goes out to grade schools throughout our nation conducted a poll of fourth graders asking, 'Would you have a VeriChip implanted in your body?' Over 2,000 kids voted—85 percent yes and only 15 percent no.

"Once the USDA makes regulations (not laws

passed by Congress—just bureaucratic regulations) that all livestock must be identified by Radio Frequency Identification to guarantee the safety of our food, is there any reason that the Department of Homeland Security won't make similar regulations requiring all humans to likewise be implanted to guarantee the security of our nation?"[252]

Fear is being used to set up a system of control that is far worse than the issues that motivate the controls. These are dangerous warning signs. A fresh message from Heaven, given by Our Lady, spoke about the signs of the times:

April 2, 2006

> **"...You ask yourself if you are following me? My children, do you not recognize the signs of the times? Do you not speak of them? Come follow me..."**

Here we are not only speaking, but writing about them. Wake up to the true reason Our Lady is coming!

Our Lady said on June 25, 1991:

> **"...If you pray, God will help you discover the true reason for my coming. Therefore, little chil-**

> **dren, pray and read the Sacred Scriptures so that through my coming you discover the message in Sacred Scripture for you..."**

Our Lady said read Sacred Scripture, read Revelation. Recognize the signs of the time. Is it not strange that Our Lady's anniversary of 25 years of apparitions fell in the same month of a significant date that occurs only once every one-thousand years and is the number of the beast? 06/06/06....6-6-6. Our Lady said:

March 25, 1990

> **"...God wants to save you and sends you messages through men, nature, and so many things which can only help you to understand that you must change the direction of your life..."**

Is it not strange that the company who sells and is behind the creation of placing computer chips in animals formed the **N**ational **I**nstitute for **A**nimal **A**griculture (NIAA). This institute is a dishonest scheme to defraud the public as a front organization. The organization was set-up to use 9/11 and Mad Cow disease to get ID systems accepted. The computer ID company, after setting up the fake screen organization of NIAA, used the organization to lobby the USDA to adopt the ID computer chip program. If this is not strange to you, then it would not be strange that the company's name, who started the front organization NIAA who lobbied USDA to adopt computer chips, is called **Digital Angel, Inc.**[253] Is the name they chose for themselves another coincidence, designed by unseen principalities? What does an angel have to do with a computer chip ID company? Nothing, from a secular worldview and a whole lot, from a Biblical worldview. lucifer is the head angel of the kingdom of darkness. In an article in the summer 2006 issue of *Paragon Magazine*, it was said that:

> *"To advance the plan and brainwash the people, the government is using the* ***'crisis management'—'problem-reaction-solution' process****. We need a problem so we will create mad-cow disease and a bird-flu pandemic. Now we must create a solution—Animal Identification. This will allow the major packers and food processors as well as the manufacturers of radio frequency identification technology who make handsome contributions to both Democrat and Republican campaigns to integrate the cattle industry and increase profit."* [254]

March 25, 1990

> **"...God wants to save you and sends you messages through men, nature, and so many things**

which can only help you to understand that you must change the direction of your life..."

God is sending us a message showing us what satan wants. he is active in putting his mark on everything that God wants, but in doing so, he also reveals his schemes.

How much more does Our Lady need to speak to us? How many more signs?

March 18, 2006

"...Only with total interior renunciation will you recognize God's love and the signs of the time in which you live. You will be witnesses of these signs and will begin to speak about them..."

April 2, 2006

"...My children, do you not recognize the signs of the times? Do you not speak of them? Come follow me..."

Look at the dates! March 18, 2006, **"You...will begin to speak about them..."** April 2, 2006, **"...Do you not speak of them?..."** April 14, 2006, Pope Benedict spoke about them:

"Lord, we have lost our sense of sin! Today a slick campaign of propaganda is spreading an inane (empty) *defense of evil, a senseless cult of*

satan, a mindless desire for transgression, a dishonest and frivolous freedom, exalting impulsiveness, immorality and selfishness as if they were new heights of sophistication.

"Lord Jesus, open our eyes: let us see the filth around us and recognize it for what it is, so that a single tear of sorrow can restore us to purity of heart and the breath of ***true freedom****. Open our eyes, Lord Jesus!"* [255]

Again, look at the date and the message. There have only been three times in all Our Lady's monthly messages when Our Lady did not start off with the words "Dear children." The message below is one of those three. Look at the first words…

March 25, 2006

"Courage, little children!…Renounce sin… Through each of your tribulations and sufferings God will find the way of joy for you…"

We are at war. If we don't renounce sin, accept and live the Commandments, we will lose peaceable living, our freedoms and our lives, as negative actions through the laws of consequences determine. Our Lady said, **"Courage,"** in March, 2006, after so much in the world had already happened. Tribulation and suffering. What kind of world are we entering? Many worldwide were shocked and shaken at the message Our Lady gave on November 2, 2006:

> **"...God is sending me to warn you and to show you the right way. Do not shut your eyes before the truth, my children. Your time is a short time..."**

These are words from Heaven – November 2, 2006!

While the working people are busy trying to make a living, there are those who are working unnoticed, building a godless system which will be against you and your family in more ways than you could ever imagine. The environmental, sustainable movement's grab for power, authority, and control is evolving into a god-like entity and rules over almost all other authority today. As it grows, it is becoming very dangerous, threatening the security of our unalienable rights and the future of our families, our homes/properties, and our faith. In regard to what structure of controls is being put into place, it is outright mortally dangerous to give power to any system or structure which is without God, without prayer, that controls every aspect of life. Nor can we accept this system, even if it is neutral, neither for or against God, for the structure will not remain neutral. It will move one way or the other, and what is neutral without prayer will move toward darkness, having no moral "stopgates" to keep it from falling. Thomas Jefferson said:

> *"Experience has shown that even the best forms,* (of authority) *those entrusted with power, have, in time and by slow operations* (step-by-step) *perverted it into tyranny."* [256]

To the degree we give power and control of our lives to any form of structure, whatsoever, which is without God and prayer, that form or structure will end up persecuting and enslaving us to the same degree. It is important to reiterate that a neutral structure which regulates man and is devoid of God will be used as a tool to crush all Christians, and both the practice and worship of Christianity. The devil's goal is neutrality of the state because he is then able to easily take possession of the neutral structures to destroy the culture. The power given to our present government, both local and national, is a grave danger for the Judeo/Christian future. If Our Lady said satan wants to destroy human life, you must realize plans are being put forth and formulated to do that through whatever means or channels he can use to do so. Our Lady said:

May 7, 1985

"...the plans which my Son and I formulated..."

And satan is busy formulating his plans as well.

CHAPTER FIFTEEN

POPULATION CONTROL.....
POPULATION REDUCTION

How does the Sabbath Commandment, our nation, animal rights, Agenda 21, the Assisi-Eco Accords, eminent domain, Our Lady's warnings, our Founding Fathers' dreams and the host of other topics that have been discussed in this book, all tie together? Does it seem these writings are all over the place, just covering disconnected topics? What you have been reading has taken years of prayer to understand, examining events through the eyes of a Christian worldview. What comes together, uniting all these events is what Our Lady said on June 25, 1989, to Ivanka, one of the six Medjugorje visionaries, that the world is in great danger and that satan is active in a 'plan' to lead us into slavery. Our Lady said:

> **"Pray because you are in great temptation and danger because the world and material goods lead you into slavery. satan is active in this plan..."**

Remember the U.N.'s Agenda 21, Sustainable, Smart Growth Development plans:

1. Global Land Use
2. Global Education
3. Global Population Control and Reduction

Numbers one and two have been covered, but what of the U.N.'s number three sustainable plan? While major headway regarding these three goals is being made, the complete achievement of them in fullness, will enslave the whole world. It is very clear that these three goals are working towards this enslavement Our Lady spoke of to Ivanka. But since it has not yet reached that point, connecting the dots may be still obscure to you.

For example, you may wonder what animal rights becoming equal to human rights have to do with the above three goals, especially population control? A prayerful overview of the world's current direction casts forth a view that becomes apparent. That the life of an "ant" and the life of a "child" should be granted equal consideration does not mean that the human child will continue with his rights to life. In fact, satan's deception is very cunning in that the life of animals, regardless of whether you're talking about ants, cattle, chimpanzees, or anything else, can never be given equal status, or have rights on par with man because his creation and place in the world cannot be equaled by any other creature. Except by one design. That is—man's rights must *degrade* to that of the animal, to be equitable. Animals around the world are killed daily for man's use in the food chain, and no one will ever be able to stop that. In addition, animal herds are often thinned out by man so to naturally keep them healthy and to protect from animal overpopulation so as to keep the eco food supply in balance; that it won't be overeaten. And so it will be for man, as if man is like all other beasts and knows not how to reap and harvest to feed his numbers. Dr. Jacqueline Kasun, in her book, The War Against Population, writes:

> *"The environmental movement, therefore, is the perfect vehicle for population control. It is popular—people do love trees and animals and beautiful scenery—and it is unequivocal in its devotion* ***to reducing human numbers."*** [257]

Dr. Kasun states that the UN's plans are "chilling" and that it is through "sustainable development" they plan to reduce human numbers:

> *"The environmental agencies of the United Nations, with their chilling blueprints for 'demographic transition' and a standardless, undefined but* ***totally planned and controlled 'sustainable development'****..."* [258]

According to the shortage ecology mind-set, man's right to life ultimately must be lowered for the good of the eco-system and all the earth. Again, it is impossible that the right to life of animals will ever be elevated to man's right to life, but man's right can be lowered so to be equitable to the rights of animals. This is the U.N.'s 3rd point: Global Population Control and Reduction. We must wake up to realize animal identification is a deception and is about control not disease. Though many believe it is good and sincerely accept it as positive, they do not see its danger. While secular worldviewists think it's a good thing, Biblical worldviewists realize it is impossible to be a good for man. It is very dangerous and will be used in the steps toward population reduction, "reduction" being the code word for "elimination" in our very *alive "culture of death."*

Man has always tended toward concentrating himself where others dwell, especially in the modern age, being nearer to commerce, social and cultural activities, jobs, healthcare, etc. In ages past, man did the same to convenience himself and his human nature, just as water takes the easiest course down a hill. The closer you move to what you want and to what you consider necessities, the closer others will also live in doing the same. This concentrating of the population gives the delusion that the earth is overrun. As populated areas grow, they distance themselves from the agrarian way of living. As population density increases more and more, it results in more and more problems that must be dealt with. It is not a population problem, it's a concentration of population problem and is related to abandoning the only occupation that God specifically ordained, found in Genesis, the agrarian lifestyle. Genesis 3:19 states, ***"By the sweat of your brow shall you eat."*** The closer one comes to agrarian living, even if only partially, the less concentration of population and the problems that come with it. The further away from the agrarian life, the greater the concentration of population and the problems that come with it. It is all in proportion to how much of the agrarian life you live. There is, of course, an advantage when man is in close proximity to each other. But we have built a whole world without God, without prayer and we are deformed in how we've developed. Objections may be made that everyone cannot farm or live that way. This is not a valid objection. The census taken in 1900 showed 90% of the people listed their primary occupation as farming! A census in 1990 listed farming only at one half of one percent![259] Nevertheless, overpopulation is not a problem. It is a delusion. As already stated "no more than 3% of the earth's ice free surface is occupied by man." That alone clearly shows it is man's development through his own creation, without seeking direction from a higher wisdom, that has created density problems, not overpopulation problems. Even 500 years before Christ, Plato and Aristotle worried about overpopulation. So did Confucious, and also Christians such as Tertullian and St. Jerome. These philosophers lived in large cities and they all were surrounded constantly by people. As a result, they began to have delusions that the land was going to run out. Dr. Kasun writes:

> *"It accounts for the recurring theme throughout history of overpopulation. Plato and Aristotle worried about it half a millennium before Christ; Athens was a great center of commerce and culture, and a very crowded city. Chinese cities were crowded centers for the exchange of products and ideas; and Confucius and other Chinese thinkers worried about "excessive" population growth. Tertullian, writing in crowded Carthage in the second century after Christ, said, 'What most frequently meets our view and occasions complaint, is our teeming population. Our numbers are burdensome to the world, which can hardly support us...In every deed, pestilence, and famine, and wars, and earthquakes have to be regarded as*

a remedy for nations, as the means of pruning the luxuriance of the human race.'

*"Saint Jerome (*who translated the Bible from Greek), *in the fourth century, wrote that 'the world is already full, and the population is too large for the soil'...None of these earlier city-dwelling philosophers could soar over the earth and see that outside of their immediate view there were almost no people at all. And so it is with us. We spend our daily lives amid crowds of people and vehicles, thronging together to conduct our mutual affairs, to trade goods and ideas, and to reap the benefits of specialization and exchange. Given the immediate impact, common to the human condition in all ages, it is easy to suppose, along with Tertullian, that 'our numbers are burdensome to the world.'"* [260]

As already quoted, the earth can sustain 8–22 times our present population and still sustain our present standard of living, still using only 50% of the land of the earth, not including the large iced areas!

Even with modern man's ability to "soar over the earth" and see the vast unpopulated landscapes outside of every city and town, the idea of overpopulation still seduces the philosophers of our day. So there are many major plans worldwide to reduce population, including massive euthanasia, abortion and birth control, curriculums indoctrinating our youth that it is not smart to have big families, together with many other subtle pressures in society that almost seem insignificant but are major planning strategies by the population control movement. Many of these ideas have become so common that we are now insensitive to them. Not only are subtle philosophies gaining influence in our culture, but the not so subtle remedies for overpopulation are boldly progressing as the influence grows that people are a "species overgrown" and in need of plans for reduction which are now manifesting.

Dr. Kasun also states,

> *"A nature-worshiping environmentalism that regards people as a species that has overgrown its 'niche' is gaining influence."* [61]

As this influence grows, so does the respectableness and acceptance of the not so subtle culture of death. In March, 2006, the Texas Academy of Science at Lamar University in Beaumont, Texas, hosted a gathering for scientists. Dr. Eric R. Pianka gave a speech in which several hundred of his scientist colleagues rose to their feet and gave a standing ovation. Dr. Pianka, a University of Texas evolutionary ecologist and lizard expert, was named and awarded, by *The Academy of Texas Scientists,* **The 2006 Distinguished Texas Scientist Award.** The central point of Pianka's speech was to condemn anthropocentrism.[262] Anthropocentrism, as touched on earlier in this writing, is defined as:

> *"The consideration of man as being the most significant entity of the universe; interpreting or regarding the world in terms of human values and experience."* [263]

Pianka condemned the Biblical order of man as stewards over creation, clarifying his belief that man does not have a privileged position in the universe through a story he told. He said his neighbor asked him what good are the lizards that he studies? He answered, "What good are you?" Pianka hammered his point home by exclaiming, "We're no better than bacteria." [264]

He went on to say that planet earth was being devastated by overpopulation since the sharp increase in population at the beginning of the Industrial Revolution and to restore the planet before it's too late, quick steps must be taken. He said the earth, as we know it will not survive without drastic measures. With over 400

Texas scientists listening intently, he then asserted the only feasible solution to saving the earth is to reduce the population to 10% of the present number. One of the scientists listening, immediately decided to turn science reporter, and began taking notes. Forest Mims realized something was up when at the beginning of Dr. Pianka's speech, he saw a scene in which a video cameraman, against the cameraman's objections, was told to turn the video camera off and point it to the ceiling. The organizers wanted to keep the speech closed for the science community. In fact, Pianka said the general public is not yet ready to hear what he was about to say. At the beginning of his speech, Forest Mims worked at his notes. Following is from the notes Mims took of Pianka's speech:

> *"War and famine would not do, Pianka explained. Instead, disease offered the most efficient and fastest way to kill the billions that must soon die, if the population crisis is to be solved...."*
>
> *"AIDS is not an efficient killer, Pianka explained, because it is too slow. His favorite candidate for eliminating 90 percent of the wor,ld's population is airborne Ebola (Ebola Reston), because it is both highly lethal, and it kills in days, instead of years. However, Professor Pianka did not mention that*

Ebola victims die a slow and torturous death, as the virus initiates a cascade of biological calamities inside the victim that eventually liquefy the internal organs. After praising the Ebola virus for its efficiency at killing, Pianka paused, leaned over the lectern, looked at us, and carefully said, ***'We've got airborne 90 percent mortality in humans. Killing humans. Think about that.'*** *The audience... had been applauding some of his statements. After a dramatic pause (of the above statements), Pianka returned to politics and environmentalism. But he revisited his call for mass death when he reflected on the oil situation.* ***'And the fossil fuels are running out,'*** *he said,* ***'so I think we may have to cut back to two billion, which would be about one-third as many people.'*** *So the oil crisis alone may require eliminating two-thirds of the world's population. How soon must the mass dying begin if Earth is to be saved? Apparently fairly soon, for Pianka suggested he might be around when the killer disease goes to work (Pianka is 67 years old)...When Pianka finished his remarks, the audience applauded. It wasn't merely a smattering of polite clapping that audiences diplomatically reserve for poor or boring speakers. It was a loud, vigorous, and enthusiastic applause..."*

"Then came the question and answer session... After noting that the audience did not represent the general population, a questioner asked, 'What kind of reception have you received as you have presented these ideas to other audiences that are not representative of us?' Pianka replied, ***'I speak to the converted!'"***

"He spoke glowingly of the police state in China that enforces their one-child policy...With this, the questioning was over. Immediately almost every scientist, professor, and college student present stood to their feet and vigorously applauded the man who had enthusiastically endorsed the elimination of 90 percent of the human population. <u>Some even cheered</u>. Dozens then mobbed the professor at the lectern to extend greetings and ask questions. It was necessary to wait a while before I could get close enough to take some photographs...Five hours later, the distinguished leaders of The Texas Academy of Science presented Pianka with a plaque in recognition of his being named ***The 2006 Distinguished Texas Scientist.*** *When the banquet hall, filled with more than 400 people, responded with enthusiastic applause, I walked out in protest."*

"Recently, I exchanged a number of e-mails with Pianka...He replied that Ebola does not discriminate, kills everyone, and could spread to Europe and the Americas by a single infected airplane passenger...(A review of) the majority of his student reviews were favorable, with one even saying, 'I worship Dr. Pianka.'...The 45-minute lecture before The Texas Academy of Science converted a university biology senior into a Pianka disciple, who then published a blog that seriously supports Pianka's mass death wish."

"Let me now remove my reporter's hat for a moment, and tell you what I think. We live in dangerous times. The national security of many countries is at risk. Science has become tainted...Must now we worry that a Pianka-worshipping former student might someday become a professional biologist, or physician, with access to the most deadly strains of viruses and bacteria? I believe that airborne Ebola is unlikely to threaten the world outside of Central Africa. But scientists have regenerated the 1918 Spanish flu virus that killed 50 million people. There is concern that smallpox might someday return. And what other terrible plagues are waiting out there in the natural world to cross

> *the species barrier, and to which scientists will one day have access? Meanwhile, I still can't get out of my mind the pleasant spring day in Texas when a few hundred scientists of the Texas Academy of Science gave a standing ovation for a speaker who they heard advocate for the slow and torturous death of over five billion human beings."* [265]

When news broke out of Pianka's speech, several tried to claim that it was taken out of context, that what he said was misconstrued, and that Mims distorted it. However, these claims are debunked because someone did tape record much of Pianka's speech which now is documented.[266] The above description of what Pianka said may sound unbelievable to you today, but again to repeat what already has been written, so would it sound unbelievable to anyone 40 years ago that soon would come a time when doctors in hospitals would birth a little child and stab it in the back of its neck to kill it in partial birth abortion. Read the words, *"partial birth."* The infant is *partially* birthed and is alive, healthy, and moving, experiencing the first instance of birth, and then a doctor kills it. It's surreal to think about it. No one would have believed this to be possible 30 or even 25 years ago and yet it has happened. Pianka, with 400 college scientists present, has advanced the satanic plan of sustainability of the earth and Smart Growth of the earth's people.

Making a direct connection to the 3rd point of the sustainable plans of global population control and reduction, Pianka also said in his speech that China "is smart" with their one child policy. He also said people who have more than one child "are not smart." To analyze who is smart and who is not, the 4-2-1 scenario is playing out all over China and is revealing how devastating and "not so smart" the one child policy is. Two sets of parents, four people give birth to only two people, one in each family. The one child from one family marries another child from another family. They give birth to one child. In just two generations, six people have arrived at the third generation. The last child born will be responsible for his two parents and four grandparents on top of providing for himself. It will be impossible for him to shoulder the burden of taking care of his parents and grandparents. China, within a generation or two is headed for a catastrophic tragedy of their elderly. There will be no ability for the work force to provide for retirement of the elderly, or for retirement plans such as social security type systems to physically accommodate the far superior numbers of aging people. It is a recipe for a time bomb, a negative consequence of years of forced abortion, sterilization, and infanticide policies that will either fruit in massive euthanasia or other forms of elimination of humans, if not starvation; a harsh impoverishment such as China could have never imagined. Even if the one child policy was reversed, it would take 20–30 years to even minutely correct the family disasters that will be occurring in the interim. So who is smart?

All the efforts of darkness, every age, points back to the same dot at the top of evil's plans. It is always population reduction and control. Charles Rice, Professor of Law at the University of Notre Dame, says:

> *"One of the best kept secrets in the world is the evil nature of the population control movement."* [267]

The United Nation's 3rd point of population control and reduction is disguised in your local city council or city commission as "Smart Growth," the code word for population control and eventually population reduction. Look at your local ordinances. It's about "Smart Growth" which has already been defined in these writings, concentrating people in small islands of land while altogether banning people from other areas, eventually forcing people off their land, into tightly packed human islands known as infill zones. This is happening more and more and will continue to happen through strategic plans, including "environmental" excuses for controls. One example of how people are being forced off their property through heavy restrictions being placed on the use of private property to create these "wilderness areas" is through the use of endangered species. Several years ago the Florida Cougar was named an endangered species and with that gained the right of protection from the government. Wherever a cougar is located, his right to exist on that property supersedes the property owner's right to use his property as he desires. If a man runs a chicken farm on his property and a cougar begins killing his chickens, by law, he cannot do anything that will harm the cougar. Not having any means of protecting his chickens, being a small farming operation, he loses his business and must sell his property. These scenarios are happening all across our country. But what has been discovered is the so "classed" "endangered" Florida Cougar is actually not an endangered species in that DNA shows it is the same cougar that roams all over Texas and other western states and is quite prolific.[268] Evidence has also been gathered to show that the so called "endangered cougar" was purposely let loose in areas of Florida [269] in which its presence is now used as the reason to restrict population or stop people altogether from using vast areas of land.

In Michigan, hunters, without realizing it, are being used to gather information that eventually will be used against them. They are being asked to bring videos and cameras on their hunts to take pictures of cougar sightings. The hunters, asked by the Michigan Wildlife Conservationists, are naively happy to comply.[270] This data, compiled by thousands of hunters is providing thousands of man hours of observation that the conservationist watchers could never afford or achieve. The data will eventually be used against not only hunting, but also those who own land. Whether these landowners use the property for business or recreational purposes, it very well may be determined as detrimental to cougars. Human use of what becomes the *so called* endangered species cougar habitat, suddenly becomes a disturbed endangered species cougar habitat. Cougars' rights are now superior over the use of your personal property, hunting leases, etc., simply by virtue that they have spread to new areas and have taken up residence. *You* cannot do that, but the animals can. With the establishment of cougar territories, a well thought out plan of conditioning is set in motion to gain acceptance through such means as the use of signs, like "Cougar Crossings." This is animal rights propaganda. Signs suddenly show up, and controls soon follow. Tactics such as placing "Cougar Crossings" signs at key locations help condition tens of thousands daily, such as the ones that can be seen on the way to Fort Meyers Airport in Florida, by everybody who flies in or out. How many people have seen cougars cross the highway on the way to the airport? And if by chance, one has, who is he? An animal rights' activist? How come cougars only show themselves to them, and no one else? Why are there two signs spaced a few hundred yards apart from each other? Why strategically placed only at a thoroughfare location? In an area that Henry Ford and Thomas Edison were winter neighbors? An area that still today draws many people who spend their winters there, flying in and out, people of great influence, as well as affluence, whose decisions affect multitudes of people? Even *if* cougars cross there, how many have been run over? The answer to all of these questions can be answered with one word...*agenda*. You are considered thoughtless and mindless, easily led to believe what these people want to condition you to believe. These signs are free advertisement by environmentalists to set up shop and controls to take your land, restrict its use, and redirect people to where *they* want you to live, through the use of oppressive regulations. The signs at Fort Meyers Airport are of great benefit to their cause in conditioning corporate owners and decision makers, knowing that they will travel back to their communities across the United States and will, step by step, accept these regulations and controls as they become more opened to environmental causes. Why not? Everyone loves nature and the environment. Even the most base and uncultured man stands in awe before one of the great Redwoods of California or at the edge of a cliff in the Grand Canyon or overviewing the great waterfalls of our land. We, as people from all walks of life, love creation, but there must be a distinction made to separate those who take advantage of our love for these things, who use animals and creation to further their warped agendas. It is a warped mind-set that man must be made equal and eventually submit to manufactured rights of creatures and the eco-systems in which they are found.

With a horse taken down and killed through a cougar attack in Southern Michigan's Jackson County in 2005,[271] who wants cougars in their backyards? If a horse can be taken down by a cougar, what chance does a child, an adult, or your pets have to escape such attacks? Who wants this anxiety when your children have to take out the garbage? Beware when a rare species is suddenly discovered in your area or backyard. It very likely has been introduced and/or is being helped to proliferate with an agenda. Beware of being told cougars are not attacking. California, Colorado, and other states are experiencing a growing number of such tragic instances of people and pets, not only being attacked but killed and eaten. One woman, riding on her bicycle on a bike trail in Whiting Ranch Park near Mission Viejo, California, was chased and pulled off by a cougar, and then severely mauled before being barely rescued by another bicylist.[272] Near to the same location, a body was found mauled and eaten from what was believed to be the same cougar. As stated, other cases exist. There is always an excuse by the experts like: "The cougar was hungry and began to see humans as easy prey." Of course he was hungry. All of them get hungry. That's the point. Anything that gets hungry that is capable of killing a man does not need to be near man. However, it's not <u>man</u> who should be forced out, regardless of whether an animal is endangered or not. Thank God that dinosaurs are extinct. At the "Dinosaur Crossings"—"Two Cars and the Passengers Were Eaten Yesterday" would be your headlines. As with dinosaurs, there comes a time when it just might be the plan of God that some creatures go extinct, at least in areas where it "endangers" man. This is not the end of the world and may improve the surviving world man lives in. That is real balance and logic. But it is just for such Scriptural logic that Christianity is so hated, that the earth and its creatures were made for man, that man is at the head of creation and is to have dominion over it and the animals that inhabit it. St. Francis of Assisi loved animals and they loved him, but he also ate 'em'. We do not need cougars, bears, wolves, etc. to repopulate areas they roamed 500 years ago. The United States, in regards to where its people have settled, does not need to be a **wild land**. The world will not end if cougars and the like are restricted from many areas of the United States. In the guide for public officials "Understanding Sustainable Development, Agenda 21", it states:

> *"Sustainable Development is a plan for global control, using land and resource restriction, social transformation through education, and other programs to accomplish this end. The land use element of Sustainable Development calls for the implementation of* ***two action plans designed to eliminate private property: 1st, the Wildlands Project, and 2nd, Smart Growth****. Upon implementation of these plans, all human action is subject to control.*
>
> *"Since all things ultimately come from natural resources on rural lands, the transfer of the landscape from citizen control to government control will make it easy for government and its partners—*

> *NGO's (Non-Government Organizations who partner with the government)—to control what we have, what we do, and where we go.*
>
> *"The rural land-use plan embodied in the Wildlands Project is inextricably tied to its urban counterpart, Smart Growth. As human beings are barred from rural land, there will be a concentration of human activity in urban areas. Through Smart Growth, the infrastructure is being created for a post-private property era in which human action is subject to centralized government control."* [273]

Animal identification is not needed for disease control. It is needed as part of the above plan to loop you into the U.N.'s plan. Animal ID-ing and Smart Growth should be opposed strongly. Inform your friends of the facts. Inform them of this book. Keep your copy for study, but give a new copy to them. Hold accountable, as well as educate local and state officials who will oppose, in law, these steps and the implementation of these programs. Many can start or fund organizations to educate and oppose these plans. Form groups to meet with your elected officials to inform them and to let them know that you expect them to fight this strongly.

But expect no victory if you do not accept the living of the Sabbath.

The first step in controlling land use, both rural and city, is through population movement/control. The second step is through population reduction. Because some are beginning to understand what Smart Growth is, there is a new code word emerging due to the negativity surrounding the term "Smart Growth." The new code word is "Quality Growth." The name change game will continue the more informed citizens learn the meanings behind sustainable terminology. Your local officials will deny all these things. Some, because they are in the dark themselves, and others because they are aware of the strong citizen opposition and to avoid confrontation they become evasive. Of these, they themselves are sold on these concepts not having investigated, for themselves, the origins of Sustainable Development and Smart Growth. Most local city councils and planners do not know or understand who is behind the sustainable smart growth plans. As stated, Agenda 21 is no secret, no conspiracy. You can research, discover and understand all that is written with only a moderate Biblical worldview. However, whatever you do, you must become enlightened. ***"My people perish for lack of knowledge."*** If you think these schemes can't happen, why is Our Lady coming for 25 years? Telling us the world is in great danger? Our Lady said:

February 17, 1984

"...The world has been drawn into a great whirlpool. It does not know what it is doing. It does not realize in what sin it is sinking..."

CHAPTER SIXTEEN

"I CALL YOU TO MAKE A CHOICE."

When the radical feminists began to lose their gains, they found how to resurrect their cause. They saw their hope was in the Catholic Church, not because of its teaching, but its universality. The purpose of the Assisi Declaration was again to use not only the Catholic Church, but all the major faiths, to spread its message, which, as already mentioned, they themselves termed "The Greening of Religion." [274] They were elated at what resulted through the gathering at St. Francis' Basilica in Assisi. But the feminist movement and the eco-movement have laid deep within it a darker side which has harmed many in the Church. satan wants to destroy particularly all of Christendom, and particularly the Catholic Church, and constantly works to parasite off the latter through its members because its reach is universal with roots throughout the world. Therefore, satan's first offense is to inflict into the Church the virus grown by him. It is simple logic that the Green Movement chose Assisi to parasite itself off the veins of Christendom. The Catholic Church, Biblically based churches, etc. do not need to be "greened" because the teachings of the Church offers the strongest means to preserve nature, human life and the planet on which we live. Being dictated to and submitting to outsiders, who desire that our morals and values be based in accordance to the "greening" philosophies of secular and socialist worldviews, is equated to satan quoting Scripture to Jesus in the desert, telling Him what Scripture means so as to get Jesus to act according to satan's desires. Our Lady said:

June 25, 1985

> **"I urge you to ask everyone to pray the Rosary. With the Rosary you will overcome all the troubles which satan is trying to inflict on the Catholic Church. Let all priests pray the Rosary. Give time to the Rosary."**

With reason, we can see all the ties forming one big knot to enslave and strangle man. Our Lady's way is different. It is one of freedom. If God is the Creator, there is no one who wants to preserve Creation and life more than God, and God the Creator wants that through freedom. Agenda 21, Sustainable Development and Smart Growth is anything but about freedom. It is the new darkness over man in *this* century, just as communism was in the last century. Perhaps, it would be beneficial to cast a backward glance to a not-so-distant past to be reminded of the horrors suffered under the banner of "socialism." In the early 1920s, Joseph Stalin declared that, *"God must be out of Russia in five years."* What happens to a nation when God is forced to leave? Margaret Werner was a young girl when her father accepted an offer from Henry Ford to help operate a new manufacturing facility in Gorky, Russia. It was 1932, and the Great Depression had hit across the United States. Carl Werner left Detroit, Michigan, with his wife, Elizabeth and daughter, Margaret, and traveled to Russia with 450 other unsuspecting American employees from the Detroit area. No one knew they were walking into a nightmare of which most would not survive. The poverty, extremely poor living conditions, lack of food and heat were difficult enough to endure, but the oppression, the fear, the frequent and sudden disappearance of neighbors, the inability to leave the country and return to America led to depression and hopelessness.

The Werner family did not escape these tragedies. Police showed up at Carl Werner's home when Margaret was 17. Her father was sentenced on trumped up charges and sent to a labor camp in Siberia where he eventually died from the work and poor living facilities.

His family never saw or heard from him again since the day he was taken away. In the face of so much injustice, something broke in Margaret. She refused to bow down to the authorities. Internally, she never lost her identity as an American and the spirit of freedom burned in her soul. She refused to let that flame die. Because of her resistance, she too was eventually arrested, at the age of 24, wrongfully accused and sentenced to 10 years hard labor in the same Siberian labor camp that her father had been sent. She served all 10 years, and shortly after her release, she escaped to Germany, with her mother and eventually they both made it back to America. She revealed how she was able to survive the horror of those years when so many thousands of others did not. The following describes the scene of Margaret being transported by train to her Siberian labor camp.

> *"...During our journey, we stopped at all the minor train depots along the way to take on more people, more prisoners. They were people like me, robbed of their youth, their entire futures contingent on this whim or that one, hanging by a thread. We were at the mercy of irrational government and political idiocy of the highest order, but their lives were not like mine for one important reason. They were not Americans. They did not*

know that life could be different. They had only experienced ongoing, lifelong despair, but I had hope. One day, I told myself, regardless of anything else that could happen to me, I would escape all this nonsense and return to the wonderful United States of America — land of the free and home of the brave!

"Deep inside I knew that one day my life would be given back to me. I don't know why, but I knew. My hope was for and in that coming day... But the other prisoners piling into our cattle car, these Russians, had no such hope. Their only hope was in their basic day-to-day ability to endure the crazy anguish of life here in their own country. They had no prospect of going elsewhere — like back to America some day. These simple Russians, good people at the core, were subject to endless oppression under these totalitarian conditions from which they were powerless to escape. The personal choices I took for granted while growing up in America — choices about health, happiness, and growth — these dear Russian people had never had. They never knew of such options, not even the simplest ones.

"They could not turn to religion for hope; atheism

was the Soviet religion. Hopelessness was deeply and permanently etched into their faces. It penetrated below the surface, into their souls. I can still see their faces clearly in my mind's eye today: men and women, young and old, with a look of total resignation, no hope whatsoever. A country without God is a terrible place. A horribly cold, harsh spirit hovered over this country, like a cloud that would not lift. It thickened the air and filled your nostrils everywhere you went. You could feel it crawl into your skin, into your pores. That was the condition of their lives and the very look upon their faces, as best I can describe it...Pain and human suffering went deep, deeper than one could imagine, and then deeper still." [275]

Reading Margaret's story, it is difficult to understand anyone surviving under so much adversity, cruelty and horror, but the dream of freedom gave her the strength to hope each day. We shake our heads and say, "This could never happen in America!" Hopefully, this writing has convinced you that, yes it can, but that we have time to reverse the path satan has us on. Our Lady speaks of freedom seven separate times in Her messages. She tells us freedom is a gift from God.

November 25, 1987

"...I desire each of you for myself, but God has given to all a freedom which I lovingly respect and humbly submit to..."

It is amazing that freedom is so sacred that Our Lady submits to it as it is indelibly a mark of God, an unalienable right of man that even God will not contradict nor can Heaven take it away. The most influential Creature made by God, the Holy Virgin Mary, says:

August 7, 1986

"...I am with you, but I cannot take away your freedom..."

Freedom is sacred and holy because its very essence is of God, Himself.

March 25, 1996

"...decide for God who is freedom and love..."

The character of God is displayed through His giving us freedom, a freedom so profound that He even allows His creatures to hate Him. Every time we sin, we give over to satan part of our freedom, reclaimed only through repentance. The greater influence of satan, the greater loss of freedom.

November 25, 1989

> **"...I desire that your decisions be free before God, because He has given you freedom. Therefore, pray so that, free from any influence of satan, you may decide only for God..."**

Does what Our Lady says in Her message pertain only to free will? Is She not referring to our physical freedom? Our Lady does say She desires our decisions to be free before God. But simply thinking, "I'm free to decide," does not necessarily mean that is true. It is within the character of God to want us to have freedom which can only be "had" through Him. If God is minused out of the equation, how then is our freedom secured? It is why the Fathers of our nation looked so intensely and strongly to God to fulfill the *"dream that they had,"* which was to create a nation in which every man had the freedom to fulfill his dreams. It is clear that satan wants to take away our freedom by not only trying to enslave our souls, but also our physical "place," and the nation in which we live. When we decide for satan, the enslaver, and his ways, in contrast to deciding for God and His ways, it puts us on the path of not only losing our freedom in decisions, but also losing freedom over our physical lives. The dream of our nation's Forefathers was for our nation to be an oasis of freedom.

We are losing our freedoms, which were first lost in our hearts through abandoning God's ways, and which now is manifesting in our nation.

August 7, 1986

> **"...you don't know that beside an oasis stands the desert, where satan is lurking and wants to tempt each one of you. Dear children, only by prayer are you able to overcome every influence of satan in your '*place*.' I am with you, but I cannot take away your freedom..."**

But satan *can and is* taking away our freedoms, and we are in a serious spiritual crisis that is manifesting in our nation, our **'place,'** as Our Lady says. We have exchanged God's freedom for love for material things. We have lost love and true values, step-by-step. An evil spirit of consumerism has enslaved us.

March 25, 1996

> **"...In this time, when due to the spirit of consumerism, one forgets what it means to love and to cherish true values, I invite you again, little children, to put God in the first place in your life. Do not let satan attract you through material things but, little children, decide for God who is**

> **freedom and love. Choose life and not death of the soul..."**

Not with death of the body, but with the death of enough souls, comes the death of a nation. Nations fall by their people and their morals, or lack thereof. We have fallen asleep in obeying God's precepts, His laws. Instead, we are responsible for having awakened in ourselves an attachment to material things. Sleep presupposes enslavement. Our Lady says:

June 25, 1989

> **"Pray because you are in *great* temptation and *danger* because the world and material goods lead you into slavery. satan is active in this plan..."**

Mark Hall, a Christian musician, set out to write new music to the Christmas hymn, "O Little Town of Bethlehem," but instead something else came out of his heart. Pause before reading the following words of the song. We invite and encourage you to call Caritas immediately and read the words as you listen to this song. At one point, reading and listening, you will be moved in your spirit as we were. Don't cheat yourself. Resist reading ahead before calling. If the words do not move your heart, your heart is too hard. You can hear the song by dialing 205-672-2000, 24 hrs. Ask for or press extension 350. To re-play, press 350 to hear the song again. You may listen to it as many times as you like. The song was found after the title of this book was given and basically written. It seems its words and title were God ordained for this book.*

While You Were Sleeping *276

By Mark Hall

Oh little town of Bethlehem, Looks like another silent night
Above your deep and dreamless sleep
A giant star lights up the sky
And while you're lying in the dark
There shines an everlasting light
For the King has left His throne
And is sleeping in a manger tonight, tonight.

Oh Bethlehem, what you have missed
while you were sleeping
For God became a Man, and stepped into your world today
Oh Bethlehem, you will go down in history
As a city with no room for its King

* *While You Were Sleeping* can be obtained through your local music store or through www.castingcrowns.com..

While you were sleeping
While you were sleeping

O little town of Jerusalem, Looks like another silent night
The Father gave His only Son
The Way, the Truth, the Life had come

But there was no room for Him
In the world He came to save

Jerusalem, what you have missed while you were sleeping
The Savior of the world is dying on your cross today
Jerusalem, you will go down in history
As a city with no room for its King
While you were sleeping
While you were sleeping

United States of America, Looks like another silent night
As we're sung to sleep by philosophies
That save the trees and kill the children
And while we're lying in the dark
There's a shout heard 'cross the eastern sky
For the Bridegroom has returned
And has carried His bride away in the night, in the night

America, what will we miss while we are sleeping?
Will Jesus come again,
And leave us slumbering where we lay?
America, will we go down in history

As a nation with no room for its King?
Will we be sleeping?
Will we be sleeping?

*United States of America, looks like another silent night…**

Our Lady comes to the world and the Nation of Light is sleeping. O America! Who will weep for you? O Nation ordained by God, who was given the Queen, the Immaculate Conception, the Patroness of your nation, Her nation conceived as a pure conception, by the Divine, is calling you to the light so to spread the light through the world and you are sleeping while She visits the earth. The final call and oh, America you have no room for Her in your heart. No room for Her in your nation. No room for Her Son, Jesus, whom She wishes for you to wake up to. One tear in repentance for violating Our Lord's day…one tear to change your heart. Who will cry for you, O America? The world hates you because you were born and foundationed in Christ's principles and the world hated Him.

John 15:18–20

"If the world hates you, realize that it hated me first. If you belonged to the world, the world

* *While You Were Sleeping* can be obtained through your local music store or through www.castingcrowns.com..

would love its own; but because you do not belong to the world, and I have chosen you out of the world, the world hates you."

This is a revelation of why America is hated, by not only the world, but by even some of its own citizens. The hatred of the United States of America is puzzling, until you understand the above verse. The hatred of Christ will certainly bring hatred to even a nation if its foundation was built on the Christian principles of the Christ.

Pause and reflect for a few moments and grasp why there is so much hatred toward our nation. Consecrate yourself, your family, and your nation to the Heart of Our Lady and to the Heart of Jesus. Make a solemn consecration to live, honor and obey the Commandment of the Sabbath and change the direction of your life.

Christians have been carried away by secular worldview philosophies. How terrible our fate if we do not change. Love the One who has loved you through the centuries.

May, 1984

"Throughout the centuries, I have given myself completely to you..."

Awake to the Virgin Queen. Learn what God's love means.

September 25, 1997

> **"...Today I call you to comprehend that without love you cannot comprehend that God needs to be in the first place in your life. That is why, little children, I call you all to love, not with a human love, but with God's love..."**

And of Jesus, Our Lady says:

June 25, 1994

> **"...I desire, little children, to guide you all to Jesus because He is your salvation..."**

Our Lady wants our hearts to triumph through Jesus, a triumph that also must include our nation, because it is instilled with Her Son's principles.

March 18, 2007

> **"Dear children! I come to you as a Mother with gifts. I come with love and mercy. Dear children, mine is a big heart. In it, I desire all of your hearts, purified by fasting and prayer. I desire that, through love, our hearts may triumph together. I desire that through that triumph you**

may see the real Truth, the real Way and the real Life. I desire that you may see my Son. Thank you."*

We must urgently awake in our time to that which the Messiah awoke the world up to 2000 years ago.

The computer chip implants in animals, the freedoms that are eroding at an alarming rate, the worldwide plans of governance, all these are a part of an evolutionary plan, that has evolved step-by-step, a complex system ripe for an antichrist to step right into. It does not take a far-fetched conspiracy or an elaborate futuristic imagined scheme to see very plainly that the system is in our midst. It is not an opinion. There are enough facts to prove such a system is under construction. The "buying and selling" of everything falls easily into this system that now exists. Should it be believed that we are living in the days of the antichrist? Through prayer and Our Lady's messages the answer is surprisingly, "No." But, again, the technology of man has reached a point where it will happen, if not stopped. How can it be stopped if Scripture foretells of these times? Just as in the days of the Tower of Babel, man had reached advancements that would have moved forward the time table of civi-

* This message of March 18, 2007 was inserted here just before this book went to press.

lization. Advancements that perhaps, by the time of Christ, would have brought about an industrial revolution, machinery, automobiles, etc., which would have superseded God's time table. Genesis tells us:

> ***"The Lord came down to see the city and the tower that the men had built. Then the Lord said: 'If now, while they are one people, all speaking the same language, they have started to do this, nothing will later stop them from doing whatever they presume to do. Let us then go down and there confuse their language, so that one will not understand what another says.' Thus the Lord scattered them from there all over the earth, and they stopped building the city. That is why it was called Babel, because there the Lord confused the speech of all the world. It was from that place that he scattered them all over the earth.*** Genesis 11:5–9

God brought confusion to their language, setting back civilization from being able to progress by disconnecting man. Today's communication races civilization ahead at light speed, paralleling the advancements of ancient man that also began happening too quickly. Except for us, we have arrived at the point that Scripture states:

"Nothing will later stop them from doing whatever they please." Genesis 11:6

Just as God had to break apart and separate man's communication to stop his advancements with the Tower of Babel, so too it will be for us. Our culture is full of "babble." From useless conversations in excessive use of cell phones to non-stop conversations on radios and televisions, endless chatter…a continuous stream of communication flowing. But when you consider the substance of these conversations, most are without purpose and value and it can even be said that they have contributed to many sins, not the least of which is the sin of wasting time, "busy idleness," as idleness is the devil's workshop. How much prayer or contemplation time is killed through non-essential conversations? While in the U.S., it is true, we speak in one language, it is still babbling, and we are suffering from the same attitudes of "doing whatever we please to do." Paralleling the communication with the physical manifestation of such a society, you can then understand why Our Lady is coming to stop the building of the Tower of Babel in our time, and to remind us that we are not free to do whatever we please in redefining laws against natural law. A list of violations against natural law today could name, far and above the sins of man in the past, including those of the Tower of Babel: from cloning with plans to grow human bodies for parts in farming labs, to the recent developments of transplanting human faces, full face transplants, including hair and ears, down to the neck; or from illicit marriage unions to the adoption of children into abominable "family" structures. These are only a few of many sins against natural law, but each one is such a serious transgression that only one in itself is enough for God to take action against man. Doctors in Cleveland, Ohio, announced in May 2006 that they have achieved enough success on cadavers to transplant faces, from dying or brain dead donors, to living patients. Nothing is sacred any longer. Anything and everything can be profaned.[277] Add to that literally thousands of violations of man, thinking he can do whatever he pleases, as if he himself is god. Next, include the system of the beast that has already been built, the technology already here, as foretold in Revelation, and then you will be able to understand that we are falling head long into that period of time which will lead to the end of the world, unless it is interrupted by a divine act of God. We will either rapidly digress towards it or the system will be dismantled for the time being. One or the other.

Our Lady is clearly coming to interrupt it. How? By a comparable event of what happened in the city of

Babel that will break the present systems from being brought into activity. Why? Because even the elect, the true believers, do not have the spiritual fiber to survive under an antichrist system. Our Lady has told us, we have forgotten the Bible. She has come to give us time to reacquaint ourselves with our Maker, and to help know Jesus in a more intimate way. Therefore, the present systems must be broken apart to stop the march of advancement so that the messages of Our Lady cannot just be read, but become rooted into a way of life, cultivated into world societies. The enculturalization of Our Lady's messages must pass into the next generations of Christians so to ready man for the time in the future when he will meet the antichrist system, face to face. This present anti-god system will be set back just as Babel was, but it will resurrect again, perhaps in a period of time as short as the end of this century or perhaps two or more. We cannot know. But then, when the antichrist system is built for the last days, true Christians will have the fiber, through Our Lady's messages, to hold out through to the end.

In the book, Requiem, Images of Ground Zero, photographer Gary Suson chronicles the clearing and clean-up of Ground Zero, from the first day of September 11, 2001, until the very end. Earning the appreciation and respect from the New York firefighters through his sensitivity in recording these events, he was granted privileged access to the site. His photographs are deeply moving as are many of his personal experiences with what and who he encountered during the year that followed September 11th. One story, in particular, was startling in its implications. Suson describes the scene:

> *"It was the last few days of January 2002 and I was standing near the North Tower area conversing with a New York Fire Department Chief, when I noticed some charred papers on the edge of a steep incline. Separating me from the papers was a Jersey barrier, erected to keep workers away from the dangerous drop-off. I asked the Chief if I could photograph the papers and he hesitantly said yes, but asked me to make it quick because it was dangerous. I shot only three frames. The first was of a charred letter from police headquarters. Barely sticking out from under the letter were some cream-colored papers. When I lifted the police letter, I found there were a few wet and charred pages from a Bible. The Bible itself was nowhere to be found. I was instantly taken aback by this find, but never had a chance to examine the pages because my coworker pulled up in his gator*

and told me to jump in, as there was a recovery in progress that we had to get to. I leaned over quickly, shot two photographs, and jumped in the back of his gator. That night there was a huge rainstorm and Ground Zero turned into a giant mud pit and had to be temporarily shut down because the trucks couldn't make it up the hill. The next day I got the proof sheets back and nearly fell off my chair when I saw that the passage on the page facing me was Genesis 11, the Tower of Babel. It was a very moving, though bizarre, find; I took the symbolism of the "11" and the "Tower" as a positive sign that God was watching over the victims in their last moments, and that He was also watching over this hallowed ground during the recovery efforts. Also, I found the page during a period when I was considering tapering off my shooting, because the things I was seeing were too much to bear. I am not trained for wartime photography and the sights that go along with it. This was a war zone and it was taking its emotional toll on me. Finding the Genesis 11 Bible page gave me the strength to continue with my duties; I felt someone 'upstairs' must have approved of what I was doing. Whether it was just some strange coincidence or divine intervention, it had important meaning to me. A group of my friends went down to look for the page the next day but it had been washed away into the mud during the storm." [278]

Another "signs of the time?" Two gigantic buildings crash to the ground, leaving little remains of anyone or anything. Five months had passed since the fateful September day. A photographer "noticed some charred papers on the edge of a steep incline," that he is inspired to get a picture of. Certainly there were a lot of wind-blown papers amongst the site. Why did these catch Suson's attention? He discovers underneath the top letter, a few Bible pages, with the Bible nowhere in sight. And it *just so happens* that the chapter of the Bible was Genesis 11...the Tower of Babel. The picture showed one verse highlighted in yellow. Verse 7 reads:

"Let us then go down and there confuse their language, so that one will not understand what another says." Genesis 11:7

From this action of God, the people were scattered and the building of their city, of their system was stopped. We must reflect upon why God left this sign at the site of the destroyed Twin Towers. From a Biblical worldview, the logical conclusion is that God, step-by-step, is revealing to our nation that we are living in a time in which a Tower of Babel is being built, a tower that is destined to fall as well. So much does God want us to understand this, that he gives us a visual...two fallen towers....along with His Word from Holy Scripture amidst the rubble.

How will this modern day Babel be torn down? From the beginning of the Medjugorje apparitions in 1981, Our Lady has foretold of chastisements, three admonitions that will happen in the lifetime of the visionaries, who are in their forties, as of 2007. These three admonitions will alter the world in a complete way, as the Great Flood did. They will be events that will be undeniably from God. They will not even be comparable with 9/11, the tsunami, or Hurricane Katrina. We don't know if they will be a physical, total world economic collapse, a horrific spiritual purification or a combination of both with the laws of nature being suspended. What we do know is that it is very probable that they will take place within the next fourteen years as of 2007, or just after the next fourteen year period.* In Fatima, Portugal, in 1917, Our Lady appeared to three children visionaries, to whom She imparted three secrets, one of which became known as the Third Secret of Fatima. The Third Secret was finally released by Pope John Paul II

* The author's basis in formulating this probability has come through 20 years of following the messages of the Virgin Mary.

on June 26, 2000. It revealed that there was an angel of God who was to strike the earth with fire but upon contact with the splendor of the Holy Virgin Mary the raining fire was stopped.[279]

Yet in another apparition in the early 1970s, in Akita, Japan, Our Lady began appearing to a nun, Sister Agnes. These apparitions have been approved by the Church. On October 13, 1973, Our Lady appeared to Sr. Agnes, and she was shown and told the following:

> *"...the Father will inflict a terrible punishment on mankind. It will be a punishment greater than the deluge, such as no one will have seen before. Fire will fall from the sky...."* [280]

The correlation of the 1917 Fatima apparition, with the angel dispensing fire from Heaven and the apparitions in Akita where Our Lady said: *"Fire will fall from the sky and will wipe out a great part of mankind,"* is unnerving in exactness; *"Fire will fall from the sky..."* Fatima's 3rd secret fortunately shows that upon contact with Our Lady's splendor it was stopped. The 25 plus years of daily apparitions and what Our Lady has done in Medjugorje, gathering the world to Her Son, certainly fills the role of "the splendor of Our Lady." When Mirjana, the Medjugorje visionary, received the

7th of ten secrets, she begged, prayed and pleaded for Our Lady to intercede to Her Son Jesus not to allow it. Later, in an apparition, Our Lady told her it would be avoided. Was this the fire? We do not know as it remains a secret. But Mirjana was told by Our Lady that other admonitions would not be avoided. Only that they could be mitigated through prayer and fasting. Mirjana revealed later that there was one other secret that was worse than the 7th.[281] These admonitions are necessary to tear down the systems that are already here and that are continuing to be built up around the world. Again, the chastisements will bring a good effect, in the necessary reprieve, so that Our Lady's messages can get rooted into the hearts of believers of the next several generations. Again, this is necessary so the next coming generations of Christians will mature and have the fiber that the early Christians had. Those future Christians will withstand the trials, maintaining their faith when the world enters the time of the antichrist, bringing about the end of the world. Yes, Our Lady's messages are that profound, and yes, these messages, echoing the Scriptures, will be the strength and source to help sustain Christians through the greatest trials the earth will ever experience, the totality of the end of the world. For the interim, however, from now until the coming admonitions, we must grow in holiness, preparing for the time when God will tear down these systems, to interrupt the time table that is advancing before it is time. Our Lady did inform us of a possibility of a century of peace:

December 25, 1999

> **"...Through your 'yes' for peace and your decision for God, a new possibility for peace is opened...this century will be for you a time of peace and well-being..."**

There are insights, within Our Lady's messages, that indicate that man is being given a time of grace, a time of conversion before the time of oppression comes from a system that is already built to oppose God and His ways; the anti-god, antichrist system of the beast.

November 25, 1997

> **"...I led and am leading you through this time of grace, that you may become conscious of your Christian vocation. Holy martyrs died witnessing: I am a Christian..."**

The main point to make is that today's Christians could not live through an antichrist system. Most are too weak, too conditioned, too comfortable and spineless. Their lives are filled with idols of money, materialism, sports, entertainment and seeking only after enjoyment, achievements, relaxation, and pleasure. They pay lip service to God's laws. Who is able to stand their ground today? The head of a health department in a large city in Alabama found success in closing down two abortion clinics through inspections. The one who held the position was a Christian who wanted to take such action, but then resistance began against him by some of the pro-choice women under his command and he moved to a position of "maybe I shouldn't rock the boat." You could describe his new position as "spineless Christianity." Few Christians have the "courage" to do what is right without considerations. Many are willing to do something until resistance comes along. We are to do what is right and not consider the consequences. Our Lady said:

May 25, 1988

> **"...Pray, little children, that satan does not sway you like branches in the wind...Pray without ceasing so that satan cannot take advantage of you..."**

We must realize that we cannot win this battle by any other means but wholly and fully committed, responsible actions in faith with exclusive allegiance to

God. Dietrich Bonhoeffer spoke of how to fight evil... and that often man, even the Christian man...will depend upon his own strength of reason, principles, conscience, duty, freedom or virtues, rather than surrender and submit himself completely to the will of God in obedient action to His calls. Man then wonders why he fails in conquering the evil surrounding him.

The Call of God

> *"Who stands his ground? The great masquerade of evil has wrought havoc with all our ethical preconceptions. This appearance of evil in the guise of light, beneficence and historical necessity is utterly bewildering to anyone nurtured in our traditional ethical systems. But for the Christian who frames his life on the Bible, it simply confirms the radical evilness of evil.*
>
> *"The failure of rationalism is evident. With the best of intentions, but the naive lack of realism, the rationalist imagines that a small dose of reason will be enough to put the world right. In his short sightedness, he wants to do justice to all sides* (for example, the retreating actions of the head of the health department to close abortion clinics) *but in the milieu of conflicting forces he gets trampled*

upon without having achieved the slightest effect. Disappointed by the irrationality of the world, he realizes at last the futility, retires from the fray and weakly surrenders to the winning side.

"Worst still is the total collapse of moral fanaticism. The fanatic imagines that his moral purity will prove a match for the power of evil. But like a bull he goes for the red rag instead of the man who carries it and grows weary and succumbs, he becomes entangled with nonessentials and falls into the trap set by the superior ingenuity of his adversary.

"Then there is the man with a conscience. He fights single-handed against overwhelming odds in situations which demand a decision but there are so many conflicts going on, all of which demand some vital choice with no advice or support save that of his own conscience and he is then torn to pieces. Evil approaches him in so many specious and deceptive guises that his conscience becomes nervous and vacillating. In the end, he contents himself with the salve instead of a clear conscience and starts lying to his conscience as a means of avoiding despair. If a man relies exclu-

sively on his conscience he fails to see how a bad conscience is sometimes more wholesome and strong than a deluded one.

"When men are confronted by bewildering variety of alternatives, the part of duty seems to offer a sure way out. They grasp at the operative as one certainty. The responsibility for the imperative rests upon its author not upon its executor. But when men are confined to the limits of duty, they never risk a daring deed on their own responsibility, which is the only way to score a bull's eye against evil and defeat it. The man of duty will, in the end, be forced to give the devil its due.

"What about, then, of the man of freedom. He is the man who aspires to stand his ground in the world. Who values the necessary deed more highly than a clear conscience or the duties of his calling, who's ready to sacrifice a barren principle for a fruitful compromise or a barren mediocrity for a fruitful radicalism. What then of him? He must beware lest his freedom become his own undoing, for in choosing the lesser of two evils, he may fail to see that the greater evil he seeks to avoid may prove to be the lesser. Here we have the raw material of tragedy.

"Some seek refuge from the rough and tumble of public life in the sanctuary of their own private virtue. Such men, however, are compelled to seal their lips and shut their eyes to the injustice around them. Only at the cost of self deception can they keep themselves pure from the defilements incurred by responsible action. For all that they achieve that which they leave undone will still torment their peace of mind. They will either go to pieces in the face of this disquiet or develop into the most hypercritical of all Pharisees.

"Who then can stand his ground? Only the person whose ultimate criterion is not merely his ***reason****, his* ***principles,*** *his* ***conscience****, his* ***duty****, his freedom or his virtue, but who is ready to sacrifice all these things when he is called to obedient and* ***responsible action in faith*** *and* ***exclusive allegiance to God.*** *The responsible person seeks to make his whole life a response to the question and 'call' of God."* [282]

Is that not why Our Lady is saying: "Thank you for having responded to my 'call'"* —meaning thank you for giving yourself wholly and completely to God

* Our Lady in Her monthly messages to the world and other messages ends them with "Thank you for having responded to my call," the call of God.

without considerations or cost? We have needed Our Lady all these years to lead us down a different "way," to "wake us up," for Christians have fallen asleep, just as the song said. The call to action, to change our nation, is urgent. It depends first and solely upon exclusive allegiance to God and His call to live obedience to the Commandments of which most Christians accept, except for one, the Sabbath. We must immediately accept this and must put God first in our lives. Many things depend upon us. We must take charge to sanctify ourselves and then to sanctify and cleanse our nation...and pray, which is our protection.

July 25, 1991

> **"...much of what will happen depends on your prayers..."**

If the three secret admonitions coming soon to the world are of a corrective measure, why should we then worry with trying to effect change now in our nation? Because what will happen, Our Lady says, depends on us. Remember, Mirjana said we can mitigate the admonitions or chastisements through prayer. Living God's precepts in fullness will help also. We must get as many people on the Ark as possible. Our Lady's mantle is the Ark of our time. Our Lady is the hope for the future and we must, therefore, take back America, to help lead the world back to holiness, through the conversion which will wake up America—individual conversion—one conversion at a time. Evil has gotten a strong foothold in our world through taking one step at a time. We must be just as persistent in taking one step at a time towards re-claiming that which is being stolen from us. Our Forefathers didn't just leave to us the Declaration of Independence and the Constitution, they left to us their "witness," for they themselves achieved the impossible, through God, by taking one step at a time.

On September 2, 2006 Our Lady spoke about the future to Mirjana. The following is the description of Mirjana's September 2, 2006 apparition.

Our Lady did not give the usual greeting message but started with the following words:

> **"You know that we have been gathering for me to help you to come to know the love of God."** *

She then spoke about the future which Mirjana cannot reveal, but added that Our Lady said:

> **"I am gathering you under my Motherly mantle to help you to come to know God's love and His**

* Our Lady has called everyone on the second of each month to pray for non-believers.

greatness. My children, God is great. Great are His works. Do not deceive yourselves that you can do anything without Him, not even to take a single step. My children, instead set out and witness His love. I am with you..."

We need to take steps to heal our nation. The first step is education of people's minds. Memorize the following statement. Put it on your refrigerator. Repeat it throughout the day as a prayer and apply it to Our Lady's ways and messages which Our Lady gives us to set a fire in our own minds and hearts.

"It does not require a majority to prevail, but rather an IRATE, TIRELESS MINORITY keen to set brush fires in people's minds." [283]

Samuel Adams

The godless have been doing this for years. It's time those who wear the title "Christian" do the same. The American Revolution began with the spreading of a pamphlet called *"Common Sense,"* a document listing the injustices that were being leveled at Americans. It spread like wildfire. Spread this book in the same way because its purpose is first to educate, setting your mind ablaze in desiring to get truth, and then moving you to act upon those truths in the transformation of our nation.

Do you know America's history? Many people would answer yes, but in fact, most do not. When was the last time you read a book on the history of our nation? Not modern revisionist books and biographies, but books close to the event makers. In our community, we are constantly reading and sharing books with each other that feed our love of what God has given to us in being Americans. Often, we seek older books, many of which are now revived by being newly republished. That way, we keep the ideals alive that were birthed by our Founding Fathers. We speak about them at the breakfast table, as we are walking to Rosary in the Field, as we tend to our work, always with our children eavesdropping on our conversations. America's history is rich with lives worthy of studying, that exemplify what made America such a great nation: faith in God, love of family, hard work, freedom fought and died for, virtues lived. The revisionists would have us all believe that America's origin is evil and is just getting what it deserves. Educate your children, your families. Spread this information to your pastors and your churches, neighbors, your friends and co-workers. Begin with step one, the first revolution in Christendom, and let the Holy Spirit light up step two, the second revolution in our nation.

Lastly, our fight is not against people in darkness but the evil in them. We must conquer them and bring them to the light of Christ. It starts with our witness being enlightened and embellished by truth. Purposely risking repetition, we cannot be enlightened as to what we must do if we do not keep the Sabbath. At the same time, it is difficult not to get angry with those who so blatantly, so arrogantly throw our freedoms out the window. We here have sat in city council meetings and have been told lies right to our faces concerning the "Sustainable, Smart Growth plans" for our own county. In Florence, Alabama, on June 12, 2006, a Sustainable, Smart Growth spokesman told civil officials how to avoid and subdue "screaming citizens." It was an attitude displayed, demonstrating to us that the government that is suppose to be of the people, for the people, and by the people is now, "over" the people. The more you do your own research and really study the documents, the angrier you will feel, especially with the continued taking of private property. Such a darkness as that can be seen in a court case where Justice Janice Brown wrote a dissenting opinion involving the San Reno Hotel U. City and the County of San Francisco, a portion of which follows:

> *"Once again a majority of this court has proved that if enough people get together and act in concert, they can take something and not pay for it...But theft is still theft. Theft is theft even when government approves of thievery...Turning a de-*

mocracy into a kleptocracy does not enhance the stature of thieves; it only diminishes the legitimacy of government."* [284]

This is in violation of the Commandment, "Thou shall not covet thy neighbors goods," as well as "Thou shall not steal." Many of the states who recently passed laws blocking eminent domain for development have a blight clause which already is being 'redefined' for any place which is not serving the tax base enough for local government. Your unalienable right to own private property is still at risk, despite new laws of protection. The just anger this causes can easily be directed towards the people who are putting themselves in this position of "God." However, Our Lady has shown us in Her messages that we are to separate the sin from the sinner. We are to love the sinner, show respect for the person, but not the sin, and put effort in educating them as well, because many have been conditioned and indoctrinated into these plans. However, at the same time, we cannot lose site that we still must hold them accountable for their actions.

General Sada,[285] who was mentioned early in this

* Justice Brown's use of the word "kleptocracy" is actually inferring that in this situation the taking of land is no different than a "kleptomaniac;" a neurotic that is overcome with persistent impulses to steal. In addition, do not be deceived by what city councils and county boards call 'redevelopment" It's a nice name for eminent domain.

writing, a Christian general serving under Saddam Hussein, was a man of deep integrity and honesty. When the invasion of Iraq caused Saddam's regime to fall, although he was a Christian, there were many leaders who wanted him to be a part of the leadership structure because of his character and trustworthiness. Because of who he was, he had not one, but a crew of bodyguards assigned to him. On one occasion, his bodyguards noticed a car driving several times in front of his house. They then noticed the passengers had a video camera and were filming his home. They knew it meant only one thing. They intended to kill Sada. The bodyguards told Sada and he gave the order to go after them. Several cars went on a chase and caught the would-be assassins. Four very young men were hauled before Sada. General Sada called Iraq's Prime Minister who told Sada to interrogate them and decide from there what to do. There was no question in anyone's mind that the four would be executed. They were trembling because they knew their deaths were imminent within a day. Upon seeing them, Sada wrote:

> *"When I saw the four young men, I knew these were not ordinary terrorists. They did have the long beards and Muslim clothing, but they were different. When I asked what they were doing,*

they admitted that they were planning to blow up my house..."

"So I asked them, 'What do you do when you're not blowing people up?' Two of them told me they were engineering students at the University of Baghdad, and the other two were in their second year of medical school. Again, I just shook my head. Here were four bright young men, obviously from good families..."

"I felt sad for them, and I knew very well what the intelligence officers would do to them when I turned them over to the police. As I was considering my options, I asked them, 'Why did you listen to these men who told you to kill me?' They said, 'They're foreigners, and they told us that it was the will of Allah for us to kill you. If we didn't do it, we would be cursing Islam.' I looked at them and I just said a silent prayer: Jesus, tell me what to do with these young men.'" [286]

Sada knew what he was expected to do and he knew there would be no mercy shown to the four who stood before him. Sada saw no defiance in them, but rather through their fear, a regret and repentance. After he prayed, Sada knew he was to let them go. He called the

Prime Minister who was stunned and then yelled at him that what he was doing was against the law. But Sada responded back:

> *"Sir, these people were trying to kill me. You know that I'm a Christian, and we're taught to practice forgiveness. Even Jesus Christ, when they hung him on the cross, said, 'Father, forgive them, because they don't know what they're doing.' So let me deal with this in my own way."* [287]

When Sada returned to the young men, he told them they were being set free. They thought it was a trick and believed they were being set-up and that once they left the house they would be killed. But Sada reassured them that no harm would come to them. They were let go. Four hours later the young men returned, but this time with their fathers and mothers, who came to thank Sada for saving their lives. Sada invited them inside his home. The parents, being so moved by his compassion, offered their sons to Sada to be his bodyguards.

> *"They were kissing me and thanking me over and over, but I said…the only thing I want from you is...These two are going to be good doctors, and the other two are going to be good engineers one day. They're our hope for the future, and Iraq*

needs them… Most of them had tears in their eyes by this time, but they were listening carefully to what I was saying. So I told the boys, (these terrorists) are losers, they're killers, and they're cowards. They won't do the dirty work themselves, but they want you to kill your fellow citizens. They're nobody, but you're somebody, because you are the future leaders of Iraq. Please don't throw your lives away for losers like that." [288]

All the boys have continued to visit Sada from time to time. They always ask if they can do anything for him in which he responds to them to work hard, and he will help them find good positions. When Sada reported this to the Prime Minister, he said:

"Georges, sometimes I don't understand you. You Christians always do things like this, but God only knows what they're going to do." And I said, "Sir... I'll put them in good positions. And I think this is the best way of making our young people whose eyes have been blinded by hate and lies to see the truth. One day you'll see what happens." [289]

Some people still say that Sada made a mistake and that these boys will come and finish the job on him one day. Sada doesn't believe that, but even if they do, he has no regrets of his decision because he believes that Jesus revealed to him what he was to do. Many people know this story and they said had Sada been a Muslim, he would have had the boys hung that same day, but because he is a Christian, he had mercy on them. Our Lady said on January 23, 1986:

> **"...If you pray with the heart, dear children, the ice of your brothers' hearts will melt and every barrier shall disappear. Conversion will be easy for all who desire to accept it. You must pray for this gift which by prayer you must obtain for your neighbor..."**

As Christians and living Our Lady's messages, as the above states, is not to say that had they been successful at killing Sada, that there should have been no retribution made. Crimes committed must have punishments equal to the seriousness of the crime. However, they didn't carry it out. Our Lady has told us that "love" is the only instrument She desires us to use. It can be "tough love," but love must be behind all our actions and motivations even when dealing with those who have become traitors to the very foundations of American Liberty.

The situation is not hopeless, but it is desperate. It clearly appears overwhelming and, in fact, it is. Plans of evil will not be stopped by human power but by God's children complying with God's law. Then God will do the rest. Our situation is too complex to leave it up to us to fix. But at the same time, we are not to sit around and do nothing. We must be active, working, and ready to "seize the moment" when God grants it. Did Gideon and his army defeat the enemy? No! Did Joshua tear down the wall of Jericho and defeat his enemy? No! God acted on their behalf and through them. They collaborated with God. God's plans always require something from us even when God is doing it for us. Even Jesus dying on the cross, paying for our sins, winning salvation for us, requires us to collaborate by accepting Him and being repentant. We are confronted with an evil so great that Our Lady is coming daily for over 27 years to show us how to behave so that God will act on our behalf, through our collaboration with Him, by crushing evil. You must first realize the seriousness of the situation to know what to do. Our Lady said:

July 25, 1991

> **"...I desire you to grasp the seriousness of the situation and that much of what will happen depends on your prayers, and you are praying a**

little bit!...begin to pray and fast seriously as in the first days of my coming..."

What will happen depends on you. A clear statement of our activity of collaboration with Our Lady with God. Lastly, it must be plainly stated that this writing is about a real revolution. This first will be accomplished not with words but the changing of mentality, the education of oneself, of our nation's situation and acting upon that wisdom. Some thinking today fears that if a revolution was to begin that there is a danger of it opening things up to hostile elements which would hijack the situation. *Understand this:* a hostile takeover has already taken place everywhere in our nation. It is we who have yet to engage on our part.

Recapping: **There must be two revolutions. First, in the Church. Pastors and all ministers of the Word must demand from the pulpits that all Christians comply with the Sabbath Commandment. All Christians must hold their clergy accountable and demand back from them not only to comply with their living the Sabbath Commandment, but also to preach it with strength and the fire of authority of the Word — shepherds giving their sheep the food that they are starving for. We must act now in implementing this. What can you as individuals do? Form groups of 5–10 people, from each parish or**

congregation, to start spreading the teaching of God's Sabbath Commandment. Business leaders can be the first to set the example. You will lose something by closing down on Sunday, but then you also will gain much more. When our nation's churches take this Commandment seriously and it spreads as fire across our nation, and Sunday becomes the day God intended it to be, then God will grant an opportunity to renew our nation. And <u>not until then</u>. The same goes for any other nation that follows suit.

It will not, it cannot happen until you fulfill this Command. It is by the authority of living this Commandment for 14 years and experiencing the fruits that have come from doing so, that this is stated so clearly and strongly. All your efforts to save our nation are in vain as a Christian until you accept, and live 100% the Sabbath Commandment. Remember, it is our broken window that Christians have not fixed that is allowing all the other windows of society to be broken. If we keep ours fixed, the others won't be broken.

The second revolution must take place in our nation. It will **not** come through the present two-party political systems, but through "we the people" whose rights are "unalienable." God will provide the circumstances and momentum for this transformation to take place. We need to pray for a structure to be in place to "**seize the moment**" when God grants it. By the positive laws of consequences, if we live the Sabbath Commandment, we will be given by God, through Our Lady as Patroness of our nation, a **"seize the moment"** opportunity to take our nation back to its founding…to the 'fathers' dreams they had.

We need not wonder whether or not all that is contained in this writing will happen. One thing is certain, something will happen. A negative or a positive outcome is quickly heading our way. The negative consequences are already manifesting. The positive will manifest when our nation's churches take the Sabbath Commandment seriously, and you put it into your life. We must do as Scripture tells us, and ***"Admonish one another"*** to keep the Sabbath if you are going to wear the title "Christian." Our future depends upon it.

CHAPTER SEVENTEEN

"SEIZE THE MOMENT"

Finally, this book cannot be completed without showing what *"a seize the moment could be and what would it appear like?"* We cannot know God's ways in which He chooses to restore a people, but we can look at some seize the moments God has granted.

In Tennessee, at the end of 1945, three thousand battle hardened veterans returned to McMinn County, located between Chattanooga and Knoxville in the eastern part of the state.[290] They were shocked and angered by what they found. Their county and towns were completely corrupted, with bribes common throughout the police and Sheriff's Department and among the political figures, along with many other illegal activities, and an entrenched political machine that openly practiced fraud that resulted in the stealing of elections. The machine guaranteed the reelection of the controlling political party and their hold on power in the years of 1940, 42, and 44 in the county. Just before the 1946 elections a G.I., in a speech at a rally opposing the political machine, said:

"The principles that we fought for in this past war do not exist in McMinn County. We fought for democracy because we believe in democracy, but not the form we live under in this county." [291]

One hundred fifty-nine G.I.'s of McMinn County petitioned the F.B.I. to send election monitors, as well as the Justice Department to investigate the 1940, 42, and 44 elections for fraud.[292] Their repeated requests were ignored. The G.I.'s decided to run for office, on a non-partisan ticket, to rid the county of corruption. Sheriff Mansfield, part of the political mob machine, brought in 200 armed deputies on the day of the election to intimidate the voters which included beating some of them with brass knuckles. The primary election was held on Thursday, August 1, 1946, and when G.I. poll watchers showed up, they were immediately beaten by the deputies. As the day wore on, force and intimidation continued. When deputies shot one voter in the back [293] for casting the wrong vote, resolve in the crowd began to rapidly swell. Because of the brutalities and because the G.I.'s were refused the right to watch the ballots being cast, tensions increased. At 4:45 p.m., a thousand people had gathered across the street of the 11th precinct. The crowd [294] was made up of many men who had just liberated Europe and the South Pacific from two of the most powerfully corrupt war machines in human history.[295] Those who fought in the war that had liberated other lands now faced having to live under intolerable oppressive conditions themselves. They decided that by no means were they going to live under tyranny in their own homeland. As two of the political machine's armed guards arrogantly came toward the crowd to intimidate them and ready to shoot, the G.I.'s, without any weapons rushed them before they could shoot a target, and put them under guard at a tire shop near the center of town.[296]

By 5:10 p.m., when one of the precincts closed early in an illegal move to stop votes being cast, the crowd rapidly grew to literally several thousand, mostly men, strung along a three block area.[297] Threats to kill some of the crowd were made by another two officers who were also overcome by the crowd and added to the other two under guard. Then three more deputies came, and again the immediate reaction of the crowd was a defensive move to overcome them, placing them also into the tire store under guard. The citizens disarmed and arrested a total of seven deputies.

By 6:35 p.m.,[298] the sheriff's men, assisted by state highway patrol and city police, took the ballot box to the McMinn County Jail. They were equipped with high-powered rifles and several hundred pistols on display. Earlier in the day, one veteran soldier said: *"Over there we had something to fight back with."* [299] Another said, *"We haven't got a chance with this Gestapo."* [300] Keys were obtained to the National Guard and State Guard Armories and weapons and ammo were "borrowed" by the G.I.'s. By 8:45 p.m., a revolutionary army of 500 armed and battle experienced G.I.'s, with a few M-1's and other weapons, converged on the jail. Seventy-five deputies had barricaded themselves inside the jail with the ballot box and three G.I. hostages. Meanwhile, the army of G.I.'s posted themselves [301] at ground level across the street, on the roof of the power company, and on other nearby buildings.

At 9:00 p.m., the full-fledge *Battle of Athens* began. Ralph Duggon, a former Navy Lieutenant Commander and a leader of the veteran G.I.'s said, *"The crowd (of G.I.'s) was 'met by gunfire' and because they had 'promised that the ballots would be counted as cast' they (the G.I.'s) had no choice but to meet fire with fire."* [302]

The G.I.'s fired back at them, making a full fledged shooting assault on the heavily fortified jail which held the deputies and three G.I. poll watchers they had taken as prisoners.[303] Heavy shooting continued and between 11 p.m. until 12:40 a.m., thousands of rounds were exchanged. The soldiers were pouring lead into every opening in the brick jail. G.I.'s cut phone lines to the jail. By the wee hours of Friday morning, 2:00 a.m., on August 2, deputies said they would kill the three G.I. hostages in the jail if the army of G.I.'s didn't stop shooting.[304] The G.I.'s, in turn, issued an ultimatum to surrender and come out with hands up. There was no compliance to the demands of the G.I.'s, so in an effort to press for a victory, they made make-shift bombs and dynamited the jail. After the fourth blast, the deputies began to yell they wanted to surrender. As officers filed out, they were understandably, roughly searched, disarmed, and then marched back into the jail cells and locked up. By sunrise, 4:00 a.m., the battle was over and as the light of day burst forth, a war zone materialized with cars upside down, smashed and burned, and the "bullet scarred jail" clearly visible alongside other buildings caught in the crossfire, telling of the previous night's *"Battle of Athens."* By 10:00 a.m., Friday, the G.I.'s were patrolling the streets and order was established. With the G.I.'s in complete control, the deputies were released from jail.

By 4:00 p.m. on Saturday, a three man commission was elected and set up a government framework.

At 9:00 p.m.[305] on Saturday, August 3, fifteen hundred citizens converged on Athens with firearms to back the new government. Telephone calls came in from neighboring cities pledging aid if needed in defense of their town. As a result of the Battle of Athens, the new non-partisan government restored order, cleaned up their county, and peace ensued. In the Congressional Record, in [306] Washington D.C., Rep. John Jennings Jr. from Tennessee, justified the revolution saying, "*The Justice Department*'s repeated failure to help the McMinn County residents" led to the actions of the citizenry, adding… *"at long last decency and honesty, liberty and law have returned to the fine county of McMinn county."* [307]

Water cannot stay water, once it passes 212 degrees. It changes to steam.

The townspeople of the county had taken their town back by "we the people," as the Declaration of Independence declares, ***"…whenever any Form of Government becomes destructive of these Ends, it is the Right of the People to alter or to abolish it, and to institute new Government…when a long train of abuses…it is their Right, it is their Duty, to throw off such Government, and to provide new Guards for their future Security…"*** This was the legal grounds for such action 230 years ago in the birth of our nation, it was the legal grounds in the Battle of Athens in 1946, and it is the legal grounds for our time today. However, few understand the legal right the Declaration gives as we have been conditioned to believe the opposite and that the Declaration's only value was for the founding of our nation. This is not what our Forefathers believed, nor Abraham Lincoln. Abraham Lincoln, in office 85 years after the Declaration of Independence was drafted, said:

> *"The government, with its institutions, belongs to the people who inhabit it. Whenever they shall grow weary of the existing government, they can exercise their constitutional right of amending it,* ***or their revolutionary right to dismember or overthrow it."*** [308]

Lincoln clearly believed, as well as our Forefathers, that there existed for the United States citizens this *"revolutionary right."* A right that is found in our first inspired document. Everyone must be educated that by the virtue of the Declaration, we have at our present time a *revolutionary right.* As was quoted previously in this writing, he called the nation to go back to the truths of the Declaration of Independence. That was almost 100 years after it was written. Lincoln obviously did not see it as a historical document, but rather that it had value for his day, as well as for our day in guiding us, especially in restoring *Christian principles.* It is the "Revisionists" who have taught, indoctrinated, and led us to believe the Declaration is only of historical value. However, again, Lincoln's words, quoted earlier in this book, shows the opposite and is most appropriate to reread.

> *"(Our father's) established these great self-evident truths that…their posterity might look up again to the Declaration of Independence and take courage to renew that battle which their FATHERS began, so that truth…and Christian virtues might not be extinguished from the land…Now, my countrymen, if you 'have been taught doctrines' conflicting with the great landmarks of the Declaration of Independence…let me entreat you to come back… come back to the truths that are in the Declaration of Independence."* [309]

"Truths?" God is truth. Lincoln said to come back to the Declaration, that *"Christian virtue might not be extinguished from the land."* The extinguishing of Christian virtues is exactly what is happening in our present time! Have you been taught doctrines conflicting with the Declaration of Independence? Yes, we all have. Every institution across the land has had revisionists change its core beliefs and principles about the Declaration of Independence and other documents of our founding by some degree or another.

We must change our mentality which has been touched and formed by the media and the educational systems which is resulting in our letting America be taken without resistance. Also, as stated previously, the moral character of the Constitution and the rights it gives comes from what is declared in the Declaration of Independence. There are many who do not want you to understand this because if you become educated to it, then their power is threatened as well as their educational efforts of instilling godless philosophies throughout governmental and institutional systems to achieve the implementing of structures that will destroy your family, your right to property and home, and peaceable living. Just as when someone else puts on your overcoat, something else has slipped into our nation's overcoat; a socialist godless system of controls which abides with immorality and corruption, along with condoning and protecting illicit behavior. Someone else in your overcoat does not make them you. It looks like your coat, feels like your coat. It is your coat. But who is in it is not you. The real overcoat of the United States does not now clothe what is and always was the United States. A surrogate system of laws, controls, and abuses is clothed underneath the U.S. overcoat. It looks like the U.S. coat, feels like the U.S. coat, but what inhabits it is not our nation. All our nation's Fathers, right up to just a few decades ago, would be horror-stricken by what is taking place in our nation. By their own words found in letters, speeches, and diaries, and by the witness of their very lives, we can be assured that they would have immediately formed a revolt. Think about what has slipped into our nation's coat? It is much worse than the wolf who disguised himself to fool Little Red Riding Hood in order to try and destroy her. A satanic infestation has clothed itself under the guise of our nation — systems such as the media and the corrupt educational and political institutions have clothed themselves with the legitimacy of the U.S. as a nation, that what they represent is what we are, while at the same time ripping apart the very fabric that has always held our nation together. Only one thing can change that. You!

With these problems, not only is the sovereignty of our nation now at risk with all that has been revealed through this writing, but we, as a nation, have also reached the summit of decadence at which point **'all'** past civilizations who had reached this same summit have fallen. Acceptance and toleration of laws and protections of abominable life styles was the last fatal straw whereby every nation in history which progressively, step-by-step, reached this point was severely purified or destroyed. It is an inevitable, historical, undeniable result of the laws of consequences.

We are moving into a phase where we can no longer rely on our voices being heard by petitioning the representatives of government or, as presently structured, casting our votes at the ballot box. Both of these are now tools used against us, so to keep us in order and to stop water from turning to steam. These two tools, collecting petitions and casting our votes as constitutional rights, have worked in the past. But we cannot continue dousing water on a fire that gives us a shorter and shorter warning time before some immoral, anti-christian and anti-American law is snuck stealthily through by lawmakers, without sooner or later being crushed by "our shepherds". The herd's "right to object" was almost outlawed January 2007, with only a lead time of 9 days to gather enough petitions to stop it. The bill that almost became law would have made it a crime, with a two hundred thousand dollar fine to object against policies of our government!! [310] We must immediately recognize and rise above a mentality that we have only these two steps of "petitioning and voting" as our means to change things. We must start thinking of another way. Are these thoughts bold? We live in a moment where boldness must rise up in our hearts now. If we wait too long, we will not have the ability to act boldly. Petitioning and voting has turned into the tool of managing the opposition, namely the Christian worldviewists, to feel they are achieving something, all the while losing more and more ground.

We are past the time of sending a message. It is time to impose a mandate. We must join together in a struggle to remove from our nation laws which will expedite and assure our ruination. No state can be allowed by its Christian citizens to have laws protecting abominable lifestyles, abominable marriages or adoptions by such unions. The issues that incited the Battle of Athens are as nothing compared to this ultimate abuse of children. The grave spiritual health of our nation aside, historically, we have arrived at the point that we will return to God through His purification or we will return to God by our humbling ourselves, repenting of our sins and giving God back His sovereignty over this nation of "we the people," His children. Our nation, in 230 years of history, has never faced such a massive amount of threatening issues, in addition to the many abominations that are present in our society today.

But how can we claim we are a peaceful people, if the Virgin Mary's title is Queen of Peace? Is the Battle of Athen's example out of touch with Our Lady's messages of peace? First, one must realize what is peace. Our Lady said what it is.

February 25, 1991

"...God is peace itself..."

If God is peace and our nation, through its institutions and laws, has more and more divorced itself from God and His laws, then as a nation we are not at peace. Our present political processes, institutions and many of our laws are against God and Christian principles. We must establish peace, first in our hearts, living holiness and then in our nation. But how do we establish it in our nation? In Washington D.C., inscribed upon a war monument is a quote that says: "The object of every war is a more perfect peace."

Is this example of what happened in Athens a call to arms? No. It is a call to live holiness and then God's 'will' will manifest into a seize the moment. Athens is an example of a seize the moment in which Christian principles, through disgusted citizens, rose up in them in indignation against immorality and righted the situation. Let it be known that past and present history shows that God is not against such actions unless it is done with malice or hate. From the birth of our nation to the Battle of Athens, honest citizens, with the desire to live in peace, in God, grasped hold of their legal "unalienable" right and took action. While not all the G.I.'s were angels in the revolution in Athens, their actions were for a right cause based in legal principles from the Declaration of Independence. The miracle was that not one person died. The Battle of Athens stands as one possible sign of what God may give as a seize the moment. But still how can the Battle of Athens be reconciled with the Queen of Peace and Her call to Peace? After all, this is a time of grace. The Athens Battle did not happen in this period. True. But Poland did. It is another seize the moment example. If you doubt that Christian principles origined and drove the Battle of Athens, you will not be able to doubt the origins of another battle, a monumental battle that took place in this "time of grace." As a boy, Pope John Paul II paused after every Mass to light a candle for the conversion of Russia.[311] Little did he know that one day, he would be a part of a Divine plan to overthrow communism in nations across the globe. Before John Paul's birth on May 18, 1920, another boy was born, February 6, 1911, and as a young boy, he, like John Paul, also grew up with deep convictions. They were born a little over eight years apart. Their birth and growing up years coincided with the birth and expansion of communism. Both of these boys would later join forces to crush the head of satan's socialist agendas. Not only did their lives run parallel with each other, but also their deaths as they died just ten months apart from each other. Instilled deeply in Ronald Reagan were the principles of Christianity through the guidance and witness of his mother's Christian faith. These principles strongly formed a confidence in his character that would eventually carry him into a direct confrontation with communist leaders worldwide which led to the eventual collapse of communism.

In the book, God and Ronald Reagan, author Paul Kengor writes of Reagan:

> *"As the Soviet Communists pressured the expansion of Marxism and Leninism and their brutal campaign against religion, the mature Reagan watched with pity, disgust, and commitment not to be silent. By the time he became president in 1981, he was ready to take action against Lenin's empire. He was committed to doing so by every means necessary."* [312]

Just as the two boys emerged in the same period of time at birth, so too did they rise at the same time in taking the office of the highest position of their respective callings. John Paul was elected Pope in October of 1978. Reagan was elected President of the United States a little over twenty-four months later.

John Paul II visited Poland a little over six months after his election. He told the Poles, "Be not afraid" and he publicly declared for all communist countries to allow freedom of conscience, individual rights, private property, and independence.[313] The largest crowd in the history of the world gathered to see one man, five million Poles heard John Paul's words.[314]

Ronald Reagan believed he had found a kindred spirit who was as courageous in speaking out as he was. Indeed two kindred spirits put upon the earth in the same time frame to "seize a moment" God would orchestrate. In 1917, Fatima, Portugal, in the apparitions, the Virgin Mary predicted the then infant Bolshevik Revolution would cause Russia to spread her errors throughout the world. Our Lady also predicted the shooting of the Pope in Vatican Square. The shooting happened on the anniversary of the Fatima apparitions, May 13, 1981, forty-three days after Ronald Reagan was shot on March 30, 1981.

The hospital's top surgeon, who would operate on the Pope, was at home when he felt an overwhelming impulse to go to the hospital. The Pope was shot when the doctor was ten minutes away from the hospital. Traffic had been so congested, that had he not left when he did, he would not have been able to go into emergency surgery to save the Pope's life, who had lost 60% of his blood.[315] Likewise, President Reagan, arriving at the hospital, was met by both the University's chief brain surgeon and chief thoracic surgeon [316] who both, by fate, happened to be meeting at the hospital, which made them instantly available to rush to the President's side. The Pope and the President both precariously missed death. Reagan's bullet stopped when it was but a fraction away from his heart. The Pope's bullet traveled through his body, miraculously missing vital organs. The Pope said, *"One hand fired the gun and another hand guided the bullet."* [317] Reagan believed God saved his life for a Divine purpose. John Paul believed the same, even stating that the Virgin Mary of Fatima protected him and saved his life.

Reagan felt after he was shot, he was spared for a Divine plan, especially to stop nuclear war.[318] After being shot, on Good Friday, Reagan was meeting with New York Cardinal Cooke. Cooke told him, "the hand of God was upon you." Reagan grew very serious, "I know. I have decided that whatever time I have left is for Him."[319] Kengor writes of a meeting with Reagan and Mother Teresa. In June, at a private meal, Reagan, with a few selected guests, hosted Mother Teresa. During the meal, she said, *"Mr. President, do you know that we stayed up for two straight nights praying for you after you were shot? We prayed very hard for you to live."* She then looked at Reagan directly and addressed him dramatically. *"You have suffered the passion of the Cross and have received grace. There is a purpose to this. Because of your suffering and pain, you will now understand the suffering and pain of the world."* This was Reagan's own belief. Mother Teresa continued, *"This has happened to you at this time because your country and the world needs you."* Nancy Reagan dissolved into tears, while the President was left almost speechless.[320]

Indeed, it was Reagan's belief that God had chosen the United States, raised it up as the hope of mankind, the shining city on the hill for all the world. John Paul II said, *"At this present moment in the history of the world, the U.S. is called, above all, to fulfill its mission in service of world peace."*[321] Reagan, before and after being elected as President, frequently quoted Pope Pius XII's statement about the United States, *"Into the hands of America, God has placed an afflicted mankind."*[322] He deeply believed this and even more so after he was shot.

June 7, 1982, twelve months after the moving meeting with Mother Teresa, the two boys who grew up with unshakable belief in 'God's will' and a shared belief about communism, met face to face. They discussed the assassination attempts, both said that they believed they had a special "Divine plan" to fulfill. Both felt their survival was miraculous. Both had been actors, John Paul in the theater and Reagan in movies. Both were very prayerful, though Reagan's prayer life was not made known to the public. It was, however, vouched for by Bill Clark, a devoted Catholic and Reagan's closest aide, as the two were often on their knees together.[323] In their first meeting, the Holy Father and the President committed themselves and the institution of the Church and America to a goal to bring down communism. From that day, the focus was to first bring it about in Poland. Poland would be the wedge to break up the communist block and make it crumble.[324] A cardinal who was one of the Pope's closest aides was quoted as saying, *"Nobody believed the collapse of communism would happen this fast or on this timetable."* [325]

Indeed the relationship between John Paul and Reagan became so close that the Pope believed Reagan was an instrument of God, that when the U.S. Bishops criticized Reaganism, the Pope prevailed upon the U.S.

Bishops to water down their criticism. When Vatican officials made a report to strongly criticize the President's Strategic Defense Initiative, the Pontiff ordered it buried. [326]

The Pope and President met several times through their terms. CIA Director, William Casey and others shuttled back and forth between Washington and the Vatican, briefing the Pope or his aides on a regular basis.[327] Cardinal Pio Laghi discreetly, at least six times, entered the White House at the South Gate, avoiding notice.[328]

Before the first meeting of the Pope and President, one of many seize the moments occurred in Poland. In August, 1980, a labor union named Solidarity, spontaneously catapulted from no members to, within three months, ten million members, one-half of the country's workmen.[329] On August 16, 1980, one of the union activists in the negotiating room, did the unthinkable. He removed Lenin's bust from the room and put in its place a black and white picture of Ronald Reagan, who was not even elected president yet.[330] *"Upon being asked who was the "last hope" for Poland, the Poles placed Reagan third, behind only the Pope and the Virgin Mary."* [331]

All of the above is stated to give evidence of God's actions in bringing down, rising up, and bringing about the transformation and renewal of nations. But still, with the messages of the Queen of Peace, how can it be claimed that Our Lady had hope or plans for this seize the moment in Poland, which led to several revolutions and the toppling of political systems and whole nations? Poland, after the Pope's visit in 1979, had growing temperatures, rising to the point of boiling over. Because of the tremendous tension in Poland, even the possibility of a potential war between the U.S. and U.S.S.R existed, the Virgin Mary was later asked by the visionaries of Medjugorje about the fate of Poland and its people. Our Lady gave an answer.

October 1981

> **"There will be great conflicts, but in the end the just will take over."** [332]

These are strange words from the **Queen of Peace**. She speaks, **"the just will take over."** What – the Queen of Peace speaks of those who are **"taking over"** as **"the just"?** It is a clear statement of where Our Lady stands in regards to the uprising of the people. They were given a seize the moment by God which caused ***great conflicts*** and many battles that would eventually overthrow the communist regime in Poland, Czechoslovakia, East Germany, Hungary, Bulgaria, Romania and eventually all of Russia. How about that for the Queen's intention for peace?

The struggle of the people of Poland was finally won in 1989 and while they prepared to hold their first elections, Reagan, who had ended his second term as President, watched from his home in California. Paul Kengor writes:

> *"...former president Reagan eagerly anticipated the moment from his home in California. A few weeks before the Polish elections, Reagan received a visit from four gentlemen: two Solidarity members and two Polish Americans hosting them. One of the hosts, Chris Zawitkowski, who today is head of the Polish-American Foundation for Economic Research and Education, asked the master campaigner if he had any words of wisdom or encouragement for the two Solidarity members as they prepared for the final stretch to the June elections. Zawitkowski was expecting to hear about political strategy, or even the invocation of Thomas Jefferson or the Founders; instead, he was taken aback by what he heard from the seasoned candidate: "Listen to your conscience," said Rea-*

gan, "because that is where the Holy Spirit speaks to you."

"With this line, what began as a political appeal became a spiritual encounter. The ex-president pointed to a picture of Pope John Paul II, which hung on his office wall. "He is my best friend," explained Reagan. "Yes, you know I'm Protestant, but he's still my best friend." Antoni Macierewicz, a Solidarity member who had been imprisoned by the communists, reciprocated by giving Reagan a Madonna that he had hand carved in a Polish gulag. Holding the gift in his hands, Reagan gladly accepted it and said that he and Nancy would be proud to have it in their home." [333]

Earlier, Ronald and Nancy Reagan had also received a gift from Pope John Paul II. It was the only gift in his eight year term that they chose to keep and pay the taxes required by law for a President if they receive a gift. It was a statue of the Virgin Mary. [334]

Ivan, one of the six visionaries of Medjugorje, relayed the taking down of communism was part of Our Lady's plans! Pope John Paul II, elected October 16, 1978, President Ronald Reagan elected November 8, 1980, all managed by the Queen of Peace who came down in the midst of this time period, June 24, 1981. Everything was in place for a seize the moment, all orchestrated by Heaven. The Pontiff wrote to Nancy Reagan upon the President's death, that there was a psychological and emotional tie between the two that he had never had with another president.[335]

The world, through Poland, was given a seize the moment by God.

Yet still, if you balk at this, that this was by Heaven's decree through Our Lady's actions, with the falling of the Berlin Wall and the total transformation of many nations, how does one explain the tenth anniversary of Our Lady's apparitions in Medjugorje? Many thought June 25, 1991 would be the last apparition. Many prepared for something monumental, just what, no one knew. But when the day came for the tenth anniversary of the apparitions, on that special day, the communist government that was still ruling over Medjugorje, Yugoslavia, suddenly dissolved and an independent nation was born with its new constitution. That very day a major civil war was sparked that would eventually cost hundreds of thousands of lives. Peace was the end result through communism being broken, and independent countries were born with freedom to worship without harassment, free elections, property rights and many other new-found liberties.

The Virgin Mary has come to draw all God's children of all beliefs back to loyalty to Him, both as individual people and as nations. As the apparitions continue, there will be more seize the moments coming. Our Lady's work of reconciling the world back to God is not yet completed. There will be more struggles. Poland's seize the moment signed up 50 percent of its work force in three months time which resulted in freeing the nation from its godless rulers. Could it not be the same for our nation to form an idea of a union for the purpose of re-establishing Christian principles and love of our nation, so to bring back the dreams of our Fathers? It could be formed into a seize the moment for the next election in which a non-partisan group could be elected through a write-in vote that would immediately transform this nation back to its moral roots, instantly mandating the end of abortion, the removal of judges who have undone and/or destroyed our nation's common laws which have always rooted its people to Christian principles; striking down all laws protecting abominable life styles; liberating the churches by reversing the restrictions placed on them against their right of free speech guaranteed by the First Amendment, and the reversal of many other perils which now befall our nation, perils that if not changed very soon will cause this nation's destruction. This is not a call to impose the Christian faith upon anyone, for that action in itself is not Christian. However, it is clearly a call back to our foundation, that this nation and its governance, laws, etc. be based and applied to all citizens the Christian principles of which are foundationed into this nation.

Poland's union helped begin driving the wedge, cracking the hold of communism upon the Eastern block nations, which transformed the world. The joining together of millions of American citizens into a non-partisan type union, to have a write-in vote, electing a non-partisan group who can transform our nation back to its founding Christian principles would by-pass the present deadlock election system which requires hundreds of millions of dollars for a candidate to be elected, thereby excluding any leader who purely seeks to do the will of God without compromise, and who would be willing to turn upside down the present corrupted surrogate system. It would be the only way in regards to electing anyone to power, who would restore and revive our Father's dreams and totally transform this nation. Do your homework. Study history. Think. Pray.

What would be the first step? First, we must realize that passivity, or doing nothing, is the tool those in power use to continue down their path unimpeded. Pope John Paul said in regards to what happened in Poland:

> *"Finally something has happened in Poland which is irreversible. People will no longer remain passive. Passivity is one of the tools of authoritarianism and now this passivity is over and so their fate is settled now (the communist). They will lose."* [336]

This nation can be changed overnight if we unite to decide our fate. On the website for the book Look What Happened While You Were Sleeping™, a survey is being taken for those who would support the starting of such a union to restore the union of the United States of America. Go to lookwhathappenedwhileyouweresleeping.com to give your yes or no support. If in three months the people of Poland could unify into the solid oneness of Solidarity and change the world, with prayer and committing to living the Sabbath as committed Godly citizens, God will give a seize the moment and He will raise up Godly leaders to rebuild our nation, placing it back on its foundation. For all who believe Scripture is true, we are guaranteed the revival of our nation.

2 Chronicles 7:14–16

> ***"And if my people, upon whom My Name has been pronounced, humble themselves and pray, and seek My presence and turn from their evil ways, I will hear them from Heaven and pardon their sins and revive their land. Now My eyes shall be open and My ears attentive to the prayer of this place. And now I have chosen and consecrated this house that My name may be there forever; My eyes and My heart also shall be there always."***

In the hope of fulfilling
the dreams our Fathers had,
A Friend of Medjugorje

P.S. Begin re-reading Look What Happened While You Were Sleeping™ a second time. You will be surprised how it will speak to you even more. This writing cannot be read only once and absorbed. It must be learned and studied to effect the change that must happen soon. Inform others and spread Look What Happened While You Were Sleeping™. Consider it a noble investment for the security of your future, your family and friends, and your nation. You can immediately start taking action by buying and giving five copies of this book away to others you know, thereby creating a tsunami across the nation to bring remedy for ourselves, our families, and our nation. As an individual or with your prayer group or group of family and friends, meet with your pastor and give him a copy. Keep close to lookwhathappenedwhileyouweresleeping.com. The site can be a tool to evolve and progress the sentiments and mentalities of "we the people" to "seize the moment" God will give to take our nation back to its founding principles of uniting it, as John Quincy Adams pronounced, *"one indissoluble bond, principles of civil government to the principles of Christianity."* [337]

Would you support a legal revolution as written about? Sign on and vote at:

lookwhathappenedwhileyouweresleeping.com

IN CONCLUSION

Finally this may be your last warning before America enters into the twilight of an irreversible decline due to delusions that we have permitted to rule over us. Delusions of accepting the loss of freedom and loss of unalienable rights, such as for the purpose and arrogance that it is up to man to save the earth. Delusions that, in our nation where 84% of its people profess Christian belief, yet shut their eyes to the truth of living the Sabbath Commandment. Delusion at who is at fault that the Ten Commandments are being attacked everywhere by those who want them taken down, when those who want them up, only want 9 out of 10 of them to be applied to their lives. America's time is a short time, unless we remove the delusions we have permitted. Our Lady said to Mirjana, one of the six visionaries:

November 2, 2006

> **"...God is sending me to warn you and to show you the right way. Do not shut your eyes before the truth, my children. Your time is a short time.**

Do not permit *'delusions'* to begin to rule over you. The way on which I desire to lead you is the way of peace and love. This is the way which leads to my Son, your God ..."

My hope is that you wake from your sleep and radically transform the Church by committing to living the Sabbath, admonishing and holding each other accountable. That spark will ignite, blowing up the strongholds that are intent on destroying our nation as the walls of Jericho fell by God's hand, thereby giving Joshua and his people a "seize the moment" as God will grant to us the same to re-declare the Declaration of Independence for a legal revolution to renew our land...It is that simple.

Webster's American Dictionary of the English Language 1828 defines delusion as:

Deception; a misleading of the mind; false representation; illusion; error or mistake proceeding from false views. [338]

You must change your mentality of false fixed beliefs.

This book, Look What Happened While You Were Sleeping™ is available at:

* *Lookwhathappenedwhileyouweresleeping.com*

* *Amazon.com*
* *Mej.com*
* *Bookstores across America*

Or phone: 205-672-2000, 24 hrs. After hrs, press ext. 318.

NOTES

CHAPTER ONE

1. *The New Century Dictionary,* Standard Reference Works Publishing Company, Inc., New York (1957), s.v. liberty
2. *An American Dictionary of the English Language,* 1828 facsimile edition, by Noah Webster. Published since 1967 by the Foundation for American Christian Education, P.O. Box 9588, Chesapeake, VA, 23321
3. William Iler Crane & William Henry Wheeler, *Wheeler's Literary Readers*, Wheeler Publishing Company, Chicago, 1924, p. 191–193
4. Ibid., p. 193–195
5. Archbishop Angelo Comastri, *"Way of the Cross of Pope Benedict XVI,"* for Good Friday, 2006, from Introduction, Office for the Liturgical Celebrations of the Supreme Pontiff
6. Ibid., Intro.
7. Ibid., Intro.
8. Ibid., 3rd Station

CHAPTER THREE

9. David Green, *More Than A Hobby*, Thomas Nelson Publishers, Nashville, TN 2005, p. 133–138
10. Ibid., p. 134
11. Ibid., p. 135
12. Ibid., p. 135
13. Ibid., p. 135
14. Ibid., p. 136
15. Ibid., p. 132
16. Ibid., p. 137
17. *Daily Oklahoman* Editorial Page, 2000
18. Michael Medved, *Right Turns: Unconventional Lessons from a Controversial Life*, Crown Forum, A Division of Random House, 2004, p. 300–302
19. Ibid., p. 301
20. Ibid., p. 314

CHAPTER FOUR

21. Archbishop Angelo Comastri, *"Way of the Cross of Pope Benedict XVI,"* for Good Friday, 2006, 3rd Station, Office for the Liturgical Celebrations of the Supreme Pontiff
22. Georges Sada, *Saddam's Secrets*, Integrity Publishers, Brentwood, TN 2006
23. Lt. Carey H. Cash, *A Table In the Presence*, W Publishing Group, Nashville, TN 2004
24. Ibid., p. 102–103
25. Ibid., p. 54
26. Ibid., p. 60
27. Ibid., p. 173–199
28. Ibid., p. 204–205
29. Ibid., p. 204
30. Ibid., p. 212
31. Ibid., p. 213
32. Ibid., p. 213–214
33. Ibid., p. 207
34. Ibid., p. 208
35. Ibid., p. 211
36. Ibid., p. 231–237
37. Ibid., p. 142–143
38. Ibid., p. 144
39. Ibid., p. 144
40. Ibid., p. 144
41. Ibid., p. 144
42. Ibid., p. 144–145
43. Ibid., p. 146
44. Caspar W. Weinberger & Wynton C. Hall, *Home of the Brave: Honoring the Unsung Heroes in the War On Terror*, A Tom Doherty Associates Book, New York, 2006
45. Ibid., p. 34
46. Ibid., p. 34
47. Ibid., p. 34–35
48. Ibid., p. 35
49. Ibid., p. 247
50. David Gates, "Sealed with a Kiss," *Newsweek*, April 17, 2006, p. 49
51. Ibid., p. 48–49
52. Ibid., p. 49
53. Michael Medved, *Right Turns: Unconventional Lessons from a Controversial Life,* Crown Forum, A Division of Random House, 2004
54. Ibid., p. 360–361
55. Ibid,. p. 361
56. Paul Kengor, *The Crusader*, ReganBooks, 2006, p. 15
57. Ibid., p. 15

58. Michael Medved, *Right Turns: Unconventional Lessons from a Controversial Life,* Crown Forum, A Division of Random House, 2004, p. 337
59. Ibid., p. 324
60. Ibid., p. 340
61. A Friend of Medjugorje, *I See Far*, SJP, 2004. A must read about why a TV-free home is a necessity for the Christian.
62. Michael Medved, *Right Turns: Unconventional Lessons from a Controversial Life,* Crown Forum, A Division of Random House, 2004, p. 419

CHAPTER FIVE

63. C.S. Lewis, *God in the Dock,* Christian Apologetics, Why Every American Christian Home Should Have the Noah Webster 1828 Dictionary, The Foundation for American Christian Education
64. *An American Dictionary of the English Language,* 1828 facsimile edition, by Noah Webster. Published since 1967 by the Foundation for American Christian Education, P.O. Box 9588, Chesapeake, VA, 23321, p. 22
65. A Friend of Medjugorje, *How To Change Your Husband*, SJP, 2006, p. 267–285
66. *An American Dictionary of the English Language,* 1828 facsimile edition, by Noah Webster. Published since 1967 by the Foundation for American Christian Education, P.O. Box 9588, Chesapeake, VA, 23321, p. 10
67. Ibid., p. 10
68. Carol Glatz & Cindy Wooden, "Pope Celebrates Easter; Urges People, Nations to Turn Away from Sin," *One Voice*, Vol. 36, No. 16
69. Archbishop Angelo Comastri, *"Way of the Cross of Pope Benedict XVI,"* for Good Friday 2006, 5th Station, Office for the Liturgical Celebrations of the Supreme Pontiff
70. Ibid., 7th Station
71. Carol Glatz & Cindy Wooden, "Pope Celebrates Easter; Urges People, Nations to Turn Away from Sin," *One Voice*, Vol. 36, No. 16, p. 3
72. Ibid., p. 3
73. Jean di Marino, "Profile: The Pope's Webmaster," *Inside the Vatican Magazine*, May 2004, p. 57

CHAPTER SIX

74. Archbishop Angelo Comastri; *"Way of the Cross of Pope Benedict XVI,"* for Good Friday, 2006, 3rd station, Office for the Liturgical Celebrations of the Supreme Pontiff
75. "Good News from the Front Lines of the Culture War," *Wallbuilder Report*, Spring 2006

76. Archbishop Angelo Comastri, *"Way of the Cross of Pope Benedict XVI,"* for Good Friday, 2006, Intro., Office for the Liturgical Celebrations of the Supreme Pontiff

CHAPTER SEVEN

77. *An American Dictionary of the English Language,* 1828 facsimile edition, by Noah Webster. Published since 1967 by the Foundation for American Christian Education, P.O. Box 9588, Chesapeake, VA, 23321, p. 12
78. *Mary Page News*, December 8, 1997, www.udayton.edu
79. Marion A. Habif, O.F.M., *"Land of Mary Immaculate,"*
80. John Adams, *Works*, Vol. X, pp. 45–46, to Thomas Jefferson on June 28, 1813
81. A Friend of Medjugorje, *Words from Heaven*® 10th Edition, St. James Publishing, 2006, p. 213–214
82. Archbishop Angelo Comastri, *"Way of the Cross of Pope Benedict XVI,"* for Good Friday, 2006, 10th Station, Office for the Liturgical Celebrations of the Supreme Pontiff
83. Pope John Paul II, *The Church in America,* Post-Synodal Apostolic Exhortation; Pauline Books and Media, Boston 1999, p. 73
84. "Letters," *Citizen Magazine*, May 2006, p. 4
85. Dale D. Buss, "Planned Parenthood Storms Pro-Life State," *Citizen Magazine*, October, 2006, p. 5–6
86. Ibid., p. 5–6

CHAPTER EIGHT

87. www.freedomkeys.com
88. Pope John Paul II, *The Church in America,* Post-Synodal Apostolic Exhortation; Pauline Books and Media, Boston 1999, p. 73
89. John Adams, *Works, Vol. X*, p. 45–46, to Thomas Jefferson on June 28, 1813
90. www.freedomkey.com/vigil.htm
91. Interview with Terri Schiavo's Family Members," FOX News Hannity and Colmes, March 24, 2005
92. Francis Ellingwood Abbot, "Nine Demands of Liberalism for Separation of Church and State," *The Annals Of America, Volume 10*, Encyclopedia Britannica, 1976, p. 299
93. Ibid., p. 299–300
94. Thomas Jefferson, Memoir, Correspondence and Miscellanies from the Papers of Thomas Jefferson, Thomas Jefferson Randolph, editor (Boston: Gray and Bowen, 1830) Vol. IV, p. 373, to Judge William Johnson on June 12, 1823
95. James Madison, The Writings of James Madison, Gaillard Hunt, editor (New York and London: G.P. Putnam's Sons, 1910) Vol, IX, p. 191, to Henry Lee on June 25, 1824

96. Reports of Committees of the House of Representatives Made During the First Session of the Thirty-Third Congress (Washington: A.O.P. Nicholson, 1854), p. 1,6,8–9
97. Story, *Commentaries*, Vol. III, p. 728, 1871
98. George Washington, Address of George Washington, President of the United States...Preparatory to His Declination (Baltimore: George and Henry S. Keatings, 1796) p. 23
99. Marshall Foster & Mary-Elaine Swanson, *The American Covenant*, The Mayflower Institute, 1992, p. 18
100. Ibid., p. 19

CHAPTER NINE

101. David Barton, *Original Intent*, Wallbuilder Press, 2005, p. 248
102. Ibid., p. 248–249
103. Ibid., p. 250
104. Abraham Lincoln: *The Works of Abraham Lincoln, Speech and Debates*, Jon H. Clifford, Editor (New York, The University Society Inc. 1908), Vol. III, August 17, 1858, p. 126–127
105. Donald T. Phillips, *Lincoln On Leadership: Executive Strategies for Tough Times,* Warner Books, 1992, p. 43–44
106. Thomas Jefferson to William Stephens Smith, 1787, Eternal Vigilance is the Price of Liberty, www.freedomkeys.com
107. William Blackstone, "Of the Nature of Laws in General," *Our Legal Heritage,* Foundation for Moral Law, Inc., November 2003, p. 15
108. Ibid., p. 15
109. "Vatican Condemns Spain Bill," BBC News, April 22, 2005, www.news.bbc.co.uk
110. *Catechism of the Catholic Church, 2nd Edition* (1994), Libreria Editrice Vaticana, p. 474
111. Ibid., p. 475
112. www.freedomkey.com
113. Archbishop Angelo Comastri, *"Way of the Cross of Pope Benedict XVI",* for Good Friday, 2006, 14th Station, Office for the Liturgical Celebrations of the Supreme Pontiff,
114. Benjamin Rush, *Letters of Benjamin Rush*, L.H. Butterfield, editor (New Jersey: American Philosophical Society, 1951), Vol. I, to John Adams on February 24, 1790, p. 532–536
115. www.freedomkey.com
116. Rush, *Letters*, Vol. II, to John Adams on September 4, 1811, p. 1103
117. David Barton, *Original Intent*, Wallbuilder Press, 2005, p. 341
118. Ibid., p. 279
119. *Random House Dictionary of the English Language* (1987). s.v. religion
120. *An American Dictionary of the English Language,* 1828 facsimile edition, by Noah Webster. Published since 1967 by the Foundation for American Christian Education, P.O. Box 9588, Chesapeake, VA, 23321

121. David Barton, *Original Intent*,Wallbuilder Press, 2005, p. 124
122. *An American Dictionary of the English Language,* 1828 facsimile edition, by Noah Webster. Published since 1967 by the Foundation for American Christian Education, P.O. Box 9588, Chesapeake, VA, 23321, p. 12
123. Benjamin Rush, *Letters of Benjamin Rush*, L.H. Butterfield, editor (Princeton, New Jersey: American Philosophical Society, 1951), Vol. I, to Elias Boudinot on July 9, 1788, p. 475
124. David Barton, *Original Intent*,Wallbuilder Press, 2005, p. 339–340

CHAPTER TEN

125. "Report of Habitat: United Nations Conference on Human Settlements," Vancouver, May 31–June 11, 1976
126. *An American Dictionary of the English Language,* 1828 facsimile edition, by Noah Webster. Published since 1967 by the Foundation for American Christian Education, P.O. Box 9588, Chesapeake, VA, 23321
127. Don Casey, "Homewood, Alabama Embraces Globalization," *Beacon Newspaper*, May 28, 2006
128. "You Gotta Pay For This View," *The Progressive Farmer*, January 2006, p. 10
129. Henry Lamb, "International Influence on Domestic Policy," *The eco-logic Powerhouse,* February, 2006, p. 7
130. Ibid., p. 10
131. www.sovereignty.net
132. Henry Lamb, "International Influence on Domestic Policy," *The eco-logic Powerhouse*, February 2006, p. 8
133. Ibid., p. 8
134. Ibid., p. 8
135. American Model United Nations International (AMUN), *"About AUMN,"* www.amun.org
136. American Model United Nations International (AMUN), *"Sample Statement Policy (3),"* www.amun.org.
137. Ibid.
138. *John Paul II, Chronicle of a Remarkable Life*, Dorling Kindersley Publishing, p. 127
139. Martha Woodall, "Father Judge Takes Top Honors at Model U.N.," *Philadelphia Inquirer*, May 23, 2006, www.macon.com
140. Henry Lamb, "International Influence on Domestic Policy," *The eco-logic Powerhouse,* February 2006, p. 9
141. Ibid., p. 9
142. *Webster's New Collegiate Dictionary,* G.&C. Merriam Company, Springfield, MA, (1980), s.v. liberty
143. *An American Dictionary of the English Language,* 1828 facsimile edition, by Noah Webster. Published since 1967 by the Foundation for American Christian Education, P.O. Box 9588, Chesapeake, VA, 23321

144. Henry Lamb, "International Influence on Domestic Policy," *The eco-logic Powerhouse,* February 2006, p. 9
145. *American Family Association of Arkansas*, 1992, Testimonry of Parent Whose Son Committed Suicide [1 of 4] After Attending the Ark. Gov's School, FreeRepublic.com
146. Ibid.
147. Ibid.
148. "So Long, Farewell Auf Wiedersehn," *Citizen Magazine*, December 2006, p. 8
149. Ibid., p. 8
150. Henry Lamb, "International Influence on Domestic Policy," *The eco-logic Powerhouse,* February 2006, p. 10
151. Ibid., p. 12
152. Ibid., p. 12
153. Jacqueline Kasun, *The War Against Population*, Ignatius Press, 1988, p. 290
154. Joseph Farah, "U.S – Mexico Merger Opposition Intensifies," *The eco-logic Powerhouse*, August 2006, p. 12
155. Robert Royal, *The God That Did Not Fail: How Religion Built and Sustains the West*, Encounter Books, 2006, p. xix–xx
156. Henry Lamb, "Sustainable Development: Transforming America," *The eco-logic Powerhouse*, December 2005, p. 8
157. Ibid, p. 9
158. Dr. S.M. Davis, *"Why Satan Wants Your Firstborn and What to Do About It,"* Vision Forum, 2003
159. Fred Gielow, "The PETA Principle," *The eco-logic Powerhouse*, May 2006, p. 22
160. Ibid., p. 22
161. Ibid. p. 22
162. Ibid. p. 22
163. Ibid. p. 22
164. *"Cultural and Spiritual Values of Biodiversity,"* United Nations Environment Programme, Intermediate Technology Publications, 1999
165. Ibid.
166 Donna Steichen, *UnGodly Rage, The Hidden Face of Catholic Feminism*, Ignatius Press, 1991, p. 29
167. Ibid., p. 36
168. Archbishop J. Michael Miller, C.S.B., *The Holy See's Teaching on Catholic Schools*, Solidarity Association, Sophia Institute Press, 2006, p. 2–3
169. Donna Steichen, UnGodly Rage, The Hidden Face of Catholic Feminism, Ignatius Press, 1991, p.60
170. Ibid., p. 23
171. *"Cultural and Spiritual Values of Biodiversity,"* United Nations Environment Programme, Intermediate Technology Publications, 1999. p. 457
172. Ibid. p. 449

173. Ibid., p. 31
174. Ibid., p. 31
175. Ibid., p. 31
176. Ibid., p. 106
177. Ibid., p. 31
178. www.keepourrights.org/sccc.html
179. *"Cultural and Spiritual Values of Biodiversity,"* United Nations Environment Programme, Intermediate Technology Publications, 1999, p. 496.
180. Ibid., p. 459
181. Ibid., p. 493
182. Ibid., p. 497
183. Ibid., p. 494
184. Ibid., p. 494
185. Ibid., p. 604
186. Dave Ziffer, *"Delphi Method Report,"* September 4, 1996, www.illinoisloop.org

CHAPTER ELEVEN

187. Arthur B. Robinson, Sallie L. Baliunas, Willie Soon, Zachary W. Robinson; *"Environmental Effects of Increased Atmospheric Carbon Dioxide,"* Oregon Institute of Science and Medicine, January 1998, p. 3–4
188. *"Nature's Extremes: Inside the Great Natural Disasters That Shape Life On Earth,"* Time Books, New York, 2006, p. 133
189. Henry Lamb, "Through the Looking Glass," December 11, 2004, www.sovereignty.net
190. Sharda Vaidyanath, "Environmental Controversy, Made in Canada," *The Epoch Times*, May 11–17, 2006 Issue
191. Global Warming Petition Project, www.oism.org, Oregon Institute of Science and Medicine, 2001
192. Arthur B. Robinson, Sallie L. Baliunas, Willie Soon, Zachary W. Robinson; *"Environmental Effects of Increased Atmospheric Carbon Dioxide,"* Oregon Institute of Science and Medicine, January 1998, p. 1
193. Ibid., p. 1
194. Global Warming Petition Project, www.oism.org, Oregon Institute of Science and Medicine, 2001, p. 4
195. Arthur B. Robinson, Sallie L. Baliunas, Willie Soon, Zachary W. Robinson; *"Environmental Effects of Increased Atmospheric Carbon Dioxide,"* Oregon Institute of Science and Medicine, January 1998, p. 1
196. Ibid., p. 5
197. Ibid., p. 4
198. Ibid., p. 2
199. Ibid., p. 2
200. Ibid., p. 1

201. Global Warming Petition Project, www.oism.org, Oregon Institute of Science and Medicine, 2001, p. 1
202. Arthur B. Robinson, Sallie L. Baliunas, Willie Soon, Zachary W. Robinson; *"Environmental Effects of Increased Atmospheric Carbon Dioxide,"* Oregon Institute of Science and Medicine, January 1998, p. 6
203. Ibid., p. 7
204. Ibid., p. 7
205. Ibid., p. 7
206. Larry Gedney, "Good Water Not Guaranteed in the North," Article #776, *Alaska Science Forum*, July 7, 1986, www.gi.alaska.edu/ScienceForum, p. 1
207. Ibid., p. 1
208. *"Visible Earth: Duststorm in South Central Alaska,"* http://visibleearth.nasa.gov
209. www.freerepublic.com
210. Ibid.
211."Our Evolutionary Enemies," *THE WEEK*, August 18, 2006
212. "Darwins Deadly Legacy," *Citizen Magazine*, December 2006, p. 11
213. Ibid., p. 11
214. Ibid., p. 11
215. Fr. Paul, "Metanoia," www.stjosephdg.org, p. 1
216. Ibid., p. 1–2

CHAPTER TWELVE

217. Maria Valtorta, The Poem of the Man-God, Vol. IV, Centro Editoriale Valtortiano, p. 824–825
218. Ibid., p. 825
219. Henry Lamb, "Sustainable Development: Transforming America," *The eco-logic Powerhouse,* December 2005, p. 11
220. Jacqueline Kason, *The War Against Population*, Ignatius Press, SanFrancisco, 1988, p. 206
221. A Friend of Medjugorje, *Twenty Years of Apparition*, 2001, p. 3–7
222. Michael Shaw, "Creating Crisis, Shortage, and a Police State," *The eco-logic Powerhouse,* February 2006, p. 16
223. Ibid., p. 17

CHAPTER THIRTEEN

224. Marlin Maddoux, *Public Education Against America*, Whitaker House Publisher, 2006, p. 174–175
225. Ibid., p. 176
226. Ibid., p. 242
227. Ibid., p. 242
228. James Dobson, Focus On the Family Broadcast, July 8–9, 2003, www.worldnetdaily.com.

229. "Dobson to Californians: Quit Public Schools," *World Net Daily*, March 30, 2002, www.worldnetdaily.com
230. Marlin Maddoux, *Public Education Against America,* Whitaker House Publisher, 2006, p. 170
231. Ibid., p. 171
232. Ibid., p. 170
233. Ibid., p. 174

CHAPTER FOURTEEN

234. Ron Sparks, "BSE Discovered in Alabama," *Alabama Farmers and Consumers Bulletin,* April 2006, Volume 54, No. 4
235. "NAIS: National Animal Identification System, The Question: Why, and at What Cost?," *The eco-logic Powerhouse*, March 2006
236. Ron Sparks, "BSE Discovered in Alabama," *Alabama Farmers and Consumers Bulletin*, April 2006, Volume 54, No. 4
237. www.freedomkey.com
238. Ibid.
239. Ron Sparks, "BSE Discovered in Alabama," *Alabama Farmers and Consumers Bulletin*, April 2006, Volume 54, No. 4
240. Dr. Mary Zanoni, "A New Threat to Rural Freedom," *The eco-logic Powerhouse*, March 2006
241. George J. Laurer, "Questions About the U.P.C. and the New Testament," p. 1
242. Charles Walters, "The Mark of the Beast," *Acres, USA*, December 2006, p. 70
243. Ibid., p. 2
244. Terry Watkins, "What About Barcodes and 666: The Mark of the Beast?," *Dial-the-Truth Ministries*, 1999, p. 7
245. *An American Dictionary of the English Language,* 1828 facsimile edition, by Noah Webster. Published since 1967 by the Foundation for American Christian Education, P.O. Box 9588, Chesapeake, VA, 23321
246. *Webster's New Collegiate Dictionary,* G.&C. Merriam Company, Springfield, MA, (1980), s.v. liberty
247. Terry Watkins, "What About Barcodes and 666: The Mark of the Beast?," *Dial-the-Truth Ministries*, 1999, p. 8
248. Ibid., p. 8
249. *An American Dictionary of the English Language,* 1828 facsimile edition, by Noah Webster. Published since 1967 by the Foundation for American Christian Education, P.O. Box 9588, Chesapeake, VA, 23321
250. Terry Watkins, "What About Barcodes and 666: The Mark of the Beast?," *Dial-the-Truth Ministries*, 1999
251. Derry Brownfield, "NAIS: National Animal Identification System," *Paragon Magazine,* Summer 2006, p. 23
252. Ibid., p. 23
253. Ibid., p. 23
254. Ibid., p. 23

255. Archbishop Angelo Comastri, *"'Way of the Cross of Pope Benedict XVI,"* for Good Friday, 2006; Office for the Liturgical Celebrations of the Supreme Pontiff
256. www.freedomkey.com

CHAPTER FIFTEEN

257. Jacqueline Kasun, *The War Against Population*, Ignatius Press, 1988, p. 289
258. Ibid., p. 289
259. U.S. Bureau of Census Statistics
260. Jacqueline Kasun, *The War Against Population*, Ignatius Press, 1988, p. 62–63
261. Ibid., p. 293
262. Forest M. Mims III, "Meeting Doctor Doom," *The eco-logic Powerhouse*, May 2006, p. 16
263. *Webster's New Collegiate Dictionary*, (1980), sv.anthropocentrism
264. Forest M. Mims III, "Meeting Doctor Doom," *The eco-logic Powerhouse*, May 2006, p. 16
265. Ibid., p. 16–17
266. J. Richard Pearcey, "Dr. 'Doom' Pianka Speaks," *The Pearcey Report*, April 6, 2006, www.pearceyreport.com
267. Jacqueline Kasun, *The War Against Population*, Ignatius Press, 1988
268. *The eco-logic Powerhouse*
269. Ibid.
270. *The Saginaw Press,* Vol. 95, No. 42, March 2007, p. 1
271. Ibid., p. 1
272. "Lion Heart," *People – Amazing Stories of Survival*, People Books, 2006, p. 20–22.
273 "Understanding Sustainable Development, – Agenda 21: Guide for Public Officials, Freedom 21 Santa Cruz, www.freedom21santacruz.net

CHAPTER SIXTEEN

274 *"Cultural and Spiritual Values of Biodiversity,"* United Nations Environment Programme, Intermediate Technology Publications, 1999, p. 497
275. Karl Tobien, *Dancing Under the Red Star*, Waterbrook Press, 2006, p. 185–187
276. Mark Hall, *While You Were Sleeping*, from Casting Crown's "Lifesong" CD, 2005 Club Zoo Music (BMI) – SWECS Music (BMI) (ADM. by EMI CMG Publishing)
277. Robert Davis, "Doctors Will Transplant a Face – But Whose?," *USA Today*, May 25, 2006
278. Gary Suson, *Requiem:Images of Ground Zero*, Barnes & Noble, 2002, p. 108

279. www.vatican.va
280. Fr. Jeije Yasuda, *Akita, The Tears and Messages of Mary*, 101 Foundation, Asbury, N.J. 1992
281. A Friend of Medjugorje, *Words from Heaven*®, 10th Edition, St. James Publishing, 2006
282 Ravi Zacharias, *"Unplugging the Truth in a Morally Suicidal Culture,"* www.rzim.org
283. www.freedomkey.com
284. "Understanding Sustainable Developement – Agenda 21: Guide for Public Officials, Freedom 21 Santa Cruz, www.freedom21santacruz.net
285. Georges Sada, *Saddam's Secrets: How An Iraqi General Defied and Survived Saddam Hussein*, Integrity Publishers, 2006, p. 293–296
286. Ibid., p. 293–294
287. Ibid., p. 294
288. Ibid., p. 295
289. Ibid., p. 295–296

CHAPTER SEVENTEEN

290. *Guns and Ammo*, October 1995, p. 50–51
291. *The Daily Post-Athenian*, Athens, Tenn., June 17, 1946, p. 1
292. *Guns and Ammo*, October 1995, p. 50–51
293. *The Chattanooga Daily Times*, Thursday, August 8, 1946
294. Ibid.
295. Stephen Byrum, *The Battle of Athens*, Paidia Productions, Chattanooga, Tenn., 1987, p. 168–169
296. *The Chattanooga Daily Times*, Thursday, August 8, 1946
297. Ibid.
298. Ibid.
299. Ibid.
300. Ibid.
301. Ibid.
302. Ibid.
303. Ibid.
304. Ibid.
305. Ibid.
306. Ibid.
307. *Congressional Record, House*; US Government Printing Office, Washington D.C., 1946, Appendix, Volume 92, Part 13, p. A4870
308. *The Daily Post-Athenian*, Athens, Tenn., June 17, 1946, p. 1, 6
309. Abraham Lincoln: *The Words of Abraham Lincoln, Speech and Debates*, Jon H. Clifford, Editor (New York, The University Society Inc. 1908), Vol. III, August 17, 1858, p. 126–127
310. "Can You Hear Us Now?," *Citizen Magazine*, April 2007, p. 18-23
311. Paul Kengor, *The Crusader*, ReganBooks, 2006, p. 88
312. Paul Kengor, *God and Ronald Reagan*, ReganBooks, 2004, p. xii
313. Paul Kengor, *The Crusader*, ReganBooks, 2006, p. 88

314. Ibid., p. 89
315. Carl Bernstein and Marco Politi, *His Holiness*, Penguin Books, 1996, p. 295
316. Paul Kengor, *God and Ronald Reagan*, ReganBooks, 2004, p. 184
317 Carl Bernstein and Marco Politi, *His Holiness*, Penguin Books, 1996, p. 296
318. Paul Kengor, *God and Ronald Reagan*, ReganBooks, 2004, p. 199
319. Ibid., p. 200
320. Ibid., p. 208–209
321. Carl Bernstein and Marco Politi, *His Holiness*, Penguin Books, 1996, p. 361
322. Paul Kengor, *God and Ronald Reagan*, ReganBooks, 2004, p. 200
323. Ibid., p. 123–124
324. Paul Kengor, *The Crusader*, ReganBooks, 2006, p. 135–136
325. Ibid., p. 134
326. Paul Kengor, *God and Ronald Reagan*, ReganBooks, 2004, p. 212
327. Paul Kengor, *The Crusader*, ReganBooks, 2006, p. 137
328. Ibid., p. 138
329. Ibid., p. 90
330. Ibid., p. 90
331. Ibid., 188
332 A Friend of Medjugorje, *Words From Heaven®, 10th Edition*, Saint James Publishing, 2006, p. 117
333. Paul Kengor, *The Crusader*, ReganBooks, 2006, p. 135–286–287
334. *Paul Harvey ABC News*, at the end of Reagan's Presidency
335. Paul Kengor, *The Crusader*, ReganBooks, 2006, p. 138
336. Carl Bernstein and Marco Politi, *His Holiness*, Penguin Books, 1996, p. 316
337. Marshall Foster & Mary-Elaine Swanson, *The American Covenant*, The Mayflower Institute, 1992, p. 18

CONCLUSION

338. *An American Dictionary of the English Language,* 1828 facsimile edition, by Noah Webster. Published since 1967 by the Foundation for American Christian Education, P.O. Box 9588, Chesapeake, VA, 23321

Footnotes from Sacred Bond, p. 195–196

*a This refers to the fact that the land that has become known as the United States of America was actually found on other occasions previous to Columbus' discovery (see *American History You Never Learned*, by A Friend of Medjugorje). However, nothing came of it, for it was not time for America to be discovered by the civilized world. The first words spoken from Columbus' mouth upon seeing the land of America before him was the "Salve Regina," or the "Hail, Holy Queen."

*b Her purpose of peace....to bring stability to all other lands. Repeatedly this has been the case. History shows that the United States is the source for stability in the world, even giving nations back to the people who had attacked us.

*c "Divided it from within" Our nation through the 1960's was in deep strife and division.

*d The apparitions in the Field in Alabama are connected to the prayer for our nation's healing and sparked the Seven Novenas to Reconcile Ourselves, Families and Nation Back to God, and several other movements to restore our nation.

*e September 11, 2001 galvanized our nation to prayer as it has not seen the likes of since before the division of the 60's and 70's. This present war, of darkness vs. light, is bringing about separation, but not like the disunity of the 60's and 70's when there was no resistance to darkness. The present war is serving to unify those towards the light, dividing them away from those who are drawn to the dark. Thus, the attacks from darkness are polarizing those who want to follow the light forming the field of battle over our nation's soul.

*f To hear a moving account of Sacred Bond, go to www.mej.com or call Caritas at 205-672-2000, ext. 352.

Index

REFERENCES

The Internet

WE DO NOT HAVE ACCESS TO the worldwide internet on the site of our mission at Caritas, nor in our homes. As mentioned earlier in this writing, we are very careful not to let technology control our lives, but rather, we control technology so that it doesn't consume our lives. Listed below are several internet sites that we recommend as you begin your own research into the many areas that are mentioned in this writing. We know that many of you do not use the internet and may actually be opposed to its use. For that reason, we will share with you our own thoughts concerning its dangers and its usefulness. One danger of the internet is that it saps time. Many plan to spend a few minutes searching for something, and then hours later, realize they lost track of time; time that should have been spent with family, at work or in prayer. For that reason, if we do research, we make access inconvenient for us by going off the premises, such as to a library, etc. We do not want even the possibility of garbage getting sent through computer lines coming into our mission and homes. We do not want even the slightest possibility of our children seeing something that would morally harm them, or ourselves—therefore, we refuse to have the worldwide hook-up for internet access on our site.

The obvious danger of the internet is that there is a world of filth that can be summoned up by anyone from just a few buttons on a keyboard. Internet abuse is taking its toll on youth, families, and society as a whole. It is tragic. Members of the church of all denominations are just as susceptible as anyone else. Jesus sent His disciples out in two's. We think it a good idea, too. In the community, if there is a need to do research on a subject, no one goes alone. We always go in pairs of two or more. It is protection and accountability with the dangers associated with the internet. Also in twos, we don't want to waste someone else's time. It disciplines us to get what we need and not linger any longer to go off on other search tangents.

The internet is also used to slander, gossip and harm the reputation of people. It happens without having to prove any sort of credibility by those doing the slandering. Just the fact that someone has a web site lends them credibility though it is often undeserved. But since it's on the internet, it is believed. Both the slanderer and those who read and spread the slander and gossip are guilty of sin. Along with slander, it is often found that the information one pulls off of the internet is not accurate, and therefore, needs to be verified before being believed. Again, just because its on the internet, doesn't mean that it is true.

With all these pit falls, why then use it? First, if you do not use it now, we are not advocating that you become an internet user. There are other ways to get first hand information, so to by-pass the middle man or 3rd party media sources. Find sources such as original writings, first hand accounts in books, etc. Interviews are not necessarily accurate in that the journalist packs the questions. Wisdom in learning how to compute the data to get truth is key to understanding what is going on around you.

What we have found with the internet is that it does give you immediate access to research and information on an unlimited amount of topics so that you can discover the truth on any number of issues and not have to be dependent upon biased 3rd party sources to try and formulate what you should believe. This particular writing discovered several useful points with research on the internet. However, we are strong in stating the internet needs to be utilized with discipline, prayer and discernment. Lastly, the internet will likely be a very important tool for a "seize the moment" in which some type of uniting could be formed overnight that could overthrow our present surrogate system.

Recommended Books:

We would like to make a brief comment about some of the books we are recommending. Some are very explicit in their description of abuses that are taking place, sighting specific cases. If some use language that we do not approve of, we get rid of the material, not wanting it on our grounds, because it is not appropriate for the Christian life. It is not necessary for Christians to be informed about what the news media and education systems are feeding you. Its for the most part a deception to keep from what really is important, like what you have just been reading in this writing. On the other hand, often Christian authors are the worst in going into graphic detail in describing sin when so much of that could be left unsaid. Some may argue that we need to know the horrible details so that our awareness of "just how bad things are getting" will be realistic and current. But that reasoning goes against the teachings of Christ who said that only the pure in spirit can see God. Our world and society are saturated with so much overemphasis of the flesh, and yet though many Christians may not be participating in it, they are taking in a daily diet of sordidness by listening and reading the reports that are always telling us "just how bad it is." It is not necessary to go into all the details of sin to get one's point across. But unfortunately, you will discover as you research that many do not heed this advice.

The purity of life in your home must be protected and while you did not read words in these writings of grave depravity, it was clearly referred to without violating the eyes, ears and thoughts of the heart and spiritual life. For too long, we've let the topic of conversation, radio, T.V., even in Christian ministry enter into our homes, cars and family of the most base, crass and lewd content. No, it is not necessary to let just anything enter the home. You are its guardian and you are it's censor. Yes, censorship is a positive good and once was the right of the governing body to protect the morals of the people. All parents should be a censor in their home. These are a few thoughts we end with to help you grow in holiness.

Sources to Further Your Education

Below is a list of books in various categories that are must-reads. This list is only a beginning. These books will give you a foundation to build upon as you continue to seek out first party sources for what is necessary for you to know and to guide you in making decisions in the future. It will be an ongoing process.

Books on Ronald Reagan

(Recommended that you read all three and in the order presented)

Reagan's War: The Epic Story of His Forty-Year Struggle and Final Triumph Over Communism
Author: Peter Schweizer
Doubleday Publishing, 2002

God and Ronald Reagan: A Spiritual Life
Author: Paul Kengor
Regan Books/HarperCollins Publishing, 2004

The Crusader: Ronald Reagan and the Fall of Communism
Author: Paul Kengor
Regan Books, a Division of HarperCollins Publishers, Inc., 2006

Recommended Reference Books

American Dictionary of the English Language
Author: Noah Webster, 1828
Foundation for American Christian Education, 1967

Original Intent: The Courts, The Constitution and Religion
Author: David Barton
Wallbuilder Press, 2005 (4th Edition)

Books on Cultural Issues

WARNING: Some of the books recommended below have very explicit and verbally graphic examples of the degradation of society. They are not books to have lying around your house, especially if children are present.

Public Education Against America: The Hidden Agenda
Author: Marlin Maddoux
Whitaker House Publishing, 2006

America Alone: The End of the World As We Know It
Author: Mark Steyn
Regnery Publishing, 2006

Minutemen: The Battle to Secure America's Borders
Authors: Jim Gilchrist and Jerome R. Corsi
World Ahead Publishing, 2006

Men in Black: How the Supreme Court Is Destroying America
Author: Mark R. Levin
Regnery Publishing, 2005

Right Turns - Unconventional Lessons From a Controversial Life
Author: Michael Medved
Crown Forum, 2004

Books on the War in Iraq

A Table in the Presence: The Dramatic Account of How a U.S. Marine Battalion Experienced God's Presence Amidst the Chaos of the War In Iraq
Author: Lt. Carey H. Cash
Thomas Nelson Publishing, 2004

Home of the Brave: Honoring the Unsung Heroes In the War On Terror
Authors: Caspar W. Weinberger and Wynton C. Hall
Forge Publishing, 2006

****

Recommended Sources to Keep Informed About Sustainable Development & Other Threats to Property Rights and American Liberties

The eco-logic Powerhouse
A Publication of the Environmental Conservation Organization, Inc.
P.O. Box 191
Hollow Rock, TN 38342
Ph. 731-986-0099
www.freedom.org

Specific articles for you to read from past Powerhouse issues that can be downloaded from their website:

"Sustainable Development: Transforming America" by Henry Lamb, December 2005
"International Influence on Domestic Policy" by Henry Lamb, February 2006

"Agenda 21 and the United Nations" by Henry Lamb, September 2006

"The NAIS Story" by Judith McGeary, June 2006

"Sovietizing America: How Sustainable Development Crushes the Individual" by Michael Shaw and Edward Hudgins, July 2005

Petition Project: Global Warming Petition
Oregon Institute of Science and Medicine
P.O. Box 1279
Cave Junction, OR 97523

www.oism.org
To view the Petition Project go to http://www.oism.org/pproject/s33p37.htm

Recommended websites:

www.americanpolicy.org

www.freedom21santacruz.net

www.keepourrights.org

www.sovereignty.net

www.vatican.va

www.mej.com

"Understanding Sustainable Development, Agenda 21: A Guide for Public Officials" is also recommended reading and can be downloaded from the freedom21santacruz.net website.

References

References

References

Over 31,072 scientists signed a petition against the threats of global warming and became part of a project entitled "Petition Project."

Global Warming Petition:

We (the following) urge the United States government to reject the global warming agreement that was written in Kyoto, Japan in December, 1997, and any other similar proposals. The proposed limits on greenhouse gases would harm the environment, hinder the advance of science and technology, and damage the health and welfare of mankind.

There is no convincing scientific evidence that human release of carbon dioxide, methane, or other greenhouse gasses is causing or will, in the foreseeable future, cause catastrophic heating of the Earth's atmosphere and disruption of the Earth's climate. Moreover, there is substantial scientific evidence that increases in atmospheric carbon dioxide produce many beneficial effects upon the natural planet and animal environments of the Earth.

The costs of this petition project have been paid entirely by private donations. No industrial funding or money from sources within the coal, oil, natural gas or related industries has been utilized. The petition's organizers, who include some faculty members and staff of the Oregon Institute of Science and Medicine, do not otherwise receive funds from such sources. The Institute itself has no such funding. Also, no funds of tax-exempt organizations have been used for this project.

The signatures and the text of the petition stand alone and speak for themselves. These scientists have signed this specific document. They are not associated with any particular organization. Their signatures represent a strong statement about this important issue by many of the best scientific minds in the United States.

Look through the following thirty-one thousand names for yourself. Find your state and ask yourself, what does this tell you about the disinformation you receive daily? Global Warming as a danger is more than a sham, it is fraudulent.

LIST OF SIGNERS OF GLOBAL WARMING PETITION BY STATE

Alabama

H. William Ahrenholz, Oscar Richard Ainsworth, PhD, John Hvan Aken, Michael L. Alexander, Robert K. Allen, MD, Ronald C. Allison, MD, Barry M. Amyx, MD, David W. Anderso, John C. Anderson, PhD, Bernard Jeffrey Anderson, PhD, Russell S. Andrews, PhD, Bobby M. Armistead, Ann Askew, Larry N. Atkinson, Alan C. Bailey, Robert Baker, Brooks H. Baker III, John Wayland Bales, PhD, James Y. Baltar, Ted B. Banner, Robert F. Barfield, PhD, Alan A. Barksdale, Richard Barnes, Samuel A. Barr, Kenneth A. Barrett, Franklin E. Bates, Ronald G. Baxley, Sidney D. Beckett, PhD, Arthur B. Beindorff, PhD, Victor Bell, Aleksandr A. Belotserkovskiy, PhD, William R. Bentley, DVM, Reginald H. Benton, M. Bersch, PhD, Raymond E. Bishop, Donald H. Blackwell, Edward S. Blair, Kevin M. Blake, Richard Lee Blanchard, PhD, Anton C. Bogaty Jr., Jonathan D. Boland, Desmond H. Bond, Terry Bonds, James H. Bonds, MD, Robert R. Boothe Jr., Dale L. Borths, Jerome Boutwell, James L. Box, William D. Boyer, PhD, William C. Bradford, Andrew E. Bradley, Michael W. Bradshaw, Bradley A. Brasfield, John F. Brass, Claude E. Breed, Thomas H. Brigham, MD, Doyle G. Briscoe, Robert Alan Brown, PhD, James Melton Brown, PhD, Alfred L. Brown, Dushan S. Bukvic, Donald F. Burchfield, PhD, Walter W. Burdin, Kim A. Burke, John E. Burkhalter, PhD, Marshall Burns, PhD, Richard C. Burnside, MD, Eddie C. Burt, PhD, Michael A. Butts, Thomas L. Cain, Arnold E. Carden, PhD, J. Cassibry, PhD, Darrell W. Chambers, Kenneth E. Chandler, MD, James D. Chesnut Jr., Charles Richard Christensen, PhD, Chad P. Christian, Otis M. Clarke, Stan G. Clayton, William Madison Clement, PhD, James H. Clements Jr., Barbara B. Clements, David N. Clum, W. Frank Cobb Jr., Frank Cobb Jr., W. A. Cochran Jr., Ernst M. Cohn, Robert M. Conry, MD, Robert Bigham Cook, PhD, Franklyn K. Coombs, Kenneth R. Copeland, MD, Clifton Couey, Robert W. Coughlin, Sylvere Coussement, Clifton E. Covey, James T. Coward, George M. Cox, Justin H. Crain, George S. Crispin, Delton G. Crosier, Delmar N. Crowe Jr., Harry Cullinan, PhD, Joseph A. Cunningham, MD, J. F. Cuttino, PhD, Thomas P. Czepiel, PhD, Robert S. Dahlin, PhD, Thomas W. Daniel Sr., Madge C. Daniel, Joe S. Darden, Julian Davidson, PhD, Donald Echard Davis, PhD, Gene Davis, Wilfred J. Davis, Allen S. Davis, Michael J. Day, PhD, David Lee Dean, PhD, Charles W. Dean, Edward E. Deason, Debra Depiano, Myron G. Deshazo Jr., Jerome R. Dickey, Warren D. Dickinson, Wouter W. Dieperink, Wenju Dong, PhD, Francis M. Donovan, PhD, Thomas P. Dooley, PhD, Gilbert F. Douglas Jr., MD, James L. Dubard, PhD, Scott A. Dunham, John R. Durant, MD, Paul G. Durr, Z'Bigniew W'Ladyslaw Dybczak, PhD, George Robert Edlin, PhD, Gabriel A. Elgavish, PhD, Rotem Elgavish, Tricia Elgavish, Rush E. Elkins, PhD, Jesse G. Ellard, Howard Clyde Elliott, PhD, Arthur F. Ellis, David A. Elrod, PhD, David J. Elton, PhD, Leonard E. Ensminger, PhD, George Epps, Robert D. Erhardt Jr., Clyde Edsel Evans, PhD, Ken Fann, William S. Farneman, Rodney G. Ferguson, Mason D. Field, MD, G. L. Fish, Don E. Fitts, Julius Fleming, William F. Foreman, William M. Forman, William R. Forrester, Philip C. Foster, Mark Fowler, Robert Dorl Francis, PhD, Richard M. Franke, Larry D. Franks, Herbert J. Furman, Bob S. Galloway, Bobby R. Ganus, Ronald Gene Garmon, PhD, Henry B. Garrett Jr., Norman A. Garrison, PhD, David J. Garvey, PhD, William F. Garvin, Nancy K. Gautier, PhD, W. Welman Gebhart, Gerard Geppert, Thomas A. Gibson, MD, Chris Gilbert, PhD, Ronald E. Giuntini, PhD, Marvin R. Glass Jr., John J. Gleysteen, MD, Alexander C. Goforth, Roger L. Golden, Bruce William Gray, PhD, James D. Gregory, Ralph B. Groome, A. M. Guarino, PhD, Wallace K. Gunnells, Leslie A. Gunter, Freddie G. Gwin, Ronald L. Haaland, PhD, Walter Haeussermann, PhD, Leroy M. Hair, Benjamin F. Hajek, PhD, Ben F. Hajek, PhD, Justin Charles Hamer, PhD, W. Allen Hammack, James W. Handley, Reid R. Hanson, PhD, Richard A. Harkins, Daniel K. Harris, PhD, Gregory A. Harris, Joseph G. Harrison, PhD, John J. Harrity Jr., Douglas G. Hayes, PhD, James L. Hayes, Charles D. Haynes, PhD, James Eugene Heath, DVM, Paul S. Heck, Ron Helms, Bobby Helms, Robert L. Henderson, John B. Hendricks, PhD, William Henry Jr., William D. Herrin, Jerry P. Hethcoat, Mitch Higginbotham, David Higgins Jr., Hermon H. Hight, David T. Hill, PhD, Brendall Hinton, PhD, Vincent L. Hodges, Joseph A. Holifield, William A. Hollerman, Frank S. Hollis, David Hood, Joseph E. Hossley, Stephen K. Howard, Keith G. Howell, James F. Howison, James W. Huff, PhD, Dale L. Huffman, PhD, James W. Hugg, PhD, John C. Huggins, Joseph P. Huie, Chih-Cheng Hung, PhD, Ray Hunter, Hassel E. Hunter, Donald J. Ifshin, Victor D. Irby, PhD, Steven K. Irvin, John David Irwin, PhD, Lyman D. Jackson, Holger M. Jaenisch, PhD, Homer C. Jamison, PhD, Donald J. Janes, Kenneth Jarrell, William W. Jemison Jr., Penelope Jester, Donald R. Johns, Frederic Allan Johnson, PhD,

Monroe H. Johnson, Frank Junior Johnson, Joseph F. Judkins, PhD, Carl D. Jumper, David A. Kallin, James M. Kampfer, Robert Keenum, Lawrence C. Keller, Arthur G. Kelly, MD, Russell R. Kerl, Paul W. King, James E. Kingsbury, Earl T. Kinzer Jr., PhD, Harold A. Kirkland, William Klein, Dorothea A. Klip, PhD, James Knight, William J. Knox, MD, Charles Marion Krutchen, PhD, David E. Labo, Joseph E. Lammon, DVM, Philip Elmer Lamoreaux, John H. Lary, MD, Lloyd H. Lauerman, PhD, John K. Ledbetter, Thomas H. Ledford, PhD, William K. Lee, DVM, John D. Leffler, Foy K. Lewis, George R. Lewis, Baw-Lin Liu, PhD, Walter Long, MD, James M. Long lll, MD, Allen Long, MD, Joyce M. Long, John F. Lozowski, Linda C. Lucas, PhD, William R. Lucas, PhD, Brian Luckianow, Randal W. Lycans, Michael A. Macfarlane, George J. Mackinaw, Robert A. Macrae, Robert A. MacRae, John F. Maddox, MD, Carl Maltese, MD, I. R. Manasco, Baldev Singh Mangat, PhD, Frank C. Mann, Sven Pit Mannsfeld, PhD, Milton Mantler, Matthew Mariano, PhD, Gordon D. Marsh, David C. Marshal, Arvle E. Marshall, PhD, Paul R. Matthews, Charles R. Mauldin, David Mays, PhD, Van Alfon McAuley, Theresa O. McBride, Mark S. McColl, W. H. McCraney, Geroge M. McCullars, PhD, Phillip I. McCullough, Randall E. McDaniel, Joe A. McEachern, William Baldwin McKnight, PhD, Curtis J. McMinn, Thomas E. McNider, Jasper Lewis McPhail, MD, B. McSpadden, Solomon O. Mester, Joseph P. Michalski, J. G. Micklow, PhD, Randall A. Mills, Benjamin K. Miree, Larry S. Monroe, PhD, Dwight L. Moody, Rickie D. Moon, Wellington Moore, PhD, Robert A. Moore, PhD, Meg O. Moore, George S. Morefield, Stephen J. Morisani, PhD, Perry Morton, PhD, Herman A. Nebrig Jr., Professor Nelson, Robert W. Neuschaeffer, James Nhool, PhD, Grady B. Nichols, PhD, Billy G. Nippert, Nathan O. Okia, PhD, Byron L. Oliver, J. F. Olivier, Jerry M. Palmer, Edward James Parish, PhD, Michell S. Pate, Roderick J. Patefield, George D. Pattillo, W. Quinn Paulk, MD, David M. Pearsall, Dom Perrotta, Nelson A. Perry, Kenneth F. Persin, Mark R. Pettitt, Tom Pfitzer, John G. Pfrimmer, Kenneth G. Pickett, Sean Piecuch, Donald S. Pierre Jr., James R. Pike, Charles Thomas Pike, Peter P. Pincura, Michael Piznar, Melvin Price, PhD, Charles W. Prince, PhD, Thaddeus H. Pruett, Jodi Purser, Danny P. Raines, Joseph Lindsay Randall, PhD, Marvin L. Rawls, Michelle B. Ray, Harold M. Raynor, Greg Reardon, Jerry Reaves, Mark Redden, Michael A. Remillard, Robert Ware Reynolds, PhD, Richard G. Rhoades, PhD, William Eugene Ribelin, DVM, Dennis Rich, George Richmond, Logan R. Ritchie Jr., Alfred Ritter, PhD, Ronnie Rivers, PhD, Hill E. Roberts, Harold Vernon Rodgriguez, PhD, Richard B. Rogers, PhD, Thaddeus A. Roppel, PhD, John W. Rouse, PhD, Eladio Ruiz-De-Molina, Leon Y. Sadler III, PhD, Adel Sakla, PhD, Andreas Salemann, PhD, James Sanford, Ted L. Sartain, D. Satterwhite, Mark Saunders, Carl Schauble, PhD, Carl Schauble, PhD, Bernard Scheiner, PhD, Peter Schwartz, PhD, Edmund P. Segner, PhD, William G. Setser, Raymond F. Sewell, PhD, Raymond Lee Shepherd, PhD, Charles H. Shivers, PhD, Carol Shreve, Don A. Sibley, PhD, Stephen T. Simpson, DVM, Wiliam F. Sims, MD, Norman Frank Six Jr., PhD, Harold Walter Skalka, MD, Daniel E. Skinner 3rd, Peter John Slater, PhD, Donald W. Smaha, Roger J. Smeenge, Obie Smith, David A. Smith, Belton Craig Snyder, Michael Sosebee, Jon J. Spano, D. Paul Sparks Jr., Michael P. Spector, PhD, Philip Speir, John T. Spraggins Jr., Lethenual Stanfield, Jarel P. Starling, Benjamin C. Stevens, Alfred D. Stevens, Dale M. Stevens, Mike Stewart, J. Stone, PhD, John W. Sumrall, Marvin Laverne Swearingin, PhD, J. M. Tagg, Thomas F. Talbot, PhD, Bruce J. Tatarchuk, PhD, Oscar D. Taunton, MD, Newton L. Taylor, Tommy L. Thompson, Zack Thompson, Eugene Delbert Tidwell, Edward R. Tietel, MD, Timothy C. Tuggle, Caades Tugwell, Ted W. Tyson, James P. Vacik, PhD, James T. Varner, Stanley S. Vasa, William W. Vaughan, PhD, Phillip G. Vaughan, Otha H. Vaughan Jr., Ohta H. Vaughan Jr., Frank L. Vaughn, Thomas Mabry Veazey, PhD, William S. Viall, William Voigt, James E. Waite, Ron C. Waites, William Waldrum Walker, PhD, John Wallace, Edward Hilson Ward, PhD, Wyley D. Ward, Raymond C. Watson Jr., PhD, Adrian O. Watson, Henry B. Weaver Jr., Donald C. Wehner, Lawrence P. Weinberger, PhD, Talmadge P. Weldon, William B. Wells Jr., Hans-Helmut Werner, PhD, Francis C. Wessling, PhD, Steven L. Whitfield, Rayburn Harlen Whorton, Leon Otto Wilken, PhD, Charles D. Wilkins, Michael Ledell Williams, PhD, Jay C. Willis, Harold J. Wilson, Walter W. Wilson, Leighton C. Wilson, Gregory Scott Windham, MD, Stanley B. Winslow, MD, Harvey B. Wright, Lewis S. Young, MD, Forrest A. Younker, Kirk R. Zimmer

Alaska

Ronald Godshall Alderfer, PhD, Donald Ford Amend, PhD, Donald Anderson, PhD, David Anderson, Duane F. Andress, Patrick J. Archey, Randall L. Bachman, Roger L. Baer, Tina L. Baker, Earl R. Barnard, Alex Baskous, Don Bassler, John M. Beitia, Eugene N. Bjornstad, John K. Boarman, William M. Bohon, James F. Boltz, Steven C. Borell, Dean C. Brinkman, Mike Briscoe, Jack A. Brockman, Carrel R. Bryant, Roger C. Burggraf, Duane E. Carson, Glen D. Chambers, Bartly Coiley, Lowell R. Crane, Michael D. Croft, Brent Crowder, Bruce E. Davison, Jonathan Dehn, PhD, Dave R. Dobberpuhl, Edward M. Dokoozian, PhD, Kathleen Douglas, Robert G. Dragnich, James Drew, PhD, Richard A. Dusenbery, PhD, William E. Eberhardt, Jeffrey D. Eckstein, John Egenholf, PhD, Robert L. Engelbach, William James Ferrell, PhD, Jeffrey Y. Foley, Monique M. Garbowicz, Jon M. Girard, Will E. Godbey, Edward R. Goldmann, Daniel C. Graham, Lawrence G. Griffin, Lenhart T. Grothe, William F. Gunderson, Brian T. Harten, David B. Harvey, Charles C. Hawley, PhD, Tommy G. Heinrich, James R. Hendershot, Steven C. Henslee, Naomi R. Hobbs, Julie K. Holayter, Kurt Hulteen, Lyndon C. Ibele, Steven K. Jones, William W. Kakel, Donald D. Keill, Edward R. Kiddle, Joseph

M. Killon, Ted R. Kinney, Christopher C. Klein, George F. Klemmick, Thomas H. Kuckertz, PhD, James F. Lebiedz, Harry R. Lee, Harold D. Lee, William E. Long, PhD, Erwin L. Long, Barrie B. Lowe, Everett L. Mabry, Monte D. Mabry, Robert F. Malouf, Bob Malowf, T. R. Marshall Jr., Donald H. Martins, PhD, Jerzy Maselko, PhD, Bruce H. Mattson, Tom E. Maunder, Justin T. Meyring, Jeff R. Michels, J. V. Miesse, William W. Mitchell, PhD, Harold R. Moeser, Jesse R. Mohrbacher, Boyd Morgenthaler, John Mulligan, Erik A. Opstad, Marvin C. Papenfuss, PhD, Pedro E. Perez, MD, Robert A. Perkins, PhD, Gret Peters, PhD, Greg Peters, PhD, Richard A. Peters, MD, Walter T. Phillips, Kenneth J. Pinard, Bruce Porter, Richard H. Reiley, Rydell J. Reints, Kermit Dale Reppond, Peter M. Ricca, PhD, Donald R. Rogers, MD, Jimmie C. Rosenbruch, Allan A. Ross, Joe L. Russell, Mortin B. Schierhorn, George Schmidt, Lynn W. Schnell, Jeffery M. Scott, Edward M. Sessions, Gaylord Shaw, PhD, Ernst Siemoneit, Todd A. Sneesby, David K. Soderlund, Damien F. Stella, Michael Storer, James W. Styler, Richard C. Swainbank, PhD, Robert C. Tedrick, Tim Terry, Kevin Tomera, MD, Michael D. Travis, Duane H. Vaagen, Dominique L. Van Nostrand, Angela C. Vassar, Ross L. Waner, Brenton Watkins, PhD, Jean S. Weingarten, Robert P. Wessels, Michael W. Wheatall, Warrack Willson, PhD, Theron C. Wilson, Frank W. Wince, Professor Yapuncich, PhD, Patrick J. Zettler

AP

Katherine B. Featherstone

Arizona

Richard E. Ackermann, Brook W. Adams, Stanley P. Aetrewicz, Larry Delmar Agenbroad, PhD, Aida M. Aguirre, Richard Ahern, Edward Ahrens, Lloyd Alaback, Leland C. Albertson, A. Amr, PhD, Sal A. Anazalone, Arthur G. Anderson, PhD, Anita Teter Anderson, James M. Andrew, John Allen Anthes, PhD, Bruce W. Apland, Ara Arabyan, PhD, Frank G. Arcella, PhD, William W. Archer, Stephen A. Arcutt, Joe R. Arechavaleta, Lew Armer, Willard Van Asdall, PhD, Mike Assad, David C. Atkins, Jerry C. Atwell, Del Austin, D. Austin, Canan D. Avela, Dirk Den Baars, PhD, T. Bahill, PhD, A. Terry Bahill, PhD, Andrew T. Bahill, PhD, David A. Bailey, J. Baker, PhD, Jonathan A. Balasa, Robert Balling, PhD, Roy Jean Barker, PhD, John E. Barkley, PhD, Ross C. Barkley, David A. Barnard, Benny B. Barnes, R. C. Barnett, Charles John Baroczy, Lawrence Dale Barr, Kenneth A. Bartal, Edward J. Barvick, John W. Bass, MD, Charles Carpenter Bates, PhD, Roger A. Baumann, Steve Baumann, Frank L. Bazzanella, Randall D. Beck, James R. Beene, W. G. Benjamin, John Bentley, Charles M. Bentzen, Arne K. Bergh, PhD, Kenneth M. Bernstein, James Wesley Berry, PhD, S. Beus, PhD, Peter F. Bianchetta, William S. Bickel, PhD, Alex F. Bissett, James R. Black, E. Allan Blair, PhD, Marlene Bluestein, MD, Charles W. Boak, Paul L. Boettcher, Bruce Bollermann, Kelsey L. Boltz, Aundra G. Booher Nix, Emil J. Bovich, Wendell Bowers, Michael Boxer, MD, John D. Brack, John J. Bradley, MD, W. Newman Bradshaw, PhD, Harold Brennan, Edward J. Breyere, PhD, Fred E. Brinker, James A. Briscoe, Albert Le Broadfoot, PhD, Beth M. Brookhouse, Fred B. Brost, John K. Brough, Richard E. Brown, MD, Stephen R. Brown, Lansing E. Brown, MD, S. Kent Brown, MD, Will K. Brown, Stephen E. Brown, Gerald R. Brunskill, John A. Brunsman, MD, Bruce Bryan, Thomas L. Bryant, Theodore Eugene Bunch, PhD, Laurie B. Burdeaux, Joe Byrne, Ken M. Byrne, Ralph E. Cadger, MD, Roger Cahill, Dennis Caird, J. B. Caird, Anthony E. Camilli, MD, John D. Camp, MD, Robert J. Campana, Robert E. Campbell, M. Durwood Canham, Joe W. Cannon, MD, Bryan J. Carder, MD, Edward H. Carey, Richard B. Carley, MD, E. N. Carlier, Charles Carrell, Jesus V. Carreon, Bruce W. Cavender, Robert T. Chapman, Gerald M. Chicoine, Lincoln Chin, PhD, Larry J. Chockie, James R. Civis, Maurice F. Clapp, James G. Clark, PhD, James W. Clark, John Wesley Clayton, PhD, La Var Clegg, LaVar Clegg, Jeffrey G. Clevenger, Raymond Otto Clinton, PhD, Elmer Lendell Cockrum, PhD, Theodore L. Cogut, Donald Coleman, Joel E. Colley, Allan W. Collins, Joanne V. Collins, Ernest W. Colwell, Thomas J. Comi, PhD, Bill J. Conovaloff, Paul Consroe, PhD, Daniel M. Conway, George W. Cook, Glenn C. Cook, Russell M. Corn, Russel M. Corn, Don Corona Jr., Roy E. Coulson, Garland D. Cox, Brian Cox, Peter J. Crescenzo, Anne E. Cress, PhD, Richard E. Cribbs, Donald E. Crowell, Gabriel Tibor Csanady, PhD, David C. Cunningham, Dewayne D. Curtis, Joseph A. Cusack, William J. Daffron, Clark J. Daggs, Charles H. Daggs Jr., James F. Dancho, Jerry Danni, Robert Darveaux, PhD, Lester W. Davis, Francisco Homero De La Moneda, PhD, JoAnn Deakin, Stuart Deakin, Tom E. Deakin, James D. Deatherage, Dirk Den-Baars, PhD, Lemoine J. Derrick, Jack L. Detrick, William Devereux, Jerome P. Dorlac, Harold J. Downey, Gregory J. Dozer, Jean B. Draper, William Dresher, PhD, Patricia Dueck, Gene E. Dufoe, Marie Dugan, Raymond J. Dugandzic, Jonathan DuHamel, J. Durham, Sher M. Durrani, Ted Earle, John T. Eastlick, Philip Anthony Emery, Glen B. Engle, T. Enloe, Lawson P. Entwhistle, A. Gordon Everett, PhD, Ted H. Eyde, Steve Fanto, MD, Robert H. Fariss, PhD, Stanley D. Farlin, PhD, Robert P. Farrell, William F. Fathauer, MD, John B. Fenger, MD, Chester G. Ferguson, MD, Sam Field, James B. Fink, PhD, Rex G. Finley, William G. Fisher, PhD, Robert T. Fitzgerald, MD, Leon Walter Florschuet, PhD, Branka P. Ford, PhD, Ron Francken, Arnold C. Frautnick, George M. Fritz, Francis R. Frola, Ron Frola, Arthur Atwater Frost, PhD, Nelson M. Funkhouser, Robert Howard Furman, MD, Floyd Fusselman, Donald Alan Gall, PhD, Clyde H. Garman, P. R. Garver, MD, Roy Lee Gealer, PhD, Glen C. Gerhard, PhD, Robert P. Gervais, MD, Henry Lee Giclas, PhD, James Giles, PhD, Donald K. Gill, Paul

C. Gilmour, PhD, Fred Gioglio, Roy L. Givens, Stephen Glacy, MD, William Glass, June Glavin, Robert L. Glick, PhD, Randy Golding, PhD, Pierce Goodman, PhD, E. J. Gouvier, Edward John Gouvier Jr., Alphonse Peter Granatek, Harold Greenfield, PhD, William M. Greenslade, George Alexander Gries, PhD, Ray Griswold, Joseph F. Gross, PhD, C. J. Gudim, Charles W. Gullikson, PhD, C. W. Gullikson, PhD, Gordon E. Gumble, Earl S. Gurley, Richard E. Guth, David B. Hackman, PhD, Anton F. Haffer, Ronald J. Hager Jr., W. Richard Hahman, William R. Hahman, Cathryn E. Hahn, Francis A. Hale, Richard C. Hall, Christy N. Hallien, Donald F. Hammer, Raymond E. Hammond, Richard W Ylie Hanks, PhD, Jerry T. Hanks, Joann Brown Hansen, PhD, Deverle Porter Harris, PhD, Ellen Harris, Elmer Otto Hartig, PhD, Hermen Hartjens, Scott E. Hartwig, W. L. Harvey, L. Hatzilambrou, PhD, Charles M. Havlik, John W. Hawley, M. W. Heath Jr., Lowell H. Heaton, John M. Heermans, Walter E. Heinrichs Jr., W. E. Heinrichs Jr., Albert K. Heitzmann, Patricia A. Helvenston, PhD, Robert S. Hendricks, Lester E. Hendrickson, PhD, Edward P. Herman, MD, Roy A. Herrington, Tom Hessler, Robin J. Hickson, D. W. Hilchie, PhD, Douglas W. Hilchie, PhD, Donald C. Hilgers, PhD, Jeffrey H. Hill, PhD, Norman E. Hill, Robert D. Hill, Bruce Hilpert, Daniel L. Hirsch, J. Brent Hiskey, PhD, Corolla K. Hoag, Alfred Joseph Hoehn, PhD, Stuart Alfred Hoenig, PhD, William C. Hoffman, PhD, R. N. Holme, G. Edward Holmes, Michael Holtfrerich, Kevin C. Horstman, PhD, Ashley G. House, James C. Hsie, William Bogel Hubbard, PhD, Richard O. Huch, Davin L. Huck, Richard R. Huebschman, Robert P. Hughes, Raymond P. Hull, Robert B. Humphrey, Kenneth L. Hunt Jr., Charles L. Hunter, Peter P. Hydrean, PhD, Sherwood B. Idso, Lawrence L. Ingram, G. W. Irvin, Dan Isbell, Kenneth K. Issacson, Teodore F. Izzo, K. A. Jackson, PhD, Douglas E. James, Thomas Jancic, Kevin L. Jardine, John H. Jarvis, MD, David E. Jeal, MD, Harry E. Jensen, Robert M. Jensen, Ralph Jewett, David C. Johnson, MD, David Johnston, Billy J. Joplin, Richard Charles Jordan, PhD, Thomas L. T. Jossem, Jim Joyce, George F. Jude, Eric Jungermann, PhD, Richard Spalding Juvet, PhD, Richard J. Kalvaitis, Ronald R. Kamyniski, Justin M. Kapla, Francis Warren Karasek, PhD, Peter P. Kay, MD, Kenneth Lee Keating, PhD, Keith M. Keating, James L. Kelly*, Shawn Kendall, Keith L. Kendall, Robert Kendrick, William A. Kennedy, PhD, Kevin M. Kenney, Harold D. Kessler, Clement Joseph Kevane, PhD, Paul M. Keyser, Paul E. Kienow, William R. Kilpatrick, MD, Professor Kingery, PhD, W. David Kingery, PhD, Dan Kirby, Clayton Ward Kischer, PhD, Roy C. Kiser, William Robert Kneebone, PhD, Vincent E. Knittel, Gregory Dean Knowlton, PhD, Paul Koblas, PhD, Leonard John Koch, Karl F. Kohlhoff, Frederick H. Kohloss, Rudolf Kolaja, Robert R. Koons, William P. Kopp, Melvin J. Kornblatt, MD, Jeff K. Kracht, Henry G. Kreis, Gerald E. Kron, PhD, Eddwin H. Krug, David J. Krus, PhD, W. Kubitsihel, MD, David L. Kuck, John G. Kuhn, W. R. Kulutachek, MD, Ihor A. Kunasz, PhD, Joseph D. Kutschka, Gary W. Lachappelle, Willard C. Lacy, PhD, Lorin G. Lafoe, Charles F. Lagergren, James L. Lake, Lynn Lalko, PhD, Lionel C. Lancaster, Wayne A. Lattin, MD, Steven B. Leeland, Randolph S. Lehn, Richard B. Leisure, Tom C. Lepley, Ron L. Levin, PhD, David W. Levinson, PhD, Seymour H. Levy, Ruth L. Leyse, PhD, Hang Ming Liaw, PhD, James A. Liggett', PhD, Urban Joseph Linehan, PhD, William G. Lipke, PhD, Ligia B. Lluria, Mark Logan, MD, James D. Loghry, Edward M. Lohman, Armand """"A.J."""" Lombard, David Lorenz, MD, Robert F. Lorenzen, MD, Robert B. Ludden, Roger J. Ludlam, Mark Ludwig, PhD, Ronald J. Lukas, PhD, Robert F. Lundin, PhD, James H. Lundy Jr., Donald E. Lynd, Clarence Roger Lynds, PhD, Robert P. Ma, PhD, Richard L. Malafa, Tom Maloney, G. S. Mander, Paul Allen Manera, PhD, James K W Mardian, PhD, William Michael Marsh, Noah W. Martin, Bijan R. Mashouf, MD, Billy F. Mathews, Thomas W. Mathewson, Donald E. Matlick, Harrison E. Matson, J. A. McAllister*, Terry McArthur, Ron McCallister, PhD, John W. McCracken, Paul McElligott, PhD, Norman E. McFate, PhD, James E. McGaha, Andrew J. McGill, Geogory E. McKelvey, Bruce A. McKinstry, R. L. McPHerson, Lorin Post McRae, PhD, John E. McVaugh Jr., Wellington Meier, PhD, Arend Meijer, PhD, Norman Anthony Meinhardt, PhD, Gary L. Melvin, Ken Melybe, Charles R. Merigold, Richard E. Merrill, MD, Robert A. Metz, Robert J. Meyers, Robert J. Meyers Jr., Harvey D. Michael, Marcus A. Middleton, Glenn Harry Miller, PhD, Kenton D. Miller, Mark A. Miller, M. Miller, James A. Moeller, Robert P. Montague, Roger L. Moody, Donald Moon, Jack W. Moore, Ramon A. Morano, Pamela A. Morford, MD, Phineas K. Morrill, John Ross Mosley, PhD, Robert Zeno Muggli, PhD, Michael C. Mulbarger, Gerald E. Munier, Earl Wesley Murbach, PhD, Fendi R. Murdock, PhD, Robert E. Nabours, PhD, Paula Nadell, Raymond Naumann, John Neff, George E. Nelms, PhD, Frank Nelson, Ronald A. Nielsen, David R. Nielsen, MD, Nyal L. Niemuth, Robert O. Nixon, PhD, Charles C. Nolan, Eric A. Nordhausen, Edward A. Nowatzki, PhD, Van Nyman, David O. Oakeson, Ernest L. Ohle, PhD, Francis Oliver, MD, Steve Orcutt, Stephen A. Orcutt, Jane M. Orient, MD, Herbert Osborn, PhD, Stephen S. Osder, Charles Lamar Osterberg, PhD, Charles Osterbury, PhD, Bernie Ott, Karl J. Palmberg, MD, Professor Panebianco, Lloyd M. Parks, PhD, Harvey G. Patterson, Doug S. Pease, E. Howard Pepper, Mike Peralta, PhD, Donald M. Percy, MD, Darlene A. Periconi-Balling, Thomas W. Phillips, Stanley P. Pietrewicz, S. Pietrewicz, Anthony Pietsch, Fred Pitman, Anthony Pitucco, PhD, John A. Plaisted, Alan P. Ploesser, James R. Plummer, Kent L. Pomeroy, MD, Fernando Ponce, PhD, William E. Poole, H. K. Poole, Jonathan D. Posner, PhD, Roderick B. Potter, George J. Potter, James A. Powell, Arnold Warburton Pratt, Robert F. Prest, Burchard S. Pruett, Robert Putnam, Thomas Pyzdek, Tom Pyzdek, Walter J. Quinlan, David D. Rabb, Kenneth D. Rachocki, PhD, Donal M. Ragan, PhD, James B. Rasmussen, Steven L. Rauzi, Kyle Rawlings, PhD, Paul R. Reay, K. Redig, Terry A. Reeves, Thomas R. Rehm, PhD, Roger A. Reich, John E. Reichenbach Jr., Kenneth G. Renard, PhD, Robert J. Reuss, C. H. Reynolds,

Harvey H. Rhodes, Warren Rice, PhD, Terry L. Rice, Ralph M. Richard, PhD, James L. Riedl, Timothy R. Robbins, Chris Robertson, Douglas L. Robinson, PhD, Thomas C. Roche Jr., T. C. Roche Jr., Michael V. Rock, MD, Ralph A. Rockow, John H. Rohrbaugh, PhD, Dwayne A. Rohweder, PhD, Garret K. Ross, Richard H. Rowe, MD, Verald K. Rowe, David Daniel Rubis, PhD, Thomas Rudy, John A. Rupley, PhD, George E. Ryberg, William R. Salzman, PhD, Robert E. Samuelson, PhD, Katherine Sanchez, John N. Sarracino, John B. Sawyer, MD, Thomas E. Scartaccini, Harvey C. Schau, PhD, Harvey C. Schau, PhD, William G. Scheck, Joseph M. Scherzer, Justin Orvel Schmidt, PhD, Conrad Schneiker, Melvin Herman Schonhorst, PhD, George K. Schuler, Michael H. Schweinsberg, Theodore Thomas Scolman, PhD, Chuck See, Hal Sefton, Mark N. Seidel, PhD, H. Selvidge, PhD, Harner Selvidge, PhD, Robert Shantz, PhD, Steven M. Shaw, PhD, Peter Sherry, Kirk W. Shubert, Thomas K. Simacek, PhD, William L. Simmermon, James D. Simpson, PhD, Mark R. Sinclair, PhD, Ernesto Sirvas, Edward Skibo, PhD, Bruce E. Skippar, W. Roy Slaunwhite, PhD, Bennett Sloan, Thomas L. Sluga, Delmont K. Smith, PhD, Alice Smith, Donald Snyder, John A. Soscia, MD, David M. Spatz, PhD, Daniel H. Spencer, Earl L. Spieles, John W. Stafford, Daniel Stamps, Royal William Stark, PhD, Travis C. Steele, Frank A. Stephenson, PhD, Lester H. Steward, PhD, Vern S. Strubeck, MD, Robert J. Stuart, Dennis L. Stuhr, Frederick E. Suhm, David Sultana, Soren J. Suver, Paul E. Swain, Gordon Alfred Swann, PhD, Moute N. Swetnam, Michael Talbot, Charles M. Tarr, Michael Teodori, MD, Marvin W. Teutsch, C. Brent Theurer, PhD, Russell W. Thiele, Jess F. Thomas, H. Stephens Thomas, MD, Glenn Thompson, PhD, Charles S. Thompson, David H. Thornton, John R. Thorson, Dennis L. Thrasher, Jacob Timmers, Spencer R. Titley, PhD, George E. Travis, Eric Tuch, Roy A. Tucker, Lee A. Tune Jr., Dennis Turner, George C. Tyler, MD, John L. Uhrie, PhD, Bobby L. Ulich, PhD, Noel W. Urban, Emmett Van Reed, C. Kenneth Vance, Albert L. Vanness, Richard V. VanRiper, Edward F. Veverka, Antonio R. Villanueva, PhD, James W. Vogler, PhD, Peter Vokac, David E. Wahl Jr., PhD, Robert C. Walish, Woodville J. Walker, Joe A. Walker, Wayne Wallace, Steven I. Walsh, Kevin Walsh, Robert C. Walsh Jr., Meredith Warner, Steven D. Washburn, MD, Roger L. Waterman, Lee R. Watkins, W. L. Wearly, PhD, William L. Wearly, Orrin John Webster, PhD, Gene Wegner, PhD, Patrick L. Weidner, Jack D. Weiss, Homer William Welch, PhD, William T. Welchert, Herbert C. Wendes, Paul J. Weser, Donald C. White, Clifford K. Whiting, Sue Whitworth, Dave E. Wick, Gordon Wieduwilt, W. Gordon Wieduwilt, John B. Wilburn, George Wilkinson Jr., Brandon C. Williams, Clifford Leon Willis, PhD, Robert E. Willow, Donald W. Wine, David Wing, PhD, John B. Winters, James C. Withers, PhD, George K. Wittenberg, PhD, Gerald Woehick, George A. Wolfe, Richard H. Wolters, Gerald L. Wood, George A. Woods, David J. Woods, Will W. Worthington, Glenn Wright, PhD, James A. Yanez, James R. Yingst, Robert A. Young, PhD, Garth L. Young, Itzak Z. Zamir, Roy V. Zeagler Jr., Charles Zglenicki, Paul W. Zimmer, Werner G. Zinn

Arkansas

Billy R. Achmbaugh, Alan J. Anderson, James R. Arce, Jerry L. Baber, Harry R. Baker, Phillip A. Barros, Lonnie G. Bassett, Ralph Sherman Becker, PhD, Randolph Armin Becker, Ford Benham, Maximilian Hilmar Bergendahl, PhD, John J. Berky, PhD, C. Dudley Blancke, Robert E. Blanz, PhD, David Bowlin, Robert Edward Bowling, PhD, Delton L. Brown Jr., Bryan Burnett, Gordon L. Burr, James P. Caldwell, Raymond Cammack, PhD, Frank Chimenti, PhD, Thomas Clark, Jeffrey M. Collar, Frederick Clinton Collins, PhD, John D. Commerford, PhD, Reggie A. Corbitt, Kenneth C. Corkum, PhD, Stanley R. Curtis, James Ed Davis, Steven E. Dobbs, PhD, Kenneth L. Duck, James A. Dunlop, Don H. Edington, James E. Erskine, William Russell Everett, PhD, Ronald Everett, PhD, Timsey L. Everett, G. Ferrer, PhD, Karen Ferrer, PhD, Richard Hamilton Forsythe, PhD, Kenneth W. French, PhD, Roland E. Garlinghouse, Walter Thomas Gloor, PhD, Francis A. Grillot Jr., John Louis Hartman, PhD, Roger M. Hawk, PhD, Larry D. Heisserer, Francis M. Henderson, MD, Chester W. Hesselbein, Ed Hiserodt, Edwin J. Hockaday, Charles J. Hoke, Erne Hume, Johnny R. Isbell, Mary E. Jenkins, MD, Charles Jones, PhD, Edward T. Jones, Matti Kaarnakari, Earnest Kavanaugh, Bill W. Keaton, David Wayne Kellogg, PhD, M. K. Kemp, Edward J. Kersey, Donald R. Keys, John W. King, PhD, Tommy C. Kinnaird, Charles H. Korns, PhD, Barry Kurth, Sterling S. Lacy, William E. Lanyon, Noel A. Lawson, Wei Li, Dennis D. Longhorn, Gary L. Low, M. David Luneau, Terry L. Macalady, Phillip A. Marak, Mary K. Marks-Wood, Lloyd D. Martin, MD, Richard Harvey Martin, MD, Kenneth L. Mazander, Clark William McCarty, PhD, Harlan L. McMillan, PhD, Thomas H. McWilliams, David G. Meador, Allan J. Mesko, Paul Mixon, PhD, Jeanne Murphy, PhD, X. J. Musacchia, PhD, Bobbie G. Musson, Danny Naegle, Charles A. Nelson, PhD, Lowell Edwin Netherton, PhD, Kelly Hoyet Oliver, PhD, Vernon L. Pate, John E. Pauly, PhD, Raymond E. Peeples, MD, John D. Pike, Joseph C. Plunkett, PhD, Larry T. Polk, Jack L. Reddin, MD, Douglas A. Rees-Evans, Allan Stanley Rehm, PhD, Al W. Renfroe, DVM, Tom E. Richards, J. Herbert Riley, Albert Robinson, PhD, Gary W. Russell, MD, William Marion Sandefur, PhD, Boris M. Schein, PhD, Paul H. Schellenberg, MD, Bruce E. Schratz, MD, B. Sherrill, David E. Sibert, Alfred Silano, PhD, Carroll Ward Smith, PhD, Wayne Smith, Jason Stewart, C. Storm, Mike Robert Strub, PhD, G. Russell Sutherland, John B. Talpas, Aubrey W. Tennille, PhD, Don M. Thomas, Buck J. Titsworth, Joseph R. Togami, George Toombs, William Walker Trigg, PhD, Daniel L. Turnbow, Alan C. Varner, Patrick D. Walker, MD, J. R. Weaver, Melvin Bruce Welch, PhD, Professor White, Stephen W. Wilson, Mary Wood, James Word, MD

California

Earl M. Aagaard, PhD, Charles W. Aami, Ursula K. Abbott, PhD, Janis I. Abele, Robert C. Abrams, Ahmed E. Aburahmah, PhD, Ava V. Ackerman, DVM, Lee Actor, Humberto M. Acuna Jr., George Baker Adams, PhD, Lewis R. Adams, William John Adams, William H. Addington, Barnet R. Adelman, John H. Adrain, MD, Jack G. Agan, Sven Agerbek, Joseph Aiello, MD, John J. Aiello, Arthur W. Akers, Gary L. Akerstrom, Wayne Henry Akeson, MD, John S. Akiyama, Philip R. Akre, MD, G. James Alaback, John A. Alai, Daniel C. Albers, Edward Albert, John C. Alden, PhD, Alex F. Alessandrini, Ira H. Alexander, Rodolfo Q. Alfonso, R. Allahyari, PhD, Louis John Allamandola, PhD, Levi D. Allen, Robert C. Allen, Charles E. Allman, John J. Allport, PhD, Ronaldo A. Almero, David Altman, PhD, Herbert N. Altneu, Frank M. Alustiza, Raymond Angelo Alvarez Jr., PhD, Antonio R. Alvarez, Zaynab Al-Yassin, PhD, Farouk Amanatullah, David Saint Amand, Carmelo J. Amato, Marvin Earl Ament, Melvin M. Anchell, MD, Wilford Hoyt Andersen, PhD, Torben B. Andersen, PhD, Joy R. Anderson, PhD, Ross S. Anderson, PhD, Orson Lamar Anderson, PhD, Chris Anderson, Conrad E. Anderson, MD, Jane E. Anderson, Roscoe B. Anderson, MD, Robert E. Anderson, Warren Ronald Anderson, Thomas P. Anderson, James Anderson, Karen Andersonnoeck, Lois Andros, Walter S. Andrus, Claude B. Anger, Gregory W. Antal, Achilles P. Anton, MD, Rolando A. Antonio, Arturo Q. Arabe, PhD, John Arcadi, Robert L. Archibald, Philip Archibald, Richard W. Armentrout, PhD, Baxter H. Armstrong, PhD, Robert Emile Arnal, PhD, Charles Arney, George V. Aros Chilingarian, PhD, Max Artusy, PhD, George J. Asanovich, Bob J. Ascherl, Edward V. Ashburn, Holt Ashley, PhD, Don O. Asquith, PhD, Everett L. Astleford, Greg J. Aten, Robert D. Athey Jr., PhD, Leonardo D. Attorre, Jerry Y. Au, Mike August, W. David Augustine, Thomas E. Aumock, Henry Spiese Aurand, Kenny Ausmus, Roger J. Austin, PhD, Philip J. Avery, Kenneth Avicola, Luis A. Avila, Theodore C. Awartkruis, PhD, T. G. Ayres, William J. Babalis, MD, Ray M. Bacchi, Gordon R. Bachlund, William E. Backes, Adrian Donald Baer, PhD, Henry P. Baier, Edmund J. Bailey, Liam P. Bailey, Benton B. Bailey, Ronald M. Bailey, Donald W. Baisch, Norman F. Baker, PhD, Don Robert Baker, PhD, Mary Ann Baker, PhD, Roland E. Baker, W. J. Baker, Orville Balcom, Ransom Leland Baldwin, PhD, Barrett S. Baldwin, PhD, David P. Baldwin, George Balella, MD, George Ball, Glenn A. Ballard, Martin Balow, John S. Baltutis, Cris C. Banaban, Herman William Bandel, PhD, Richard M. Banister, Ronald E. Banuk, Neil J. Barabas, Ronald Barany, PhD, James W. Barcikowski, Norman E. Barclay, Brian S. Barcus, Randolph P. Bardini, Morrie Jay Barembaum, Grigory Isaakovich Barenblatt, PhD, Horace A. Barker, PhD, Francis J. Barker, William B. Barksdale, PhD, Richard K. Barksdale, Mary J. Barlow, MD, Durton B. Barnes, Russell H. Barnes, Paul R. Barnes, Albert R. Barnes, Burton B. Barnes, James Robert Barnum, PhD, James P. Barrie, Bruce M. Barron, Robert H. Barron, MD, Gary D. Barry, Bruce C. Bartels, Don A. Bartick, Janeth Marie Bartlett, PhD, Bob W. Bartlett, PhD, Richard C. Barton, W. Clyde Barton Jr., Don Bartz, Cecil O. Basenberg, John E. Basinski, PhD, H. Smith Bass, Seyed A. Bastani, PhD, Samuel Burbridge Batdorf, PhD, Barbara Batterson, Edward C. Bauer, PhD, Kurt Baum, PhD, Frank J. Baumann, Hans P. Bausch, Peter Bausch, E. Beaton, David Beaucage, PhD, Robert A. Beaudet, PhD, Christine Beavcage, PhD, Horst Huttenhain Bechtel, Robert F. Bechtold, Niels John Beck, PhD, N. John Beck, PhD, Roy T. Beck, Tom G. Beck, Donald J. Beck, Milton Becker, PhD, William H. Beckley, Arnold Orville Beckman, PhD, James P. Beecher, Donald W. Beegle, Mark Beget, Nicholas Anthony Begovich, PhD, Rudi Beichel, Jean E. Beland, PhD, Ralph Belcher, PhD, Charles Vester Bell, PhD, John Bell, Barbara Belli, PhD, Thomas J. Bellon Jr., Robert K. Bellue, Francis J. Belmonte, John W. Ben, David J. Benard, PhD, Robert D. Benbow, Paul F. Bene, Barry P. Benight, Kurt A. Benirschke, MD, John Benjamin, PhD, Istvan S. Benko, William G. Benko, Kenneth W. Benner, PhD, Harold E. Bennett, PhD, Sidney A. Bensen, PhD, Andrew A. Benson, PhD, Sidney W. Benson, PhD, Herbert H. Benson, MD, John D. Benson, Rober Benson, Margaret W. Benton, Philip H. Benton, John A. Bentsen, John A. Berberet, PhD, Louis Bergdahl, Lev I. Berger, PhD, Augustus B. Berger, Otto Berger, Leo H. Berk, MD, Ami E. Berkowitz, PhD, William I. Berks, Ted Gibbs Berlincourt, PhD, Baruch Berman, Louis Bernath, PhD, Dave Berrier, Lester P. Berriman, Edwin X. Berry, PhD, Carl E. Berry, David J. Berryman, Richard G. Berryman, Georgw J. Bertuccelli, Thomas E. Berty, Bruce A. Berwager, James A. Bethke, John C. Bettinger, MD, Ernest Beutler, MD, Vladislav A. Bevc, PhD, Dimitri Beve, PhD, Vincent Darell Bevill, John H. Beyer, PhD, Ashok K. Bhatnagar, Fred V. Biagini, Carl J. Bianchini, George A. Bicher, Michael D. Bick, PhD, Donald B. Bickler, Donald G. Bickmore, Lauren K. Bieg, Richard V. Bierman, Arthur C. Bigley Jr., Jerry C. Billings, Kenneth William Billman, PhD, Charles J. Billwiller, Paul A. Bilunos, MD, R. L. Binsley, Norman Birch, Kenneth Bird, PhD, James Louden Bischoff, PhD, Kim Bishop, PhD, John William Bishop, PhD, Clifford R. Bishop, Harlan Fletcher Bittner, PhD, Linman O. Bjerken, Lars L. Bjorkman, MD, Paul A. Blacharski, Melvin L. Black, Charles M. Blair, PhD, Francis Louis Blanc, Dean M. Blanchard, Leroy E. Blanchard, Donald W. Blancher, Michael S. Blankinship Jr., Joseph S. Blanton, Dean A. Blatchford, Karl T. Blaufuss, John Blethen, PhD, Zegmund O. Bleviss, PhD, Warren M. Bliss, Max R. Blodgett, C. James Blom, PhD, Christian James Blom, PhD, Leonard C. Blomquist, David L. Blomquist, John Bloom, PhD, G. Bluzas, Warren P. Boardman, Carl Bobkoski, Gene Bock, Keith R. Bock, Richard M. Bockhorst, Gene E. Bockmier, William E. Boettger, Dale V. Bohnenberger, Eugene Bollay, Ellen D. Bolotin, PhD, Donald H. Boltz, Charles

M. Bolus, MD, Joseph C. Bonadiman, PhD, Stephen Alan Book, PhD, E. S. Boorneson, Iris Borg, PhD, W. K. Borgsmiller, MD, Manfred D. Borks, PhD, William R. Bornhorst, Gerald F. Borrmann, Anthony G. Borschneck, Robert B. Bosler Jr., Harold O. Boss, Keith A. Bostian, PhD, Danil Botoshankasky, Gerald W. Bottrell, Michel Boudart, PhD, Robert L. Boulware, Robert H. Bourke, PhD, Kenneth P. Bourke, Douglas A. Bourne, Paul K. Bouz, MD, George I. Bovadiieff, Peter F. Bowen, Warren H. Bower, David Bower, John Bowers, William M. Bowers, Doug R. Bowles, Jan Bowman, C. Stuart Bowyer, PhD, Wilson E. Boyce, Willis Boyd Sr., Delbert D. Boyer, Ralph L. Boyes, William F. Bozich, PhD, Jerry A. Bradshaw, Derek Bradstreet, F. P. Brady, PhD, Matthew E. Brady, William B. Brady, Walton K. Brainerd, MD, J. C. Brakensiek, John W. Bramhall, Francis A. Brandt, Albert Wade Brant, PhD, Wesley J. Braun, Thomas E. Braun, Ben G. Bray, PhD, Warren D. Brayton, James C. Breeding, James D. Brehove, Robert L. Breidenbaugh, Ted Breitmayer, C. H. Breittenfelder, A. C. Breller, Walter B. Brewer, Theodore C. Brice, Alan G. Bridge, PhD, Stephen G. Bridge, Robert M. Bridges, James E. Briggs, PhD, Robert Briggs, Allan Briney, MD, Donald F. Brink, PhD, Tyler Brinker, Francis Everett Broadbent, PhD, Sue Broadston, Ivor Brodie, PhD, Woody Brofman, PhD, Ronald J. Bromenschenk, Charles E. Bronson, Lionel H. Brooks, PhD, Ronald D. Brost, Robert John Brotherton, PhD, Kenneth Taylor Brown, PhD, James R. Brown, PhD, Linton A. Brown, Howard J. Brown, Hal W. Brown, Raymond E. Brown, D. Brownell, Don Brownfield, Peter Brubaker, Gene Bruce, David Bruce, MD, Carl Bruice, Steve Brunle, Harvey F. Brush, Donald L. Brust, DVM, A. Bryan, Glenn H. Bryner, Michael J. Buchan, MD, Steven M. Buchanan, John H. Buchholz, PhD, Smil Buchman, Carl J. Buczek, PhD, Donald R. Buechel, MD, Ronald M. Buehler, Fred W. Bueker, Walter R. Buerger, MD, Mary M. Buerger, Robert R. Buettell, Oscar T. Buffalow, Sterling Lowe Bugg, Robert J. Bugiada, Victor Buhrke, PhD, William Murray Bullis, PhD, Ronald Elvin Bullock, Eric Buonassisi, Jacob Burckhard, Harvey Worth Burden, PhD, Herbert S. Burden Jr., Willard Burge, Milton N. Burgess, James E. Burke, PhD, Richard Lerda Burke, PhD, Billy F. Burke, Walter L. Burke, Gary Burke, Lawrence H. Burks, James R. Burnett, PhD, J. R. Burnett, PhD, Thomas K. Burnham, MD, Victor W. Burns, PhD, Leslie L. Burns, PhD, Roger L. Burtner, PhD, Kittridge R. Burton, Douglas D. Busch, Francis R. Busch, Rick Buschini, Edwin F. Bushman, Mark M. Butier, David V. Butler, Thomas Austin Butterworth, PhD, Sidney Eugene Buttrill, PhD, Gary S. Buxton, Richard G. Byrd, MD, Algyte R. Cabak, Patricia R. Cabral, Trish Cabral, William P. Cade, Ben Cagle, William M. Cahill, MD, David Stephen Cahn, PhD, Delver R. Cain, MD, Larry Caisuin, Richard E. Cale, Fred L. Calkins, Gary N. Callihan, Chris Calvert, PhD, Henry W. Campbell, Malcolm D. Campbell, Nick Campion, Marsha A. Canales, George D. Candella, Robert E. Caniglia, Thomas F. Canning, Peter Cannon, PhD, Arlen E. Cannon, Garry W. Cannon, Harvey L. Canter, Ronald J. Cantoni, Manfred Cantow, PhD, Charles A. Capp Spindt, PhD, Albert J. Cardosa, William Thomas Cardwell, Audrey M. Carlan, George A. Carlson, PhD, Carl E. Carlson, C. E. Carlson, Lloyd G. Carnahan, PhD, Lester E. Carr Iii, PhD, Richard Carr, Edward Mark Carr, Jeffery L. Carroll, Gilbert C. Carroll, Walter R. Carrothers, Mary E. Carsten, PhD, David Carta, PhD, Willie J. Carter, PhD, Jim Carter, John G. Carver, PhD, Tony K. Casagranda, Ronald F. Cass, George Cassady, MD, Anthony A. Cassens, MD, Valen E. Castellano, James B. Castles, Jim A. Castles, Kenneth B. Castleton Jr., Henry P. Cate Jr., Russel K. Catterlin, W. L. Caudry, Thomas Kirk Caughey, PhD, Jerry Caulder, PhD, James E. Cavallin, James A. Cavanah, Chuck J. Cavanaugh, Neal C. Caya, Lee B. Cecil, Carl N. Cederstrand, PhD, Thomas U. Chace, Rowand R. Chaffee, PhD, Pamela Chaffee, Dilworth Woolley Chamberlain, PhD, Carlton Chamberlain, John S. Chambers, MD, Oliver V. Chamness, Scott O. Chamness, Sunney L. Chan, PhD, Sham-Yuen Chan, PhD, Arthur D. Chan, Steven Chandler, MD, Berken Chang, PhD, Freddy Wilfred L. Chang, PhD, Charles S. Chang, Nicholas D. Change, Mien T. Chao, George Frederick Chapline Jr., PhD, Ross T. Charest, Bruce R. Charlton, Frank D. Charron, E. Cheatham, Boris A. Chechelnitsky, Kun Hua Chen, PhD, Donald Chen, Robin S. Chen, Alwin C. Chen, Ming K. Chen, MD, Fred Y. Chen, Wade Cheng, PhD, Dallas L. Childress, George V. Chilingar, PhD, Hong Chin, PhD, Jerry L. Chodera, Shary Chotai, Tai-Low Chow, PhD, Emmet H. Christensen, Howard L. Christensen, Kent T. Christensen, John D. Christensen, Steven L. Christenson, MD, George B. Christianson, Kent B. Christianson, Allison L. Christopher, Donald O. Christy, PhD, John E. Chrysler, Daryl Chrzan, PhD, Andy C. Chu, Constantino Chua, Craig P. Chupek, Steven Ralph Church, PhD, Stanford Church, Paul Ciotti, Joseph A. Cipolla, Fernando F. Cisneros, Lawrence P. Clapham, Javier F. Claramunt, Charles R. Clark, PhD, Sharron A. Clark, Richard W. Clark, John Francis Clauser, PhD, Gordon Claycomb, Robert R. Claypool, Bruce Clegg, Carmine Domenic Clemente, PhD, Arnie L. Cliffgard, Amie L. Cliffgard, Watson S. Clifford, H. B. Clingempeel, Mansfield Clinnick, Thomas L. Cloer Jr., Joseph F. Cloidt, Ronald E. Clundt, Harold E. Clyde, Paul Jerry Coder, Allen C. Codiroli, C. Robert Coffey, Karl Paley Cohen, PhD, Norman S. Cohen, Sam Cohen, Harry Cohnger, Anthony W. Colacchia, Stefan Colban, Kenneth R. Cole, Robert G. Coleman, PhD, Miles L. Coleman, Joseph D. Coletta, Donald Colgan, John H. Collier, Thomas F. Collier, Dennis R. Collins, PhD, Irene B. Collins, DVM, Carlos Adolfo Colmenares, PhD, William B. Colson, PhD, Andre Coltrin, Robert Neil Colwell, PhD, William Tracy Colwell, PhD, Brian Comaskey, PhD, David R. Comish, MD, Jacob C. Compton, Wayne M. Compton, Wayme M. Compton, Stephen A. Confort, PhD, Harry M. Conger, John T. Conlan, Stephen W. Conn, Robert H. Conner, MD, Claud C. Conners, Mahlon C. Connett, MD, Victoria O. Conway, Patrick J. Conway, Bob A. Conway, Thomas B. Cook Jr., PhD, Frank R. Cook, PhD, Karl Cook, Charles C. Cook, James Barry Cooke, James W. Cooksley, Thomas Cooper, PhD, Robert C. Cooper, PhD, Ginette J.

Cooper, Clarence G. Cooper, MD, Martin Cooper, John D. Copley, Stephen F. Corcoran, Bruce M. Cordell, PhD, Chris D. Core, John A. Corella, John L. Corl, Joe D. Corless, MD, Roy S. Cornwell, PhD, Nicholas J. Corolis, Wayne T. Corso, Humberto S. Corzo, George J. Cosmides, PhD, Antonio Costa, Harry Cotrill, James R. Coughlin, Danny R. Counihan, George D. Couris, MD, Arnold Court, PhD, Robert E. Covey, William G. Cowdin, Daniel L. Cox, Carrol B. Cox, Kenneth R. Coyne, Daniel J. Cragin, Kenneth B. Craib, James E. Craig, PhD, Richard F. Craig, Donald James Cram, PhD, Eugene N. Cramer, Walter E. Crandall, PhD, Leroy L. Crandall, Chris L. Craney, PhD, Greg T. Cranham, John D. Craven, MD, Thomas V. Cravy, Myron N. Crawford, Dean Crawford, Dale Creasey, C. Raymond Cress, PhD, Tom Creswell, James Creswell, Phillip O. Crews, PhD, Robert W. Cribbs, Dennis M. Crinnion, Richard G. Crippen, Alipio B. Criste, Luanne S. Crockett, James H. Cronander, James G. Crose, PhD, Ajmes G. Crose, Kevin P. Cross, Deane L. Crow, MD, Herbert E. Crowhurst, Frank R. Crua, Richard Cruce, Duane Crum, PhD, Professor Cubre, William K. Culbreth, Donald M. Culler, Floyd Leroy Culler, Peter A. Culley, Murl F. Culp, David Cummings, PhD*, John Cummings, Richard A. Cundiff, A. Cunningham, Edwin L. Currier, Walter E. Curtis, Detlef K. Curtis, Damon R. Curtis, Kenneth H. Cusick, Donald F. Cuskelly, John M. Cuthbert, Leonard Samuel Cutler, PhD, Robert C. Cutone, Allen F. Dageforde, Himatlal B. Dagli, Daniel P. Dague, Gregory A. Dahlen, MD, Dennis J. Daleiden, Richard Daley, PhD, Lloyd R. Dalton, Robert L. Daly, Philip G. Damask, Hubert A. Dame, Marvin V. Damm, PhD, William E. Daniel, Warren Daniels, Raisfeld I. Danse, Moh Daoud, Henry T. Darlington, Gary L. Darnsteadt, Renato O. Dato, Clarence Theodore Daub, PhD, Phillip D. Dauben, Arthur A. Daush, Lynn Blair Davidson, PhD, William Davies, Bruce W. Davis, PhD, Larry Alan Davis, PhD, H. Turia Davis, Lawrence W. Davis, MD, James P. Davis, Harriette Davis, W. Kenneth Davis*, Don F. Dawson, Paul J. de Fries, Angelo De Min, H. A. De Mirjian, David A. G. Deacon, PhD, John M. Deacon, Willett C. Deady, Douglas L. Dean, Donald Deardorff, PhD, Gerald A. Debeau, Daniel B. Debra, PhD, Ronald J. Debruin, Robert Joseph Debs, PhD, Paul R. Decker, Curtis Kenneth Deckert, Kent Dedrick, PhD, Paul J. Defries, Edward B. Delano, J. M. Delano Jr., Cheryl K. Dell, PhD, Marc Dell'Erba, Charles C. DeMaria, Harold D. Demirjian, Howard D. Denbo, MD, Warren W. Denner, PhD, William J. Denney, Ronald W. Dennison, Wesley M. Densmore, Andrew Denysiak, PhD, Ralph T. Depalma, MD, Joseph George Depp, PhD, Ronny H. Derammelaere, Robert K. Deremer, PhD, Todd C. Derenne, Charles L. Des Brisay, Riccardo DeSalvo, PhD, Don Desborough, Brian J. Deschaine, Harold Desilets, Christopher R. Desley, MD, Alvin M Arden Despain, PhD, Steven A. DeStefano, MD, Robert E. Detrich, MD, Donald P. Detrick, James Edson Devay, PhD, Howard P. Devol, Robert V. Devore, PhD, Edmond M. Devroey, PhD, Thomas Gerry Dewees, Parivash P. Dezham, Marian C. Diamond, PhD, Arthur S. Diamond, Francis P. Diani, James D. Dibdin, MD, Wade Dickinson, Otto W. Dieffenbach, Rodney L. Diehl, Eugene L. Diepholz, Joseph Brun Digiorgio, Russell A. Dilley, Ben E. Dillon, DVM, John W. Dini, Judy Dirbas, David G. Dirckx, Ray Dirling Jr., Kenneth J. Discenza, Byron F. Disselhorst, Kent Diveley, MD, Steven J. Dodds, PhD, Richard A. Dodge, PhD, Marvin Dodge, PhD, Ernest E. Dohner, Roy Hiroshi Doi, PhD, Geoffrey Emerson Dolbear, PhD, Renan G. Dominguez, Chuck Donaldson, Igor Don-Doncon, T. Donnelly, PhD, Kerry L. Donovan, PhD, Robert F. Doolittle, PhD, Timothy B. D'Orazio, PhD, David C. Doreo, Kelly A. Doria, Lowell C. Dorius, DVM, Bernhardt L. Dorman, PhD, Ronald J. Dorovi, Weldon B. Dorris, William R. Dotson, Richard L. Double, Steven G. Doulames, Hanania Dover, Douglas B. Dow, Steven Dow, Charles P. Downer, Henry R. Downey, Alexandria Dragan, PhD, Titus H. Drake, Daniel D. Drobnis, Richard A. Drossler, Edward A. Drury, Stanley A. Drury, Richard S. Dryden, C. F. Duane, C. Ducoing, Richard D. Dudley, Margaret Dudziak, William T. Duffy, PhD, Paul N. Duggan, Peter Paul Dukes, PhD, William J. Dulude, Arnold N. Dunham, John G. Dunlap, James R. Dunn, Leo P. Dunne, John Ray Dunning, PhD, Thomas G. Dunning, Robin K. Durkee, Gordon B. Durnbaugh, Mark R. Dusbabek, Sophie A. Dutch, John A. Dutton, James G. Duvall III, PhD, A. J. Duvall, James R. Duvall, Jack Dvorkin, PhD, Paul Dwyer, Denzel Leroy Dyer, PhD, George O. Dyer, J. T. Eagen, Donald G. Eagling, Francis J. Eason, MD, Eric G. Easterling, A. T. Easton, Kenneth K. Ebel, Richard Eck, Paul R. Edris, Dennis Dean Edwall, J. Gordon Edwards, PhD, Eugene H. Edwards, PhD, David F. Edwards, PhD, Wilson R. Edwards, Robert L. Edwards, William R. Edwards, Charles Edwards, Maurice R. Egan, PhD, John P. Ehlen, Kenneth Warren Ehlers, PhD, Walter Eich, Robert E. Eichblatt, Robert Leslie Eichelberger, PhD, Herbert H. Eichhorn, PhD, Donald I. Eidemiller, PhD, D. I. Eidemiller, PhD, David Eitman, Guindy Mahmoud Ismail El, PhD, Dennis Eland, Wm C. Elhoff, Cindy Eliahu, PhD, Uri Eliahu, Shalom K. Eliahu, Kendrick R. Eliar, PhD, Thomas G. Elias, MD, James Elkins, Bert V. Elkins, William J. Ellenberger, Jules K. Ellingboe, M. Edmund Ellion, PhD, Robert D. Elliott, Jim E. Ellison, Hugh Ellsaesser, PhD, Ismat E. El-Souki, MD, G. W. Elvernum, Frank E. Emery, PhD, Cedric B. Emery, MD, Norman Harry Enenstein, PhD, Rodger K. Engebrethson, Franz Engelmann, PhD, Douglas M. Engh, MD, Wrms Engineering, Harold M. Engle, Grant A. Engstrom, James E. Enstrom, PhD, Bruce Enyeart, Professor Enyeart, Dennis A. Erdman, Wallace J. Erichsen, Alfred A. Erickson, MD, Myriam R. Eriksson, Christine Erkkila, F. H. Ernst Jr., MD, Rodney L. Eson, George Esquer, John J. Etchart, DVM, Robert H. Eustis, PhD, Marjorie W. Evans, PhD, Charles Andrew Evans, PhD, George W. Evans, Charles R. Evans, Charles B. Evavns, Dale Everett, David S. Fafarman, Robert S. Fagerness, Jack J. Fahey, John C. Fair, PhD, Raymond M. Fairfield, Clay E. Falkner, Steven L. Fallon, Mark W. Fantozzi, Earl L. Farabaugh, Wells D. Fargo, Jim O. Farley, Clayton C. Farlow, Robert Farmer, Emory W. Farr, Gregory L. Farr, James P. Fast, Charles Raymond Faulders, PhD,

John R. Favorite, Raymond J. Fazzio, Juergen A. Fehr, John D. Feichtner, PhD, Eugene P. Feist, Betty B. Feldman, W. O. Felsman, David Clarke Fenimore, PhD, Paul Roderick Fenske, PhD, Donald Fenton, PhD, Robert B. Fenwick, PhD, Richard K. Fergin, PhD, David B. Ferguson, PhD, Kenneth Edmund Ferguson, PhD, Linn D. Ferguson, Richard L. Ferm, PhD, Louis R. Fermelia, John A. Feyk, William J. Fields, Dale H. Fietz, Donald L. Fife, William Gutierrez Figueroa, MD, Alexandra T. Filer, Mark Filowitz, PhD, Reinald Guy Finke, PhD, Frederick T. Finnigan, William Louis Firestone, PhD, Bryant C. Fischback, Dwayne F. Fischer, PhD, Raymond F. Fish, Kathleen Mary Flynn Fisher, PhD, Donald Fisher, Russell L. Fisher, MD, William M. Fishman, PhD, Lanny Fisk, PhD, Jeremy W. Fitch, Richard A. Fitch, Thomas P. Fitzmaurice, William J. Fitzpatrick, PhD, James L. Fitzpatrick, Richard H. Fixler, Loren W. Fizzard, Klaus Werner Flach, PhD, Robert F. Flagg, PhD, Horacio S. Fleischman, MD, Alison A. Fleming, PhD, Donald H. Flowers, Paul H. Floyd, Edward Gotthard Foehr, PhD, Eldon Leroy Foltz, MD, Robert Young Foos, DVM, Michael J. Foote, Samuel W. Fordyce, Paul L. Forester, Charles J. Forquer, Robert R. Forsberg, Robert John Foster, PhD, John A. Foster, Henry E. Fourcade, MD, Douglas J. Fouts, PhD, Elliott J. Fowkes, PhD, Brian D. Fox, Wade Hampton Foy, PhD, Donald W. Frames, Donald Frames, Dale M. Franchak, Clifford Frank, Maynard K. Franklin, Randy E. Frazier, Reese L. Freeland, Walter J. Freeman, MD, Matt J. Freeman, Reola L. Freeman, H. Friedemann, Serena M. Friedman, MD, Earl E. Fritcher, Herman F. Froeb, MD, David Fromson, PhD, Roger J. Froslie, Charles W. Frost, Charles M. Fruey, Si Frumkin, Wilton B. Fryer, George Fryzelka, Frederick A. Fuhrman, PhD, Robert Alexander Fuhrman, Ed D. Fuller, Willard P. Fuller Jr., Lawrence W. Funkhouser, Rene G. Fuog, David William Furnas, MD, Ron Gabel, John W. Gabelman, PhD, Jerry D. Gabriel, Michael T. Gabrik Jr., Richard A. Gaebel, John Gagliano, Lorenzo A. Gaglio, Gilbert O. Gaines, John R. Galat, Robert G. Galazin, Darrell L. Gallop, PhD, Yakob V. Galperin, PhD, Kurt Gamara, PhD, Harold D. Gambill, MD, Kurt E. Gamnra, PhD, Luis A. Ganaja, Perry S. Ganas, PhD, Shirish M. Gandhi, Clark W. Gant, Tony S. Gaoiran, Carl W. Garbe, Richard Hammerle Garber, PhD, Allen J. Garber, Alejandro Garcia, PhD, Wayne Scott Gardner, PhD, Walter Garey, PhD, Jack Garfinkel, Joseph F. Garibotti, PhD, Jay M. Garner, Thomas M. Garrett, PhD, William H. Garrison, Thomas D. Gartin, MD, Justine Spring Garvey, PhD, J. W. Gasch, Jerrie W. Gasch, Nicholas D. Gaspar, Robert W. Gassin, Robert H. Gassner, Barry Gassner, R. H. Gassner, Bob Gassner CNS, Gerald Otis Gates, PhD, Thomas C. Gates, MD, Frederick Gates, George L. Gates, Charles F. Gates, G. R. Gathers, PhD, Phillips L. Gausewitz, MD, Steven D. Gavazza, PhD, Richard L. Gay, PhD, Joseph Gaynor, PhD, Bill A. Gearhart, Colvin V. Gegg, PhD, Dennis Gehri, PhD, Paul Jerome Geiger, PhD, Paul J. Gelger, PhD, Mike Gemmell, Michael S. Genewick, Michael L. Gerber, Renee T. Gerry, Paul R. Gerst, Edward C. Gessert, Alex Gezzy, John W. Gibbs, Joseph P. Gibbs, Reed Gibby, PhD, A. Reed Gibby, PhD, Warren C. Gibson, PhD, Ronald C. Gibson, Dominick R. Giglini, Larry L. Gilbert, MD, Paul T. Gilbert, Lyman F. Gilbert Sr., Susan Gillen, Wm. R. Gillen, William N. Gillespie, Paul A. Gillespie, Benjamin A. Gillette, Bruce B. Gillies, Sherwyn R. Gilliland, Robert J. Gilliland, Mike Gilmore, Dale P. Gilson, Dezdemona M. Ginosian, William F. Girouard, PhD, Silvio A. Giusti, Dain S. Glad, Dan L. Glasgow, Jerome E. Glass, Stephen M. Glatt, Thomas Glaze, John P. Gleiter, John H. Glenn, Renee V. Glennan, John D. Glesmann, John B. Glode, Vladimir M. Glozman, PhD, Aric Gnesa, Robert W. Goddard, Susan Godwin, Robert O. Godwin, Ludwig Edward Godycki, PhD, Robert W. Goedjen, David Jonathan Goerz, James A. Goethel, MD, David J. Goggin, PhD, Alfred Goldberg, PhD, Brian J. Golden, DVM, Steven D. Goldfien, Alan Goldfien, Kenneth J. Goldkamp, Bruce Goldman, John Paul Goldsborough, PhD, Norman E. Goldstein, PhD, Vladimir Golovchinsky, PhD, Michel Gondouin, PhD, D. Gonle, MD, Esteban G. Gonzales, Alexander E. Gonzalez, Ronald Keith Goodman, Roy G. Goodman, Byron Goodrich, James D. Goodridge, James W. Goodspeed, Mikel P. Goodwin, James K. Goodwine Jr., PhD, Robert Gordon, PhD, Rex B. Gordon, Gary E. Gordon, DVM, William H. Gordon J, MD, Milton J. Gordon, Nelson G. Gordy, Donald B. Gorshing, Keith E. Gosling, R. W. Gosper Jr., Wilbur Hummon Goss, PhD, Quentin L. Goss, John Ray Goss, Martin S. Gottlieb, Robert George Gould, Robert D. Gourlay, Darrell Gourley, Arthur Goyne, MD, Lawrence I. Grable, Harald Grabowsky, Ben G. Grady, PhD, Richard W. Graeme, Leroy D. Graff, Kerry M. Gragg, Gary C. Graham, PhD, Dee McDonald Graham, PhD, Alex T. Granik, PhD, Jerry Grant, Walter L. Graves, Lauren H. Grayson, MD, Joseph M. Green, PhD, Leon Green Jr., PhD, Hue T. Green, Russell H. Green Jr., Charles R. Greene, PhD, Eugene Willis Greenfield, PhD, Charles August Greenhall, PhD, Edward C. Greenhood, John Edward Greenleaf, PhD, Jeffrey Greenspoon, MD, David Tony Gregorich, PhD, Thomas J. Gregory, Gennady H. Grek, Kurt G. Greske, David R. Gress, Travis Barton Griffin, PhD, Rogert D. Griffin, Donald N. Griffin, Roy S. Griffiths, PhD, Thomas J. Grifka, MD, Donald Wilburn Grimes, PhD, Leclair Roger Grimes, Charles Groff, Alan B. Gross, DVM, Morton Grosser, PhD, Eric Gruenler, Raymond H. Gruetert, Mike A. Grundvig, Michael Gruntman, PhD, Mike Gruntman, PhD, Ross R. Grunwald, PhD, Louis E. Grzesiek, Michael R. Guarino Sr., Richard Austin Gudmundsen, PhD, Jacques P. Guertin, PhD, Gareth E. Guest, PhD, John O. Guido, MD, Darryl E. Gunderson, Richard R. Gundry, Robert Charles Gunness, PhD, Riji R. Guo, Dwight F. Gustafson, Kermit M. Gustafson, Eugene V. Gustavson, Daniel A. Gutknecht, Steven L. Gutsche, Michael D. Gutterres, John V. Guy-Bray, PhD, Michael A. Guz, Geza Leslie Gyorey, PhD, Bjorn N. Haaberg, Glenn Alfred Hackwell, PhD, Brian L. Hadley, Charlie Haener, Arno K. Hagenlocher, PhD, Chuck R. Haggett, Hashem Haghani, Richard B. Hagle, DVM, Robert A. Hagn, Pierre Vahe Haig, MD, Samir N. Haji, PhD, Marlund E. Hale, PhD, Paul F. Halfpenny, Kenneth Lynn

Hall, PhD, Sylvia C. Hall, Robert J. Hall, Daniel P. Haller, Albert A. Halls, PhD, Herbert H. Halperin, Martin B. Halpern, PhD, Lee Edward Ham, Frank C. Hamann, Ronald O. Hamburger, Edward E. Hamel, PhD, Matt J. Hamilton, Bruce Dupree Hammock, PhD, Anthony James Hance, PhD, Taylor Hancock, Professor Hand, PhD, David A. Hand, John W. Hanes, Peter Hangarter, Dale L. Hankins, Gerald M. Hanley, Dean A. Hanquist, Allan G. Hanretta, MD, Peder M. Hansen, PhD, Robert Clinton Hansen, PhD, Warren K. Hansen, Ethlyn A. Hansen, L. J. Hansen, Rowland Curtis Hansford, Lloyd K. Hanson, James C. Hanson, Richard Hanson, John Warvelle Harbaugh, PhD, Ralph Harder, MD, John A. Hardgrove, Edgar Erwin Hardy, PhD, Vernon E. Hardy, Kenneth A. Harkewicz, PhD, Terry W. Harmon, PhD, Roger N. Harmon, John Harper, Kevin J. Harper, John Harper, John E. Harper, David Harriman, Bryan J. Harrington, S. P. Harris, PhD, Kent Harris, Rita D. Harris, Tyler Harris, MD, Robert O. Harris, John David Harrison, PhD, Robin Harrison, Burton Harrison, Marvin Eugene Harrison, Philip T. Harsha, PhD, James B. Hart, M. G. Hartman, Darrell W. Hartman, Maurice Hartman, Maurice G. Hartman, George L. Hartmann, William L. Hartrick, Meredith P. Harvan, Ted F. Harvey, PhD, Jack L. Harvey, Dieter F. Haschke, Darr Hashempour, PhD, Hashaliza M. Hashim, Jiri Haskovec, PhD, Robert D. Hass, MD, Steven J. Hassett, Ronald R. Hatch, George Hathaway, PhD, Alson E. Hatheway, Mark Hatzilambrou, John C. Haugen, Kenneth E. Haughton, PhD, Donald G. Hauser, John E. Hauser, MD, Arthur Herbert Hausman, Alfred H. Hausrath, PhD, Warrnen M. Haussler, Walter B. Havekorst, Anton J. Havlik, PhD, Michael D. Hawkins, Brice C. Hawley, Dale R. Hayden Sr., Bill J. Hayes, Robert M. Hayhurst, Carl H. Hayn, PhD, William E. Haynes, Beth Haynes, MD, Paul E. Hazelman, R. Nichols Hazelwood, PhD, Dean Head, Harold Franklin Heady, PhD, David L. Heald, PhD, Albert Heaney, PhD, Stephen D. Heath, George E. Heddy III, Solomon R. Hedges, Larry E. Hedrick, Lee Opert Heflinger, PhD, Frank C. Heggli, Bettina Heinz, PhD, Richard L. Heinze, William D. Heise, Ralph A. Heising, MD, William B. Heitzman, George W. Heller, Denise M. Helm, William F. Helmick, Carl N. Helmick Jr., John W. Helphrey, Raymond G. Hemann, F. R. Hemeon, John E. Hench, PhD, Kenneth P. Henderson, Curtis E. Hendrick, Joseph E. Henn, Carol E. Henneman, MD, Joseph Hennessey, Gary L. Hennings, Donald M. Henrikson, MD, R. R. Heppe, John A. Herb, PhD, Noel Martin Herbst, Bruce J. Herdrich, Don D. Herigstad, Ronald C. Herman, PhD, Elvin Eugene Herman, Robert W. Hermsen, PhD, Charles L. Hern, Brian K. Herndon, Leo J. Herrerra Jr., James L. Herrick, MD, David I. Herrington, Christian Herrmann Jr., MD, Roger R. Herrscher, John William Baker Hersey, PhD, Robert T. Herzog, PhD, Chris A. Hesse, Christian A. Hesse, David A. Hessinger, PhD, Norman E. Hester, PhD, Paul G. Hewitt, William B. Hight, Barry J. Hildebrand, Warren W. Hildebrandt, Mahlon M.S. Hile, PhD, Robert Hill, PhD, Alan T. Hill, John H. Hill, Larry Hill, David Hillaker, John R. Hilsabeck, MD, E. B. Hilton, Hubert L. Himes, Carl Hinners, Kenneth A. Hitt, Charles A. Hjerpe, DVM, L. C. Hobbs, Peter B. Hobsbawn, Robert A. Hochman, MD, Elizabeth M. Hodgkins, DVM, David Hodgkins, Paul T. Hodiak, William B. Hoeing, Robert S. Hoekstra, William B. Hoenig Jr., Robert G. Hoey, Phil Hoff, PhD, C. Hoff, Marvin Hoffman, PhD, Howard Torrens Hoffman, PhD, Jeffrey E. Hofmann, Roger C. Hofstad, Clarence Lester Hogan, PhD, Roy W. Hogue, Doug Hoiles, Arnold H. Hoines, Franklin K. Holbrook, David Holcberg, Joy R. Holdeman, George R. Holden, Richard Holden, Robert E. Holder, C. H. Holladay Jr., Dennis R. Hollars, PhD, Charles L. Hollenbeck, Delbert C. Hollinger, Brent E. Hollingworth, David F. Holman, William H. Holmes, W. H. Holmes, Wendell Holmes, Harold T. Holtom Jr., Vincent H. Homer Jr., Andrew L. Hon, Richard Churchill Honey, PhD, John D. Honeycutt, PhD, Aaron Hong, PhD, James F. Hood Jr., Ronald M. Hopkins, PhD, Gary H. Hoppe, Donald F. Hopps, Thomas G. Horgan, Lee W. Horn, John R. Horn, MD, Erwin William Hornung, PhD, Fred L. Hotes, David L. Houghton, Leland Richmond House, MD, Loren J. Hov, Max M. Hovaten, Conrad Howan, Walter Egner Howard, PhD, S. Dale Howard, George O. Howard, Stanley G. Howard, John P. Howe, PhD, George F. Howe, PhD, Ward W. Howland, Eric S. Hoy, PhD, C. Hoyt, Chien H. Hsiao, PhD, Hani F. Hskander, J. Hsu, PhD, Robert Y. Hsu, PhD, James P. Hsu, Cynthia Hsu, Henry H. Hsu, Limin Hsueh, PhD, Kuang J. Huang, PhD, Harmon William Hubbard, PhD, Jason P. Hubbard, Wheeler L. Hubbell, MD, Cyril E. Huber, David Huchital, PhD, Stephen A. Hudson, David E. Hueseman, Hermann F. Huettemeyer, Jim D. Huff, Thomas J. Huggett, Reginald C. Huggins, Robert A. Huggins, Michael D. Hugh, Roxanne C. Hughes, Larry C. Hughes, Melville P. Hughes, Paul Hull, Charles R. Hulquist, MD, John L. Hult, PhD, Joseph W. Hultberg, Eric A. Hulteen, William E. Humphrey, PhD, Brian Humphrey, John Humphrey, Steven J. Hunn, John P. Hunt, PhD, George C. Hunt, William J. Hunter, James R. Hurd, Edward T. Hurley, Randy Hurst, Michael C. Husinko, Glen E. Huskey, PhD, Andrew Huszczuk, PhD, Lee Hutchins, E. S. Hutchison, Eric R. Hyatt, PhD, Alan W. Hyatt, PhD, Ralph Hylinski, MD, Umberto C. Iacuaniello, Samuel J. Iarg, Gerald B. Iba, MD, Harold B. Igdaloff, Kenneth T. Ingham, Rodney H. Ingraham, PhD, Donald J. Inman, William Beveridge Innes, PhD, Kaoru Inouye, Dodge Irwin, Donald G. Iselin, Don L. Isenberg, PhD, Robert Isensee, PhD, Byron M. Ishkanian, George Ismael, Farouk T. Ismail, PhD, Guindy Mahmoud Ismail El, PhD, Larry Israel, Olga Ivanilova, PhD, Lindsay C. Ives, King H. Ives, Judy Jacklich, Claude A. Jackman, Dale S. Jacknow, Harold Jackson, PhD, Warren B. Jackson, PhD, Robert A. Jackson, DVM, Kingbury Jackson, Bruce Jackson, Bruce Jackson, Sharon Jacobs, John E. Jacobsen, Albert H. Jacobson Jr., PhD, Fred J. Jacobson, Leslie J. Jacobson, Michael E. Jacobson, Kenneth D. Jacoby, Syed I. Jafri, H. S. James, Everett Williams Jameson Jr., PhD, Robert W. Jamplis, MD, Kenneth S. Jancaitis, PhD, Clarence W. Janes, Larry Jang, PhD, Norman C. Janke, PhD, John C. Jaquess, Robert Jastrow,

PhD*, George W. Jeffs, Sean Jenkins, Jack D. Jenkins, David E. Jenkins, Richard G. Jenness, Edwin B. Jennings, David Jennings, Pete D. Jennings, Frederick A. Jennings, Gerard M. Jensen, PhD, Paul E. Jensen, Denzel Jenson, PhD, Norman E. Jentz, Herbert C. Jessen, James W. Jeter Jr., PhD, Nicolai A. Jigalin, Robert M. Jirgal, Zoenek Vaclav Jizba, PhD, Niles W. Johanson, Craig A. Johanson, MD, Karl Richardq Johansson, PhD, Erik Johnson, PhD, Bryce W. Johnson, PhD, H. A. Johnson, PhD, William R. Johnson, PhD, Duane Johnson, PhD, Gerald W. Johnson, PhD, Horace Richard Johnson, PhD, G. E. Johnson, Bertram G. Johnson, Steven M. Johnson, MD, Theodore R. Johnson, P. Johnson, William P. Johnson, Walter F. Johnson, Mark A. Johnson, Raymond E. Johnson, Jim Johnson, Richard R. Johnson, George M. Johnston, Viliam Jonec, PhD, Rajinder S. Joneja, Taylor B. Jones, PhD, Claris Eugene Jones Jr., PhD, Merrill Jones, PhD, Egerton G. Jones, Robert E. Jones, Kyle B. Jones, Edgar J. Jones, Paul D. Jones, Alan B. Jones, Christopher H. Jones, Pete Jonghbloed, Peter E. Jonker, Charles Jordan, PhD, L. Jordan, Peter D. Joseph, PhD, Lyman C. Josephs III, Richard L. Joslin, Ronald F. Joyce, Macario G. Juanola, Robert H. Julian, Bruce B. Junor, Charles E. Kaempen, PhD, Robert W. Kafka, PhD, Richard L. Kahler, Richard Lee. Kahler, MD, Calvin D. Kalbach, David Kalil, Loren D. Kaller, PhD, Lisa V. Kalman, PhD, Martin D. Kamen, PhD*, Andrew J. Kampe, Sarath C. Kanekal, PhD, Thomas Motomi Kaneko, PhD, Ho H. Kang, PhD, Thomas A. Kanneman, PhD, Paul Thomas Kantz, PhD, Mark S. Kapelke, Alvin A. Kaplan, Hillel R. Kaplan, Eugene J. Karandy, MD, Sid Karin, PhD, Arthur Karp, PhD, Victor N. Karpenko, Ronald A. Kasberger, Harold Victor Kaska, Daniel E. Kass, Carl J. Kassabian, Jack T. Kassel, William S. Kather, Stanley L. Katten, Fred E. Kattuah, George Bernard Kauffman, PhD, Thomas Kauffman, Alvin Beryl Kaufman, Robert Eugene Kay, PhD, David W. Kay, PhD, Andrew J. Kay, Myron Kayton, PhD, Richard H. Keagy, DVM, John R. Keber, Patrick A. Keddington, James Richard Keddy, Ross C. Keeling Jr., Walter F. Kelber, William T. Kellermann Sr., Charles Thomas Kelley, PhD, Kevin D. Kelley, Dennis Kelley, Profressor Kelly, Leroy J. Kemp, Robert E. Kendall, Martin William Kendig, PhD, Peter H. Kendrick, Tom A. Kenfield, Michael T. Kennedy, MD, John M. Kennel, PhD, Brian M. Kennelly, PhD, Stephen W. Kent, Clifford Eugene Kent, Kathleen M. Kenyon, DVM, Josef Kercso, Clifford Dalton Kern, PhD, Quentin A. Kerns, Anna M. Kerrins, Andrew C. Ketchum, Jesse F. Keville, Tejbir S. Khanna, Simon A. Kheir, MD, Kathleen Kido-Savino, Karl E. Kienow, David C. Kilborn, Kent B. Killian, DVM, Jerry Killingstad, Lawrence K. Kim, MD, David E. Kim, MD, D. Kimball, Amon Kimeldorf, William C. Kimpel, MD, Hartley Hugh King, PhD, Joseph E. King, William S. King, Chester L. King, William L. Kingston, James W. Kinker, John J. R. Kinney, Gerald Lee Kinnison, PhD, John Kinzell, PhD, E. K. Kirchner, PhD, Tom P. Kirk, Carl S. Kirkconnell, PhD, Richard D. Kirkham, Harry H. Kishineff, Ernest Kiss, Terence M. Kite, PhD, Michael T. Kizer, Lorentz A. Kjoss, Nicholas Paul Klaas, PhD, Eugene G. Klein, Thomas Klein, Aurel Kleinerman, Robert E. Klenck, Walter Mark Kliewer, PhD, Steve J. Klimowski, Sidney Kline, Thomas J. Kling, Gilbert E. Klingman, Edwin E. Klingman, Edwin E. Klingman, William Klint, Fred L. Kloepper, Edwin E. Klugman, PhD, Richard M. Klussman, MD, James W. Knapp, MD, Penelope K. Knapp, MD, Richard Hubert Knipe, PhD, Larry P. Knowles, Charles R. Knowles, Devin Knowles, Floyd Marion Knowlton, Stephen A. Kobayashi, MD, Robert D. Kochsiek, Bertram S. Koel, MD, Hans Koellner, Gina L. Koenig, Robert Cy Koh, PhD, Joe B. Kohen, MD, George O. Kohler, PhD, R. J. Kolodziej, Kazimierz Kolwalski, PhD, Fred W. Koning, DVM, B. E. Kopaski, Rudolph William Kopf, Richard E. Koppe, John Kordosh, N. Korens, Harrison J. Kornfield, MD, John L. Kortenhoeven, Bart Kosko, PhD, Charles C. Kosky, Mark J. Koslicki, Edward Garrison Kost, PhD, Allen T. Koster, Nagy Hanna Kovacs, PhD, Sankar N. Koyal, PhD, Mitchell M. Kozinski, William R. Krafft, P. Krag, PhD, Peter W. Krag, PhD, Jerry Kraim, Keith Krake, Roman J. Kramarsic, PhD, Norbert E. Kramer, PhD, Gordon Kramer, William H. Krebs, William J. Kreiss, PhD, Ruth E. Kreiss, MD, Richard Kremer, PhD, William B. Krenz, Joseph Z. Krezandski, PhD, E. Kriva, John Led Kropp, PhD, Steven T. Krueger, Loren L. Krueger, Gai Krupenkin, E. C. Krupp, PhD, Harvey A. Krygier, MD, Mitsuru Kubota, PhD, Alexander Kucher, Frank I. Kuklinski, Eugene M. Kulesza, Kenneth W. Kummerfeld, Joseph Kunc, PhD, Guy Kuncir, Willard D. Kunz, Gary Kupp, Peter Kurtz, PhD, Paul Kutler, PhD, Leon J. Kutner, PhD, Timothy La Farge, PhD, James La Fleur, Mitchell J. LaBuda, PhD, Leonard L. Lacaze, Kurt D. Ladendorf, Franklin Laemmlen, PhD, Eugene C. Laford, PhD, Bruce Lagasse, Thomas W. LaGrelius, Milton Laikin, Cleve Watrous Laird, PhD, John W. Lake, Ron R. Lambert, Edward W. Lambing Jr., Robert A. Lame, H. D. Landahl, PhD, Richard Leon Lander, PhD, William K. Lander, William Charles Landgraf, PhD, Frank L. Landon, Charles S. Landram, PhD, William G. Landry, Archie Landry, F. Lane, Darrell W. Lang, MD, Gregory A. Langan, Thomas H. Lange, PhD, Rolf H. Langland, PhD, Philip G. Langley, PhD, Ward J. Lantier, George R. LaPerle, Gary G. Lapid, MD, Kurt A. Larcher, Lisa W. Larios, Norbert D. Larky, David F. Larochelle, MD, Bruce E. Larock, PhD, Henry Larrucea, David L. Larsen, William E. Larsen, Russell C. Larson, Harry T. Larson, Roderick M. Lashelle, DVM, Bill Lee Lasley, PhD, Jason Lau, James Bishop Laudenslager, PhD, James W. Laughlin, Garry E. Laughlin, James H. Laughon, Jim Lauria, Archibald M. Laurie, A. M. Laurie, Arbhiadl M. Laurie, Michael J. Lavallee, Thomas E. Lavenda, Charles E. Law, MD, Bill Lawler, D. John L Lawless Jr., PhD, John John Lawless Jr., PhD, William H. Lawrence, Edward B. Lawson, Bill R. Lawver, Charles E. Layne, Thomas W. Layton, PhD, Grant H. Layton, Gerry V. Lazzareschi, MD, William F. Leahy, PhD, Julie Leahy, David F. Leake, William D. Leake, James B. Lear, Joseph P. Leaser, MD, Paul Matthew Leavy, Joseph E. Ledbetter, PhD, Robert S. Ledendecker, Min L. Lee, PhD, Bum S. Lee, PhD, Long Chi Lee, PhD, Kai Y. Lee, Bryan D. Lee,

Philip R. Lee, Keun W. Lee, Carl B. Leedy, Marjorie B. Leerabhandh, PhD, Robert H. Leerhoff, Franklin E. Lees, Harry A. Leffingwell, Victor E. Leftwich, William C. Lehman, MD, Walter Lehman, James N. Lehmann, Robert F. Lehnen, Edward T. Leidigh, Algrid G. Leiga, PhD, Jerry S. Leininger, Robert B. Leinster, George W. Leisz, Ronald J. Lejman, Dan LeMay, Vernon L. Leming, Eric Lemke, Don H. Lenker, John Lenora, PhD, Billy K. Lenser, MD, Robert C. Lentzner, MD, Richard D. Leonard, Peter C. LePort, MD, Robert L. Lessley, James L. Lessman, Robert W. Lester, Max M. Lester Jr., Thuston C. LeVay, Lamberto A. Leveriza, Walter Frederick Leverton, PhD, Robert Ernest Le Levier, PhD, Howard Bernard Levine, PhD, Roger E. Levoy, DVM, J. V. Levy, PhD, Hal Lewis, PhD, William P. Lewis, PhD, Shing T. Li, PhD, Huilin Li, PhD, Thomas T. Liao, Frank Licha, Donald K. Lidster, MD, Kap Lieu, Michael L. Lightstone, PhD, Wayne P. Lill Jr., Ray O. Linaweaver, Wilton Howard Lind, Kim R. Lindbery, Robert O. Lindblom, PhD, Charles Alexander Lindley, PhD, Robert R. Lindner, Peter F. Lindquist, PhD, Laurence Lindsay, Robert Lindstrom, Leo C. Linesch, John J. Linker, Paul H. Linstrom, Darrell Linthacum, PhD, Jerome L. Lipin, MD, Arthur L. Lippman, MD, Arthur C. Litheredge, W. M. Liu, PhD, Josep G. Llaurado, MD, Verl B. Lobb, Fred P. Lobban, Timothy A. Lockwood, PhD, Lewis S. Lohr, Donald O. Lohr, Gabriel G. Lombardi, PhD, Robert Ahlberg Loney, PhD, James D. Long, Neville S. Long, Howard F. Long, Paul Alan Longwell, PhD, Clay A. Loomis, Hendricus G. Loos, PhD, David A. Lorenzen, Robert S. Lorusso, Brad M. Losey, Frank H. Lott, Stuart Loucks, Michael E. Lovejoy, C. James Lovelace, PhD, Judith K. Lowe, MD, Alvin Lowi Jr., PhD, Maurice H. Lowrey, John Kuew Hsiung Lu, PhD, Paul S. Lu, Michael D. Lubin, PhD, Anthony G. Lubowe, PhD, Raymond K. Luci, Samuel R. Lucia, Denise G. Luckhurst, H. Ludwig, Raymond J. Lukens, PhD, William Watt Lumsden, PhD, Walter F. Lundin, Jorgen V. Lunding, Theodore R. Lundquist, PhD, Pamela G. Lung, Owen Raynal Lunt, PhD, Harold Richard Luxenberg, PhD, Warren M. Lydecker, Dennis Lynch, Kevin G. Lyons, Robert S. Lyss, MD, Robert S. Mac Alister, Mike S. Macartney, Howard Maccabee, PhD, Alexander Daniel MacDonald, PhD, David V. MacDonald, John W. Mace, MD, Mario A. Machicao, John D. Mack, Donald S. Macko, PhD, John C. Maclay, Lee M. Maclean, Edward H. Macomber, Duane E. Maddux, A. Madison, Akhilesh Maewal, PhD, Frank Maga, Michael W. Magee, John L. Magee*, Hans F. Mager, Edward Thomas Maggio, PhD, Tom Alan Magness, PhD, Robert A. Maier, Walter P. Maiersperger, Douglas J. Malewicki, Michael A. Malgeri, Jim G. Malik, PhD, Calvin Malinka, William Robert Mallett, PhD, Joseph D. Malley, PhD, Albert J. Mallinckrodt, PhD, Kenneth Long Maloney, PhD, George E. Maloof, MD, Neil A. Malpiede, Enrico R. Manaay, Nikola A. Manchev, Isaak Mandelbaum, Nelson L. Mandley, Kent M. Mangold, Anna M. Manley, Nancy Robbins Mann, PhD, C. David Mann, George L. Mann, Scheana Mannes, Philip Mannes, Robert W. Mannon, PhD, William H. Mannon, James Mansdorfer, Greayer Mansfield-Jones, PhD, A. Marasco, George Raymond Marcellino, PhD, Michael Marchese, Stephen C. Marciniec, William C. Marconi, Carol Silber Marcus, PhD, A. J. Mardinly, PhD, Alan Mare, Elwin Marg, PhD, Brian Maridon, Mike J. Marienthal, Michael J. Marinak, William P. Markling, Jack Marling, PhD, Wilbur Joseph Marner, PhD, Patrick M. Maroney, David Marquis, PhD, Marilyn A. Marquis, PhD, Don Marquis, Vee L. Marron, Henry L. Marschall, Sullivan Samuel Marsden, PhD, David E. Marshburn, Lorenzo I. Marte, Richard G. Martella, Rodney J. Martin, Vurden T. Martin, Ralph F. Martin, Eric K. Martin, Lincoln A. Martin, R. Martin, Richard E. Martin, L. A. Martin, Emil L. Martin, Stanley Buel Martin, Ernest A. Martinelli, PhD, Fredrick W. Marx, MD, Joseph Maserjian, PhD, R. Kemp Massengil, MD, Paul S. Masser, PhD, Alberto G. Masso, PhD, Edgar A. Mastin, PhD, Herbert Franz Matare, PhD, Vincent A. Matera, MD, Charles R. Mathews, Eckart Mathias, Ronald F. Mathis, PhD, Harold C. Mathis, Gene L. Matranga, Kyoko Matsuda, PhD, Jacob P. Matthews 3d, Bill B. May, PhD, German R. Mayer, Edward H. Mayer, David F. Maynard, PhD, G. Mazis, Stephen Albert Mazza, Richard L. McArthy, David M. McCann, William J. McCarter, Edward W. McCauley, PhD, Jon McChesney, PhD, Chester McCloskey, PhD, William Owen McClure, PhD, David L. McClure, R. J. McClure, John M. McCluskey, MD, John V. McColligan, Billy Murray McCormac, PhD, Philip Thomas McCormick, PhD, Thomas E. McCown, Herbert I. McCoy, MD, Ray S. McCoy, Louis Ralph McCreight, Thomas G. McCreless, PhD, James B. McCrumb, Sandra L. McDougald, Edward R. McDowell, PhD, Barry R. McElmurry, William C. McFadden, William C. McFradden, Malcolm M. McGawn, William H. McGlasson, J. F. McGouldrick, Jack McGouldrick, Richard J. McGovern, John P. McGuire, Lawrence McHargue, PhD, Vernon J. McKale, Roger E. McKarus, Charles G. McKay, William Dean McKee, PhD, Joe A. McKenzie, Donald J. McKenzie, William K. McKim, Jerry McKnight, Stephen M. McKown, Steven McLean, Charles A. McLean, Debra McMahan, John D. McMahon, Lester R. McNall, PhD, Gregory R. McNeil, Michael J. McNutt, PhD, Daniel McPherson Jr., L. D. McQueen, PhD, Cyril M. McRae, Gerard J. McVicker, Homer N. Mead, Joseph Meade, Robert C. Meaders, Beverly Meador, Richard A. Meador, Herbert J. Meany, Susan L. Mearns, PhD, M. G. Mefferd, Merlin Meisner, Stanley Meizel, PhD, Gloria Melara, PhD, Robert Frederick Meldav, Rodney Melgard, Stanley C. Mellin, Alex S. Meloy, Marvin E. Melton, Bobby J. Melvin, Xian-Qin Meng, MD, Steven M. Menkus, William F. Menta, Alan C. Merchant, Leo Mercy, Paul M. Merifield, PhD, Vincent C. Merlin, Marshal F. Merriam, PhD, John Lafayette Merriam, George B. Merrick, Ronald E. Merrill, PhD, William R. Merrill, Seymour Merrin, PhD, Ross A. Merritt, Arthur L. Messinger, MD, Robert Meyearis, Rudolf X. Meyer, PhD, Marvin G. Meyer, Jewell L. Meyer, Matthew D. Meyer, Harold F. Meyer, Steven J. Meyerhofer, Richard E. Meyers, Charles J. Meyers Jr., Gerald James Miatech, PhD, E. Don Michael, Robert C. Michael, Lawrence A. Michel, Lloyd R. Michels, PhD, Michael A.

Michelson, Scott J. Mighell, Daniel F. Mika, Nagib T. Mikhael, PhD, Duane Soren Mikkelsen, PhD, Paul G. Mikolaj, PhD, Ralph Franley Miles, PhD, Gerald A. Miles, John B. Millard, PhD, Jose B. Millares, Cecil Miller, PhD, Sol Miller, PhD, Alan D. Miller, PhD, Allan Miller, PhD, James Avery Miller, PhD, Dick Miller, PhD, Kenneth J. Miller, H. L. Miller, Stanley Leo Miller, George Miller, Wilson N. Miller, C. Miller, Timothy Miller, John S. Miller, Robert L. Miller, Daryl D. Miller, Le Edward Millet, PhD, Charles E. Millett, Robert C. Mills, George P. Milton, Thomas Mincer, PhD, Robert E. Minear, Ronald L. Miner, Susie M. Ming, David R. Minor, MD, Tom L. Mintun, John M. Mintz, PhD, Srecko Mirko Mircetich, PhD, Harold Mirels, PhD, Arjang K. Miremadi, MD, Mohammad R. Mirseyedi, Theodore C. Mitchell, Arup P. Mitra, Edward Mittleman, MD, Harry F. Mixon, K. L. Moazed, PhD, Julie A. Mobley, Randy A. Moehnke, Allen A. Moff, John K. Moffitt, John George Mohler, MD, Daniel E. Mohn, Faramarz Mohtadi, MD, George E. Mohun, MD, Niculae T. Moisidis, PhD, Rogelio A. Molina, Albert James Moll, PhD, John L. Moll, PhD, Terrence V. Molloy, Robert E. Moncrieff, MD, Carl L. Monismith, Myles P. Monroe, Loren Monroe Jr., Ernesto M. Monteiro, Theodore Ashton Montgomery, MD, Henry L. Moody, Eugene R. Moore, PhD, Rodney R. Moore, Michael Morcos, Ned Morehouse, William B. Moreland, Richard Leo Moretti, PhD, Robert W. Morford, D. R. Morford, Dean R. Morford, Thomas Kenneth Morgan, PhD, Donald Earle Morgan, PhD, Lucian L. Morgan, Leon Frank Morgan, Victor G. Morgen, Michael Moroso, Philip J. Morrill, Paul E. Morris, MD, Jeffrey A. Morrish, Allen D. Morrison, Richard J. Morrissey, Dan Morrow, Frances Morse, George A. Morse, John Robert Morton, PhD, Paul K. Morton, Dennis B. Morton, Ray S. Morton, H. David Mosier, MD, Malcolm Mossman, Ronald J. Mosso, Gail F. Moulton Jr., Paul Mount II, Barbara Mroczkowski, PhD, Richard C. Much, Jerome Robert Mueller, William L. Mueller, Sig Muessig, PhD, Siegfried Joseph Muessig, PhD, Debasish Mukherjee, PhD, Butch Mulcahey, Fred R. Mulker, Kenneth I. Mullen, L. Frederic Muller, John F. Mulligan, Kary B. Mullis, PhD, Mark B. Mullonbach, T. Munasinge, PhD, David V. Mungcal, MD, Albert G. Munson, PhD, Emil M. Murad, Akira Murakami, Sean Murphy, PhD, Alexander James Murphy, PhD, Gary L. Murphy, Emmett J. Murphy, Frank Murray, PhD, Bruce Murray, Richard L. Murray, Willard G. Myers, PhD, Albert F. Myers, Dale D. Myers, Donald L. Mykkanen, PhD, Harry E. Nagle, Kenneth A. Nagy, PhD, Yervant M. Nahabedian, Yathi Naidu, PhD, Takuro S. Nakae, Glenn M. Nakaguchi, Dennis B. Nakamoto, M. Nance, A. Naselow, PhD, J. Greg Nash, PhD, Merlin Neff Jr., MD, Thomas C. Nehrbas, Richard Douglas Nelson, PhD, Victor Nelson, Lorin M. Nelson, Robert L. Nelson, Donald G. Nelson, Bruce H. Nesbit, Harold Neufeld, MD, Sylvia M. Neumann, DVM, Temple W. Neumann, Donald E. Neuschwander, Frank M. Nevarez, James Ryan Neville, PhD, J. Ryan Neville, PhD, Stanley D. Newell, Richard E. Newell, John M. Newey, Phil W. Newman, Bernard D. Newsom, PhD, H. Newsom, PhD, Kerwin Ng, Thuan V. Nguyen, PhD, Liz Niccum, Edward S. Nicholls, MD, Richard A. Nichols, PhD, Jack C. Nichols, MD, Mark E. Nichols, Richard E. Nicholson, MD, Mathew L. Nickels, MD, Marvin L. Nicola, MD, Albert H. Niden, MD, Tom F. Niedzialek, R. Nieffenegger, Kurt Nielsen, Gilbert O. Nielsen, Mark Niemiec, Rodulfo C. Niere, Joseph A. Nieroski, Edwawrd A. Nieto, Danta L. Nieva, James E. Nightingale, Jim B. Nile, Soottid Nimitsilpa, Donald A. Nirschl, Kazunori Nishioka, Gilbert A. Nixon, Michael L. Noel, Ella Mae Noffsinger, James C. Nofziger, PhD, Richard Nolthenius, PhD, Eugene L. Nooker, Jack D. Norberg, H. A. Noring, Brent C. Norman, MD, John L. Norris, Tharold E. Northup, Ferdinard J. Nowak, Wesley Raymond Nowell, PhD, Stanley J. Nowicki, Maurice Joseph Nugent Jr., PhD, Leonard James Nugent, PhD, Erwin R. Null, Robert B. Nungester, James K. Nunn, Amos M. Nur, PhD, Joseph A. Nussbaum, George A. Nyamekye, PhD, Hubert J. Nyser, Michael Nystrom, Harry Alvin Oberhelman, Theodore M. Oberlander, PhD, Rafael H. Obregon, Dale O'Brien, MD, Arlo L. Oden*, Dominick Odorizzi, Michal Odyniec, PhD, John D. Oeltman, Jacob J. Offenberger, MD, Naomi Neil Ogimachi, PhD, N. Neil Ogimachi, PhD, H. M. Ogle, J. Ogren, PhD, Joon C. Oh, Franklin T. Ohgi, Kurt N. Ohlinger, PhD, Kent A. Ohlson, William Ohm, Arthur F. Okuno, Fred B. Oldham, Arnold N. Oldre, MD, Edward A. Oleata, Edward Eugene Oliphant, PhD, Donald B. Oliver, PhD, Roy R. Oliver, E. Jerry Oliveras, Kenneth L. Olivier, PhD, Bernard J. O'Loughlin, PhD, Carl Olson, Jan B. Olson, Kevin D. Olwell, PhD, Rosalie Omahony, PhD, Willard D. Ommert, DVM, Ryan D. O'Neal, Donald E. O'Neill, Anatoli Onopchenko, PhD, Lee B. Opatowsky, PhD, Philip H. Oppenheim, MD, William L. Oppenheim, John J. Oram, PhD, Rolf O. Orchard, Fernando Ore, PhD, David R. Orfant, Mahmoud M. Oriqat, Cornel G. Ormsby, Harold A. Orndorff, Hans I. Orup, MD, Emil A. Osberg, James Osborn, Professor Osborn, Bert Osen, James E. Oslund, James R. Oster, MD, Al B. Osterhues, Theodore O. Osucha, Douglas K. Osugi, Arnold Otchin, Haruko Otoshi, Gary M. Otremba, Wayne Robert Ott, PhD, William M. Otto, Oswald L. Ottolia, John W. Overall Jr., Scott A. Owen, Dennis Owen, Thomas W. Owens, William W. Owens, Kazimiera J L Paciorek, PhD, Lorenzo M. Padilla, Jeffry Padin, PhD, Seaver T. Page, MD, Ruth Painter, Coburn Robbins Painter, Thomas Palmer, Patrick E. Pandolfi, Daniel W. Pangburn, Sergio R. Panunzio, Robert C. Paoluccio, Charles Herach Papas, PhD, Michael L. Pappas, Shashikant V. Parikh, Edward Parilis, PhD, Norman F. Parker, PhD, Calvin Alfred Parker, PhD, Kenneth D. Parker, Theodore C. Parker, David W. Parker, Dennis L. Parker, Ted Parker, Robert Parkhurst, PhD, R. M. Parkhurst, Malcolm F. Parkman, Merton B. Parlier, Lowell Carr Parode, Christopher M. Parry, PhD, Michael L. Parsons, PhD, Chester Partridge, C. R. Partridge, Stan P. Parvanian, Angelo A. Pastorino, James M. Paterson, PhD, Charles M. Patsch, Gaylord Penrod Patten, PhD, Everett R. Patten, Brenda J. Patterson, Alec M. Patterson, Richard M. Patton, James W. Paul, Raymond L. Paulson, Ferene F. Pavlics, Eleftherios B. Pavlis, Hagai Payes, James

Payne, PhD, Dalian V. Payne, Andy Peabody, David N. Peacock, PhD, Robert T. Peacock, Gerald F. Pearce, John Pearson, Robert A. Pease, Douglas P. Pedersen, Richard A. Pedersen, Louis E. Pelfini, David Gerard Pelka, PhD, W. S. Penn Jr., PhD, Paul H. Pennypacker, MD, Richard S. Penska, Jeffery Penta, Allen P. Penton, Linda H. Pequegnat, PhD, Thomas M. Perch, Irma T. Pereira, Robert V. Peringer, Arthur S. Perkins, James Jerome Perrcault, Gerald M. Perry, George Persky, PhD, Alois Peter Jr., Marvin Arthur Peters, PhD, Ralph H. Peters, Norman W. Petersen, Patricia J. Petersen, Gary Lee Peterson, PhD, Jack E. Peterson, PhD, Glenn R. Peterson, Arthur W. Peterson, James D. Peterson, Victor Lowell Peterson, Donald J. Peterson, Thomas G. Petrulas, Ray H. Pettit, PhD, Ronald W. Petzoldt, PhD, Bernard L. Pfefer, R. Fred Pfost, PhD, Robert F. Phalen, PhD, Debra Phelps, Lloyd Lewis Philipson, PhD, John P. Phillips, MD, Ronald T. Piccirillo, MD, Benjamin M. Picetti, MD, William Pickett, John H. Pickrell, Bill D. Pierce, PhD, Matthew Lee Pierce, PhD, Vincent Joseph Pileggi, PhD, Laurence Oscar Pilgeram, PhD, Kurt F. Pilgram, Irwin J. Pincus, MD, Edmund Pinney, PhD, Raymond G. Pinson, Robert G. Piper, Bernard Wallace Pipkin, PhD, Janet C. Piskor, Earl L. Pitkin, A. Lincoln Pittinger, Raluca M. Pitts, Michael A. Plakosh, Robert V. Plank, Stephen L. Plett, Joseph S. Plunkett, Randy Pochel, Gregory E. Polito, MD, Glen D. Polzin, Robert L. Pons, James B. Ponzo, Richard J. Porazynski, Fred C. Porter, David Dixon Porter, Robert Potosnak, Charle E. Pound, Robert D. Pounds, M. L. Powell, James P. Power, Jack Pratt, Martin William Preus, PhD, Gerald O. Priebe, Robert Clay Prim III, PhD, George B. Primbs, MD, Robert K. Prince, R. K. Prince, David Prinzing, Lewis W. Pritchett, Winston H. Probert, Thomas Proctor, Richard James Proctor, Oscar J. Proesel, J. Proffitt, John R. Prosek, Brian S. Prosser, Thomas Prossima Jr., Jerry A. Pruett, Fernand H. Prussing, MD, Kenneth E. Pruzinsky, Teodore C. Przymusinski, PhD, Teodor Przymusiushi, PhD, Timothy G. Psomas, Laurie D. Publicover, MD, Leamon T. Pulley, PhD, Everett W. Purcell, Bruce H. Purcell, Robert G. Purgington, Robert G. Purington, Jennifer D. Pursley, Thankamama J. Puthiaparampil, MD, John Ward Putt, Ramon S. Quesada, MD, Florentino V. Quiaot, John M. Quiel, Rae E. R., Louis C. Raburn, Donald Rado, Robert W. Ragen Jr., James K. Rainforth, James W. Raitt, MD, James A. Ramenofsky, MD, Apolinar Z. Ramiro, Simon Ramo, PhD, Roy E. Ramseier, Lawrence Dewey Ramspott, PhD, Shahida I. Rana, James Rancourt, PhD, Greenfield A. Randall, P. Randall, Thomas J. Rankin, Henry Rapoport, PhD, Daren H. Raskin, Miriam Rasky, Ned S. Rasor, PhD, Howard E. Rast Jr., PhD, Tom C. Rath, Egan J. Rattin, Michael S. Ratway, Stephen Rawlinson, Anatoly D. Ray, Monte E. Ray, Everett L. Raymond, Leonard A. Rea, Robert G. Read, Richard L. Reason, Douglas W. Reavie FACS, George J. Rebane, PhD, Jose G. Rebaya, Andreas Buchwald Rechnitzer, PhD, John G. Reddan III, Damoder P. Reddy, PhD, Allan G. Redeker, MD, David A. Reed Jr., Lester R. Reekers, Harold G. Reeser, Donald Reeves, D. F. Reeves, Steven A. Regis, Charles J. Reich, Kenneth Brooks Reid, PhD, Kyrk D. Reid, Jeff Reimche, Richard D. Rein, Fred W. Reinhart, Mark B. Reinhold, PhD, Marlin E. Remley, PhD, Charles R. Rendall, Daniel F. Renke, Nicholas A. Renzetti, PhD, Josef W. Repsch, Gerard Reski, Robert Walter Rex, PhD, Arthur A. Reyes, PhD, Diana C. Reyes, Armond G. Rheault, Dennis A. Rhyne, Richard Rice, PhD, Gary R. Rice, Neal A. Richardson, PhD, Ispoone Richlin, PhD, Harry G. Richter, Philip J. Richter, Hannes H. Richter, Corwin Lloyd Rickard, PhD, Joan D. Rickard, Douglas W. Ricks, PhD, R. J. Riddell, PhD, Richard R. Riddell, MD, Michael Riddiford, Fred M. Riddle, John L. Ridell, Adolphus A. Riewe, James W. Riggs, PhD, George P. Rigsby, PhD, Gary T. Riley, G. Riley, Lyrad Riley, John A. Rinek, Thomas A. Ring, Robert Ringering, MD, Richard L. Ripley, David Ririe, PhD, Martin W. Ritchie, PhD, Robert Brown Ritter, Jack B. Ritter, Arnold P. Ritter, Manuel S. Rivas, R. A. Rivas, James E. Robbins, Roy L. Roberson, Stephen F. Roberts, Jim D. Robertson, Donad B. Robertson, Richard C. Robinson, Karen S. Robinson, Robert B. Roche, Peter A. Rock, PhD, Adam Rocke, Leon H. Rockwell, PhD, James W. Rodde, Jonathan P. Rode, PhD, Fredrich H. Rodenbaugh, MD, Bertram J. Rodgers Jr., Glenard W. Rodgers, Anthony F. Rodrigues, Dan V. Rogers, D. R. Rogers, Carl A. Rohde, Gerhard Rohringer, PhD, Jack W. Rolston, Ephraim Romesberg, Wendell Hofma Rooks, Steven D. Root, Eugene John Rosa, PhD, Dennis G. Rose, Denis G. Rose, Allan B. Rose, Eric C. Roseen, Alan Rosen, PhD, Steven Loren Rosenberg, PhD, Dan Yale Rosenberg, Donald Edwin Rosenheim, Kermit E. Rosenthal, Jack W. Rosenthal, Rollie D. Rosete, MD, Jonathan P. Rosman, MD, Ted E. Ross Jr., Stephen Ross, MD, Suzi Ross, William E. Ross, Mario E. Rossi, A. David Rossin, PhD, Bryant William Rossiter, PhD, Thomas J. Rosten, J. Paul Roston, Adolph Peter Roszkowski, PhD, Ariel A. Roth, PhD, Gerald S. Rothman, William Stanley Rothwell, PhD, Stan A. Rotnwell, Nicholas Rott, PhD, Jerome A. Rotter, MD, James E. Roulstone, James M. Rowe, PhD, William R. Rowe, Leroy H. Rowley, George M. Roy, David C. Royer, G. Roysdon, John Rozenbergs, PhD, Balazs F. Rozsnyai, PhD, Leonard Rubenstein, Benjamin D. Rubin, MD, Allen G. Rubin, Efim S. Rudin, Gerard Rudisin, Thomas P. Rudy, PhD, John V. Rudy, W. Ruehle, Edward Rugel, Howell Irwin Runion, PhD, Richard A. Runkel, PhD, Jack E. Runnels, Robert C. Rupert, R. C. Rupert, B. Rush, PhD, Lewis B. Russell, Edmund L. Russell, Andrew Russell, Paul G. Ruud, PhD, Ed J. Ruzak, Philip L. Ryall, Joe Ryan, PhD, Bill Chatten Ryan, PhD, Kevin M. Ryan, Daberath Ryan, Elliott Ryder, PhD, Kathleen Rygiel, Alfredo H UA S Ing, PhD, Patrick Saatzer, PhD, Joseph D. Sabella, MD, William W. Sable, Frank Sacco, Edgar Albert Sack, PhD, B. Sadri, Frederick M. Sagabiel, William F. Sager, Richard A. Sager, Professor Saghafi, PhD, Kanwar V. Sain, Nirmal S. Sajjan, Roy T. Sakamoto, Eugene Salamin, Robert E. Salfi, PhD, Mikal Endre Saltveit, PhD, Paul K. Salzman, PhD, Larry Sample, Grobert D. Sanborn, William C. Sanborn, Ray O. Sandberg, Jay C. Sandberg, Richard P. Sandell, Thomas L. Sanders Jr., Burton B. Sandiford, James K. Sandin, Steven D.

Sandkohl, Marvin M. Sando, MD, James S. Sands, Enrique Sanqui, George T. Santamaria, Henry E. Santana, Tom Santillan, Kenneth W. Sapp, Amir M Sam Sarem, PhD, A. Sam Sarem, PhD, Greg Sarkisian, Raymond Edmund Sarwinski, PhD, Melvin W. Sasse, J. Satko, Richard S. Satkowski, Hugh M. Satterlee, PhD, Walt Saunders, Robert E. Saute, PhD, Basil V. Savoy, Austin R. Sawvell, MD, Frederick George Sawyer, PhD, Charles W. Sayles, PhD, Charles R. Saylor, James Scala, PhD, Michael P. Scarbrough, Carolyn A. Scarbrough, Michael P. Scardera, Lido Scardigli, Lawrence A. Schaal, Erwin A. Schaefer, Jeffrey Schaffer, Edward M. Schaschl, John F. Schatz, PhD, George E. Schauf, MD, Donald E. Scheer, David H. Scheffey, Paul Otto Scheibe, PhD, Thomas J. Scheil, Perry Arron Scheinok, PhD, Michael W. Schell, Deborah S. Schenberger, PhD, Don Van Schenck, Clifton S. Schermerhorn, MD, Don Ralph Scheuch, PhD, Paul G. Scheuerman, Stanley J. Scheurman, MD, Ted M. Schiller, Mark Schiller, MD, Guenter Martin Schindler, PhD, Rudolf A. Schindler, Richard H. Schippers, Hassel C. Schjelderup, PhD, Wilbert H. Schlimmeyer, Evert Irving Schlinger, PhD, Erika M. Schlueter, PhD, John H. Schmedel, Rudi Schmid, PhD, Francis R. Schmid, Kurt C. Schmidt, Alfred C. Schmidt, John W. Schmidt, Richard L. Schmittel, Henry A. Schneider, George L. Schofield Jr., PhD, Kurt A. Scholz, Martin R. Schotzberger, Robert Schrader, Klaus G. Schroeder, PhD, Ed J. Schryver, Donald Schuder, Adolph T. Schulbach, Daniel Herman Schulte, PhD, Robert K. Schultz, PhD, Theodore C. Schultze, Roger W. Schumacher, Joseph F. Schuman, Peter T. Schuyler, Samuel G. Schwab, Steven C. Schwacofer, Alan B. Schwartz, Gary W. Schwede, PhD, Raymond L. Schwinn, MD, Donald R. Scifres, PhD, Kevin M. Scoggin, DVM, Richard A. Scollay, Franklin Robert Scott, PhD, Deborah J. Scott, PhD, Elizabeth Scott, MD, John F. Scott, Harrison S. Scott, Paul Scribner, D. G. Scruggs, Jeffrey Scudder, Christopher L. Seaman, PhD, W. H. Seaman, Paul A. Sease, Robert L. Seat, Bruce E. Seaton, Randall J. Seaver, Leslie I. Sechler, MD, Donald B. Sedgley, Michael L. Seely, PhD, Erwin Seibel, PhD, Edward W. Seigmund, Glenn A. Sels, John R. Selvage, N. T. Selvey, Jospeh Semak, Frederick D. Sena, George W. Sening, James C. Senn, Oscar W. Sepp, Alexander Sesonske, PhD, John D. Severns, Bradley E. Severson, Ordean G. Severud, Archie F. Sexton, Patricia Marie Shaffer, PhD, James W. Shaffer, Jayendra A. Shah, MD, Arsen A. Shahnazarian, Lloyd Stowell Shapley, PhD, Gary Duane Sharp, PhD, Clifford A. Sharpe, Roland L. Sharpe, Clay Marcus Sharts, PhD, Marvin E. Shaver, Black Shaw, MD, Reece F. Shaw, Warren D. Shaw, Ian Shaw, I. D. Shaylor-Billings, Dennis Shea, Richard Shearer, George F. Sheets, Zubair A. Sheikh, Kent L. Shepherd, John L. Sheport, David A. Sheppard, Russell Sherman, Dalton E. Sherwood, Wilbert Lee Shevel, PhD, George L. Shillinger, Kaz K. Shintaku, Calvin Shipbaugh, PhD, Michael L. Shira, Ralph E. Shirley, Arthur W. Shively, Gary Shoemaker, PhD, Robert S. Shoemaker, Oliver B. Sholders, John J. Shore III, Michael A. Short, PhD, Christopher R. Shubeck, Rex Hawkins Shudde, PhD, Patrick James Shuler, PhD, Douglas C. Shumway, Dinah O. Shumway, Sidney G. Shutt, Raymond E. Sickler, Kurt Sickles, Joseph A. Siegel, MD, John P. Siegel, William Siegfried, Steven M. Siegwein, Brent C. Siemer, Hans R. Sifrig, Paul L. Sigwart, Michael Silbergh, Henry W. Silk Ret, Robert T. Silliman, Armando B. Silva, Daniel D. Silva, Gregory P. Silver, Jacob Silverman, PhD, Herbert Philip Silverman, PhD, Herschel W. Silverstone, Craig A. Silvey, William J. Simek, P. John Simic, MD, Michael N. Simidjian, Javid J. Siminou, William W. Simmons, PhD, Ira B. Simmons, E. Lee Simmons, Keith Simmons, Edgar Simons, Jack Simonton, Donald C. Simpson, Gordon G. Sinclair, Iqbal Singh, MD, Vernon Leroy Singleton, PhD, Juscelino M. Siongco, Harold T. Sipe, William D. Siuru, PhD, Stanley L. Sizeler, MD, Fritiof S. Sjostrand, PhD, Paul S. Skager, Sidney E. Skarin, PhD, Robert E. Skelton, PhD, Arlie D. Skelton, George I. Skoda, Bernard G. Slavin, PhD, Mikhail E. Slepak, PhD, Marina Slepak, PhD, Richard Slocum, PhD, Robert Gordon Smalley, PhD, Gary Smart, Ronald T. Smedberg, Helen M. Smedbery, Rick G. Smelser, Michael J. Smith, PhD, Donald R. Smith, PhD, S. Clarke Smith, MD, Eric Smith, Eric Smith, Geoffrey R. Smith, DVM, Donald C. Smith, DVM, Dana L. Smith, Charlee Smith, Gary Smith, MD, Donna E. Smith, MD, Donald A. Smith, Jeff Smith, Walter J. Smith, James R.E. Smith, Eileen Smithers, Peter Smits, Neil R. Smoots, Walter L. Snell, William Rossenbrook Snow, PhD, Donald Philip Snowden, PhD, Stephen J. Snyder, Donald R. Snyder, Richard C. Soderholm, James R. Soderman, R. T. Soledberg, Bertram C. Solomon, MD, Ronald C. Sommerfield, John R. Sondeno, Harold S. Song, MD, Loren R. Sorensen, Frank S. Sorrentino, MD, Marco J. Sortillon, Everett R. Southam, PhD, Charles L. Spaegel, Michael E. Spaeth, PhD, William L. Sparks, Russell T. Spears, MD, Aaron B. Speirs, Lawrence C. Spencer, Pierrepont E. Sperry Jr., Arlo J. Spiess, Robert Joseph Spinrad, PhD, John Robert Spreiter, PhD, Rodger W. Spriggs, George S. Springer, PhD, Gerard J. Sprokel, PhD, James P. Srebro, Pierre St. Amand, PhD, David St. Armand, William Stable, Kenneth E. Stager, PhD, Harold Keith Stager, Kim W. Stahnke, Mark A. Stalzer, PhD, Anthony C. Stancik, Clarence H. Stanley, Timothy N. Stanton, Scott R. Stanton, Rosemarie Stanton, Chauncey Starr, PhD, Darrel W. Starr, Edward R. Starr, MD, Mike Starzer, Raymond Stata, PhD, Harrison L. Staub, John F. Steel, MD, Thomas C. Steele, Arnold Edward Steele, Albert J. Stefan, Edward M. Steffani, Richard J. Stegemeier, Michael Steger, Howard Steinberg, PhD, Morris Albert Steinberg, PhD, Richard L. Stennes, MD, Stuart Stephens, PhD, Ralph L. Stephens, David A. Stepp, Edward E. Sterling, MD, John A. Stern, Sidney Sternberg, Alvin R. Stetson, David L. Stetzel, Milan R. Steube, Frank Stevens, Lewis A. Stevens, Robert Stevenson, PhD, Robert Lovell Stevenson, PhD, Albert E. Stevenson, Homer J. Stewart, PhD, Gordon Ervin Stewart, PhD, Kathleen M. Stewart, MD, Wayne L. Stewart, Chris Stier, Gerald G. Still, PhD, Howard A. Stine, Daniel P. Stites, MD, Richard P. Stock, Norman D. Stockwell, PhD, Larry J. Stoehr, Richard Stone, PhD, Tabby L. Stone, PhD, W. Ross Stone, PhD, Lin Stone, David Stone, Mark Storms, Jay C. Stovall,

David Stowell, Erwin Otto Strahl, PhD, Edward D. Strassman, Paul M. Straub, Joe M. Straus, PhD, James R. Strawn, Herbert D. Strong Jr., Allen Strother, PhD, Wilfred Stroud, Kenneth A. Stroup, Mark W. Strovink, PhD, Harold K. Strunk, PhD, John H. Struthers, Allen Stubberud, PhD, Perry L. Studt, PhD, Justin Stull, Gunther L. Sturm, Donadl Sturmer, M. Subramanian, PhD, Ravi Subramanian, Marek A. Suchenek, PhD, Mark A. Suden, James Carr Suits, PhD, Thomas J. Sullivan, PhD, John F. Sullivan, Robert J. Sultan, Sally S. Sun, MD, Andrew D. Sun, MD, Vane E. Suter, Mark E. Sutherlin, John Svalbe, Robert J. Swain, Alan A. Swanson, Linda S. Swanson, MD, Robert Nols Swanson, William Alan Sweeney, PhD, Peter Swerling, PhD, Chauncey Melvin Swinney, PhD, Leif Syrstad, George B. Szabo, Walter S. Szczepanski, Andrew Y. Szeto, PhD, Edwin E. Szymanski, PhD, Spencer L. Tacke, Charles E. Tackels, David Dakin Taft, PhD, Bill H. Taggart, Steve J. Taggart, MD, Samuel Isaac Taimuty, PhD, Girdhari S. Taksali, David B. Talcott, Donald D. Talley, Ralph G. Tamm, Harry H. Tan, PhD, Y. Tang, PhD, James B. Tapp, Waino A. Tapple, Anthony Tate, Richard L. Taw, MD, Eric R. Taylor, PhD, George F. Taylor, Neil L. Taylor, Edward Taylor, William G. Taylor, MD, Michael K. Taylor, John J. Taylor, Donald E. Taylor, Frank C. Tecca, Athey Technologies, PhD, Edward A. Tellefsen, Edward Teller, PhD*, Orlando V. Telles, Robert Templeton, John T. Tengdin, Jacob Y. Terner, MD, Richard D. Terry, PhD, Steven R. Terwilliger, Henry J. Tevelde, DVM, Richard W. Tew, PhD, Edward Teyssier, Michael G. Thalhamer, Joshua M. Tharp Jr., M. R. The Smiths, PhD, Gordon H. Theilen, DVM, Jerold Howard Theis, PhD, J. H. Theis, PhD, James D. Thissell, Roderick W. Thoits, Gerald A. Thomas, PhD, Charles A. Thomas Jr., PhD, C. A. Thomas Jr., PhD, Russ H. Thomas, James Thomas, Garfield J. Thomas, Dean Thomas, Kevin L. Thomas, Michel A. Thomet, PhD, Warren Thompson, PhD, Dennis P. Thompson, MD, Ken Thompson, Kenneth A. Thompson, K. A. Thompson, William J. Thornhill, Lewis Throop, PhD, Henrik C. Thurfjell, John P. Tibbas, Gerald F. Tice, Karen M. Tierney, William Arthur Tiller, PhD, Edward K. Tipler, Arthur Robert Tobey, PhD, Joseph D. Tobiason, PhD, Brent Tolend, Gerald V. Toler, David C. Toller, MD, Maher B. Toma, MD, John Toman, Crisanto R. Tomongin, John C. Toomay, Wilfred Earl Toreson, PhD, Eric D. Torguson, Felipe N. Torres, John P. Toth, MD, Charles H. Touton, David C. Tower, MD, Jeffrey G. Towle, PhD, Edward L. Townsend, Norton R. Townsley, Donald Frederick Towse, PhD, Rosalyn Tran, MD, Elbert W. Trantow, Timothy L. Trapp, Mitchell Trauring, William Brailsford Travers, PhD, Frank C. Trayer, B. V. Traynor, Raymond Treder, John D. Trelford, MD, William H. Trent, PhD, Richard L. Trimble, Patrick A. Tripe, MD, Curtis W. Tritchka, Glenn C. Troman, Craig J. Trombly, Bretton E. Trowbridge, Eddy S. Tsao, A. N. Tschaeche, Tai Po Tschang, MD, Manuel Tsiang, PhD, Theodore Yao Tsu Wu, PhD, Dean B. Tuft, PhD, Raymond Tulkki, Richard Eugene Tullis, PhD, Bryan Tullis, B. R. Tunai, Andy Tung, Willis E. Tunnell, MD, Robert L. Turk, MD, Richard E. Turk, MD, Robert E. Turner, PhD, Ted H. Tuschka, PhD, Henry A. Tuttle, Ross W. Tye, PhD, Glenn A. Tyler, PhD, Vincent H. Uhlenkott, Harold B. Uhlig, Joseph J. Unger, Randall Unthank, Erik Unthank, Robert R. Upp, PhD, James L. Uptegrove, Donadl C. Urfer, Eldon L. Uverne Knuth, PhD, Richard Vacherot, Frank H. Vacio, MD, J. O. Vadeboncoeur, John A. Vaillancourt, MD, J. Peter Vajk, PhD, A. Valdos-Meneses, Richard M. Valeriote, Bernard A. Vallerga, Jacob E. Valstar, Job van der Bliek, J. Van Der Bliek, James R. Van Hise, PhD, J. R. Van Hise, PhD, Naola Van Orden, PhD*, John H. VanAmringe, Peter Vanblarigan, PhD, Mark Vande Pol, Arthur VanDeBrake, Wilem Vander Bil, PhD, Chris J. Vandermaas, Larry E. Vanhorn, Walker S. Vaning, Ruth A. vanKnapp, Barry M. Vann, Vito August Vanoni, PhD, Vagarshak V. Vardanyan, PhD, Larry Vardiman, PhD, Perry H. Vartanian Jr., PhD, Bangalore Seshachalam Vasu, PhD, T. D. Vaughan, Arlie D. Vaughn, King F. Vaughn, James Vavrina, Steven W. Vawter, Kenneth S. Vecchio, PhD, Alejandro T. Vega, Edward E. Velarde, Margarita B. Velarde, MD, Daniel W. Velasquez, Wencel J. Velicer, Louis Veltese, Theodore E. Veltfort, Anthony J. Verbiscar, PhD*, Robert J. Verderber, Jared Verner, PhD, Dmitry Vernik, PhD, Daniel J. Vesely, Peter Vessella, Thomas H. Vestal, Louis Vettese, Charles L. Vice, Joan Vickery, Andrew S. Vidikan, Susan L. Vigars, Carlos F. Villalpando, Roberto Villaverde, PhD, Norbert F. Vinatieri, Edgar L. Vincent, Jonathan R. Vinci SE, R. C. Visser, Petro Vlahos, Roger Frederick Vogel, Randy L. Vogelgesang, Kevin G. Vogelsang, Robert M. Volpe, Richard L. Volpe, Karl Vonderlinden, PhD, Suresh H. Vora, Frederick H. Vorhis, Earl H. Vossenkemper, Frederick C. Vote, Henry P. Voznick, Daniel L. Vrable, PhD, William R. Wachtler, PhD, William Howard Wade, PhD, Glen Wade, PhD, Robert Harold Wade, PhD, Don Wade, MD, Donald Wadsworth, PhD, Mark A. Wagner, James K. Wagner, Kenneth E. Wagner, MD, Lewis D. Wagoner, Howard W. Wahl, Scott G. Wahl, Dennis L. Wahl, David P. Wahl, Richard I. Waite Jr., George Wakayama, R. Stephen Waldeck, Jason S. Waldrop, Richard T. Wales, Dennis Kendon Walker, PhD, Raymond W. Walker, Verbon P. Walker, Jay H. Walker, Patrick M. Walker, John C. Walker, Milton B. Walkup, Edward M. Wall, Edwin Garfield Wallace, PhD, Tom S. Wallace, Eleanor A. Wallen, MD, Henry A. Waller, John E. Wallis, Joel D. Walls, PhD, Darrel N. Walter, Herbert G. Walter, MD, Gregg D. Walters, Austin G. Walther, Donald M. Waltz, Bohdan I. Wandzura, T. Wang, PhD, Zhi Jing Wang, PhD, Dale Ward, James J. Ward, Paul H. Ward, MD, Jay L. Ward, Charlene L. Wardlow, Ronald S. Wardrop, Richard V. Warnock, Jack S. Warren, Richard Warriner, John P. Waschak, Halbert S. Washburn, Harry L. Washburn, Robert M. Washburn, Claude Guy Wasterlain, PhD, Glenn L. Wasz, Milton N. Watanabe, Dean A. Watkins, PhD, William W. Watson, Guy E. Watson, Charlie E. Watson, Gary W. Watson, R. E. Watts, Walter L. Way, Todd Weatherford, PhD, Robert A. Weatherup, Robert D. Weaver, Albert Dinsmoor Webb, PhD, William P. Webb, PhD, Creighton A. Webb, Jack W. Webb, Harry V. Webber, MD, Bruce Warren Webbon, PhD, William P. Weber, PhD, Erich C. Weber, Barrett H. Weber, MD,

David Webster, John Robert Webster, Mark B. Webster, D. J. Wechsler, William J. Wechter, PhD, Saul Wechter, William H. Weese, Lloyd Weese, Robert L. Wehrli, Rudolph W. Weibel, Glen F. Weien II, Hans Weil-Malherbe, PhD, Carl Martin Weinbaum, PhD, William M. Weinstein, MD, Daniel G. Weis, PhD, Russell J. Weis, Max T. Weiss, PhD, Robin Ivor Welch, PhD, Frank Joseph Welch, PhD, Hugh E. Wells, Lisa M. Welter, PhD, Lee Welter, MD, Gunnar Wennerberg, R. C. Wentworth, PhD, Robert P. Wenzell, Robert H. Wertheim, Donald A. Wesley, PhD, A. Wessman, Clinton L. West, Robert E. West, Jack H. West, Rod D. Westfall, Travie J. Westlund, Kenneth Harry Westmacott, PhD, Henry Griggs Weston Jr., PhD, Robert J. Wetherall, Mike A. Whatley, Carlos Wheeler, Joseph G. Whelan, Vernon T. Whitaker, Robert Lee White, PhD, Gerry W. White, Richard L. White, David J. White, Joel E. White, MD, Sterling F. White, Kenneth E. Whitehead, Kent G. Whitham, Stephen A. Whitlock, David V. Whitmore, Dennis B. Whitney, Robert C. Whitten, PhD, R. Whitting, Derek A. Whitworth, PhD, Eyvind H. Wichmann, PhD, John G. Wichmann, DVM, George J. Widly, Arthur F. Widtfeldt, Daniel W. Wiedman, Francis P. Wiegand, Robert L. Wiegel, Doug Wiens, John S. Wiggins, PhD*, John Henry Wiggins, PhD, Don A. Wiggins, David W. Wilbur, PhD, Corbert E. Wilcox, Orland W. Wilcox, Michael R. Wilcox, Carroll Orville Wilde, PhD, James W. Wilder, Frederick R. Wiley, Fred R. Wiley, Wilbur F. Wilhelm, Donald W. Wilke, Charles L. Wilkins, Harold E. Wilkins, MD, Ross C. Wilkinson, Bennington J. Willardson, Van William, PhD, Forrest R. Williams, Austin M. Williams, Edgar P. Williams, Garth H. Wilson, PhD, David W. Wilson, PhD, Robert A. Wilson, MD, Royce D. Wilson, Melvin N. Wilson, Jerome M. Wilson, Maurice L. Wilson, Michael A. Wilson, Linda W. Wilson, MD, William E. Wilson, Donald E. Wilson, Jack Wilson, George D. Wiltchik, MD, Edward J. Wimmer, Jack A. Winchell, Ernest O. Winkler, Robert Winslow, Roger G. Winslow, Guy W. Winston, Wray Laverne Winterlin, Harry Winterlin, Philip Rex Winters, Bruce A. Winters FACS, MD, Donald F. Winterstein, PhD, W. T. Wipke, PhD, Wesley L. Wisdom, Eric V. Witt, Kenneth A. Witte, PhD, Robert F. Witters, Lawrence R. Wlezien, Virgil O. Wodicka, PhD, Milo Wolf, PhD, Paul M. Wolff, PhD, Milo M. Wolff, PhD, John H. Wolthausen, Fred W. Womble, Otto Wong, PhD, Sun Y. Wong, Ka-Chun Wong, Willis Avery Wood, PhD, Jason N. Wood, Don E. Wood, Bruce Wood, Kevin G. Wood, David L. Wood, MD, Walter H. Wood, MD, James M. Wood II, Michael L. Woodard, Michael D. Woods, Robert J. Woodward, Richard C. Woodward, Gene A. Worscheck, Margaret Skillman Woyski, PhD, Melville T. Wright, David G. Wright, Michael E. Wright, William W. Wright, Harold V. Wright, Chris J. Wrigley Jr., Jack G. Wulff, Richard A. Wunderlich, Charles R. Wunderlich, Stephen Walker Wunderly, PhD, Philip J. Wyatt, PhD, David E. Wyatt, MD, Jeff Wyatt, Bruce M. Wyckoff, Robert A. Wyckoff, Thomas S. Wyman, Leslie K. Wynston, PhD, Y. Xie, PhD, Albert R. Yackle, Bohdan M. Yacyshyn, Paul F. Yaggy, Walter M. Yamada, PhD, Jack A. Yamauchi, John S. Yankey III, John Lee Yarnall, PhD, Anthony Yarosky, Scott Raymond Yates, PhD, John L. Yates, Melvin B. Yates, Robert W. Yates, Francis Eugene Yates, John C. Yeakley, Carlton S. Yee, PhD, Paul Pao Yeh, PhD, Kuo-Tay P. Yeh, Michael W. Yeoman, Ki Jeong Yi, Sherwin D. Yoelin, Denison W. York, Wei Young, PhD, Jackson Young, Stephen G. Young, MD, Robert D. Young, Richard Young, G. Young, John C. Youngdahl, Dennis E. Youngdahl, Mohamad A. Yousef, PhD, Mary Alice Yund, PhD, D. Yundt, Sulhi H. Yungul, PhD, Kirk A. Zabel, David R. Zachary, Kamen N. Zakov, Carlos A. Zamano, Alex Zapassoff, J. Edward Zawatson, Joe E. Zawatson, Jason D. Zeda, Yuan Chung Zee, PhD, Howard C. Zehetner, Ken R. Zeier, Sanford S. Zeller, Kerry Zemp, Robert H. Zettlemoyer, Yi Zhad, PhD, Sigi Zierling, PhD, Elmer LeRoy Zimmerman, PhD, David L. Zimmerman, Douglas A. Ziprick, MD, Harold Zirin, PhD, Keith Zondervan, PhD, Louis M. Zucker, MD, Lewis Zucker, Yury Zundelevich, PhD, Joe Zupan, Soloman Zwerdling, PhD

Canada, British Columbia

David Naugler, PhD

Canada, United Kingdom

Damon Green, PhD

Colorado

Wilbur A. Aanes, David M. Abbott Jr., Joseph M. Abell, Paul Achmidt, Steven W. Adams, Wayne F. Addy, T. Adkins, Jacques J.P. Adnet, John Aguilar, Alfred Ainsworth 3rd, Frank J. Alder, Franklin Dalton Aldrich, PhD, Gary L. Allison, Kevin R. Allison, Kevin E. Allisonn, Victor Dean Allred, PhD, Bruce W. Allred, Robert C. Alson, Greg A. Altberg, Ashton Altieri, Anthony B. Alvarado, Kenneth S. Ammons, Adolph L. Amundson, David Anderson, PhD, Walton O. Anderson, Glenn L. Anderson, Tom Anderson, James P. Anderson, Mark J. Andorka, George Andreiev, Russell A. Andrews, Stephen P. Antony, James K. Applegate, PhD, Steven B. Aragon, Sidney O. Arola, Charles E. Atchison, William J. Attwooll, Mark Atwood, PhD, James K. August, Kurt L. Austad, Michael N. Austin, Steven G. Axen, Lee R. Bagby, William F. Bagby, Steve G. Bagley, R. V. Bailey, Dana Kavanaugh Bailey, Jack R. Baird, PhD, Daniel Bakker, Alfred Hudson Balch, PhD, Brund Balke, MD, Leslie Ball, DVM, Art Barber, George Arthur Barber, Gerald L. Barbieri, Stephen W. Barnes, Ralph M.

Barnett, Charles J. Baroch, PhD, Lance R. Barron, William E. Barton, PhD, Richard L. Bate, Albert Batten, PhD, Martin A. Bauer, Bertrand J. Bauer, Ralph B. Baumer, Eric Paul Baumgartner, David Paul Baumhefner, Robert L. Bayless Jr., William H. Bayliff, George W. Bayne, Shelby R. Bear, Dennis E. Beaver, Gayle D. Bechtold, Kenneth A. Beegles, Wayne R. Beeks, Wallace Bell, PhD, Donald P. Bellum, R. L. Benjamin, Cade L. Benson, Edgar L. Berg, Rodney H. Bergholm, Brian Berman, Leonard Bertagnolli, Cornelius E. Berthold, Gregory W. Bertram, Howard H. Bess, MD, Carl E. Beutler, Robert G. Beverly, Wallace J. Bierman, Doug N. Biewitt, D. G. Bills, PhD, Edward R. Binglam, E. F. Birdsall, PhD, Ramon E. Bisque, PhD, Daniel Bisque, Matthew L. Bisque, John P. Biswurm, Christopher R. Black, Thomas E. Blackman, Barry Blair, Robert B. Blakestad, James C. Blankenship, Thomas L. Blanton, PhD, Ronald K. Blatchley, Victor V. Bliden, Duane N. Bloom, PhD, Donald R. Bocast, Jane Haskett Bock, PhD, Bernard L. Bogema, Cody B. Bohall, Richard A. Bohling, Mike Boland, Robert L. Bolmer, Dudley Bolyard, Lee J. Bongirno, Charles S. Bonnery, MD, Jack N. Boone, PhD, Travis J. Boone, Larry Q. Bowers, Jean A. Bowles, PhD, Steven C. Boyce, PhD, Lester L. Boyer Jr., PhD, Brian J. Boyle, DVM, Bob D. Brady Jr., Carl F. Branson, Jeff D. Braun, John E. Brehm Sr., Michael B. Brewer, Luther W. Bridges, PhD, James A. Brierley, PhD, Corale Louise Brierley, PhD, Corale L. Brierley, PhD, Mont J. Bright Jr., Michael W. Brinkmeyer, James Brinks, PhD, Michael Brittan, PhD, George William Brock, Lawrence R. Brockman, Dean C. Brooks, James R. Brooks, John M. Brown, PhD, Ben D. Brown, DVM, Lynne A. Brown, Charles Robert Bruce, PhD, Thomas J. Bruno, PhD, Thomas T. Bruns, PhD, John L. Brust, Kenton J. Bruxvoort, Donald G. Bryant, PhD, Nathan B. Bryant, Joel W. Buck, James S. Bucks, PhD, Perry Buda, David J. Bufalo, C. James Bulla Jr., Stephen D. Bundy, Michael A. Burgess, Leonard F. Burkart, PhD, Dean S. Burkett, Robert H. Bushnell, PhD, Frank J. Buturla, Fredrick G. Calhoun, Mathhew D. Calkins, Jay Callaway, Terry J. Cammon, H. D. Campbell, Rayford R. Canada, John Canaday, John A. Canning, PhD, Andrew J. Capra, Curtis D. Carey, Charles E. Carlson III, William A. Carlson, Scott Carpenter, Robert Carpenter, Thomas M. Carroll, Mason Carlton Carter, PhD, Lew Casbon, Joseph Cascarelli, Dennis C. Casto, Eugene N. Catalano, P. Ceriani, PhD, Paul D. Chamberlin, Donald R. Chapman, William L. Chenoweth, Robert H. Chesson, Hsien-Hsiang Chiang, PhD, Milton Childers, PhD, Sarah J. Chilton, MD, Chris Chisholm, Wiley R. Chitwood, Odin D. Christensen, PhD, Richard L. Christiansen, PhD, Robert Milton Christiansen, PhD, J. W. Christoff, Ivan L. Clark, Catherine A. Clark, John F. Clarke Jr., James S. Classen, Curtis S. Clifton, Peter R. Clute, Leighton Scott Cochran, PhD, William T. Cohan, Lawrence E. Coldren, Lee Arthur Cole, PhD, David R. Cole, Gary W. Collins, Nina T. Collum, PhD, Arthur F. Colombo, PhD, Richard F. Conard, Martin E. Coniglio, Michael S. Connelly, David F. Coolbaugh, PhD, Harvey L. Coonts, Louis W. Cope, Robert J. Coppin, David Corbin, David B. Corman, Arlen C. Cornett, Rodney H. Cornish, PhD, Garryd D. Cornish, Charles E. Corry, PhD, George E. Cort, Benjamin Costello, Charles K. Cothem, Thomas P. Courtney, Arthur W. Courtney, Thomas R. Couzens, Louis Cox Jr., PhD, Cecil J. Craft, Bruce D. Craig, PhD, Don J. Craig, DVM, Dexter Hildreth Craig, Marla Criss, David L. Crouse, Alfred John Crowle, PhD, Wolney C. Cunha, Robert L. Curruthers Jr., Michael S. Cuskelly, Aaron T. Cvar, Carl W. Dalrymple, Kevin M. Daly, Valeria Damiae, PhD, Henry W. Danley, William M. Danley, Eugene A. Darrow, Donald Davidson, PhD, Edward J. Davies, PhD, John A. Davis Jr., PhD, Daryl W. Davis, James L. Davis, Michael Davison, William Daywitt, John W. Deberard, Peter George Debrunner, PhD, Jeff L. Deeney, Steven L. DeFeyter, Gerald H. Degler, Susan M. Deines, B. J. Delap, Richard A. Denton, William Davis Derbyshire, PhD, Lawrence E. Dernabach, Jeffrey H. Desautels, W. R. Dettmer, John L. Devitt, Rudolph John Dichtl, Douglas Dillon, PhD, Jerry R. Divine, Robert Clyde Dixon, Gene P. Dodd, Lee A. Dodgion, Thomas C. Doe, Eugene Johnson Doering, Erin R. Dokken, Richard D. Dolecek, Michael W. Donley, PhD, Arthur F. Donoho, David R. Donohue, Kiernan O. Donovan, Terry W. Donze, Gerald R. Dooher, MD, Robert J. Doubek, R. J. Doubek, Edward C. Dowling Jr., PhD, Mancourt Downing, PhD, William Fredrich Downs, PhD, Jerry D. Droppleman, PhD, Emerson K. Droullard, Murray Dryer, PhD, Harold R. Duke, PhD, Alan Ronald Dump, Thomas J. Dumull, Paul M. Duncan, Harry E. Duprey, Benny R. Dusenbery, William T. Dusterdick, Donald R. East, Dennis M. Eben, Donald P. Ebright, Anita Eccles, Dana A. Echter, Paul F. Eckstein, Ronald K. Edquist, Julie A. Edwards, Thomas B. Egan, Linda L. Ehrlich, William H. Eichelberger, Keith W. Eilers, H. Richard Eisenbeis, PhD, Robert L. Elder, James Eley, PhD, Richard C. Enoch, Alexander Erickson, Christopher Erskine, Thomas M. Erwin, Rudy Eskra, Rudolph Eskra, Ronald L. Estes, Donald Lough Everhart, PhD, Joseph P. Fagan Jr., Thomas G. Fails, Frank Farnham, Duane D. Fehringer, Stuart R. Felde, John L. Fennelly, Arthur Thomas Fernald, PhD, Clinton S. Ferris Jr., PhD, James W. Ferry, Dale A. Fester, Charles J. Fette, Thomas G. Field, PhD, Dennis C. Finn, Carl V. Finocchiaro, Harlan Irwin Firminger, MD, Roland C. Fischer, Werner E. Flacke, MD, Peter A. Fleming, MD, Clarence W. Fleming, Jay E. Foley, Jon R. Ford, Deon T. Fowles, Glenn M. Frank, DVM, Andrew P. Franks, Ronald D. Franks, Harry D. Frasher, James E. Frazier, Richard J. Frechette, Ryan D. Frederick, William E. Freeman, Tim F. Friday, H. Howard Frisinger, PhD, William R. Fritsch, Norm Froman, L. W. Frowbridge, PhD, Suzanne M. Fujita, Connie Gabel, PhD, Richard A. Gabel, PhD, Joseph Galeb, PhD, Donald L. Gallaher, Anthony J. Galterio, Patrick S. Galuska, Pat Galuska, Charles L. Gandy, Paul W. Gard Jr., Paul W. Gard Jr., Edward E. Gardner, PhD, Homer J. Gardner, Andrew J. Garner, Thomas R. Gatliffe, William M. Gemmell, Andre A. Gerner, Cynthia A. Gerow, PhD, Douglas O. Gibbs, Elizabeth L. Gibbs, Delbert V. Giddings, Paul N. Gidlund, John M. Giesey, Walter Charles Giffin, PhD, Brian W. Gilbert, Leland E. Gillan, Alan D. Gillan, Leland E.

Gillan, Rick J. Gillan, Jack D. Gillespie, James R. Gilman, John Gishpert, Dan G. Gleason, Hartley C. Gleason, Earl T. Glenwright, Christine Gloeckler, Robert A. Glover, George G. Goble, PhD, Ronald B. Goldfarb, PhD, Scott L. Gomer, David V. Gonshor, John M. Goodrich, Jeff P. Goodwin, Alfred F. Gort, Mark H. Gosselin, John W. Goth, D. F. Gottron, Donald F. Gottron, Walter Carl Gottschall, PhD, Gary L. Gough, Thomas L. Gould, PhD, Gordon Gould, PhD, Ronald J. Gould, Robert J. Governski, Robert E. Gramera, PhD, Lee B. Grant Jr., MD, Lewis O. Grant, Kenneth Donald Granzow, William M. Gray, PhD, Robert C. Gray, Steven R. Gray, Deborah C. Greenwall, MD, Alfred Griebling, James K. Griffin, W. R. Griffitts, PhD, Paul K. Grogger, PhD, Alfred W. Grohe, Stephen J. Grooters, Michael P. Gross, Eugene L. Grossman, Paul M. Gruzensky, PhD, Ross L. Gubka, Lyle A. Gust, Ronald G. Gutru, R. G. Gutru, Donald Haas, Lawrence N. Hadley, PhD*, Richard Frederick Hadley, Frank A. Hadsell, PhD, Pablo Hadzeriga Jr., Gregory A. Hahn, Michael J. Hall, Timothy J. Halopoff, Saheed Hamid, Don D. Hamilton, PhD, Warren B. Hamilton, PhD, Stanley K. Hamilton, PhD, Marvin A. Hamstead, PhD, Joe John Hanan, PhD, Howard W. Hanawalt, Ray A. Hancock, John W. Hand Sr., Lawrence Handley, PhD, Donald L. Hanlon Jr., Barry J. Hansen, Chris E. Hansen, Lowell H. Hansen, MD, Sergius N. Hanson, Carl D. Hanson, Elwood Hardman, W. Henry Harelson, Mark F. Harjes, Stephen T. Harpham, Kevin D. Harrison, Elbert Nelson Harshman, PhD, Donald D. Hass, Charles N. Hatcher, Rav P. Hattenbach, Christpher N. Hatton, Niels B. Haubold, Ray L. Hauser, PhD, Consuelo M. Hauser, Michael E. Hayes, Eugene D. Haynie, DVM, Eugene C. Head Jr., Jenifer Heath, PhD, Robert Bruce Heath, DVM, Dale Heermann, PhD, Leonard Heiny, Leslie V. Hekkers, Marvin W. Heller, PhD, Roger A. Heller, William D. Helton, Courtney C. Hemenway, Frank Heming, PhD, Phil W. Henderson, Daniel F. Henderson, Raymond L. Henderson, Ralph L. Henderson, Charles J. Hendricks, Raymond P. Henkel, PhD, Charles S. Henkel, PhD, Thomas W. Henry, PhD, G. Herbert, Gary A. Herbert, Jeff Herrle, Martin Hertzberg, PhD, Neal Van Heukelem, Phillip E. Hewlett, Edward D. Hice, Ronald Higgins, Margaret A. Hill, Charles L. Hill, Bill L. Hiltscher, William J. Hine, John S. Hinman, Lee D. Hinman, John Hinton, John S. Hird, Brian G. Hoal, PhD, Noel Hobbs, Farrel D. Hobbs, Marcus D. Hodges, Marty Hodges, Roy A. Hodson, Arthur P. Hoeft, Harald Hoegberg, Robert J. Hoehn, MD, John Raleigh Hoffman, PhD, Christopher J. Hogan, PhD, Ronnie E. Hogan, David Clarence Hogg, PhD, Douglas G. Hoisington, Erik Holck, Frank J. Holliday, Victor T. Holm, David A. Holmes, Edmond W. Holroyd, PhD, Richard D. Holstad, James C. Holzwarth, Russell M. Honea, PhD, John Hoorer, William E. Hopkinds, Andrea S. Horan, Joseph M. Hornback, PhD, Isaac Horowitz, Kim Horsley, PhD, Richard F. Horsnail, PhD, William W. Hoskins, Douglas L. House, James O. Houseweart, Larry B. Howard, PhD, Dennis M. Howe, PhD, Craig A. Howell, Earl L. Huff, Julie Huffman, PhD, Ronald W. Huffman, Travis Hughes, PhD, Timothy J. Hughes, Frederick O. Humke, William D. Humphrey, Mack W. Hunt, Gary Hunt, Leland L. Hurst, Jerome Gerhardt Hust, Robert E. Husted, Robert B. Huston, Eric J. Hutchens, John G. Hutchens, R. W. Hutchinson, PhD, Gary L. Hutchinson, Francis Hutto, PhD, Mark D. Ibsen, Kenneth D. Ibsen, Eugene Ignelzi, Duane Imhoff, Robert J. Irish, Larry A. Irons, Scott R. Irvine, William W. Irving, James A. Ives ll, John B. Ivey, Stewart A. Jackson, PhD, Manly L. Jackson, M. L. Jacobs, PhD, Jay M. Jacobsmeyer, Jimmy Joe Jacobson, PhD, Bahram A. Jafari, PhD, Marek Jakubowski, PhD, Frederick J. Janger, Gustav Richard Jansen, PhD, Duane A. Jansen, George J. Jansen, Karen F. Jass, Seymour Jaye, William F. Jebb, Joe A. Jehn, Eivind B. Jensen, James D. Jessup, Thomas J. Jobin, Carl T. A. Johnk, PhD, Robert Britten Johnson, PhD, Blane L. Johnson, PhD, Donal Dabell Johnson, PhD, Clinton B. Johnson, Curtis L. Johnson, Thomas L. Johnson, Abe W. Johnson, Michael S. Johnson, Walter E. Johnson, M. S. Johnson, Robert C. Johnson, Steve D. Jolly, PhD, G. R. Jones, Paul C. Jones, Robert S. Joy, Ray L. Jukkola, Rodger A. Jump, James E. Junkin, George W. Jury, Dale C. Kaiser, MD, F. Kamsler, Raymond C. Kane Jr., Joe Kaplen, Gretchen A. Kasameyer, Todd R. Kaul, Alvin Kaumeyer, Michael Keables, PhD, Philip D. Kearney, PhD, Cresson H. Kearny, Richard A. Keen, PhD, Kenneth L. Keil, Stephen R. Keith, Frederick A. Keller, PhD, Sean P. Kelly, Walter O. Kelm, Graham Elmore Kemp, Robert C. Kendall*, Larry Kennedy, Charles L. Kerr, Michael L. Kiefer, Richard E. Kiel, Terry Kienitz, Thomas G. Kimble, Scott M. Kimble, Barry A. King, Thomas A. Kingdom, Monty C. Kingsley, PhD, John Kirkpatrick, Peter H. Kirwin, Hugh M. Kissell, Donald N. Kitchen, PhD, W. Kitdean, PhD, Sharon J. Klipping, Thomas Mathew Kloppel, PhD, Norman C. Knapp, Martin E. Knauss, Duane Van Kniebes, John K. Knop, Kirvin L. Knox, PhD, Kenneth Wayne Knutson, PhD, Nicholas F. Koch, Donald E. Koenneman, Wilbur L. Koger Jr., David L. Kohlman, PhD, William A. Koldwyn, PhD, Arvin L. Kolz, Kenneth D. Kopke, Nicholas C. Kortekaas, Thaddeus S. Kowalik, Jan Krason, George Krauss, PhD, Lee E. Krauth, Robert E. Kribal, PhD, Douglas H. Krohn, Fred J. Kroll, William R. Kroskob, Keith Krugh, John W. Labadie, PhD, Conrad M. Ladd, John P. Lafollette, Michael A. Laird, Robert A. Lamarre, Allen B. Lamb, Bruce Landreth, George L. Lane, Stephen S. Lange, Arthur L. Lange, Greg A. Larsen, Larry L. Larsen, Byron W. Larson, Roy E. Larson, Kenneth M. Laura, Linda E. Lautenbach, Leroy D. Lawson, Daryl E. Layne, Jozef Lebiedzik, PhD, Kennon M. Lebsack, Bob L. Lederer, MD, Arthur C. Lee, DVM, Robert Allen Lefever, PhD, Gail Legate, William Lehmanu, Michael G. Leidich, Richard W. Lemke, Robert Lentz, Jim Leslie, Barbara B. Lewis, Charles George Liddle, Fred H. Lightner, Richard B. Liming, Peter K. Link, PhD, Kurt O. Linn, PhD, Jeffrey D. Linville, Richard E. Lippoth, Jay Lipson, Donald L. Little, Daniel W. Litwhiler, PhD, Thomas O. Livingston, George A. Livingston, Willem Lodder, PhD, Eric Lodewijk, Eric Lodewyk, George O. Lof, PhD, Dave Lofe, Leonard V. Lombardi, PhD, W. Warren Longley, PhD, H. M. Losee, Harlie M. Love,

Robert W. Lovelace, Delwyn J. Low, T. D. Luckey, PhD, Frank L. Ludeman, Ralph Edward Luebs, PhD, Lilburn H. Lueck, Kenneth Luff, Forest V. Luke, Larry Lukens, PhD, Robert A. Lunceford, Carl Lyday "Col, USAF(RET)", Gerald Lyons, Robert D. Macdonald, Jerry MacLoughlin, PhD, Logan T. MacMillan, James A. Macrill, MD, Kent I. Mahan, PhD, Michael W. Mahoney, Thomas P. Mahoney, George Joseph Maler, Richard Maley, Anthony L. Malgieri, James Leighton Maller, PhD, James D. Mallorey, Keith N. Malmedal, David E. Malmquist, Jerome J. Malone Jr., Leo J. Maloney, Richard H. Mandel Jr., Peter A. Mandics, PhD, Robert A. Manhart, PhD, Jay A. Manning, Edward D. Manring, MD, Sam W. Maphis II, Samuel P. March, George J. Marcoux, Jay G. Marks, PhD, William E. Marlatt, PhD, Anthony D. Marques, L. K. Marshall, Charles F. Marshall, Jack E. Martin, PhD, Randall K. Martin, T. Scott Martin, James A. Martinez, Neal R. Martinez, John B. Maruin, Fredrick J. Marvel, Richard Frederick Marvin, Charles B. Masters, MD, Terry Mather, PhD, Michael R. Matheson, MD, J. Paul Mathias, Donald A. Mathison, Bruno A. Mattedi, Weston K. Mauz, Donald E. May, Edwarde R. May, John D. Mayhoffer, James E. Mayrath, PhD, Joseph F. McAleer, Howard S. McAlister, Stewart S. McAlister, Eddie W. McArthur, Lon A. McCaley, John S. McCallie, Shawn W. McCarter, Robert P. McCarthy, Calvin H. McClellan, Tim D. McConnell, Joe M. McCord, PhD, Jerry N. McCowan, Dirk W. McDermott, Robert McDonald, Larry G. McDonough, Marion Edward McDowell, MD, James D. McFall, Frank E. McGinley, Linda M. McGowan, Stuart D. McGregor, Norman L. McIver, PhD, William J. McKelvey, Quentin McKenna, Floyd McKinnerney, Brenda K. McMillan, Richard B. McMullen, MD, Charles S. McNeil, William McNeill, PhD, Ken Meisinger, PhD, Kenneth R. Meisinger, PhD, Eric W. Mende, Keith P. Mendenhall, Alan E. Menhennett, Jack M. Merritts, Warren H. Mesloh, James T. Metcalf, James R. Van Meter, Ken Metzer, Walter D. Meyer, PhD, Harvey J. Meyer, PhD, Troy L. Meyer, Ralph Meyertons, Leonard V. Micek, Eugene Joseph Michal, PhD, Eugene J. Michel, PhD, Michael C. Mickley, PhD, Theodore W. Middaugh, William J. Miles, PhD, Leo J. Miller, PhD, Robert J. Miller, PhD, Harold W. Miller, David T. Miller, Glenn E. Miller, George Miller, Paul R. Millet, Stephen L. Milller, James H. Mims, Michael J. Minkel, Paul Miskowicz, Bruce S. Mitchell, Gary C. Mitchell, Robert K. Mock, Carroll J. Moench, P. Michael Moffett, MD, Gunter B. Moldzio, PhD, Frank P. Molli, James R. Mondt, Kenneth W. Monington, PhD, Christopher Monroe, PhD, David Coit Moody, PhD, Richard Moolick, Lawrence Y. Moore, PhD, Roger Moore, John F. Moore, Jay P. Moore, Jonathan C. Moore, Frank D. Moore, Allan J. Mord, PhD, Duane E. Moredock, Robert C. Morehead, Kenneth O. Morey, W. Lowell Morgan, PhD, Timothy P. Morgen, Lawrence C. Morley, PhD, Bruce E. Morrell, Lisa M. Morris, Richard L. Morris, Dick Morroni, Jerome Gilbert Morse, PhD, John Jacob Mortvedt, PhD, Vladimir K. Moskver, MD, Larry R. Moyer, Bill L. Mueller, James R. Muhm, Thomas U. Mullen Jr., Kelly J. Murphy, James R. Musick, PhD, Randall L. Musselman, PhD, Jan Mycielski, PhD, Burt S. Myers, MD, Misac Nabighian, PhD, Yoshio Nago, James Nagode, Gene O. Naugle, DVM, John D. Nebel, Loren D. Nelson, PhD, John Nelson, PhD, Thomas A. Nelson, Al L. Nelson, Toby S. Nelson, Larry K. Nelson, David L. Nelson, Wayne W. Nesbitt, Valmer H. Ness, Roger C. Neuscheler, Roger Newell, PhD, John B. Newkirk, John Newman, Thomas Newman, James M. Newton, Preston L. Nielsen, Richard L. Nielson, PhD, Gordon Dean Niswender, PhD, James Nolan, Cliff Nolte, Matt R. Nord, Gary Nordlander, C. L. Nordstrom, John D. Norgard, PhD, Stephen N. Norris, Gary Nydegger, Chris M. Nyikos, David Claude O'Bryant, Robert Odien, PhD, Robert T. O'Donnell, Walter G. Oehlkers, Elvert E. Oest, PhD, Eldon L. Ohlen, Ralph L. Ohlmeier, George Ojdrovich, Richard C. Oliver, PhD, Daniel Olsen, PhD, Brent Olsen, Norval E. Olson, James Oltmans II, Victor C. Oltrogge, Michael T. Orsillo, Joseph T. Osmanski, James R. Ottomans II, Willard G. Owens, Thomas D. Oxley, Ralph S. Pacini, MD, Michael L. Page, Louis A. Panek, PhD, Arthur J. Pansze Jr., PhD, Ben H. Parker Jr., PhD, Pierce D. Parker, PhD, John M. Parker, Neil F. Parrett, Richard S. Passamaneck, PhD, H. Richard Pate, James Winton Patton, PhD, Gary M. Patton, William Paucrisler, PhD, Thomas R. Paul, Kenneth R. Paulsen, John J. Paulus, Louis A. Pavek, PhD, Mike J. Peacock, Galen L. Pearson, S. Ivar Pearson, John D. Peebles, Michael R. Peelish, Alfred H. Pekarek, PhD, M. J. Pellillo, Robert W. Pennak, PhD*, Daivd Peontek, Luke A. Perkins, Reagan J. Perry, Eric Perry, Michael S. Perry, Zell E. Peterman, PhD, Max S. Peters, PhD, Douglas C. Peters, Joseph Claine Petersen, PhD, Alan Herbert Peterson, PhD, George C. Pfaff Jr., Ryan A. Phifer, Michael R. Piotrowski, PhD, John J. Pittinger, Byron L. Plumley, Henry Pohs, Charles B. Pollock, Larry Pontaski, George J. Popovich Jr., Lynn K. Porter, PhD, Bruce D. Portz, Madison J. Post "NOAA, ESr.L", PhD, Richard Postma, PhD, Stephan N. Pott, Kathleen M. Power, Kenneth L. Presley, Donald R. Primer, Ron W. Pritchett, Ronald W. Pritchett, Dick A. Prosence, Russell J. Qualls, PhD, Albert J. Quinlivan Jr., Patrick D. Quinney, Terence T. Quirke, PhD, Edward L. Rademacher Jr., John G. Raftopoulos, DVM, Ted Rains, John Ruel Rairden III, John M. Rakowski, William Ramer, Alan M. Rapaport, MD, David E. Rapley, Alvin L. Rasmussen, Donald O. Rausch, PhD, Shea B. Rawe, Michael Rawley, David Thomas Read, PhD, James G. Reavis, PhD, David N. Rebol, James A. Reddington, Jack Redmond, PhD, Thomas Binnington Reed, PhD, Bruce B. Reeder, Robert G. Refvem, Scott J. Reiman, Elmar Rudolf Reiter, PhD, Keith A. Rensberger, John J. Reschl Sr., Melvin Rettig, Gordon F. Revey, John R. Reynolds, J. J. Richard, James W. Richards, Everett V. Richardson, PhD, Kenton Riggs, Cody Riley, Dan H. Rimmer, D. Allan Roberts, James L. Robertson, PhD, James A. Robertson, PhD, Raymond S. Robinson, PhD, Charles S. Robinson, PhD, Dale W. Rodolff, Brian D. Rodriguez, Scott G. Roen, Raylan H. Roetman, William L. Rogers, John A. Rohr, Charles T. Rombough, PhD, Albert J. Rosa, PhD, John G. Roscoe, Lawrence J. Rose, Sam Rosenblum, Lewis C. Rossman, Charlie Rossman, Ora H. Rostad,

David L. Roter, MD, George Rouse, PhD, Raymond L. Ruehle, Donald Demar Runnells, PhD, Susan S. Rupp, MD, William J. Ruppert, Michael T. Rusesky, Cynthia B. Russell, Michael J. Ryan, Michael A. Rynearson, Burns Roy Sabey, PhD, Harry A. Sabin, Julius Jay Sabo, Alberto Sadun, PhD, Eugene Saghi, PhD, Kenneth C. Saindon, Edward A. Samberson, Justin Sandifer, Mark K. Sarto, Frank Satterlee, Eldon P. Savage, PhD, Larry T. Savard, Robert B. Sawyer, MD, Karl G. Schakel, John A. Schallenkamp, Michael R. Schardt, Randolph E. Scheffel, Erwin T. Scherich, Jonathan D. Scherschligt, William D. Scheuerman, Andre H. Schlappe, Gerald J. Schlegel, Robert F. Schmal, Gregory S. Schmid, Paul G. Schmidt, Douglas R. Schmidt, Henry J. Schmitt, MD, Robert W. Schrier, PhD, Donald E. Schroeder Jr., Russell Schucker, Myron R. Schultz, Steven R. Schurman, Ronald G. Schuyler, J. O. Scott, Terry A. Scott, Richard T. Scott, Samuel A. Scott, Linda M. Searcy, Robert Seklemian, D. W. Sencenbaugh, D. W. Sencerbaugh, William H. Sens, Randolph L. Seward, George H. Sewell Jr., Alan William Sexton, PhD, Steven R. Shadow, Clarence Q. Sharp, Kenneth Sharp, Alan Dean Shauers, Roy W. Shawcroft, PhD, Daniel R. Shawe, PhD, Eugene M. Shearer, Grant L. Shelton, William M. Sheriff, George M. Sherritt, Kenneth Shonk, William A. Shrode, PhD, Craig E. Shuler, PhD, Edward F. Shumaker, Curtis A. Shuman, PhD, Russell W. Shurts, Jim A. Siano, Herb W. Siddle, Kenneth E. Siegenthaler, PhD, Eugene Glen Siemer, PhD, Miles Silberman, PhD, Nancy Jane Simon, PhD, Brian E. Simpson, Kenneth J. Simpson, Erwin Single, Ray L. Sisson, William D. Siuru, PhD, Gary W. Sjolander, PhD, Andrew D. Sleeper, PhD, Darryl Eugene Smika, PhD, Francis J. Smit, Earl W. Smith, PhD, Clarence Lavett Smith, PhD, John Ehrans Smith, PhD, Darryl E. Smith, PhD, Duane H. Smith, Merritt E. Smith, Glenn S. Smith, Scotty A. Smith, Robert M. Smith, Tim L. Smith, Loren E. Smith, Wallace A. Sneddon, MD, Gary D. Snell, James J. Snodgrass, William H. Snyer, Laurence R. Soderberg, John E. Soma, Ronald W. Southard, Antonio Spagna, PhD, Robert L. Speckman, Jim Spellman, Charles Spencer, John Spezia, Andrew Spiessbach, PhD, Charles W. Spieth, Brian B. Spillane, Derik Spiller, Ralph U. Spinuzzi, MD, Melvin Spira, MD, William J. Spitz RG, Charles L. Spooner, Roy D. Sprague, Kirk A. Sprague, Douglas S. Sprague, Robert L. Sprinkel Jr., Edwin H. Spuhler, Robert P. Spurck, PhD, Harold W. Stack, Douglas S. Stack, Michael Keith Stahl, Joel R. Stahn, Gregory E. Stanbro Jr., Robert I. Starr, PhD, Jennifer Staszel, Jack B. Stauffer, Robert A. Stears, Karl H. Stefan, Michael H. Steffens, Keith M. Stehman, Walter E. Steige, William D. Steigers, PhD, Richard A. Steineck, Gerry Steiner, PhD, Frank M. Stephens Jr., PhD, Frank A. Stephens, Lou Stephens, Jeff Stevens, Mary Stevenson, Daryl Stewart, Paul R. Stewart, Gordon K. Stewart, Richard E. Stiefler, MD, Harold Stienmeier, Richard H. Stienmier, MD, Fred B. Stifel, PhD, Julie A. Stiff, Cheryl A. Stiles, Gustav Stolz Jr., Brad W. Stone, Bill A. Stormes, Vladimir Straskraba, Jimmie J. Straughan, Bruce A. Straughan, Lawrence V. Strauss, Theron L. Strickland, Arthur W. Struempler, PhD, Howard F. Stup, Wayne Summons, Sherman Archie Sundet, PhD, Joseph D. Sundquist, Harry Surkald, Edward J. Suski, Mark D. Swan, Vernon F. Swanson, Vincent P. Sweeney Jr., Christopher L. Sweeney, Jerry L. Sweet, PhD, Henry C. Szymanski, Ronald Dwight Tabler, PhD, George C. Tackels, Kenneth G. Tallman, Joseph U. Tamburini, Charles R. Tate, David A. TenEyck, Ted L. Terrel, PhD, Kendell V. Tholstrom, John P. Thomas, MD, M. Ray Thomasson, PhD, Tommy Burt Thompson, PhD, Gerald E. Thompson, Michael B. Thomsen, Curtis G. Thomson, Jack Threet, Gaylen A. Thurston, PhD, Bruce Tiemann, PhD, K. Laus D. Ieter Timmerhaus, PhD, Fred S. D. Toole, Brenndan P. Torres, Terrence J. Toy, PhD, Thomas M. Tracey, Zung UU Tran, PhD, James M. Treat, John R. Troka, Leslie Walter Trowbridge, PhD, Wade Dakes Troxell, PhD, Harry A. Trueblood Jr., Paul A. Tungesvick, Kenneth D. Turnbull, Alistair R. Turner, Alfred H. Uhalt Jr., E. H. Ulrich, David J. Ulsh, George M. Upton, Julio E. Valera, PhD, Phillip D. Van Law, James R. Van Meter, Martha Van Seckle, Tim J. Van Wyngarden, Tracy L. Vandaveer, David D. Vanderhoofven, Alwyn J. Vandermerwe, PhD, Gordon H. Vansickle, Kenneth D. Vanzanten, Roy G. Vawter, Delton E. Veatch, Chris J. Veesaert, Richard Veghte, Roger N. Venables, Stan F. Versaw, Steven G. Vick, Lilly Vigil, Boris L. Vilner, James David Vine, Richard J. Vonbernuth, Tim J. Vrudny, Robert L. Wade, Jerome A. Waegli, David A. Wagie, PhD, Charles F. Wagner, MD, Cherster A. Wallace, PhD, Denny M. Wallisch, Kent D. Walpole, DVM, W. A. Walther Jr., Douglas L. Walton, George G. Walton, Frederick Field Wangaard, PhD, Keith K. Wanklyn, Jeff Ware, John F. Ware, Edward M. Warner, Darrell R. Warren, MD, Simon P. Waters, Donald K. Wathke, Tim Watson, PhD, Shaunna J. Watterson, Frank B. Watts, Dale Watts, William J. Way, Leo Weaver, John F. Weaver, Rodney L. Weber, Douglas H. Wegener, James A. Wehinger, Irving Weiss, PhD, Kirk R. Weiss, Joseph Leonard Weitz, PhD, John C. Welch, MD, Thomas Wellborn, Lawrence D. Wells, Philip B. Wells, Donald A. Welsh, Robert H. Welton, Harold C. Welz, Anthony J. Wernnan, Cecil B. Westfall, Richard L. White, Ann L. White, Christopher P. Whitham, Robert W. Whitt, Claude Allan Wiatrowski, PhD, Peter L. Wiebe, MD, Albert H. Wieder, Loren Elwood Wiesner, PhD, Charles G. Wilber, PhD, Donald Wilde, John D. Wilkes, PhD, Wayne E. Wilkins, Jewel E. Willborn, Ted F. Wille, Ronald M. Willhite, Glen Williams, Richard E. Williamson, Michael D. Wilson, PhD, Alvin C. Wilson, Wilmer W. Wilson, Laurence M. Wilson, Denis J. Winder, MD, Robert C. Winn, PhD, Jack E. Winter, DVM, David Wire, David J. Wirth, David J. Wirtz, Floyd A. Wise, Chester E. Wisner, Robert L. Wiswell, Franklin P. Witte, PhD, James D. Wolf, Laird S. Wolfe, PhD, Adrian L. Wolfe, PhD, Bruce R. Wolfe, Charles V. Wolfers, Steven A. Wolpert, DVM, Cyrus F. Wood, Robert P. Woodby, Steven Woodcock, Frank Woodward, Tyler Woolley, PhD, Richard F. Worley, Birl W. Worley, Christopher Wright, Jim M. Wroblewski, Harrison C. Wroton, Richard V. Wyman, PhD, Robert B. Wyman, Dan A. Yaeger, Randy R. Yeager, David R. Yedo, PhD, Gene Yoder, Jay L. York, PhD, Douglas W. York, Masami Yoshimura, PhD, Thomas J. Young, MD,

William W. Yust, Stephen G. Zahony, Gerald W. Zander, James G. Zapert, Duane Zavadil, Timothy Dean Ziebarth, PhD, Milton A. Ziegelmeier, Robert Zimmerman, Sally G. Zinke

Connecticut

Robert K. Adair, PhD, Robert P. Aillery, Philip D. Allmendinger, MD, James L. Amarel, Thomas F. Anderson, PhD, Janis W. Anderson, David B. Anderson, Manuel Andrade, Steven M. Andreucci, Angela N. Archon, Philip T. Ashton, James R. Barrante, PhD, Paul Bauer, PhD, Jack W. Beal, PhD, Edward J. Beauchaine Jr., Paul D. Bemis, Robert Beringer, PhD, Eugene Berman, PhD, Ervin F. Bickley Jr., Charles D. Bizilj, R. G. Blain, Alan L. Blake, Professor Boa The Chu, PhD, Steven Allan Boggs, PhD, Karl R. Boldt, Laszlo J. Bollyky, PhD, Walter A. Bork, Harvey B. Boutwell, Norman E. Bowne, Robert S. Bradley, Randolph Henry Bretton, David Allan Bromley, PhD, Andrew B. Burns, Dennis H. Burr, William Patrick Cadogan, PhD, Leonard J. Calbo, PhD, William T. Caldwell, Zoe N. Canellakis, PhD, Joseph H. Cermola, Robert M. Christman, Boa-The Chu, PhD, William H. Church, PhD, Eric P. Cizek, Steven K. Clark, Greg P. Clark, J. David Coakley, Henry B. Cole, James N. Colebrook, George Collins, William F. Condon, PhD, Ralph D. Conlon, Eugene Anthony Conrad, PhD, Robert Joseph Cornell, PhD, Robert W. Cornell, PhD, Cynthia Coron, PhD, Paul J. Cortesi, William Allen Cowan, PhD, Alan L. Coykendall, Ernest L. Crandall, Edward D. Crosby, Zoltan Csukonyi, Charles C. Cullari, Dwight Hills Damon, PhD*, Edward Dana, Rocco N. Dangelo, Michael J. Darre, PhD, Lee Losee Davenport, PhD, Kenneth A. Decarolis, MD, Eddie Del Valle, Frank Deluca, Anthony J. Dennis, PhD, Hans R. Depold, Raymond J. Dicamillo, J. F. Dinivier, Edward W. Diskavich, Charles H. Doersam Jr., Charles H. Doersan Jr., Barbara B. Doonan, PhD, Valerie B. Duffy, PhD, K. H. Dufrane, Eliot Knights Easterbrook, PhD, Edwin George Eigel Jr., PhD, Henry J. Ellenbast Jr., Richard A. Eppler, PhD, Paul McKillop Erlandson, PhD, Daniel J. Evans, Jason P. Farren, Ernest H. Faust Jr., Robert Feingold, Steve Ferraro, William M. Foley, PhD, Herman J. Fonteyne, John C. Forster, George E. Fournier, G. Sidney Fox, Henry E. Fredericks, Arnold E. Fredericksen, Charles Richard Frink, PhD*, George P. Fulton, Joseph T. Furey, Wayne R. Gahwiller, Louis M. Galie, Ernest B. Gardon, PhD, Ernest B. Gardow, PhD, M. R. Gedge, Albert L. Geetter, MD, Robert Charles Geitz, PhD, Mark Gerstein, PhD, Roger R. Giler, Charles M. Gilman, John W. Glomb, PhD, Efim I. Golub, PhD, Robert Boyd Gordon, PhD, Laurence Gould, PhD, Vincent R. Gray, PhD, Mario A. Grippi, Fred J. Gross, Gottfried Haacke, PhD, Robert E. Haag, Sigvard Hallgren, Robert D. Halverstadt, Arthur L. Handman, John Haney, MD, Caryl P. Harkins, PhD, Howard Hayden, PhD, David L. Hedberg, MD, James Heidenreich, David E. Henderson, PhD, William B. Henry, MD, Jack L. Herz, PhD, Kenneth A. Hiller, Clyde D. Hinman, Jonathan Hoadley, Douglas Hoagland, John A. Hofbauer, George Robert Holzman, PhD, John Hoover, Donald Husted, James C. Hutton, Alfred Ingulli, Gideon Isaac, Gideon E. Isaac, Harry A. Jackson, Eva Vavrousek Jakuba, PhD, Jesse C. Jameson, W. W. Jarowey, Elliot E. Jessen, John William Johnstone Jr., Morton R. Kagan, PhD, Frank P. Kalberer, David W. Keefe, Marvin Jerry Kenig, PhD, Dan T. Kinard, Ravi Kiron, PhD, Paul Gustav Klemens, PhD, Bruce G. Koe, Anthony P. Konopka, William M. Kruple, Donald Kuehl, Harold Russell Kunz, PhD, H. Russell Kunz, PhD, Edward P. Kurdziel, Jai L. Lai, PhD, Robert Carl Lange, PhD, Professor Langeland, PhD, Robert A. Lapuk, John Larson, S. Benedict Levin, PhD, James J. Licari, PhD, John Liutkis, PhD, John Liutkus, PhD, Robert W. Loomis, Bernard W. Lovell, PhD, Alvin Higgins Lybeck, Tso-Ping Ma, PhD, James J. Macci, James MacDonald, Thomas Magee, David J. Mailhot, Harold J. Malone, MD, Richard G. Mansfield, Jack J. Marcinek, William C. Martz, Ceslovas Masaitis, Donald Matthews, Paul G. Mayer, Robert J. J. Mayerjak, PhD, Donald Mayo, PhD, William Markham McCardell, William Ray McConnell, PhD, L. McD. Schetky, PhD, J. W. McFarland, PhD, Hugh McKenna, James P. Memery, Robert B. Meny, Dean and Lois D. Miller, John Milne, Jeffrey N. Mobed, David S. Moelling, Michael Monroe, PhD, Richard Moravsik, Timothy A. Morck, PhD, John P. Moschello, MD, Saeid Moslehpour, PhD, Francis Joseph Murray, PhD, Ronald Fenner Myers, PhD, Norman A. Nadel, Peter Nalle, John Nasser, Edward S. Ness, PhD, Charles Henry Nightingale, PhD, Brian O'Brien, Robert L. O'Brien, Ronald R. Oneto, Raymond L. Osborne Jr., MD, John Harold Ostrom, PhD, Joseph R. Pagnozzi, Francis Rudolph Paolini, PhD, Laurine J. Papa, David Frank Paskausky, PhD, Mark R. Pastore, Alfred N. Paul, Zoran Pazameta, PhD, Raul T. Perez, MD, Al Peterson, Ronald Piccoli, Daniel Joseph Pisano, PhD, Thomas Plante, Inge Pope, Robert W. Powitz, PhD, John B. Presti, B. Prokai, PhD, Michael J. Pryor, PhD, Ken J. Pudeler, John A. Raabe, PhD, Arthur L. Rasmussen, DVM, John A. Reffner, PhD, Harold Bernard Reisman, PhD, Hans Heinrich Rennhard, PhD, Anna V. Resnansky, William C. Ridgway III, PhD, Francis J. Riley, Charles A. Rinaldi, Felice P. Rizzo, Frank Roberts Jr., Donald Wallace Robinson, J. David Robords, Fred L. Robson, PhD, Robert Henry Roth, PhD, William R. Rotherforth, William R. Rotherporth, Robert A. Rubega, PhD, George Rumney, PhD, John P. Sachs, PhD, Robert Howell Sammis, Reinhard Sarges, PhD, Emilio A. Savinelli, PhD, John R. Schafer, Ronald G. Schlegel, M. E. Schwiebert, Howard E. Schwiebert, Clive R. Scorey, PhD, Andrew E. Scoville, Thomas Seery, PhD, Ronald Sekellick, Chester J. Sergey Jr., Harry Sewell, PhD, Richard C. Sharp, Mark Shlyankevich, PhD, Linton Simeri, PhD, Linton Earl Simerl, PhD, Jaime Simkovitz, MD, E. L. Sinclair, Bolesh Joseph Skutnik, PhD, George N. Smilas, Elwin E. Smith, Bruce Sobol, MD, Lon E. Solomita, Andrzej Stachowiak, Bernard A. Stankevich, William R. Stanley, Steven C. Stanton, Joseph Sternberg, PhD, Charles Lysander Storrs, PhD,

Joseph R. Stramondo, David Swan, Charles J. Szyszko, John Tanaka, PhD, Robert G. Tedeschi, Robert H. Thompson, PhD, Frederick G. Thumm, Sargent N. Tower, Robert L. Trapasso, MD, Richard F. Tucker, Marvin Roy Turnipseed, PhD, Alan K. Vanags, Geprge Veronos, PhD, Daniel Vesa, John S. Wagner, Terramce J. Walsh, Robert G. Weeles, Edward B. Wenners, Richard Wildermuth, Roger F. Williams, Robert F. Williams, George C. Wiswell Jr., John E. Yocom, Robert L. Yocum, Edward A. Zane, MD, Claude Zeller, PhD, William Arthur Ziegler, Charles T. Zrakas

Delaware

Earl Arthur Abrahamson, PhD, Albert W. Alsop, PhD, Giacomo Armand DI, PhD, Joseph Bartholomew Arots, PhD, Charles Hammond Arrington, PhD, Andre JS Baidins, PhD, Andrejs Bajdins, PhD, Lewis Clinton Bancroft, Theo C. Baumeister, Paul Becher, PhD, Scott K. Beegle, Oswald R. Bergmann, PhD, Robert Paul Bigliano, William A. Bizjak, William L. Blackwell, Charles G. Boncelet, PhD, Frank R. Borger, Ernest R. Bosetti, John Harland Boughton, PhD, Charles J. Brown Jr., PhD, Thomas S. Buchanan, PhD, Bruce M. Buker, Charles B. Buonassisi, Donovan C. Carbaugh, PhD, Louise M. Carter, William B. Carter, Leonard B. Chandler, PhD, Robert John Chorvat, PhD, Emil E. Christofano, Alexander Cisar, A. Cisar, Ian Clark, George Rolland Cole, PhD, Albert Z. Conner, Nancy H. Conner, Harry Norma Cripps, PhD, R. D. Crooks, William H. Day, PhD, Daniel M. Dayton, William E. Delaney III, PhD, Pamela J. Delaney III, Dennis O. Dever, Seshasayi Dharmavaram, PhD, Armand Digiacomo, PhD, William A. Doerner, PhD, Walter Domorod, Charles Dougherty, Roland G. Downing, PhD, Francis J. Doyle, Arthur Edwin Drake, PhD, Elizabeth W. Fahl, PhD, Stephen R. Fahnestock, PhD, Eric R. Fahnoe, Enrico Thomas Federighi, PhD, Thomas Aven Ford, PhD, Dennis Light Funck, PhD, John Frederick Gates Clark, PhD, William J. Geimeier, MD, Joseph Edmund Gervay, PhD, Wayne Gibbons, PhD, David A. Glenn, William H. Godshall, John E. Greer Jr., Alfred Gruber, Lachhman D. Gupta, Earl T. Hackett Jr., R. M. Hagen, PhD, Thomas K. Haldas, Charles W. Hall, Thomas W. Harding, PhD, Charles R. Hartzell, PhD, James R. Hodges, Winfried Thomas Holfeld, PhD, Anthony R. Hollet, Roger L. Hoyt, Chin-Pao Huang, PhD, Robert G. Hunsperger, PhD, Mir Nazrul Islam, PhD, Harold Leonard Jackson, PhD, Vladislav J. Jandasek, Paul R. Jann, Charles S. Joanedis, John Eric Jolley, PhD, Louise Hinrichsen Jones, PhD, Robert John Kallal, PhD, Robert James Kassal, PhD, John T. Kephart, Charles O. King, PhD, Joseph Jack Kirkland, PhD, Henry Kobsa, PhD, Theodore Augur Koch, PhD, Robert F. Kock, Bruce David Korant, PhD, Carl George Krespan, PhD, Palaniappa Krishnan, PhD, Wo Kong Kwok, PhD, Bernard Albert Link, PhD, Royce Zeno Lockart, PhD, Francis M. Logullo, PhD, H. Y. Loken, PhD, Rosario Joseph Lombardo, PhD, Ruskin Longworth, PhD, Carl Andrew Lukach, PhD, Jeffrey B. Malick, PhD, Creighton Paul Malone, PhD, Philip Manos, PhD, Charle Eugene Mason, PhD, W. Mc Cormack, PhD, Margaret A. Minkwitz, PhD, Donald M. Mitchell, Edward Francis Moran, PhD, William E. Morris, Calvin Lyle Moyer, PhD, Marcus A. Naylor Jr., PhD, Howard E. Newcomb, Edmund Luke Niedzielski, PhD, Michael Nollet, Lilburn Lafayette Norton, PhD, Louis P. Olivere, Robert D. Osborne, Alfred Horton Pagano, PhD, Albert A. Pavlic, PhD, Rowan P. Perkins, Michael E. Pilcher, Raymond S. Pusey, Ann Rave, PhD, Richard L. Raymond, Charles Francis Reinhardt, PhD, John Reitsma, Robert D. Ricker, PhD, Louis H. Rombach, PhD, Leonard Rosenbaum, MD, Richard A. Rowe, PhD, Mark Russell, PhD, David Frank Ryder, PhD, Bryan B. Sauer, PhD, Robert Andrew Scala, PhD, Jerome C. Sekerke Sr., Robert Smiley, PhD, Jack Austin Snyder, PhD, Frank E. South, PhD, Harold F. Staunton, PhD, Xavier Stewart, PhD, Douglas C. Stewart, James W. Stingel, George Joseph Stockburger, PhD, Richard W. Stout, Milton Arthur Taves, PhD, William Russell Thickstun, PhD, James R. Thomen, PhD, Siva Vallabhaneni, Tina K. Vandyk, Deadaws Ventures, J. G. Vermeychuk, PhD, Vernon G. Vernier, MD, Owen W. Webster, PhD, John T. Wellener, Thomas Whisenand, PhD, Professor Whisenand, PhD, Arthur Whittemore, Joseph S. Woodhead, DVM, Ihor Zajac, PhD

Washington D.C.

Philip H. Abelson, PhD*, Nicholas A. Alten, Todd Barbosa, MD, Marlet H. Benedick, Donna F. Bethell, John D. Bultman, PhD, Adrian Ramond Chamberlain, PhD, Ronald E. Cohen, PhD, Marguerite Wilton Coomes, PhD, James M. Cutts, Walter R. Dyer, PhD, Howard L. Egan, PhD, Paul Herman Ernst Meijer, PhD, John B. Fallon, Martin Finerty Jr., Donna Fitzpatrick, Bruce Flanders, PhD, Nancy Flournoy, PhD, Edmund H. Fording Jr., Robert F. Fudali, PhD, Marjorie A. Garvey, Clarence Joseph Gibbs, PhD, David John Goodenough, PhD, Caryl Haskins, PhD*, Niki Hatzilambrou, PhD, Robert L. Hirsch, PhD, John Thomas Holloway, PhD, William S. Hughes, MD, Charles J. Kim, PhD, Thomas Adren Kitchens, PhD, John Cian Knight, PhD, Richard L. Lawson, Frank X. Lee, PhD, Donald R. Lehman, PhD, Devra C. Marcus, MD, Gerald Noah McEwen, PhD, Charles J. Montrose, PhD, F. Ksh Mostofi, MD, Stanley Nesheim, Errol C. Noel, PhD, Frederick J. Pearce, PhD, James S. Potts, Bhakta Bhusan Rath, PhD, Thomas Leonard Reinecke, PhD, Alexander F. Robertson, PhD, Malcolm Ross, PhD, Malcom Ross, PhD, Mark A. Rubin, Joaquin A. Saavedra, Jeffery D. Sabloff, MD, Frank Shalvey Santamour, PhD, Walter Schimmerling, PhD, Nina Scribanu, MD, Frank Senftle, PhD, Anatole Shapiro, PhD, Thomas Elijah Smith, PhD, Thomas R. Stauffer, PhD, Marjorie R.

Townsend, Kyriake V> Valassi, PhD, Robert Walter, James D. Watkins, Carl W. Werntz, PhD, Frank Clifford Whitmore, PhD, William Phillips Winter, PhD, William Yamamto, MD, Daniel V. Young, MD, Lorenz Eugene Zimmerman, MD

Florida

M. Robert Aaron, Frank D. Abbott, Jose L. Abreu Jr., Austin R. Ace, John Adams, Jorge T. Aguinaldo, Tom J. Albert, Evelyn A. Alcantara, PhD, Thomas Alderson, PhD, Samuel Roy Aldrich, PhD, Luis A. Algarra, Mark J. Alkire, MD, Eric R. Allen, PhD, Pampselo Allen, George L. Allgoever, Richard E. Almy, Ramon J. Alonso, PhD, Virgilio E. Alvarez, Raymond J. Anater, Barry D. Anderson, Vincent Angelo, PhD, Herbert D. Anton, Henry W. Apfelbach, MD, W. H. Appich Jr., Orlando A. Arana, R. Kent Arblaster, Antonio E. Arce, William Bryant Ard, PhD, Vittorio K. Argento, PhD, Ross Harold Arnett, PhD, Jack N. Arnold, James T. Arocho, MD, Rhea T. Van Arsdall, Charles R. Ashford, Victor Asirvatham, PhD, Robert C. Asmus, Lynn Atkinson, Robert C. Atwood, Kathi A. Aultman, MD, Alfred Ells Austin, PhD, Andrew B. Avalon, Mark Averett, Donald Avery, Bonnie Jean Wilson Bachman, PhD, Ed Bailey, Travis Bainbridge, Earl W. Baker, PhD, Theodore Paul Baker, Joseph H. Baker, MD, William M. Baldwin, Ferdi M. Baler, Ronald C. Ballard, DVM, Lloyd Harold Banning, Peter R. Bannister, Donald E. Barber, Paul D. Barbieri, Andrew M. Bardos, Walter E. Barker Jr., Ellis O. Barnes, Kenneth J. Barr, J. H. Barten, Niles Bashaw, Mark J. Bassett, PhD, Michael A. Bassford, Sam P. Battista, PhD, Max G. Battle Sr., Don J. Bauer, Arthur Nicholas Baumann, Lisa L. Baumbach, PhD, Timothy H. Beacham, James M. Beall, Elroy W. Beans, PhD, James H. Beardall, Mhamdy H. Bechir, PhD, Theodore Wiseman Beiler, PhD, Alfred J. Beljan, Leonard W. Bell, Dee J. Bell, Robert J. Bellino, MD, Armando L. Benavides, Deodatta V. Bendre, MD, Carroll H. Bennett, Clayton A. Bennett, Henry L. Bennett, Rudy J. Beres, John W. Bergacker, Robert D. Berkebile, MD, Donald C. Berkey, Elliot Berman, PhD, Oran L. Bertsch, Arthur F. Betchart, Ervin F. Bickley Jr., David A. Bigler, Robert W. Birckhead, Alfred F. Bischoff, Burt James Bittner, James K. Blaircom, Joel J. Blatt, PhD, Ralph C. Bledsoe, Ernest L. Bliss, DVM, Robert R. Blume, Wayne Dean Bock, PhD, Peter Boer, PhD, Colleen H. Boggs, Harry Joseph Boll, PhD, Sam Bolognia, Nicholas H. Booth, PhD, Robert M. Borg, Walter S. Bortko, Joseph F. Boston, PhD, Leroy V. Bovey, Clifford R. Bowers, Gale Clark Boxill, PhD, Joseph C. Bozik, George Bradshaw, Jerry A. Brady, MD, Richard H. Braunlich, Thomas N. Braxtan, MD, Lloyd J. Bresley, Peter R. Brett, Joe E. Brewer, Greg A. Bridenstine, Edwin C. Brinker, Anne M. Briscoe, PhD, Joe P. Brittain, Wayne Brittian, Buford L. Brock, Hampton Ralph Brooker, PhD, John Brooks, N. P. Brooks, Bahngrell W. Brown, PhD, Fredrick G. Brown, MD, Gary L. Brown, Kenneth B. Bruckart, Bernard O. Brunegraff, Gerald W. Bruner, Richard L. Brutus, DVM, Frederick T. Bryan, PhD, Bobby F. Bryan, Gary L. Buckwalter, PhD, David A. Buff, Mark A. Bukhbinder, PhD, Ervin Trowbridge Bullard, PhD, Edward J. Buonopane, MD, Paul Philip Burbutis, PhD, Stanley Burg, PhD, James H. Burkhalter, PhD, Charles Burns, MD, Philip J. Burnstein, Thomas R. Busard, MD, Philip Alan Butler, PhD, Clair E. Butler, DVM, John J. Byrnes, MD, Barry M. Bywalec, Charles R. Cabiac, Robert Cadieux, Mary M. Cadieux, Marilee Whitney Caldwell, PhD, Patrick E. Callaghan, MD, Jeffrey D. Caltrider, James B. Camden, PhD, John R. Cameron, Joseph Campbell, PhD, Clifford A. Campbell, Jose A. Campoamor, Carlos A. Camps, Jorge A. Camps, Paul Canevaro, Julian E. Cannon, Hugh N. Cannon, Daniel James Cantliffe, PhD, William J. Carson, DVM, Arthur L. Carter, Harvey P. Carter, MD, Fred S. Carter, MD, William J. Caseber Jr., Wiley·M. Cauthen, Robert Cavalleri, PhD, Steven Chabottle, Robert Champlin, Howard E. Chana, William M. Chandler, MD, Donald G. Chaplin, Gregory W. Chapman, M. J. Charles, MD, Augustus Charos, Fernando G. Chaumont, Robert S. Chauvin, PhD, Mary E. Chavez, DVM, Craig F. Cheng, Genady Cherepanov, PhD, Paul A. Chervenick, MD, Roger B. Chewning, Sen Chiao, PhD, R. Chiarenzelli, Henry D. Childs, MD, Craig Chismarick, David Chleck, Mandj B. Chopra, PhD, Wen L. Chow, PhD, Bent Aksel Christensen, PhD, James R. Clapp, Richard Allen Claridge, James R. Clarke, James T. Clay, James D. Cline, Paul L. Clough, Clarence Leroy Coates, PhD, Keith H. Coats, PhD, Leroy M. Coffman, DVM, C. Eugene Coke, PhD, Gregory Cole, Samuel Oran Colgate, PhD, Glenn E. Colvin, Franklin J. Cona, James T. Conklin, James R. Connell, Fountain E. Conner, Walter Edmund Conrad, PhD, Alberto Convers, MD, James J. Conway, PhD, Anne M. Cooney, Denise R. Cooper, PhD, Raymond David Cooper, PhD, Ernest B. Cooper, Mark S. Cooper, Emmett M. Cooper, MD, George P. Cooper, Dawson M. Copeland, Eugene Francis Corcoran, PhD, Graydon F. Corn, Leon Worthington Couch II, PhD, Richard J. Councill, Robert O. Covington, John Cowden, Vincent Frederick Cowling, PhD, Francis M. Coy, MD, Warren S. Craven, James F. Crawford, Buford Creech, G. Kingman Crosby, David G. Cross, MD, William C. Cross, Tom L. Crossman, David Crowe, D. L. Crowson, David L. Crowson, Jose R. Cuarta Jr., Matteo A. Cucchiara, Donald A. Cuervo, William M. Cullen, Russell E. Cummings, Gene L. Curen, Peter J. Curry, Fred W. Curtis Jr., Rosario E. Cushera, Walter J. Czagas, Donald W. Czubiak, George Clement Dacey, PhD, John A. Dady, Bao D. Dang, Andrew W. Dangelo, Jean H. Darling, MD, Albert N. Darlington, Thomas L. Davenport, PhD, Charlie R. Davenport, Duanne M. Davis, PhD, Duane M. Davis, PhD, Janice R. Davis, Noorbibi K. Day, PhD, Duke Dayton, James W. De Ruiter, Nathan W. Dean, PhD, Stanley Deans, PhD, B. D. Debaryshe, Wayne Deckert, PhD, Albert M. DeGaeta, James A. deGanahl, Quentin C. Dehaan, MD, Robert T. Dehoff, PhD, Glenn A. DeJong, Gary J. Dellerson, Harold Anderson

Denmark, Kenneth Derick, Gary D. Dernlan, Edward Augustine Desloge, PhD, Ronald P. Destefano, PhD, Lawrence E. Deusch, Martha S. Deweese, Charles S. Dexter, MD, C. Dexter, MD, Charles M. Dick, Philip A. Dick, John A. Dickerson, James C. Diefenderfer, John R. Dieterman II, Julie Y. Dieu, PhD, Norman G. Dillman, PhD, Richard H. Dimarco, Robert L. Dimmick, Howard Livingstone Dinsmore, PhD, Roy H. Dippy, James P. Diskin, William L. Dixon, MD, N. Djeu, PhD, Gerald D. Dobie, Jerry L. Dobrovolny, PhD, Robert W. Dobson, Michael Dodane, John E. Dolan, William R. Dolbier, PhD, Eugene E. Dolecki, L. Guy Donaruma, PhD, John R. Doner, PhD, Frederick G. Doran, MD, Keith L. Doty, PhD, Daniel A. Doty, W. Campbell Douglass 3rd, MD, Spencer Douglass, Larry J. Doyle, PhD, Edward F. Drass, MD, Neil I. Dreizen, David M. Drenan, DVM, F. J. Driggers, Vojtech A. Drlicka, MD, Roger W. Dubble, Joseph E. Duchateau, Loring Duff, Edward T. Dugan, PhD, James M. Dunford, Russell F. Dunn, PhD, James L. Dunnie, Steven Jon Duranceau, PhD, Fred P. Dwight, Julian Jonathan Dwornik, PhD, Joseph Jackson Eachus, PhD, James B. Earle, Hamel B. Eason, MD, Amy E. Eason, James J. Edmier, Dean Stockett Edmonds Jr., PhD, Warren R. Ehrhardt, Howard George Ehrlich, PhD, Paul Ewing Ehrlich, PhD, Esther B. Eisenstein, MD, Luis R. Elias, PhD, David F. Elliott, John O. Elliott, Scott Ellis, Lamont Eltinge, PhD, Frederick H. Elwell, William A. Engel, John M. England, Jack L. Engleman, John Enns, PhD, Frederick B. Epstein, PhD, Larry R. Erickson, Samuel E. Eubank, Ralph L. Evans, James Legrand Everett, Norm R. Every, John M. Evjen, PhD, Martin Fackler FACS, MD, Atir Fadhli, PhD, Larry E. Fairbrother III, Peter M. Fallon, MD, Scott D. Farash, Robert L. Farnsworth, Robert C. Faro, PhD, Donald D. Farshing, PhD, Donald Featherman, Henry A. Feddern, PhD, Louis Feinstein, PhD, Jean F. Feldman, DVM, Emmett B. Ferguson, MD, Patrick J. Ferland, Henry T. Fielding, Carl E. Fielland, Joshua A. Fierer, MD, Norton E. Fincher, Robert D. Finfrock, Ronald L. Finger, Barney W. Finkel, MD, Charles W. Finkl Jr., PhD, Gerald R. Fishe, George H. Fisher, PhD, Charles H. Fisher, MD, John C. Fisher, William J. Flick, William H. Flowers, PhD, John C. Floyd, Timothy A. Focht, Peter John Fogg, PhD, James H. Fogleman, MD, Paul D. Folse, Candido F. Font, Anderson M. Foote 3rd, Marion Edwin Forsman, PhD, Irving S. Foster, PhD, Norman G. Foster, Rob Foster, Robert G. Foster, Don Fournier, Gerald Fox, Russell E. Frame, Sidney Frank, Allan J. Frank, Anthony D. Frawley, PhD, S. Frazier, PhD, Stephen Earl Frazier, PhD, Andrew W. Frech, Thomas V. Freiley, Arthur Lee Fricke, PhD, Raymond Friedman, PhD, Dan C. Frodge, Higinio J. Fuentes, Robert Louis Fullman, PhD, Clark W. Furlong, Ronald M. Fussell, George Gabanski, George Gabanski, Robert Earl Gabler, John C. Galen, Robert M. Gallen, Boris Galperin, PhD, Joseph E. Gannon, William Lee Garbrecht, PhD*, Harry E. Gardner Jr., Carl C. Garner, Charles J. Garrett, Don L. Garrison, Jose R. Garrote, MD, Geoffrey W. Gartner Jr., John J. Gaughan, Eugene R. Gaughran, PhD, John F. Gaver, Douglas M. Gebbie, MD, Steve Geci, Anthony F. Gee, James E. Geiger, John Geiger, Paul G. Geiss, MD, Karl R. Geitner, Edmund A. Geller, MD, George T. Genneken, Lawrence D. Gent Jr., Larry Gerahiau, Milo P. Gerber, MD, Eugene Jordan Gerberg, PhD, Walter M. Gerhold, MD, Umberto Ferdinando Gianola, PhD, Kurt R. Gies, Fred Giflow, Peter Gilbert, Edward R. Gillie, June Gillin, William Gilmore Jr., George A. Gimber, W. E. Girton, Johanna M. Glacy-Araos, Richard E. Gladziszewski, Thomas Alexander Gleeson, PhD, Anatol A. Glen, MD, Ronald Gluck, Richard H. Gnaedinger, PhD, C. J. Gober, Robert Owen Godwin, Louis D. Gold, PhD, Alan S. Goldfarb, PhD, Lionel Solomon Goldring, PhD, Gary J. Goldsberry, Yitzhak Goldstein, Ely Gonick, PhD, Ed E. Gonzalez, Lewis F. Good Jr., Ted A. Goodman, Brett P. Goodman, Robert Stouffer Gordee, PhD, Theodore B. Gortemoller Jr., David Gossett, Henry Gotsch, Charles F. Gottlieb, PhD, Karl Gould, Gerald Geza Gould, Hans C. Graber, PhD, Howard E. Graham, F. R. Grant, M. R. Grate, MD, Frank Grate, Wayne C. Graves, Chester W. Graves, George F. Green, PhD, Willie H. Green, Donald J. Gregg, Charles W. Gregg, Frank E. Gregor, Bert L. Grenville, Donald K. Grierson, R. Howard Griffen, Gordon E. Grimes, Chester F. Grimsley, William B. Grinter, Frank Grote, Gerry Gruber, PhD, Ivan Grymov, Ernest A. Gudath, Cnelson Guerriere, MD, Robert O. Guhl, Joseph W. Guida, Jean R. Gullahorn, Michael E. Gunger, Phillip W. Gutmann, Thomas J. Gyorog, Mutaz Habal, PhD, James A. Hagans, PhD, Jeffrey S. Haggard, Donald R. Hagge, James T. Haggerty, MD, Warren A. Hahn, Theodore W. Hahn, MD, Oussama Halabi, Douglas K. Hales, John F. Hallahan, Harry Hamburger, MD, Brenton M. Hamil, PhD, Darryl J. Hamilton, Professor Hamilton, Douglas K. Hammann, Thomas G. Hammond Jr., Larry D. Hamner, M. Hancock, Robert William Hanks, PhD, Donald C. Hanto, Kevin G. Harbin, DVM, William Hardy, Jeffrey L. Harmon, PhD, Professor Eric Harms, Eric A. Harms, Joseph J. Harper, Gary G. Harrison, Robert Hartley, William H. Hartmann, MD, Ronald F. Hartung, Eldert Hartwig Jr., Ed Harwell, Alden G. Haskins, Charles L. Hattaway, Arthur J. Haug, PhD, Ralph E. Hayden, Michael E. Hayes, PhD, Ralph L. Hayes, John A. Hayes, John F. Hazen, Ronald Alan Head, PhD, Robert S. Hearon, George M. Hebbard, Boyd R. Hedrick Jr., Roy W. Heffner, Brian E. Heinfeld, David F. Heinrich, Cecil Helfgott, PhD, James F. Helle, Richard B. Hellstrom, Robert L. Helmling, MD, James Brooke Henderson, PhD, J. N. Hendrix, MD, Jim Hennessy, Carl H. Henriksen, Jonathan Henry, PhD, James F. Hentges, PhD, Alvin C. Hernandez, Alberto Hernandez, Irwin Herman Herskowitz, PhD, David E. Hertel, Richard L. Hester, Richard P. Heuschele, Thomas B. Hewton, David K. Hickle, Kathryn Hickman, PhD, Gregory D. Hicks, MD, Thomas M. Hicks, Gregory D. Hicks, Clarence Edward Hieserman, C. E. Hieserman, Eric V. Hill, PhD, Richard F. Hill, Robert E. Hillis, PhD, Helmuth E. Hinderer, PhD, Carla J. Hinds, George T. Hinkle, PhD, George M. Hinson, Daniel J. Hirnikel, Thomas James Hirt, PhD, Robert Warren Hisey, PhD, H. Ray Hockaday, John T. Hocker, Edward Hoffmann, James P. Hogan, PhD, L. E. Hoisington, PhD, Lawrence E.

Hoisington, PhD, David G. Holifield, PhD, Allen B. Hollett, Richard A. Hollmann, Eugene H. Holly, MD, Michael D. Holm, Donald A. Holmer, PhD, H. Duane Holsapple, Larry H. Hooper, MD, E. Erskine Hopkins, Lewis Milton Horger, PhD, David Hornsby, Evelio N. Horta, PhD, Paul A. Horton, PhD, Hamid Hosseini, John H. Hotaling, William B. Houghton, Charles M. House, MD, Larry Housel, Gordon P. Houston, Louis R. Hovater, James Howze, Roger Hrudy, Sung Lan Hsia, PhD, Robert J. Hudek, George R. Hudson, Russell Henry Huebner Sr., PhD, Gaylord Huenefeld, Arvel Hatch Hunter, PhD, Jamie Hunter, Ronald L. Hurt, Scotty M. Hutto, Kenneth Hyatt, Carly H. Hyland, Terrence L. Ibbs, Phillip M. Iloff Jr., PhD, Paul E. Ina, William L. Ingle, David Irvin, Robert M. Ivey, Bruce G. Jackson, MD, J. G. Jackson III, Wes S. Jacobs, Michael T. Jaekels, MD, Paul C. Jakob, Clifford H. James, John C. Janus, Samuel E. Jaquinta, Karen C. Jaroch, Hanley F. Jenkins, MD, Paul A. Jennings, PhD, Clayton Everett Jensen, PhD, Anthony E. Jernigan, Howard R. Jeter, Eileen D. Johann, PhD, Virgil Ivancich Johannes, PhD, James Robert Johnson, PhD, T. Johnson, Anthony Johnson, David A. Johnson, Gerald B. Johnson, Charles W. Johnson, H. C. Johnson, J. William Johnson, MD, Frederick W. Johnston Jr., Harold E. Johnstone, MD, R. H. Jones, PhD, Roy Carl Jones, PhD, Marcia Jones, Barbara C. Jones, MD, Claude D. Jones, Edward Joseph, MD, Edwin A. Joyce Jr., Patrick A. Joyce, Hiram Paul Julien, PhD, H. P. Julien, PhD, Brian J. Just, PhD, Martin J. Kaiser, Bernard J. Kane, Ramanuja Chara Kannan, Robert Karasik, William J. Kardash Sr., Delmar W. Karger, Robert R. Karpp, PhD, Jeffery J. Karsonovich, Kenneth Stephen Karsten, PhD, A. J. Kassab, PhD, Michael J. Kaufman, PhD, Michael E. Kazunas, Kar M. Keil, MD, Carroll R. Keim, Richard K. Keimig, Daniel C. Kelley, John E. Kemp, Francis J. Kendrick, PhD, Dallas C. Kennedy II, PhD, Robert W. Kennedy AF (Ret), James A. Kennelley, PhD, Charles W. Kennison, James G. Keramas, PhD, Robert Kergai, John E. Kerr, Keith M. Kersch, John M. Kessinger, MD, Ronald J. Kessner, Charles R. Keyser, Suresh K. Khator, PhD, Roosey Khawly, MD, Jennifer L. Kibiger, Richard L. Kiddey, David E. Kiepke, Robert R. Kilgo, Hueston C. King, MD, McLeroy King, Randy L. King, Stan A. Kinmouth, Dalton L. Kinsella, MD, James R. Kircher, Henry W. Kirchner, Michael K. Kirwan, Wendell G. Kish, DVM, Abbott Theodore Kissen, PhD, Geza Kisvarsanyi, PhD, Eva B. Kisvarsanyi, Waldemar Klassen, PhD, Steven K. Klecka, Willard R. Kleckner, PhD, Karl M. Klein Jr., Karl G. Klinges, PhD, Benny Leroy Klock, PhD, Glenn S. Kloiber, Daniel E. Kludt, Ian G. Koblick, Lee E. Koepke, Lawrence K. Koering, Paul A. Kohlhepp, MD, Donald H. Komito, George J. Kondelin Jr., George E. Konold, John Kopec Sr., Richard J. Kossman, MD, Sidney Kovner, Stanley Krainin, Donald R. Kramer, John Krc Jr., Istvan M. Krisko, PhD, John M. Krouse, MD, Walter Hillis Kruschwitz, PhD, Dennis J. Kulondra, PhD, Frank Turner Kurzweg, MD, Bogdan Ognjan Kuzmanovic, PhD, Tung-Sing Kwong, Edward G. Kyle, Charles Lager, Henry J. Lamb, Donald H. Lambing, Michael C. Lamure, Albert L. Land, B. Edward Lane, Brian Lane, Paul J. Langford, JoAnne Larsen, PhD, Reginald Einar Larson, Edwin D. Lasseter, Mark T. Lautenschlager, David Lawler, Peter K. Lazdins, PhD, Frank W. Leach, George R. Lebo, PhD, John p. Leedy, Irving Leibson, PhD, Gordon F. Leitner, Carl Lentz, MD, Kenneth Allen Leon, PhD, Philip B. Leon, Dennis J. Leonard, PhD, Donald E. Lepic, Michael A. Leuck, Samuel Levin, Stanley S. Levy, PhD, Thomas F. Lewicki, Thomas Lick, PhD, Jon L. Liljequist, Bruce A. Lindblom, Bruce G. Lindsey, PhD, Raul A. Llerena, Vern Lloyd, Salvadore J. Locascio, PhD, S. J. Locascio, PhD, Emil P. Loch, Richard F. Lockey, Bruce A. Loeppke, Ernest E. Loft, R. Loftfield, Crispino E. Lombardi, R. W. Long, PhD, James A. Long, Don D. Lorenc, Robert A. Loscher, Julio G. Loureiro, Richard G. Loverne, Gordon Lovestrand, Robert W. Loyd, Steven A. Lubinski, John W. Luce, Richard R. Ludlam, Bobby R. Ludlum, S. J. Ludwig, Henry C. Luke, Ronald A. Lukert, MD, Arthur Lyall, Victoria S. Lyon, DVM, Paul Macchi, MD, Theodore S. Macleod, Robert K. Macmillan, Orville E. Macomber, Robert L. Magann, James G. Magazino, James Mahannah, Raymond C. Mairson, Ray C. Mairson, Edmund R. Malinowski, PhD, Edmund M. Malone, Joe H. Maltby, DVM, Eugene H. Man, PhD, Jesse R. Manalo, Robert J. Mandel, MD, Anthony P. Mann, Walter Manning, Joseph Robert Mannino, PhD, W. E. Manry Jr., MD, Robert S. Mansell, PhD, Juliano Maran, Vladimir K. Markoski, Gerardo L. Marquez, Homer L. Marquit, MD, John J. Marra, A. E. Marshall Jr., Roger W. Marsters, PhD, Paul R. Martel, Jose L. Martin, PhD, William W. Martin, Ralph Harding Martin, Mason E. Marvel, PhD, Harry L. Mason, Wayne A. Mather, Robb R. Mathias, Maria B. Matinchev, MD, Guy C. Mattson, PhD, James W. Maurer, MD, Florentin Maurrasse, PhD, John G. Mavroides, PhD, Marion S. Mayer, PhD, George T. McAllister, Joseph James McBride, PhD, J. J. McBride Jr., PhD, Clarence H. McCall, Edward E. McCallum, Carolyn A. McCann, MD, Ron L. McCartney, MD, R. McCarty, G. J. McCaul, Walter H. McCluskey, Daniel F. McConaghy, Daniel G. McCormick, Donald S. McCorquodale, PhD, Scott A. McCoy, Stephen C. McCranie, Robert L. McCroskey, PhD, Victor McDaniel, PhD, Lee Russell McDowell, PhD, Stuart E. McGahee, Anthony McGoron, PhD, David F. McIntosh, Darrell W. McKinley, Michael McKinney, PhD, Professor McKisson, George Hoagland McLafferty, Charles D. McLelland, Malcolm E. McLouth, Harold R. McMichael, Donald W. McMillan, MD, Donald F. McNeil, PhD, Clyde W. McNew, Edwin R. McNutt, Glenn L. McNutt, Marion L. Meadows, Rolando Meireles, Tonya S. Mellen, Henry Paul Meloche, PhD, Darrell E. Melton, Robert William Menefee, PhD, Gunter Richard Meng, MD, Jerry Merckel, PhD, Daniel N. Mergens, MD, Andrew H. Merritt, PhD, Henry Neyron Merritt, PhD, Duane R. Merritt, Lawrence E. Mertens, PhD, James H. Messer, Aldo J. Messulam, PhD, Jack Messulam, MD, Aldo J. Messulan, PhD, Alexandru Mezincescu, PhD, Oskar Michejda, PhD, Harold S. Mickley, PhD, Judith A. Milcarsky, DVM, Sylvester S. Milewski, John F. Milko, William Knight Miller, PhD, Kenneth J. Miller, MD, Scott Milroy, PhD, Robert

Mitchell Milton, PhD, R. Edward Minchin Jr., PhD, Malcolm G. Minchin, N. Misconi, PhD, Patricia Mitchell, John B. Mix, PhD, Jeffrey N. Mock, Stanley S. Moles, PhD, Ralph Moradiellos, Christopher A. Morgan, PhD, Robert A. Morrell, Harold N. Morris, James H. Moss, Lee W. Mozes, PhD, Charles L. Mraz, Rosa M. C. Muchovej, PhD, John T. Muller, Robert C. Mumby, MD, John F. Murphy, PhD, William Parry Murphy, MD, Frank A. Musto, Jay Muza, PhD, Leslie A. Myers, PhD, Mark T. Myers, Daniel A. Myerson, MD, Harry E. Myles, Don R. Myrick, Roger P. Natzke, PhD, Donald K. Nelson, Hugo D. Neubauer Jr., James E. Neustaedter, George F. Nevin, Waldo Newcomesz, Jesse R. Newell, McFadden A. Newell, Richard W. Newell, Arthur W. Newett, Carl S. Newman, William A. Newsome, MD, Bill H. Nicholls, David S. Nichols, Kenneth W. Nickerson, Paula W. Nicola, Edward Niespodziany, PhD, Herbert Nicholas Nigg, PhD, Margaret M. Niklas, Edward G. Nisbett, John C. Nobel, MD, Michael J. Noesen, William G. Norrie, Ronelle C. Norris, Peggy A. Northrop, Albert Notary, Carlos G. Nugent, Robert L. Oatley, James J. O'Brien, PhD, Thomas W. O'Brien, PhD, T. F. Ochab, Frederic C. Oder, PhD, Norbert W. Ohara, PhD, J. W. O'Hara, PhD, Kenneth R. Olen, PhD, Ronald V. Olsen, Oluf E. Olsen, Lewis E. Olson, Robert J. Olson, Ray Andrew Olsson, MD, Robert Milton Oman, PhD, Don O'Neal, Adrain P. O'Neal, Albert E. O'Neall, Gene F. Opdyke, James F. Orofino, Donald Orr, David A. Orser, William Albert Orth, PhD, Harold Osborn, Matthew J. Ossi, Wendall K. Osteen, PhD, John P. Osterberg, Augustua C. Ouano, PhD, Robert Franklin Overmyer, Terence Cunliffe Owen, PhD, Jerry M. Owen, Henry Yoshio Ozaki, PhD, Glenda B. Pace, Thomas J. Padden, PhD, Fred Paetofe, Edward C. Page, Edward Palkovic, Jay Palmer, PhD, Ralph Lee Palmer, Gyan Shanker Pande, PhD, Patrick J. Di Paolo, Charles J. Papuchis, Georges Pardo, PhD, Marie J. Parenteau, Charles L. Park, MD, Cyril Parkanyi, PhD, Anthony T. Parker, David H. Parsons, Richard L. Pase, Garland D. Patterson, Ben W. Patz, PhD, Gary W. Pauley, Charles H. Paxton, Robert M. Peart, PhD, Richard Stark Peckham, PhD, Edward A. Pela, Winston Kent Pendleton, PhD, Robert E. Peppers, Horacio F. Perez, Stanley E. Permowicz, MD, Thomas E. Perrin, James B. Perry, MD, Edward R. Pershe, PhD, Irvin Leslie Peterson, DVM, Fred Petito, Wallace M. Philips, MD, Jim M. Phillips, Wayne A. Pickard, MD, Brett H. Pielstick, Frank A. Pierce, James J. Pierotti, Robert F. Pineiro, PhD, Victor J. Piorun, R. Clinton Pittman, MD, Ronald Plakke, PhD, Charles D. Plavcan, David Pocengul, Frederick J. Pocock, Robert C. Pollard, Richard G. Pollina, Alan Y. Pope, Hugh Popenoe, Dorian J. Popescu, Richard R. Popham, Louis B. Popovich, Ronald R. Porter, Mary B. Portofe, Bonnie W. Posma, Denzil Poston, PhD, Priscilla J. Potter, PhD, P. Mark Powell, Lee A. Powell, Sandra S. Powers, Faustino L. Prado, Kenneth L. Pratt, MD, Steve L. Precourt, Betty Peters Preece, Irwin M. Prescott, R. Preston, Charles W. Price, Katherine L. Price, Claude C. Priest, Kermit L. Prime Jr., Thomas P. Propert, Lumir C. Proshek, MD, Charles B. Pults, Charles W. Putnam, Bodo E. Pyko, PhD, Ma Qin, H. Paul Quicksall, Robert H. Quig, Jesus F. Quiles, Donald Joseph Radomski, James A. Ralph, Andrea L. Ramudo, Patricia Ramudo, Charles Addison Randall, PhD, Carlisle Baxter Rathburn, PhD, Gregory K. Ratter, Morgan G. Ray Sr., John M. Reardon, MD, Walter T. Rector, William M. Redding, Immo Redeker, John W. Redelfs, MD, Sherman Kennedy Reed, PhD, Gerhard Reethof, PhD, James A. Reger, George Kell Reid, PhD, Gerald R. Reiter, MD, Bruce G. Reynolds, PhD, Ernest J. Rice, William Joseph Richards, PhD, Bruce A. Richards, MD, Carl B. Richardson, Richard Wilson Ricker, PhD, Robert R. Righter, Gene A. Rinderknecht, DVM, Franklin G. Rinker, Harold L. Riser, George Ritter, MD, Christopher Rizzolo, James J. Roark, George W. Robbins, Kenneth M. Robert, Robert S. Roberts, MD, George A. Roberts, Kenneth Roberts, Roger L. Robertson, Donald K. Robertson, F. Herbert Robertson, Gary J. Robinson, Charles L. Robson, Michael W. Rochowiak, PhD, James C. Roden, DVM, Billy R. Rodgers, PhD, Jorge A. Rodriguez, Felix Rodriguez-Trelles, PhD, Walter H. Rogers Jr., Winston Rogers, Francis C. Rogerson, Richard C. Ronzi, Isaac F. Rooks, William S. Roorda, Peter P. Rosa, Mary C. Roslonowski, PhD, Lenard H. Ross, Jack Rossman, Ronald P. Rowand, Robert Seaman Rowe, PhD, Bob R. Rowland, Joseph A. Roy, Ronald A. Rudolph, Paul W. Runge, Devon S. Rushnell, A. Yvonne Russell, PhD, Roger L. Russell, David E. Russell, Joseph C. Russello, Byron E. Ruth, PhD, Ralph R. Ruyle, Terrell B. Ryan, DVM, Frank Sabo, Alfred Saffer, PhD, Alexander A. Sakhnovsky, A. A. Sakhnovsky, Israel Salaberrios, Fernando M. Salazar, MD, Richard J. Salk, MD, Arthur S. Salkin, Robert E. Samara, Donald S. Sammis, D. S. Sammis, Ronald E. Samples, Daniel C. Samson, Thomas H. Samter, MD, Oscar A. Sanchez, MD, William E. Sanders, Kenneth L. Sanders, Miguel A. Santos, Herbert P. Sarett, PhD, Noray Sarkisian, Joachim Sasse, PhD, Edward A. Saunders, PhD, Samuel O. Sawyer III, Eugene D. Schaltenbrand, David O. Scharr, Jay R. Schauer, Zbigniew I. Scheller, MD, Frederick W. Schelm, Richard A. Scheuing, PhD, Blair H. Schlender, Donald J. Schluender, Robert Schmeck, Hubert F. Schmidt, Richard A. Schmidtke, PhD, Karl H. Schmitz, Robert Schroeder, PhD, Peter Schroeder, PhD, Charles Schroeter, John K. Schueller, PhD, Larry E. Schuerman, Robert P. Schuh, John H. Schumertmann, PhD, David J. Schuster, PhD, Eunice C. Schuytema, PhD, John Warner Scott, PhD, Scott E. Scrupski, Walter Tredwell Scudder, PhD, John W. Seabury, Richard A. See, Christopher Seelig, Barry D. Segal, Harvey N. Seiger, PhD, John O. Selby, Luther R. Setzer, Earl William Seugling, PhD, Kenneth N. Sharitz, J. B. Sharp, M. L. Sharrah, PhD, Bob Sheldon, Preston F. Shelton, Donald M. Shepherd, Walter L. Sherman, Gregory C. Shinn, DVM, Valentin Shipillo, PhD, Aleksey Shipillo, John W. Shipley, PhD, Neil Shmunes, MD, James Edward Shottafer, PhD, Eric S. Shroyer, Orren B. Shumaker, John M. Siergiej, Carl Signorelli, Ernest S. Silcox, Paul W. Silver, Fred G. Simmen, Joel M. Simonds, Harry S. Sitren, PhD, Andrew Sivak, PhD, Arthur C. Skinner Jr., E. F. Skoczen, Robert P. Skribiski, Dave Skusa, Philip Earl

Slade, PhD, William Donald Smart, Jery Smieinski, William H. Smiley, Paul Vergon Smith, PhD, Alexander G. Smith, PhD, Diana F. Smith, DVM, Michael Smith, Augustine Smith, Clifton R. Smith, Samuel W. Smith, MD, Silke G. Smith, Dale A. Smith, Rudolph C. Smith II, Theodore A. Smith, T. J Lee Smith Jr., Bruce W. Smith, Bob A. Smith, Robert C. Smythe, John T. Snell, James M. Snook, George Snyder, PhD, Warren S. Snyder, Marc P. Sokolay, MD, Omelio JR Sosa Jr., PhD, Parks Souther, Donald E. Spade, James A. Spagnola, C. R. Spencer, Richard Jon Sperley, PhD, Norman P. Spofford, Michael D. Sprague, Robert Carl Springborn, PhD, Robert H. Springer, PhD, Donald Platte Squier, PhD, Mark A. Stahmann, PhD, John P. Stancin, PhD, Gregory F. Stanley, Harvey J. Stapleton, PhD, Cecil R. Stapleton, Walter L. Starkey, PhD, Roger A. Starner, Jan D. Steber, Theodore M. Stefanik, Thomas M. Steinert, Osmar P. Steinwald, John E. Stelzer, Russell A. Stenzel, Jesse Jerald Stephens, PhD, Robert D. Stephens, Kerry K. Steward, PhD, Ivan Stewart, PhD, Edgar K. Stewart, John Stewart, William W. Stewart, Werner K. Stiefel, Irvin G. Stiglitz, PhD, Donald Stilwell, Paul R. Stodola, Timothy D. Stoker, Joseph B. Stokes Jr., MD, Kenneth J. Stokes, Leonard Stoloff, P. Stransky, Randy P. Stroupe, Kelly C. Stroupe, Duane H. Strunk, Eugene Curtis Stump, PhD, Frank Milton Sturtevant, PhD, Jacob W. Stutzman, PhD, J. W. Stutzman, PhD, Spiridon N. Suciu, PhD, Edward J. Sullivan, Chades F. Summer Jr., Frederick C. Sumner, John C. Sundermeyer, Peter R. Sushinsky, Howard Kazuro Suzuki, PhD, Laurie A. Swanson, Ronald Lancelot Sweet, PhD, Burton L. Sylvern, Walter Symons--, James Imre Szabo, MD, Michael Szeliga, Barrett L. Taft, John F. Takacs, Gabor J. Tamasy, William Francis Tanner, PhD, John P. Tanner, J. P. Tanner, Robert Tanner, Donald E. Tannery, Frederick Drach Tappert, PhD, Armen Charles Tarjan, PhD, Amy T. Tatum, Philip Teitelbaum, PhD, Aaron J. Teller, PhD, Jeffrey Tennant, PhD, Harold Aldon Tenney, David S. Teperson, MD, Edward B. Thayer, David T. Therrien, Thomas J. Thiel, Richard William Thomas, PhD, Lovic P. Thomas, David Morton Thomason, PhD, Neal P. Thompson, PhD, Bill H. Thrasher, PhD, Lee F. Thurner, Pat T. Tidwell, Jennifer L. Tillman, William E. Tipton, Victor J. Tofany, MD, Robert S. Tolmach, MD, Manolis M. Tomadakis, PhD, Gene T. Tonn, Professor Torres, James A. Treadwell, Joseph Trivisonno Jr., PhD, Byron C. Troutman, Charles H. True, Duane J. Truitt, Steven K. Trusty, Walter Rheinhardt Tschi, PhD, R. C. Tucker Jr., PhD, Geoff W. Tucker, DVM, Stela Tudoran, MD, Leroy L. Turja, Thomas K. Turner, Ralph J. Tursi, Tom W. Utley, PhD, Donna Utley, PhD, Raj B. Uttamchandani, PhD, Augustus Ceniza Uvano, PhD, David P. Vachon, Robert L. Valliere, Horn Harold H. Van, PhD, Raymond Van Pelt, Maria Ventura, William Vernetson, PhD, Daniel F. Vernon, DVM, Raymond A. Verville, Shane Vervoort, MD, Fernando Villabona, Mark Villoria, PhD, Thomas R. Visser, Ronald S. Vogelsong, PhD, James Vollmer, PhD, Dale L. Voss, John C. Vredenburgh, William N. Waggener, Nnaette P. Wagner, PhD, Arthur C. Waite, Donald J. Wakely, Stephen D. Waldman, DVM, J. David Walker, Harold Dean Wallace, PhD, Joseph M. Walsh, Professor Wanliss, PhD, James Wanliss, PhD, Diane Ward, Ralph E. Warmack, PhD, Bertram S. Warshaw, Lawrence K. Wartell, Gerald R. Wartenberg, L. W. Warzecha, Charles Henry Watkins, PhD, C. Watson, Britt Watson, John W. Wayne, Howard W. Webb, MD, Lloyd T. Webb, George W. Webster, David Stover Weddell, PhD, John D. Weesner, Stephen L. Wehrmann, DVM, Stephen L. Wehrmann, DVM, John H. Weiler, Mitchell A. Weiner, MD, George A. Weinman, David Weintraub, PhD, Steven Weise, Aaron W. Welch Jr., PhD, Thomas B. Welch, Professor Wells, PhD, Daniel R. Wells, PhD, Buford E. Wells, MD, Steven P. Wells, Douglas F. Welpton, MD, Patrick T. Welsh, PhD, Jim C. Welsh, Robert J. Werner, Ronald R. Wesorick, Lewis H. West, R. S. Westberry, Richard S. Westberry, Donald H. Westermann, Edwin F. Weyrauch, George F. Whalen Jr., Frank Carlisle Wheeler, PhD, William R. Whidden, John I. White, PhD, Jacquelyn A. White, Albert C. White, George T. Whittle, MD, Alfred A. Wick, MD, Marvin L. Wicker, David Wickham, Donald J. Wickwire, Joseph R. Wiebush, PhD, Kurt L. Wiese, MD, James W. Wiggin, MD, Richard L. Wiker, Dale S. Wiley, Harvey Bradford Willard, PhD, Tom Vare Williams, PhD, David Williams, Ralph C. Williams, MD, George E. Williams, Charles T. Williams, Robert Elwood Wilson, PhD, Tun Win, MD, Frank R. Winders, James D. Winefordner, PhD, Les Winston, Lesley Winston, Raymond L. Winterhalter, Hugh E. Wise Jr., PhD, Robert S. Wiseman, PhD, James T. Wittig, Howard G. Womack, Irwin Boyden Wood, PhD, Richard P. Woodard, PhD, Roderick F. Woodhouse, David P. Woodhouse, Christopher L. Woofter, James A. Woolley, William C. Woolverton, MD, James G. Worth, James G. Worth, Donald J. Worthington, David H. Wozab, Dane C. Wren, Floyd D. Wright, William E. Wright, Tien-Shuenn Wu, PhD, Anton M. Wypych, Theodore E. Yaeger 4th, MD, Ted Yaeger, David E. Yarrow, Charles Yeh, John V. Yelvington, DVM, Frank Yi, Richard R. Yindra, Ted S. Yoho, DVM, Guy P. York, PhD, Richard A. Yost, PhD, Frank Young, PhD, Cindy M. Young, Douglas J. Yovaish, Professor Zamor, David Aaron Zaukelies, PhD, Fred G. Zauner, Ernest E. Zellmer, Donald M. Zelman, MD, Melanie P. Ziemba, Richard A. Ziemba, MD, Jay Zimmer, Peter H. Zipfel, PhD, Parvin A. Zisman, John Zoltek, PhD, Eli Zonana, MD, Harry David Zook, PhD, Robert M. Zuccaro

Georgia

William G. Adair Jr., William P. Adams, L. A. Adkins, Frank Jerrel Akin, PhD, Robert H. Allgood, Mike E. Alligood, Bruce Martin Anderson Jr., Byron J. Arceneaux, Robert Arnold Jr., DVM, Doyle Allen Ashley, PhD, R. Lee Aston Esq, PhD, James Atchison, Keith H. Aufderheide, PhD, C. Mark. Aulick, PhD, Paul E. Austin, Dany Ayseur, Charles L. Bachman, Robert Leroy Bailey, PhD, James A. Bain, PhD, George C. Baird,

Dana L. Baites, Bill Barks, Larry K. Barnard, Ralph M. Barnes, Gary Bartley, Frank A. Bastidas, Thomas L. Batke, George L. Batten, PhD, Joseph E. Baughman, PhD, Joseph H. Baum, PhD, William Pearson Bebbington, PhD, Gordon Edward Becker, PhD, Wilbur E. Becker, Terrence M. Bedell, James E. Bell, Robert Bell, William A. Bellisle, Steve J. Bennet, Denicke Bennor, Jack C. Bentley, James M. Berge, Gary C. Berliner, Christopher K. Bern, Ray A. Bernard, PhD, Vicky L. Bevilacqua, PhD, Don Black, M. Donald Blue, PhD, Barry Bohannon, J. R. Bone, Jim Bone, Charles D. Booth, Arthur S. Booth Jr., MD, Edward M. Boothe, Richard E. Boozer, Sorin M. Bota, James Ellis Box, PhD, Harry R. Boyd, Paul R. Bradley, George B. Bradshaw, Edward L. Bragg Sr., Elizabeth Braham, Greg R. Brandon, J. Allen Brent, PhD, William M. Bretherton Jr., Robert N. Brey, PhD, F. S. Broerman, Jerome Bromkowski, MD, Paul C. Broun, MD, Robert E. Brown, Bill D. Browning, William Bruenner, Paul J. Bruner, Sibley Bryan, Richard W. Bunnell, James Lee Butler, PhD, Sabrina R. Calhoun, Ronnie Wayne Camp, Thomas M. Campbell, James Cecil Cantrell, PhD, Patricia D. Carden, PhD, Laura H. Carreira, PhD, Peter J. Carrillo, MD, Wendell W. Carter, Marshall F. Cartledge, Robert E. Carver, PhD, Billy R. Catherwood, Michael Cavanaugh, Matilde N. Chaille, MD, Kevin L. Champion, John Champion, Jack H. Chandler Jr., Chung-Jan Chang, PhD, Chung Jan Chang, PhD, Edmund L. Chapman Jr., Chellu S. Chetty, PhD, Ken Chiavone, Raghaven M. Chidambaram, MD, George Andrew Christenberry, PhD, Alfred E. Ciarlone, PhD, James A. Claffey, PhD, James William Clark, Mark A. Clements, PhD, Arthur E. Cocco, PhD, Harland E. Cofer, PhD, Charles Erwin Cohn, PhD, Gene Louis Colborn, PhD, James C. Coleman Jr., Francis E. Coles, Frank E. Coles, Platon Jack Collipp, MD, P. J. Collipp, MD, Clair Ivan Colvin, PhD, Leon L. Combs, PhD, Henry P. Conn, David Constans, James H. Cook, Allen Costoff, PhD, Marion Cotton, PhD, R. E. Courtney, Jack D. Cox, Joe B. Cox, John A. Cramer, PhD, Howard Ross Cramer, PhD, Valerie Voss Crenshaw, Robert A. Cuneo, Thomas Curin, PhD, Alan G. Czarkowski, Geoffrey Z. Damewood, Ernest F. Daniel, MD, Anne F. Daniels, Charlie E. Daniels, Jagdish C. Das, Shelley C. Davis, PhD, James F. Dawe, DVM, Harry F. Dawson, Reuben Alexander Day, PhD, Juan C. De Cardenas, Richard E. Dedels, Johnny T. Deen, PhD, Robert E. Deloach Jr., G. E. Alan Dever, PhD, G. E. Dever, PhD, David Walter Dibb, PhD, John I. Dickinson, MD, John W. Diebold, John Dieterman, Herbert V. Dietrich Jr., MD, Charles J. Dixon, Hugh F. Dobbins, Harry Donald Dobbs, PhD, Thomas P. Dodson, Clive Wellington Donoho Jr., PhD, John Dorsey, PhD, Douglas P. Dozier, MD, Thomas E. Driver, Dennis P. Drobny, Earl E. Duckett, Robert L. Dumond, R. E. Dunnells, John W. Duren, James R. Eason, Donald D. Ecker, Teresa Ecker, Stephen W. Edmondson, MD, Marvin E. Edwards Jr., Gary L. Elliott, Gary M. Ellis, Frampton Ellis, I. Nolan Etters, PhD, W. E. Evans, Martin Edward Everhard, PhD, H. Facey, Joan H. Facey, Wayne Reynolds Faircloth, PhD, Miguel A. Faria Jr., MD, Charles Farley, Christopher J. Farnie, Thomas Farrior, Royal T. Farrow, Michael A. Faten, Mike D. Faulkenberry, John C. Feeley, PhD, Lorie M. Felton, Brent Feske, PhD, Robert Henry Fetner, PhD, Burl M. Finkelstein, PhD, Joanna Finkelstein, William R. Fisher, MD, Reed Edward Fisher, J. Ed Fitzgerald, PhD, Carl W. Flammer, Eugene L. Fleeman, K. Fleming, PhD, G. Craig Flowers, PhD, Robert E. Folker, Walter R. Fortner, Gary D. Fowler Jr., Thomas G. Frangos, PhD, Dean R. Frey, Ralph Fudge, Thomas R. Gagnier, A. Gahr, PhD, Tinsley Powell Gaines, Richard E. Galpin, Gary John Gasche, PhD, George S. Georgalis, Reinhold A. Gerbsch, PhD, Istvan B. Gereben, Lawrence C. Gerow, Georgina Gipson, Charles G. Glenn, Clyde J. Gober, Maria Nelly Golarz de Bourne, PhD, Eugene P. Goldberg, PhD, Earl S. Golightly, Thomas L. Gooch, Monty P. Goolsby, Walter Waverly Graham, PhD, John B. Gratzek, PhD, John B. Gratzek, PhD, James S. Gray, PhD, Robert M. Gray, Clayton Houstoun Griffin, Edward M. Grigsby, Ramon S. Grillo, PhD, William F. Grosser, Erling JR Grovenstein Jr., PhD, Krishan G. Gupta, MD, Robert E. Hails, Kent W. Hamlin, John R. Haponski, Clyde D. Hardin, James Lombard Harding, PhD, Cliff Hare, Kenneth E. Harper, MD, Joseph Belknap Harris, PhD, Raymond K. Hart, PhD, Lynn J. Harter, Roger Conant Hatch, Yuichi B. Hattori, Harry T. Haugen, MD, J. Hauger, PhD, William D. Haynes, Thomas D. Hazzard, Charles Jackson Hearn, PhD, Norman L. Heberer, Kenneth F. Hedden, PhD, Walter A. Hedzik, Jeffrey J. Henniger, Gustav J. Henrich, John M. Hester Jr., Craig U. Heydon, Donald G. Hicks, PhD, Terry K. Hicks, Harold Eugene Hicks, Thomas J. Hilderbrand, Kendall W. Hill, Roland W. Hinnels, Robert Francis Hochman, PhD, Dewey H. Hodges, PhD, Kirk Hoefler, Ross Hoffman, W. Hogge, Cornelia Ann Hollingsworth, PhD, Leonard Rudolph Howell Jr., PhD, Chenyi J. Hu, Richard L. Hubbell, James R. Hudson, Brad Huffines, John Hughes, William C. Humphries, Hugh F. Hunter, Richard Hurd Jr., MD, William John Husa Jr., PhD, Al J. Hutko, R. D. Ice, PhD, Walter Herndon Inge, PhD, Donald A. Irwin, James W. Ivey, Thomas W. Jackson, MD, Dabney C. Jackson, David I. Jacob, Stephen B. Jaffe, Vidyasagar Jagadam, Kenneth S. Jago, Jiri Janata, PhD, Robert H. Jarman, MD, Stanley J. Jaworski, Roger D. Jenkins, MD, Wayne Henry Jens, PhD, David R. Jernigan, Robert H. Johnson, PhD, Ben S. Johnson, James P. Jollay, Alan Richard Jones, PhD, Dick L. Jones, James K. Jones, MD, E. C. Jones, Miroslawa Josowicz, PhD, Paul F. Jurgensen, MD, Gerald L. Kaes, Donald Kaley, Judith A. Kapp, PhD, M. Katagiri, Ray C. Keause, Raymond J. Keeler, William L. Kell Jr., Craig Kellogg, PhD, Gerald D. Kennett, Warren W. Kent, DVM, Joyce E. Kephart, Boris M. Khudenko, PhD, Cengiz Kicic, Cengiz M. Kilic, C. Louis Kingsbaker Jr., R. C. Kinzie, Adrian F. Kirk, Steven Knittel, PhD, Mark A. Knoderer, Juha P. Kokko, PhD, Jenny E. Kopp, Tsu-Kung Ku, Frederick Read Kuc, PhD, Steven B. Kushnick, W. Jack Lackey, PhD, Alexander O. Lacsamana, Myron D. Lair, Trevor G. Lamond, PhD, Willis E. Lanier, Paul H. Laughlin, MD, Leo R. Lavinka, Brian K. Lawrence, Gerald W. Lawson, John C. Leffingwell, PhD, John P. Leffler, Philip I.

Levine, Edward L. Lewis, MD, Kermit L. Likes, Dennis Liotta, PhD, Robert L. Little, PhD, Fred Liu, PhD, Robert Gustav Loewy, PhD, Robert Loffredo, PhD, Stanley Jerome Lokken, PhD, William L. Lomerson, PhD, Earl Ellsworth Long, Larry Lortscher, Jerry Loupee, G. A. Lowerts, PhD, John Lauren Lundberg, PhD, Sarah R. Mack, Joseph Edward MacMillan, PhD, Patrick K. Macy, David A. Madden, James M. Maddry, L. T. Mahaffey, John B. Malcolm, Philip L. Manning, Dale Manos, David E. Marcinko, PhD, Natale A. Marini, John R. Martinec, Arlene R. Martone, MD, Henry Mabbett Mathews, PhD, Walter K. Mathews, PhD, Mike Matis, Curry J. May, Georges S. McCall II, Neil Justin McCarthy, PhD, Morley Gordon McCartney, PhD, James R. McCord III, PhD, Burl E. McCosh Jr., Sean McCue, MD, Malcolm W. McDonald, PhD, Charles W. McDowell, MD, Larry F. McEver, Ray McKemie, D. K. Mclain, PhD, Archibald A. McNeill, MD, Larry G. McRae, PhD, David Scott McVey, PhD, Thomas R. McWhorter, Andrew J. Medlin Jr., Jacob I. Melnik, Ronald E. Menze, Walter G. Merritt, PhD, Allen C. Merritt, PhD, Karne Mertins, Glenn A. Middleton, Miran Milkovic, PhD, Jean P. Millen, W. Jack Miller, PhD, R. W. Milling, PhD, Carey R. Mitchell, Brett A. Mitchell, G. C. Mitchell Jr., Carl Douglas Monk, PhD, W. Dupree Moore, Iraj Moradinia, PhD, Thomas D. Moreland, Stephen T. Moreland, Robert G. Morley, PhD, Seaborn T. Moss, MD, Don L. Mueller, Juan A. Mujica, MD, Karl W. Myers, George Starr Nichols, PhD, Jonathan H. Nielsen, Frec C. Nienaber, Fred C. Nienaber, Ray A. Nixon, Prince M. Niyyar, Stephen R. Noe, MD, Susan J. Norwood, Sidney L. Norwood, James Alan Novitsky, PhD, Wells E. Nutt, Stanley Miles Ohlberg, PhD, Philip D. Olivier, PhD, William L. Otwell, Frank B. Oudkirk, William E. Owen, Jerry Owen, Brent W. Owens, Joseph L. Owens, MD, J. Pace, PhD, Ganesh P. Pandya, MD, Les Parker, James Parks, John H. Paterson, William R. Patrick, Daniel D. Payne, Franklin E. Payne, MD, William F. Payne, Terry Peak, Ira Wilson Pence Jr., PhD, Mel E. Pence, DVM, Edgar E. Perrey, Parker H. Petit, Peter J. Petrecca, David W. Petty, Calvin Phillips, John R. Pickett, PhD, Arthur John Pignocco, PhD, Gus Plagianis, Robert V. Plehn, MD, Gayther Lynn Plummer, PhD, Robert A. Pollard Jr., Joseph W. Porter, Jerry V. Post, Cordell El Prater, Russell Pressey, PhD, Milton E. Purvis, Michael Pustilnik, PhD, Robert E. Rader, Bradford J. Raffensperger, Michael R. Rakestraw, MD, Periasamy Ramalingam, PhD, Stephen C. Raper, Oscar Rayneri, Earnest H. Reade Jr., James L. Rhoades, PhD, Robert A. Rhodes, PhD, Peter Rice, Terrence L. Rich, Allan A. Rinzel, Paul W. Risbin, Ken E. Roach, Dirk B. Robertson, PhD, John S. Robertson, PhD, David D. Robertson, PhD, Douglas W. Robertson, David G. Robinson, PhD, Wilbur R. Robinson, Willie S. Rockward, PhD, Gwenda Rogers, Stephen A. Roos Jr., W. Jeffrey Row, William J. Rowe, George F. Ruehling, Michael K. Rulison, PhD, James H. Rust, PhD, James Ryan, Marcus Sack, Thomas F. Saffold, George Sambataro, B. Samples, Ronald E. Samples, Gary L. Sanford, PhD, Deborah K. Sasser, PhD, Herbert C. Saunders, William E. Sawyer, Henry Frederick Schaefe, PhD, James R. Schafner, Thomas J. Schermerhorn, PhD, William Schierholz, Robert C. Schlant, Michael Charles Schneider, PhD, Cecil W. Schneider, Terril J. Schneider, Barry P. Schrader, Randy C. Schultz, Robert John Schwartz, PhD, Florian Schwarzkopf, PhD, David Frederick Scott, PhD, Gerald E. Seaburn, PhD, Oro C. Seevers, Robert Seitz, PhD, Morton O. Seltzer, Premchard T. Shah, W. A. Sheasin, MD, Andrew J. Shelton, Louis C. Sheppard, PhD, Chung-Shin Shi, PhD, William G. Shira, Joseph John Shonka, PhD, Ronald W. Shonkwiler, PhD, John V. Shutze, PhD, Valery Shver, Steven W. Siegan, MD, Samia M. Siha, PhD, John A. Slaats, Herbert M. Slatton, Earl Ray Sluder, PhD, Morris Wade Smith, PhD, Ralph Edward Smith, PhD, Joel P. Smith Jr., MD, Tom Smoot, PhD, Charles C. Somers Jr., Richard C. Southerland, Jon A. Spaller PG, Guy K. Spicer, Firth Spiegel, MD, Charles Hugh Stammer, PhD, Carey T. Stark, Ralph Steger, Fredric Marry Steinberg, MD, John Edward Steinhaus, PhD, Robert J. Stewart, Michael J. Stieferman, Richard C. Stjohn, Geo L. Strobel, PhD*, Bill Styer, Thomas G. Swanson, Eric Swett, Darrell G. Tangman, Robert Techo, PhD, Robert L. Terpening, Robert A. Theobald, Peter R. Thomas, M. D. Thompson, PhD, William Oxley Thompson, PhD, L. H. Thomson, Francis N. Thorne, PhD, Aloysius Thornton, PhD, Wilfred E. Tinney, Mark Tribby, PhD, Nancy Turner, R. W. Turner, Richard Suneson Tuttle, PhD, Noble Ransom Usherwood, PhD, Ahmet Uzer, PhD, James H. Venable, MD, Matthew J. Verbiscer, Jim Vess, Herbert Max Vines, PhD, Terry L. Viness, John Vogel USAF Ret, Susan Voss, PhD, Carroll E. Voss, Donald L. Voss, William C. Walker, PhD, Russell Wagner Walker, PhD, Peter Walker, Gregory C. Walter, MD, Daniel F. Ward, MD, Fred F. Warden, Raymond Warren, Roland F. Wear, MD, Charles Edward Weaver, PhD, Warren M. Weber, MD, Robert M. Webster, MD, Donald C. Wells, Richard Whalen, PhD, Mike D. Whang, PhD, James Q. Whitaker, MD, Arlon Widder, Richard L. Wilks, Paul T. Willhite, Dansy Williams, Jeffrey P. Wilson, PhD, Carlos A. Wilson, Herbert Lynn Windom, PhD, Ward O. Winer, PhD, Alan R. Winn, Robert H. Wise Jr., Robert J. Witsell, Monte Wolf, PhD, Edward Wolf, Monte W. Wolfe, PhD, Scott Wood, James H. Wood, MD, Gerald Bruce Woolsey, PhD, Jerry K. Wright, PhD, Neill S. Wyche, Hwa-Ming Yang, PhD, Raymond H. Young, PhD, Andrew T. Zimmerman, Clarence Zimmerman, Glenn A. Zittrauer, Marvin H. Zoerb, D. Zuidema, PhD

Hawaii

Curtis Beck, Charles Bocage, James Brewbaker, PhD, James Brewbaker, PhD, Richard Brill, Edmond D. Cheng, PhD, Salwyn S. Chinn, John Corboy, MD, Michael Cruickshank, PhD, Anders P. Daniels, PhD, Harry Davis, PhD, Walter Decker, Guy H. Dority, PhD, Arlo Wade Fast, PhD, Masanobu R. Fujioka, Susan K. Gingrich, Brian L. Gray, Lloyd Grearson, James A. Griffith, MD, Benjamin C. Hablutzel, Mark Hagadone,

PhD, John C. Hamaker, PhD, Kirk Hashimoto, Philip Helfrich, PhD, Philip D. Hellreich, MD, Fred Hertlein III, Yoshitsugi Hokama, PhD, David R. Howton, PhD, Lester M. Hunkele lll, James Ingamells, PhD, Gary Ishikawa, Glenn Jensen, Richard A. Jurgensen, T. Theodore Kadota, PhD, Yong-Soo Kim, PhD, Ronald H. Knapp, PhD, Adelheid R. Kuehnle, PhD, Michael Lane, Joel S. Lawson, PhD, Bill Lech, Alan Lloyd, John A. Love, Claus Berthold Ludwig, PhD, Charles Lavern Mader, PhD, Lee A. Mansfield, Charles K. Matsuda, Edward R. McDowell, PhD, Martin McMorroa, James Mertz, MD, John P. Mihlbauer, Dave Miller, Gabor Mocz, PhD, David R. Moncrief, William F. Moore, MD, Justus A. Muller, Paul D. Nielson, MD, Richard L. O'Connell, Steven Emil Olbrich, PhD, Carlos A. Omphroy, MD, Panagioti Prevedouros, PhD, Edison Walker Putman, PhD, Raymond C. Robeck, Charles G. Rose, Jim Russell, James C. Sadler, Arthur A. Sagle, PhD, Narendra K. Saxena, PhD, Jon H. Scarpino, MD, Benjamin R. Schlapak, Steven Seifried, PhD, Rogert Sherman, Shoji Shibata, PhD, Ramon K. Sy, MD, Michelle Teng, PhD, S. A. Whalen, Gary White, Stephen Wilson, MD, Oliver Wirtki, William K. Wong, MD, Cleveland C. Wu, MD, Alexander Wylly, PhD, Klaus Wyrtki, PhD, Klau Wyrtki, PhD, Alfred A. Yee

Idaho

Stephen B. Affleck, PhD, Kimbol R. Allen, Wilfred L> Antonson, Elton E. Arensman, Marvin D. Armstrong, PhD, Adrian Arp, PhD, Jim F. Ashworth, Carl Fulton Austin, PhD, J. Brent Bagshaw, Craig Riska Baird, PhD, LeRoy N. Barker, PhD, Brent O. Barker, Douglas D. Barman, Justin P. Bastian, Wiley F. Beaux, Matthew A. Beglinger, Donald R. Belville, MD, Julius R. Berreth, Darvil K. Black, PhD, Willis J. Blaine, Wilson Blake, PhD, Richard C. Bland, George Bloomsburg, PhD, Joe Bloomsburg, Carl R. Boehme, Carl R. Boehme, John Roy Bower Jr., PhD, David Boyce, Fred W. Brackebusch, Timothy J. Brewer, Ken N. Brewer, Randall A. Broesch, James L. Browne, Shelby H. Brownfield, Merlyn Ardel Brusven, PhD, Brent J. Buescher, PhD, William M. Calhoun, David Lavere Carter, PhD, Thomas Cavaiani, PhD, William R. Chandler, L. F. Cheng, PhD, Grant S. Christenson, Randil L. Clark, PhD, James W. Codding, Guy M. Colpron, Michael Cook, Carl Corbit, Ronald C. Crane, PhD, Richard A. Cummings, Raymond C. Daigh, Kim B. Davies, Karl Dejesus, PhD, Robert F. Denkins, Thomas R. Detar, Mel Dewsnup, Melvin L. Dewsnup, Mark C. Dooley, Stanley L. Drennan, MD, Larry A. Drew, PhD, Merlyn C. Duerksen, MD, O. Keener Earle, William J. Farrell, MD, Matthew Fein, Donald N. Fergusen, Roger Ferguson, Ferol F. Fish, PhD, Richard E. Forrest, DVM, Harry Kier Fritchman, PhD, Robert L. Geddes, Paul L. Glader, Doug J. Glaspey, Donald W. Glenn, V. L. Goltry, MD, Hans D. Gougar, PhD, John G. Haan, Lloyd Conn Haderlie, PhD, Richard Hampton, PhD, Julie J. Hand, Leonid Hanin, PhD, Bill M. Hann, Evan Hansen, PhD, Gerald H. Hanson, Robert N. Hanson, Roger Wehe Harder, Herbert E. Harper, Tim Harper, Herbert J. Hatcher, PhD, John B. Hegsted, Richard Charles Heimsch, PhD, Brian G. Henneman, Robert A. Hibbs, PhD, Richard C. Hill, MD, Robert F. Hill, Larry Hinderager, Kenneth M. Hollenbaugh, PhD, Clifford Holmes, Harold E. Horne, Case J. Houson, K. B. Howard, John E. Howard, Arthur R. Hubscher, Allan S. Humpherys, Richard M. Hydzik, C. Thomas Jewell, MD, Janard J. Jobes, Timothy J. Johans, Donald Ralph Johhnson, PhD, L. P. Johns, James B. Johnson, PhD, Kent R. Johnson, PhD, Lawrence Harding Johnston, PhD, James J. Jones, Jitendra V. Kalyani, Robert W. Kasnitz, Gary J. Kees, Fenton Crosland Kelley, PhD, Paul C. Kowallis, Stephen Kronholm, MD, Philip M. Krueger, PhD, John S. Kundrat, MD, Tim M. Lawton, George J. LeDuc, John W. Leonard, Leroy Crawford Lewis, PhD, William Little, PhD, Robert A. Luke, PhD, Richard Luke, Patricia A. Maloney, Billy L. Manwill, Jon L. Mason, Ralph W. Maughan, Jeremiah Mc Carthy, PhD, Kent R. McGarry, Mark A. McGuire, PhD, Bill McIlvanie, Twylia J. McIlvanie, Michael E. McLean, Brent A. McMillen, Scott G. McNee, Reg Meaker, Reginald E. Meaker, Donald L. Mecham, Travis W. Mechling, William L. Michalk, Ellis W. Miller, PhD, James A. Miller, Dile J. Monson, John L. Morris, PhD, Steven Moss, Jack Edward Mott, PhD, George Murgel, PhD, Thomas J. Muzik, PhD, Michael J. Myhre, MD, Roger Donald Nass, Thomas C. Neil, PhD, Doug W. New, Daniel Nogales, PhD, Randy Noriyaki, Mark J. Olson, William Joseph Otting, PhD, Gerald G. Overly, Aida Patterson, Ed L. Payne, PhD, Raymond M. Petrun, Gene W. Pierson, Harold A. Powers, Vernon Preston, Alan L. Prouty, Thomas R. Rasmussen, Bill Richards, Robert E. Rinker, PhD, Eric P. Robertson, Arthur P. Roeh, Jodie Roletto, Jerry F. Sagendorf, Charles Sargent, Rex Schorzman, David Laurence Schreiber, PhD, Carl W. Schulte, Sidney J. Scribner, Francis Sharpton, PhD, Glen M. Sheppard, George H. Silkworth, Claude Woodrow Sill, John Wolfgang Smith, PhD, Jay Hamilton Smith, PhD, Wesley D. Smith, PhD, Roger F. Sorenson, Ross A. Spackman, John C. Spalding, Barbara Spengler, Thomas Speziale, PhD, Gene Start, Raymond J. Stene, Bruce W. Stoddard, Wilfried J. Struck, Dale Stukenholtz, PhD, Donald C. Teske, Eugene Theios, Gary K. Thomas, MD, Warren N. Thompson, James P. Todd, Del Traveller, Francois D. Trotta, MD, Leland Wayne Tufts, John H. Turkenburg, Edmund Eugene Tylutki, PhD, Joseph James Ulliman, PhD, Randy K. Uranes, Bingham H. Vandyke Jr., PhD, Chien Moo Wai, PhD, Thornton H. Waite, Leslie M. Walker, Mont M. Warner, PhD, Jon H. Warner, D. T. Westermann, PhD, John E. Wey Jr., Jack Weyland, PhD, Robert N. Wiley, George L. Wilhelm, S. Curtis Wilkins, Oliver S. Williams, Roy L. Wise, George D. Wood, Austin L. Young, Mark Yuly, PhD, Stephen P. Zollinger, PhD

Illinois

Refaat A. Abdel-Malek, PhD, Eric R. Adolphson, Kenneth Agnes, Vincent M. Albanese, Rudolph C. Albrecht, Albert L. Allred, PhD, Kent A. Alms, Bradley A. Aman, Duane R. Amlee, Dewey Harold Amos, PhD, Thomas A. Amundsen, David A. Anderson, Joel Anderson, Kevin P. Ankenbrand, Herbert S. Appleman, Douglas E. Applequist, PhD, Anatoly L. Arber, PhD, Ed Arce, Robert W. Arends, Lawrence Ariano, MD, Ralph Elmer Armington, PhD, Jaime N. Aruguete, MD, Joseph J. Arx, Warren Cotton Ashley, PhD, Luben Atzeff, MD, Darrel D. Auch, Frank Averill, PhD, Teresita D. Avila, MD, Arthur J. Avila, Alison M. Azar, Harold Nordean Baker, PhD, Louis Baker, PhD, Marion John Balcerzak, PhD, Andrew Ateleo Baldoni, PhD, R. M. Bales, Seymour George Bankoff, PhD, Ernest Barenberg, PhD, Charles Barenfanger, John Barney, Lawrence J. Barrows, PhD, Eugene Barth, Douglas B. Bauling, Linda L. Baum, PhD, Richard C. Baylor, MD, Gary Beall, PhD, Rhett Bearmont, Craig A. Beck, Robert P. Becker, PhD, O. Beggs, Albert J. Behn, PhD, Ihor Bekersky, PhD, Gary Lavern Beland, PhD, Thomas E. Bellinger, George Bennett, PhD, G. Bennett, PhD, Lawrence Uretz Berman, Curtis L. Bermel, Daniel S. Berry, Debanshu Bhattacharya, PhD, John W. Bibber, PhD, Gregg Bierei, Roger A. Billhardt, M. J. Birck, J. L. Bitner, Eli W. Blaha, PhD, Thomas E. Blandford, William Blew, W. R. Blew, Robert L. Blood, MD, Loren E. Bode, PhD, Daniel G. Bodine, Robert J. Boehle, Thomas M. Bohn, Mark S. Boley, PhD, A. Bollmeier, Patrick V. Bonsignore, PhD, Lewis D. Book, David L. Booth, PhD, Edgar A. Borda, MD, Harold Joseph Born, PhD, Joseph Carles Bowe, PhD, Robert E. Boyar, R. Braatz, PhD, Robert Giles Brackett, PhD, Dorothy L. Bradbury, Eric M. Bram, Thomas Brandlein, William H. Bray, MD, William Thomas Brazelton, PhD, Manuel Martin Bretscher, PhD, Joseph L. Brewer, PhD, Gregory J. Brewer, PhD, Mark O. Brien, Steve Briggs, PhD, Robert B. Brigham, Bruce Edwin Briley, PhD, Ed A. Brink, Douglas A. Brockhaus, Mark Bronson, David P. Brown, PhD, William Brown, John S. Brtis, Eldon J. Brunner, Gary G. Bryan, Ronald C. Bryenton, Greg Buffington, Philip G. Buffinton, Michael Bundra, Ivan L. Burgener, Marty Burke, Peter G. Burnett, Donald S. Burnley, Mike Burnson, William C. Burrows, PhD, Rodney L. Burton, PhD, Robert Busing, Duane J. Buss, PhD, Margaret K. Butler, Gary J. Butson, PhD, Ralph O. Butz Jr., James Albert Buzard, PhD, Roy Byrom, Fernando and Cynthia Caburnay S. Caburnay, MD, Manual Calzada, Marvin E. Camburn, PhD, Howard Suckling Cannon, PhD, William L. Carper, MD, Robert C. Casagranda, Phillip M. Caserotti, J. Steven Castleberry, Stanley Changnon Jr., Stanley Alcide Changnon, William Charowhas, Michael Andrew Chaszeyka, A. Cheney, J. A. Cifonelli, PhD, Leroy Clardy, Russell H. Clark, MD, Robert Clark, David G. Clay, James M. Clifford, Alan Clodfelter, Jim Cloud, Benjamin T. Cockrill Jr., Fritz Coester, PhD, William C. Cohen, PhD, Allan H. Cohen, PhD, Paul D. Coleman, PhD, Keith A. Collins, DVM, Paul J. Concepcion, MD, John Conconnan, Dennis D. Conner, Gail Rushford Corbett, PhD, Rebecca Corbit, Stephen Watson Cornell, PhD, Thomas Corrigan, PhD, Khalid Cossor, Gordon E. Craigo, Frederick L. Crane, PhD, Donald W. Creger Sr., John Edwin Crew, PhD, Gregory A. Crews, George A. Criswell, Michael Summers Crowley, PhD, Andrew A. Cserny, PhD, John Robert Culbert, Peter L. Cumerford, Russell A. Dahlstrom, Heinz H. Damberger, PhD, Morris Juda Danzig, PhD, Kaz Darzinskis, Jeff David, Robert H. Dean, Lyndon L. Dean, Frank Deboer, PhD, Edward Dale Deboer, Charles S. Dehaan, Robert F. Deibel Jr., Manuel J. Delerno, Thomas G. Denton, T. G. Denton, Edward M. Desrochers Jr., Donald Dewey, PhD, James Dewey, Justin E. Dewitte, Charles Edward Dickerman, PhD, Bryan J. Dicus, Kenneth Diesburg, PhD, Ray C. Dillon, Timothy W. Dittmer, Omer H. Dix, W. Brent Dodrill, Theodore Charles Doege, MD, Michael F. Dolan, Richard J. Dombrowski, Otello P. Domenella, Wayne Donnelly, John E. Dowis, Gerald L. Downing, David R. Doyle, William K. Drake, MD, G. L. Dryder, PhD, John T. Dueker, Carl D. Dufner, John D. Dwyer, MD, Michael Dwyer, Steven Dyer, Philip J. Dziuk, PhD, Philip Eugene Eaton, PhD, Lawrence Thornton Eby, PhD, Bernard Ecanow, PhD, Charles Ecanow, PhD, Donald E. Eckmann, W. Kent Eden, Paul H. Egbers, Donald A. Eggert, PhD, Kevin S. Elam, James O. Ellis Sr., George Emerle, Louis Emery, PhD, David Engwall, PhD, Jack H. Enloe, Edward Bowman Espenshade, PhD, R. Evans, Don J. Fanslow, PhD, Wells E. Farnsworth, PhD, Marjorie Whyte Farnsworth, PhD, David A. Fehr, Imre M. Fenyes, MD, Joseph Fidley, PhD, Joanne K. Fink, PhD, Patricia Ann Finn, PhD, Ross Francis Firestone, PhD, Robyn Fischer, Steve Fiscor, Emalee G. Flaherty, MD, Donald R. Fletcher, James M. Fox, Stephen Joseph Fraenkel, PhD, Julian Myron Frankenberg, PhD, Raymond Frederici, David M. Frederick, DVM, Richard C. Frederick, MD, Allan L. Freedy, Donald Nelson Frey, PhD, Herbert C. Friedmann, PhD, Andrew R. Frierdich, Wesley Fritz, PhD, Karl J. Fritz, PhD, Aaron E. Fundich, Jim Gadwood, John Gaither, Thomas R. Galassi, Charles O. Gallina, PhD, Daniel G. Ganey, Robt J. Garner, Douglas L. Garwood, PhD, Eduardo Gasca, George Gasper, PhD, Roger W. Geiss, MD, William O. Gentry, PhD, Boyd A. George, PhD, George J. Getty, Camillo Ghiron, PhD, Frederick W. Giacobbe, PhD, Larry V. Gibbons, PhD, Kernon M. Gibes, Jeff Gillespie, John R. Gilmore, PhD, Kenneth J. Ginnard, George Isaac Glauberman, PhD, William D. Glover, William Gong, PhD, William Good, Harold J. Goodman, MD, Joseph Gorsic, PhD, Chris D. Gosling, George Robert Goss, PhD, David G. Gossman, Samuel P. Gotoff, MD, Marcus S. Gottlieb, Robert J. Graham, PhD, Ted R. Gray, Frank D. Graziano, PhD, D. W. Greger, David Gregg, Gregg T. Greiner, DVM, James Edward Griffin, PhD, Edward Lawrence Griffin, Harold Lee Griffin, Ronald E. Groer, Eugene E. Gruber, PhD, Andrew F. Guschwan, MD, Philip Felix Gustafson, PhD, Kenneth A.

Gustafson, David Solomon Hacker, PhD, Richard H. Hagedorn, Reino Hakala, PhD, Ken Hall, Suleiman M. Hamway, Daniel F. Hang, Mark E. Hansen, MD, A. O. Hanson, PhD, Robert K. Harbour, Thomas D. Harding, Danny L. Hare, Ben Harrison, PhD, Thomas R. Harwood, MD, John A. Hasdal, PhD, Hans Hasen, Robert Havens, Douglas B. Hayden, Robert J. Heaston, PhD, David Robert Hedin, PhD, Todd Hedlund, Mihaela Hegstrom, Lawrence C. Heidemann, Stan F. Heidemann, Paul K. Heilstedt, Ron Heisner, James Raymond Helbert, PhD, J. Raymond Helbert, PhD, Roy J. Helfinstine, Joseph B. Helms, DVM, William C. Helvey, John F. Helwig, Jeannine L. Henderson, Alfred J. Hendron Jr., PhD, Lester Allan Henning, Richard Henry, PhD, Arthur A. Herm, PhD, Edward Robert Hermann, PhD, Ernest Carl Herrmann, Karl Hess, PhD, Cynthia Hess, PhD, Kenneth E. Hevner, Menard George Heydanek Jr., PhD, Warren R. Higgins, Raymond M. Hinkle, PhD, Terry L. Hird, Joseph C. Hirschi, Richard A. Hirschmann, MD, Bill J. Hlavaty, Vincent Hodgson, PhD, Timothy J. Holcomb, Gary L. Hollewell, DVM, Betsy L. Holli, PhD, Franklin Ivan Honea, PhD, Arie Hoogendoorn, PhD, Doc Horley, PhD, Doc Horsley, PhD, Craig Horswill, PhD, George E. Hossfield, Kathleen Ann House, PhD, Robert M. House, Ronald L. Howard, T. E. Hsiu, PhD, Charles Fu Jen Hsu, PhD, Jean Luc Hubert, Craig S. Huff, Donald C. Huffaker, PhD, Dennis Huffaker, Stanley R. Huffman, MD, James A. Huizinga, DVM, John Gower Hundley, PhD, Stephen A. Hutti, Icko JR Iben Jr., PhD, Mac Igbal, Nick Iliadis, Cecil W. Ingmire, DVM, Ronald S. Inman, Mitio Inokuti, PhD, Herbert O. Ireland, PhD, Gary J. Isaak, Anthony D. Ivankovich, PhD, David Eugene James, PhD, Lynn M. Janas, PhD, Frank Henry Jarke, Gerald G. Jelly, DVM, William J. Jendzio, Stewart C. Jepson, Milton Raymond Johnson, PhD, Glenn Richard Johnson, PhD, Irving Johnson, PhD, Rodney B. Johnson, Helen S. Johnstone, MD, John Lloyd Jones, PhD, Les Jones, Daniel R. Juliano, PhD, William A. Junk, PhD, George T. Justice, Dennis D. Kaegi, John E. Kaindl, John M. Kalec, MD, Manfred Stephan Kaminsky, PhD, Elisabeth M. Kaminsky, MD, Harvey Sherwin Kantor, MD, George Kapusta, PhD, Dorkie Kasmar, Joseph J. Katz, PhD, R. Gilbert Kaufman, PhD, Michael Kazarinov, PhD, Frederick D. Keady, Clint J. Keifer, Walter R. Keller, Charles D. Kellett, Frank N. Kemmer, Francis S. Kendorski, Albert Joseph Kennedy, PhD, Robert Kepp, PhD, Naaman Henry Keyser, Gregory B. Kharas, PhD, G. B. Kharas, PhD, G. Khelashvili, PhD, John W. Kiedaisch, PhD, John W. Kieken, Myoung D. Kim, MD, S. M. King, PhD, Sanford MacCallum King, PhD, Timothy P. Kinsley, John D. Kinsman, Betty W. Kjellstrom, DVM, Harold E. Klemptner, MD, James C. Klouda, Edward Andrew Knaggs, Norm Knights, James Otis Knobloch, PhD, James W. Knox, James Start Koehler, PhD, Janice H. Koehler, David E. Koehler, Carol R. Koehler, Richard W. Koester, Randall Kok, PhD, Tim Koller, Professor Kongpricha, PhD, Virgil J. Konopinski, Mark J. Konya, Kevin D. Kooistra, Gerald L. Kopischke, Dennis N. Kostic, John J. Krajewski, PhD, John F. Krampien, James J. Krawchuk, Arthur A. Krawetz, PhD, Robert E. Kreutzer Jr., Kevin Krist, PhD, Arthur T. Kroll, Moyses Kuchnir, PhD, Eugene James Kuhajek, PhD, Moira Kuhl, Samar K. Kundu, PhD, Walter E. Kunze, Peter Kusel, PhD, Kenneth M. Labas, James R. Lafevers, PhD, Charles Ford Lange, PhD, Ralph Louis Langenheim, PhD, John L. Lapish, Andre G. Lareau, Seymour Larock, Carl S. Larson, PhD, Wayne O. Larson, PhD, Bruce Linder Larson, PhD, James L. Leach, PhD, Dennis R. Lebbin, PhD, Jean-Pierre Leburton, PhD, Richard V. Lechowich, PhD, Do B. Lee, Charles Lee, Gregory E. Lehn, Charles Leland, James D. Lenardson, Terrence A. Leppellere, Dennis Leppin, Ronald G. Leverich, Terrence G. Leverich, Lawrence T. Lewis, PhD, Steven R. Lewis, Ted E. Lewis, Robert D. Libby, David L. Licht, Rebecca A. Lim, PhD, Henry Robert Linden, PhD, William E. Liss, Kenneth J. Little, Derong Liu, PhD, Qian Liu, PhD, Chian Liu, PhD, Stephen R. Lloyd, PhD, John T. Loftus, Roger A. Logeson, J. S. Loomis Jr., John S. Loomis Jr., Herb Lopatka, Janet A. Lorenz, PhD, Paul Albert Lottes, PhD, John E. Lovell, Walter S. Lucas, Spomenka M. Luedi, Thomas J. Lukas, PhD, Channing Harden Lushbough, PhD, Mark R. Lytell Jr., Richard W. Lytton, MD, E. Jerome Maas, PhD, Roy P. Mackal, PhD, Arvind J. Madhani, PhD, Alexander B. Magnus Jr., James Magnuson, Om Prakash Mahajan, PhD, Eric L. Malaker, MD, Francis M. Mallee, PhD, Leszek L. Malowanski, Christian John Mann, PhD, Carl A. Manthe, Dennis L. Markwell, Ronald Lavern Martin, PhD, Richard Martiñez, Edward L. Marut, Donald Frank Mason, PhD, Richard I. Mateles, PhD, John Mathys, PhD, Michael Matkovich, Robert R. Mazer, Professor McAneny, PhD, Ed McCanbe, Charles R. McCconnel, PhD, Ann E. McCombs, DVM, Charles R. McConnell, PhD, Sherwood W. McGee, Michael J. McGirr, MD, Randall K. McGivney, Ellen A. McKeon, DVM, Peter McKinney, MD, James R. McVicker, DVM, Ralph D. Meeker, PhD, Joseph C. Mekel, Kenneth E. Mellendorf, PhD, Edgar L. Mendenhall, Richard C. Meyer, PhD, Stuart Lloyd Meyer, PhD, Gary L. Miles, Thomas J. Miller, David Mintzer, PhD, Alex Mishulovich, PhD, Vyt Misiulis, Robert H. Mohlenbrock Jr., PhD, Jeff Monahan, PhD, Raymond W. Monroe, Robert A. Morris, Professor Morris, Gary E. Mosher, Herman E. Muller, Paul E. Mullinax, Dan J. Muno, Alan E. Munter, Bichara B. Muvdi, PhD, John L. Nanak Jr., David Ledbetter Nanney, PhD, Thomas F. Nappi, Richard M. Narske, PhD, Joseph J. Natarelli, J. Timothy Naylor, Dale D. Nelson, Harry J. Neumiller Jr., PhD, Richard William Neuzil, Thomas W. Nichols, Marcella G. Nichols, John Nicklow, PhD, John D. Noble, PhD, Jeffrey J. Nodorft, Michael L. Norman, PhD, Richard Daviess Norman, Jack D. Noyes, DVM, Alan H. Numbers, Bernard C. Ogarek, Fredric C. Olds, Lawrence Oliver, PhD, Farrel John Olsen, PhD, Michael P. O'Mara, MD, William Dennis Oneill, PhD, William C. Orthwein, PhD, Professor Oskoorouchi, PhD, Joseph M. O'Toole, Jacques Ovadia, PhD, Carl F. Painter, PhD, Nicholas J. Pappas, MD, Eugene N. Parker, PhD, James D. Parker, DVM, Kirit Patel, Natu C. Patel, Clinton P. Patterson, Val E. Peacock, PhD, Barry E. Pelham, David W. Pennington, Roscoe L. Pershing, PhD, Peter Paul Petro, PhD,

Dave Pettit, Tom Phipps, PhD, Susan K. Pierce, PhD, Charles Edward Pietri, Glen A. Piland, Dean A. Pilard, Richard A. Pilon, Roger D. Pinc, MD, Mark A. Pinsky, PhD, Chris Piotrowski, Ed Piszynski, Rus Pitch, Philip Andrew Pizzica, Robert J. Podlasek, PhD, Richard Polad, Donald W. Potter, MD, Susan Powell, Robert C. Powell, MD, John E. Powell Jr., Gary Preston, George W. Price, Michael R. Prisco, PhD, William H. Prokop, David L. Puent, Kay M. Purcell, Eugene Pyrcioch, Kathy Qin, Jim Quandt, Charles E. Quentel, Robert D. Quinn, Carl G. Rako, George Ramatowski, James Rasor, Andrew A. Rathsack, Kent Rausch, PhD, Richard G. Rawlings, Sylvian Richard Ray, PhD, Fred Reader, Professor Reader, Craig R. Reckard, Harold Frank Reetz, PhD, Gary K. Regan, Leonard Reiffel, PhD, Vincent Reilms, PhD, Paul G. Remmele, Joseph C. Renn, James M. Richmond, PhD, Bill Tom Ridgeway, PhD, Roy Ringo, PhD, George Roy Ringo, John V. Roach, Arthur Roberts, PhD, Jene L. Robinson, Jacob Van Roeckel, James A. Roecker, George A. Roegge, DVM, Donna Rook, D. L. Rook, Kelly Roos, PhD, Andrew H. Rorick, Albert R. Rosavana, MD, David Rose, PhD, Eric J. Rose, Richard A. Rosenberg, PhD, Peter S. Rosi, MD, Gordon Keith Roskamp, PhD, Andrew Rothsack, Timothy Rozycki, George G. Rudawsky, Thomas A. Rudd, Thomas A. Rudelms, MD, Edward Evans Rue, John Ruhl, Mark Ruttle, Julian G. Ryan, Debra J. Rykoff, PhD, Gregory Ryskin, PhD, George D. Sadler, PhD, M. M. Said, PhD, James A. Samartano, Dennis R. Samuelson, MD, Paul D. Sander, PhD, Mykola Saporoschenko, PhD, Satish Chandra Saxena, PhD, Angelo M. Scanu, Harold E. Scheid, Jay Ruffner Schenck, PhD, Roger M. Schiavoni, Alexander B. Schilling, PhD, Robert Arvel Schluter, PhD, William A. Schmucker, Charles David Schmulbach, PhD, Richard Schockley, Felix Schreiner, PhD, Richard J. Schuerger, PhD, Garmond Gaylord Schurr, Robert W. Schwaner, MD, John J. Sciarra, Paul A. Seaburg, PhD, J. Glenn Sean, J. Glenn Seay, Bruce R. Sebree, PhD, Otto F. Seidelman, Lewis S. Seiden, PhD, Richard G. Semonin, Lee Hanley Sentman, PhD, Gordon E. Sernel, Charles Shabica, PhD, Alan R. Shapiro, John D. Shepherdson, Charles P. Sheridan, Arthur J. Sherman, Douglas B. Sherman, Joseph Cyril Sherrill, PhD, Robert L. Shone, PhD, Sanjeev G. Shroff, PhD, James C. Shults, Lawrence G. Sickels, Kent Sickmeyer, Arthur Siegel, Chester Paul Siess, PhD, Gaston N. Siles, Walter Lawrence Silvernail, PhD, Ralph O. Simmons, PhD, Joseph H. Simmons, Gerald Simon, MD, Donald E. Sims, Matthew D. Sink, Amor Sison, John R. Skelley, Gary M. Skirtich, Francis J. Slama, PhD, Arthur Smith, Roger C. Smith*, Ned L. Snider, MD, Richard H. Snow, PhD, Duane Snyder, Milton A. Sobie, Harry J. Soloway, MD, Dennis B. Solt, PhD, Robert E. Sorensen, Peter Sorokin, MD, Chris Soule, Edmund S. Sowa, Brian Spencer, James W. Spires, Mark W. Sprouls, William R. Staats, PhD, Stephen S. Stack, Thomas R. Stack, Paul Stahmann, J. E. Stanhopf, E. J. Stanton, Peter J. Stanul, Stephen E. Stapp, Timothy W. Starck, John J. Staunton, Enrique D. Steider, MD, Frank Jay Stevenson, PhD, Raymond Fred Stevenson, D. Scott Stewart, PhD, Robert G. Stewart, Robert Llewellyn Stoffer, PhD, Bob Storkman, Glenn E. Stout, PhD, Nathan Stowe, Randy E. Strang, James F. Stratton, PhD, Stephen A. Straub, PhD, Edward A. Streed, Joseph W. Stucki, PhD, Benjamin G. Studebaker, Alan M. Stueber, PhD, John Stueve, Frank C. Suarez, Thomas E. Sullivan, Armando Susmano, MD, Christine Sutton, R. Kent Swedlund, MD, Jerry Sychra, PhD, Steven A. Szambaris, Ajit C. Tamhane, PhD, Rita Tao, Robert E. Teneick, PhD, Lee C. Teng, PhD, Marius C. Teodorescu, PhD, Ram P. Tewari, PhD, W. Tharnish, Carol Tharp, MD, Lawrence Eugene Thielen, Otto G. Thilenius, PhD, Kris Thiruvathukal, PhD, Brian G. Thomas, PhD, John D. Thomas, Don E. Thompson, Stacy T. Thomson, Thomas A. Thornburg, DVM, Peter E. Throckmorton, PhD, E. Timson, August P. Tiritilli, Cyril M. Tomsic, Kenneth James Trigger, Alkesh N. Trivedi, Edwin S. Troscinski, Alvah Forrest Troyer, PhD, Richard Trzupek, Donald Tuomi, PhD*, Anthony Turkevich, PhD, James J. Ulmes, Ronald T. Urbanik, Larry D. Vail, PhD, Albert P. Van der Kloot, Edward Van Drunen, William Van Lue, DVM, Donald O. Van Ostenburg, PhD, William Brian Vander Heyden, PhD, Donald D. Vanfossan, PhD, Edmund Vasiliauskas, PhD, Ira J. Vaziri, MD, John G. Victor, PhD, Larry L. Vieley, Francis J. Vincent, MD, Robert W. Voedisch, Edward D. Vojack, Edward W. Voss, PhD, Mike Wadlington, Howard L. Wakeland, Jack Wakeland, Jeff Walker, Rodger Walker, John Walker, Daniel J. Walters, Soo-Young C. Wanda, R. Wanke, PhD, Evelyn Kendrick Wantland, PhD, Brent A. Ward, Toby Ward, Lewis R. Warmington, David D. Warner, James Warner, Jim Warner, Bruce Warren, Donald L. Watson, Jason A. Watters, George E. Webb Jr., David Fredrick Weber, PhD, James A. Weber, Olaf L. Weeks, William B. Welch, MD, Eric Welles, Daniel Wenstrup, John R. Wesley, MD, Hans U. Wessel, PhD, Douglas Brent West, PhD, Paul J. West, MD, James William Westwater, PhD, Robert Lloyd Wetegrove, PhD, Grady A. White, Laurie C. Wick, Timothy H. Wiley, Jack M. Williams, PhD, Thomas Williams, PhD, Jack R. Williams, Arthur R. Williams, R. Wilson, PhD, Lorenzo Wilson, Alan P. Wilson, Carman P. Winarski, Ronald John Wingender, PhD, Robert W. Wingerd, Lester H. Winter, Dale M. Winter, Robert Wisbey, David C. Witkins, Lloyd David Witter, PhD, Dale Wittmer, PhD, George D. Wolf, Gene H. Wolfe, Clarke K. Wolfert, Sylvia Wolfson, Sophie M. Worobec, Virgil A. Wortman, Judy L. Wright, MD, Leo A. Wrona, MD, Jaroslav Wurm, PhD, Robert L. Wwetegrove, PhD, Peter S. Wyckoff, William P. Yamnitz, X. Terry Yan, PhD, John Herman Yopp, PhD, Don York, Susan D. Younes, Donald E. Young, PhD, Wanda C Soo Young, Forrest A. Younker, Hany H. Zaghloul, Edward P. Zahora, Zhonggang Zeng, PhD, Arthur J. Zimmer, PhD

Indiana

Bernaard J. Abbott, PhD, Paul Abbott, Riaz F. Abdulla, PhD, Chris Adam, Robert Aldridge, Gabriel C.

Aldulescu, MD, Joshua C. Allen, Madelyn H. Allen, DVM, Jonathan Alley, MD, Lawrence D. Andersen, Walter C. Anglemeyer, Morris Herman Aprison, PhD, John Arch, Thomas G. Armbuster, MD, Delano Z. Arvin, PhD, Joe E. Ashby, PhD, Romney A. Ashton, MD, Robert Aten, PhD, M. Atkins, Matt Atkinson, Christian C. Badger, Tim Baer, James Bailey, Edward J. Bair, PhD, Dale I. Bales, PhD, David L. Banta, Mark A. Bartlow, Steven Craig Bass, PhD, Norris J. Bassett, Walter Frank Beineke, PhD, Mark R. Bell, PhD, Paraskevi Mavridis Bemiller, PhD, James Noble Bemiller, PhD, Edward J. Benchik, John M. Bentz, MD, Rod Bergstedt, William P. Best, Lawrence M. Bienz, Robert Francis Bischoff, Kenneth A. Bisson, Raymond J. Black, Jon Blackburn, Paul V. Blair, PhD, George B. Boder, W. Bordeaux, Andrew Chester Boston, PhD, Steve Boswell, Edmond Milton Bottorff, PhD, James L. Bowman, D. Boyd, PhD, Frederick Mervin Boyd, PhD, Richard A. Boyd, MD, Redford H. Bradt, PhD, John T. Brandt, MD, Harold W. Bretz, PhD, Tom P. Brignac, Raymond Samuel Brinkmey, PhD, Thomas R. Brinner, PhD, Herbert Brown, PhD, Arlen Brown, PhD, James Brown, John W. Brown, Cornelius Payne Browne, PhD, W. George Brueggemann, MD, Robert F. Bruns, PhD, Russell Allen Buchanan, Stuart Buckmaster, Professor Burchett, PhD, John Burwell, Tom Busch, Ernest Edward Campaigne, PhD, Randy S. Cape, Michael E. Caplis, PhD, Eric S. Carlsgaard, Donald D. Carr, PhD, Jerry Allan Caskey, PhD, Stanley W. Chernish, Dhan Chevli, PhD, David L. Christmas, John P. Chunga, MD, Waller S. Clements, David L. Clingman, Roberto Colella, PhD, Christina M. Collester, Don Collier, Andy R. Collins, P. Connolly, Addison G. Cook, PhD, Donald Jack Cook, PhD, Tracy Correa, PhD, Peter A. Costisick, Mike Cox, Donald K. Craft, Donald K. Craft, Tom Crawford, PhD, Thomas M. Crawford, PhD, Robert Crist, David F. Crosley, Marsha L. Culbreth, Stephen L. Cullen, J. William Cupp, PhD, John T. Curran, Theodore Wayne Cutshall, PhD, James M. Czarnik, Marie E. Dasher, Bruce R. Dausman, David G. Davidson, DVM, Harold William Davies, PhD, Paul F. Davis, Harry G. Day, Mark E. Deal, David J. Dean, Steve Denner, PhD, Kenneth R. Deremer, Kenneth R. Devoe, MD, Shree S. Dhawale, PhD, Dave Dicksor, Dallas Lee Dinger, Tom Dingo, H. Marshall Dixon, PhD, Henry Marshall Dixon, PhD, Gerald Ennen Doeden, PhD, Joe Dotzlaf, David W. Dragoo, Underwood Dudley, PhD, David R. Duffy, Samuel D. Dunbar, John J. Durante, Martin C. Dusel, Robert L. Dyer, James P. Dykes, C. Dykstra, PhD, Jae Ebert, Ronald L. Edwards, Weldon T. Egan, MD, Richard Egly, PhD, John L. Emmerson, PhD, Calvin W. Emmerson, Terry L. Endress, Gary L. England, Brian D. Erxlebon, Ed Escallon, Craig T. Evers, PhD, Edward A. Fabrici, Mitchel D. Fehr, Norman G. Feige, John C. Fenoglio, Steven E. Ferdon, Virginia Rogers Ferris, PhD, Paul A. Feszel, MD, Greg Filkovski, Bruce Fiscus, Elson Fish, William B. Fisher, MD, Edward W. Fisher, Richard J. Flores, John D. Foell, Eugene Joseph Fornefeld, PhD, Dwaine Fowlkes, James W. Frazell, Jim Friederick, Alfred Keith Fritzsche, PhD, Meredith W. Fry, Eric Fry, Philip L. Fuchs, PhD, Forst Donald Fuller, PhD, Stephen E. Funkhauser, Arnold R. Gahlinger, Gustavo E. Galante, MD, Roy E. Gant, Don Gard, PhD, Sudhakar R. Garlapati, MD, David E. Gay, William A. Geary, PhD, Perry J. Gehring, PhD, Gordon H. Geiger, PhD, Doyle Geiselman, PhD, Phillip Gerhart, PhD, John S. Gilpin, DVM, Robert W. Glasscock, Dan Gleaves, DVM, Robert Hamor Gledhill, PhD, Hugh S. Glidewell, DVM, Matthew F. Gnezda, PhD, Victor W. Goldschmidt, PhD, William Raymond Gommel, PhD, James P. Graf, Douglas Grahn, PhD, Lawrence Grauvogel, Norman W. Gray, Richard Grenne, Susan S. Grenzebach, Steven H. Griffith, Tom U. Grinslade, Larry R. Groves, Joseph C. Gruss, Albert Guilford, Gerald Edward Gutowski, PhD, John E. Haines Jr., David W. Haines, MD, Harold T. Hammel, PhD, Robert F. Hand, Charles Hantzis, James Hardesty, Robert B. Harnoff, Clark Hartford, James M. Hartshorne, William H. Hathaway, Bruce A. Hayes, Darrell R. Hazlewood, James C. Heap, Dwight H. Heberer, Thomas J. Helbing, John P. Henaghan, Stanley M. Hendricks II, Ronald D. Hentz, Wallace E. Hertel, Harold R. Hicks, W. B. Hill, PhD, Donald E. Hilton, Loren John Hoffbeck, PhD, Joseph D. Holder, DVM, John E. Holdsworth, John T. Hopwood, Randolph R. Horton, William J. Hosmon, James E. Hough, Karl J. Houghland, Hub Hougland, Don Morgan Huber, PhD, Roger J. Hull, Carl D. Humbarger, DVM, Charles C. Huppert, PhD, John M. Igelman, D. Igou, PhD, Donald K. Igou, PhD, Gregory J. Ilko, Rosario Indelicato, E. William Itell, Robert B. Jacko, PhD, Bill G. Jackson, PhD, David E. Jahn, Aloysius A. Jaworski, Robert L. Johnson, Wyatt Johnson, Howard D. Johnston, Ken A. Jones, John D. Jones, John Jones, Eric J. Jumper, PhD, Donald J. Just, Dimitar Kalchev, W. B. Karcher, Gregory A. Katter, Daniel Kaufman, Jim Kent, Steven P. Kepler, B. Charles Kerkhove Jr., Edward T. Keve, Dan Kieffner, Winfield S. Kiester, Dennis D. Kilkenny, Professor Kilpinen, PhD, Jon Kilpinen, PhD, Gary A. Kimberlin, Norma A. Kinsel, PhD, Glen J. Kissel, PhD, Ronald E. Kissell, Peter T. Kissinger, PhD, Lassi A. Kivioja, PhD, Howard Joseph Klein, PhD, John C. Klingler, Williams G. Knorr, James Paul Kohn, PhD, Steven Kontney, William A. Koontz, MD, Edmund Carl Kornfeld, PhD, Aaron David Kossoy, PhD, Thomas F. Kowalczyk Jr., Michael J. Koyak, Richard Kraft, Bruce L. Lamb, DVM, C. Elaine Lane, MD, E. E. Laskowski, Ralph F. Lasley, William S. Laszlo, David Lawson, Marisa S. Leach, Brent Leatherman, Timothy A. Lee, Richard Leidlein, Andrew Lenard, PhD, A. Lenard, PhD, Peter E. Liley, PhD, Ronald H. Limbach, William C. Link, MD, Donald Linn, PhD, Tim A. Litz, Andrew Lonard, PhD, Robert L. Longardner, James S. Lovick, DVM, Philip J. Lubensky, Melvin Robert Lund, MD, Neil P. Lynch, Martin Maassen, John C. Mackey, John C. Mackey, Jeffrey Maguire, John August Manthey, William Markel, PhD, Terry W. Marsh, MD, Terry Marsh, Bill L. Martz, MD, James Marusek, James A. Marvsek, Jojseph B. Materson, Tats Matsuoka, DVM, Robert Mayemick, Larry R. Mayton, Allan J. McAllister, MD, Roger D. McClintock, Edwin D. McCoy, James T. McElroy, MD, Orville L. McFadden, DVM, John D. McGregor, Edward A. McKaig, PhD, William J.

McKenna, James C. McKinstry, Robert A. McKnight Jr., Duncan R. McLeish, Professor McMonigal, PhD, Chuck McPherson, Mark R. Meadows Sr., James R. Meier Sr., Wilton Newton Melhorn, PhD, Gary Merkis, Mark B. Messmer, Emil W. Meyer, DVM, Sandra Miesel, Anthony J. Mihulka, John A. Mikel, Douglas Gene Mikolasek, PhD, Robert Douglas Miles, Dane A. Miller, PhD, Stephen L. Miller, George R. Miller, Robert T. Miller, Bradley G. Mills, Norman T. Mills, Kenneth L. Minett, T. Miranda, PhD, Thomas J. Miranda, PhD, Michal Misiurewicz, PhD, Donald H. Mohr, John G. Mohr, Kenneth R. Moore Jr., Alfred L. Morningstar, Raymond L. Morter, PhD, James L. Mottet, John R. Mow, Joel E. Mowatt, Daniel H. Mowrey, PhD, Thomas J. Mueller, PhD, Barry B. Muhoberac, PhD, Jeff K. Munger, Haydn Herbert Murray, PhD, Michael L. Nahrwold, Wade L. Neal, Joseph J. Neff, Steven H. Neucks, MD, Charles C. Ney, Kenneth E. Nichols, PhD, George D. Nickas, PhD, Henry Frederick Nolting, Robert C. Novak, John Lewis Occolowitz, George O. P. O'Doherty, PhD, Michael H. O'Donnell, Winston Stowell Ogilvy, PhD, John Olashuk, Timothy C. O'Neill, Jonathan M. Oram, John Robert Osborn, PhD, G. Out, PhD, Albert Overhauser, PhD, Mock Overton, Willis M. Overton IV, C. Subah Packer, PhD, Jim F. Pairitz, Wayne Parke, Charles S. Parmenter, PhD, George A. Payne, Kenneth D. Perry, Doug Perry, Robert G. Phillips, Robert L. Pigott ll, Professor Pine, PhD, Ronald C. Pinter, Jeffery J. Poole, Jerry Prescott, Kenneth Price, PhD, Marvin E. Priddy, MD, Gary J. Proksch, PhD, Charles L. Provost, Robert R. Pruse, Phillip G. Przybylinski, Lawrence T. Purcell, MD, L. Purcell, MD, David Puzan, Forrest W. Quackenbush, PhD, Beat U. Raess, PhD, Jeffrey T. Rafter, Professor Ramers, PhD, John E. Ramsey, Phillip Gordon Rand, PhD, Mamunur Rashid, PhD, Lee Raue, Francis Harvey Raven, PhD, James V. Redding, Roger G. Reed, Jack Reed, David W. Reherman, Paul F. Reszel, MD, Paul A. Reszel, MD, Brian F. Ricci, Doug A. Richison, David F. Ring, Paul Rivers, PhD, B. D Nageswara Roa, PhD, Larry Roach, Fred E. Robbins, Allan Roberts, Ira J. Roberts, Charles A. Robinson, C. A. Robinsons, Jean-Christophe Rochet, PhD, Nancy Rodgers, PhD, Milton W. Roggenkamp, MD, Thomas K. Rollins, MD, Michael G. Rossmann, PhD, R. E. Rothhaar, PhD, John W. Rothrock Jr., James Lincoln Rowe, PhD, Fred Rubbins, Boris Rudkevich, Don E. Ruff, Robert G. Rydell, Michael Sain, PhD, Philip Kent Salitros, Donald G. Scearce, Donald Joseph Scheiber, PhD, Alfred Ayars Schilt, PhD, Alvin Schmucker, Stephen J. Schneider, George A. Schul, DVM, David Schultz, PhD, Ronald L. Schwanke, Bobby J. Sears, George Sears, Mark F. Seifert, PhD, Phillip Sensibaugh, Andrew Sexton, Dennis N. Sheets, Mary A. Sheller, PhD, Steve Shepherd, Kevin M. Sherd, W. Sherman II, Thomas W. Sherman Jr., Ronald W. Shimanek, Vernon Jack Shiner, PhD, A. Cornwell Shuman, PhD, J. Shung, PhD, Edward Harvey Simon, PhD*, James G. Skifstad, PhD, Robert H. Slagel, C. B. Slagle, Roger Smith, Danny Smith, William H. Smith Jr., Parviz Soleymani, Quentin Francis Soper, PhD, Robert J. Sovacool, Edward Eugene Sowers, PhD, Larry D. Spangler, John M. Spears, MD, John A. Spees, Bill Spindler, William Jacob Stadelman, PhD, Ralph Stahl, Michael C. Stalnecker, S. M. Standish, Alan G. Stanley, Gerald R. Stanley, John M. Starkey, PhD, Donn Starkey, Frank R. Steldt, PhD, William Stevenson, William R. Stiefel, W. R. Stiefel, William H. Stone, Ronald S. Straight, Catherine Strain, Richard N. Streacker, Edgar F. Stresino, Ronald Stroup, Stanley Julian Strycker, PhD, Jeffrey James Stuart, PhD, Victor Sturm, Carol S. Stwalley, PhD, James S. Sweet, Carey Swihart, John A. Synowiec, PhD, Albin A. Szewczyk, PhD, Virginia Tan Tabib, MD, Elpidio V. Tan, Harold L. Taylor, PhD, Harold Mellon Taylor, PhD, Scott A. Taylor, DVM, C. L. Taylor, James A. Taylor, Curtis Taylor, Lowell George Tensmeyer, PhD, Howard F. Terrill, DVM, Nayana B. Thaker, MD, Thomas Delor Thibault, PhD, Martin J. Thomas, PhD, Marlin U. Thomas, PhD, Jerry A. Thomas, Larry G. Thompson, MD, Christina Z. Thompson, Leo Thorbecke, J. Bradley Thurston, MD, Bryan M. Tilley, Glen Cory Todd, PhD, Charles Edward Tomich, William R. Tompkins, Daniel J. Toole, Ruperto V. Trevino, John E. Trok, PhD, Jerry A. True, Robert C. Tucker, PhD, Lawrence D. Tucker, Tim N. Tyler, PhD, John Joseph Uhran, PhD, Tadeusz M. Ulinsnki, Joseph L. Unthank, PhD, Strien R E Van, PhD, Richard Edward Van, PhD, Bertram Van Breeman, Professor Vandemerwe, PhD, Vern C. Vanderbilt, PhD, Robert Dahlmeier Vatne, PhD, Spencer Max Vawter, Darrell A. Veach, Arthur A. Verdi, James H. Vernier, Richard Anthony Vierling, PhD, Raymond Viskanta, PhD, Karl J. Vogler, PhD, Donald F. Voros, Duc Vu, Vladeta Vuckovic, PhD, Susan M. Waggoner, Norman O. Wagoner, Jerry C. Walker, PhD, James L. Walters, David R. Wanhatalo, Robert W. Weer, John H. Weikel, PhD, George W. Welker, PhD, Lowell Ernest Weller, PhD, Tom Wells, Robert Joseph Werth, PhD, Aubrey L. Wesson, Winfield B. Wetherbee, PhD, Bill Wetherton, Alfons J. Wetzel, Dave L. Wheatley, Larry A. Wheelock, Roy Lester Whistler, PhD, Joe Lloyd White, PhD, Lawrence Wiedman, PhD, Charles Eugene Wier, PhD, Gene Wild, PhD, James C. William, PhD, Carl J. Williams, Tony D. Wilson, John R. Wingard, Frank A. Witzmann, PhD, William E. Woenker, You-Yeon Won, PhD, Gary K. Woodward, Gregory M. Wotell, Lee E. Wright, Jerry Wright, T. J. Wright, Yao Hua Wu, PhD, Neil Yake, Jason W. Yeager, Richard Yoder, DVM, Andres J. Zajac, Michael W. Zeller, Albin A. Zewczyk, PhD, Paul L. Ziemer, PhD, John E. Zimmerman, Steven L. Zirkelback, MD, Earl J. Zwick, PhD

Iowa

Stephen B. Affleck, PhD, Kimbol R. Allen, Wilfred L> Antonson, Elton E. Arensman, Marvin D. Armstrong, PhD, Adrian Arp, PhD, Jim F. Ashworth, Carl Fulton Austin, PhD, J. Brent Bagshaw, Craig Riska Baird, PhD, LeRoy N. Barker, PhD, Brent O. Barker, Douglas D. Barman, Justin P. Bastian, Wiley F. Beaux, Matthew A.

Beglinger, Donald R. Belville, MD, Julius R. Berreth, Darvil K. Black, PhD, Willis J. Blaine, Wilson Blake, PhD, Richard C. Bland, George Bloomsburg, PhD, Joe Bloomsburg, Carl R. Boehme, Carl R. Boehme, John Roy Bower Jr., PhD, David Boyce, Fred W. Brackebusch, Timothy J. Brewer, Ken N. Brewer, Randall A. Broesch, James L. Browne, Shelby H. Brownfield, Merlyn Ardel Brusven, PhD, Brent J. Buescher, PhD, William M. Calhoun, David Lavere Carter, PhD, Thomas Cavaiani, PhD, William R. Chandler, L. F. Cheng, PhD, Grant S. Christenson, Randil L. Clark, PhD, James W. Codding, Guy M. Colpron, Michael Cook, Carl Corbit, Ronald C. Crane, PhD, Richard A. Cummings, Raymond C. Daigh, Kim B. Davies, Karl Dejesus, PhD, Robert F. Denkins, Thomas R. Detar, Mel Dewsnup, Melvin L. Dewsnup, Mark C. Dooley, Stanley L. Drennan, MD, Larry A. Drew, PhD, Merlyn C. Duerksen, MD, O. Keener Earle, William J. Farrell, MD, Matthew Fein, Donald N. Fergusen, Roger Ferguson, Ferol F. Fish, PhD, Richard E. Forrest, DVM, Harry Kier Fritchman, PhD, Robert L. Geddes, Paul L. Glader, Doug J. Glaspey, Donald W. Glenn, V. L. Goltry, MD, Hans D. Gougar, PhD, John G. Haan, Lloyd Conn Haderlie, PhD, Richard Hampton, PhD, Julie J. Hand, Leonid Hanin, PhD, Bill M. Hann, Evan Hansen, PhD, Gerald H. Hanson, Robert N. Hanson, Roger Wehe Harder, Herbert E. Harper, Tim Harper, Herbert J. Hatcher, PhD, John B. Hegsted, Richard Charles Heimsch, PhD, Brian G. Henneman, Robert A. Hibbs, PhD, Richard C. Hill, MD, Robert F. Hill, Larry Hinderager, Kenneth M. Hollenbaugh, PhD, Clifford Holmes, Harold E. Horne, Case J. Houson, K. B. Howard, John E. Howard, Arthur R. Hubscher, Allan S. Humpherys, Richard M. Hydzik, C. Thomas Jewell, MD, Janard J. Jobes, Timothy J. Johans, Donald Ralph Johhnson, PhD, L. P. Johns, James B. Johnson, PhD, Kent R. Johnson, PhD, Lawrence Harding Johnston, PhD, James J. Jones, Jitendra V. Kalyani, Robert W. Kasnitz, Gary J. Kees, Fenton Crosland Kelley, PhD, Paul C. Kowallis, Stephen Kronholm, MD, Philip M. Krueger, PhD, John S. Kundrat, MD, Tim M. Lawton, George J. LeDuc, John W. Leonard, Leroy Crawford Lewis, PhD, William Little, PhD, Robert A. Luke, PhD, Richard Luke, Patricia A. Maloney, Billy L. Manwill, Jon L. Mason, Ralph W. Maughan, Jeremiah Mc Carthy, PhD, Kent R. McGarry, Mark A. McGuire, PhD, Bill McIlvanie, Twylia J. McIlvanie, Michael E. McLean, Brent A. McMillen, Scott G. McNee, Reg Meaker, Reginald E. Meaker, Donald L. Mecham, Travis W. Mechling, William L. Michalk, Ellis W. Miller, PhD, James A. Miller, Dile J. Monson, John L. Morris, PhD, Steven Moss, Jack Edward Mott, PhD, George Murgel, PhD, Thomas J. Muzik, PhD, Michael J. Myhre, MD, Roger Donald Nass, Thomas C. Neil, PhD, Doug W. New, Daniel Nogales, PhD, Randy Noriyaki, Mark J. Olson, William Joseph Otting, PhD, Gerald G. Overly, Aida Patterson, Ed L. Payne, PhD, Raymond M. Petrun, Gene W. Pierson, Harold A. Powers, Vernon Preston, Alan L. Prouty, Thomas R. Rasmussen, Bill Richards, Robert E. Rinker, PhD, Eric P. Robertson, Arthur P. Roeh, Jodie Roletto, Jerry F. Sagendorf, Charles Sargent, Rex Schorzman, David Laurence Schreiber, PhD, Carl W. Schulte, Sidney J. Scribner, Francis Sharpton, PhD, Glen M. Sheppard, George H. Silkworth, Claude Woodrow Sill, John Wolfgang Smith, PhD, Jay Hamilton Smith, PhD, Wesley D. Smith, PhD, Roger F. Sorenson, Ross A. Spackman, John C. Spalding, Barbara Spengler, Thomas Speziale, PhD, Gene Start, Raymond J. Stene, Bruce W. Stoddard, Wilfried J. Struck, Dale Stukenholtz, PhD, Donald C. Teske, Eugene Theios, Gary K. Thomas, MD, Warren N. Thompson, James P. Todd, Del Traveller, Francois D. Trotta, MD, Leland Wayne Tufts, John H. Turkenburg, Edmund Eugene Tylutki, PhD, Joseph James Ulliman, PhD, Randy K. Uranes, Bingham H. Vandyke Jr., PhD, Chien Moo Wai, PhD, Thornton H. Waite, Leslie M. Walker, Mont M. Warner, PhD, Jon H. Warner, D. T. Westermann, PhD, John E. Wey Jr., Jack Weyland, PhD, Robert N. Wiley, George L. Wilhelm, S. Curtis Wilkins, Oliver S. Williams, Roy L. Wise, George D. Wood, Austin L. Young, Mark Yuly, PhD, Stephen P. Zollinger, PhD

Kansas

Dwight L. Adams, MD, Stephen R. Alewine, Donald R. Andersen Jr., Thornton Anderson, William L. Anderson, Harrison Clarke Anderson, MD, Ernest Angino, PhD, Amalia R. Auvigne, MD, James F. Badgett, D. Bahm, Richard C. Bair, Nathan S. Baldwin, Larry Bale, Cliff Bale, Mark J. Bareta, Neal Barkley, Campbell C. Barnds, Lynn Shannon Bates, PhD, Curtis M. Beecham, PhD, Delfin J. Beltran, MD, John S. Black, Charles Blatchley, PhD, Robert G. Boling, Lawrence Glenn Bradford, PhD, Don L. Braker, Brian W. Braudaway, Wesley G. Britson, Robert A. Brooks, PhD, Bruce C. Brooks, Ward W. Brown, DVM, Dail Bruce, Joan Brunfeldt, MD, Ralph W. Bubeck, MD, William M. Byrne, PhD, Jon M. Callen, Earl D. Carlson, Charles T. Chaffin, PhD, James E. Connor, Ted L. Cooper, Max E. Cooper, Murray D. Corbin, MD, Patrick Ivan Coyne, PhD, Kent Craghead, Phillip T. Cross, Robert Hamblett Crowther, Glenn Crumb, PhD, James R. Daniels, Chad Davies, PhD, Eugene William Dehner, PhD, Ronald A. Dial, J. W. Dohr, Leslie J. Doty, John Doull, PhD, Rod Duke, David W. Dukes, Marilyn Duke-Woodside, MD, A. F. Dyer, Joe R. Eagleman, PhD, Donald R. Eidemiller, Darrel Lee Eklund, PhD, Al Erickson, Michael J. Eslick, Roger W. Evans, MD, Eugene Patrick Farrell, Gregory A. Farrell, Gene Richard Feaster, PhD, Roger Fedde, PhD, Stephen L. Ferry, Theodore C. Finkemeier, John R. Floden, Carl A. Fowler, Steve Frankamp, Dale E. Fulcher, David W. Garrett, Dick A. Geis, MD, Donald R. Germann, MD, James N. Glenn, MD, Clifford Glenn, Earl F. Glynn, Bruice Gockel, Kenneth L. Goetz, PhD, Peter J. Gorder, PhD, Robert C. Gorman, Albert J. Gotch, PhD, Douglas D. Graver, Lewis L. Gray, Jerry Green, Mary Ann Grelinger, M. Griffin, PhD, William C. Groutas, PhD, John T. Growney, MD, Larry Haffey, Stephen F. Hagan, MD, Quinlan Halbeisen, Wesley H. Hall, MD, Otto Hallier, William W.

Hambleton, PhD, Mark A. Hamilton, Robert M. Hammaker, PhD, Scott E. Hampel, T. Harder, PhD, Geoffrey O. Hartzler, Kirk Hastings, Douglas H. Headley, Dennis R. Hedke, Sandy Herndon, B. Heyen, PhD, Robert J. Hodes, Brett A. Hopkins, PhD, Robert Hopkins, Marta Howard, William C. Hutcheson, DVM, Roscoe G. Jackson II, PhD, Michael D. Jackson, MD, Byron E. Jacobson, Dale P. Jewett, Leland R. Johnson, PhD, David W. Kapple, Kim Karr, PhD, Suzanne Kenton, Michael Kerner, John Kettler, Cecil M. Kingsley, Philip G. Kirmser, PhD, Kenneth J. Klabunde, PhD, Robert W. Klee, Burke B. Krueger, Jack K. Krum, PhD, Daniel O. Kuhn, James E. Kullberg, Michael J. Lally, Roger O. Lambson, PhD, David L. Lamp, Mark Larson, Richard Leeth, Richard Leicht, E. C. Lester, Jingyu Lin, PhD, Glenn Liolios, John B. Loser, James Loving, Leon Lyles, PhD, Keith D. Lynch, PhD, Franklin F. Mackenzie, Susan L. Mann, Robert A. Martinez, Gayle Mason, Keith Mazachek, PhD, Thomas McCaleb, Robert J. McCloud, Richard E. McCoy, James L. McIlroy, George M. McKee Jr., Alvin E. Melcher, DVM, Dwight F. Metzler, Frank Midkiff, Clinton F. Miller, Leon J. Mills, PhD, Eldon F. Mockry, Reginald B. Moore, Norman R. Morrow, DVM, Fred Moss, DVM, Vincent U. Muirhead, E. A. Munyan, MD, Vincent U. Murihead, Joseph K. Myers, Jay F. Nagori, C. Nobles, Charles Arthur Norwood, PhD, Carl E. Nuzman, Verda Nye, Rocky Nystom, Daniel J. Obrien, PhD, Steven P. O'Neill, Thomas E. Orr, Dennis D. Ozman, Randy C. Parker, Kyle Parker PG, Dean Pattison, Charles W. Pauls, Wayne Penrod, Bill Perry, Heide Petermann, Leroy Lynn Peters, PhD, David Pflum, Max E. Pickerill, PhD, Danny L. Piper, Don Plisek, Jack J. Polise, Arthur F. Pope, Donald L. Poplin, Robert Pratt, John J. Ramm, Thomas E. Ray, Dean D. Reeves, MD, David Relihan, James C. Remsberg, Robert L. Reymond Jr., Charles A. Reynolds, PhD, Brian K. Richardet, Larry J. Richardson, David Allan Ringle, PhD, Kenneth Roane, Edward H. Roberts, James W. Rockhold, Richard L. Ronning, Karl K. Rozman, PhD, Kenneth Russell, James M. Ryan, PhD, Frederick Eugene Samson, PhD, Fred Samson, PhD, L. A. Sankpill, Larry V. Satzler, Michael J. Sauber, Kelly B. Savage, Robert R. Schalles, PhD, Charles Schmidt, J. Richard Schrock, PhD, Robert Samuel Schroeder, PhD, Warren D. Schwabauer Jr., Charles M. Schwinger, James E. Sears, Paul A. Seib, PhD, Arnold W. Shafer, MD, Dexter Brian Sharp, PhD, Brett E. Sharpe, Brian A. Sheets, Leland M. Shepard, Lloyd W. Sherrill, Merle Dennis Shogren, Mark A. Shreve, Ray Shultz, Glen L. Shurtz, PhD, James Van Sickle, William E. Simes, Larry Skelton, Edward Lyman Skidmore, PhD, Bruce G. Smith, Randall K. Spare, DVM, Feliz A. Spies, Robert P. Spriggs, Jerry L. Stephens, William T. Stevenson, PhD, Jeffrey Smith Stevenson, PhD, Robert R. Stolze, Robert Stolzle, Richard L. Stoppelmoor, Doug T. Stueve, Bala Subramaniam, PhD, James W. Suggs, Stuart Endsley Swartz, PhD, Saeed Taherian, PhD, Marcus K. Taylor, Leslie Thomas, Timothy C. Tredway, Richard S. Troell, James M. Tullis, Steven G. Turner, Richard M. Vaeth, M. Van Swaay, PhD, Gary Vogt, Rosmarie von Rumker, PhD, Bruce L. Wacker, Wilber B. Walton, Dennis L. Wariner, Robert K. Wattson Jr., Laurence R. Weatherley, PhD, Allan R. Weide, MD, Ronald L. Wells, PhD, Kenneth R. Wells, Jerry R. Werdel, Steve S. Werner, Tom J. Westerman, Eric R. Westphal, PhD, Carol J. Whitlock, Wendell Keith Whitney, PhD, W. Keith Whitney, PhD, William Wiener, James C. Wiley, Jim Wiley, Don K. Wilken, Robert L. Williams Jr., Thomas Williams, Allen K. Williams, Lonnie D. Willis, DVM, Robert G. Wilson, PhD, Steven J. Wilson, Earl C. Windisch, Elmer J. Wohler, Russell L. Woirhaye, Jim Wolf, Charles Hubert Wright, PhD, Ralph G. Wyss, Shawn Young, Dwight A. Youngberg, Mario K. Yu, MD, Michael T. Zimmer, Adam D. Zorn, Glen W. Zumwalt, PhD

Kentucky

Neil Adams, PhD, Dell H. Adams, Howard W. Althouse, Bryron Alvey, R. Byron Alvey, Michael R. Amick, Robert L. Amster, DVM, Donald Applegate, DVM, Donald Archer, A. Ashley, PhD, Richard A. Aurand, Thomas H. Baird, John P. Baker, PhD, Randal Baker, Lee A. Balaklaw, MD, Paul A. Barry, Bonnie L. Bartee, Walter G. Barth, Charles I. Bearse III, Lloyd Beck, Daniel D. Beineke, PhD, Charles D. Bennett, R. Berson, PhD, Michael Binzer, Mary L. Blair, John G. Bloemer, Richard S. Bonn, Roscoe C. Bowen, PhD, Reginald J. Breeding, Jeffrey D. Brock, Fred A. Brooks, William F. Brothers Jr., Thomas Dudley Brower, MD, Gerald Richard Brown, PhD, Philip T. Browne, MD, Harry A. Bryan, Barry J. Burchett, MD, Frank C. Campbell Jr., Robert E. Campbell, Alan A. Camppli, PhD, Thomas D. Carder, Jeffrey S. Caudill, Robert Lee Caudill, William K. Caylor, Bill K. Caylor, James Charles, Richard Cheeks, Lijian Chen, PhD, Professor Chen, PhD, John Albert Clendening, PhD, Thomas R. Coffey, James L. Cole, DVM, Donald W. Collier, Stanley W. Collis, MD, Todd Colvin, Shawn W. Combs, Thad F. Connally, MD, Henry E. Cook Jr., Professor Corley, Linda G. Corns, James Cramer, Rhonda Creech, Philip G. Crnkovich, W. D. Cubbedge, William B. Cubbedge, John J. Czarniecki, Frank N. Daniel, Roger A. Daugherty, Gilber De Cicco, Paul E. Dieterlen, Philip W. Disney, Philip W. Disney, Billy Dobbs, George Charles Doderer, William B. Dougherty, James W. Drye, Donald B. Dupre, PhD, Gregory A. Durffent, Lee G. Durham, MD, Victor E. Duvall, Thomas E. Eaton, PhD, Gary Eberly, Harvey Lee Edmonds Jr., PhD, William D. Ehringer, PhD, P. Eichenberger, Donald R. Ellison, William K. Elwood, PhD, Thomas W. Emly, William G. Emmerling, Jim L. End, Dennis W. Enright, MD, Michael B. Erp, Russell J. Fallon, Lynda R. Farley, Allan George Farman, PhD, David Ray Finnell, Ken W. Fishel, Tommie E. Flora, Paul C. Fogle, David C. Foltz, James Lynn Fordham, Gene P. Fouts, Rebecca Franke, Mary Feltner Futrell, PhD, Fletcher Gabbard, PhD, F. Gabbard, PhD, Theodore H. Gaeddert Jr., Stanley A. Gall, MD, Theo H. Gammel, Ronald F. Gariepy, PhD, Albert S. Garofalo, Daniel L. Garrison, Lawrence K. Gates, MD, Lewis

G. Gay, Thomas Edward Geoghegan, PhD, Robert B. George, Earl Robert Gerhard, PhD, Jonathan Gertz, Peter P. Gillis, PhD, Bobby G. Gish, Gordon C. Glass, Peter D. Goodwin, Clifford D. Goss, Kenton J. Graviss, PhD, Ara Hacetoglu, Richard P. Hagan, PhD, Paul F. Haggard, W. Hahn, Ted D. Haley, Robert Halladay, Harold D. Haller, Charles Edward Hamrin Jr., PhD, W. Han, Charles Hardebeck, MD, Byron C. Hardinge, Dean O. Harper, PhD, Roswell A. Harris, PhD, Dennis R. Hatfield, Aaron Haubner, PhD, John H. Havron, Erv Hegedus, Regina C. Henry, Wiley Hix Henson, PhD, Carl W. Hibscher, Don Hise, R. W. Holman, PhD, Kenneth R. Holzknecht, MD, Alan W. Homiak, Ricky Honaker, PhD, Professor House, Kevin Houston, James F. Howard, PhD, David W. Howard, J. William Huber, Donald W. Hunter, Ralph E. Jackson, Leo B. Jenkins, PhD, Randolph A. Jensen, Elaine L. Jocobson, PhD, Ray Edwin Johnson, PhD, Omar M. Johnson, DVM, James H. Justice, Norman E. Karam, Leslie E. Karr, MD, Kenneth F. Keller, PhD, Kurt A. Keller, Ann M. Keller, William W. Kelly Jr., John Elmo Kennedy, PhD, Riley Nelson Kinman, PhD, Riley N. Kinners, PhD, W. S. Klein, David Kling, Nancy F. Kloentrup, PhD, Riley N. Kminer, PhD, James E. Krampe, Clarence R. Krebs, Steve Kristoff, PhD, Wasley Sven Krogdahl, PhD, John E. Kuhn, PhD, Garth Kuhnhein, John P. Lambert, Harold Legate, Syd H. Levine, Charles L. Lilly, Merlin D. Lindemann, PhD, Noel W. Lively, Susan Logsdon, James Longo, George E. Love, John Lowbridge, PhD, Charles S. Lown, Gerald J. Lowry, PhD, Phillip Lucas, Robert M. Lukes, PhD, George W. Luxbacher, PhD, William Charles MacQuown, PhD, Dannys Maggard, Alan T. Male, PhD, Robert C. Mania, PhD, Ronald A. Mann, PhD, William J. Mansfield, MD, Dan Marinello, Maurice K. Marshall, Ronald L. Marshall, M. Masthay, PhD, Richard S. Mateer, PhD, Vincent E. Mayberry, Wayne R. McCleese, Terry McCreary, PhD, Bill McGowan, PhD, John Long Meisenheimer, PhD, Phil M. Miles, David B. Miller, Franklin K. Miller, Ronald R. Monson, Dory D. Montzaemi, Glenn I. Moore, MD, Duane Moore, Charle E. Mosgrave, Steven W. Moss, F. Allen Muhl, Fitzhugh Y. Mullins, James K. Neathery, PhD, Jerry S. Newcomb, David A. Newman, PhD, Lynn Ogden, MD, Bernie D. Oliver, Steve Ott, Joseph C. Overmann, B. K. Parekh, PhD, Earl F. Pearson, PhD, Arthur P. Peel, Jeff Peters, Douglas W. Peters, Jeffrey L. Peters, Glenn Pfendt, John E. Plumlee, MD, Michael Portman, Ronald T. Presbys, Phil Quire, William Quisenberry, Craig Rabeneck, Manny K. Rafla, PhD, Stephen C. Rapchak, Erick L. Redmon, Frederick C. Rehberg, Phillip J. Reucroft, PhD, Gary Reynolds, J. E. Rhoades, Bart E. Richley, John Thomas Riley, PhD, David Roach, PhD, James O. Roan, Stewart W. Robinson, PhD, Thomas J. Roe, Jason K. Romain, Paul B. Rullman, Mary Ruwart, PhD, James M. Rynerson, MD, Thomas A. Saladin, MD, Robert Alois Sanford, PhD, Mark S. Sapsford, Thomas A. Saygers, Charles M. Saylor III, Larry Saylor, Donald J. Scheer, PhD, Frank M. Schuster, George W. Schwert, PhD, Randolph J. Scott, Daniel M. Settles, PhD, Richard W. Sewell, TE Sheffield, Michael Sherlock, Robin N. Siewert, John A. Sills, PhD, Professor Sitarski, PhD, Marek A. Sitarski, PhD, Frank Sizemore, Hayden Smith, Avery E. Smith, Anne Cameron Snider, James D. Sohl, Gerard T. Sossorg, Joseph Sottile, PhD, Gary L. Southerland, Gary G. Sowards, Donald G. Spach, PhD, Donald G. Spaeth, PhD, Werner E. Speer, Robert Wright Squires, PhD, Harry P. Standinger, Douglas E. Stearns, Dennis M. Stephens, Darcy Stewart, Richard C. Stocke, Bill Stoeppel, Alan Stone, Richard W. Storey, S. R. Subramani, Tommy L. Sutton, George H. Swearingen Jr., Morris A. Talbott, Daniel Tao, PhD, Daniel V. Terrell III, Gregory R. Thiel, M. P. Thorne, DVM, Paul E. Tirey, Albert M. Tsybulevskiy, PhD, Robert S. Tucker, Kot V. Unrug, PhD, Joseph Van Zee, William York Varney, PhD, Rodney D. Veitschegger Jr., Jim Volz, Konstanty F. von Unrug, PhD, George Vourvopoulos, PhD, William J. Waddell, MD, Bruce E. Waespe, David W. Wallace, MD, Danny R. Ward, Alva C. Ward, Michael Webb, Larry Wells, PhD, William Wetherton, Roy E. Whitt, Rudy Wiesemann, Robert O. Wilford, James Cammack Wilhoit, PhD, Bill R. Wimpelberg, Dennis C. Withey, Douglass W. Witt, Farley R. Wood, Earl C. Wood, Alice J. Woosley, Donald R. Yates, Professor Yost, PhD, Ralph S. Young, Peter S. Zanetti, Richard Jerry Van Zee, PhD, Robert Zik, David J. Zorn

Louisiana

Leonard Caldwell Adams, PhD, Tim Addington, Mark R. Agnew, Steven L. Ainsworth, Paul W. Allen, PhD, Christopher G. Allen, Arthur E. Anderson, Roy E. Anderson, James R. Anderson, Robert E. Angel, Lowell N. Applegate, Lou Armstrong, Daniel J. Aucutt, Bryan Audiffred, William E. Avera, Hugh Bailey, Kernen Banker, Wallace H. Barrett, E. Baudoin, Rick Bauman, Edward W. Beall, Joseph A. Beckman, PhD, Charles Bedell, Edward Lee Beeson Jr., PhD, C. Allen Bell, James M. Bell, E. Paul Bercegeay, PhD, Dan Berry, R. Dale Biggs, PhD, David L. Billingsley Jr., Ron J. Blanton, Virgil L. Boaz, PhD, Larry P. Bodin, Frank R. Boehm Jr., Gerald S. Boesch Jr., Lawrence G. Bole, MD, James E. Boone, PhD, Professor Borsari, John Boulet, Arnold Heiko Bouma, PhD, Timothy M. Boyd, Samuel B. Brady IV, Ernest Breaux, Larry Breeding, Karen Brignac, Matthew Broussard, Francis W. Broussard, Mary J. Broussard, Tim Brunson, David W. Bryant, David William Bunch, PhD, Ronald Butler, Augustus George Caldwell, PhD, Gene Callens, PhD, Sidney Campbell, Louis J. Capozzoli, PhD, Bobby L. Caraway, PhD, Edward Carriere, PhD, Oran R. Carter, James Clark Carver, PhD, Thomas E. Catlett, Thomas W. Cendrowski, John N. Cetinich, Bruce Chamberlain, Angelo Chamberlin, Doyle Chamgers, PhD, Jhn Chandler, Harlan H. Chappelle, Emery R. Chauvin, Huimin Chen, PhD, Danny J. Clarke, Chris M. Cobb, J. M. Coffield, R. D. Coles, Ted Z. Collins, MD, James G. Connell, William J. Connick Jr., Kenneth R. Copeland, Kevin Corbin, Walter H. Corkern, PhD, Frank A. Cormier, Michael R. Coryn,

Judith Coston, Vincent F. Cottone, Ronald A. Coulson, PhD, Ronald Reed Cowden, PhD, Lawson G. Cox, MD, Joel B. Cromartie, Gene Autrey Crowder, PhD, John Hicdford Cunniff, Harold B. Curry, Chopin Cusachs, PhD, Louis Chopin Cusachs, PhD, Burt L. St. Cyr, Rita Czek, Russell E. Dailey, L. R. Dartez Jr., Shawn P. Daugherty, Dennis J. Dautreuil, James H. Davidson, Robert C. Dawson, Harry H. Dawson, Donal Forest Day, PhD, John H. Dekker, Anthony J. DeLucca, Charles N. Delzell, PhD, Thomas A. Demars, PhD, Tom Demars, MD, Winston Russel deMonsabert, PhD, William DePierri, PhD, Tom DePierri, William G. DePierry, PhD, Marcio Dequeiroz, PhD, Herbert C. Dessauer, PhD, David F. Dibbley, Elizabeth S. Didier, PhD, Paul A. Dieffenthaller, Timothy J. Dore, Larry Dorris, Carl L. Douglas Jr., Harry Vernon Drushel, PhD, Patrick Dubois, C. J. Duet, Terry M. Duhon, Genet Duke, PhD, Raymond J. Dunn, Henry J. Dupre, MD, Sidney J. Dupuy III, MD, Eugene F. Earp, D. Elliott, PhD, W. Engle, Thomas L. Eppler, PhD, John R. Eustis, Dabney M. Ewin, MD, Donald C. Faust, MD, Gary Z. Fehrmann, D. Bryan Ferguson, John Ferguson, Jorge M. Ferrer, Jack Field, PhD, Gary L. Findley, PhD, Robert G. Finkenaur, Marlon R. Fitzgerlad, Robert Wilson Flournoy, PhD, Michael A. Fogarty, Martin M. Fontenot, Rudolph M. Franklin, Benjamin D. Fremming, Jeffrey W. French, U. George Frondorf, Roger D. Fuller, Frank P. Gallagher, Jonathan C. Garrett, Raymond F. Gasser, PhD, Edward William Gassie, PhD, Richard L. Gates, Paul Robert Geissler, PhD, Alexander A. Georgiev, PhD, T. C. Gerhold, Peter John Gerone, PhD, Robert T. Giles, Bob Gillespie, Jeffrey D. Ginnvan, Marvin G. Girod, MD, Nicholas E. Goeders, PhD, John T. Goorley, PhD, V. L. Goppelt, George Gott, Robert J. Gouldie, Joseph C. Graciana, Eric Greager, Randolph K. Greaves, Donald L. Greer, PhD, Alan B. Grosbach, Ronald R. Grost, Frank R. Groves Jr., PhD, Roland J. Guidry Jr., William T. Hall, MD, Bruce A. Hallila, John H. Hallman, PhD, M. Wayne Hamson, PhD, Abraham S. Hananel, PhD, D. E. Hansen, Marvin Wayne Hanson, PhD, Ted N. Harper, Clarence C. Harrey Jr., Albert D. Harvey 3rd, PhD, Kim L. Harvey, Kerry M. Hawkins, V. R. Hawks Sr., William G. Hazen, Phillip C. Hebert, Harold Gilman Hedrick, PhD, Richard E. Heffner, J. Hemstreet, PhD, G. C. Hepburn Jr., Stephen R. Herbel, John J. Herbst, MD, Roger N. Hickerson, F. M. Hill Jr., John C. Holliman, Paul K. Holt, Lloyd G. Hoover, Sylvester P. Horkowitz, Edwin Dale Hornbaker, PhD, Nancy A. Hosman, Walter A. Hough, PhD, Stephen C. Hourcade, John E. Housiaux, Michael S. Howard, PhD, William T. Howell, Fritz Howes, F. Markley Huey, Woodie D. Huffman, K. Huffman, Barry Hugghins, Robert L. Hutchinson, PhD, Terry E. Irwin II, Edward A. Jeffreys, Dale R. Jensen, Edwin N. Jett, Emil S. Johansen, Adrian Earl Johnson Jr., PhD, Thomas J. Johnson, Jack E. Jones, PhD, William H. Jones, Douglas L. Jordan, Paul A. Jordan, MD, John Andrew Jung, PhD, Michael Lee Junker, PhD, M. L. Junker, PhD, Robert J. Justice, J. Justiss Jr., Charles Kahn, Richard D. Karkkainen, Olgerts L. Karklins, PhD, J. B. Karpa, Kevin Kelly, PhD, Stephen J. Kennedy, Walter Paul Kessinger Jr., PhD, Michael L. Kidda, Charles A. Killgore, John King, Charles Leo Kingrea, PhD, K. Klingman, PhD, Thomas R. Klopf, Mark A. Knoblach, Daniel E. Knowles, Stanley Phelps Koltun, Anton Albert Komarek, Christopher La Rosa, R. G. Lacallade, Dale J. Lampton, Vicki A. Lancaster, PhD, Ricky M. Landreneau, DVM, L. Landry, Ronald J. Landry, H. Norbert Lanners, PhD, John LaRochelle, PhD, Dana E. Larson, James A. Latham, Edwin H. Lawson, MD, Lynn L. Leblanc, PhD, Bill Ledford, Grief C. Lee, Joseph M. Leimkuhler, James C. Leisk, Samuel A. Leonard, Gregory Scott Lester, James C. Lin, PhD, William Henry Long, PhD, Arthur L. Long, William E. Long, Jerry A. Louviere, MD, John R. MacGregor, MD, William T. Mahavier, PhD, Vincent T. Mallette, Carl W. Mangus, Alvin V. Marks, John Luis Martinez, Campo Elias Matens, Barbara L. Matens, J. L. Mathews, Rex Leon Matlock, PhD, Neil F. Matthews, Charles M. May Jr., David R. Mayfield, Bobby Mayweather, Michael L. McAnelly, Danny W. McCarthy, PhD, Mickey McDonald, John P. McDonnell, Robert G. McGalmery, R. D. McGee, Michael McIntosh, J. T. McQuitty, MD, Alan L. McWhorter, PhD, Tammy S. Meador, Jimmy L. Meier Sr., Jerry J. Melton, William W. Merrill, MD, Robert Merrill, Charles R. Merrimen, PhD, Robert A. Meyer, Dennis Meyer, Michael S. Mikkelson, Kelley F. Miles, Robert H. Miller, PhD, Harvey I. Miller, PhD, Joseph Henry Miller, PhD, Arnout L. Mols, Christy A. Montegur, MD, Douglas Moore, J. Stephen Moore, Richard Newton Moore, Paul H. Morphy, Harry Edward Moseley, PhD, Peter V. Moulder, Clifford Mugnier, Douglas V. Mumm, Donald D. Muncy, Jack P. Murphy, MD, John D. Murry, Adil Mustafa, Rocco J. Musumeche, Peter C. Mutty, Lynn J. Myers, DVM, Billy J. Neal, William J. Needham, Joseph Navin Neucere, Robert H. Newll, Charles H. Newman, PhD, Rogers J. Newman, PhD, Conrad E. Newman, James R. Nichols, Martin R. Nolan, Richard Dale Obarr, PhD, Liang S. Ocy, PhD, Donald A. Olivier, Dean S. Oneal, Addison Davis Owings, PhD, Richard Milton Paddison, Muriel Signe Palmgren, PhD, Richard Parish, PhD, Kirt S. Patel, MD, Frank M. Pattee, John W. Paxton, Julian Payne, Armand Bennett Pepperman, PhD, John H. Pere, James L. Peterson, George E. Petrosky, Chester Arthur Peyronnin Jr., James E. Pfeffer, John R. Pimlott, Richard M. Pitcher, Morris C. Place, Larry Plonsker, PhD, Timothy M. Power, Irving J. Prentice, Charles W. Pressley, R. L. Prichard, William A. Pryor, PhD, Elliott Raisen, PhD, Ganesier Ramachandran, Charles L. Rand, Clinton M. Rayes, William Rehmann, Alfred Douglas Reichle, PhD, Robert T. Reimers, PhD, Leslie H. Reynolds, Lee J. Richard, Leonard Frederick Richardson, PhD, Neil Richter, Herman H. Rieke, PhD, Jim Rike, Kent R. Rinehart, Terry D. Rings, Bruce A. Rogers, Gerard A. Romaguera, MD, Richard Rosenroetter, M. Rosenzweig, Lawrence James Rouse, PhD, Steve Rowland, Gillian Rudd, PhD, Kelli Runnels, PhD, Louis L. Rusoff, PhD, Richard A. Sachitano, PhD, Charles M. Sampson, Ronald G. Sarrat, Ralph J. Saucier, Robert Joseph Schramel, Roy W. Schubert, PhD, Otto R. Schweitzer, PhD, Albert Edward Schweizer, PhD, Michael J. Screpetis, Richard D.

Seba, PhD, Joseph E. Sedberry Jr., PhD, Rowdy L. Shaddox, Lawrence H. Shaw, Gordon Shaw, David Preston Shepherd, PhD, Frederick F. Shih, PhD, Muhammad D. Shuja, Karen L. Shuler, Mark Sibille, Don A. Sibley, PhD, Harold D. Siegel, William Carl Siegel, Larry Sifton, Lucila Silva, John D. Silvernail, William E. Simon, PhD, A. Craig Simpson, Howard F. Sklar, Denny L. Small, James M. Smith, MD, Larry Smith, Thomas M. Snow, Kepner D. Southerland, Elmer N. Spence, Donald Sprowl, PhD, Paul A. Stagg, Kevin Stanley, Eric States, G. Sterling, Arthur E. Stevenson, Rune Leonard Stjernholm, PhD, Edward H. Stobart, Theresa D. Stokeld, Robert C. Stone Jr., James P. Storey, William T. Straughan, PhD, Roland A. Sturdivant, Alberto Suarez, MD, Richrad Sullivan, Ruth Sundeen, Frank J. Sunseri, Tony E. Swisher, Katherine Talluto, PhD, Orey Tanner Jr., Eric R. Taylor, PhD, Erik D. Taylor, Paul R. Tennis, MD, Frank J. Tipler, PhD, Wallace K. Tomlinson, MD, James E. Toups, MD, J.E Toups, MD, Ed Trahan, Ann F. Trappey, John H. Traus, Melvin L. Triay lll, Peter J. Van Slyke, Anthony R. Venson, PhD, John R. Vercellotti, PhD, Marc Vezeau, Clemens J. Voelkel, Eugene von Rosenberg, Charles Henry Voss Jr., PhD, Harold V. Wait, John Wakeman, PhD, Nell Pape Waring, MD, F. J. Warren Jr., Edis W. Warrif, W. P. Weatherby, Luke T. Webb, Anthony J. Weber, Donald J. Weintritt, Shane Wells, Juergen Wesselhoeft, Richard M. West, Tom West, Russ Westerhaus, Albert J. Wetzel, James Henry Wharton, PhD, Paul R. Whetsell, Tadeusz Karol Wiewiorowski, PhD, Monty Wilkins, Louis E. Willhoit Jr., PhD, Oneil J. Williams Jr., Chester G. Wilmot, PhD, Leslie C. Wilson, PhD, Kathleen S. Wiltenmuth, Edmund W. Winston, William J. Woessner, MD, William H. Wohler, Andrzej Wojtanowicz, PhD, Laurence Wong, PhD, J. Stuart Wood, PhD, Mike Wood, Adonna M. Works, Roger M. Wright, David B. Wurm, PhD, Tom Wyche, Bruce C. Wyman, PhD, David Allou Yeadon, Michael C. Yohe, L. L. Yoho, Gerald M. Young, Ronnie M. Youngblood, Chester E. Zawadzki, Juan C. Zeik, MD, Fred C. Zeile, Edward J. Zisk, Marvin L. Zochert

Maine

Roger B. Allen, PhD, Clayton H. Allen, PhD, James R. Bellenoit, Charles G. Beudette, James V. Bitner, Henry H. Blau, PhD, Robert Perry Bosshart, PhD, Peter B. Brand, John Bridge, R. S. Chamberlin, Andrew Jackson Chase, Joseph M. Chirnitch, Michael Coffman, PhD, H. Douglas Collins, MD, Carl Cowan, Mark R. Daigle, Lee C. Devito, Donald Dobbin, Herbert W. Dobbins, William L. Donnellan, MD, Stephen Doye, Kenneth M. Eldred, Stephen G. Eldridge, Robert C. Ender, John W. Fitzpatrick, Randall C. Foster, Robert C. Frederich, Joseph M. Genco, PhD, Clark A. Granger, PhD, Steven R. Grant, Douglas Griffin, DVM, Raymond E. Hammond, R. W. Hannemann, Wilkes B. Harper, Earnest M. Hayes, Grove E. Herrick, PhD, Alan E. Hitchcock, Aaron L. Hoke, William G. Housley, PhD, H. Blane Howell, Terence J. Hughes, PhD, Laurence N. Johnson, Herbert C. Jurgeleit, MD, Kathy A. Kaake, Roger F. Karl, Roland Lebel, PhD, Richard R. Lecompte, Dulcie Lishness, Alan B. Livingstone, Albert F. Lopez, Sylvia B. Lowry, John P. Lynam, Peter L. Madaffari, Charles E. Maguire, Robert Lawrence Martin, PhD, Cairbre C. McCann, MD, Ivan Noel McDaniel, PhD, Ralph R. McDonough, Clark Nichols, Jackson Nichols, David Sanborne Page, PhD, Richard A. Parker, Doris S. Pennoyer, MD, Burce E. Philbrick, Carl R. Poirier, Waldo C. Preble, Glenn Carleton Prescott, Malcolm H. Ray, PhD, Charles Davis Richards, PhD, Everett V. Richardson, PhD, Thomas L. Richardson, MD, Harold A. Rosene, MD, Robert B. Russell Jr., Richard Sama, Razi Saydjari, Peter Schoonmaker, Mark D. Semon, PhD, Timothy G. Shelley, Paul L. Sherman, Thomas F. Shields, MD, Charles William Shipman, PhD, Donald M. Stover, James H. Stuart, PhD, David B. Thurston, John A. Tibbetts, Frank Trask, Erik J. Wiberg, Arthur F. Wilkinson, H. Hugh Woodbury, PhD, Robert E. Zawistowski, Jay Zeamer

Maryland

Roger L. Aamodt, PhD, Donald W. Abbott, Wayne L. Adamson, Winford R. Addison, Perry Baldwin Alers, PhD, Frederick C. Althaus, Melvyn R. Altman, PhD, Edward J. Ames III, Martin R. Ames, Kenneth J. Anderer, Leif H. Anderson, Ivan J. Andrasik, Walter Robert Van Antwerp, J. B. Aquilla, MD, Joseph Armstrong, PhD, Casper J. Aronson, Raymond J. Astor Sr., M. Friedman Axler, PhD, Azizollah Azhdam, James A. Ball, George P. Bancroft, Carroll Marlin Barrack, PhD, Stephen S. Barranco, Carol J. Bartnick, PhD, Warren J. Bayne, Rowland Bedell Jr., Harold E. Beegle, Roger A. Bell, PhD, Robert C. Beller, Warren Walt Berning, Joseph M. Bero, Charles Frank Bersch, Arlen D. Besel, Harry E. Betsill, Brooke A. Beyer, MD, Andrew L. Biagioni, William Elbert Bickley, PhD, Barbara O. Black, Thomas T. Blanco, Gilbert Sanders Blevins, PhD, Ralph N. Blomster, PhD, Samuel Blum, Paul W. Boldt, Morris Reiner Bonde, PhD, Warren J. Boord, Wayne E. Booth, Alexej B. Borkovec, PhD, George Bosmajian, PhD, Robert Clarence Bowers, Frank J. Bowery Jr., Emanuel L. Brancato, Allan R. Brause, PhD, John P. Brennan, Abner Brenner, PhD, Edward Breyere, PhD, Owen P. Bricker III, PhD, Philander B. Briscoe, MD, John D. Bruno, PhD, Jeffrey W. Bullard, PhD, Philip Gary Burkhalter, Richard Burkhart, Thomas Butler, Paul M. Butman, William L. Cameron, Frederick W. Camp, PhD, Robert J. Cangelosi, Robert N. Carhart, Donald E. Carlson, PhD, C. Jelleff Carr, PhD, Lynn K. Carta, PhD, David G. Carta, PhD, John Paul Carter, Vincent O. Casibang, PhD, Peter Castruccio, PhD, Joel V. Caudill, Nancy L. Centofante, PhD, David Leroy Chamberlain, PhD, John T. Chambers, Yung Feng Chang, PhD, Yung-Feng Chang, PhD, Lloyd M. Charles, MD, Zachary L. Chattler, David W. Christensen, Richard G. Christensen,

Ross D. Christman, Alfred Lawrence Christy, PhD, Paul Chung, Bill Pat Clark, PhD, Leo J. Clark Jr., John B. Clark, Charles Frederick Cleland, PhD, David A. Cline, Gideon Marius Clore, PhD, John B. Coble, Robert Cohn, MD, James D. Coleman, Todd A. Collins, DVM, William Henry Collins, Marco Colombini, PhD, Charles D. Conner, PhD, Robert S. Cooper, PhD, Jules M. Coppel, William Sydney Corak, Rebecca B. Costello, PhD, Ross Couwenhoven, PhD, William Crawford, Joseph Presley Crisler, PhD, Thomas Benjamin Criss, PhD, John Cullom, Robert D. Culver, Lawrence E. Cunnick, Ralph L. Cunningham, Dalcio Kisling Dacol, PhD, Charles Dwelle Daniel, PhD, Jayant J. Darji, Wes R. Daub, Leroy Edward Day, Forest C. Deal Jr., PhD, Thakor M. Desai, Kamalinee V. Deshpande, Armand Desmarais, Ronald Dewit, PhD, Edmund Armand Dimarzio, PhD, Cecil Malmberg DiNnuno, Kent C. Dixon, David B. Doan, David B. Dobson, Abel M. Dominguez, PhD, James E. Drummond, PhD, Thomas E. Dumm, Frederick C. Durant III, Sajiad H. Durrani, PhD, Assaf J. Dvir, Thomas W. E Jr., Donald Eccleshall, PhD, Joseph D. Eckard Jr., PhD, Charles N. Edwards, William Frederick Egelhoff, PhD, Gerald I. Eidenberg, Geral Eidenberg, Jokomo A. Ekpaha-Mensah, PhD, Stephen D. Elgin, MD, Emil Elinsky, Bruce L. Elliott, PhD, John Elsen, George F. Emch, Philip H. Emery Jr., PhD, Sarah Eno, PhD, Duane G. Erickson, PhD, Charles M. Ernst, Michael J. Ertel, Neal C. Estand, Norman Frederick Estrin, PhD, Albert Edwin Evans, PhD, William Evans, Phyllis B. Eveleth, PhD, Mostafa A. Fahmy, PhD, Alva R. Faulkner, Maria Anna Faust, PhD, Wayne D. Fegely, David M. Feit, Ronald L. Felsted, PhD, Mary K. Felsted, Charles M. Ferrell, Aldo Ferretti, PhD, David Fischel, PhD, Eugene Charles Fischer, PhD, William W. Fitchett Jr., Hugh Michael Fitzpatrick, Lewis W. Fleischmann, Joseph H. Flesher, Jeffrey S. Flesher, Alvin R. Flesher, John E. Folk, PhD, Allan L. Forbes, MD, Vaughn M. Foxwell Jr., William E. Franswick, Joseph C. Fratantoni, Bernard. A. Free, Ernest Robert Freeman, Ronald S. Fry, Sabit Gabay, PhD, William George Galetto, PhD, Bernard William Gamson, PhD, Robert Vernon Garver, Godfrey R. Gauld, Joseph C. Gerstner, Thomas George Gibian, PhD, Eric Giosa, James A. Given, George Gloeckler, PhD, Christine Gloeckler, Constance Glover, PhD, Dale P. Glover, James Glynn, PhD, William R. Godwin, Mark J. Gogol, Mikhail Goloubev, PhD, John Roland Gonand, PhD, Donald A. Gooss Sr., DVM, William B. Gordon, PhD, Willis Gore, PhD, John W. Gore Jr., Gio Batta Gori, PhD, Owen P. Gormley, William M. Gould, MD, C. Grabowski, Harvey W. Graves, Lucy M. Gray, George Linden Greene, PhD, Gerald Alan Greenhous, PhD, Reynold Greenstone, Claude W. Gregory, Joseph R. Greig, PhD, Linda M. Gressitt, Tom Griffiths, Sidney Grollman, PhD, Sigmund Grollman, PhD, H. Guenterberg, Mustafa Guldu, Cloyd Dake Gull, Alvin Guttag, Rooney Neal Hader, Albert Felix Hadermann, PhD, John Haffner, Richard David Hahn, MD, Mary B. Hakim, Martha L. Hale, PhD, Timothy A. Hall, PhD, Diane K. Hancock, PhD, E. M. Hansen, Lawrence R. Harding, George E. Harmening, DVM, Bruce W. Harrington, B. L. Harris, PhD, Benjamin L. Harris, PhD, Edward R. Harris, Greg A. Harrison, PhD, Michael H. Hart, PhD, Lumbert U. Hartle, Robert A. Hartley, MD, Francis Hauf, Frank L. Haynes, PhD, Earl Larry Heacock, Donald J. Healy, PhD, John B. Hearn, MD, Robert E. Hedden, Joseph Mark Heimerl, PhD, Philip B. Hemmig, Ronald Hencin, PhD, Andrew L. Henni, Richard Allison Herrett, PhD, Frank F. Hertsch III, Jeffrey L. Hess, PhD, Sol Hirsch, Viet Hoang, Robert W. Hobbs, PhD, Stephen Hochman, Herbert Hochstein, PhD, Frederick A. Hodge, PhD, Paul Hogroian, Russell Holland, PhD, Otto A. Homberg, PhD, Donald Paul Hoster, PhD, Riley Dee Housewright, PhD, Russell D. Howard, PhD, Franklin P. Howard, Dwight D. Howard, Sue Huck, PhD, John Stephen Huebner, PhD, Sean P. Hunt, David L. Hursh, Anthony L. Imbembo, MD, John Edwin Innes, PhD, Peter D. Inskip, Patricia A. Irwin, Terri Isakson, Bruce Jacobs, James J. Jaklitsch, Neldon Lynn Jarvis, PhD, John P. Jastrzembski, Kuan-The Jeang, PhD, Joseph Victor Jemski, PhD, Arthur Seigfried Jensen, PhD, LeeAnn Jensen, PhD, Stephen Johanson, Robert V. Johnson, PhD, Harold B. Johnsson III, Gerald S. Johnston, Emmet Jones, Alan D. Jones, David Joseph, PhD, Stanley Robert Joseph, PhD, John Juliano, Peter V. Juvan, MD, Joseph A. Kaiser, PhD, Stanley Martin Kanarowski, Gerson N. Kaplan, MD, Olgerts Longins Karklins, PhD, Herman F. Kaybill, PhD, Patrick Norman Keating, PhD, Robert Kelly, Ronald G. Kelsey USA Ret, Dennis A. Kennedy, James G. Kester, Harry W. Ketchun Jr., David R. Keyser, PhD, Chul Kim, PhD, Ralph C. Kirby, Henry Klein, Karl C. Klontz, MD, Frederick R. Knoop, William F. Kobett, Alex Kokolios, William A. Korvin, Robert J. Kostelniki, PhD, Eugene George Kovach, PhD, Allen A. Kowarski, Kenneth Koziol, Kenyon K. Kramer, MD, Robert W. Krauss, PhD, Joseph Henry Kravitz, PhD, Lawrence C. Kravitz, PhD, Ron Kreis, PhD, Edward A. Kriege, Jacob K. Krispin, PhD, John R. Krouse, Donald M. Krtanjek, Ann Marie Krumenacker, Lorin Ronald Krusberg, PhD, Chris E. Kuyatt, PhD, Andrew J. Kuzmission, Charles T. Lacy Sr., Jaynarayan H. Lala, PhD, Robert J. Lambird, John P. Lambooy, PhD, Malcolm Daniel Lane, PhD, Mike Lauriente, PhD, James A. Lechner, PhD, Matthew A. Lechowicz, Clarence E. Lee, Charles H. Lee, James Lewis Leef, PhD, Herwig Lehmann, PhD, Gregory S. Leppert, PhD, James D. Lesikar, PhD, Howard Lessoff, Gilbert V. Levin, PhD, Alexander D. Leyderman, PhD, Milton Joshua Linevsky, PhD, Robert W. Lisle, MD, G. D. Little Jr., Douglas E. Lohmeyer, Donlin Martin Long, PhD, Gerald W. Longanecker, David Loninotti, Philip E. Luft, PhD, William Hamilton Lupton, PhD, Franklin D. Maddox, Carl W. Magee, B. Maghami, Richard Magno, PhD, Andrew E. Mance, MD, Naga Bhushan Mandava, PhD, Stephen W. Manetto, Phillip Warren Mange, PhD, Lawrence Raymond Mangen, Wayne Martin, Edward J. Martin, Steven M. Martin, Donald Massey, Richard E. Matz, Jean Mayers, Paul Henry Mazzocchi, PhD, Bruce E. McArtor, PhD*, Jeffrey P. McBride, Frank Xavier McCawley, Daniel G. McChesney, PhD, David H. McCombe, Samuel R. McConoughey, John Dennis McCurdy, PhD, Wilbur Renfrew McElroy, PhD, Richard B. McMullen, Bryce H.

McMullen, William L. Mehaffey, Robert S. Melville, PhD, Robert J. Melvin, John. N. Menard, Peter L. Metcalf, PhD, M. Kent Mewha, MD, Frederick G. Meyer, PhD, George B. Michel, James E. Mielke, PhD, Wyndham Davies Miles, PhD, Donald B. Miller, PhD, Brian C. Miller, George H. Milly, PhD, Michael H. Mirensky, Wayne Mitzner, PhD, Matthew H. Moles, MD, W. Bryan Monosmith, PhD, Marcia M. Moody, PhD, Henry F. Moomau, Robert Avery Moore, PhD, Peter T. Mora, PhD, Alice B. Moran, PhD, Leonard Mordfin, PhD, Jim Morentz, PhD, Joe W. Moschler Jr., Arthur B. Moulton, Gary M. Mower, Joseph J. Mueller, Charles Lee Mulchi, PhD, Jim Mullen, John Irvin Munn, PhD, Wayne K. Murphey, PhD, John Cornelius Murphy, PhD, Scott Myers, Norbert Raymond Myslins, PhD, Zane Elvin Naibert, PhD, Robert A. Neff, George D. Nesbitt, MD, Nicolas G. Nesteruk, William J. Neville, Richard Nieporent, PhD, David T. Nies, Danny E. Niner, Mark A. Noblett, Jim Noffsinger, PhD, Thomas E. Nolan, Richard B. North, MD, Nicholas J. Nucci, Robert W. Olwine, MD, Roger P. Orcutt, PhD, Johathan H. Orloff, PhD, T. O'Toole, PhD, Edward T. O'toole, PhD, William G. Palace, T. T. Palmer, PhD, Timothy T. Palmer, PhD, Spyridon G. Papadopoulos, Albert C. Parr, PhD, Dale Wayne Parrish, PhD, Marshall F. Parsons, Malcolm Patterson, David Chase Peaslee, PhD, Samuel Penner, PhD, Robert Edward Perdue Jr., PhD, Russel G. Perkins, Charles A. Pessagno, Stephen G. Petersen, George D. Peterson, PhD, Frank C. Pethel, William Leo Petrie, Edward M. Piechowiak, Kirvan H. Pierson Jr., Arthurs H. Piksis, PhD, Lester Y. Pilcher, Robert A. Piloquin, Joseph T. Pitman, Karl W. Plumlee, PhD, George Pollock, Myron Pollycove, Robert F. Poremski, Richard F. Porter, Louis Potash, PhD, James Edward Potzick, Kendall Gardner Powers, PhD, Hullahalli Rangaswamy Prasan, PhD, H. Price, Donald William Pritchard, PhD, Leon Prosky, PhD, William M. Pulford, Herman Pusin, Earl Raymond Quandt, PhD, Bernard Raab, PhD, Mohsen Khatib Rahbar, PhD, John W. Ranocchia Sr., Richard L. Rebbert, PhD, Sterlin M. Rebuck, Charles W. Rector, PhD, James D. Redding, Frank J. Regan, William G. Regotti, Fred M. Reiff, Hugh T. Reilly, Chad Reiter, PhD, Hee M. Rhee, PhD, James K. Rice, Joseph Dudley Richards, Nancy Dembeck Richert, PhD, Michael Richmond, Melvin W. Richter, Claude Frank Riley Jr., Lauro P. Rochino, Theodore Rockwell, David F. Rogers, PhD, Frederick A. Rosell, David A. Rossi, Anthony Richard Ruffa, PhD, Kevin C. Ruoff, Jeffrey W. Ryan, Alicja M Kirkien Rzeszotarsk, PhD, M. Kirkien Rzeszotarsk, PhD, Waclaw Janusz Rzeszotarski, PhD, Frank D. Sams, Jerrell L. Sanders, Paul Santiago, Badri N. Satwah, David R. Savello, PhD, William A. Scanga, Mark Schaefer, Charles W. Scheck, Imorton M. Schindler, Joseph J. Schmidt, Philip L. Schmitz, George J. Schonholtz, MD, Ethan Joshua Schreier, PhD, W. L. Schweisberger, Robert G. Sebastian, Frank David Seydel, PhD, Thomas P. Sheahen, PhD, Gennady M. Sherman, Howard S. Shieh, Kevin J. Shields, Kandiah Shivanandan, PhD, K. Shivanandan, PhD, John B. Shumaker, PhD, Paul T. Shupert, Edwin B. Shykind, PhD, Ronald E. Siatkowski, PhD, Payson U. Sierer, Jerry Silhan, J. Silverman, PhD, Joseph Silverman, PhD, Joseph D. Silverstein, PhD, William Simmons, Harjit Singh, MD, Ruth Kressbey Sisler, Dale Dean Skinner, Paul Slepian, PhD, Richard L. Smith, PhD, Gilbert Howlett Smith, PhD, David A. Smith, PhD, Bruce H. Smith, MD, Joseph Collins Smith, Robert J. Snoddy, Michael R. Snyder, Edward D. Soma, MD, Richard M. Sommerfield, John N. Sorensen, Leo E. Soucek USA Ret, W. B. Spivey, Pete R. Spuler, Gregory A. Staggers, Charles J. Stahl III, MD, Robert C. Stanley, John Starkenberg, PhD, Jerry E. Steele, William Henry Steigelmann, Louis E. Stein, Howard Odell Stevens, Peter Beekman Stifel, PhD, Scott R. Stiger, Thomas L. Stinchcomb, Vojislav Stojkovic, PhD, John C. Stokes, Robert R. Strauss, PhD, Edward Strickling, PhD, Bruce C. Strnad, PhD, Alan Strong, PhD, Rolland E. Stroup, Gene Strull, PhD, Harry H. Suber, PhD, James E. Sundergill, Martin Surabian, Hilmar W. Swenson, PhD, Barbara J. Syska, Donald Roy Talbot, John C. Tankersley, Robert Ernest Tarone, PhD, Tom Tassermyer, Tyler Tate, Hari P. Tayal, Louis Terenzoni, Nick van Terheyden, MD, Glenn A. Terry, PhD, John Aloysius Tesk, PhD, Rod S. Thornton, Alan Thornton, Glenn E. Tisdale, PhD, James G. Topper, Dan E. Tourgee, Edmund C. Tramont, MD, M. J. Travers, Joseph M. Tropp, Herbert M S Uberall, PhD, Kenneth S. Unruh, PhD, George F. Urbancik Jr., O. Manuel Uy, PhD, Andrew Van Echo, Lawrence J. Vande Kieft, PhD, James G. Vap, MD, Lyuba Varticouski, PhD, Marc Vatin, James Ira Vette, PhD, James Hudson Vickers, DVM, Arthur Viterito, PhD, William E. Wallace, Clifton O. Wallace Jr., Robert Jerome Walsh, John Fitler Walter, PhD, Charles E. Walter, John S. Walter, Rudolf R. Walter 3d, Donald K. Walter, William Walters, PhD, Barbara S. Walters, Paul John Waltrup, PhD, John Huber Wasilik, PhD, Thomas L. Watchinsky Sr., David J. Waters, PhD, Richard Milton Waterstrat, PhD, Frank M. Watkins, MD, George H. Way, Howard H. Weetall, PhD, Eugene C. Weinbach, PhD, Professor Weinert, PhD, Gerald C. Wendt, Richard P. Wesenberg, Larry L. West, James C. Wharton, Philip J. Whelan, MD, Edmund William White, PhD, Reed B. Wickner, Dennis A. Wilkie, Vernon L. Williams, Scott R. Williams, James E. Wilson, Clarence A. Wingate, John M. Winter Jr., PhD, Ernest Winter, Thomas Wisniewski, John B. Wolff, PhD, Winnie Kwai Wah Wong Ng, PhD, Keith Woodard, John N. Woodfield, Walter E. Woodford Jr., Rita J. Wren, George M. Wright, PhD, Carol G. Wright, Sidney Yaverbaum, PhD, Robert Gilbert Yeck, PhD, Hubert Palmer Yockey, PhD, George. A. Young, PhD, William Nathaniel Zeiger, PhD, Robert George Zimbelman, PhD, John Gordon Zimmerman, PhD, Paul Carl Zmola, PhD, Edwin Zucker

Massachusetts

Ann S. Adams, Albert H. Adelman, PhD, Norman Adler, PhD, Vincent Agnello, MD, Mumtaz Ahmed, PhD, Sol Aisenberg, PhD, Harl P. Aldrich, PhD, Charles D. Alexson, Richard Alan Alliegro, Edward E. Altshuler,

PhD, Wayne P. Amico, Dean P. Amidon, Jonathan Arata, PhD, Neil N. Ault, PhD, Bob J. Aumueller, Joseph Avruch, Peter R. B, MD, Frederic S. Bacon Jr., Joseph Anthony Baglio, PhD, James l. Baird, Andrew D. Baker, Sallie Baliunas, PhD, William Warren Bannister, PhD, Fioravante A. Bares, PhD, Allen Vaughan Barker, PhD, Debra Barngrover, PhD, Wylie W. Barrow Jr., Samuel M. Barsky, Peter J. Barthuly, F. R. Barys, Carl H. Bates, PhD, Herbert Beall, PhD, Timothy L. Beauchemin, Richard J. Becherer, PhD, Harry Carroll Becker, PhD, John C. Becker 3rd, John J. Benincasa, Sharon Benoit, Edward J. Benz, MD, Daniel Berkman, Robert L. Bertram, Richard J. Bertrand, Robert E. Beshara, Georgy Bezkorovainy, Maneesh Bhatnagar, Joseph D. Bianchi, Conrad Biber, PhD, Yan Bielek, Klaus Biemann, PhD, Seymour J. Birstein, Aaron Led Bluhm, PhD, Bruce Plympton Bogert, PhD, Norman Robert Boisse, PhD, John A. Bologna, Gregory M. Bonaguide, Laszlo Joseph Bonis, PhD, Robert S. Borden, MD, Kenneth Jay Boss, PhD, John F. Bovenzi, PhD, H. Kent Bowen, PhD, Clifford W. Bowers, Sidney A. Bowhill, PhD, Colin Bowness, PhD, Karl W. Boyer, John J. Brady, Robert J. Breen, Sean P. Brennan, Lawrence S. Bright, Ernest F. Brockelbank, Ronald F. Brodrick, Delos B. Brown, Wilson L. Brown, Walter Redvers John Brown, Robert G. Brown, Alex A. Brudno, PhD, Barry W. Bryant, PhD, Arnold R. Buckman, Auraam J. Budman, Avraam Budman, H. Franklin Bunn, Michael D. Burday, Charles Burger, Stephen E. Burke, E. A. Burke, Ronald T. Burkman, MD, George H. Burnham, Jennifer Burrill, James H. Burrill Jr., Joyce Burrill, Richard S. Burwen, Inez L. Busch, MD, Scott E. Butler, PhD, E. B. Buxton, Valery K. Bykhovsky, PhD, Frank Cabral Jr., Michael S. Cafferty, Daniel L. Cahalan, PhD, Dan Cahalan, PhD, Daniel E. Caless, Wendell J. Caley Jr., PhD, John M. Calligeros, Allan Dana Callow, PhD, Nicholas A. Campagna Jr., Harry F. Campbell, Donald A. Carignan, Arthur Carpenito, Jack William Carpenter, PhD, Jerome B. Carr, PhD, James C. Carroll, Jeffrey A. Casey, PhD, Renata E. Cathou, PhD, Joseph F. Chabot, DVM, Antohny J. Chamay, Kenneth Champion, PhD, Charles H. Chandler, Robin Chang, PhD, Robert A. Charpie, PhD, Dennis William Cheek, PhD, Zafarullah K. Cheema, PhD, Chi Hau Chen, PhD, Chi-Hau Chen, PhD, C. H. Chen, PhD, Mark R. Chenard, Ronald B. Child, Alm Christensen, Robert T. Church, Donald John Ciappenelli, PhD, Daniel E. Clapp, MD, Richard H. Clarke, PhD, John T. Clarno, James J. Cleary, John P. Cocchiarella, MD, Michael Coffey, Lawrence B. Cohen, Jonathan Cohler, Jerry M. Cohn, Professor Cole, PhD, Martin Cole, Anthony J. Colella, Sumner Colgan, Robert J. Conrad, Robert D. Cotell, Eugene E. Covert, PhD, John Merrill Craig, John B. Creeden, Peter Crimi, PhD, Edward Crosby, Robert P. Cunkelman, Maria A. Curtin, PhD, Cameron H. Daley, George F. Dalrymple, Anthony D. D'Ambrosio, Patricia Ann D'Amore, PhD, Balkrishna S. Dandekar, PhD, John T. Danielson, PhD, Joseph Branch Darby Jr., PhD, Leo G. Darian, Eugene Merrill Darling Jr., Thonet Charles Daughine, Donald J. David, PhD, Charles F. De Ganahl, Ronald K. Dean, Frank D. Defalco, PhD, John A. Defalco, Carlo J. DeLuca, PhD, Kevin A. Demartino, PhD, Don W. Deno, PhD, Eolo D. Derosa, MD, Martin A. Desantis, David P. Desrosiers, Marshall Emanuel Deutsch, PhD, Robert M. Devlin, PhD, Pedro Diaz, Pasquale Diciaccio, Robert A. Donahue, PhD, Alejandro M. Dopico, PhD, James Merrill Douglas, PhD, Westmoreland J. Douglas, PhD, George T. Dowd, Margaret Driscoll, Robert C. Dubois, John Dulchinos, Roland R. Dupere, Harold Fisher Dvorak, Stephen M. Dyer, DVM, Bruce P. Eaton, Eric B. Eby, George F. Edmonds Jr., Andrew E. Ellis, Sherif Elwakil, PhD, L. R. Engelking, PhD, John E. Engelsted, PhD, Richard A. Enos, Nancy Enright, Klaas Eriks, PhD, Alvin Essig, MD, Robert Everett, T. Farber, Richard J. Farris, PhD, James T. Fearnside, Robert D. Feeney, PhD, Zdenek F. Fencl, William Andrew Fessler, PhD, Edward Mackay Fettes, PhD, Kenneth G. Fettig, Fred F. Feyling, John Fierke, Melvin William First, PhD, Fred Fisher, Edward L. Fitezmeyer Jr., Maurice E. Fitzgerald, PhD, John Ferard Flagg, PhD, Carl E. Flinkstrom, John L. Flint, Harold W. Flood, David Flowers, Timothy Fohl, PhD, John H. Folliott, Clifford J. Forster, Christopher H. Fowler, Irving H. Fox, MD, Myles A. Franklin, Martin S. Frant, PhD, Al A. Freeman, Hanna Friedenstein, Peter Friedman, PhD, Melvin Friedman, Francis S. Furbish, PhD, Neil A. Gaeta, Christopher P. Gagne, John P. Gallien, Richmond Gardner, Joseph M. Gately, Robert F. Gately, Grantland W. Gelette, Vlasios Georgian, PhD, Elliot L. Gershtein, Adolf J. Giger, PhD, Steven D. Gioiosa, Horst E. Glagowski, Homer Hopson Glascock II, PhD, Julie Glowacki, PhD, Valery Anton Godyak, Richard Goessling, Jeff M. Goldsmith, Leonid Goloshinsky, Maya Goloshinsky, Alex Gonik, Brian G. Goodness, Scharita Gopal, Marina J. Gorbunoff, PhD, Alan B. Goulet, James T. Gourzis, PhD, Nicholas John Grant, PhD, Jurgen Michael Grasshoff, PhD, John F. Gray, Howard Green, MD, Anton C. Greenland, PhD, William T. Greer, James B. Gregg, Joseph W. Griffin Jr., PhD, Reginald M. Griffin, PhD, Linda Griffith, PhD, Rosa Grinberg, PhD, David P. Gruber, Nicholas J. Guarino, John E. Guarnieri, Peter H. Guldberg, Joseph M. Gwinn, Robert Simspon Hahn, PhD, Douglas C. Hahn, Charles W. Haldeman III, PhD, John R. Hall, PhD, Priscilla O. Hamilton, PhD, John C. Hampe, Linda C. Hamphill, Bruce E. Hanna, Charles S. Hatch, James W. Havens, Robert L. Hawkins, PhD, John Heard, Milton W. Heath Jr., Thomas S. Hemphill, Richard G. Hendl, PhD, Jozef Hendriks, Brian B. Hennessey, Karl P. Hentz, Hans Heinrich Wolfgang Herda, PhD, David J. Herlihy, Thomas F. Herring, Jeffrey L. Herz, George Herzlinger, PhD, Carl E. Hewitt, PhD, Richard E. Hillger, PhD, Charles H. Hillman, Charles J. Hinckley, Harold Hindman, John C. Hoagland, J. D. Hobbs, Melvin Clay Hobson, PhD, Lon Hocker, PhD, George Raymond Hodgins, Donald J. Hoft, Joseph L. Holik, PhD, Lawrence R. Holland, Frederick Sheppard Holt, PhD, F. Sheppard Holt, PhD, Lowell Hoyt Holway, PhD, Francis J. Hopcroft, Harold H. Hopfe, Donald P. Horgan, Ken Hori, Mark Lee Horn, PhD, John E. Huguenin, PhD, George William Ingle, Lucy Ionas, Martin Isaks, PhD, Gerald William Iseler, PhD, Kenneth M. Izumi, PhD,

James G. Jacobs, Lenard Jacobs, Joseph H. Jessop, H. William Johansen, PhD, Alan W. Johnson, Richard B. Johnson, H. M. Jones, PhD, Harry B. Jones, George J. Kacek, Robert A. Kalasinsky, Antoine Kaldany, MD, James B. Kalloch, Matthew S. Kaminske, Paul D. Kearns, James W. Keating, Maura E. Keene, MD, Charles Kelley, PhD, Mason E. King, Edwin G. Kispert, PhD, John F. Kitchin, PhD, Michael J. Kjelgaard, Donald J. Kluberdanz, A. G. Kniazzeh, PhD, Bryan S. Kocher, PhD, Robert D. Kodis, F. Theodore Koehler, Edward C. Koeninger, Janos G. Komaromi, Dennis J. Kopaczynski, Harold J. Kosasky, Michael F. Koskinen, Kerry L. Kotar, PhD, Paul Krapivsky, PhD, Christopher P. Krebs, Henry C. Kreide, John Gene Kreifeldt, PhD, Jacqueline Krim, PhD, Boris B. Krivopal, PhD, Louis Kuchnir, MD, Amarendhra M. Kumar, PhD, Thomas Henry Kunz, PhD, Jing-Wen Kuo, PhD, Glenn H. Kutz, Robert W. Kwiatkowski, Ludmila K. Kyn, Melvin Labitt, Martin R. Lackoff, PhD, Louis D. Laflamme, John Lahoud, Richard R. Langhoff, Ernest T. Larson, L. Lasagna, MD, Eric J. Lastowka, Robert L. Laurence, PhD, Robert A. Lavache, Jerome M. Lavine, PhD, Gilbert R. Lavoie, PhD, Paul D. Lazay, PhD, Louis A. Ledoux, Kenneth M. Leet, PhD, David Leibman, Andrew Z. Lemnios, PhD, John F. Lescher, Robert E. Levin, PhD, Yuri Levin, Karen N. Levin, Linda J. Levine, Howard L. Levingston, Phil Levy, Robert P. Leyden, Barry J. Liles, PhD, William Tenney Lindsay, PhD, Richard S. Lindzen, PhD, Stuart J. Lipoff, Janet M. Lo, DVM, John H. Lok, Morgan J. Long, DVM, Albert W. Lowe, Umass Lowell, PhD, J. Lowenstein, PhD, Henry E. Lowey, Howard W. Lowy, MD, Richard E. Lundberg, Gordon F. Lupien, MD, Sidney John Lyford, PhD, Scott Lyle, Leah Lyle, Jenner Maas, DVM, Brian MacDonald, Charles L. Mack Jr., Charle Aram Magarian, John S. Magyar, Joseph D. Malek, David H. Mallalieu, Nicholas J. Mandonas, Harold J. Manley, J. Mannion, John A. Manzo, Richard W. Marble, Robert W. Marculewicz, Mikhail D. Margolin, Richard M. Marino, PhD, William A. Marr, PhD, Peter D. Martelly, Eric Martz, PhD, James V. Masi, PhD, Mihkel Mathiesen, PhD, Charles F. Mattina, PhD, Thomas E. Mattus, Robert S. Mausel, MD, John Elliott May, PhD, Ernst Mayr, PhD, Siegfried T. Mayr, PhD, Janes W. McArthur, MD, David W. McCabe, Russell F. McCann, John Joseph Gerald McCue, PhD, Kilmer S. McCully, Sean D. McEnroe, Leonard J. McGlynn Jr., James B. McGown, Gary H. McGrath, Peter D. McGurk, Edward J. McNiff, Kenneth Earl McVicar, Donald K. Medeiros Sr., E. K. Megerle, Frank J. Meiners, Ivars Melingailis, PhD, Roland W. Michaud, Joseph J. Mickiewicz, Klaus A. Miczek, PhD, Joseph J. Miliano, Fanny I. Milinarsky, Richard James Millard, Robert C. Miller, PhD, Philip G. Milone, John R. Mirabito Jr., Ralph Monacohan, PhD, Ralph Monaghan, Harold W. Moore, David A. Morano, PhD, Richard D. Morel, Raymond C. Morgan, Walter J. Mozgala, Michael J. Mufson, MD, J. Mishtu A Mukerjee, George F. Mulcahy, Richard F. Mullin, John D. Munno, Rafael I. Mushkat, Rafael Mushkat, Luba Mushkat, Romen M. Nakhtigal, Robert R. Nersasian, PhD, Paul Nesbeda, PhD, Walter P. Neumann 2nd, Phillip E. Neveu, Paul M. Newberne, PhD, Sydney I. Newburg, Walter R. Niessen, Donald W. Noble, James A. Nollet, Carole M. Noon, John C. Ocallahan, PhD, Daniel J. O'Connor, Kenneth C. Ogle, Bernard X. Ohnemus, Thomas O'Leapy Jr., William P. Oliver, PhD, Curtis R. Olsen, PhD, Ludmica Olshan, Alexander Olshan, Dexter A. Olsson, Austin S. Omalley, Peg Opolski, Robert I. Orenstein, Charles Ormsby, PhD, Demetrius George Orphands, PhD, Robert Osthues, M. M. Palmer, Robert T. Palumbo, Dana M. Pantano, PhD, Leonard Parad, W. N. Parsons, PhD, Bhupendra C. Patel, Mangal Patel, Brian Patten, PhD, Charles J. Patti, Robert J. Pawlak, Raymond Andrew Paynter, PhD, Edward J. Peik, Ronald Peik, Steven J. Pericola, Stig Persson, Mikhail I. Petaev, PhD, Paul R. Petcen, Roland O. Peterson, Samuel Petrecca, Louis John Petrovic, PhD, Eleanor Phillips, PhD, Richard Arlan Phillips, PhD, Sanborn F. Philp, PhD, Charles A. Pickering, Allan Pierce, PhD, William J. Pietrusiak, Joseph L. Polidoro, Jay M. Portnow, PhD, David L. Post, Pranav M. Prakash, MD, Susan M. Prattis, PhD, David S. Prerau, PhD, G. Price, Ronald L. Prior, PhD, Daniel Puffer, Evan R. Pugh, PhD, James R. Qualey, PhD, Ryan D. Quam, Prosper E. Quashie, Arthur Robert Quinton, PhD, Steve Rabe, Harold R. Raemer, PhD, Keen A. Rafferty, PhD, Nicholas D. Raftopoulos, Alvin O. Ramsley, David Rancour, PhD, Thomas Raphael, PhD, Amram Rasiel, PhD, Dennis Rathman, PhD, John A. Recks, Robert Harmon Rediker, PhD, Philip O. Redway, David W. Rego, Arnold E. Reif, PhD, Oded A. Rencus, MD, Harris Burt Renfroe, PhD, Charles T. Reynolds, MD, John R. Rezendes, Frederic Richard, PhD, Allyn St. Clair Richardson, PhD, Allyn St. Clair Richardson, Edward J. Rickley, Donald E. Ridley, Stephen Joseph Riggi, PhD, Paul B. Rizzoli, MD, Robert S. Rizzotto, Charles D. Robbins, Francis Donald Roberts, PhD, Robert W. Rodier, Peter Rogers, PhD, Randy Rogers, Peter D. Roman, Thomas Ronay, PhD, Peter E. Roos, Anthony V. Rosa, Byron Roscoe, Philip Rosenblatt, Stuart Rosenthal, MD, Jamesneil JR Ross Jr., PhD, Sanford Irwin Roth, MD, William Clinton Roth, Raymond A. Rousseau, Robert T. Rubano, Paula A. Ruel, DVM, Richard F. Russo, Jean L. Ryan, PhD, Carroll J. Ryskamp, Faina Ryvkin, PhD, Richard J. Salmon, Erdjan Salth, PhD, Alan M. Salus, Dominick A. Sama, PhD, Sarmad Saman, PhD, George W. Sampson, Oli A. Sandven, PhD, Joseph B. Sangiolo, Michele S. Sapuppo, Richard Sasiela, PhD, Paul S. Satkevich, Daniel R. Saunders, Carol L. Savage, MD, Samuel Paul Sawan, PhD, Charles J. Scanio, PhD, Jeffrey Schenkel, Allan L. Scherr, PhD, Martin Schetzen, PhD, Elliot R. Schildkraut, Mikhail Schiller, Warner H. Schmidt, William Harris Schoendorf, PhD, Bradford R. Schofield, Nick R. Schott, PhD, Stephen Schreiner, PhD, Hartmut Schroeder, PhD, Paul K. Schubert, Manfred B. Schulz, PhD, Yael A. Schwartz, PhD, Henry G. Schwartzberg, PhD, Bruce W. Schwoegler, Stylianos P. Scordilis, PhD, Ryan S. Searle, Norman E. Sears, George Seaver, PhD, Walter Sehuchard, Salvatore J. Seminatore, Sal J. Seminatore, Edward C. Shaffer, PhD, Frank G. Shanklin, Edward Kedik Shapiro, PhD, Ralph Shapiro, PhD, S. Shayan, Dov J.

Shazeer, PhD, Vedat Shehu, PhD, Daniel H. Sheingold, Paul S. Shelton, Thomas B. Shen, PhD, Hao Ming Shen, PhD, Vivian Ean Shih, MD, George A. Shirn, PhD, Steven E. Shoelson, PhD, Werner E. Sievers, Maya Simanovsky, MD, Leo Siminavosky, PhD, Christpher Simpson, Robert I. Sinclair, Joseph J. Singer, William M. Singleton, Richard Henry Sioui, PhD, Norman Sissenwine, Cary Skinner, Gilbert Small Jr., PhD, Douglas E. Smiley, Nathan Lewis Smith, PhD, Verity C. Smith, Edna H. Sobel, MD, Monique S. Spaepen, Howard C K Spears, Timothy Alan Springer, PhD, W. van de Stadt, Archibald D. Standley Jr., Mark A. Staples, PhD, James C. Stark, PhD, Frank A. Stasi, Hermann Statz, PhD, Herman Statz, PhD, Thomas N. Stein, Peter Stelos, PhD, James Irwin Stevens, Harold E. Stinehelfer, James H. Stoddard, PhD, Donald B. Strang, E. Whitman Strecker, Jerrold H. Streckert, Paul J. Suprenant, Laurence R. Swain, Oscar P. Swecker, George J. Szecsei, Geza Szonyi, PhD, John R. Taft, Daniel Joseph Tambasco, PhD, Jeffery P. Tannebaum, MD, Peter E. Tannewald, PhD, Allan F. Taubert Jr., Kenneth J. Tauer, PhD, Kenneth E. Taylor, John W. Telford, PhD, Joseph Ignatius Tenca, Robert J. Thompson, George W. Thorn, MD, Serge Nicholas Timasheff, PhD, Nancy S. Timmerman, Dean Tolan, PhD, Kurt Toman, PhD, Vladimir Petrovich Torchilin, PhD, Diogenes R. Torres, PhD, Ildiko Toth, PhD, Paul S. Tower, Paul J. Trafton, PhD, T. C. Trane, James Trenz, Edwin P. Tripp III, Donald E. Troxel, PhD, Brian Edward Tucholke, PhD, Ben Tuval, Yuri Tuvim, PhD, David I. Tweed, David Tweedy, Jim F. Twohy, James F. Twohy, George W. Ullrich, Eric Edward Ungar, PhD, Robert O. Valerio, MD, Robert P. Vallee, PhD, Larry Van Heerdan, Thomas J. Vaughan, Eugene D. Veilleux, Erich Veynl, Alfred Viola, PhD, Otto Vogl, PhD, Michael A. Volk, Edward A. Vrablik, Janet M. Walrod, Myles A. Walsh, PhD, Peter R. Walsh, Kurt D. Walter, Michael D. Walters, PhD, Roy F. Walters, John F. Wardle, PhD, Alan A. Wartenberg, MD, P. C. Waterman, PhD, James L. Waters, John F. Waymouth, PhD, Raymond N. Wear, William P. Webb, Bruce Daniels Wedlock, PhD, Roger P. Wessel, Kenneth Steven Wheelock, PhD, Burton Wheelock, Douglas White, PhD, William R. White, Richard H. Whittle, Mel Wiener, George Friederich Wilgram, PhD, Leonard Stephen Wilk, Denise Williams, Byron H. Willis, PhD, James W. Winkelman, MD, Dave Withy, George M. Wolfe, James A. Wolstenholme, Kenneth S. Woodard, Donald Prior Wrathall, PhD, Robert D. Wright, John M. Wuerth, Geert J. Wyntjes, John C. Yarmac III, Marvel J. Yoder, PhD, William C. Young, Chester W. Zamoch, MD, Gregory G. Zarakhovich, PhD, Inna Y. Zayas, Harold Zeckel, PhD, Ming Zhang, PhD, Dong Er Zhang, PhD, Alexander Zhukovsky, PhD, Thomas E. Zipoli, MD, Martin Vincent Zombeck, PhD, Vincent M. Zuffante

Michigan

Douglas R. Abbott, Wayne Aben, Harry Adrounie, PhD, V. Harry Adrounie, PhD, Henry Albaugh, Dave Alexander, Amos Robert Anderson, PhD, Professor Anderson, Craig A. Anderson, Jon C. Anderson, MD, Mitchell Anderson, R. L. Anderson, Peter R. Andreana, PhD, Mohammed R. Ansari, Robert Lee Armstrong, PhD, Clifford B. Armstrong Jr., Charles G. Artinian, MD, Tom Asmas, PhD, Donald W. Autio, Charles R. Bacon, PhD, Mary Bacon, Lloyal O. Bacon, Terry Baker, George Bakopoulos, Carr W. Baldwin, Ronald L. Ballast, Dan W. Bancroft, Rudolph Neal Band, PhD, Richard A. Barca, Thomas Barfknecht, PhD, Michael J. Barjaktarovich, Daniel D. Barnard, Tom Barnard, Josh T. Barnes, Donald J. Barron, Frederick Bauer, PhD, Ceo E. Bauer, Thomas Bauer, Barry A. Bauermeister, Wallace E. Beaber, Bruce A. Beachnau, DVM, Joseph M. Beals, MD, William Boone Beardmore, PhD, Wayne D. Beasley, DVM, William Beaton, Carl G. Becker, Bob W. Belfit, Thomas G. Bell, PhD, Dwight A. Bell, Daniel Thomas Belmont, PhD, John V. Bergh, Ernest Bergman, Jeffrey J. Best, Robert Bilski, J. Bishop, Tomas H. Black, Charles E. Black, Luther L. Blair, John R. Blaisdell, Dav Blakenhagen, Barbara Blass, PhD, Carl Bleil, PhD, Brian Bliss, Larry D. Blumer, John G. Bobak, Lawrence C. Boczar, David Edwin Boddy, PhD, Willard A. Bodwell, Wladimir E. Boldyreff, Scott Boman, William Bond, Lawrence P. Bonicatto, Philip Borgending, David P. Borgeson, James L. Borin, Dwight D. Bornemeier, PhD, Steven L. Bouws, Alan D. Boyer, David Brackney, Gary L. Bradley, DVM, Peggy A. Brady, PhD, Mark S. Braekevelt, Alan David Brailsford, PhD, James A. Brandt, Albert J. Brant, Webb Emmett Braselton, PhD, Harvey H. Braun, James I. Breckenfeld, MD, Ross J. Bremer, Bart J. Bremmer, Michael J. Brennan, MD, William A. Brett, Darlene Rita Brezinski, PhD, Dale Edward Briggs, PhD, Blaschke Briggs, Phil N. Brink, Paul Brittain, B. J. Broad, Tammy A. Brodie, DVM, William J. Broene, Richard K. Bronder, James S. Brooks, John W. Broviac, MD, J. Brower, Richard B. Brown, PhD, Richard Brown, Roy T. Browning, Burton Dale Brubaker, PhD, Douglas B. Brumm, PhD, Paul O. Buchko, Charles D. Bucska, Stephen G. Buda, David E. Bullock, David Richard Buss, PhD, Stephen L. Bussa, Ceil Bussiere, Frank L. Butts, DVM, Forrest K. Byers, Charles Cain, PhD, Louis Capellari, Darrel E. Cardy, F. L. Carlsen Jr., Peter E. Carmody, MD, E. Louis Caron, Glenn S. Carter, MD, Steven K. Casey, William J. Cauley, Robert Champlin, PhD, Daniel W. Chapman, Luis Charbonier, MD, C. Robert Charles, MD, Benjamin Frederic Cheydleur, Lawrence O. Chick, Dale J. Chodos, Sue C. Church, MD, Gene S. Churgin, Joseph R. Cissell, Robert Malden Claflin, PhD, William Clank, MD, Tim Clarey, PhD, John Alden Clark, PhD, d. R. Clark PC, Kent Clark, John C. Clark, Richard P. Clarke, PhD, Bill Cleary, Paul W. Clemo, William G. Clemons, M. Gerald Cloherty, MD, Samuel W. Coates, PhD, James L. Coburn, PhD, Chester Coccia, Flossie Cohen, MD, Paul L. Cole, A. Collard, Ralph O. Collter, William B. Comai, John F. Conroy, Robert C. Cook, Daniel M. Cooper, Bahne C. Cornilsen, PhD, John D. Cowlishaw, PhD, R. E. Craigie Jr., David Craymes, Ronald Cresswell, PhD, Dale Scott Cromez, Dean A. Cross, C. Richard

Crowther, PhD, Warren B. Crummett, PhD, Kenneth D. Cummins, Merlyn Curtis, Charles Eugene Cutts, PhD, Robert C. Cyman, Werner J. Dahm, PhD, Paul D. Daly, Nicholas Darby, PhD, Forrester B. Darling, Kent R. Davis, Ralph Anderson Davis, H. M. DeBoe, Dennis B. Decator, Jim L. Delahanty, E. F. Delitala, John A. DeMattia, Frank Willis Denison, PhD, Robert Dennett, Glenn O. Dentel, David R. Derenzo, Larry D. Dersheid, Maruthi N. Devarakonda, PhD, Jaap B. Devevie, MD, Marco J. Di Biase, MD, Macdonald Dick II, MD, Aaron M. Dick, Reynold J. Diegel, PhD, Jerry A. Dieter, PhD, Alma Dietz, David Ross Dilley, PhD, Pryia C. Dimantha, Jim V. Dirkes, James D. Dixon, PhD, Thomas A. Doane, Herbert Dobbs, PhD, Glen R. Dodd, Dale E. Doepker, John Domagala, PhD, Thomas Donahue, B. Donin, Thomas MC Donnell, Theron Downes, PhD, Michael Cameron Drake, PhD, Michael T. Drewyor, James F. Driscoll, PhD, S. C. Dubios, S. C. Dubois, LeRoy Dugan, PhD, Gary Rinehart Dukes, PhD, L. Jean Dunegan, MD, Duane F. Dunlap, Harold Dunn, William A. Dupree, James A. Durr, Beecher C. Eaves, Earl A. Ebach, PhD, Gordon Eballardyce, Floyd S. Eberts, PhD, Dale P. Eddy, Robert Egbers, Val L. Eichenlaub, PhD, Jacob Eichhorn, PhD, Paul J. Eisele, PhD, Jack R. Elenbaas, Hans George Elias, PhD, Richard I. Ellenbogen, MD, Robert W. Ellis, PhD, Duane F. Ellis, Rodney Elmore, Gordon H. Enderle, Don J. Erickson, Lars Eriksson, Shanonn E. Etter, De James J. Evanoff, Leonard Evans, PhD, David Hunden Evans, PhD, Bradley Evans, MD, Eugene C. Fadler, Robert Feisel, William John Felmlee, Robert Fenech, Howard Ferguson, James H. Fernandes, Verno Fernandez, PhD, Marion S. Ferszt, MD, Terence M. Filipiak, Terence M. Filiplak, Charles Richard Finch, PhD, John Bergeman Fink, PhD, Donald W. Finney Jr., Henry P. Fleischer, Gary R. Foerster, Jay Ernest Folkert, PhD, Dwain Ford, PhD, Gary L. Foreman, Mary R. Forintos, Ingemar Bjorn Forsblad, PhD, Guy J Del Franco, Bruce A. Frandsen, Douglas Frantz, Lewis G. Frasch, Nile Nelson Frawley, PhD, Vincent I. Frazzini, James L. Frey, MD, Wilfred Lawson Freyberger, Robert Edsel Friar, PhD, Thomas W. Fritchek, James H. Frye, MD, Stephen L. Funk, Lyle E. Funkhouser, James A. Gallagher, PhD, Harendra Sakarlal Gandhi, PhD, Kent Gardner, H. Richard Garner, Jay B. Gassel, Geoffrey C. Geisz, Charles Gelwall, Charles Gentry, John W. Gesink, PhD, Lawrence J. Giacoletto, PhD, Randy Gibbs, Timothy P. Gilberg, Warren D. Gilbert, Tony Gill, Thomas D. Gillespie, PhD, Gary Gillespie, MD, Tim Gilson, Dan Glazier, Robert I. Goldsmith, MD, Herbert H. Goodwin, Gary J. Gorsalitz, Stephen R. Gorsuch, Vincent J. Granowicz, Geraldine Green, PhD, Marvin L. Green, Henry V. Greenwood, David Henry Gregg, PhD, John D. Grier, Robert F. Gurchiek, Robert J. Gustin, Robert A. Haapala, Herald A. Habenicht, William C. Haefner, DVM, William Carl Hagel, PhD, Russell H. Hahn, Forest E. Haines, PhD, Raymond M. Halonen, George J. Hambalgo, MD, Ralph E. Hamilton, Philip Hampton, Martin J. Hanninen, Daniel L. Hanson, Stewart T. Harman, Timothy A. Harmsen, Helen Harper, Keith H. Harris, Arthur B. Harris, Bruce V. Harris, Kenneth Harris, B. Harris, James Edward Harris, William A. Harrity, MD, Albert Hartman, William Louis Hase, PhD, Irwin O. Hasenwinkle, Richard E. Haskell, PhD, Bruce D. Hassen, Gregory J. Havers, James P. Hebbard, Donald B. Heckenlively, PhD, John Heckman, PhD, James B. Heikkinen, Kevin G. Heil, Ed W. Hekman, Alan K. Hendra, MD, Owen A. Heng, PhD, Raymond L. Henry, PhD, William J. Henry, Neal Hepner, Jerry L. Herrendeen, Luis F. Herrera, MD, Todd W. Herrick, Robert A. Herzog, John C. Hill, PhD, J. C. Hill, PhD, Raymond Hill Jr., W. G. Hines, PhD, Marshall Hines, Gregory D. Hines, John R. Hines, Jack T. Hinkle, PhD, Jack Wiley Hinman, PhD, Jivig Hinman, PhD, Roger R. Hinshaw, Kenneth Hinze, Ralph J. Hodek, PhD, Charles P. Hodgkinson, MD, Kenneth M. Hoelst, David V. Holli, Don H. Holzhei, PhD, William John Horvath, PhD, Robert L. Hosley, Eric C. Houze, Scott Hover, Robert George Howe, PhD, Thomas J. Hrubovsky, Eugene Yuching Huang, PhD, John A. Hudak, Larry Hudson, Harold L. Hughes, Bradley Eugene Huitema, PhD, Calvin T. Hulls, MD, Frank Hussey, John M. Hutto, MD, David Peter Hylander, Bradley S. Hynes, Marvin H. Ihnen, Raymond Ingles, David C. Irish, Donald Richard Isleib, PhD, Asaad Istephan, PhD, John F. Itnyre, MD, Thomas R. Jackson, Richard G. Jacobs, Ray Jaglowski, Arnold Jagt, C. C. Jakimowicz, Daryl N. James, Borek Janik, PhD, Edward S. Jankowski, Dennis C. Jans, John A. Jaszczak, PhD, Guy C. Jeske, Gordon E. Johnson, Gerald E. Johnson, James S. Johnson, Frank Norton Jones, PhD, Raymond P. Joseph, Bernard William Joseph, Richard Harvey Kabel, Michael G. Kalinowski, Jeremy M. Kallenbach, PhD, Brian D. Kaluzny, Margaret A. Kaluzny, Joseph M. Kanamueller, PhD, Alexander A. Kargilis, Neil R. Karl, Lawrence A. Kasik, Raymond J. Kastura, Jack H. Kaufman, MD, Thomas H. Kavanagh, DVM, Charles Kelly, Peter Kelly, Mike Kendall, Wilbur W. Kennett, William G. Kern, Majiid Khalatbari, J. S. King, PhD, Horst Kissel, Karel Kithier, PhD, Edgar W. Kivela, PhD, Rolf E. Kleinau, Gerald J. Kloock, Charles Philip Knop, PhD, Wayne Knoth*, Chung-Yu Ko, Ludovik F. Koci, William P. Koelsch, DVM, John C. Koepele, Adam J. Kollin, Michael K. Kondogiani, Joseph P. Konwinski, Dale W. Koop, Raoul Kopelman, PhD, R. Kosarski, Robert Allen Koster, PhD, Louis C. Kovach, James E. Kowalczyk, Adam Kozma, PhD, Ted Kozowyk, Kenneth Kramer, Tom J. Krasovec, Clyde Harding Kratochvil, PhD, David J. Krause, PhD, John Belshaw Kreer, PhD, Matthew P. Kriss, Kenneth S. Kube, MD, David J. Kubicek, Edward P. Kubiske, Richard E. Kuelske, Andrew Kujawiak, Gerard J. Kulbieda, Norman R. Kurtycz, Martin D. Kurtz, Edward R. Lady, PhD, Thomas J. Laginess, Kenneth Lagrand, Donald Joseph Lamb, PhD, Jeffrey C. Lamb, Richard W. Lambrecht Jr., Harold H. Lang, PhD, Ronald A. Lang, George R. Lange, Richard L. Lanier, DVM, James J. Laporte, Vernon L. Larrowe, PhD, Eric R. Larsen, PhD, Elisabeth Larsen, Kenneth Larson, Elisabeth Larson, Michael G. Last, Ruth C. Laugal, Daniel G. Laviolette, Walter E. Lawrence, Edward J. Lays, Ruben C. Legaspi, MD, John M. Leinonen, F. Lemke, PhD, Geoffrey Lenters, PhD, Joseph W. Leone, Bruno Leonelli, Frederick

C. Levantrosser, Roy W. Linenberg, John C. Linton, Michael Forrester Lipton, PhD, Kurt R. List, Georgetta S. Livingstone, PhD, Edward T. Lock, James E. Lodge, Steve Loduca, PhD, Lawrence Hua Hsien Louis, PhD, Don L. Loveless, Cole Lovett, PhD, Marvin Lubbers, Frederick E. Lueck, Mike Lueck, F.E. Lueck, Donald R. Lueking, PhD, Robert Luetje, Randolph M. Luke, Dwight E. Lutsko, Dick J. Macadams, John F. Macgregor, MD, John T. Madl, Wiliam Thomas Magee, PhD, Edward W. Maki, Eugene R. Maki, Ernest W. Malkewitz, David J. Maness, Lub B. Mann, Nasrat George Mansoor, William D. Marino, George E. Marks, George E. Maroney, PhD, Norman B. Marshall, PhD, Richard Marshall, Dennis Marshall, George H. Martin, PhD, Ronald H. Martineau, Conrad Jerome Mason, PhD, John L. Massingill Jr., PhD, Mark L. Matchynski, Mundanilkuna A. Mathew, PhD, David C. Matzke, Augustin D. Matzo, Daniel W. May, S. Mazil, PhD, Shaun Leaf McCarthy, PhD, Leslie Paul McCarty, PhD, Neil McClellan, Edward L. McConnell, Donald Alan McCrimmon, PhD, Michael C. McDermit, William J. McDonough, Robert D. McElhaney, MD, Jeffrey A. McErlean, MD, Daniel R. McGuire, Richard J. McMurray, MD, Ruth D. McNair, PhD, Dennis McNeal, Dan B. McVickar, PhD, Ken Mead, Kenneth W. Mead, Rodney Y. Meade, Loida S. Medina, MD, Dale J. Meier, PhD, Robert J. Meier Jr., PhD, Peter D. Meister, PhD, Joseph Meites, PhD, George W. Melchior, PhD, Bohdan Melnyk, Albert R. Menard, PhD, George D. Mendenhall, PhD, Roberto Merlin, PhD, James S. Merlino, Herman Merte, PhD, Heinz Friedrich Meyer, PhD, Donald Irwin Meyer, PhD, Robert F. Meyer, PhD, Howard J. Meyer, Eugene Mezger, MD, Joseph M. Michalsky, David Michelson, Carol J. Miller, PhD, Steven J. Miller, DVM, Herman L. Miller, Jack F. Mills, PhD, Francis J. Mills III, James A. Mills, Mark M. Miorelli, Philip V. Mohan, Lydia Elizabeth Moissides-Hines, PhD, Lawrence J. Moloney II, David G. Mooberry, Eugene Roger Moore, PhD, Thomas S. Moore, PhD, Leonard O. Moore, PhD, Richard Anthony Moore, PhD, Ronald Morash, PhD, Eduardo A. Moreira, Gene E. Morgan, Mark A. Moriset, Charles R. Morrison, Timothy B. Mostowy, Bob Mottice, Peter Roy Mould, PhD, Craig Brian Murchison, PhD, Pamela W. Murchison, PhD, Sean T. Murphy, PhD, Raymond Harold Murray, MD, Donald Louis Musinski, PhD, James G. Musser, Wesley F. Muthig, Marvin Myers, Michael J. Nadeau, Edward M. Nadgorny, PhD, Robert F. Nagaj, Champa Nagappa, PhD, Ray Nalepka, Robert J. Nankee, Mark R. Napolitan, Terry T. Neering, Gary R. Neithammer, Keith Nelson, Jan G. Nelson, Kenneth W. Nelson, Carl C. Nesbitt, PhD, A. David Nesbitt, Martin Newcomb, PhD, Russell D. Newhouse, Theresa Newton, DVM, Joseph P. Newton, Jerome C. Neyer, Roberta J. Nichols, PhD, Kathleen M. Nicholson, Kenneth W. Nickerson, Alfred Otto Niemi, PhD, James M. Nieters, Harmon Nine, PhD, Harman S. Nine, PhD, Harmon D. Nine, Ivan Conrad Nordin, PhD, J. Nordin, Jim T. Nordlund, David C. Norton, Raymond F. Novak, PhD, William R. Nummy, PhD, Richard R. Nunez, Richard Allen Nyquist, PhD, Leroy T. Oehler, Le R. Oehler, Walter K. Ogorek, Stanley P. Oleksy, MD*, Stanley P. Olesky, MD, Earl D. Ollila, Duane A. Olson, Gary Orvis, George F. Osterhout, Gary Ovans, Thomas L. Paas, John Pace, Jorge A. Pacheco, Karur R. Padmanabhan, PhD, William Pals, DVM, Jack S. Panzer, Jack Parker, Gary Pashaian, Bharat K. Patel, MD, Michael K. Paul, MD, James Marvin Paulson, PhD, Alfred A. Pease, Roger Peck, William T. Pelletier, PhD, Paul S. Pender, J. Percha, William J. Peters, Calvin R. Peters, James B. Peters, Edward Charles Peterson, Valeri Petkov, PhD, Frederick Martin Phelps, PhD, F. M. Phelps, PhD, Perry T. Piccard, Anton J. Pintar, PhD, James C. Plagge, PhD, Alan Edward Platt, PhD, Daniel E. Pless, Susan Pless, Charles E. Plessner, Robert E. Plumley, Howard K. Plummer, James W. Pollack, Joseph M. Post, Darrell L. Potter, Harold Anthony Price, PhD, Kenneth Prox, Andrzej Przyjazny, PhD, Siegfried Pudell, E. Dale Purkhiser, PhD, Rena H. Quinn, Todd L. Rachel, Michael T. Radvaw, Charles F. Raley, PhD, Dario Ramazzotti, Sonia R. Ramirez, MD, Eero Ranta, MD, Robert E. Rapp, MD, John W. Rebuck, PhD, Foster Kinyon Redding, PhD, William M. Redfield, C. Reed, PhD, Bart J. Reed, Tom Reed, Robert R. Reiner, Richard F. Reising, PhD, Richard H. Reitz, PhD, Robert F. Reynolds, Kathy A. Rheaume, Anthony J. Rhein, William Bennett Ribben, PhD, Jeffrey E. Richards, Allan Richards, Gregory B. Rickmar, Otto K. Riegger, PhD, Paul E. Rieke, PhD, Stanley K. Ries, PhD, James Rigby, PhD, Bernard Jerome Riley, James H. Rillings, PhD, Beverly Riordan, Harlan Ritchie, PhD, Glen A. Roberts, Bernard I. Robertson, George Henry Robinson, Mary T. Rodgers, PhD, Karen J. Roelofs, DVM, Ignatius A. Rohrig, Norman L. Root, Douglas N. Rose, PhD, Leonard Rosenfeld, Paul E. Rosten, Jean E. Russell, PhD, Michele M. Ryan, Timothy M. Ryan, Charles Joseph Ryant Jr., PhD, Lal Pratap S. Singh, PhD, Carol Saari, Steven T. Salli, Vernon Ralph Sandel, PhD, John F. Sandell, PhD, Peter P. Sandretto, Greg Savasky, Todd S. Schaedig, Carl Schafer, Albert L. Schaller, Carl Alfred Scheel, PhD, Francis Matthew Scheidt, PhD, Alexander W. Schenck, Edgar H. Schlaps, Professor Schlichting, PhD, Robert A. Schmall, PhD, Curtis S. Schmaltz, Earl A. Schmidt, Helen Schols, Keith Schreck, Paul E. Schroeder, MD, Arthur W. Schubert, Norman W. Schubring, Robert W. Schubring, Albert Barry Schultz, PhD, Donald D. Schuster, Richard C. Schwing, PhD, Philip A. Seamon, Cathie Jo Seamon, Frank R. Seidl, Martin F. Seitz, Richard R. Seleno, Arthur Seltmann, Robert Seng, Shirish A. Shah, PhD, David Shah, Donald H. Shaver, Mark C. Shaw, Stephen R. Sheets, Dan Shereda, Richard D. Show, Martin Sichel, PhD, Charles H. Sidor, Larry D. Siebert, Kent Siegel, Michael D. Singer, PhD, Julie A. Sinnott, John E. Skidmore, Harold T. Slaby, PhD, David F. Slater, Nelson S. Slavik, PhD, Joh Slaybaugh, T. Wentworth Slitor, George Slomp, PhD, James Blair Smart, PhD, Herbert J. Smedley, Paul Dennis Smith, PhD, Hadley James Smith, PhD, Rick Smith, Ron Smith, Louis G. Smith, C. R. Snider, Robert James Sokol, MD, Don V. Somers, Richard E. Sonntag, PhD, Nick Sorko-Ram, James H. Sosinski, Gary W. Sova, Steven Tremble Spees, PhD, John Leo Speier, PhD, Robert F. Spink, Henry J. Spiro, MD, John G.

Spitzley, Kenneth E. Spray, Peter Springsteen, Gordon W. Squires, Dave Stamy, Charles Stanich, Reed R. Stauffer, David A. Steen, PhD, Kevin J. Steen, J. Stephanoff, Robt L. Stern, PhD, George L. Stern, William C. Stettler, PhD, Al Worth Stinson, Donald Lewis Stivender, Howard Stone, PhD, Richard C. Stouffer, James Shive Strickland, PhD, Edwin Joseph Strojny, PhD, John H. Stunz Jr., MD, Darrel G. Suhre, James A. Surrell, MD, Todd W. Sutton, Jon R. Swanson, PhD, J. A. Sweet, LeRoy Swenson, Don Eugene Swets, Ronald J. Swinko, Joseph Vincent Swisher, PhD, B. J. Szappanyos, MD, Greg A. Szyperski, PhD, Michael Tarrant, Carl I. Tarum, Frank J. Taverna, B. Ross Terry, Raymond Thacker, PhD, Dilli J. Thapa, Alan W. Thebert, John Thebo, Don L. Theis, Sean Theisen, MD, Joe C. Thomas, Steve Thomas, Ted Thompson, Ned Thompson, Thomas Thornton, Richard Perry Tison, Stephen Winter Tobey, PhD, Mary Ann Tolker, David W. Tongue, Calvin Douglas Tormanen, PhD, Pascual E. Tormen, William N. Torp, Paul Eugene Toth, Mike Touchinski, Donald J. Treder, Tom Troester, James Trow, PhD, Judith Lucille Truden, PhD, Michael A. Tubbs, William Arthur Turcotte, Richard R. Turkiewicz, Roy C. Turnbull, Almon George Turner Jr., PhD, Joan L. Tyrrell, Peter I. Ulan, Charles R. Ulmer, Kurt E. Utley, PhD, Rheenan Verlan H. Van, PhD, Richard L. Van De Polder, Richard Michael Van Effen, PhD, Clayton Edward Van Hall, PhD, Keith D. Van Maanen, Kamala J. Vanaharam, Thomas L. Vanmassenhove, William Vecere, Roger F. Verhey, PhD, Paul A. Volz, PhD, John P. Von Plonski, Howard Voorhees, PhD, Jaroslav J. Vostal, MD, A. R. Wagner, Richard E. Wainwright, Donald Waite, F. A. Walas, Rick S. Wallace, John Walther, Jan A. Wampuszyc, Peter O. Warner, PhD, Brian Warner, Alfred B. Warwick, Frederick H. Wasserman, Michael T. Wattai, Gary S. Way, Walter J. Weber Jr., PhD, Michael Weber, Alfred R. Webster, Gordon J. Webster, James W. Weems, William J. Weinmann, Allan Orens Wennerberg, Stanley J. Wenzlick, Leslie Morton Werbel, PhD, James L. Wesselman, Edgar Francis Westrum, PhD, Norris C. Wetters, Thomas J. Whalen, PhD, Joseph W. Whalen, PhD, Russell P. Whitaker, Alan B. Whitman, PhD, Gregg B. Wickstrom, MD, Anthony J. Widenman, Anthony Widenmann III, Thomas D. Wiegman, Tom V. Wilder, Robert A. Wilkins, PhD, Gary J. Wilkins, Peirre A. Willermet, PhD, Donald H. Williams, PhD, Jefrey F. Williams, PhD, William W. Willmarth, PhD, Douglas J. Wing, Martin J. Wininger, R. D. Wood, PhD, Christoper S. Wood, Robert T. Woodburn, Richard D. Woods, PhD, Greg J. Woods, Clark D. Woolpert, DVM, K. Worden, Gordon Wright, PhD, Weimin Wu, PhD, Walter P. Wynbelt, Ning Xi, PhD, Stuart Yntema Sr., David Caldwell Young, PhD, Joseph A. Zagar, Eugene F. Zeimet, Albert Fontenot Zellar, PhD, Jiri Zemlicka, PhD, Roger Ziemba, Richard J. Zimmer, Paul W. Zimmer

Minnesota

Terry D. Ackman, Bryan C. Adams, Paul Bradley Addis, PhD, Ronald R. Adkins, PhD, Gene P. Andersen, Ingrid Anderson, PhD, Ken Anderson, Nathan Anderson, B. M. Anose, PhD, Dana Arndt, Orv B. Askeland, Bryan Baab, Ronald R. Bach, PhD, Paul A. Bailly, PhD, A. Richard Baldwin, PhD, Douglas W. Barr, Blaine W. Bartz, Milton Bauer, Wolfgang J. Baumann, PhD, Brian P. Beecken, PhD, Richard Behrens, PhD, Andrew H. Bekkala, PhD, David M. Benforado, Jody A. Berquist, DVM, Jack N. Birk, Rolland Laws Blake, PhD, Rodney L. Bleifull, PhD, William R. Block, Todd E. Boehne, Clay B. Bollin, Maurice M. Bowers, Susan H. Bowers, MD, Raymond J. Brandt, Arvid J. Braun, E. J. Bregmann, Charles W. Bretzman, Roderick B. Brown, Allan D. Brown, Stephen M. Brzica, MD, Richard L. Buchheit, Donald Burke, Mary E. Butchert, James Calcamuggio, Elwood F. Caldwell, PhD, Herbert L. Cantrill, MD, David Carlson, Dave Carlson, Orwin Lee Carter, PhD, M. Castro, Victor M. Castro, Jim Caton, Eugene Chao, John W. Chester, Terry R. Christensen, PhD, Arnold A. Cohen, PhD, Mark W. Colchin, Professor Cole, PhD, Mariette Cole, PhD, James A. Collinge, MD, Kent W. Conway, Robert Kent Crookston, PhD, Donald D. Dahlstrom, MD, Moses M. David, PhD, Thomas Jonathan Delberg, PhD, Fletcher G. Driscoll, PhD, Terrance W. Duffy, Wayne K. Dunshee, Dedi Ekasa, Wayne G. Eklund, James H. Elleson, Paul John Ellis, PhD*, Richard F. Emslander, MD, Arthur E. Englund, Douglas J. Erbeck, PhD, John Gerhard Erickson, PhD, Jack A. Eriksen, John A. Eriksen, Lee M. Espelan, MD, Robert W. Everett, PhD, Craig T. Evers, PhD, Michael Fairbourne, Eric E. Fallstrom, Homer David Fausch, PhD, Daniel A. Feeney, DVM, Keith Fellbaum, Herbert John Fick, Stephen D. Fisher, Eugene Flaumenhaft, PhD, Eugene Flaumenhaft, PhD, Carolyn R. Fletcher, DVM, Dean G. Fletcher, Terrence F. Flower, William R. Forder, David William Fox, PhD, Melvin Frenzel, Melchior Freund*, Frank D. Fryer, John Gaffrey, Mary Carol Gannon, PhD, Frank Germann, Harold E. Goetzman, Lawrence Eugene Goodman, PhD, Max Green, Gregory Greer, Troy Gregory, Carl L. Gruber, PhD, Sam Gullickson, Kelleen M. Gutzmann, Jeff Hallerman, Arthur Hamburgen, George Charles Hann, Steven Hanson, Jonathan Hartzler, PhD, Peter Havanac, Dean J. Hawkinson, DVM, Neil R. Helming, Tara Henrichsen, Ryan Henrichsen, Donald W. Herrick, MD, Fred G. Hewitt, PhD, Frederick George Hewitt, PhD, David A. Himmerich, Charles D. Hoyle, PhD, Mark D. Huschke, Valentin M. Izraelev, PhD, Wayne D. Jacobson, Rodney Jasmer, Mark T. Jaster, Jean Jenderlco, Timothy Berg Jensen, PhD, Robert P. Jeub, Scott Johnson, Richard W. Joos, PhD, Frank D. Kapps, MD, Michael Peter Kaye, Charles Keal, Allan H. Kehr, Patrick L. Kelly, Paul T. Kelly, Frank W. Kemp, MD, James L. Kennedy, Bridget R. King, DVM, Donald W. Klass, William P. Klinzing, PhD, Roger C. Klockziem, PhD, Charles Kenneth Knox, PhD, David Kohlstedt, PhD, Richard A. Kowalsky, Michael S. Kuhlmann, Joseph M. Kuphal, John J. Lacey Jr., Robert F. Lark, Ashley V. Larson, Allen Latham, Wayne Adair Lea, PhD, R. Douglas Learmon, Scott

A. Lechtenberg, Brian W. Lee, PhD, Bruce Legan, PhD, Ernest K. Lehman, Mike Lehman, E. K. Lehmann, Ernest K. Lehmann, Wendell L. Leno, Roland E. Lentz, Donald A. Letourneau, Benjamin Shuet Kin Leung, PhD, Wyne R. Long, Donald Hurrell Lucast, PhD, Mariann Lukan, Rufus Lumry, PhD, Richard G. Lunzer, MD, William Macalla, Mac Macalla, James D. MacGibbon, MD, Jay Mackie, John Maclennan, John R. Manspeaker, Jean A. Marcy-Jenderko, William N. Marr, W. N. Mayer, WT Mac McCalla, John McCauley, Tom McNamara, William H. McNeil, Igor Melamed Sr., David Shirley Mellen, Maurice W. Meyer, PhD, Frank Henry Meyer, Daniel W. Mike, DVM, K. Milani, Stephen A. Miller, David W. Miller, Lawrence D. Miller, Robert Moe, Robert Leon Moison, Glenn D. Moore, PhD, David L. Mork, PhD, Howard Arthur Morris, PhD, Dave Mueller, Edward S. Murduck, PhD, Richard C. Navratil, Kenneth H. Nebel, Kevin F. Nigon, DVM, Wayland E. Noland, PhD, Frank Q. Nuttall, PhD, Richard P. Nyberg, August J. Olinger, Mark G. Olson, PhD, Leonard G. Olson, Joseph Wendell Opie, PhD, Charlotte Ovechka, PhD, John S. Owens, Gordon Squires Oxborrow, Richard Palmer, Robert E. Palmquist, Guy R. Paton, Timothy A. Patterson, John W. Paulsen, Alfred Pekarek, PhD, Michael Pestes, Steven F. Peterson, MD, Donald G. Peterson, Douglas D. Pfaff, John N. Pflugi, Frederic Edwin Porter, PhD, Russell C. Powers, Thomas F. Prehoda, Randy M. Puchet, Steven M. Quinlan, Byron K. Randall, Steven T. Ratliff, PhD, Nancy C. Raven, Timothy J. Reilly, Richard J. Reilly, Kristin Riker-Coleman, David Joel Rislove, PhD, Janis Robins, PhD, Robert G. Robinson, PhD, Robert Rosene, Janet M. Roshar, PhD, Olaf Runquist, PhD, Peter A. Rzepecki, PhD, Wilmar Lawrence Salo, PhD, Wade D. Samson, Richard M. Sanders, PhD, Peter K. Sappanos, Jay Howard Sautter, PhD, Paul Savaryn, MD, Curt C. Schmidt, Tony Schmitz, Thomas W. Schmucker, Oscar A. Schott, Gerald Schramm, Kevin Schulz, PhD, James W. Seaberg, Dave Seibel, James M. Sellner, James C. Sentz, PhD, James B. Serrin, PhD, Arlen Raynold Severson, PhD, Dennis F. Shackleton, G. P. Shaffner, Mark W. Siefken, PhD, William E. Skagerberg, Frank J. Skalko, PhD, Neil A. Skogerboe, MD, Ivan Hooglund Skoog, PhD, Norman Elmer Sladek, PhD, Kenneth Sletten, Aivars Slucis, Chad J. Smith, Bryan Smithee, David Perry Sorensen, PhD, Harold G. Sowmam, PhD, Dale R. Sparling, PhD, D. Dean Spatz, Edward Joseph Stadelmann, PhD*, Leon Stadtherr, PhD, Larry A. Stein, Truman M. Stickney, Sandy Stone, Bart A. Strobel, Patrick Suiter, Bruce M. Sullivan, Arlin B. Super, PhD, Frederick Morrill Swain, PhD, David R. Swanberg, Brian M. Swanson, Robert M. Swanson, Brion P. Szwed, Robert T. Tambornino, Gerald T. Tasa, Gregory D. Taylor, Greg Taylor, Walter Eugene Thatcher, PhD, Brenda J. Theis, James A. Thelen, DVM, Mark Thoma, Herbert Bradford Thompson, PhD, Mary E. Thompson, PhD, Richard David Thompson, Arnold William Thornton, PhD, Edward A. Timm, Patrick A. Tuzinski, John R. Tweedy, Oriol Tomas Valls, PhD, William R. Vansloun, MD, Gloria E. Verrecchio, DVM, George M. Waldow, David R. Wallace, James R. Waller, PhD, E. C. Ward, Robert Wardin, PhD, Douglas Eugene Weiss, PhD, Rod Wells, Jerome R. Welnetz, James E. Wennen, James E. Wenner, James F. Werler, Clarence L. Wesenberg, Darrell J. Westrum, Robert W. Whitmyer, John F. Wilkinson, Daryl P. Williamson, MD, Richard D. Williamson, Dick Williamson, Ronn A. Winkler, Jerry Witt, PhD, Mark Wolf, Bruce Frederick Wollenb, PhD, Professor Woller, John Woods, MD, Richard R. Zeigler, Nancy Zeigler, William J. Zerull, Daryl E. Zuelke

Mississippi

Hamed K. Abbas, PhD, William W. Adams, Phillip S. Ahlberg, Richard G. Ahlvin, Timothy A. Albers, Robert T. Van Aller, PhD, William M. Ashley, Charles Edward Bardsley, PhD, Lawrence R. Baria, Rolon Barnes, F. Scott Bauer, Fred H. Bayley, James T. Bayot, PhD, Henry Joe Bearden, PhD, H. Joe Bearden, PhD, Fred E. Beckett, PhD, albert G. Bennett, PhD, Roy A. Berry, PhD, Curt G. Beyer, Harold L. Blackledge, M. L. Blackwell, Michael Blackwell, Hamid Borazjani, PhD, Steven T. Boswell, John C. Bourgeois, William E. Bowlus, MD, Cynthia R. Branch, John R. Brinson, Ronald A. Brown, PhD, George A. Brunner, Stanley F. Bullington, PhD, Harry Dean Bunch, PhD, Rufus T. Burges, William P. Burke, MD, Charles C. Bush, Carolyn M. Buttross, Paul D. Bybee Jr., Charles E. Cain, PhD, Curtis W. Caine, S. Pittman Calhoun, James E. Calloway, PhD, Christopher P. Cameron, PhD, John J. Carley, Kenneth G. Carter, MD, Garland L. Cary, Sidney Castle, Paul David Cate, David L. Chastain, J. Mike Cheeseman, Alfred P. Chestnut, PhD, Leroy H. Clem, PhD, Charles B. Cliett, Avean Wayne Cole, PhD, Billy E. Colson, F. Dee Conerly Jr., Sara J. Cooper, DVM, Gordon E. Cordes, Sidney G. Cox, Robert M. Crout, Kay Crow, David B. Crump FACS, Verne L. Culbertson, Robert William Cunny, Marion E. Davenport, Donald D. Davidson, Don Davis, Sandra Davis, Paul Day, Ken Dillard, Wanda L. Dodson, PhD, Donald Warren Emerich, PhD, Rick L. Ericksen, Professor Estalote, PhD, Henry P. Ewing, PhD, Thomas C. Ewing, Clarance S. Farmer, Robert William Farwell, PhD, Harold D. Fikes, Theodore H. Filer, PhD, William E. Finne, Robert Rodney Foil, PhD, William R. Ford, MD, Marcial D. Forester, Arley G. Frank, PhD, Melvin H. Franzen, Richard T. Furr, MD, James B. Furrh Jr., Lanelle Guyton Gafford, PhD, Robert S. Gaston, B. J. Gilbert, Roy Glenn, Allan Guymon, PhD, John D. Haien, Duane E. Haines, PhD, David Hancek, Carey F. Hardin, Julian C. Henderson, MD, Clifton L. Hester Jr., MD, John Pittman Hey, PhD, John P. Hey, MD, Robert M. Hildenbrand, William G. Hillman, Jack D. Hilton, James R. House III, Gary A. Huffman, DVM, Dudley J. Hughes, Arthur Scott Hume, PhD, Harold R. Hurst, PhD, Stephen L. Ingram Sr., Jonathan Janus, PhD, Johnny E. Jones, Christopher W. Jones, Paul Jurik, Harold E. Karges, Gerald W. Kinsley, Wilbur Hall Knight, Richard S. Kuebler, MD, Bobby D. Lagrone, Willem Lamartine Lamar, Elmer W. Landess, DVM,

Tommy Leavelle, PhD, Leslie Leigh, Nelson J. Letourneau, PhD, Clarence D. Lipscombe Iii, PhD, Henry R. Logan, Mark J. Losset, Allen Lowrie, Dennis L. Lundberg, PhD, Kenneth R. Magee, Angel Kroum Markov, MD, W. Maret Maxwell, MD, Phillip W. McDill, MD, Calvin P. McElreath, Louis D. Meegehee, Maurice A. Meylan, PhD, Donald Piguet Miller, PhD, Dalton L. Miller, Cindy Miller, Dale C. Mitchel, Ray E. Mitchell, Dale C. Mitchell, John L. Montz, Thomas C. Moore, Kenneth W. Moss, William L. Nail, Grey L. Neely Jr., Isaac A. Newton, MD, Stephen Oivanki, Marvin L. Oxley, Henry L. Parker, Blakeslee A. Partridge, Bernard Patrick, MD, Richard Patton, PhD, Emil H. Pawlik, Tom L. Pederson, John P. Pittman, PhD, Biuy R. Powell, James W. Pressler, Edward W. Puffer, John A. Pybass, Frank A. Raila, MD, Charles C. Randall, James W. Rawlins, PhD, James H. Rawls, Armando Ricci Jr., Karl A. Riggs, PhD, Robert Wayne Rogers, PhD, A. Kirk Rosenhan, Thomas E. Rosser, Stephen P. Rowell, Ernest Everett Russell, PhD, Jacob B. Russell, Edward C. Schaub, Amy M. Schmidt, Robert Schneeflack, Thomas Schwager, Lawrence L. Seal, Francis G. Serio, MD, John Herbert Shamburger, Bernard L. Shipp, MD, Joseph A. Shirer, Gary Shupp, Robert E. Shwager, Harold A. Simmons, PhD, Carl Simms, James Winfred Smith, PhD, Donald L. Smith, Gary Sneed, Harry V. Spooner Jr., Vance Glover Sprague Jr., Maitland A. Steele, James O. Stephens, William A. Stewart, Darryl Stewart, Robson F. Storey, PhD, Jeffrey Summers, MD, Thomas G. Tepas, James A. Thornhill, H. Thornton, Michael M. Tierney, A. C. Tipton Jr., MD, Roger Townsend, Glover Brown Triplett, PhD, E. H. Tumlinson, Manson Don Turner, PhD, Michael M. Turner, Waheed Uddin, PhD, John M. Usher, PhD, George B. Vockroth, Thurman C. Waller, Joe D. Warrington, Zahir U. Warsi, PhD, Charles L. Wax, PhD, Charles W. Werner, PhD, Lyle D. Wescott, PhD, Raymond Westra, PhD, Randall H. White, Stacy White, Gene D. Wills, PhD, Gene D. Wills, PhD, Wilbur William Wilson, PhD, Robert Womack Jr., E. Greg Wood III, MD, Donald E. Yule

Missouri

Anthony W. Adams, MD, Richard L. Adams, C. William Ade, Richard John Aldrich, PhD, Robert W. Allgood, Robert W. Andersohn, Richard Alan Anderson, PhD, Mary Anderson, Richard M. Andres, PhD, Mel Andrews, Charles Apter, PhD, Marcia L. Arnold, John P. Atkinson, Robert J. Bachta, John J. Bailey Jr., Lee J. Bain, PhD, Robert D. Baker, PhD, Connie L. Baldwin, Lorry T. Bannes, Cory W. Barron, Charles L. Barry, DVM, Dane G. Battiest, John G. Bayless, Carl L. Beardeh, Louis S. Becker, David A. Beerbower, Donald T. Behrens, MD, Abdeldjelil Belarbi, PhD, Max Ewart Bell, PhD, David E. Bemath, Roger Berger, Robert C. Beste, Daniel R. Billbrey, Charles F. Bird, Wayne Edward Black, PhD, Michael M. Blaine, Joseph Terril Bohanon, PhD, Carl D. Bohl, Craig H. Boland, Mark S. Boley, Dean Bolick, J. B. Boren, PhD, Thomas G. Borowiak, Louis Percival Bosanquet, PhD, John W. Botts, Gary Boyer, PhD, Erwin F. Branahl, Anne F. Bransoum, DVM, Brian L. Brau, Stanton H. Braude, PhD, Robert L. Breckenridge, MD, Monroe F. Brewer, William J. Bridgeforth, Steven R. Brody, Robert E. Brown, PhD, Olen Ray Brown, PhD, Jeff E. Browning, John J. Bruegging, Don D. Brumm II, Lester G. Bruns, PhD, Billy L. Bruns, David A. Bryan, PhD, Michael R. Buckheit, DVM, Jim E. Buckley, Eugene B. Buerke, Matt J. Bujewski, Martin Bunton, Larry Burch, Joe T. Burden, Joel G. Burken, PhD, George F. Burnett, Joe D. Burroughs, John Frederick Burst, PhD, Stan Butt, Stanley J. Butt, Eugene C. Bvbee, Christopher I. Byrnes, PhD, Raymond J. Caffrey, Lynn B. Calton, Paul Cameron, Martin Capages Jr., PhD, Will Dockery Carpenter, PhD, Hugh Carr, Marino Martinez Carrion, PhD, John Carroll, PhD, J. K. Cassil, John Arthur Caughlan, Harold Chambers, PhD, Kenneth P. Chase, Robert L. Cheever, Kuang Lu Cheng, PhD, Lou Chenot, Henry H. Chien, PhD, Larry B. Childress, David T. Chin, PhD, Troy L. Chockley, Professor Choi, PhD, Rich Christianson, Sally Clark, Kent H. Clotfelter, Calvin E. Coates, David K. Cochran "LTC, MC, USAR", PhD, Jane E. Collins, Keith R. Conklin, Jack L. Conlee, Gheorghe M. Constantinescu, PhD, Alfred A. Cook, Creighton N. Cornell, Raymond C. Cousins, PhD, Micheal A. Cowan, Braden S. Cox, John M. Cragin, PhD, Ronald W. Craven, Clara D. Craver, Bradford R. Crews, Thomas Bernard Croat, PhD, Stephen Crouse, Frazier Curt, MD, D. Dankel, Kenton T. Davidson, James A. Davis, PhD, Brent Davis, John A. Deal, Jack Dederich, Lynn I. Demarco, MD, Randall G. Dempsey, Jeffery R. Derrick, Kevin A. Deschler, R. Deufel, PhD, James D. Dexter, MD, Shawn M. Diederich, Charles Dietrick, Nicholas T. Dimercurio, Mark A. Ditch, Donald A. Ditzler, Marvin P. Dixon, PhD, Jim Doehla, William Waldie Donald, PhD, Nirunjan K. Doshi, Eric Doskocil, PhD, Robert R. Dossett, Michael Gilbert Douglas, PhD, George Douglas Douglas, William L. Drake Jr., MD, Matthew G. Dreifke, Randall G. Dreiling, Raymond L. Driscoll, G. L. Dryden, PhD, Gil Dryden, PhD, Richard Edward Dubroff, PhD, Paul J. Dumser, B. B. Dunagan, Henry H. Dunham, PhD, Robert G. Dunn Jr., Jamese Durig, PhD, Reginald W. Dusing, MD, Ronald R. Dutton, Roger W. Dutton, Donovan A. Eberle, Tom M. Edelman, Jozef W. Eerkens, PhD, William C. Eggers, Barry R. Eikmann, Michael J. Elli, Edward Mortimer Emer, PhD, Edgar G. H. Emery, Adolph M. Engebretson, PhD, A. M. Engebretson, PhD, Ron A. Engelken, DVM, Charles P. Etling, James L. Fallert, Milo M. Farnham, MD, Mark E. Farnham, MD, Carl H. Favre, A. N. Feelem, Walter C. Feld, David M. Felkner, Dean R. Felton, Frederic L. Fenier, Kenneth P. Ferguson, Byron Dustin Field, Quay G. Finefrock, James L. Fletcher Jr., Steven T. Fogel, MD, Denis Forster, PhD, Frank Cavan Fowler, PhD, Todd and Blanche Fraizer, David M. Fraley, PhD, Harold J. Frank, Gordon R. Franke, PhD, George E. Franke, Karen S. Frederich, Max Freeland, PhD, Gary W. Friend, Clark H. Fuhlage, Wm. Terry Fuldner, Michael E. Gaddis, Robert Gene Garrison, PhD, Ray A. Gawlik, Daryl D. George, PhD, James C.

Gerdeen, PhD, Damian J. Gerstner, Jerry D. Gibson, Ken Giebe, Leo Giegzelmann, James W. Gieselmann, Melvin E. Giles, Howard D. Gillin, Steven P. Gilmore, DVM, Homer F. Gilzow, Richard Joel Gimpelson, MD, Mark Ginoling, Conway Goehman, Royal D. Goerz, MD, Terry L. Gooding, Norman E. Goth, Todor K. Gounev, PhD, Gary Graeser, George Stephen Graff, Tom R. Grass, Mary S. Graves, DVM, James Greenhaw, MD, Mary A. Grelinger, Kurt L. Gremmler, Mike Griese, Brian S. Griffen, Virgil Vernon Griffith, PhD, Louis John Grimm, PhD, Barbara Grimm, Arthur N. Griswold, DVM, Herb W. Gronomeyer, Fred H. Groves, PhD, Elaine Guenther, Paul E. Guidry, Earl R. Hackett, Brian T. Hackett, Jacqueline Hackett, R. C. Hafner, Henry E. Haggard, Johnnie E. Hall, Eugene W. Hall, MD, James W. Hamilton, PhD, Adrian J. Hampshire, Lewis F. Hancock, John P. Hansen, PhD, Ronald A. Hansen, Willis Dale Hanson, Lawrence R. Happ, Nicholas Konstan Harakas, PhD, William B. Hardin, MD, Christopher Harman, Brian Harrington, Pam C. Hart, Melissa Hart, Randall E. Hart, Clay E. Haynes, Ross Melvin Hedrick, PhD, Roger Heiland, Roger Heitland, Duane Helderlein, James C. Hemeyer, Bruce C. Hemming, PhD, Steve D. Hencey, Stephen J. Henderson, Marty C. Henson, John Frederick Herber, PhD, Carl K. Herkstroeter, Troy L. Hicks, PhD, Gene H. Hilgenberg, Jack Filson Hill, PhD, Jerry L. Hofman, K. Hogan, Troy J. Hogsett, David Eldon Hoiness, PhD, D. Hoiness, PhD, Tammy Holder, Robert L. Hormell, Edward E. Hornsey, PhD, William Burtner House, PhD, Jack E. Howard, James P. Howard, DVM, Tina M. Howerton, Craig R. Huber, Robert B. Hudson, Wayne Huebner, PhD, James B. Hufham, PhD, Randy L. Hughes, Michael D. Hurd, Victor E. Hutchison, Jeffrey A. Imhoff, Vincent J. Imhoff, Walter L. Imm, Hobart L. Jacobs, Jerome S. Jacobsmeyer, Leon U. Jameton, Clifford S. Jarvis, Theresa Jeevanjee, PhD, Max Jellinek, PhD, Guy E. Jester, PhD, James W. Johnson, PhD, Richard Dean Johnson, PhD, Peter F. Johnson, Robert G. Johnson, MD, George Johnston, Robert W. Jonasen, R. W. Jonesen, Phillip A. Jozwiak, William Jud, Frederick J. Julyan, PhD, Hemendra A. Kalbamna, Doris Kalita, Salma B. Kamal, PhD, Alan A. Kamp, Fred Kampmans, Earl J. Kane, Arnold F. Kansteiner, PhD, Raymond Kastendieck, John D. Keich, Ed Kekec, Roy Fred Keller, PhD, Amy L. Kelly, Marion Alvah Keyes IV, Ali M. Khojasteh, MD, John B. Kidney, Charles N. Kilo, MD, Justin A. Kindt, Jerome W. Kinnison, Jeffrey Kiviat, MD, Raymond Kluczny, PhD, Ronald A. Knight, PhD, Charles E. Knight, Bedford F. Knipschild, MD, Donald J. Kocian, Richard W. Koenig, David M. Koenig, Ernest J. Koestering, Ronald A. Kohser, PhD, Alois J. Koller Jr., Kenneth J. Kopp, PhD, Otto R. Kosfeld, Leslie R. Koval, PhD, Vincent J. Kovarik, Raymond J. Kowalik, Bob Kraemer, Lawrence Krebaum, PhD, Roy Krill, Joseph F. Krispin, Frank G. Kriz, Lester H. Krone 3d, Joseph T. Krussel, Donald E. Kuenzi, MD, Lowell L. Kuhn, Stanley P. Kuncaitis, David W. Kuneman, Vicent E. Kurtz, PhD, Henry Kurusz, Tom Lacey, David H. Lah, William M. Landau, MD, Stacy O. Landers, Brownell W. Landes, Stephen R. Langford, Edward Lanser, Michael A. Lawson, Bob Lee, Randy W. Lehnhoff, Joshua M. Leise, PhD, Leslie Roy Lemon, Donald W. Lett, Steven K. Lett, Marc S. Levin, Kenneth L. Light, Arthur Charles Lind, PhD, John F. Lindeman, MD, Jesse B. Lininger, Ellen Kern Lissant, PhD, Kenneth Jordan Lissant, PhD, Henry Liu, PhD, Robert S. Livingston, PhD, Peter F. Lott, PhD, Allan R. Louiselle, Forrest G. Lowe, F. Lowe, Anthony Lupo, PhD, Robert J. Macher, Alexander E. Macias, Michael A. Madonna, Robert E. Mady, Dillon L. Magers, Robert Maher, PhD, Philip W. Majerus, Bob Mallory, PhD, Carole J. Maltby, PhD, Warren O. Manley, Lena M. Mantle, Ronald E. Markland, Clifford Marks, Thomas R. Marrero, PhD, Thomas E. Marshall, PhD, Wm. N. Marshall, Edwin J. Martin, PhD, Byron L. Martin, Stanley E. Massey, Balakrishnan Mathiprakasam, PhD, Charles R. Mattox Jr., Joe May, James L. McAdamis, Joseph C. McBryan, Edwin B. McBurney Jr., Martin H. McClurken, M. McCorcle, PhD, Hulon D. McDaniel, Kerry McDonald, PhD, Hector O. McDonald, PhD, William S. McDowell, Kenneth Laurence McHugh, PhD, William M. McLaurine, Joseph U. McMillan, Kathleen A. McNelis, Leo J. Menz, PhD, Roger J. Mercer, Dean Edward Metter, PhD, D. Joseph Meyer, Frank W. Meyers, John A. Mihulka, David R. Miller, PhD, Dennis Miller, Carol R. Mischnick, MD, Eugene L. Mleczko, Gary L. Montgomery, D. G. Moore, PhD, Francis E. Moore Jr., Robert D. Moore Jr., Bernard J. Moormann, William T. Morgan, PhD, Randy S. Morris, Willard Morton, Brad Moseley, Melvyn Wayne Mosher, PhD, William H. Mount, Kevin M. Mowery, Wayne K. Mueller, John E. Mullins, Sarah M. Mundy, Archie Lee Murdock, PhD, Orin L. Murray, Scott H. Muskopf, Vivek Narayanan, PhD, Robert Nash, Robert Overman Nellums, David J. Nelsen, G. Barry Nelson, Robert E. Nevett 3rd, Eugene Haines Nicholson, PhD*, Paul J. Nord, PhD, Robert Nothdurft, PhD, Darwin A. Novak Jr., PhD, Laurence M. Nuelle, Deborah O'Bannon, PhD, Marvin Loren Oftedahl, PhD, Richard B. Oglesby, MD, Andrew Oldroyd, PhD, Mark A. Ousnamer, Donald S. Overend, MD, Sastry V. Pappu, PhD, Robert B. Park, Joseph Gilbert Patterson, Elroy J. Peters, PhD, Philip C. Peterson, Randall Petresh, Randy Petresh, George W. Petri, Larry T. Pettus, Donald L. Pfost, PhD, Harry M. Philip, Bruce B. Phillips, PhD, Lawrence Pilgram, Jerry P. Place, PhD, Ronald J. Poehlmann, M. E. Postlethwaite, Neil E. Prange, Daphne Press, R. H. Prewitt Jr., Melvin H. Proctor, John E. Rabbitt, Dennis P. Rabin, PhD, Jerome D. Radar, Rodney Owen Radke, PhD, Donald Rapp, H. C. Rechtien Jr., Norman Van Rees, James A. Reese, Richard B. Renz, Walter L. Reyland, George W. Reynolds, Vic Reznack, Gene M. Rice, Graydon Edward Richards, PhD, Bill M. Rinehart, Frank S. Riordan Jr., PhD, Ernest Aleck Robbins, PhD, Warren A. Roberts, Rodney A. Robertson, Daniel Rode, PhD, Michael Rodgers, PhD, Dustin J. Rogge, Dan Rohr, Dallas W. Rollins, Marston Val Roloff, PhD, Max E. Roper, Bruce David Rosenquist, PhD, Harold Leslie Rosenthal, PhD, Donald Kenneth Ross, PhD, James A. Ross, John E. Roush Jr., Charles F. Row, MD, David M. Rucker, Gerald Bruce Rupert, PhD, Richard E. Ruppert, Theodore A. Ruppert, Paul J. Russ, Robert Raymond

Russell, PhD, Robert B. Russell, Paul H. Rydlund, Edwin L. Ryser, J. Evan Sadler, PhD, Daniel K. Salisbury, Mohammad Samiullah, PhD, Leslie S. Samuels, Fred J. Sanders, Richard D. Sands, Thomas J. Sawarynski, Gutherie Scaggs, Barrett Lerner Scallet, PhD, Kenneth B. Schechtman, PhD, Carl R. Scheske, Edward P. Schneider, E. P. Schneider, Lloyd E. Schultz, Ignatius Schumacher, PhD, Elroy E. Schumacher, DVM, Gerald V. Schwalbe, Gary W. Schwartz, Kirk G. Schweiss, Kerry G. Scott, Chuck Seger, Jan Segert, PhD, David L. Seidel, Jay Shah, Robert Ely Shank, PhD, Franklin H. Sharp, Bob D. Shaw, Ralph Waldo Sheets, PhD, Harvey D. Shell, George Calvin Shelton, PhD, Michael F. Shepard, DVM, Ronnie C. Shy, Daniel Robert Sidoti, Oliver W. Siebert, Robert H. Sieckhaus, Dennis J. Sieg, MD, Marc S. Silverman, Virgil Simpson, Joseph J. Sind, Charles Carleton Sisler, Harvey D. Small, Haldon E. Smith, Clara Diddle Smith Craver, Wes Sorenson, PhD, Jack P. Spenard, Wayne K. Spillner, Alfred Carl Spreng, PhD, Michael E. Spurlock, PhD, Paul F. Stablein, PhD, Roger D. Steenbergen, Theo J. Steinmeyer, Robert E. Stevens, Norman D. Stickler, Charles A. Stiefermann, James Osber Stoffer, PhD, Mel J. Stohl, Daniel F. Stokes, William Stoneman, MD, Don B. Storment, Keith A. Stuckmeyer, Gary Stumbaugh, George Sturmon, Dan T. Sullivan, MD, Amy D. Sullivan, Daniel T. Sullivan, John E. Sullivan, Xingping Sun, PhD, Salvatore P. Sutera, PhD, Mark E. Swanson, Peter H. Sweeney, Jason R. Szachnieski, David Tan, Tzyh-Jong Tarn, PhD, Jerry W. Tastad, Joseph R. Tauser, Kenneth R. Teater, Mark W. Tesar, Guy G. Thacker, Vernon James Theilmann, PhD, Richard C. Theuer, PhD, Marc G. Thomas, Granville Berry Thompson, PhD, Kenneth C. Thomson, PhD, Stephen D. Tiesing, Dudley Seymour Titus, PhD, Douglas M. Tollefsen, PhD, Merrill M. Townley, DVM, Clarence A. Trachsel, Frank E. Tripp, Sheryl Tucker, PhD, John E. Turnage, Donald J. Turner, Zbylut Jozef Twardowski, PhD, Blaine A. Ulmer, Frank D. Utterback, William P. Vale, Cornelius Van Dyke, Michael E. Vandas, Walter F. Vandelicht, Jerry G. VanderTuig, PhD, Allen L. Vandeusen, J. J. Ventura, Stanley Viglione, David N. Visnich, C. L. Voellinger, Michae F. Vogt, Michael F. Vogt, Frederick W. Vonkaenel, James R. Waddell, DVM, Billy C. Wade, Elizabeth L. Walker, PhD, Timothy J. Walsh, Richard C. Waring, Don Warner, PhD, James A. Warnhoff, Jay Weaver, Mark C. Wehking, Charles W. Wehking Jr., A. R. Weide, Frank G. Weis, Richard E. Wendt, PhD, Roger Michael Weppelman, PhD, Samuel A. Werner, PhD, Terry L. Werth, John P. Werthman, James F. Westcott, Dallas G. Wetzler, Charles K. Whittaker, MD, Jon H. Wiggins, PhD, James M. Williams, Roger W. Williams, Joh W. Wilson, PhD, Clyde Livingston Wilson, PhD, Royce A. Wilson, David Wilson, MD, Robert Winder, David F. Winter, James J. Wissman, Michael Witt, Edward W. Wolfe, William A. Wolff, DVM, Jared J. Wolters, Randall Wood, PhD, Marvin S. Wool, George T. Wootten, Paul N. Worsey, PhD, George G. Wright, John Scott Yaeger, Libby Yunger, PhD, Marvin Leon Zatzman, PhD, Chad E. Zickefoose, Thomas W. Ziegler, Ferdinand B. Zienty, PhD, Gary Zimmermann, Joseph E. Zweifel, Howard A. Zwemer

Montana

David J. Abbott, Frank Addison Albini, PhD, Corby G. Anderson, PhD, William Ballard, PhD, David W. Ballard, Wayne Bauer, George L. Baughman, Monte P. Bawden, PhD, Haley Beaudry, Pat Behm, Curtis M. Belden, Wade L. Bellon, Robert A. Bellows, PhD, Douglas N. Betts, Albert R. Blair, William V. Bluck, Jason W. Boeckel, Harold L. Bolnick, MD, Fred M. Bonnett, Professor Bozlee, PhD, Jeff Briggs, Lawrence E. Bronec, Garry J. Carlson, A. Lee Child, James W. Crichton, MD, Jerry Croft, Chris A. Cull, Gregory N. Cunniff, Thomas A. Dale, Nigel L. Davis, Ward Dewitt, MD, Wade T. Diehl, Dennis Dietrich, MD, Patrick J. Downey, Edward A. Dratz, PhD, J. Robert Dynes, PhD, Fred N. Earll, PhD, H. Richard Fevold, PhD, Lee H. Fisher, MD, Fess Foster, PhD, Bob W. Fulton, LeRoy Gebhardt, PhD, Larry W. Geisler, David F. Gibson, John E. Grauman Jr., Mike Greger, Leland Griffin, Evan L. Griffith, Robert J. Guditis, James F. Hammill, MD, Lowell C. Hanson, James C. Hansz, Earl Ray Harrison Jr., MD, Charles M. Hauptman, Leo A. Heath, Alfred Hendrickson, Conrad R. Hilpert, PhD, Larry C. Hoffman, C. R. Hunkins, Ronald D. Isackson, MD, Charlie M. Jackson Jr., William C. Jenkins, B. Johnke, John P. Jones, R. E. Juday, PhD*, John M. Jurist, PhD, John H. Kennah, Jarvis R. Klem, Stephen J. Knapp, Stephan T. Kujawa, PhD, Michael L. Laird, Gerald J. Lapeyre, PhD, Wayne E. Lee, Robert S. Macdonald, William C. Maehl, Robert Audley Manhart, PhD, Daniel E. March, Morry Markovitz, Jim Mendenhall, MD, Ira Kelly Mills, PhD, Lyle Leslie Myers, PhD, Kenneth Nordtvedt, PhD, Michael J. Oard, Michael J. Oard, Patricia H. Paulson-Ehrhardt, John P. Pavsek, George R. Powe, Frank Radella, Keith A. Rae, Clark S. Robinson, Frank Rosenzweig, PhD, John H. Rumely, PhD, William R. Sacrison, Philip K. Salitros, James R. Scarlett, Darrell Scharf, Fred P. Schilling, PhD, Robert E. Schumacher, Robert M. Schweitzer, Mike Schweitzer, MD, Fred Schwendeman, MD, Larry R. Seibel, Robert K. Sengl, Ray W. Sheldon, Steven L. Shelton, James C. Simmons, MD, Earl O. Skogley, PhD, Gordon E. Sorenson, Gilbert Franklin Stallknecht, PhD, George D. Stanley, PhD, Peter F. Stanley, Michael J. Stevermer, Ralph F. Stockstad, Arthur L. Story, Kyle Strode, PhD, John Edgar Taylor, PhD, Trevor Taylor, James E. Taylor, Deniz Tek, MD, Donald L. Tennant, Forrest D. Thomas II, PhD, Melinda Tichenor, Bradley S. Turnbull, Charles E. Umhey Jr., Wayne Paul Van Meter, PhD, Saralee Neumann Visscher, PhD, Cory Vollmer, Russ Wahl, Kevin K. Walsh, Mike Wentzell, J. Michael Wentzells, Adam Whitman, D. J. Williams, Wesley R. Womack, David Eugene Worley, PhD, Thomas J. Worring, Randi W. Wytcherley, Courtney Young, PhD, Greg D. Zeihen, Gordon F. Ziesing, A. L. Zimmerman, Aaron L. Zimmerman, Donald G. Zink, PhD

Nebraska

Robert J. Anderson, MD, R. Arnold, PhD, Donald R. Arrington, Leroy E. Baker, Ronald Bartzatt, PhD, Don Becker, Paul Bekarik, Tiffany Bendorf, Lloyd Benjamin, Ray Bentall*, William M. Berton, MD, John R. Brady, Professor Bratzatt, PhD, Albert L. Brown, PhD, Lloyd B. Bullerman, PhD, John Bryan Campbell, PhD, James A. Carroll, PhD, Raymond W. Conant, MD, C. Michael Cowan, PhD, Clifford H. Cox, PhD, Jon P. Dalton, Douglas A. Delhay, PhD, Jerry A. Doctor, Frank J. Dragoun, James F. Drake, PhD, Vincent Harold Dreeszen, William N. Durand, Allen Ray Edison, Jeffrey A. Ehler, James G. Ekstrand, Jeff H. Erquiaga, PhD, Merlin Feikert, Gerald C. Felt, MD, Arthur F. Fishkin, PhD, Glenn Wesley Froning, Elisha J. Fuller, David Gambal, PhD, James Garretson, Fred M. Gawecki, MD, Ron Gawer, M. Glasser, Bradley A. Gloystein, DVM, Robert Dwight Grisso, PhD, Terry Grubaugh, Myron E. Haines, Ray J. Hajek, John F. Hartwell, Dwight Haworth, PhD, Robert Mathew Hill, PhD, Ronald D. Hoback, Loren G. Hoekema, Steve N. Hoody, MD, Ken Hucke, Kermit Jacobsen, Sherwin W. Jamison, Fritz E. Kain, Paul Karr, PhD, Dan L. Keiner, Bradley N. Keller, Floyd C. Knoop, PhD, Duane G. Koenig, MD, James G. Krist, Phillip Laroe, Dwight L. Larson, MD, Leon D. Leishman, Louis I. Leviticus, PhD, Max W. Linder, MD, Daryl C. Long, PhD, William W. Longley Jr., PhD, Lawrence H. Luehr, Douglas E. Lund, PhD, Jeffrey E. Malan, Douglas W. Mallenby, PhD, John P. Maloney, PhD, C. Wayne Martin, PhD, Charles Wayne Martin, PhD, Bob C. McFarland, Thomas R. McMillan, David B. Mead, James Mertz, Gary D. Michels, PhD, Therese Michels, PhD, James P. Millard, Gail L. Miller, Larry E. Moenning, DVM, Chanin Monestero, Michael C. Mulder, PhD, Lyle W. Nilson, Richard A. Onken, James T. O'Rourke, PhD, David Paik, George Phelps, William Poley, William J. Provaznik, Kent W. Pulfer, PhD, Henry J. Quiring, MD, John W. Reinert, Keith Riese, Paul D. Roberts, Neil Wilson Rowland, PhD, Melvin Dale Rumbaugh, PhD, Wayne L. Ryan, PhD, C. B. Ryan, Morris Henry Schneider, PhD, J. Shield, PhD, James B. Siebken, Professor Skluzacek, PhD, Eugene W. Skluzacek, PhD, Tim J. Sobotka, Franklin L. Stebbing, Staphen N. Stehlak, Stephen Stehlik, Herschel E. Stoller, MD, Noble L. Swanson, MD, Thomas Tibbels, MD, John Toney, David George Tunnicliff, PhD, Norman Russell Underdahl, Glenn Underhill, PhD, Ronald E. Waggener, PhD, Frederick William Wagner, PhD, Laurie Walrod, Dean D. Watt, PhD, Dwight J. Williams, Richard Barr Wilson, MD, Jake Winemiller, Gene Wubbels, PhD, S. A. Zarbano, MD, Sebastian A. Zarbano, MD, Thomas Herman Zepf, PhD

Nevada

Opal Adams, Howard J. Adams, Leslie Anderson, PhD, J. S. Armijo, PhD, Timothy D. Arnold, Orazio J. Astarita, C. David Baer, Matthew P. Bailey, PhD, Leland B. Baldrick, Richard L. Balogh Jr., William M. Bannister, DVM, Ted Barben, Theodore R. Barben, Jon Barth, Scott Beckstrand, John Bennetts, Kenton E. Bentley, PhD, Bernard D. Benz, Rahul S. Bhaduri, Arden E. Bicker, E. Boehmer, Raul H. Borrastero, Richard P. Bowen, Charles Arthur Bower, PhD, Sydney D. Bowers, William J. Brady, Alan D. Branham, Timothy J. Bray, MD, Doug Brewer, Steve H. Brigman, James A. Brinton, MD, Robert C. Broadbent, Russell K. Brunner, Donald H. Buchholz, Paul Buller Jr., Richard A. Calabrese, Roy Eugene Cameron, PhD, Paul B. Canale, MD, Richard S. Carr III, Michael R. Cartwright, John W. Catledge, Marc Cave, Bob A. Chambers, Ken Chambers, Fred Charette, PhD, Henry Chessin, MD, Bertrand Chiasson, PhD, Randy Chitwood, Lawrence S. Chun, MD, Edward M. Cikanek, Paul B. Clark, Ronald W. Clayton, John G. Cleary, James W. Cole, J. R. Colgan, James Collier, PhD, Sharon L. Commander, Teresa A. Conner, Neil D. Cos, PhD, Sheldon F. Craddock, Dale E. Crane, Michel W. Creek, Kurt E. Criss, Marla A. Criss, Marla A. Criss (Osborne), Steven R. Custer, Jaak J. K. Daemen, PhD, Fred J. Daniels Jr., John H. DeTar, PhD, Howard W. Dickson, Steve Dixon, Paul Dobak, Donald C. Dobson, PhD, Richard M. Dombrosky, Patrick J. Dougherty, Ralph C. Dow, Stephen D. Dow, MD, Doyle J. Dugan, W. P. Duyvesteyn, PhD, Carrie M. Eddy, Howard Lyman Ellinwood, PhD, Edi K. Engeln, Larry R. Engle, Karl C. Fazekas, MD, Carmen Fimiani, PhD, Robert D. Fisher, MD, David C. Fitch, W. Darrell Foote, PhD, Wilford Darrell Foote, PhD, Robert T. Forest, Helen L. Foster, PhD, Neil Stewart Fox, PhD, Forrest L. Fox, Corri A. Fox, Gary Fullington, Steven Alexander Gaal, PhD, Roy M. Gale, Peter E. Galli, Charles R. Galloway, Larry Joe Garside, James P. Gerner, Thomas E. Gesick, R. L. Giacomazzi, Peter F. Giddings, Dewayne Everett Gilbert, PhD, James M. Gills, James S. Goft, Patrick Goldstrand, PhD, Ernesto A. Gonzaga, Robert E. Gordon, C. Thomas Gott, PhD, William P. Graebel, PhD, Mihail I. Grigore, Robert E. Gross, MD, Kathleen J. Gundy, Lewis B. Gustafson, PhD, M. Craig Haase, Jeffrey M. Haeberlin, C. Troy Haggard, Robert W. Handford, Elsie L. Harms, Floyd T. Harris, Larry W. Hatcher, William R. Henkle Jr., Michael Henson, Barbara P. Hillier, James J. Hodes, James J. Hodos, K. E. Hodson, Thomas Edward Hoffer, PhD, Lee E. Hoffman, James B. Holder, Robert C. Horton, Dan Howard, Joseph E. Howland, PhD, Liang Chi Hsu, PhD, E. L. Hunsaker, Ernest L. Hunsaker, John H. Huston, Craig Hutchens, MD, John Walter Hylin, PhD, E. Carl Hylin, PhD, Arshad Iqbal, Jeffrey Janakus, Lynn Jaussi, Terry L. Jennings, Donald K. Jennings, Don Jennings, Marc Z. Jeric, PhD, Scott Jimmerson, William P. Johnston, PhD, Robert A. Jones, PhD, Dick Jones, Edward P. Jucevic, Kirk K. Kaiser, MD, Thomas R. Kalk, William J. Kane, MD, Kathryn

E. Kelly, PhD, Raymond C. Kelly, PhD, Charles P. Kelly, Robert Ray Kinnison, PhD, Stephene C. Kinsky, PhD, Herbert A. Klemme, Paul W. Knoop, MD, Robert J. Kopp, PhD, Larry D. Kornze, Mary Korpi, Curtis Kortemeier, Charle Kotulski, Robert M. Koval, Peter A. Krenkel, PhD, Dale D. Kulm, Charles A. Lacugna, Jan B. Lamb, Debbie Laney, David J. Langston, Richard G. Laprairie, Judd Larowe, MD, Clark D. Leedy, PhD, Peter E. Lenz, Thomas M. Leonard, Alfred Letcher, Carl R. Leviseur, MD, Kenton M. Loda, Vance Longley, David Lorge, Richard B. Loring, C. Barton Loundagin, Kenneth A. Lucas, MD, Paul Lumos, Farrel Wayne Lytle, Mel G. Maalouf, Joseph M. Maher, Robert L. Mann, John Craige Manning, PhD, Martin J. Manning, Lindley Manning, Carl R. Manthei, Edward F. Martin, William C. Mason, William H. Matchett, PhD, David C. Mathewson, Lauren H. Mattingly, Robert J. McConkie, Lee B. McConville, Karl W. McCrea, Dayton T. McDonald, John C. McHaffie, Harold P. Meabon, Robert F. Merchant Jr., MD, G. Messenger, PhD, George Clement Messenger, PhD, George J. Miel, PhD, Greg Millspaugh, M. Myd Min, Cynthia R. Moore, Paul V. Morgan, Neil J. Mortensen, Kenneth L. Moss, Ralph D. Mulhollen, David L. Mumford, MD, Ralph G. Musick Jr., Richard F. Nanna, John Neerhout Jr., Michael L. Neeser, Owen N. Nelson, R. William Nelson, Genne M. Nelson, Daniel P. Neubauer, William N. Neumann, Joe D. Newton, Donald R. Nichols, Thomas L. Nimsic, Elray S. Nixon, PhD, Ann T. Nunnemaker, Samuel G. Nunnemeker, Mark A. Odell, Frederick Kirk Odencrantz, PhD, Gary L. Oppliger, PhD, William V. Orr, Thomas Paskowski, Sergio Pastor, Gilbert W. Patterson, Robert Paul, Durk Pearson, Alan Embree Peckham, Alan C. Peitsch, Frank M. Pelteson, Robert A. Perkins, Richard M. Perry, Mitchel Phillips, David M. Pike, John Polish, John Porterfield, Alan T. Power, Neal J. Prendergast, MD, Robert F. Prichett, Victor H. Prodehl, Ralph Quosig, Charles G. Ranstrom, Kent Redwine, PhD, Fredrick K. Retzlaff, Brian Ridpath, Kevin J. Riley, Bradley R. Rising, Daniel E. Robertson, Raymond F. Robinson, R. S. Rodda, Frank A. Rogers, MD, Franklin J. Ross, Zsolt F. Rosta, Edwin S. Rousseau, Robert H. Ruf, PhD, Kim J. Runk, Myrl J. Saarem, Alva E. Saucier, Stanley F. Schmidt, PhD, William Schrand, Thom J. Seal, David W. Seeley, Sandy Shaw, Wen Shen, Bernie J. Sherin Jr., Lisa Shevenell, PhD, Michael E. Silic, Michael B. Simpson, Doug J. Siple, Olin K. Smith, John Snow, Charles D. Snow, M. Bradford Snyder, PhD, Scott E. Soderstrom, James P. Solaro, Lyle C. Southworth, Robert M. St. Louis, William R. Stanley, David J. Starbuck, Kenneth L. Steffan, Don W. Stevens, Harry B. Stoehr, John Grover Stone, PhD, Kevin W. Sur, Edward J. Sutich, Charles A. Sweningsen, Edgar R. Terlau, Tommy Thompson, PhD, David B. Thompson, PhD, Richard Thompson, Rory Tibbals, George P. Timinskas, Robert W. Titus, Luis A. Topete, Richard R. Tracy, PhD, Robert J. Trauger, John G. Trulio, PhD, Paul T. Tueller, PhD, Glenn W. Tueller, MD, Michael G. Turek, Phil L. Ulmer, Nancy Vardiman-Hall, Darrell E. Wagner, John D. Walter, PhD, Quinten E. Ward, W. Layne Weber, Walter F. Wegst, PhD, James M. Wehrman, DVM, Carl M. Welch, Herbert C. Wells, John D. Welsh, Henri Wetselaar, MD, Keni Whalen, Gordon R. Wicker, John B. Wigglesworth, Scott W. Wiljanen, Clavin E. Willoughby, Sylvan Harold Wittwer, PhD, Daniel J. Wonders, Morris T. Worley, Richard V. Wyman, PhD, Peter F. Young, Ken Zaike, Danny Zampirro, Robert L. Zerga

New Hampshire

Henry J. Adams, Arthur Edward Albert, PhD, Lynn C. Anderson, DVM, Ernest F. Angelicola, Ralph H. Baer, Walter Barquist, MD, Kenneth H. Barratt, Hans D. Baumann, PhD, Wayne Machon Beasley, Paul R. Beswick, Peter Bird, Harvey J. Bloom, Frank T. Bodurtha, PhD, Philip D. Bogdonoff, PhD, Ray Book, Raymond H. Book Jr., Thomas A. Bover, Andrew J. Breuder, Ray O. Bristol, Bruce L. Brown, James A. Browning, Lawrence F. Buckland, Charles Rogers Buffler, PhD, John C. Burgeson, Roland Polk Carreker, PhD, Robert M. Chervincky, John A. Clements, Dennis Coburn, Norm G. Cote, Edmund T. Cranch, Jesse F. Crump, Thomas John Curphey, PhD, Bendit Cushman-Roisin, PhD, Joseph S. D'Aleo, Robert Desmarais, MD, George Dunnavan, Andrew L. Eastman, Richard N. Erickson, George Fallet, Daniel J. Filicicchia, Thomas L. Fowke, Roy R. Frampton, PhD, Edwin Francis Fricke, PhD, Joe Gagliardi, Leon H. Geil, Katherine J. Getchell, Wayne J. Getchell, Michael D. Gilbert, PhD, William T. Golding, Robert B. Gould*, Kevin J. Gray, PhD, David L. Gress, PhD, Gordon W. Gribble, PhD, Carlton W. Griffin, Jay S. Grumbling, David R. Hall, William A. Hamill, Stephen Hansen, Robert Duane Harter, PhD, Norman H. Heinze, Rick Hickerson, Lawrence Hoagland, PhD, Scott D. Hobson, S. Hobson, Tim Horton, John S. Howland, Fred R. Huber, Everett Clair Hunt, PhD, Albert H. Huntoon, Karl Uno Ingard, PhD, Uno Ingard, PhD, Lawrence R. Jeffery, Carl N. Johnson, PhD, Arthur Robert Kantrowitz, PhD, Gerson Kegeles, PhD, Anthony J. Kelley, James F. Kerivan, Michael Klingler, Louis H. Klotz, PhD, Robert G. Koch, MD, Dennis A. Lauer, Marcel Elphege LaVoie, PhD, John W. Leech, PhD, Semon M. Lilienfeld, MD, Daniel Sidney Longnecke, Russell W. Maccabe, William G. Machell, C. J. Manning, Albert V. Martore, James Maynard, Kenneth E. Mayo, Kevin M. McEneaney, Eugene D. Mellish, Edward J. Merrell, David O. Mulgrew, John Muller, PhD, George A. Oldham, Karle Sanborn Packard, R. Palmer, Radi Pejouhy, Howard G. Pritham, MD, Jonathan S. Remillard, Harold C. Ripley, Gilbert S. Rogers, Barbara Rucinska, PhD, Jason J. Saunderson, PhD, Ronald E. Scott, PhD, Robert Seaman, John J. Segedy, PhD, Faye Slift, Bernard G. E. Stiff, David E. Strang, MD, Augustine R. Stratoti, Robinson Marden Swift, PhD, Morgan Chuan Yuan Sze, PhD, Donald M. Taylor, Lawrence J. Varnerin, PhD, Charles Wagner, Richard W. Waldron, PhD, Maynard C. Waltz, William T. West, PhD, James R. Weth, George R. Winkler, Stephen S. Wolf, Yin Chao Yen, PhD

New Jersey

Daniel T. Achord, PhD, Phillip Adams, PhD, Richard Ernest Adams, Ben J. Addiego, Anthony J. Adrignolo, PhD, Robert Aharonov, Andrew J. Alessi, Roger Casanova Alig, PhD, Casanova Alig, PhD, Emma Allen, PhD, A. Frank Alsobrook, Martin E. Altis, Pushpavati S. Amin, G. Anderle, PhD, George H. Andersen, John Robert Andrade, PhD, Eva Andrei, PhD, Frederick T. Andrews, Charles H. Antinori, PhD, P. J. Apice, Alan Appleby, PhD, Earl F. Arbuckle 3rd, Zaven S. Ariyan, PhD, John V. Artale, Robert Artz, Frederick Addison Bacher, Bruce E. Bachman, Alan G. Backman, MD, James H. Bailey Jr., William Oliver Baker, PhD, Robert J. Baker, Benjamin H. Bakerjian, Nicholas N. Baldo Jr., Arthur Ballato, PhD, Zinovy I. Barch, PhD, Jeffrey D. Barczak, Yeheskel Bar-Ness, PhD, Douglas G. Bartels, Alton H. Bassett, PhD, Acton Bassett, Nayan K. Basu, Richard Baubles, Eric Baum, PhD, John W. Bauman, PhD, Robert M. Bean, PhD, Harold J. Becker Jr., Herbert Ernest Behrens, Raymond L. Bendure, PhD, James A. Benjamin, PhD, David R. Benner, Gordon D. Benson, MD, Daniel D. Bertin, Harry M. Betzig, Rowland Scott Bevans, PhD, Karin Bickford, Joseph W. Bitsock, MD, David Blewett, Robert W. Blocker, Rodney J. Blouch, Claire Bluestein, PhD, Sheri L. Blystone, PhD, Anthony Vincent Boccabella, PhD, Richard F. Bock, Seymour M. Bogdonoff, Nicholas Bohensky, Kees Boi, PhD, Gaston A. Boissard, William V. Booream, William G. Borghard, PhD, William K. Boss Jr., MD, Robert W. Bosse, Henry Bovin, Roger L. Boyell, Paul S. Boyer, PhD, Matthew A. Braccio, Robert Brady, Robert H. Brakman, William Brennan, Kurt Brenner, Charles O. Brostrom, PhD, William M. Brown, PhD, James Brown, Richard L. Brown, Paul Eugene Brubaker, PhD, Gregory J. Brunetta, James A. Bruni, Charles Frank Bruno, PhD, Ralph Bruzzichesi, Carl J. Buck, PhD, David Richard Burley, PhD, Samuel R. M. Burton, Richard S. Butryn, Michael J. Byrne, Edwin Caballero, James L. Calderella, John D. Calvert, Douglas J. Campbell, Daniel T. Canavan, Peter J. Canterino, Walter J. Canzonier, Timothy J. Carlsen, David Carter, Alan Caruba, Lilana I. Cecan, PhD, Bernard H. Chaiken, MD, Partitosh M. Chakrabarti, PhD, Chun K. Chan, PhD, Ronald R. Chance, PhD, Donald Jones Channin, Victor S. Cheng, Roy T. Cherris, Arthur Warren Chester, PhD, Ye C. Choi, PhD, Chang H. Chung, Eugene L. Church, PhD, Anthony J. Cirillo Jr., Otto M. Clemente, J. Clemente, Mary P. Coakley, PhD, Paul H. Cohen, Harvey H. Cohen, Francis Colace, MD, Roger T. Cole, Donald E. Collins, Robert B. Comizzoli, PhD, George J. Conrad, Maryann A. Conte, Edward M. Cooney, Thomas E. Cope Jr., Lois J. Copeland, MD, Deborah A. Corridon, Bernard J. Costello, Val Francis Cotty, PhD, James C. Coyne, PhD, Frank Cozzarelli, John P. Craig, MD, Carolyn S. Crawford, MD, Kenneth Alan Crossner, PhD, Edwin Patrick Crowell, William J. Cruice, Donald C. Cuccia, MD, Richard Williamson Cummins, PhD, Michael A. Cuocolo Jr., Janet C. Curry, Eugene J. Daly, Theo C. Damen, Wayne E. Daniel, Henry D. Dankenbring, Matthew A. Danza, Robert F. Dauer, Edward Emil David Jr., PhD, Thomas A. Davis, PhD, William F. Davis, Arthur Donovan Dawson, PhD, Albert Dazzo, Stephen Dazzo, Tom V. Debrock, Donald R. Degrave, James R. Deland Jr., Joseph A. Delvers, Michael R. Demcsak, David T. Denhardt, PhD, Eric Dennis, Felix M. Depinies, PhD, Dimitris Dermatis, PhD, Vijaya S. Desai, MD, Salvatore J. Desalva, PhD, R. Detig, PhD, Anthony J. Devivo, Thomas F. Devlin, PhD, F. D. Dexter, Franklin D. Dexter, William J. Dieal, Ray DiMartini, PhD, Earl M. Dipirro, MD, William A. Dittrich, Richard W. Dixon, PhD, George F. Doby, Emerson B. Donnell Jr., Sandra Steranka Donovan, PhD, Patrick Dorgan, Milos A. Dostal, PhD, Nancy M. Doty, Nicholas J. Driscoll, Donald C. Dunn, James A. Dusenbury, Dushan Dvornik, PhD, Freeman John Dyson, Wayne F. Eakins, Harold W. Earle, Alieta Eck, MD, Peter Egli, Robert Ehrlich, PhD, I. Robert Ehrlich, PhD, Saundra M. Ehrlich, Richard Edward Elden, Shaker H. El-Sherbini, PhD, Youichi Endo, PhD, William J. Engelhard, Seymour Epstein, PhD, Joshua A. Erickson, John G. Esock 3rd, Ramon L. Espino, PhD, Glen A. Evans, Alexander Fadeev, PhD, Peter W. Failla, Robert J. Farquharson, Michael L. Fasnacht, Charles E. Fegley 3rd, Abraham S. Feigenbaum, PhD, Paul M. Feinberg, PhD, Frederick P. Fendt, Eric V. Fernstrom, Robert M. Feuss, Paul Finkelstein, PhD, Gordon H. Fish, T. Burnet Fisher, Richard E. Foerster, Dennis Fost, PhD, Philip Franco, Peter M. Franzese, Daniel W. Frascella, PhD, Inge Friedrich, MD, Gerhard J. Frohlich, PhD, Roland Charles Fulde, PhD, Shun Chong Fung, PhD, John C. Gabriel, L. John Gagliardi, PhD, George Gal, PhD, Anthony Gallo, Paul H. Garnier, Thomas L. Geib, MD, Celine Gelinas, PhD, Gary Gerardi, PhD, Norbert Gerlach, Raymond P. Germann, Theodore A. Giannechini, Anne M. Giedlinski, Albert M. Giudice, Sivert Herth Glarum, PhD, Ronald N. Glass, Werner B. Glass, Frederick G. Glatter, MD, Robert A. Gleason, Douglas J. Glorie, Stephen Gold, PhD, Xavier F. Gonzalez, Lewis S. Goodfriend, Jerome D. Goodman, PhD, Martin Leo Gorbaty, PhD, Eugene Gordon, PhD, Edward A. Gorka, Jerome J. Gramsammer, Jeffrey E. Grant, Ashby A. Grantham, Wayne P. Grau, Martin Laurence Green, PhD, Marvin I. Greene, Frederic C. Grigg, Richard G. Grisky, PhD, Don J. Grove, PhD, Y. Guberer, PhD, James G. Guider, Vajira K. Gunawardana, Stuart S. Gut, DVM, Berwin A. Guttormsen, George Hacken, PhD, Stephanos S. Hadjiyannis, Erich L. Hafner, PhD, James J. Hagan, PhD, James M. Hammell, Sunil P. Hangal, PhD, I. Hapij, PhD, William Happer, PhD, John R. Harding, Wayne A. Harmening, Peter Hartwick, Clifford Harvey, PhD, Frank C. Hawk, PhD, Philip F. Healy, Sylvester B. Heberlig, James B. Heller, Edwin Hendler, PhD, Tom A. Hendrickson, Uri Herzberg, PhD, Jack Hickey, Thomas J. Hicks, Mark J. Higgins, Walter L. Hinman Jr., Arthur Hirsch, PhD, Michael J. Hnat, PhD, Frederick J. Hofmann, Austin W. Hogan, PhD, Thomas C. Holcombe, Charles B. Hopkins Jr., Harry M. Horn,

PhD, Alan J. Horowitz, Zdenek Hruza, PhD, Taras P. Hrycyshyn, Roy E. Hunt, William E. Hymans, PhD, Arnold Gene Hyndman, PhD, K. Hyun, PhD, Bradley Ingebrethsen, PhD, Basil J. Ingemi, MD, Criton George S. Inglessis, PhD, Nicholas A. Ingoglia, PhD, Shabana Insaf, PhD, Shahid Insaf, MD, Michelle L. Jablons, Johan Jaffe, PhD, Kenneth Irwin Jagel, PhD, Paul J. Jakubicki, Robert R. Jamieson, Akshay Javeri, Hugh F. Jenkins, Max F. Jenne, Luis E. Jimenez, PhD, Amos E. Joe, Leo Francis Johnson, PhD, Scott R. Johnston, John G. Johnstone, A. D. Jones, Liutas K. Jurkis, Leonard Juros, Liutas K. Jurskis, Raymond F. Kaczynski, Michael Z. Kagan, PhD, Sergei L. Kanevsky, Stanley F. Kantor, Guido George Karcher, Bennett C. Karp, PhD, Frederick C. Kauffman, PhD, Yuri Kazakevich, PhD, John H. Kearney, Horst H. Keasdy, PhD, Craig T. Keeley, David B. Keller, Joseph J. Keller, Joseph Kelley, PhD, Craig T. Kelley, John Kellgren, PhD, George Cantine Kent, PhD, Michael John Keogh, PhD, Thomas J. Kesolits, Mark Otto Kestner, PhD, Z. Khan, Charles W. Kilgore II, Snezana Kili-Dalafave, PhD, Aejin Kim, Robert M. Kipperman, PhD, Hartmann J. Kircher, Steven G. Kisch, Walter B. Kleiner, PhD, Lawrence Paul Klemann, PhD, Robert C. Kluthe, Richard J. Knopf, William J. Koehl Jr., PhD, William J. Koenecke, Norm C. Koller, Catherine Koo, PhD, George Eugene Kosel, John Norman Kraeuter, PhD, Walter H. Kraft, Ralph H. Kramer, Michael S. Krepky, Geddy J. Krul, MD, Stephen A. Kubow, PhD, James Edgar Kuder, PhD, Stephen J. Kuritz, PhD, Frank Michael Labianca, PhD, Paul Albert Lachance, PhD, John F. Laidig, James C. Lane, Robert L. Langerhans, Robert Charles Langley, Ralph Lanni, Geoffrey R. Lanza, John P. Larocco, Jack Samuel Lasky, PhD, Alan R. Latham, PhD, Robert J. Laufer, PhD, Ralph John Leary, PhD, Bob Lefelar, Robert Lefelar, Richard O. Leinbach, Mario Leone, Thomas E. Leonik, Allan L. Levey, Sidney B. Levinson, J. Levy, Jacek K. Leznicki, PhD, Wayne W. Lippincott, John E. Littlefield, John M. Lix, William Lockett Jr., Charles W. Lofft, G. M. Loiacono, Carlos A. Londono, Alfredo M. Lopez, PhD, Donald H. Lorenz, PhD, Jan Lovy, PhD, John J. Lowney, Brian Lubbert, Peter J. Lucchesi, PhD, Professor Lucelari, PhD, Frank P. Lunn III, Luigi Lupinacci, Patrick B. Lynam, Charles S. Lyon, Margaret J. Lyons, Wilfred J. Mabee, Douglas J. MacNeil, PhD, Alfred Urquhart MacRae, PhD, Chandra P. Mahadass, George F. Mahe, John Philip Maher, Robert Maines, Robert C. Maleeny, Joseph T. Maloy, PhD, James Manfreda, George J. Manik, Louis J. Mankowski, August Frederick Manz, Betty L. Marchant, MD, Stanley S. Marcus, MD, Herman Lowell Marder, PhD, Andrew C. Marinucci, PhD, James W. Martin, Ramon Martinelli, PhD, Albert Masetti, Harry L. Masten, R. Mastracchio, Norman J. Matchett, Melvin K. Mathisen, Richard A. Matula, PhD, Kenneth Maxwell, Bryce Maxwell, Robert W. McAdams, Robert J. McCabe, Francis D. McCann, John Price McCullough, PhD, Richard J. McDermott, Wilbur Benedict McDowell, PhD, Edward R. McFarlan, Peter McGaughran, Kenneth J. McGuckin, George Francis McLane, PhD, Pat McMahon, William A. McMahon Jr., H. McVeigh, PhD, Sidney S. Medley, PhD, George Megerle, PhD, Charles T. Melick, James Richard Mellberg, Neri Merlini, PhD, Frank J. Mescall, George F. Meshia, Joseph N. Miale, Wayne Michaelchuck, Paul Charles Michaelis, Paul Michaels, William J. Mikula, Dick M. Miller, Dale F. Milsark, William B. Mims, PhD, Robert S. Miner Jr., PhD, Jerry B. Minter, Charles W. Moehringer, H. Walter Moeller, Edward J. Moller, Mark D. Morgan, PhD, Antonio Moroni, PhD, Lester D. Morris, DVM, M. E. Morrison, PhD, Edward G. Moss, Helmut Mrozik, PhD, Charles Norment Muldrow Jr., PhD, Jeffrey S. Mumma, Richard C. Murgittroyd, Charles H. Murphy, PhD, Joseph A. Musci, Ernest M. Myhren, Joseph O. Myslinski, Michael J. Napoliello, MD, John T. Nardone, Franklin Richard Nash, PhD, Errol S. Navata Sr., Edward G. Nawy, PhD, John P. Neglia CHMM, Lasalle L. Nolin, Frank R. Nora, Wayne J. Norman, Jerry J. Notte, William J. Novick, PhD, Susan R. Obaditch, Dennis O. Odea, Hans Oesau, Edward A. Ohm, PhD, Vilma E. Oleri, Horace G. Oliver Jr., Gregory L. Olson, Charles S. Opalek, Anthony M. Ordile, Gerald J. Orehostky, Donald H. Ort, Paul W. Osborne, PhD, Tom J. Osborne Jr., Dan A. Ostlind, PhD, Richard C. Otterbein, Sally Bulpitt Padhi, PhD, M. Robert Paglee, Felice Charles Palermo, Richard Walter Palladino, Lawrence G. Palmer, Virendra N. Pandey, PhD, Gabriel J. Paoletti, Pat A. Papa, Laura Z. Papazian, MD, Robert P. Parisi, Arthur Parks Sr., Robert A. Pascal, PhD, Raymond A. Patnode, Walter B. Paul, PhD, Rolf Paul, PhD, William Peet, Edward R. Pennell, Samuel C. Perks, PhD, Anthony James Petro, PhD, Raymond J. Pfeiffer, PhD, Francis A. Pflum, John Philipp, Wendell Francis Phillips, Joseph F. Pilaro, August W. Pingpank, Steven S. Plemenos, John Polcer, Robert D. Popper, Reddeppa N. Pothuri, PhD, Robert C. Potter, DVM, Kurt Pralle, David Pramer, PhD, Bernard L. Prince, James R. Prisco, Charles John Prizer, Eugene M. J. Pugatch, PhD, Peter T. Queenan, Jack G. Rabinowitz, MD, Attilio Joseph Rainal, PhD, Karel Frantisck Raska Jr., PhD, Susanne Raynor, PhD, Horace A. Reeves, Richard G. Reeves, Franklin G. Reick, Kenneth E. Resztak, George Henry Reussner, Edward T. Rhode, Bruce C. Rickard, Martin Max Rieger, PhD, James Louis Rigassio, R. Rivero, George H. Robertson, Michael J. Rohal, Louis D. Rollmann, PhD, Lee Rosenthal, PhD, John A. Rotondo, PhD, Arthur Israel Rubin, Ralph A. Runge, Irving I. Rusoff, PhD, George M. Rynkiewicz, John W. Ryon, PhD, Edward Stephen Sabisky, PhD, Frithiof N. Sagerholm Jr., Raymond J. Salani, Solomon J. Salat, Joseph J. Salvatorelli, Robert H. Salvesen, PhD, R. E. Sameth, Edward W. Sapp, John W. Sarappo, Eric F. Sarshad, Louis J. Sas, Charles M. Sather, Matthew J. Schaeffer, Harold C. Schanck, Garrett C. Schanck, Charles T. Schenck, DVM, Layton Schlafly, MD, Steven I. Schneider, Robert Edwin Schofield, PhD, Mary Gervasia Schreckenberg, PhD, Gervasia M. Schreckenberg, PhD, William Lewis Schreiber, PhD, Peter Schroder, Eric Schuler, Donald Frank Schutz, PhD, Fred A. Schwizer, Thomas J. Scully, Fred Seeber, PhD, John M. Segelken, Gray F. Sensenich Jr., Nicholas M. Setteducato, Mahmoud P. Shahangian, Junaid R. Shaikh, MD, Michael L. Shand, PhD, Thomas J. Sharp,

Richard H. Sharrett, MD, Milton C. Shedd, Everett O. Sheets, MD, Joshua Shefer, PhD, James Churchill Shelton, PhD, Mark V. Sheptock, Peter B. Sheridan, Dennis Shevlin, PhD, Kathleen M. Shilling, Frank Shinneman, Andrew L. Shlafly, Taposh K. Shome, David A. Shriver, PhD, Donald Bruce Siano, PhD, John Philip Sibilia, PhD, Hsien Gieh Sie, PhD, Frederick Howard Silver, PhD, Karl Leroy Simkins, PhD, Frederick H. Singer, Gainmattie Gail Singh, Roy J. Sippel, PhD, Leon J. Skvirsky, Jim R. Slate, Alvin Slomowitz, Patrick L. Smiley, Mariah Jose Smith, PhD, Albert Smith, Marvin F. Smith Jr., Bryan J. Smith, Eric S. Smith, William Smith, Joseph Smock, Angela Snow, PhD, Harold J. Sobel, MD, Frank B. Sorgie, George F. Spagnola, J. C. Spitsbergen, PhD, Marie T. Spoerlein, PhD, Ralph Joseph Spohn, PhD, Andrew P. Srodin, Gilbert Steiner, PhD, Timothy D. Steinhiber, William D. Stevens, PhD, Charles Steward, PhD, N. Stiglich, Bruce D. Stine, Tom Stinnett, Ronald S. Strange, PhD, Anthony W. Strano, Robert Stubblefield, PhD, Szymon Suckewer, PhD, S. Suckewer, PhD, Donald Supkow, PhD, Norman Sutherland, Jan O. Svoboda, Karl P. Svoboda, James R. Sweeney, Joseph M. Tak, Alan Wayne Tamarelli, PhD, George P. Tanczos, Robert J. Tarantino, David Taylor, Richard M. Taylor, Patrick H. Terry, Sant S. Tewari, PhD, Warren Alan Thaler, PhD, John L. Thein, Lowell Charles Thelin, William L. Thoden, Gordon A. Thomas, PhD, William Baldwin Thompson, PhD, Ellen K. Thompson, Henry C. Tillson, PhD, John H. Tinker, MD, William C. Tintle, John M. Toto, Donald R. Tourville, PhD, Ralph Trambarulo, PhD, Ralph A. Treder, PhD, Jeffrey Charles Trewella, PhD, Jane Tsai, Stephen Tsingas, Stephen P. Tyrpak, P. Roy Vagelos, MD, James P. Van Hook, PhD, Steven Vanata, Thomas Henry Vanderspurt, PhD, William Vandersteel, Christina VanderWende, PhD, Francis J. Vassalluzzo, MD, Andreas H. Vassiliou, PhD, Philip J. Vecere Sr., Patrick G. Vemacchia, Karl G. Verebey, PhD, John A. Vigelis, Francis V. Villani, Frank A. Vinciguerra, Luciano Virgili, PhD, Dale E. Vitale, PhD, George Viveiros, Gert P J Volpp, PhD, Gert Volpp, PhD, Paul Justus Volpp, PhD, Gerald N. Wachs, MD, Richard C. Walling, Walter M. Walsh Jr., PhD, Arthur Ernest Waltking, Stanley Frank Wanat, PhD, Hsueh Hwa Wang, W. Steven Ward, PhD, Clifford A. Warren, Frank Warren Jr., Frank R. Warshany, Madeline S. Wasilas, Stuart L. Weg, MD, Walter F. Wegst, PhD, Roy W. Weiland, George Austin Weisgerber, PhD, William G. Weissman, Barry R. Weissman, Warren D. Wells, Jack Harry Wernick, PhD, George M. Wheeler, John Michael Whelan, PhD, Joseph Marion Wier, PhD, Kenneth C. Wilding Jr., Jos B. Wiley Jr., Karla E. Williams, Neal Thomas Williams, Frederick Willis, Robert K. Willmot Jr., Lloyd Winsor, Anthony E. Winston, Donald F. Wiseman, Peter Joseph Wojtowicz, PhD, Chi-Yin Wong, Joseph Eliot Woodbridge, PhD, Patrick J. Wooding, John R. Woodruff, Von Worthington, Paul E. Wyszkowski, Jim Yarwood, Dennis K. Yoder, Richard H. Young, Stephen A. Yuhas, Robert F. Yuro, Egon J. Zadina, A. Zamolodchikov, PhD, Professor Zbuzek, PhD, Debi Y. Zeno, John Benjamin Ziegler, PhD, David Zudkevitch, PhD, Melvin L. Zwillenberg, PhD

New Mexico

Carl M. Abrams, Donald Adams, Stuart R. Akers, Frederick I. Akiya, M. Dale Alexander, PhD, Charles C. Allen, Lynford Lenhart Ames, PhD, James F. Andrew, PhD, Harold V. Argo, PhD, Robert L. Armstrong, PhD, Charles Arnold, PhD, Walter R. Ashwil, Walter R. Ashwill, Erik Aspelin, Dustin M. Aughenbaugh, Gerald V. Babigian, Lester Marchant Baggett, PhD, Lara H. Baker, PhD, Arden Albert Baltensperger, PhD, James A. Baran, PhD, Franklin Brett Barker, PhD, Scott L. Beardemphil, David F. Beck, A. D. Beckerdite, A.D. Beckerdite, Glenn W. Bedell, PhD, Rettig Benedict, PhD, H. W. Benischek, Kaspar G. Berget, M. Berkey, Marshall Berman, PhD, Frances M. Berting, PhD, Andrew J. Betts, John Beyeler, William Edward Blas , Clay Booker, PhD, Kevin W. Boyack, PhD, Ben M. Boykin, Richard J. Boyle, Patrick Boyle, Ben Brabb, PhD, Charles D. Braden, Martin Daniel Bradshaw, PhD, Frederick S. Breslin, PhD, Robert E. Bretz, PhD, Clifton Briner, Kay Robert Brower, PhD, James S. Brown, Donnie E. Brown, James R. Buchanan, MD, J. F. Buffington, Merle E. Bunker, PhD, Frank Bernard Burns, PhD, Suzanne C. Byrd, Robert C. Byrd, Fernando Cadena, PhD, Fernando Cadena-C, PhD, Howard Hamilton Cady, PhD, Dennis R. Cahill, George Melvin Campbell, PhD, John S. Campbell, Gregory Cannon, Frederick Herman Carl Schultz, PhD, Peter R. Carlson, John Granville Castle, PhD, Roy Dudley Caton Jr., PhD, Charles W. Causey, Philip Ceriani, MD, P. Ceriani, MD, Peter E. Christensen, Petr Chylek, PhD, Kenneth W. Ciriacks, PhD, William F. Clark, Frank Welch Clinard, PhD, Michael R. Clover, PhD, Richard Lee Coats, PhD, Allen H. Cogbill, PhD, Michael W. Coleman, Kenneth B. Collins, Albert D. Corbin, Samuel Douglas Cornell, PhD, Maynard JR Cowan Jr., Morgan Cox, Jerry Ferdinand Cuderman, PhD, John E. Cunningham, PhD, Dirk A. Dahlgren, PhD, James P. Daley, John C. Dallman, PhD, Michael Daly, Richard Aasen Damerow, PhD, George Damon, PhD, Edward George Damon, PhD, James M. Davidson, PhD, Frank W. Davies, Herbert T. Davis, PhD, Robert D. Day, PhD, Michael J. Dietz Sr., Malcolm Dillon, Robert Hudson Dinegar, PhD*, Steven K. Dingman, Eugene H. Dirk, PhD, Paul Dobak, B. Donaldson, PhD, D. Donaldson, PhD, Gary B. Donart, PhD, Rae A. Dougherty, John R. Doughty, PhD, Charles O. Dowell, Richard T. Downing, Clifton Russell Drumm, PhD, Leonard Duda, PhD, Patricia M. Duda, Sherman Dugan, Thomas A. Dugan, Herbert M. Dumas, C. M. Duncan III, Thomas G. Dunlap, Jed E. Durrenberger, J. E. Durrenberger, Lawrence G. Dykers, Robert John Eagan, PhD, Tim E. Eastep, George W. Eaton Jr., Janes M. Edgecombe, Keith Ehlert, Chris S. Ellefson, Albert George Engelhardt, PhD, Raymond Engelke, PhD, Steve R. England, DVM, Roger Charles Entringer, PhD, Andy C. Erickson, Jay Erikson, PhD,

Mary Jane Erikson, R. W. Erwin, William R. Espander, PhD, Eugene Henderson Eyster, PhD, Ron Farmer, Douglas Fields, PhD, Morris Dale Finkner, PhD, Philip C. Fisher, PhD, Fred F. Fleming Jr., Stuart Flicker, K. Randy Foote, Clarence Q. Ford, PhD, Robert F. Ford, PhD, David Wallace Forslund, PhD, Eric Beaumont Fowler, PhD, Harry James Fox, Julian R. Franklin, Michael Frese, PhD, J. M. Fritschy, Paul Fuierer, PhD, Julie Fuller, Michael S. Fulp, Irwin M. Gabay, MD, Bruce E. Gaither, Quentin Galbraith, Ri Garrett, John Eric Garst, PhD, J. C. Garth, PhD, Jackson Gilbert Gay, Arthur Gebean, Raymond S. George, PhD, Timothy Gordon George, C. M. Gillespie, PhD, Claude Milton Gillespie, PhD, David L. Gilmer, H. Scott Gingrich, Thomas H. Giordano, PhD, Earl R. Godwin, MD, Terry Jack Goldman, PhD, James Wylie Gordon, PhD, Walter L. Gould, PhD, David G. Grabiel, Mathew O. Grady, Charles Thornton Gregg, PhD, Clifton E. Gremillion, Reid Grigg, PhD, A. G. Griswold, Walter Wilhelm Gustav Lwowsk, PhD, Arnold Hakkila, PhD, Eero Arnold Hakkila, PhD, Frank C. Halestead, Charles Ainsley Hall, PhD, V. A. Hamilton, James T. Hanlon, PhD, Harry C. Hardee, PhD, Daniel E. Harmeyer, Richard A. Harris, PhD, E. Frederick Hartman, Eric W. Hatfield, Robert F. Hausman Jr., PhD, K. Havernor, PhD, Russell Haworth, Dennis B. Hayes, PhD, Dale B. Henderson, PhD, Mary Jane Hicks, PhD, Jon D. Hicks, Michael Hicks, Dwight S. Hill, Fred L. Hinker, Terry D. Hinnerichs, PhD, Charles Henry Hobbs, DVM, Stephen M. Hodgson, David K. Hogan, Gregory A. Hosler, Michael G. Houts, PhD, Volney Ward Howard Jr., PhD, James M. Hylko, J. Charles Ingraham, PhD, Mehraboon S. Irani, MD, David H. Jagnow, George Jarden, MD, Andrew John Jason, PhD, Ronald L. Jepsen, Robert Johannes, PhD, Ken L. Johnson, Wesley Morris Jones, PhD, Richard D. Juel, MD, Jon P. Kahler, C. Keenan, PhD, William E. Keller, PhD, John Daniel Kemp, PhD, David R. Kendall, Claude Larry Kennan, PhD, H. Grant Kinzer, PhD, John H. Kolessar III, Fleetwood R. Koutz, Gary R. Kramer, PhD, William Joseph Kroenke, PhD, Lillian A. Kroenke, Paul Kuenstler, PhD, Roger W. Lamb, Leo J. Lammers, James G. Lareau, Signa Larralde, PhD, Tom B. Larsen, PhD, Laurence Lattman, PhD, Roger X. Lenard, Lary R. Lenke, Frank L. Lichousky, William C. Lindemann, PhD, H. Jerry Longley, PhD, Gabriel P. Lopez, PhD, Radon B. Loveland, Bruce P. Lovett, MD, Kenneth Ludeke, PhD, Mark J. Ludwig, Jesse Lunsford, Raymond A. Madson, Jeffrey Mahn, Norman Malm, PhD, Bob Malone, Gary M. Malvin, PhD, Dorinda Mancini, Joseph Bird Mann, PhD, Charles Robert Mansfield, PhD, Greg Mansfield, Jose Eleazar Martinez Jr., David S. Masterman, Mark A. Mathews, PhD, James W. Mayo 3rd, Douglas K. McCullough, Patrick D. McDaniel, PhD, Kirk McDaniel, Luther F. McDougal, Thomas D. McDowell, PhD, Heath F. McLaughlin, Virginia McLemore, PhD, Reed H. Meek, James H. Metcalf, Andre F. Michaudon, PhD, Edmund Kenneth Miller, PhD, Peter W. Milonni, PhD, James J. Mizera, R. C. Mjolsness, PhD, Raymond C. Mjolsness, PhD, Charles E. Moeller, Michael Stanley Moore, PhD, Joan M. Moore, Joe P. Moore, Tamara K. Morgan, Henry Thomas Motz, PhD, Joseph Mraz, Arthur Wayne Mullendore, Darrell Eugene Munson, PhD, Daniel Neal, PhD, Leland K. Neher, PhD, Burke E. Nelson Sr., PhD, Burke E. Nelson, PhD, R. T. Nelson, Jim Niebaum, James Niebaum, Clyde John Marshall Northrup, PhD, Robert Norton, Bob Norton, Henry C. Nowail, Edward E. O'Donnell, PhD, William Ohmstede, Paul J. Ortwerth, PhD, Robert C. O'Shields, David K. Overmier, Thomas G. Parker, William L. Partain, PhD, Stanley J. Patchet, PhD, James Howard Patterson, PhD, Randy Patterson, Robert H. Paul, PhD, David C. Pavlich, Tamara E. Payne, PhD, Daniel N. Payton III, PhD, Jeffrey Peace, Jerry L. Peace, Ralph B. Peck, PhD, Lester D. Peck, Jeffrey Philbin, PhD, James A. Phillips, PhD, Rex D. Pieper, PhD, Gordon E. Pike, PhD, Pam Pinson, Pamela D. Pinson, James D. Plimpton, PhD, Paul Pompeo 3rd, William Morgan Porch, PhD, Nolan Probst, Irving Rapaport, J. R. Ratcliff, Leonard Raymond, Gary D. Rayson, PhD, George R. Reddy, Joe W. Reese, Paul A. Rehme, John Douglas Reichert, PhD, Mark M. Reif, PhD, William E. Reifsnyder, Anita S. Reiser, Norbert T. Rempe, Elliott A. Riggs, PhD, Jim Riker, PhD, Arnold Robinson, David A. Rockstraw, PhD, Larry D. Rodolph, John D. Roe, G. Rollet, Gary R. Rollstin, Gary R. Rollstin, Benny H. Rose, PhD, Daniel G. Rossbach, B. A. Rosser, Darryl D. Ruehle, Kenneth Sabo, PhD, Richard John Salzbrenner, PhD, George Albert Samara, PhD, Ian A. Sanders, Michael A. Sandquist, MD, Donald James Sandstrom, Alcide Santilli, David P. Sauter, Thomas S. Scanlon Jr., Frank R. Schenbel, Scott A. Schilling, Jeffrey S. Schleher, Theodore R. Schmidt, PhD, Glen L. Schmidt, PhD, David A. Schoderbek, Charles R. Schuch, Joseph Albert Schufle, PhD, L. Schuster, John Seagrave, PhD, Robert D. Sears, Gary L. Seawright, PhD, Jack Behrent Secor, PhD, Dwight Sederholm, David W. Seegmiller, PhD, Fritz A. Seiler, PhD, James Shaffner, Thomas L. Shelley, Lawrence Sher, Arnold John Sierk, PhD, Kenneth Sinks, Wilbur A. Sitze, Joseph L. Skibba, PhD, Florentine Smarandache, PhD, Maynard E. Smith, PhD, Clay T. Smith, PhD, Garmond Stanley Smith, PhD, Harvey M. Smith, Jon E. Sollid, PhD, Michael Scott Sorem, PhD, Professor Sparks, PhD, Morgan Sparks, PhD, David J. Sperling, James Kent Sprinkle, Vincent W. Steffen, Stephen M. Sterbenz, PhD, Philip J. Sterling, Billy Stevens, Regan W. Stinnett, PhD, Leo W. Stockham, PhD, James William Straight, PhD, Thomas F. Strattom, PhD, William R. Stratton, PhD, Thomas Fairlamb Stratton, PhD, Leonard Richard Sugerman, Donald Lee Summers, A. Einar Swanson, Einar Swanson, Donald M. Swingle, PhD, D. Swingle, PhD, Mariano Taglialegami, Willard Lindley Talbert, PhD, David R. Tallant, PhD, Glen M. Tarleton, Gene W. Taylor, PhD, Michael M. Thacker, Edward Frederic Thode, PhD, James L. Thomas, PhD, James L. Thomas, Angela Thomas, John R. Thompson, PhD, Seth J. Thompson, Billy Joe Thorne, PhD, Gary Tietjen, Robert Allen Tobey, PhD, Leonard A. Traina, PhD, Anthony J. Trennel, Charles V. Troutman, Patricio Eduardo Trujillo, John T. Tysseling, John D. Underwood, Jurgen H. Upplegger, PhD, Bruce Harold Van Domelen, PhD, Ron Van Valkenburg,

Don R. Veazey, Charles G. Vivion, MD, George Leo Voelz, MD, James Von Husen, Frederick Ludwig Vook, PhD, Arden L. Walker, Francis J. Wall, PhD, Robert F. Walter, PhD, Roddy Walton, PhD, Norman R. Warpinski, PhD, Mial Warren, PhD, James D. Waters, William W. Weiss, William J. Whaley, Gerald W. Whatley, David Wheeler, H. E. Whitfacre, Larry K. Whitmer, Raymond V. Wick, PhD, James Wifall, Gary R. Williams, Gene Wilson, Donald E. Wilson, Norman G. Wilson, Bob Winn, Kenelm C. Winslow, Donald Lester Wolberg, PhD, Robert O. Woods, PhD, Eric J. Wrage, Harlow Wright, Harlow Wrishe, John L. Yarnell, PhD, Frank Yates Jr., George W. York Jr., PhD, Lloyd M. Young, PhD, Jeffrey L. Young, Phillip L. Youngblood

New York

Ralph F. Abate, Alan V. Abrams, MD, Paul B. Abramson, PhD, John K. Addy, PhD, Siegfried Aftergut, PhD, M. C. Agress, Robert J. Alaimo, PhD, Rogelio N. Alama, Jay Donald Albright, PhD, Zeki Al-Saigh, PhD, Randy J. Alstadt, Vincent O. Altemose, Peter Christian Altner, MD, Burton Myron Altura, PhD, Ronald F. Amberger, PhD, Leonard Amborski, PhD, Richard Amerling, MD, Robert C. Amero, Moris Amon, PhD, H. C. Anderson, Felixe A. Andrews, Dan Antonescu-Wolf, MD, John Archie, William J. Arion, PhD, Alfred Arkell, PhD, Gertrude D. Armbruster, PhD, Seymour Aronson, PhD, Clement R. Arrison, James S. Arthur, PhD, Alvin Ashman, Charles W. Askins, Winifred Alice Asprey, PhD, Walter Auclair, PhD, Louis A. Auerbach, Rosario D. Averion, Walton T. Ayer, John M. Babli, Christopher J. Bablin, Henry Lee Bachman, Richard G. Badger, Lcdr Paul Baham, Betty L. Bailey, Randall L. Bakel, Joseph M. Ballantyne, PhD, Debendranath Banerjee, PhD, Donald E. Banzhaf, MD, Octavian M. Barbu, Charleton C. Bard, PhD, Robert Barish, PhD, Jeremiah A. Barondess, MD, Louis Joseph Barone, Benjamin Austin Barry, Thomas G. Bassett, Robert William Batey, Frances Brand Bauer, PhD, Henry H. Baxter, Mark K. Beal, David Beckner, David F. Bedey, PhD, Allan Lloyd Bednowitz, PhD, Dan Beldy, Robert G. Bellinger, DVM, Gerald William Bennett, PhD, Douglas A. Bennett, Jay Manton Berger, PhD, Herbert Weaver Berry, PhD, Kenneth Del Bianco, Jean M. Bidlack, PhD, Kenneth L. Bielat, PhD, Joseph F. Bieron, PhD, Jean M. Bigaouette, J. E. Bigelow, John Edward Bigelow, Rodney Errol Bigler, PhD, William Bihrle, Arthur Bing, PhD, George Birman, David L. Black, PhD, Donald E. Black, J. Warren Blaker, PhD, Nik Blaser, Sheldon Joseph Bleicher, MD, Marvin E. Blumberg, M. Blumenberg, PhD, Fred G. Bock, Mary M. Bockus, J. Neil Boger, Haig E. Bohigian, PhD, Donald A. Bolon, PhD, Shirley C. Bone, Robert M. Booth, Sunder S. Bora, PhD, David Borkholder, PhD, George Boulter, Mohamed Boutjdir, PhD, Leo J. Brancato, Mike Brannen, Sydney Salisbury Breese, Jan Leslie Breslow, Rainer H. Brocke, PhD, John W. Brook, PhD, Robert R. Brooks, PhD, Walter Brouillette, PhD, Allen S. Brower, Melvin H. Brown, Samuel S. Browser, PhD, Eugene John Brunelle, Howard Bryan, Edward Harland Buckley, PhD, Herbert Budd, PhD, Richard F. Burchill, James M. Burlitch, PhD, David W. Burnett, Lawrence E. Burns, Robert A. Buroker, DVM, Steve Burrell, Tracee A. Burzycki, Timothy P. Bushwell Jr., PhD, K. B. Cady, PhD, Angelo Cagliostro, Stephen R. Cain, PhD, Robert Ellsworth Calhoo, PhD, Gerald Allan Campbell, PhD, Antonio Mogro Campero, PhD, Enrico M. Camporesi, MD, A. Van Caneghem, MD, Thomas J. Carpenter, John L. Carroll, Robert B. Case, MD, Anthony S. Caserta, Chris Cash, Edward Cassidy, Joseph Cassillo, Alan William Castellion, PhD, Lawrence M. Cathles, PhD, Robert E. Cech, PhD, Lawrence J. Cervellino, Charles C. Chamberlain, PhD, Shu Fun Chan, PhD, Alison E. Charles, PhD, Richard Joseph Charles, PhD, Jacob Chass, Stuart S. Chen, PhD, Tak-Ming Chen, Relly Chern, MD, A. Cheung, PhD, Joseph F. Chiang, PhD, Yuen Sheng Chiang, PhD, Robert L. Christensen, PhD, Kenneth G. Christy, Phillip S. Cimino, Emil T. Cipolla, Michael Circosca, Stephen F. Claeys, Earlin N. Clarke, Nicholas L. Clesceri, PhD, Theodore James Coburn, PhD, Paul Cochran, William D. Coe, Anthony Cofrancesco, PhD, Ezechiel Godert David Cohen, PhD, Randall Knight Cole, PhD, Philip J. Colella, Lawrence Colin, Hans Coll, PhD, George H. Collins, Robert J. Conciatori, MD, Norman I. Condit, John P. Coniglio, Dennis Conklin, PhD, John Joseph Connelly, PhD, John A. Constance, William S. Cooley, MD, Harry B. Copelin, Arthur J. Cosgrove, Wilfred Arthur Cote, PhD, Eric W. Cowley, Robert Stephen Craxton, PhD, Robert J. Cresci, PhD, Nicholas G. Cristy, Alfred G. Cuffe, John S. Cullen, Edoardo S. Cuniberti, Ira B. Current, Darisuz Czarkowski, PhD, Lawrence B. Czech, Vincent F. D'Agostino, Barton Eugene Dahneke, PhD, William Dalton, Charles A. Daniel, Wayne Daniels, Professor Dannenberg, PhD, Zafar I. Dar, DVM, Ray L. Darling Jr., Baldev B. Das, MD, Ellen S. Dashefsky, DVM, Edward Daskam, Raymond Davis, PhD, John R. Davis Jr., Ivana P. Day, PhD, Alain de La Chapelle, MD, Nixon de Tamowsky CSP, Robert E. DeBrecht, Gilbert DeCicco, Erwin Delano, PhD, John W. Delano, PhD, William M. Delaware, Jon Delong, Albert M. Demont, Charles Desbordes, Michael C. Detraglia, PhD, Vincent T. Devita, MD, Gregory J. Devlin, Robert C. Devries, PhD, William B. Dickinson, PhD, Professor Dimeglio, Carlos M. Dobryn, Edwin S. Dojka, Bruce J. Dolnick, PhD, Robert M. Domke, Robert W. Doty, PhD, Lawrence G. Doucet, Patricia Doxtader, PhD, Professor Doxtader, PhD, John Droz Jr., Bernard S. Dudock, PhD, Jim Dunn, PhD, James R. Dunn, PhD, George J. Dvorak, PhD, Robert H. Easton, Constantino Economos, PhD, James P. Edasery, PhD, Robert Flint Edgerton, PhD, John A. Edward, Kurt F. Eise, Richard J. Engel, Charles Edward Engelke, PhD, Louis James Esch, PhD, Theodore Walter Esders, PhD, Levent Eskicakit, James Estep, PhD, John H. Estes, PhD, Howard Edward Evans, PhD, Woodrow W. Everett, Abraham Eviatar, MD, Craig Fahrenburg, PhD, Carl Fahrenkrug, PhD, Carl Fahrenkrugh, Amedeo

Alexander Fantini, PhD, Gerald N. Fassell, Ralph A. Favale, MD, Anthony John Favale, Jay M. Feder, MD, Tom Feil, George Feinbaum, MD, Martin Felicita, Archie D. Fellenzer Jr., Charles P. Felton, MD, John W. Fenton II, PhD, Maj Virgil F. Ficarra, MD, Robert H. Fickies, Bradley J. Field, James R. Fienup, PhD, Anthony Salvatore Filandro, Peter Stevenson Finlay, PhD, Arnold G. Fisch, Grahme P. Fischer, Nancy Deloye Fitzroy, Delbert Dale Fix, PhD, John Edward Fletcher, PhD, Irving M. Fogel, Charles E. Frank, Dorothea Zucker Franklin, MD, Andrew Gibson Frantz, MD, Donald M. Fraser, MD, Gilbert Friedenreich, Gilbert Friedenreich, Gerald M. Friedman, PhD, Maria I. Galaiko, Eugene H. Galanter, PhD, Gregory W. Gallagher, Richard D. Galli, Franics M. Gallo, Rosa M. Gambier, PhD, Gerard C. Gambs, Donald D. Garman, Robert Harper Garmezy, Howard B. Gates, Raymond E. Gaus, Robert Frank Gehrig, PhD, Gunther Richard Geiss, PhD, James G. Geistfeld, PhD, Herbert Leo Gelernter, PhD, Dale M. George, Angelos S. Georgopoulos, J. P. Gergen, PhD, Anne A. Gershon, MD, Eric B. Gertner, Mellor A. Gill, Robert Gillcrist, Lawrence B. Gillett, PhD, Ernest Rich Gilmont, PhD, Helen S. Ginzburg, Ronald M. Gluck, Charles J. Godreau, MD, Leslie I. Gold, PhD, Malcolm Goldberg, PhD, Michelle Goldschneider, PhD, Edward B. Goldstein, PhD, Leonard Gordon, Steven Grassl, PhD, Saul Green, PhD, Alex Gringauz, PhD, Herbert Grossman, C. Edward Grove, PhD, Timothy R. Groves, PhD, Johathan R. Gruchala, Bruce B. Grynbaum, MD*, Robert F. Guardino, Heinrich W. Guggenheiher Sc D, PhD, Heinrich Walter Guggenheimer, PhD, Paul F. Gugliotta, PhD, Michael A. Guida, Raj K. Gupta, PhD, Susan Gurney, James Guyker, PhD, Daniel Habib, PhD, Albert Haim, PhD, Thomas Haines, PhD, Mike Hale, PhD, Norm Hall, Joseph Halpern, PhD, Jack A. Hammond, Stanley E. Handman, Sultan Haneed, PhD, Leon Dudley Hankoff, MD, Kevin Joseph Hanley, George E. Hansen, Gordon Charles Hard, PhD, George Bigelow Hares, PhD, Henry Gilbert Harlow, Dean Butler Harrington, Donald R. Harris, PhD, Bruce Harris, Ramon P. Harris, Sylvan Hart, Delmer L. Hart, Richard W. Hartmann, PhD, Roger Haskell, PhD, Frederick C. Hass, PhD, Floyd N. Hasselrlis, Maximilian E. Hauser, Wayne Haushnecht, William W. Havens Jr., PhD, G. Wayne Hawk, Daniel P. Hayes, PhD, F. Terry Hearne, Ira Grant Hedrick, Charles Gladstone Heisig, PhD, Mark Heitz, PhD, David Helfand, Harold R. Hellstrom, MD, Lloyd Emerson Herdle, PhD, Zvi Herschman, Zri Herschman, MD, Kenneth H. Hershey, Ralph Allan Hewes, PhD, Patrick Hickey, Walter A. Hickox, Robert E. Hileman, PhD, James O. Hillis, H. O. Hoadley, Stanley H. Hobish, Roger Alan Hoffman, PhD, Theodore P. Hoffman, PhD, Merrill K. Hoffman, Walter H. Hoffmann, John C. Holko, Alfred C. Hollander, MD, Harold A. Holz, Kenneth E. Hoogs PC, MD, Robert H. Hopf, Harvey Allen Horowitz, Mark G. Horschel, Malcolm D. Horton, Barbara J. Howell, PhD, Jan Hrabe, PhD, Lawrence R. Huntoon, PhD, Michael John Iatropoulos, PhD, Marvin L. Illingsworth, PhD, A. Rauf Imam, PhD, Charles G. Inman, A. M. Irving, Erich Isaac, PhD, Zafar A. Ismail, PhD, Patrick Thomas Izzo, PhD, Joseph P. Jackson, James Jacob, PhD, Theodore G. Jacobs, Jules Jacquin, William Julian Jaffe, PhD, Thomas E. Jensen, PhD, George A. Jensen, George A. Jenson, Henry Louis Jicha Jr., PhD, M. Jin, PhD, Karel Jindrak, PhD, Professor Joerz, Sune Johansson, Francis Johnson, PhD, Horton A. Johnson, MD, Andrew E. Jones, PhD, Larry Josbeno, Jack J. Kahgan, Robert O. Kalbach, PhD, Norman Wayne Kalenda, PhD, Moses K. Kaloustian, PhD, Robert M. Kamp, Walter Reilly Kane, PhD, Walter T. Kane, Munawar Karim, PhD, Bertil J. Kaudern, George Kaufman, MD, Donald Bruce Keck, PhD, Zvi Kedem, PhD, Robert Adolph Keeler, Jerome Baird Keister, PhD, D. Steven Keller, PhD, Spencer II Kellogg II, Margaret M. Kelly, J. Kelly, Donald Laurens Kerr, PhD, S. F. Kiersznowski, Robert William Kilpper, PhD, Kenneth M. King, Paul I. Kingsbury, PhD, P. I. Kingsbury Jr., PhD, Janet M. Kirsch, Paul R. Kirsch, George Stanley Klaiber, PhD, Bruce Holmes Klanderman, PhD, Vasilios Kleftis, Ludwig Klein, PhD, Eugene M. Klimko, PhD, Sylvia K. Knowlton, MD, Elisa Konofagou, PhD, Howard J. Kordes, Karl F. Korfmacher, PhD, Jack I. Kornfield, PhD, Lee Ming Kow, PhD, Professor Kraft, PhD, Robert W. Kress, Valentina R. Kulick, PhD, Rudolph K. Kulling, PhD, Max Kurtz, Theodore W. Kury, PhD, Peter La Celle, PhD, Paul L. Lacelle, PhD, Joann Lachut, Sanford Lacks, PhD, Robert J. Laffin, PhD, Peter L. Laino, MD, David E. Landers, R. L. Lane, PhD, Richard L. Lane, PhD, Arthur M. Langer, PhD, Frank Lanzafame, PhD, Joseph M. Lanzafame, PhD, Peter Lanzetta, PhD, Evelyn P. Lapin, PhD, Charles Conrad Larson, PhD, Keith F. Lashway, Kent P. Lawson, PhD, John F. Lawyer, Jeffrey C. Lawyer, Norman Lazaroff, PhD, Robert J. Lecat, PhD, Andre Leclair, PhD, N. A. Legatos, August Ferdinand Lehman, Nathaniel S. Lehrman, MD, Herbert August Leupold, PhD, Richard D. Levere, MD, Jane R. Levine, Herbert August Levpold, PhD, Harold W. Lewis, PhD, Yong J. Li, PhD, Emanuel Y. Li, MD, Cathy Licata, Irwin A. Lichtman, PhD, James A. Liggett, PhD, Ralph Linsker, PhD, Arnold A. Lipton, MD, Clayton Lee Liscom, Bruce A. Lister, Richard G. Livingston, Clyde R. Locke, MD, Joseph Carl Logue, Anna K. Longobardo, Jerome J. Looker, PhD, John Looney, Ronald J. Lorenz, Jerry A. Lorenzen, PhD, David Lorenzen, MD, Thomas Lowinger, PhD, Gerald Luck, George W. Luckey, PhD, Frederick J. Luckey, Carol J. Lusty, PhD, Bruce MacDonald, John Fraser Macdowell, Elbert F. Macfadden Jr., MD, Robert E. Madden, MD, Robert E. Madden, Robert W. Madey, PhD, Edward F. Magnusson, Leathem Mahaffey, PhD, Hug David Maille, PhD, Jay Maioli, Timothy M. Maloney, William Muir Manger, PhD, Ruben Manuelyan, Karl Maramorosch, PhD, G. Marie Agnew Marcelli, Morris J. Markovitz, Paul Marnell, PhD, Robert E. Marrin, Vincent F. Marrone, PhD, James A. Marsh, PhD, Elliott R. Marsh, L. Gerald Marshall, Irving Marvin, John J. Mastrangelo, Donald E. Mathewson, David Matthew, Paul R. Mattinen, Paul B. Mauer, Robert E. Maurer, PhD, A. Frank Mayadas, PhD, Theodor Mayer, PhD, Denis G. Mazeika, John R. Mcbride, PhD, Thomas A. McClelland, PhD, J. R. D.

McCormick, PhD, John P. McGuire, William R. McLean, William McNamara, PhD, Paul F. McTigue, Winthrop D. Means, PhD, John Medavaine, Allen G. Meek, Karin W. Megerle, K. Megerle, Karl R. Megerle, Lester Meidenbauer, Otto Meier Jr., Daniel T. Meloon, PhD, Emest Menaldino, MD, Paul Barrett Merkel, PhD, David L. Messenger, John D. Metzger, PhD, Robert P. Meyer, PhD, Richard H. Meyer Jr., John C. Midavaine, Kevin J. Miley, Allan F. Miller, Gary S. Mirkin, MD, Gerald Jude Mizejewski, PhD, Robert P. Moehring, Henry W. Moeller, PhD, Joseph C. Mollendorf, PhD, Leo F. Monaghan, Salvatore J. Monte, Richard T. Mooney, John Moran, Thomas C. Morgan, Paul W. Morris, PhD, William Guy Morris, PhD, Roger Alfred Morse, PhD, Kenneth Ernest Mortenson, PhD, Edward P. Mortimer, Wayne Morton, Lloyd Motz, PhD, Eldridge Milford Mount, PhD, Charles F. Mowry, Shakir P. Mukhi, MD, L. Muller, Charles Munsch, Shyam Prasad Murarka, PhD, Daniel B. Murphy, PhD, Victor L. Mylroie, Victor L. Myroie, Eric Nary, Hugh M. Neeson, Jarda D. Nehybka, Charles A. Nelson, PhD, Sven Nelson, Wendell Neugebauer, Hans P. Nichols, Richard Nickerson, MD, Joseph F. Noon, R. A. Norling, William T. Norton, PhD, Julian Nott, Jerzy Nowakowski, PhD, Tom O'Brien, PhD, Matthew F. O'Connell, Robert T. Ohea, Tonis Oja, PhD, Joanne M. Ondrako, PhD, Dino F. Oranges, Michael J. O'Rourke, PhD, Brian P. O'Rourke, Ernest Vinicio Orsi, PhD, Harold R. Ortman, Paul C. Oscanyan, PhD, Maurice J. Osman, C. M. Oster, Hans Walter Osterhoudt, PhD, Professor Otu, PhD, Murali Krishna Pagala, PhD, Donald G. Paish, MD, Christopher R. Palma, PhD, Giorgio Pannella, PhD, Lawrence D. Papsidero, PhD, Hemant Bhupendra Parikh, David J. Parker, Zohreh Parsa, PhD, Richard E. Partch, PhD, Robert William Pasco, PhD, Kenneth Pass, PhD, Harini Patel, PhD, Sandra Patrick, Gregory J. Patterson, Michael V. Pavlov, George John Pearson, PhD, Erik Mauritz Pell, PhD, Joseph C. Pender, MD, John P. Pensiero, Theodore Peters Jr., PhD, John H. Peterson, MD, Dana M. Pezzimenti, Tuan Duc Pham, PhD, Herbert R. Philipp, PhD, Neal Phillip, PhD, Ernest E. Phillips, Erling Phytte, PhD, Carlson Chao Ping Pian, Richard N. Pierson, MD, Valter Ennis Pilcher, PhD, Vernor A. Pilon, MD, Walter Thornton Pimbley, PhD, David Pimentel, PhD, William R. Pioli, Anthony W. Pircio, PhD, Rahn G. Pitzer, Wendy K. Pogozelski, PhD, V. Pogrebnyak, PhD, Wilson Gideon Pond, PhD, Om P. Popli, Gerhard Popp, PhD, George Henry Potter, PhD, Ernest Ppospischil, R. Priefer, PhD, Svante Prochazka, PhD, Richard P. Puelle, Donald H. Puretz, PhD, D.C. Putman, Orrea F. Pye, PhD, James Roger Quinan, PhD, Richard L. Racette, Joseph Wolfe Rachlin, PhD, Michael Ram, PhD, Madeline K. Ramsey, Paul Ellertson Ramstad, PhD, Hugh Rance, PhD, Navagund Rao, PhD, Arthur A. Rauth, Stanley R. Rawn Jr., Geoffrey Recktenwald, PhD, Michael L. Reichard, Jerome A. Reid, MD, Anthony A. Reidlinger, PhD, Norman E. Reinertsen, Edwin Louis Resler Jr., William E. Rew, William T. Rhea, John T. Rice, PhD, Guercio Louis Richard, MD, Elmer A. Richards, Charles M. Richardson, C. H. B. Richardson, Selma Richman, Malcolm M. Riggs, MD, James Lewis Ringo, PhD, Walter Lee Robb, PhD, Leslie Earl Robertson, Terence Lee Robinson, PhD, Maxine Lieberman Rockoff, PhD, James D. Rodems, Robert M. Roecker, PhD, Lloyd Sloan Rogers, MD, Herman O. Rogg, Robert C. Rohr, PhD, Mario F. Romagnoli, David M. Rooney, PhD, Robert L. Rooney, Milton Jacques Rosen, PhD, Joseph Rosi, John Rostand, R. A. Roston, Ronald D. Rothchild, PhD, Elliot M. Rothkdpf, PhD, E. Rothkopf, PhD, Lewis P. Rotkowitz, MD, William N. Rotton, MD, Gaylord Earl Rough, PhD, Ibrahim Rubeiz, PhD, Len Rubenstein, Leonard Rubenstein, Arthur L. Ruoff, PhD, William F. Ryan, Richard 0. S, Frederick Sachs, PhD, John Salvador Jr., Jay Salwen, MD, Robert S. Samson, Jose Sanchez, PhD, Juan Sanchez, Jon Henry Sanders, PhD, Andrew M. J. Sandorfi, PhD, Edward James Sarcione, PhD, Balu Sarma, PhD, Frank Scalia, PhD, Marc A. Scarchilli, Len Schaer, Simon Schaffel, PhD, Anthony J. Schaut, Alan J. Schecter, PhD, Edward J. Schmeltz, Frederick W. Schmidlin, PhD, Richard F. Schneeberger, Samuel Ray Scholes Jr., PhD, Gerald Schulte, James J. Schultheis, Gerald Schultz, W. E. Schwabe, John Schwaninger, Frederick A. Schweizer, Daniel Sciarra, MD, Wright H. Scidmore, Terrence R. Scott, Brian E. Scully, MD, David R. Seamen, Boris M. Segal, MD, Robert Seider, Sharon Seigmeister, Frederick Seitz, PhD*, Professor Seleem, PhD, Domenick A. Serrano, Bryon R. Sever, PhD, Wayne K. Shaffer, Professor Shapiro, Professor Sharkey, PhD, Clifford J. Shaver, Richard Gregg Shaw, PhD, Robert Shaw, MD, Chester Stephen Sheppard, PhD, Malcolm J. Sherman, PhD, Robert M. Shields, PhD, Avner Shilman, PhD, Steve Shoecraft, John Shotwell, John O. Shotwell, Avanti C. Shroff, PhD, Eugene E. Shube, Barbara Shykoff, PhD, Richard W. Siegel, PhD, J. Siegenthaler, John Siegenthaler, James Ernest Siggins, PhD, John Sigsby, Albert Simon, PhD, John M. Simpson, Emil D. Sjoholm, Victor Skormin, PhD, J. A. Slezak, PhD, Jane Ann Slezak, PhD, Harry Kim Slocum, PhD, Frederick W. Smith, PhD, Cedric M. Smith, MD, Roy C. Smith J, Neil M. Smith, Albert A. Smith, Bronislaw Smura, PhD, Herman Soifer, Robert Soley, MD, Chester P. Soliz, MD, John Robert Sowa, PhD, Paul William Spear, MD, William E. Spears Jr., Abraham Spector, PhD, Stanley B. Spellman, MD, William J. Spezzano, Michael J. Spinelli, John M. Spritzer 3rd, Alfred E. Stahl, Laddie L. Stahl, Zygmunt Staszewski, D. E. Steeper, Martin F. Stein, MD, Larry C. Stephans, Harry Stevens Jr., Carleton C. Stewart, William Andrew Stewart, MD, Gerhard Stohrer, PhD, Norman Stanley Stoloff, PhD, John S. Stores, PhD, Stewart P. Stover, Fred Strnisa, PhD, Forrest C. Strome, PhD, Raymond G. Stross, PhD, Henry Stry, Leon S. Suchard, Michael Surgeary, Bob Sutaria, Paris D. Svoronos, PhD, John M. Swab, Charles Swain, Donald Percy Swartz, MD, Donald Sykes, PhD, Joseph Szczesniak, MD, Robert Szego, PhD, Boleslaw K. Szymanski, PhD, Charles Peter Talley, PhD, Mehmet Y. Tarhan, Pamela A. Tarkington, MD, Nixon De Tarnowsky, Aaron M. Taub, PhD, James E. Taylor, PhD, Kenneth J. Teegarden, PhD, Stephen Whittier Tehon, PhD, Aram V. Terchwian, George Terwilliger, PhD, David K. Thom, Edward Sandusky

Thomas, PhD, G. J. Thorbecke, PhD, Craig E. Thorn, PhD, Larry Tilis, MD, Tore Erik Timell, PhD, William Timm, Lu Ting, PhD, Sathyan C. Tivakaran, Thomas B. Tomasi, PhD, Joseph Torosian, Joseph M. Tretter, Robert Bogue Trimble, PhD, Anthony Trippe, PhD, Professor Troupe, PhD, Min-Fu Tsan, PhD, Herbert F. Tschudi, Robert Joseph Tuite, PhD, James B. Turchir, William Joseph Turner, PhD, Arthur Glenn Tweet, PhD, John Urdea, Charles F. Vachris, Marius P. Valsamis, MD, Vida K. Vambutas, PhD, Ruth VanDeusen, R. V. Vanhoweistine, PhD, Michael O. Varner, Thomas S. Velz, Carl J. Verbanic, PhD, David Augustus Vermilyea, PhD, Morrill Thayer Vittum, PhD, Kalman N. Vizy, PhD, Alexander V. Vologodskii, PhD, Richard W. Vook, PhD, Leonid Vulakh, PhD, Ernest N. Waddell, Thomas J. Wade, PhD, John M. Wadsworth, Salome Gluecksohn Waels, PhD, Salome G. Waelsch, PhD, Richard Joe Wagner, PhD, A. Wagner, Anne M. Wagner, Christopher Walcek, PhD, Joseph Walters, MD, Robert L. Walton, James E. Wanamaker, Robert S. Ward, Howard C. Ward Jr., Barbara E. Warkentine, PhD, Arthur P. Weber, PhD, Julius Weber, Brent M. Wedding, PhD, Paul M. Wegman, Edward David Weil, PhD, Leonard Harlan Weinstei, PhD, Herbert Weinstein, Leonard Weisler, PhD, Harvey Jerome Weiss, R. B. Wenger, MD, Jack Hall Westbrook, PhD, Elizabeth M. Whelan, PhD, Donald Robertson White, PhD, Carl F. Whitehead, David C. Widrig, James Wiebe, Grace M. Wieder, PhD, W. H. Williams, PhD, William H. Williams, PhD, Kevin Williams, Nik Willmore, PhD, Nicolaos Daniel Willmore, PhD, Jack Belmont Wilson, PhD, Janet W. Wilson, DVM, Frank W. Wise, PhD, Charles E. Wisor, MD, Paul C. Witbeck, Mark Witowski, Harold Ludwig Witting, PhD, Robert C. Wohl, PhD, Paul Wojnicz, Arthur J. Wolf, Peter Wolw, John T. Wozer, Robert W. Wright, PhD, Konran T. Wu, PhD, John E. Wylie, Dmeter Yablonsky, PhD, Kenneth R. Yager, Scott Yanuck, William D. Young Jr., Wen Shi Yu, PhD, Luke Dhia Liu Yuan, PhD, Chia Liu Yuan, PhD, Anthony M. Yurchak, MD, Richard Yuster, Marco Zaider, PhD, Ethel Suzanne Zalay, PhD, Andreas A. Zavi, PhD, Allen Zelman, PhD, Frank F. Zhang, PhD, Edward N. Ziegler, PhD, Jehuda Ziegler, PhD, Hirsch J. Ziegler, Ronald F. Ziolo, PhD, Richard J. Ziomkowski, Thomas A. Zitter, PhD, David Zuckerberg, Carl William Zuehlke, PhD, Peter Zuman, PhD

North Carolina

Eugene Adams, Walter F. Adams, Rolland W. Ahrens, PhD, Allan J. Albrecht, William D. Albright, Moorad Alexanian, PhD, Charles M. Allen, PhD, Reevis Stancil Alphin, PhD, John Pruyn Van Alstyne, Robert H. Appleby, Webster J. Arceneaux Jr., Robert L. Austin, Max Azevedo, Rodger W. Baier, PhD, Lloyd W. Bailey, Jim Bailey, Richard J. Baird, John L. Bakane, Charles R. Baker, PhD, D. K. Baker, PhD, R. Baker, Walter E. Ballinger, PhD, Steven Bardwell, PhD, Stanley O. Barefoot, James A. Bass, Norman J. Bedwell, Carl Adolph Beiser, PhD, John C. Bemath, William Benson, Edward George Bilpuch, PhD, Jack C. Binford, Larry G. Blackburn, Stephen T. Blanchard, Catherine E. Blat, Arthur Palfrey Bode, PhD, Charles Edward Boklage, PhD, E. Arthur Bolz, PhD, Everett A. Bolz, MD, Arthur Bolz, MD, Margurette E. Bottje, PhD, William George Bottjer, PhD, Daniel P. Boutross, Richard D. Bowen, James L. Bowman, Stephen G. Boyce, PhD, Dale W. Boyd Sr., MD, Lyle A. Branagan, PhD, David K. Brese, Charles B. Breuer, PhD, Charles B. Brever, PhD, Richard L. Brewer, Philip M. Bridges, David W. Bristol, John Oliver Brittain, PhD, James E. Brookshire, Henry S. Brown, PhD, Ben Brown, Robert C. Brown, MD, David Brown, M. Frank Brown, Brett H. Bruton, Donald Buckner, Francis P. Buiting, Leonard Seth Bull, PhD, Paul Leslie Bunce, MD, James J. Burchall, PhD, Hugh J. Burford, PhD, Rollin S. Burhans, John Nicholas Burnett, PhD, Loy R. Burris, Neal E. Busch, PhD, Domingo E. Cabinum, MD, Dixon Callihan, PhD, David D. Calvert Jr., Harry B. Cannon Jr., J. David Carlson, PhD, David W. Carnell, Benjamin Harrison Carpenter, PhD, Randall L. Carver, Charles D. Case, Anthony J. Castiglia, MD, Frank P. Catena, Gregory P. Chacos, Raymond F. Chandler, John Judson Chapman, PhD, Brad N. Chazotte, PhD, John Garland Clapp, PhD, Howard Garmany Clark, PhD, William M. Clark, MD, Larry Clarke, Raymond E. Clawson, Kenneth W. Clayton, Frank Clements, Warren Kent Cline, PhD, Todd Cloninger, PhD, Donald Gordon Cochran, PhD, Bertram W. Coffer, MD, William L. Cogger Jr., Chris Coggins, PhD, Richard Paul Colaianni, Stephen K. Cole, PhD, Elwood B. Coley, MD, Clifford B. Collins, John R. Cone, Paul Kohler Conn, PhD, John M. Connor, Maurice Gayle Cook, PhD, Anson Richard Cooke, PhD, Jackie B. Cooper, Alfred R. Cordell, MD, John W. Costlow, PhD, Frederick Russell Cox, John T. Coxey 3rd, Terry A. Cragle, Ely J. Crary, MD, David F. Creasy, Ronald P. Cronogue, DVM, John M. Crowley*, Alan L. Csontos, Bradford C. Cummings, William S. Currie, George B. Cvijanovich, PhD, Anthony A. Dale, Tony Dale, Walter E. Daniel,

PhD, Jose Joaquim Darruda, PhD, Dean Daryani, Tony Dau, Howard C. Davenport, Clayton L. Davidson, W. H. Davidson, MD, Harold Davies, William Robert Davis, PhD, Warren B. Davis, Dana E. Davis, Eugene De Rose, PhD, Robert J. Dean, MD, Nancy E. Dechant, Donald W. Dejong, PhD, James B. Delpapa, Adam B. Denison, Gregory W. Dickey, Raymer G. Dilworth, Michael Dion, Nama Doddi, PhD, Hugh J. Donohue, MD, G. Double, PhD, E. Douglass, Donald A. Dowling, Thomas R. Drews, Earl G. Droessler, William DuBroff, PhD, Joseph M. Ducar, Donald John Duoziak, PhD, Kevin D. Durs, Paul B. Duvall, Robert S. Eckles, Jim Edgar, Steve S. Edgerton, Douglas F. Eilerston, Professor Ejire, PhD, Norma S. Elliott Jr., William H. Elliott Jr., John Joseph Ennever, George E. Erdman, Harold P. Erickson, PhD, Paul S. Ervin, M. Frank Erwin, Joseph J. Estwanik, MD, David P. Ethier, Ralph Aiken Evans, PhD, Marshall L. Evans, John O. Everhart, Herman A. Fabert Jr., Alan L. Falk, David W. Fansler, Michael Farona, PhD, William Joseph Farrissey Jr., PhD, John James Felten, PhD, V. Hayes Fenstermacher, Courtney S. Ferguson, PhD, Herman White Ferguson, James Fiordalisi, PhD, Joseph W. Fischer, MD, David C. Fischetti, Ken Flurchick, PhD, Thomas P. Foley, Roger A. Foote, Michael J. Forster, PhD, Mac Foster, PhD, Robert Middleton Foster, MD, Neal Edward Franks, PhD, Scott French, Pete G. Friedman, Robert S. Fulghum, PhD, Louis Galan, A. Ronald Gallant, PhD, Clifton A. Gardner Jr., Donald M. Garland, MD, Watson M. Garrison, Daniel S. Garriss, Mark P. Gasque, Edward F. Gehringer, PhD, John C. Geib, William T. Geissinger, MD, Forrest E. Getzen, PhD, Harry F. Giberson, Michael J. Gibson, PhD, Gerald W. Gibson, Gray T. Gilbert, Nicholas W. Gillham, PhD, John H. Gilliam, MD, Thomas R. Gilliam, Tom Gilliam, Elizabeth H. Gillikin, Lucinda H. Glover, Eric Charles Gonder, PhD, Tim Good, Robert Goodman, Donald Gorgei, Bill Grabb, Tommy Grady, Robert B. Gregory, Edward Griest, PhD, Tim A. Griffin, Eugene W. Griner, James J. Grovenstein, Robert M. Gruninger, Frederic C. Gryckiewicz, Harold A. Guice, Robert J. Gussmann, Joseph A. Gutierrez, Kevin Hackenbruch, Kenneth Doyle Hadeen, PhD, John V. Hamme, PhD, Charles Edward Hamner, PhD, N. Bruce Hanes, PhD, Steve Hansen, PhD, James E. Hardzinski, Charles M. Harman, PhD, Michael A. Harpold, PhD, Joe Harris, PhD, Bernard C. Harris, Heath Harrower, Paul J. Harry, James Ronald Hass, PhD, Thomas W. Hauch, MD, Gerald B. Havenstein, PhD, Richard J. Hawkanson, Leland E. Hayden, John Lenneis Haynes, George L. Hazelton, Jane K. Hearn, Ralph C. Heath, Jonathan Daniel Heck, PhD, Edward M. Hedgpeth, MD, Luther W. Hedspeth, Carl John Heffelfinger, PhD, John A. Heitmann, PhD, Henry Hellmers, PhD, Anna Miriam Morgan Henson, PhD, M. M. Henson, PhD, Teddy T. Herbert, PhD, John Key Herdklotz, PhD, James E. Hester, Thomas R. Hewitt, William J. Hindman Jr., James H. Hines Jr., William B. Hinshaw, PhD, Willie L. Hinze, PhD, Maureane R. Hoffman, PhD, Kenneth W. Hoffner, Anatoli T. Hofle, Richard Thornton Hood Jr., Michael L. Hoover, Philip J. Hopkinson, Charles R. Hosler, John L. Hubisz, PhD, Colin M. Hudson, PhD, Allen S. Hudspeth, MD, B. Huggins, C. G. Hughes, Harold Judson Humm, PhD, Francis X. Hurley, PhD, William R. Hutchins, William Hutchins, Richard Ilson, Albert M. Iosue, PhD, James Bosworth Irvine, Rosemary B. Ison, F. K. Iverson, Robert A. Izydore, PhD, Hank Z. Jackson Jr., J.A. Jackson, Mordecai J. Jaffe, PhD, Robert Janowitz, Chueng R. Ji, PhD, Melvin C. Jones, Friedlen B. Jones, MD, Edward Daniel Jordan, PhD, Donald G. Joyce, MD, Karl Kachadoorian, Thomas R. Kagarise, Antone J. Kajs, Victor V. Kaminski, PhD, A. J. Karalis, Emmett S. King, Oscar H. Kirsch, Duane L. Kirschenman, Sam D. Kiser, R. Klein, PhD, Thomas Rhinehart Konsler, PhD, John T. Kopfle, Jeffrey L. Kornegay, Lemuel W. Kornegay, MD, John M. Kramer, Howard R. Kratz, PhD, Steven Kreisman, Frederick William Kremkau, PhD, Lance Whitaker Kress, PhD, George James Kriz, PhD, Raymond Eugene Kuhn, PhD, James Richard Kuppers, PhD, Walter W. Lace, Evan Dean Laganis, PhD, Dennis J. Lapoint, PhD, Robert E. Lasater, William E. Laupus, MD, Douglas M. Lay, PhD, Suzanne M. Lea, PhD, Harvey Don Ledbetter, PhD, Richard A. Ledford, PhD, Keith E. Leese, Dennis M. Leibold, Michael L. Leming, PhD, Robert Murdoch Lewert, PhD, Gordon Depew Lewis, PhD, George W. Lewis, MD, Chia-yu Li, PhD, John B. Link, Mark D. Lister, PhD, Harold W.

Lloyd Jr., Charles H. Lochmuller, PhD, Harry G. Lockaby, Richard A. Loftis, John B. Longenecker, PhD, Ian S. Longmuir, Kyle W. Loseke, Jeff S. Lospinoso, Doug Loudin, Sadler Love, Jeffery D. Loven, Holly E. Lownes, David L. Lucht, Arthur Lutz, David S. Lutz, John Henry MacMillan, John Henry MacMillian, Cecil G. Madden, Rodney K. Madsen, Jethro Oates Manly, PhD, William Robert Mann, PhD, P. K. Marcon, Gerald R. Marschke, MD, Harold L. Martin, Professor Martin, Bryon E. Martin, Leila Martin, MD, Robert C. Matejka, Joe K. Matheson, Thomas D. Mattesonn, Nils E. Matthews, Eric J. Matzke, Kenneth Nathaniel May, PhD, Michael S. Maynard, PhD, Robin S. McCombs, Philip Glen McCracken, PhD, Jennifer McDuffie, PhD, Dale A. McFarland, Kenneth G. McKay, PhD, Hugh M. McKnigh Sr., Hugh M. McKnight, Nathan H. McLamb, Nicole B. McLamb, Beverly N. McManaway, M. S. Medeiros Jr., Richard Young Meelheim, PhD, Bill R. Merritt, B. R. Merritt, Genevieve T. Michelsen, Donald V. Micklos, Allan Millen, Alan Millen, Daniel Newton Miller, PhD, Robert James Miller, PhD, James R. Miller, Jesse R. Mills, James F. Mills, James W. Mink, PhD, Gary N. Mock, PhD, Mary V. Moggio, Masood Mohiuddin, PhD, Paul Richard Moran, PhD, Edward G. Morris, Willard L. Morrison Jr., Thomas M. Morse, Don R. Morton, Susan R. Morton, Parks D. Moss, Christopher B. Mullen, Jamie Murphy, Raymond L. Murray, PhD, Kenneth E. Neff, Hesam O. Nekooasl, Richard D. Nelson, A. Carl Nelson Jr., John T. Newell, PhD, John Merle Nielsen, PhD, Alan H. Nielsen, Larry Nixon, D. B. Nothdurft, Robert A. Novy, PhD, Donald E. Novy, Joe Allen Nuckolls, Sylvanus W. Nye, MD, Calvin M. Ogburn, Mitchell M. Osteen, Kevin D. Ours, Robert J. Owens, Virgeon A. Pace, Teresa W. Page, Bert M. Parker, PhD, George W. Parker, Bernard L. Patterson, MD, Orus F. Patterson III, Dennis R. Paulson, Ira W. Pearce, George Wilbur Pearsall, Mary Alice Penland, Ralph Matthew Perhac, PhD, Derrick O. Perkins, Peter Petrusz, PhD, Dwayne Phillips, Cu Phung, PhD, Mark S. Pierce, William C. Piver, Harvey Pobiner, Mark A. Pope, Thomas D. Pope, MD, Kevin T. Potts, PhD, Roger Allen Powell, PhD, Eugene A. Praschan, Gary C. Prechter, MD, Mark L. Prendergast, William Pulyer, Peter M. Quinn, Karl Spangler Quisenberry, PhD, Charles W. Raczkowski, PhD, Jay M. Railey, James Arthur Raleigh, PhD, Colin Stokes Ramage, Walter B. Ramsey, James A. Reagan, Jamie Redenbaugh, Bernice E. Redmond, MD, Michael R. Reesal, PhD, William O. Reeside, G. George Reeves, PhD, Nancy Reeves, Stanley E. Reinhart, PhD, Stephen G. Richardson, PhD, Jerry F. Rimmer, Benjamin L. Roach, Paul J. Robert, C. Gordon Roberts, PhD, Joe L. Robertson, MD, Norman Glenn Robison, PhD, John M. Roblin, PhD, Neill E. Rochelle, John M. Rodlin, PhD, Michael E. Rogers, John H. Rohde, PhD, O. Rose, PhD, Joseph W. Rose, John D. Ross, PhD, John Ross, Thomas M. Royal, Sohindar S. Sachdev, PhD, Robert L. Sadler, Walter Carl Saeman, Joseph R. Salem Sr., Francis L. Sammt, William August Sander, PhD, Foster J. Sanders, MD, Peter Thomson Sarjeant, PhD, Jerry Satterwhite, Vinod Kumar Saxena, PhD, Howard John Schaeffer, PhD, J. T. Scheick, PhD, Keith Schimmel, PhD, Laurence W. Schlanger, Howard A. Schneider, PhD, Douglas G. Schneider, William S. Schwartz, James Alan Scott, Allen J. Senzel, PhD, Alan J. Senzel, PhD, Charlie C. Sessoms Jr., Stephen T. Sharar, Lewis J. Shaw, Joe H. Sheard, Donald Lewis Shell, PhD, Kevin A. Shelton, Bruce A. Shepherd, Lamar Sheppard, PhD, Moses Maurice Sheppard, PhD, William C. Sides, Charles N. Sigmon, Dorothy Martin Simon, PhD, Anthony D. Simone, Richard E. Slyfield, Warren A. Smith, Norman Cutler Smith, George Smith, James R. Smith, Robert L. Smyre, Stanley Paul Sobol, Ken Soderstrom, PhD, Ronald G. Soltis, Jan J. Spitzer, PhD, James B. Springer, PhD, James L. Spruill, Alexander Squire, Hans H. Stadelmaier, PhD, Sanford L. Steelman, PhD, Bern Steiner, Charles T. Steinman, DVM, Paul B. Stelzner, Gene Stephenson, Richard M. Stepp, DVM, Richard H. Stickney, Henry A. Stikes, William T. Stockhausen, Waldemar D. Stopkey, Ralph D. Stout, William R. Stowasser, Richard Strachan, PhD, Roger D. Stuck, William Alfred Suk, PhD, Lyman E. Summerlin, Kim H. Tan, PhD, Marshall C. Taylor, MD, Stanley Thomas, PhD, John Pelham Thomas, PhD, Stan J. Thomas, PhD, Steven G. Thomasson, Thomas Tighe, Ronald W. Timm, Samuel Weaver Tinsley, PhD, Arthur Toompas, Alvis Greely Turner, PhD, William J. Turpish, Frank M. Tuttle, Robert K. Tyson,

PhD, David L. Uhland, Laura Valdes, John A. VanOrder, Paul Varlashkin, PhD, Denniss E. Voelker, Robert A. Vogler, H. Von Amsberg, PhD, Nicholas C. Vrettos, William Delany Walker, PhD, Jie Wang, PhD, Mansukhlal C. Wani, PhD, W. C. Warlick, Mark R. Warnock, David Warwick, David B. Waters, Jack Watson, Robert B. Watson, James D. Waugh, Norman L. Weaver, Jerome Bernard Weber, PhD, David Weggel, PhD, James T. Welborn, MD, Gregory V. Welch, Frank Welsch, PhD, Edward L. Wentz, Kenneth T. Wheeler, PhD, Stuart R. White, Thomas W. Whitehead Jr., PhD, Brooks M. Whitehurst, James N. Wilkes, Louis A. Williams, MD, Roberts C. Williams Jr., Candler A. Willis, PhD, Cody L. Wilson, PhD, Perry S. Windsor, Gary M. Wisniewski, Richard Lou Witcofski, PhD, Peter Witherell, PhD, Karol Wolicki, MD, G. C. Wolters, J. Lamar Worzel, PhD, Charles A. Yost, Gregory C. D. Young, PhD, Stanley Young, PhD, Thomas R. Zimmerman, Bruce John Zobel, PhD

North Dakota

Joseph E. Adducci, MD, Richard A. Adsero, Robert F. Agnew, MD, James L. Alberta, C. Allard, Donald A. Andersen, PhD, Timothy W. Bartel, Robert J. Bartosh Jr., Armand Bauer, PhD, James H.M. Beaudry, Duane R. Bentz, George Bibel, PhD, Timothy A. Bigelow, PhD, Mike Briggs, Richard E. Broschat, Jeremy J. Brown, Justin Burggroff, Edward C. Carlson, PhD, Jon M. Carroll, Greg D. Dehne, Alan Dexter, PhD, William Erling Dinusson, PhD, John C. Duffey, Mary A. Durick, John W. Eng., PhD, Joe T. Fell, Joe Friedlander, Mark A. Gonzalez, PhD, Robert S. Granlund, James J. Gress, Harvey Gullicks, PhD, Wayne M. Haidle, Steven H. Harris, Harry Lee Holloway, PhD, Bruce Imsdahl, Francis Albin Jacobs, PhD, Dennis R. James, Larry C. Katcher, Ronald C. Koehler, Mark S. Kristy, Troy J. Leingay, O. Victor Lindelow, Kathleen M. Lucas, Rodney G. Lyn, PhD, Calvin G. Messersmith, PhD, Calvin D. Messesmith, PhD, Cameron B. Mikkelsen, DVM, Donald A. Moen, PhD, Duane R. Myron, PhD, John Dennis Nalewaja, PhD, Joel K. Ness, PhD, Randal Ness, James R. Olson, Jim L. Ozbun, PhD, Kellan Pauly, Terry L. Rowland, Casey J. Ryan, David P. Schaaf, Brett Schafer, E. Brett Schafer, Timothy A. Schmidt, Bruce D. Seelig, PhD, Garry Austin Smith, PhD, Leroy A. Spilde, PhD, Dean R. Strinden, MD, Harold Sundgren, Professor Torgenson, Carl S. Vender, Robert J. Werkhoven, John F. Wheeler, Alicia A. Wisnewski, DVM

Ohio

Robert E. Abell, Gene H. Abels, MD, Harold Elwood Adams, PhD, Richard W. Adams, MD, Verne E. Adamson, Kevin Ahlborg, Roy A. Albertson, Steven J. Alessandro, George C. Alexander, DVM, Mary E. Alford, Jennifer M. Alford, Ben C. Allen, PhD, Robert G. Allen, DVM, Carl J. Allesandro, Timothy L. Altier, Patrick Aluotto, PhD, Charles David Amata, PhD, Paul Gerard Amazeen, PhD, Ernest J. Andberg, John P. Anders, MD, Doug E. Andersen, Randa;; H. Anderson, Christopher Anderson, Charles S. Andes, William D. Ankney, Stuart H. Anness, Robert D. Anthony, Clarence R. Apel, MD, Carl Apicella, Kenneth P. Apperson, Richard Apuzzo II, Howard Arbaugh, Mark Armstrong, Harold H. Arndt, Bob Ashworth, Otilia J. Asuncion, MD, William J. Atherton, PhD, Lester C. Auble, Frederick N. Aukeman, Bruce S. Ault, PhD, Neil C. Babb, Kenneth A. Bachmann, PhD, Frank Rider Bacon, Maurice F. Baddour, Keith J. Bagarus, Donald R. Bahnfleth, Roger P. Baker, Robert L. Baker, Benny H. Baker, Gary E. Baker, Fredrick B. Ball, D. Ballal, PhD, William L. Ballis, Evan S. Baltazzi, PhD, William R. Banman, Elmer Alexander Bannan, Zot Barazzotto, Kurt L. Barbee, Donald O. Barici, Anthony Barlow, PhD, Steven J. Barlow, Herbert G. Barth, Robert F. Bartholomew, MD, Benjamin M. Bartilson, James W. Bartos, David L. Bartsch, Samuel J. Basham Jr., Roland E. Bashore, Richard Basinski, Robert Dean Battershell, PhD, Robert Bauman, Donald Beasley, PhD, J. Donald Beasley, PhD, Daniel E. Beasley, Tom B. Bechtel, PhD, Giselle Beeker, Stephen W. Bell, David F. Bellan, John F. Beltz, John Wilfrid Benard, James Harold Benedict, PhD, Ronald G. Benneman, William W. Bennett, George Benzing, MD, Hugh Berckmueller, Alexander T. Berkulis, Andre Bernier, Albert C. Bersticker, Kevin J. Bertermann, James H. Bertke, Larry W. Best, MD, Dennis W. Bethel, William F. Beuth, Lawrence Romaine Bidwell, PhD, Daniel C. Bieberitz, Bill J. Bielek, Donald Bigg, PhD, Ted F. Billington, George Edward Billman, PhD, Layton C. Binon, Matthew C. Birch, Dennis W. Bishop, Michael G. Bissell, MD, James J. Bjaloncik, John F. Blackmer, Marc E. Blankenship, John R. Blasing, Charles William Blewett, PhD, Raymond Blinn, Dexter W. Blome, PhD, James W. Blue, PhD, Paul J. Boczek, Howard Boeing, John E. Bohl, DVM, Edward H. Bollenger, PhD, Edward Harry Bollinger, PhD, Irwin H. Bollinger, DVM, Michael T. Bonnoitt, Peter Frank Bonventre, PhD, Samia Borchers, MD, William Borchers, Dan Borganes, PhD, Dan Borgnaes, PhD, William E. Bosken, Kenwood A. Botzner, Jim D. Boucher, Gerardus D. Bouw, PhD, Richard O. Bowerman, Scott C. Boyer, John H. Boyles Jr., MD, Lincoln L. Braden, Thomas Brady, PhD, Robert E. Brandt, Arthur M. Brate, Jennifer L. Braun, David Braun, Johnny A. Brawner, MD, Bruce H. Brazelton, Merlin Breen, PhD, Jerald R. Brevick,

PhD, Joseph Brinck, Thomas A. Brisken, Gloria C. Britton, Gloria C. Britton, Robert Walter Broge, PhD, John M. Bronstein, PhD, Gordon Brooks, Lawrence U. Brough, Karen Brown, Robert Brown, Timothy H. Brown, Thane A. Brown, Thomas V. Brown, Roy W. Brown, P.T. Brown, Larry D. Brown, John J. Brumbaugh, Kenneth K. Brush, DVM, John B. Brush, Mark R. Bruss, MD, Tom Bryan, Kenneth J. Brzozowski, PhD, Ken Brzozowski, PhD, Gregory J. Brzytwa, Tom Buckleitner, Ronald E. Buckley, Kevin Buddie, Edwin V. Buehler, PhD, David C. Burgess, Martin P. Burke Jr., Amy L. Burke, Robert David Burns, PhD, Jerry W. Burns, John R. Burns, Richard S. Burrows, PhD, B. Burton, PhD, Alan G. Burwinkel, MD, Robert L. Bush, Jeff N. Butler, Richard H. Byers, Garth Arthur Cahoon, PhD, Mike Cameron, John Campagna, Leo V. Campbell, Larry Campbell, David R. Canterbury, Ronald E. Cantor, MD, R. S. Carbonara, PhD, Robert S. Carbonara, PhD, Brenda L. Carr, Gwendowyn B. Carson, PhD, Richard M. Carson, Chuck Carson, Richard Cartnal, PhD, William O. Cass, MD, Thomas J. Castor, Michael Caudill, PhD, Tito Cavallo, MD, Rosemary Louise Centner, William L. Chalmer, PhD, Edwin B. Champagne, PhD, Chiou S. Chen, PhD, Peter Chesney, Paul W. Chester, Joseph S. Chirico, Shyamala Chitaley, PhD, Patricia S. Choban, Frank W. Chorpenning, PhD, Kenneth D. Christman, MD, Ryan A. Chrysler, John E. Cicillian, Kimball Clark, Shane F. Clark, Peter Clarke, James F. Clements, Douglas J. Clow, Steven D. Coder, Steven J. Cohen, Edward Eugene Colby, Clarence Cole, PhD, Christopher J. Cole, John Cole, Edward A. Collins, PhD, Horace Rutter Collins, E. Keith Colyer, David M. Combs, Floyd Sanford Conant, Paul D. Conkel, James K. Conlee, Wayne Mo Connor, William E. Conway, William Edward Cooley, PhD, Jack L. Coomer, Harry C. Cooper, Christopher T. Cordle, PhD, Billy D. Cornelius, Dale R. Cornett, DVM, David George Cornwell, PhD, Norman R. Cox, Aaron S. Coyan, Richard A. Crago, Richard S. Cremisio, PhD, R. S. Cremisio, PhD, Larry G. Criswell, Eugene E. Crosby, Robert Franklin Cross, PhD, D. B. Crouch, Frank Cutshaw Croxton, PhD, Ralph G. Crum, PhD, Richard Lee Cryberg, PhD, Tom E. Ctvrtnicek, Hongjuan Cui, PhD, Bruce A. Currie, Tom P. Currie, Mary J. Custer, James R. Cutre, Joseph M. Czajka, James Thomas Dakin, PhD, James J. Dale, Raphael D'Alonzo, PhD, Henry J. Dammeyer, Richard John Danke, PhD, S. Dantiki, PhD, Rodney C. Darrah, Charles R. Daub, Pierre H. Dauby, PhD, Julian Anthony Davies, PhD, Brian D. Davis, James H. Davis, MD, Mark Davis, Douglas A. Dawes, William W. Dawson, Mike P. Day, Robert E. Dean, Charles W. Dearmon, Ronald W. Decamp, Anthony A. Dechiara, Clarence Ferdinand Decker, PhD, Arthur John Decker, PhD, Rowan B. Decoster, Gerald Degler, Charles D. Degraff, Ken Dejager, John Dejager, Everett DeJager, Robert Mitchell Delcamp, PhD, Joseph F. Denk Sr., Cecil F. Desai, MD, Ravi S. Devara, MD, Paul D. Deverteuil, Edward J. Devillez, PhD, Thomas E. Devoe, James K. Devoe, Richard J. Dick, Winifred Dickinson, PhD, Henry A. Diederichs, John D. Dietsch, MD, Harold L. Dimond, PhD, James S. Dittoe, DVM, Roy Richard Divis, Brown M. Dobyns, PhD, Robert Dodd, Stephen R. Doe, Erich D. Dominik, Charles P. Dorian, David H. Douglas, Robert W. Douglass, PhD, Jeffrey D. Downing, Michael L. Dransman, Harry J. Driedger, Ned E. Druckenbrod, Earl W. Duck, Thomas Joseph Dudek, PhD, Richard E. Dugan, John Durig, D. Durkee, PhD, Michael W. Durner, Professor Dutta, PhD, Leonard A. Duval, T. Dzik, PhD, Jimmy P. Easley, Jared C. Ebbing, Arthur C. Eberle, Paul Edmiston, PhD, Brian Edwards, Gary L. Eilrich, PhD, William Anthony Eisenhardt Jr., PhD, J. David Ekstrum, Klaus Emil Eldridge, PhD, Sylvan D. Eller, W. S. Elliott, Frank E. Ellis, MD, James C. Ellsworth, Richard H. Engelmann, Dale Ensminger, John K. Erbacher, PhD, Robert H. Erdmann, Ted Erickson, Carl Eriksson, George Ernst, PhD, John T. Eschbaugh, Robert H. Essenhigh, PhD, Gustave Alfred Essig, Daniel Esterline, PhD, Frances C. Esteve, Brian K. Fabel, W. J. Fabish, James P. Fadden, David M. Faehnle, William O. Fahrenbruck, Howard Fan, PhD, John M. Farley, David E. Farrell, PhD, David N. Fashimpaur, Sherwood Luther Fawcett, PhD, Leonid Z. Fedner, Robert William Fenn, PhD, Larry Fernandez, Rene Fernandez, Richard J. Fidsihum, Conrad William De Fiebre, PhD, Rex N. Figy, MD, Richard P. Fink, John Martin Finn, PhD, John Fischley, Ira B. Fiscus, David L. Flannery, PhD, Raymond J. Flasck, MD, Russell W. Flax, Wolfgang H. Fleck, James R. Fletcher Jr., Richard Kirby Flitcraft II, M. R. Flitcraft, John Flynn, Dale Force, John Forman, Eric N. Forsberg, Norman A. Fox, Walter J. Frajola, PhD, Charles E. Frank, PhD, Michael Frank, MD, R. Thomas Frazee, Andrew M. Freborg, Anton Freihofner, Billy W. Friar, PhD, John Albert Fridy, PhD, Alfred E. Friedl, Miriam F. Friedlander, MD, Dale J. Friemoth, Hilda K. Frigic, Bret A. Fry, Thomas C. Furnas, PhD, Dennis J. Fuster, Ronald M. Gabel, Frederick Worthington Gage, John H. Galla, MD, Heather Gallacher, PhD, Joan S. Gallagher, PhD, Ethan Charles Galloway, PhD, Stephen J. Ganocy, Harry Richard Garner, Jeanette M. Garr, PhD, Daniel L. Garver, Dan L. Garver, A. D. Gate, Carl Gausewitz, David M. Gausman, Stephen A. Geers Jr., Alexander Salim Geha, Walter B. Geho, PhD, W. Blair Geho, Philip A. Geis, PhD, Elton W. Geist, Nick Genis, Jerome J. Gerda, Ulrich H. Gerlach, PhD, Richard Paul Germann, PhD, Glenn R. Gersch, John E. Getz, Louis Charles Gibbons, PhD, Thomas E. Giffels, Stephen Warner Gilby, PhD, T. J. Gilligan, PhD, W. J. Girdwood, Norbert S. Gizinski, MD, Travis W. Glaze, Daniel Glover, PhD, Myra A. Gold, Richard Goldthwait, PhD, John C. Goon, Manuel E. Gordillo, MD, E. D. Gordon, Scott Gordon, John R. Gorham, PhD, Charles E. Gottschalk, Edward J. Gouvier, Lawrence F. Gradwell, Bob Graham, Otto G. Gramp, Bruce Howard Grasser, Mark A. Gray, David C. Greene, John J. Greene, Dane W. Gregg, N. E. Grell, Frank E. Gren, Daniel R. Grieser, Walter M. Griffith Jr., PhD, Otto Grill, Martin J. Grimm Jr., Raymond L. Grismer, Thomas Albin Grooms, PhD, Percy J. Gros Jr., Percy C. Gros, Steven L. Grose, William C. Grosel, Leo C. Grosser, Henry M> Grotta, PhD, James B. Grow, Andrew P. Grow, Shannon Grubb, William J. Grunenwald, Paul W. Gruner, Douglas A. Gruver, Terry Guckes,

PhD, Robert F. Guenther, Yann G. Guezennec, PhD, Bruce P. Guilliams, Carl P. Gulla, Rand A. Gulvas, Don R. Gum, Atul A. Gupte, Donald T. Guthrie, Ronald Gutwiller, George J. Guzauskas, Robert Morton Haber, PhD, Paul S. Hadorn, PhD, Ron Haeffer, Don C. Haeske, G. Richard Hagee, PhD, George Richard Hagee, Thomas J. Hager, Judd Lewis Hall, PhD, G. P. Hall, Joseph L. Hall, Kent Hall, Matthew R. Halter, Jeffrey V. Handorf, David E. Haney, Wilbur Leason Hankey Jr., PhD, James Hanlon, John J. Hannan, DVM, Sandra Hardy, Richard Harkins, Ronald O. Harma, Steven Harmath, W. T. Harmon, Mary L. Harmon, B. Harper, PhD, Richard E. Hartle, MD, Robert R. Hartsough, Robert Rice Haubrich, PhD, Andrew F. Haumesser, Hans Hauser, Arthur B. Havens, Paul W. Haverkos, Thomas J. Hawk, MD, Robert Hawthorne, Professor Haycox, U. P. Hayduk, Fred Hayduk, Gregory S. Hazlett, George L. Heath, Art L. Hecker, PhD, William H. Hedley, PhD, Edward H. Heineman, Robert J. Heintz Jr., J. Heisey, Kenneth J. Hemmelgarn, Klaus H. Hemsath, PhD, Jerry S. Henderson, Shawn Heneghan, PhD, Hugh M. Henneberry, Paul M. Henry, Al Hepp, PhD, Charles Edward Heredendoff III, PhD, William Lee Hergenrother, PhD, Vernon J. Hershberger, John A. Hersman, Evelyn V. Hess, Mary Lee Hess, Don J. Heuer, Chares R. Hewitt Jr., PhD, Howard Minor Hickman, E. S. Hicks 3rd, Mark S. Hill, Dexter W. Hill, Bob Hill, Don R. Hiltner, Ashley Stewart Hilton, PhD, Bradley T. Hina, R. J. Hipple, Robert T. Hissong, Gary E. Hoam, Richard T. Hoback, MD, Michael Hoch, PhD, David A. Hoecke, Harry R. Hoerr, Bob Hoffee, Mark W. Hoffman, Ralph B. Hoffman, Thomas Hoffman, Scott B. Hoffmann Jr., William A. Hohenstein, Charles M. Hohman, Allen Hoilanson, Thomas J. Holderread, John H. Hollis, Thomas P. Holloran, Edward Hopkins, Howard Horne, Myer George Horowitz, PhD, Lloyd A. Horrocks, PhD, Ralph L. Hough, David D. Houston, Edgar L. Howard, Edward J. Hren, Wilbert N. Hubin, PhD, Norman Thomas Huff, PhD, Dave Huffman, Donald H. Hughes, PhD, Walter P. Huhn, Bruce Lansing Hull, DVM, John H. Hull, Ronald E. Hulsey, Steve A. Hunter, Frank D. Huntley, John O. Hurd, Shakir Husain, PhD, Ira B. Husky, MD, Keith Arthur Huston, PhD, John T. Huston, Darrell A. Hutchinson, Ahmed A. Ibrahim, Douglas K. Iles, Ronald H. Isaac, PhD, Milton S. Isaacson, R. Jackman, John W. Jacob, George D. Jacobs, John W. Jacox, Ralph R. Jaeger, PhD, Alexander A. Jakubowycz, MD, Richard J. Jambor, Jerry James, Blair F. Janson, PhD, F. Jarka, Charles St. Jean, DVM, Lisa A. Jeffrey, Peter Jerabek, George G. Jetter, Vinton H. Jewell, Stanley W. Joehlin, Dennis M. Johns, PhD, Ronald Gene Johnson, PhD, Robert Oscar Johnson, PhD, Lars R. Johnson, William E. Johnson, Wendell Johnson, Fre T. Johnston, Matt Johnston, Kenneth L. Jonas, Don Jones, Daniel J. Joseph, Blaine R. Joyce, R. M. Judy, Frank E. Kalivoda Jr., Harold Kalter, PhD, Antony Kanakkanatt, PhD, James Karom Jr., Victor G. Karpov, PhD, Lewis P. Kasper, Rosalind Kasunick, Vladimir Katovic, PhD, Robert L. Katz, MD, Christopher W. Keefer, Terrence P. Keenan, Harold Marion Keener, PhD, Calvin W. Keeran, Hubert Joseph Keily, PhD, John Eugene Keim, PhD, George E. Kelbly Jr., Joseph H. Keller, Parry J. Keller, Joseph H. Keller, DVM, Joe Keller, Albert Kelly, Thomas A. Kenat, PhD, Jeffrey S. Kennedy, Thomas C. Kennicott, Harold Benton Kepler, Harold E. Kerber, PhD, James Gus Kereiakes, PhD, Vincent J. Kerscher Jr., Jack D. Kerstetter, Ricky D. Kesig, Tom Kesler, Mel Keyes, PhD, John E. Kiefer Jr., Richard W. Kieffer, Donald W. Kifer, Paul John Kikolai, PhD, Arthur M. Killin, Hyun W. Kim, PhD, Harry S. King, PhD, John Frederick Kircher, PhD, James W. Kirchner, Chester Joseph Kishel, PhD, Craig A. Kister, Ronald W. Klenk, Robert Kline, PhD, Lee A. Klopfenstein, MD, David Kloppenburg, Albert Leonard Klosterman, PhD, Kent Knaebel, PhD, Matthew D. Knecht, Slavko Knezevic, MD, Dennis D. Knowles, MD, Arthur T. Koch, PhD, Kevin J. Kock, Ken E. Kodger, Stan Koehlinger, Clint Kohl, PhD, Bernard R. Kokenge, PhD, Frank Komorowski, MD, Daniel R. Kory, PhD, Joseph J. Kotlin, Frank Louis Koucky, PhD, Peter Kovac, J. L. Kovach, PhD, Kenneth W. Krabacher, Deborah J. Krajicek, Eric Russell Kreidler, PhD, Julius Peter Kreier, PhD, Mark L. Kreinbihl, Warren C. Kreye, PhD, William G. Krochta, PhD, David J. Krupp, James R. Krusling, James Kulick, Gordon Kuntz, PhD, Professor Kunz, PhD, Frederick L. Kuonen, David W. Kurtz, PhD, Leonard G. Kutney, James Walter Lacksonen, PhD, Jerry P. Lahmers, DVM, Russell J. Lahut, Alan Van Lair, PhD, George W. Lambrott, Norman J. Lammers, PhD, G. D. Lancaster, Scott A. Landgraf, Jerome B. Lando, PhD, Robt Lane, PhD, Robert Larson, PhD, Robert P. Lattimer, PhD, Duane E. Lau, Robert J. Lauer, Elbert D. Lawrence, MD, Hugh J. Leach, Stephen J. Lebrie, PhD, Lawrence M. Lechko, Michael T. Lee, DVM, James Frederick Leetch, PhD, Kevin Lefler, Jay H. Lehr, PhD, Mark Leifer, MD, Jon Leist, John C. Leite, Bernard J. Leite, Paul W. Leithart, Terry L. Lemley, PhD, John A. Lengel Jr., Mary A. Lenkay, MD, Dean J. Lennard, Ralph Lennerth, Gary A. Lensch, John A. Leonatti, Joseph Leonelli, PhD, Arkadii I. Leonov, PhD, Arkady I. Leonuso, PhD, Fred E. Leupp, Stanley M. Levers, Peter A. Lewis, PhD, Hudnall J. Lewis, MD, Thomas E. Lieser, Charles G. Lindeman, Jonathon P. Llewellyn, Harold R. Lloyd, Shane A. Locke, David A. Lockmeyer, Dwight N. Lockwood, John R. Long, PhD, Roland V. Long, Lawrence E. Long, Daniel Longo, Dan C. Lostoski, Martha Loughlin, Gerard A. Loughran, Rodney R. Louke, Donald F. Lowry, Alan H. Lubell, Hugh H. Lucas, Caroline N. Luhta, Thomas Elwin Lynch, J. Machen, Alex L. MacInnis, Peter Mackenzie, James B. Macknight, Richard Mahard, PhD, Leo R. Maier, PhD, Edward F. Maleszewski, Eugene Malinowksi, PhD, John Malivuk, Irving Malkin, Lancing P. Malusky, PhD, Neil W. Mann, Ronald W. Manus, PhD, David R. Marcus, MD, Joseph Marhefka, Daniel F. Marinucci, Philip C. Marriott, Jack Marshall, Martin D. Marsic, Daniel William Martin, PhD, Frank P. Martin, Jay W. Martin, Joseph P. Martino, PhD, Andrew J. Maslowski, Lester George Massay, PhD, Jim E. Masten, Joseph B. Masternick, B. Matty, John M. Maxfield, MD, Michael Maximovich, PhD, Robert Mayhan, PhD, Terry J. Mazanec, PhD, August C. Mazza, MD, Glenn W. McArdle,

Emerson O. McArthur III, Greg McCall, Gregory W. McCall, Joseph F. McCarthy, Brenda C. McCune, Harry C. McDaniel, Tim W. McDaniel, James N. McDougal, PhD, Kevin C. McGann, MD, James A. McGarry, Robert P. McGough, Philip McGuinness, Gene McKenzie, Irven J. McMahon, Robert H. McMaster, MD, Pearson D. McWane, PhD, Earle M. Mead, Ronald G. Meadows, Dean Meadows, Mitchell I. Meerbaum, Carl P. Meglan, W. Meilander, Walter Meinert, Paul W. Meisel, Steve Meisel, Ame T. Melby, MD, C. Benjamin Meleca, PhD, Mike Melnick, Max G. Menefee, PhD, Harry Winston Mergler, PhD, Robert Edward Merritt, Robert Mertens, PhD, William A. Metcalf, Kenneth A. Metz, A. R. Metzer, Dave Meyer, PhD, Thomas G. Meyer, Fritz D. Meyers, Andrew J. Meyers, Dwight W. Michener, M. B. Mick, Tim K. Mickey, Gerald P. Migletz, George F. Mihalich, Louis C. Mihaly, Frederick John Milford, PhD, Todd Milick, David Miller, PhD, C. Miller, PhD, Raymond E. Miller, PhD, Marlen L. Miller, Laverne L. Miller, Laura S. Miller, Timothy P. Miller, George A. Minges, Dale Minor, Flora Miraldi, PhD, David A. Miskimen, Jay P. Mitchell, David J. Mitchell, MD, Howard R. Mitchell Jr., MD, Ben G. Mitchell, Pradip K. Mitra, Marvin J. Mohlenkamp, PhD, Lars E. Molander, Karl H. Moller, Stephen P. Molnar, PhD, Michael W. Monk, Michael M. Montgomery, Scott M. Moody, PhD, Young I. Moon, PhD, John A. Moraites, John P. Morelock, Stanley L. Morgan, Dave Morgan, P. J. Mormile, Edward C. Morris, Lynn A. Morrison, Brad G. Morse, Richard F. Mortensen, PhD, T. R. Morton, Stewart Wayne Moser, Thomas E. Moskal, PhD, Pual W. Mossey, John D. Mowery, Wayne E. Moyer, Jeffery L. Moyer, Gordon Mark Muchow, PhD, Robert L. Mullen, PhD, David Munn, PhD, Philip C. Munro, PhD, Richard August Muntean, PhD, Robert L. Murdoch, Joel Muse Jr., PhD, Dale W. Musolf, Chrisy M. Myers, DVM, Sam A. Myers, Richard R. Nadalin, Sonia Najjar, PhD, Sang Boo Nam, PhD, John Christopher Nardi, Bhaskara R. Narra, MD, Harry C. Nash, PhD, Ronald O. Neaffer, PhD, John E. Nebergall, Daniel W. Nebert, Glen Ray Needham, PhD, John T. Nenni, Neal M. Nesbitt, James F. Neuenschwandor, Jesse V. Newburn, Simon L. Newman, PhD, Mark A. Newman, Richard S. Newrock, PhD, Thomas Nichols, Dennis A. Nie, John A. Niebauer, Harry D. Niemczyk, PhD, Alan J. Niemira, Samuel Nigro, MD, Henry Nikkel, William E. Noble, MD, Hallan Costello Noltimier, PhD, David B. Norby, Peter J. Nord, PhD, Tim L. Norris, Gregory J. Nortz, Thomas E. Noseworthy, A. Novak, PhD, Edward F. Novak, William E. Nutter, PhD, Elmer J. Obermeyer, Allan O'Brien, MD, Herbert A. Odle, Richard W. Oehler Jr., Robert A. Oetjen, PhD, Pearl Rexford Ogle, PhD, Jack M. Ohmart, Jerry C. Olds, Richard C. Organ, James E. Orwig, Robert R. Osterhout, Dave Osterhout, James Oziomek, PhD, Gilbert E. Pacey, PhD, Frank Patrick Palopoli, PhD, Bob J. Palte, Richard E. Panek, Salvatore R. Pansino, PhD, H. L. Parks, Alice B. Parsons, Stuart Parsons, Charlie Patchett, Geraldine C. Patman, Bruce H. Pauly, Charles W. Pavey, MD, Anthony J. Pearson, PhD, Michael J. Pechan, PhD, Lyman Colt Peck, PhD, Bruce Pedersen, Robert G. Peed, Larry J. Pemberton, Earl R. Pennell, Joel W. Percival, DVM, Joseph C. Perin Jr., Michael D. Perrea, George Perry, PhD, James C. Petrosky, PhD, J. A. Petrusha, Robert W. Pfaff, William H. Pfaff, Douglas R. Pfeiffer, PhD, John R. Pfieffer, Ronald John Pfohl, PhD, Keith Phillips, Clarence R. Piatt, Kathi A. Piergies, Richard E. Pietch, Jeffrey T. Pietz, MD, Charles F. Pilati, PhD, Richard W. Pine, MD, David G. Pinney, Ervin L. Piper, John A. Plenzler, B. Poling, PhD, Donald S. Poole, Herbert G. Popp, Terry Potter, Louis A. Povinelli, PhD, Jean D. Powers, PhD, William G. Preston, William H. Prior, David G. Proctor, PhD, Richard A. Proeschel, Zenon C. Prusas, PhD, Jamie Przybylski, T. O. Purcell, PhD, Abbott Allen Putnam, Leon L. Pyzik, Kristine J. Raab, DVM, M. J. Rabinowitz, PhD, Roger L. Radeloff, Thomas S. Raderstorf, Marvin C. Raether, David E. Rainer, Robert P. Raker, MD, John Ramus, Robert T. Randall, Roberta B. Randall, Oscar Davis Ratnoff, MD, James P. Rauf, Joseph R. Raurora, Park Rayfield, PhD, Harold H. Reader Jr., Larry K. Reddig, Richard L. Reddy, Robert F. Redmond, PhD, Roy Franklin Reeves, PhD, Dean J. Reichenbach, MD, Richard H. Reinhardt, Eugene Reiss, David A. Retterer, R. H. Reuter, PhD, David Stephen Reynolds, MD, Young W. Rhee, MD, Daniel Rhodes, Perry J. Ricciardi, Bernard L. Richards, PhD, Aimee M. Richmond, MD, Thomas Ricketts, N. R. Ricks Jr., Ralph E. Ricksecker, Harold P. Rieck, John Samuel Rieske, PhD, Frederick J. Riess, Ali Rihan, William M. Rike, Doyd T. Riley, PhD, Michelle M. Rising, Malcolm L. Ritchie, PhD, Charles I. Ritchie, Edgardo H. Rivera, MD, Jerald Robertson, Robert L. Robke, Alex F. Roche, PhD, Professor Rodenburg, PhD, Boley J. Rog, DVM, Thomas R. Rolfes, Floyd Eugene Romesberg, PhD, Eldon E. Ronning, PhD, I. C. Rorquist, Frederick R. Rose Jr., William E. Rosenberg, Melvin S. Rosenthal, MD, Mark A. Rosenzweig, Arthur L. Ross, Professor Rostek, PhD, Lloyd B. Roth, John Rottenborn, David L. Rouch, PhD, William R. Rousseau, MD, Trent Rowe, Melinda Rowe, William C. Rowles, Brian Rowles, Csaba Rozsa, PhD, Neil S. Rubin, Stephen A. Ruehlman, Dan J. Rundell, Mark V. Runyon, Charles Runyon, Harry C. Russell, George B. Rutkowski, Willis C. Ryan, Elmer T. Sabo, Edward Sabo, David Sachs, PhD, George S. Sajner, Stephen G. Salay, Seppo Ossian Salminen, PhD, Stuart C. Salmon, PhD, S. C. Sandusky, Sam Sangregory, John R. Sans, PhD, Richard L. Sanson, Michael D. Santry, Fred Saris, PhD, Frank J. Sattler, Rudolph A. Sattler, Lee A. Scabeck, Patrick J. Scarpitti, MD, Rudolph J. Scavuzzo, PhD, Gary A. Schackow, James K. Schaffer, Daniel Scheffel, Timothy William Schenz, PhD, Roger Scherer, PhD, Philip Eowin Schick, PhD, Charles T. Schieman, Richard Schiewetz, Robert E. Schilling, John Schlaechter, Don L. Schlegel, James A. Schlunt, Donald J. Schmitt, Gordon T. Schmucker, Karl. A. Schnapp, Ronald E. Schneider, PhD, Steven M. Schneider, PhD, Joan Matthew Schneider, PhD, David Schneider, John Schneider, Erwin Schnetzer, Mark T. Scholl, Albert William Schreiner, MD, Leo Schrider, Charles R. Schroeder, James W. Schroeder, Franklin D. Schrum Jr., Steve Schulte, Stphen Schulte, Frank Schultz, Thomas A. Schultz, Donalo R. Schuster, Robert R. Schutte, Karl A.

Schwape, Robert C. Schwendenman, James A. Schwickert, Professor Scofield, PhD, James L. Seals, Robert Secor, MD, Jorge F. Seda, Warren George Segelken, PhD, Robert Seigneur, James A. Selasky, Maurie Semel, PhD, James P. Serber, Mark Setele, Christopher E. Shadewald, David A. Shadoan, William Shafer, Jane J. Shaffer, MD, George P. Shaffner, Jeffrey S. Shane, Fred J. Sharn, Fredrick G. Sharp, Robert Shaw, Elwood R. Shaw, Lyle D. Sheckler, Steven A. Shedroff, Paul Sheil, Nadia M. Shenouda, PhD, Douglas A. Sheridan, Paul Griffith Shewmon, PhD, Lee R. Shiozawa, PhD, Leila Shiozawa, Larry Shivak, Andrew Shkolaik, Ted H. Short, PhD, Glenn Sickles, Jerome M. Siekierski, Michael Peter Siklosi, PhD, Arthur Dewitt Sill, PhD, Lester C. Simmons, Hugh W. Simpson, Robert S. Simpson, Allen W. Singer, DVM, Paul E. Sisco, Michael L. Sitko, PhD, Ron Sizemore, Hugh B. Skees, Marek J. Skoskiewicz, MD, Robert B. Skromme, A. Skrzyniecki, PhD, Jerry L. Slama, Raymond J. Slattery, Francis Anthony Sliemers Jr., Allan M. Smillie, PhD, David K. Smith, PhD, Ivan K. Smith, PhD, Mark A. Smith, PhD, Myron R. Smith, Watson C. Smith, Rick A. Smith, Kevin T. Smith, Davey L. Smith, Professor Smithrud, PhD, George Ray Smithson Jr., Cloyd Arten Snavely, PhD, David T. Snelting, Rodney K. Snyder, Joe Snyder, Gifford G. Solem, Thomas A. Somerfield, Thomas M. Sopko, William T. Southards, Larry M. Southwick, Philip Andrew Spanninger, PhD, Richard Clegg Spector, Robert R. Speers, PhD, Hermann A. Spicker, Ernest G. Spittler, PhD, Robert Bruce Spokane, PhD, Richard M. Sprang, Robert Harold Springer, PhD, Allan Springer, PhD, Lindsay E. Spry, Professor Sroub, Thomas M. Stabler, Murray D. Stafford, Larry C. Stalter, Ronald L. Stamm, Norman Weston Standish, PhD, Dann Stapp, Fred Starheim, PhD, Walter Leroy Starkey, PhD, Peter Staudhammer, PhD, D. Stefanescu, PhD, John W. Steinberger, MD, John C. Steiner, MD, David George Stephan, PhD, James P. Stephens, Henry C. Stevens, PhD, Mark Stewart, Ron Stieger, C. Chester Stock, PhD, Brent T. Stojkov, Michael R. Stone, Robert A. Straker, Randall L. Stratton, Carl Richard Strauss, PhD, Gary D. Streby, Richard A. Strong, Warren Stubblebine, PhD, John Stubbles, PhD, C. D. Stuber, PhD, Mark A. Stuever, George E. Sutton, PhD, James Lowell Sutton, Arden W. Swanson, Ronald E. Symens, Widen Tabakoff, PhD, Mowafak M. Taha, Sherwood G. Talbert, Richard F. Tallini, Louis Anthony Tamburino, PhD, Richard R. Tattoli, Thomas L. Taubken, Douglas Hiram Taylor, PhD, David M. Tennent, PhD, Martha Melay Tennent, Lou Testa, Nicholas J. Teteris, MD, James R. Theaker, Lawrence E. Thieben, John B. Thomas, Dudley G. Thomas, Thomas Thompson, PhD, Roger D. Thornton, Paul Thurman, Anthony D. Ticknor, Clyde Raymond Tipton Jr., Kenneth M. Tischler, Sarah A. Tjioe, PhD, Michael J. Toffan, Paul E. Tomes, Daniel Tonn, PhD, Peter J. Torvik, PhD, Daniel Town, PhD, D. A. Towner, William L. Trainor, John H. Trapp, Leora A. Traynor, MD, Michael J. Trimeloni, Charles F. Trivisonno, William Trommer, David V. Trostyanetsky, Harris C. True, Igor Tsukerman, PhD, Mary Ann Tucker, Richard C. Tumbleson, Robert C. Turner, Joseph Tutak, Tony Tye, Russell A. Ulmer, Thomas J. Ulrich, Israel Urieli, PhD, Dave Petrovich Uscheek, Johammes M. Uys, PhD, Johannes M. Uys ScD, PhD, Stephen J. Vamosi, David Van Sice, Sam Vandivort, Brian S. Vandrak, Richrad S. Varga, John A. Varhola, Joseph M. Varvaro, Gregory S. Vassell, Steve Vatovec, Jeff Vaughn, Richard P. Veres, William J. Veroski, Ronald James Versic, PhD, Kent Vickie, Thomas P. Viggiano, Keith E. Vilseck, Robert L. Vitek Sr., James W. Voegele, Joseph C. Vogel, Walter E. Vonau, Lois B. Wachtman, Raymond S. Wagner, W. B. Walcott, John J. Waldron, Michael Wallace, Brent Wallace, Richard F. Wallin, PhD, Eugene J. Walsh, John K. Walsh, Edward P. Waltz, Lance G. Wanamaker, Graham T. Wand, Douglas Eric Ward, PhD, Roscoe Fredrick Ward, Donald E. Washkewicz, Chatrchai Watanakunakorn, MD, Maurice E. Watson, PhD, Timothy E. Weaver, PhD, William M. Weaver, PhD, Allen E. Webster, Donald K. Wedding, Thomas A. Weedon, Brenda Wehner, Brenda Wehnermuck, Carl S. Wehri, MD, Frank Carlin Weimer, PhD, Daniel Weiss, Friedlander D. Weiss, Michael Welch, Elbert J. Weller, John Fengpinct Wen, PhD, Marlin L. Wengerd, Carl Werhi, MD, John C. Werner, David B. West, Clark D. West, Fred Westerman, PhD, Tammy Westerman, Fred Ernst Westermann, PhD, Harry Whitney Wharton, PhD, Robert E. Wheeler, R. E. Whitam, Eugene A. White, MD, Douglas S. White, Thomas J. Whitney, PhD, Charles E. Wickersham, PhD, William T. Wickham, PhD, Lawrence H. Wickstrom, James A. Wiechart, Edward William Wiederhold, Robert Wieneke, Robert George Wiese, PhD, Jesse H. Wilder, Dwight R. Wiles, L. B. Willett, PhD, Paul Williams, Daniel G. Williams, Craig F. Williams, MD, Thomas A. Willke, PhD, Alan J. Willoughby, Robert W. Wilmott, MD, Chester Caldwell Winter, MD, Frederick S. Wintzer, Richard Melvin Wise, PhD, Herbert A. Wise Jr., James M. Withrow, James K. Woessner, Andrew W. Wofford, Donald R. Wogaman, S. Raymond Woll, J. D. Wood, PhD, Jackie Dale Wood, PhD, Malcolm Wood, Jim Woodford, Ted Woods, Professor Woodworth, Gene E. Wright, MD, Nathan A. Wright, Milton Wyman, DVM, R. A. Wynueca, PhD, R. A. Wynveen, PhD, Kefu Xue, PhD, Riad Yammine, Gilbert Yan, Anthony J. Yankel Jr., William Harry Yanko, PhD, Donald J. Yark, Ronald A. Yates, Wilbur Yellin, PhD, Terrill Young, Fred Young, Edward A. Yu, Stanley Zager, PhD, Joseph Zappia, Lawrence E. Zeeb, James W. Zehnder II, R. A. Zeuner, Perry H. Ziel, Steven A. Zilber, Tom L. Zimmerman, PhD, Tommy L. Zimmerman, PhD, Steven P. Zody, Raymond N. Zoerkler, Gary B. Zulauf, John F. Zurawka

Oklahoma

Ernest R. Achterberg, Brian D. Adam, PhD, Albert W. Addington, Robert M. Ahring, PhD, Brian R. Ainley, William L. Albert, James C. Albright, PhD, Ben Alderton, John C. Alexander, Kenneth L. Allen, Craig Allison,

Ivan D. Allred, Ronny G. Altman, Terrell Neils Andersen, PhD, James K. Anderson, Jack R. Anthony, William H. Audley, John B. Aultmann Jr., Dennis D. Baggett, Daniel M. Baker, PhD, Newton C. Baker, Richard B. Banks, Lindsey B. Barnes, MD, David T. Basden, Haskell H. Bass, MD, Robert Batay, David George Batchelder, T. Mack Baugh, Brian Bean, Edward A. Beaumont, Bennett E. Bechtol, Benny E. Bechtol, Bruce M. Bell, PhD, Thomas C. Bennett, Glen L. Berkenbile, MD, Charles W. Bert, PhD, James M. Beyl, Professor Bigelow, PhD, James Biggs, PhD, John Lawrence Bills, PhD, Michael A. Birch, Marshall D. Bishop, Brian H. Blackwell, Larry J. Bledsoe, Robert Blevins, Edward Forrest Blick, PhD, Jack E. Bobek, Terry Bobo, John M. Bohannon, Victor Bond, PhD, Howard William Bost, PhD, John N. Botkin, Clarence Bowers, B. W. Box, Chris Boxell, MD, Barth Bracken, Shawn Braden, Edward Newman Brandt, PhD, Bruce G. Lenn Bray, PhD, Lindell C. Bridges, David A. Brierley, James P. Brill, PhD, Bob Diggs Brown, C. A. Brown, John H. Bryant, Brad D. Burks, Jay B. Burner, Vaud A. Burton, MD, Lee C. Burton, James Robert Burwell, PhD, Gary Buser, P. Edward Byerly, PhD, W. D. Byrd, Warren D. Cadwell, William S. Cagle, Peter K. Camfield, PhD, Jerry L. Camp, John Morgan Campbell, PhD, Jesse Campbell, Philip Jan Cannon, PhD, Alan Carlton, Robert K. Carpenter, Bruce M. Carpenter, John Cassidy Jr., Gene C. Cates, Kenneth F. Cathey, John M. Cegielski Jr., PhD, Raymond Eugene Chapel, Robert C. Charles, R. C. Charles, Jim C. Chase, Kenneth M. Clark, Ken K. Clark, Harris A. Clay, J. C. Clemmer, Terry Cluck, PhD, James H. Cobbs, Joseph B. Cole, William B. Collier, PhD, Kenneth Edward Conway, PhD, Michael C. Cook, Lowell L. Coon, William L. Coppoc, Donald L. Crain, PhD, Rex C. Cramer, Kenneth S. Cressman, Curtis W. Crowe, Billy Crynes, R. Dafoe, Duane C. Dahlgren, Glenn Hilburn Dale, Rodnoosh R. Davari, Herbert G. Davis, Michael J. Davis, Dale E. Dawson, John R. Dean, Roy Dennis, Larry Denny, Lawrence A. Denny, Henry N. Deshazo II, John Robert Dille, MD, Ross J. Dixon, Elliott P. Doane, PhD, Kenneth J. Dormer, PhD, William F. Dost Jr., Professor Dudt, PhD, Professor Dudt, PhD, Donald T. Duke, Larry Dunn, Marcus Durham, PhD, D. Dutton, Jeffrey L. Dwiggins, R. C. Earlougher, Jason Egelston, Abdalla M. Elias, Lloyd S. Elliott, David Allen Ellis, PhD, Robert S. Ellis, MD, Charles F. Engles, Jack F. Epley, Ralph H. Espach, Craig R. Evans, MD, F. Monte Evens, PhD, Arthur C. Falkler, Charles H. Farr, PhD, S. D. Farrar, Clarence Robert Fast, Robert O. Fay, PhD, James K. Fayard, J. Roberto Feige, Robert Fergusen, Louis G. Fernbaugh, Craig Ferris, Franklin E. Fields, Warren V. Filley, Leon Fischer, PhD, Wayne W. Fish, PhD, J. W. Fishback II, John Berton Fisher, PhD, John I. Fisher, Raymond E. Fletcher, Jack Fly, Melton L. Fly, James M. Forgotson, PhD, Bill E. Forney, Lee C. Francis, James M. Franklin, Joes R. Friedman, Profeesor Friess, H. Robert Froning, PhD, S. W. Fruehling, Maryann C. Fuchs, John Gallagher, PhD, Ornald L. Gambrell, Tony G. Gardner, Charles R. Garner, Harvey L. Gaspar, MD, George Hiram Gass, PhD, Rick D. Gdanski, PhD, William C. Geary, Robert L. Geyer, PhD, William A. Giffhorn, Bertis Lamon Glenn, PhD, Kent J. Glesener, Wilmer E. Goad, Leroy Goodman, Scott D. Gordon, Robert G. Graf, Dick Greenly, Dick Greonly, I. Vincent Griffin, Billy D. Griffin, Brandon Griffith, Mark Grigsby, PhD, James I. Grillot, Richard S. Grisham, MD, Fred Grosz, PhD, Dane Gruben, Elard L. Haden, Pablo Hadzeriga, William D. Hake, M. H. Halderson, Thomas G. Halfast, Rick Hall, Phillip M. Hall, Kevin Halstead, Justin Hamlin, Daniel L. Hansen, PhD, Harold Cecil Harder, PhD, Barry A. Hardy, Bryant J. Hardy, Gerald R. Hare, Charles E. Harmon, Charles R. Harvey, C. N. Haskell, Philip J. Hawkins, Anthony V. Hayes, Kendall Hays, Kenneth Heacock, George B. Heckler, James H. Hedges, PhD, Richard Warren Hedlund, PhD, Vinson D. Henderson, Stuart W. Henderson, Henry W. Hennigan, Timothy L. Hermann, Chesley C. Herndon Jr., Barry E. Herr, John P. Herzog, Neil C. Hightower, Irving A. Hill, George W. Hillman, Donald O. Hitzman, Tong Yun Ho, PhD, Joe M. Hodgson, Carl C. Holloway II, PhD, Harvey Holman, James A. Holt, David M. Holy, Wendell A Van Hook, Doug Horton, Rodney T. Houlihan, PhD, Ray A. Howell, Steven P. Huddleston, David A. Hudgins, Kenneth James Hughes, Jerry Hughes, Deanne D. Hughes, W. Bryan Hughes, Ronald Hull, Hubert B. Hunt, Luverne A. Husen, Michael D. Huston, Walter E. Hyde, Rodney D. Ice, PhD, John R. Imel, Lisa Funkhouser Ingle, Donald C. Jacks, Richard J. Jambor, Chet H. Jameson Jr., Vincent Francis Jennemann, PhD, Michael W. Jezercak, PhD, Harlin Dee Johnson, PhD, Terry E. Johnson, H. Dee Johnston, PhD, Harlin D. Johnston, PhD, Bill Johnston, Ralph S. Jones, Pat Joyce, Richard L. Jueschke, Brian O. Keefer, Dan F. Keller, MD, A. L. Kelley, Arthur L. Kelley, W. J. Kelly, PhD, Jim M. Kelly, Tim Kennemer, DVM, John F. Kerr, David R. Kimes, Francis W. King, John G. Kinsey, H. Kleemeier, Gary C. Knight, Jeffrey R. Knoles, Katherine M. Kocan, PhD, Eunsook Tak Koh, PhD, Kurtis Koll, PhD, R. H. Krumme, J. Michael Lacey, J. A. Landrum, Robert B. Lange, Jon LaRue, PhD, Reginald M. Lasater, Kenneth E. Laughrey, Richard Lawson, J. T. Lee, Leo V. Legg, Robert E. Lemmon, PhD, James H. Lieber, James B. Lockhart, Lyle G. Love, Dale D. Lovely, William R. Low III, Justin Lowry, Samuel E. Loy 3rd, Sam E. Loy III, Robert C. Lucas, William Glenn Luce, PhD, Frank Lucenta, C. Luger, Scott E. Lugibihl, Mike S. Mabry, Scott E. Maddox, Bruce H. Mailey, Martin D. Malahy, Scott Maley, T. A. Manhart, Phillip Gordon Manke, PhD, Francis S. Manning, PhD, Sam S. Marbry Jr., Douglas L. Marr, Richard Martin, PhD, Jerry Martin, PhD, Samuel T. Martner, PhD, Ted P. Matson, Wallace I. May, Kevin M. Mayes, David L. McCarley, Douglass A. McClure, Bob M. McCraw, Max P. McDaniel, PhD, Leslie Ernest McDonald, PhD, M. McElroy, PhD, Gregory B. McGowen, Stephen Edward McGuire, PhD, W. D. McIntosh, Cameron R. McLain, Wilfred E. McMurphy, PhD, James M. Mcusic, Ralph M. McVay, Verlin G. Meier, Neal E. Mercer, Dean H. Mikkelson, Larry O. Miller, Gary Miller, Michael G. Mills, Claude E. Mised, Paul L. Mitchell, Bj J. Moon, MD, Donald N. Mooney, David K. Moore, Ronnie G. Morgan, PhD, Jon L. Morgan, Oscar P. Morgan

Jr., O. P. Morgan Jr., Teruo Morishige, PhD, W. Mike Morrison, O. Charles Morrison, W. A. Morse, Ora M. Moten, Michael G. Mount, Joseph F. Mueller, Stephen Nelson, John Nichols, PhD, Leo A. Noll, PhD, Doug Norton, John E. Norvell, PhD, Richard C. Obee, Randy M. Offenberger, Kenneth D. Oglesby, S. J. Orloski, J. Orloski, James Robert Owen, PhD, Bill G. Owen, Fredric Newell Owens, PhD, Bruce Robert Palmer, PhD, Jerald Parker, PhD, Gary L. Parks, Stephen Laurent Parrott, PhD, Pradeep V. Patel, PhD, Charles A. Paulson, R. Payne, H. Peace, Herbert E. Pearson, Ray E. Penick, Raymond E. Penick, Frederic J. Penner, Charles C. Perry Jr., PhD, Raj Phansalkar, PhD, Don A. Phillips, Wallace C. Philoon, PhD, Gerald Pierson, George Pierson, Raymond E. Pletcher, Dennis L. Poindexter, William Jerry Polson, PhD, David E. Powley, Victoria Prevatt, PhD, Geoffrey L. Price, PhD, James E. Pritchard, PhD, Barry Profeta, James K. Purpura, Richard W. Radeka, Benjamin F. Ramsey, Spencer G. Randolph, Gujar N. Rao, PhD, J. B. Red, Harold J. Reddy, Thomas R. Redman, Larry Redmon, PhD, Max E. Reed, PhD, Philip W. Reed, Harold J. Reedy, Homer Eugene Reeves, PhD, Carl J. Regone, B. J. Reid, Don J. Remson, Thomas W. Reynolds, Tom Reynolds, Ken J. Richards, PhD, J. Mark Richardson, PhD, Verlin Richardson, PhD, Olen L. Riggs Jr., PhD, David Rippee, Jerry Lewis Robertson, PhD, Wilbert Joseph Robertson, PhD, Stanley L. Robertson, PhD, Robert L. Rorschach, Jeffrey S. Ross, Dighton Francis Rowan, PhD, Donal E. Ruminer, Larry J. Rummerfield, Geo Rushton, Mamdouh M. Salama, PhD, John T. Sanner, Charles Gordon Sanny, PhD, James E. Schammerhorn, Frank W. Schemm, Dwayne A. Schmidt MD>, Carl F. Schneider Jr., James G. Schofield, Robert G. Schroeder, Roland Schultz, PhD, Charles R. Schwab, Radny Schwab, Charles N. Scott, Robert L. Scott, John H. Seader, Walter E. Seideman, PhD, Lawrence R. Seng, Charles Shackelford, Jack A. Shannon, Brian S. Shaw, William W. Sheehan, MD, Jon P. Sheridan, Adolph Calveran Shotts, John P. Siedle, PhD, Sofner Smith, Jay K. Smith, Sherman E. Smith, Kevin L. Smith, Professor Snavely, Theodore Snider, PhD, Wallace W. Souder, PhD, Thomas C. Spear, Glenn E. Speck, Harry Spring, Robert M. St. John, PhD, John Stark, Gary Franklin Stewart, PhD, Edwin Tanner Still, P. Doug Storts, J. Story, Dennis E. Stover, PhD, George G. Strella, Raymond Walter Suhm, PhD, Gary D. Sump, PhD, Lyll S. Surtees, William D. Sutton, E. W. Sutton, Earl W. Sutton, James A. Svetgoff, Shaun H. Sweiger, DVM, Allen G. Talley, Terry F. Tandy, James R. Taylor, MD, William N. Thams, Cullen Thomas, Barbara J. Thomas, William Hugh Thomason, PhD, Robert R. Thompson, PhD, Timothy R. Thompson, W. H. Thompson Jr., Jimmy L. Thornton, Michael B. Tibbits, Robert Totusek, PhD, Lawrence H. Towell, Harry P. Trivedi, Joe L. Troska, MD, Steven M. Trost, PhD, Billy Tucker, PhD, Bill B. Tucker, PhD, James M. Tully, Charles L. Turner, Brian Turner, Lynn D. Tyler, PhD, Mark W. Valentine, MD, John Warren Vanderveen, PhD, James Milton Vanderwiele, Gary V. Vanmeter, James R. Vaughan, Joseph C. Vaughn, James P. Vaughn, Laval M. Verhalen, PhD, Suzanne Vincent, PhD, Ed Wagner, William D. Wakley, PhD, Charles Wall, Lew Ward, Kenneth K. Warlick, William E. Warnock Jr., Lawrence A. Warzel, PhD, George A. Waters, J. R. Webb, Curtis W. Weittenhiller, Irving P. West, Delmar G. Westover, Gene L. Whitaker, James D. White, PhD, James R. Whiteley, PhD, Joe V. Whiteman, PhD, Thomas L. Whitsett, MD, Michael L. Wiggins, PhD, Keith P. Willson, Timothy M. Wilson, PhD, David B. Wilson, David M. Wilson, Donn Braden Wimmer, William K. Winter, PhD, Richard B. Winters, Thomas H. Wintle, Kenneth Wolgemuth, PhD, K. Wong, PhD, I. K. Wong, PhD, C. Wootton, Wm. P. Wortman, Paul McCoy Wright, PhD, John L. Wright, Bill J. Wright, Demetrios V. Yannimaras, PhD, Donald Yaw, Marvin E. Yost, PhD, Donald F. Zetik, PhD, Donald Frank Zetjk, PhD, Charles W. Ziemer, PhD, John C. Zink, PhD

Oregon

Gail D. Adams, PhD, Fred A. Allehoff, Arthur W. Allsop, Allen A. Alsing, Elmer A. Anderson, PhD, Loran K. Anderson, Kenneth E. Anderson, Micheal J. Anhorn, Stig A. Annestrand, Lynn Apple, Edward E. Ashley, Owen H. Auger, Cyril G. Bader, Eric S. Ball, Brian F. Barnett, Cary N. Barrett, PhD, Earl M. Bates, Bruce L. Bayley, Thomas Erwin Bedell, PhD, Sheeny Behmard, Frederick H. Belz, Ronald Berg, Richard A. Bernhard, Siegried R. Berthelsford, MD, James J. Besemer, Stephen E. Binney, PhD, Guy William Bishop, PhD, Warren M. Bliss, Vern Allen Blumhagen, Sergey Boblcov, Dennis B. Bokovoy, S. Bonar, Susan Boner, Daniel C. Boteler, Dan C. Boteler, William J. Brady, MD, William Henry Brandt, PhD, David Briggs, Karel M. Broda, William J. Brody, MD, James R. Brunner, John D. Bryan, Charles M. Buchzik, John P. Buckinger, Hallie Flowers Bundy, PhD, Edgar M. Burton Jr., Robert E. Bynum, Donald D. Calvin, MD, Steve M. Carlson, A. Eugene Carlson, MD, Glenn Elwin Carman, PhD, Richard A. Carpenter, Richard N. Carter, MD, David Owen Chilcote, PhD, Donald Ernest Chittick, PhD, Duane Christensen, David Thurmond Clark, PhD, C. K. Claycomb, PhD, Cecil K. Claycomb, PhD, Vyvyan S. Clift, Ray W. Clough, John D. Coates, D. W. Coleman, Jerry Colombo, Erik E. Colville, F. N. Cooke, PhD, Rebecca A. Coulsey, Edward A. Crane, Michael A. Creager, Arthur D. Crino, William Craig Cullen, PhD, Stanley E. Cutrer, Michael Daly, PhD, Harold Datfield, Jay C. Davenport, Kirk C. Davis, Fred W. Decker, PhD, Martin J. Dehaas, William David Detlefsen, PhD, William J. DeVey, Lee G. Dickinson, Edward Joseph Dowdy, PhD, Nicholas Drapela, PhD, Arthur B. Drescher, Robert W. Du Priest, John Durbetaki, Owen W. Dykema, Rodney D. Elmore, David M. Enloe, Richard F. Erpelding PC, PhD, Steven P. Eudaly, Clinton Faber, Fred W. Fahner, Gary Farmer, William Farnham, David G. Farthing, PhD, Andrew J. Fergus, Cyrus West Field, PhD, Professor Findorff, Robert

Findorff, D. Findorff, James W. Fitzsimmons, MD, Richard H. Fixott, Bruce Ingram Fleming, PhD, J. Ford, PhD, Steve Fordyce, Dwayne T. Friesen, PhD, Herbert Farley Frolander, PhD, Herbert G. Gascon, Otto M. Gobina, PhD, Jerry J. Gray, Thomas B. Gray, Garrison W. Greenwood, PhD, James Robb Grover, PhD, M. S. Gurney, Christopher T. Haffner, Paul Ellsworth Hammond, PhD, Raymond J. Hardiman, Floyd A. Harrington, John P. Harville, PhD, Paul L. Hathaway, William M. Heerdt, Stanley O. Heinemann, Robert H. Heitmanek, Charles A. Hen, Tom R. Herrmann, PhD, Dennis E. Hess, Clayton Hill, John Donald Hill, DVM, John Holbrook, Norman B. Holman, James Frederick Holmes, PhD, Ronald G. Holscher, Robert D. Hunsucker, PhD, Douglas Hunt, Brad L. Hupy, W. E. Hutley, John F. Hutzenlaub, PhD, Brian J. Imel, Merlyn Isaak, Robert E. Jamison, MD, Ryan M. Jefferis, Yih-Chyun Jenq, PhD, Terrance Johnson, PhD, Karl J. Johnson, Jenri B. Joyaux, Edward Lynn Kaplan, PhD, Larry Kapustka, PhD, Dennis J. Kavanaugh, Ronald W. Kelleher, Robert C. Kieffer, Tatyana P. Kilchugina, PhD, Marion E. Kintner, MD, Donald Kinzer, Gregory F. Kohn, Loren D. Koller, PhD, Carl R. Kostol, MD, Robert W. Koza, David A. Kribs, Leonard J. Krombein, Donald L. Lamar, PhD, Andrew Lambie, Don LaMunyon, PhD, Robert Larsell, Eric Larsen, PhD, Bryan C. Larson, Harold M. Lathrop, DVM, William Orvid Lee, PhD, Guy L. Letourneau, Kenneth W. Lewin, Mark A. Liebe PD, PhD, Kurt D. Liebe, W. J. Lindblad, Garry N. Link, Robert K. Linn, Adam Lis, PhD, Daniel C. Lockwood, Michael Love, Herbert F. Lowe, R. Kent Lundergan, Douglas Mackenzie, MD, J. Malcom, Niels L. Martin, PhD, Philip O. Martinson, Richard R. Mason, PhD, Curtis R. Matteson, Mark W. Matthes, Jerome A. Maurseth, Michael D. McCaffery, Mary McCarthy, MD, Henry F. McKenney, Harold A. McSaaden, MD, Harry H. Mejdell, PhD, Deering D. Melin, Daniel Merfeld, PhD, Paul Louis Merz, PhD, Cameron D. Mierau, Larry D. Miller, Professor Minkin, PhD, Leonid Minkin, PhD, J. Minoff, PhD, Johnny D. Mitchell, Robert H. Mitchell, William A. Mittelstadt, Donovan B. Mogstad, Javid Mohtasham, PhD, Darrell W. Monroe, Larry Wallace Moore, PhD, Joseph T. Morgan, MD, Emile C. Mortier, Jane E. Mossberg, Clifford John Murino, PhD, Ruth Naser, Victor Thomas Neal, PhD, Steven L. Neal, MD, David Michael Nelson, PhD, Harold W. Nichols, William Nisbet, Richard E. Noble, Maya M. Nowakowski, R. L. Nowlin, Gerald O'Bannon, PhD, Laurence B. Oeth, Roger D. Oleeman, PhD, Roger Dean Olleman, Loren K. Olson, Cherri Pancake, PhD, Donald H. Parcel, Albert Marchant Pearson, PhD, Joseph C. Peden lll, MD, Wendell Pepperdine, PhD, Heriberto Petschek, Richard F. Pfeifer, Lincoln Phillippi, Dennis Phillips, PhD, Leroy D. Poindexter, Serge Preston, PhD, J. J. Price III, Casey Jo Price, William E. Purnell, MD, William J. Randall, PhD, Bob Raser, Alfred Ratz, PhD, Jerry Re, Kenneth R. Reed, Joseph Arthur Reed, MD, Michael E. Rehmer, James W. Richards, Jerry O. Richartz, William J. Robinet, Noah E. Robinson, PhD, Arthur B. Robinson, PhD, Joshua A. Robinson, Bethany R. Robinson, Zachary W. Robinson, Arynne L. Robinson, James D. Rodine, PhD, Francis Rogan, Charles Raymond Rohde, PhD, Chris Rouser, K. Rudestam, Lee Chester Ryker, PhD, Michael A. Sandguist, Dennis A. Schantzen, Rolf Schaumann, PhD, Larry Scheckter, PhD, Chester A. Schink, PhD, Dyrk H. Schlingman, Clifford Leroy Schmidt, PhD, Roman A. Schmitt, PhD, Robert M. Schwarze, Doug P. Schwin, Richard N. Seemel, Eric Sharpnack, DVM, Donald K. Shields, Terry Shortridge, Larry D. Shuttlesworth, Jerry A. Siemens, Richard Ernest Siemens, Bruce Siepak, Ronald Smelt, PhD, Deboyd Smith, Troy L. Smith Jr., Everett Southam, PhD, Ronald P. Staehlin, Paul Edward Starkey, Scott M. Steckley, Robert C. Stones, PhD, William L. Strangio, PhD, Robert Leonard Straube, PhD, Charles Strohkirch, Danuta Szalecka, Wojciech Szalecki, PhD, Carson William Taylor, Jerry Tobin, William L. Toffler, Albert L. Tormey, Dah Weh Tsang, PhD, David B. Tyson, Hassel Henry John Van, PhD, R. A. Vollar, James Arthur Vomocil, PhD, Mike Vossen, Orvin Edson Wagner, PhD, A. D. Watt, Susan L. Wechsler, Dennis H. Wessels, MD, Jack A. Weyandt, Richard V. Whiteley Jr., PhD, Chuck F. Wiese, Robert Stanley Winniford, PhD*, C. N. Winningstad, Mark C. Wirfs, George F. Wittkopp, Peter Wolmut, Peter Wyzinski, Jeffry T. Yake, Elisabeth S. Yearick, PhD, Nicholas J. Yonker, Jeffrey Zachman, Donald J. Zarosinksi, Donald J. Zarosinski

Pennsylvania

Joe L. Abriola Jr., David A. Acerni, John R. Ackerman, Roy Melville Adams, PhD, Lionel Paul Adda, PhD, George Aggen, PhD, Thomas I. Agnew, PhD, David J. Akers, Munawwar M. Akhtar, Greg Alan, Eric K. Albert, PhD, James T. Albert, Robert Lee Albright, PhD, Fred Ronald Albright, PhD, Reuben J. Aldrich, Joseph J. Alex, Joe Alex, Harold R. Alexander, Danrick W. Alexander, George L. Allerton, Robert Q. Alleva, Gary W. Allshouse, R. A. Allwein, James A. Aloye, Joseph R. Ambruster, Richard D. Amori, Fred Amsler, MD, David Robert Anderson, PhD, Arvid Anderson, J. Hilbert Anderson, Raynal W. Andrews, Harry N. Andrews, Timothy Andreychek, Edward A. Andrus, Francis M. Angeloni, PhD, Howard P. Angstadt, PhD, Bradley C. Antanaitis, PhD, Bradley C. Anthanaitis, PhD, David R. Appel, Bill Archer, Diane Archer, Desiree A. Armstrong, PhD, James R. Armstrong, DVM, Randall W. Arnold, C. Arnold, Charles W. Arnold, Jerome P. Ashman, Philip R. Askman, Andrew P. Assenmacher, Victor Hugo Auerbach, PhD, Dale A. Augenstein, PhD, Joe Augspurger, PhD, J. Todd Aukerman, Kent P. Bachmann, Walter J. Bagdon, PhD, David George Bailey, PhD, Egon Balas, PhD, W. Loyd Balderson, PhD, W. Lloyd Balderston, PhD, Paul F. Balint, Antonio P. Ballestero Jr., Kent F. Balls, MD, Chad J. Bardone, Philip A. Barilla, Barry L. Barkley, Larry E. Barnes, DVM, L. Bruce Barnett, PhD, Robert M. Barnoff, PhD, James E. Barrick, PhD, Paul Barton, PhD, Patrica W.

Bartusik, Jonathan Langer Bass, PhD, Robert L. Batdorf, PhD, Joe Battista, Carl August Bauer, PhD, Kerry E. Bauer, Michael H. Bauer Jr., Wolfgang Baum, PhD, Kenneth L. Baumert, PhD, A. W. Baumgartner, Richard W. Bayer, Theodore H. Bayer, Buddy A. Beach, James Monroe Beattie, PhD, Frank V. Beaumont, Ellington McHenry Beavers, PhD, Thomas F. Beck, Robert S. Becker, PhD, Robert B. Beelman, PhD, Cari R. Beenenga, David B. Behar, MD, John Behun, PhD, Alan R. Beiderman, William W. Bele, Stanley C. Bell, PhD, George C. Bell, John A. Bellak, Erwin Belohoubek, PhD, David J. Bender, PhD, Daniel W. Bender, Ashley Bengali, PhD, Allen William Benton, PhD, Edward John Benz, Charles R. Bepler, MD, Santo C. Berasi, Alan Berger, William G. Berlinger, David Berry, PhD, Robert Walter Berry, PhD, Christopher Anthony Bertelo, PhD, Joseph M. Beskit, Tirlochan S. Bhat, Paul D. Bianculli, MD, Stanley J. Biel Jr., Richard J. Bielicki, George J. Bierker, Keith L. Bildstein, PhD, Dan A. Billman, Terrence L. Bimle, Lisa Binkley, William W. Bintzer*, James A. Bishop Jr., Richard E. Bishop, Curtis S. Bixler, Jerry M. Blackmon, Douglas R. Blais, DVM, Paul R. Blankenhorn, PhD, Paul J. Blastos, MD, Robert C. Blatz, Harold Frederick Bluhm, Edward S. Bober, David Bochnowich, Bohdan K. Boczkaj, PhD, Kenneth E. Bodek, Gerald R. Bodman, Arthur W. Boesler 3rd, William Emmerson Boggs, N. Charles Bolgiano, PhD, Nicholas Charles Bolgiano, PhD, James C. BolliBon, Jeffery L. Bolze, James M. Bondi, Oliver P. Bonesteel, Charles M. Bonner, Bruce W. Booth, PhD, Frederick Bopp III, PhD, Stuart Boreen, Theodore T. Borek II, Robert Bores, PhD, Paul N. Bossart Jr., Thomas H. Bossler, Aksel Arnold Bothner, PhD, Paul Andre Bouis, PhD, William C. Bowden, Mark Bowen, Dennis L. Bowers, Paul R. Bowers, Ed Bowersox, L. W. Bowman, PhD, Lewis Wilmer Bowman, PhD, Robert S. Bowman, PhD, Gerald L. Bowman, Arthur F. Bowman, Robert Allen Boyer, PhD, John J. Boyle, William Earle Bradley, Keneth A. Brame, Bruce Livingston Bramfitt, PhD, Patrick G. Brannac, Frank J. Braun, James P. Brazel, Darwin Brendlinger, Joseph N. Breston, PhD, Robert N. Brey, P. L Thibaut Brian, PhD, Pierre Leonce T Brian, PhD, C. Carroll Brice, Paul P. Bricknell, MD, Kevin V. Bridge, Randall A. Brink, R. Brisbin, Frederick N. Broberg, E. J. Brock, PhD, Edward C. Broge, PhD, Richard P. Brookman, F. L. Brown, Fitzhugh Lee Brown, James Brubaker, Daniel E. Bruce, Linda Bruce-Gerz, Glenn G. Bruckno, Roger R. Brumbaugh, Jacomina A. Bruno, MD, Jeffrey W. Brunson, Frederick Vincent Brutcher Jr., PhD, Walter T. Bubern, Ralph S. Bucci, Robert C. Buckingham, MD, Daniel E. Bullard, PhD, Jacob Burbea, PhD, Herbert A. Burgman, David M. Burkett, Cynthia A. Burr, John F. Burr, Edward G. Busch, Elsworth R. Buskirk, PhD, James S. Butcofski, MD, Phillip E. Butler, James J. Butler, R. Lee Byers, PhD, Mike Cabirac, John L. Caddell, MD, Craig R. Calabria, PhD, David R. Calderone, Lawrence A. Caliguiri, MD, David S. Callaghan, William R. Camerer 3rd, Robert Camero, Frederick W. Camp, PhD, Shirley Campbell, Robert Campo, PhD, James N. Canfield, Joseph M. Cannella, MD, Frederic S. Capitosti, Anthony P. Caprioli, Steven Carabello, Mario Domenico Carelli, PhD, John Carey, George F. Carini, PhD, Harold Edwin Carley, PhD, Ralph Carlson, PhD, Douglas Carlson, Professor Carlson, Charles Patten Carpenter, PhD, Brad H. Carpenter, Michael J. Carrera, Roger E. Carrier, PhD, Ron A. Carrola, Robert J. Carroll, MD, J. Randall Carroll, Thomas C. Carson, Joanne M. Caruno RW, Floyd L. Cassidy, Ronald E. Castello, Anthony J. Castellone, Robert L. Catherman, MD, David Cattell, PhD, Joseph J. Catto, William J. Cauffman, MD, Edward L. Caulkins, Paul Cazier, Gilbert J. Celedonia, Chris Cellucci, PhD, Nick Cemprola, Zoltan Joseph Cendes, PhD, John J. Cenkner, Samuel Cerni, PhD, George G. Cervenka, John Chadbourne, PhD, Ronald A. Chadderton, PhD, John Chappell, Kenneth Chaquette, Stanley H. Charap, PhD, Edward M. Charney, Edward Chastka, MD, Chi-Yang Cheng, PhD, Kuang Liu Cheng, PhD, John M. Chenosky, Kenneth P. Chepenik, PhD, Joseph R. Chessario, Peter Cheung, PhD, V. Chiappardi, James P. Childress, DVM, D. S. Choi, PhD, Janet C. Christiansen, DVM, Alan Christman, PhD, Kyung Y. Chung, MD, Jon A. Ciotti, Michele A. Cipollone, John S. Clark, Duane Grookett Clarke, PhD, Robert L. Clouse, David A. Cobaugh, Carl Cochrane, Charles W. Coe Ii, David B. Coghlan, Jennifer M. Cohen, PhD, Michael R. Cohen, PhD, Merrill Cohen, MD, James M. Coleman, PhD, Robert E. Coleman, PhD, William Coleman, Wm. E. Coleman, David B. Collins, Christopher J. Commans, Leonard Conapinski, James J. Concilla, Harold Conder, PhD, Albert Carman Condo Jr., Rex B. Conn, MD, Garret H. Conner, MD, Paul W. Conrad, Donald R. Conte, Nicholas N. Coppage, Robert B. Corbett, PhD, John Corcoran, MD, Vincent F. Cordova, William E. Cormier, John Cornell, Kevin Cotchen, Larry Coudriet, Robert A. Cousins, Fred Covelli, Brent W. Cowan, Jeffrey L. Coward, Glenn E. Cowher, Michael F. Cox, Robert L. Cragg, Jonathan Crawford, Michael J. Cribbins, Robert D. Cryer, Dezso L. Csizmadia, Donald E. Cummings, Howard Cunningham, PhD, Francis M. Curran, Ken E. Cutler, George F. Daebeler, W. V. Dailey, James M. Daley, Roy W. Danielsen, Victro M. Danushevsky, PhD, D. K. Davies, PhD, Mark Davis, Frank Robert Dax, Sheldon W. Dean Jr., PhD, Joseph Deblassio, PhD, David R. Debo, William M. Decker, Paul E. DeCusati, PhD, Emil W. Deeg, PhD, Jonh D. Defelice, Vincent A. Degiusto, Andrew Dekker, MD, Paul Dellevigne, John J. DeLuccia, PhD, George T. Demoss, Louis J. Denes, PhD, William E. Dennis, PhD, Norman C. Deno, PhD, Fred E. Derks, T. Derossett, PhD, Bhasker C. Desai, Daniel Frank Desanto, PhD, George R. Desko, Ryan Desko, Neal D. Desruisseaux, PhD, Maurice Deul, Frederick William Deuries, Robert Dewitt, PhD, Ronald K. Dickey, Rodger L. Diehl, Frederick M. Dietrich, Edward J. Diggs III, E.J. Diggs III, Jeffrey A. Dille, Frederick R. Dimasi, Edward R. Dobson, Ronald P. Dodson Jr., James B. Doe, Ralph O. Doederlein, Robert C. Doerr, Michael J. Doherty, MD, Gregory Dolise, Donald E. Dorney, Frank A. Dottore, W. D'Orville Doty, PhD, Charles B. Dougherty, Patrick A. Dougherty, Thomas J. Dowling, Bruce D. Drake, PhD, David F. Drinkhouse, Richard M. Drisko, PhD, Ronald H. Duckstein Jr., Ken

Dudeck, Michael J. Duer, William O. Dulling, Charles Lee Duncan, PhD, Lawrence A. Dunegan, MD, David P. Dunlap, Jack M. Durfee, Henry W. Durrwachter, Dennis J. Duryea, John B. Duryea, J. F. Duvivier, PhD, Jean Fernard Duvivier, James Philip Dux, PhD, Arthur H. Dvinoff, PhD, Judith M. Dvorsky, Francis Gerard Dwyer, PhD, Alan C. Dyar, John C. Dzurino, Russell E. Earle, Douglas A. East, PhD, Richard J. Ebert, Charles Eckman, Charles K. Edge, PhD, H. Paul Ehrlich, PhD, Dion R. Ehrlich, Michael John Elkind, Richard J. Ellis, PhD, K. Donald Ellsworth, Don C. Ellsworth, Franklin T. Emery, PhD, Thomas J. Emory, Robert J. Ennings Heinsohn, PhD, J. Michael Enyedy, Robert Allan Erb, PhD, Richard R. Erickson, PhD, Jan Erikson, PhD, Terry Ess, Ben Edward Evans, PhD, George H. Evans, James M. Eways, Michael William Fabian, PhD, Thomas John Fabish, PhD, Leonard J. Facciani, David R. Fair, Frank G. Falco, Joe Falcone, PhD, Phillip A. Farber, PhD, Robert L. Fark, Mike Farmer, Raymond G. Fasiczka, PhD, Dennis A. Faust, Jerry W. Faust, Donald P. Featherstone, Thomas V. Febbo, James F. Feeman, PhD, Michael L. Fenger, Ronald W. Fenstermaker, Albert B. Ferguson, MD, Michael W. Ferralli, PhD, David E. Field, Albert J. Fill, Michael Fink, James W. Finlay, MD, Frances M. Finn, PhD, Leonard W. Finnell, Robert P. Fischer, Grace Mae Fischer, Douglas A. Fisher, PhD, Wade L. Fite, PhD, Henry J. Fix, R. M. Fleig, Charles W. Fleischmann, PhD, Harry Fleming, Scott J. Fletcher, Robert Flicker, Anthony Foderaro, PhD, James F. Foley, James S. Fontaine Jr., Robert T. Forbes, John W. Foreman, Albert J. Forney, James L. Foster Jr., Timothy J. Fox, Bennett R. Fox, J. Fox, Sandra W. Francis, PhD, Dimitrios N. Frangiadis, William Frankl, MD, Norbert W. Franklin, August R. Freda, PhD, Glenn C. Frederick, Wallace L. Freeman, PhD, L. L. French, Robert L. Frey Sr., Professor Frey, Larry S. Friedline, S. Scott Frielander, Alfred E. Fuchs, Robert B. Fulton, PhD, William R. Funk, Harold R. Fuquay, Samuel T. Furr, Gabriel C. Fusco, PhD, P. S. Gaal, PhD, Peter Gaal, Steven R. Gage, James R. Gage, William A. Gallus, James J. Gambino, Donald J. Gandenberger, Joseph E. Gantz, Richard J. Garbacik, George F. Garcelon, Celso-Ramon Garcia, MD, Albert S. Garofalo, Jennifer J. Garrett, Donald W. Gauntlett, James Gaynor, Donald Gebbie, David Geeza, Roland P. Gehman, Evelyn M. Gemperle, Alfonso R. Gennaro, PhD, Professor Gennaro, PhD, Richard J. Genova, F. Jay Gerchow, Ronald E. Gerdeman, J. Calvin Gerhard, George William Gerhardt, PhD, Henry Dietrich Gerhold, PhD, William P. Gibbons, MD, W. P. Gibbons, MD, Donald G. Gibson, Charles Burroughs Gill, PhD, C. Burroughs Gill, PhD, Michael S. Gillan, Daniel Gillen, Harry K. Gillespie, MD, Thomas E. Gillingham, PhD, Jacques Gilloteaux, PhD, Joseph A. Giordano, MD, Ernie Giovannnitti, Melvin H. Gitlitz, PhD, James S. Glessner, Barbara W. Glockson, PhD, Jonathan C. Goble, Frederick A. Goellner, Thomas W. Goettge, Theodore Philip Goldstein, PhD, Walter J. Goldsworthy, Jonathan M. Golli, Ralph Golta, PhD, Michael S. Goodman, MD, John H. Goodworth, MD, Robert B. Gordon, Henry B. Gorman, Scarlette Z. Gotwals, DVM, Fred L. Graf, Jamieson Graf, Jim Graham, Michael W. Graham, Norman Howard Grant, PhD, D. Gray, PhD, Richard E. Gray, Ronald D. Gray, Kim W. Graybill, Claudius A. Greco, Patricia A. Green, J. D. Green, George M. Greene II, PhD, Miles G. Greenland, Ronald H. Greenwood, Howard M. Greger, Richard A. Gress, Jean Griffin, J. Tyler Griffin, Jonathan M. Grohsman, William G. Gross, Timoth Grotzinger, Joseph S. Grubbs, Gerald William Gruber, PhD, G. W. Gruber, PhD, Geza Gruenwald, PhD, Reed H. Grundy, Gavin G. Guarino, William G. Gunderman, Hans Heinrich Gunth, PhD, Wolfgang H H Gunther, PhD, Ropert E. Gusciora, William A. Gustin, David Lawrence Gustine, PhD, William C. Guyker, James T. Gwinn, George J. Haberman, John A. Habrle, Ross A. Hackel, Richard S. Hackman, Andree H. Hadden, Carl W. Haeseler, PhD, Joseph H. Hafkenschiel, MD, Oskar Hagen, PhD, Jack W. Hager, John A. Haiko, David A. Hair, James L. Hales, John P. Halferty, Kenneth R. Ham, MD, James V. Hamel, PhD, Erwin F. Hamel, Gordon Andrew Hamilton, PhD, Bruce S. Hamilton, James G. Haney, Jerry E. Hankey, Michael L. Haraczy, Michael P. Harasym, Henry Reginald Hardy, PhD, Robert Ian Harker, PhD, Col. E.G. Harper, John A. Harris, PhD, Ernest A. Harrison, PhD, Don E. Harrison, PhD, Clark D. Harrison, T. W. Harshall, George R. Hart, Edward L. Hartmann, Nathan L. Hartwig, PhD, W. P. Hartzell, Richard Harwood, PhD, Michael K. Hatem, Peter L. Hatgelakas, James N. Hauff, Helga Francis Havas, PhD, Eugene J. Hebert, Neil Hedrick, James J. Heger, Donald L. Heim, Walter N. Heine, Paul E. Heise, Wesley E. Heisley, Mike D. Helmlinger, Robert P. Helwick, James C. Henderson, William R. Henning, PhD, David S. Hepler, Roger Myers Herman, PhD, Phillip D. Herman, J. Wilson Hershey, PhD, John E. Herweh, Robert P. Heslop, Eugene L. Hess, PhD, Marilyn E. Hess, PhD, Thomas E. Hess, William John Adrian Vanden Heuvel III, PhD, Kenneth D. Hickey, PhD, Richard T. Hilboky, Hilton F. Hinderliter, PhD, Bruce J. Hinkle, MD, Jan D. Hinrichsen, Millard L. Hinton, Raymond Price Hinton, Raymond G. Hobson, J. Hochendoner, Paul G. Hofbauer, Richard J. Hoffert, Charles F. Hoffman, Thomas F. Hoffman, Joseph L. Hoffmann, Deborah Hokien, PhD, Rodney E. Holderbaum, Philip M. Holladay, PhD, Werner J. Hollendonner, MD, Robert Holleran, Ronald Holmes, Ken A. Holtz, Jerry E. Holtzer, Robert C. Holzwarth, Richard A. Hoover, David A. Hopkins, Richard A. Horenburger, James Hosgood, James W. Howard, Jason Howe, Benjamin F. Howell Jr., PhD, Paul J. Hoyer, PhD, Nicholas C. Hrnjez, Kuo Hom Lee Hsu, PhD, Dale A. Hudson, PhD, John Laurence Hull, John Kenneth Hulm, PhD, Frank Hultgren, PhD, Philip Wilson Humer, PhD, Philip R. Hunt, DVM, Jason S. Hustus, J. J. Huth III, Andre M. Iezzi, Bruce E. Ilgen, DVM, Alvin Richard Ingram, PhD, Patricia A. Innis, Philip George Irwin, PhD, Richard W. Irwin, George Isajiw, MD, Sheldon Erwin Isakoff, PhD, Gordon A. Israelson, William M. Jacobi, PhD, Donald Jaffe, PhD, Shadrach James, MD, Will B. Jamison, Mark Jancin, Ken M. Janke, Samuel M. Jenkins 3rd, Raymond W. Jensen, William A. Jester, PhD, Benjamin L. Jezovnik, Spurgeon S. Johns, M. W.

Johnson, PhD, Alan W. Johnson, PhD, Melvin Walter Johnson, PhD, Dale Johnson, Robert M. Johnson, William Dwight Johnston, PhD, David H. Jones, PhD, Hadley H. Jones, Richard Patterson Jones, Roger F. Jones, Thomas E. Jordan, Robert Kenneth Jordan, Pisica H. Joseph, Donald Joye, PhD, Joseph Malcahi Judge, PhD, Thomas J. Junker, Walter J. Jurasinski, Stephen A. Justham, PhD, Robert Kabel, PhD, George C. Kagcer, PhD, Joh R. Kalafut, Beth Kalmes, James Herbert Kanzelmeyer, PhD, Norman G. Kapko, Naum M. Kaplan, M. Kapolka, PhD, George A. Kappenhagen, Eskil Leannart Karlson, PhD, John J. Karpowicz, Thomas W. Karras, PhD, Ronald L. Kasaback, Thomas Kasuba, Michael J. Kaszyski, Joel Kauffman, PhD, Leo F. Kaufhold, Robert L. Kay, PhD, J. M. Kazan, James D. Keith, Jay H. Kelley, PhD, George R. Kemp Jr., Robert J. Kendra, Edward J. Kenna, Phil L. Kershner, Donald L. Kettering, MD, Z. Khatchadourian, Andrew Kicinski, Anthony Stanley Kidawa, Maclean Kirkwood, Pamela D. Kistler, PhD, Amy G. Klann, PhD, Louis T. Klauder, PhD, John Klein, Donald R. Kleintop, Stanley J. Kletch, Irvin C. Klimas, Gary P. Klipe, Kenneth A. Kloes, James J. Knapik, Dale B. Knepper Jr., Reinhard H. Knerr, PhD, F. James Knight, Thomas E. Kobrick, Donald J. Koestler, Robert N. Kohler, William C. Kohnle, Paul M. Kolich, Paul J. Konkol, Robert Philip Koob, PhD, Joseph Korch, Edward Korostoff, PhD, Randolph M. Kosky, Kishen Koul, PhD, William P. Kovacik, PhD, Edward R. Kovanic, Theodore J. Kowalysayn, Theodore J. Kowalyshan, MD, Theodore J. Kowalyshyn, John G. Kraemer, Drew A. Kramer, Douglas J. Kramm, Thurman R. Kremser Sr., PhD, Arthur F. Krieg, MD, Scott Kriner, Elbert V. Kring, PhD, Professor Krivak, Joseph F. Kroker, Paul H. Krumrine, PhD, Regis W. Kubit, George Kugler, PhD, Casimir A. Kukielka, Andrei Kukushkin, Francis R. Kull, Jeff Kumer, Robert F. Kumpf, Irving B. Kun, Sean T. Kuplean, Scott T. Kupper, Robert John Kurland, PhD, Peter Labosky, PhD, Joseph Thomas Laemmle, PhD, Dale B. Lancaster, PhD, Ronald E. Land, George P. Lang, John M. Langloss, PhD, Thomas S. Larko, Stanley B. Lasday, Joseph Lasecki, John C. Lathrop, Gordon Fyfe Law, Joethel T. Lawler, Eugene J. Lawrie, Robert W. Lawson, Richard D. Leamer, PhD, Paul W. Lebarron, David C. Leber, MD, Donald D. Lee, PhD, Kuo Hom Lee Hsu, PhD, E. J. Leffler, Edward F. Leh, Paul H. Lehman, PhD, Joseph M. Lehman, Ronald G. Lehman, Richard K. Lehman, Harry J. Lehr, David Leiss, Daniel Leiss, Stanley L. Leitsch, Craig Lello, DVM, George W. Leney, Jim W. Lennen, Ronald S. Lenox, PhD, Stephen Lentz, PhD, Stephen K. Lentz, George W. Leroux, David M. Lesak, Richard E. Lesher, Hans E. Leumann, Mark Levi, PhD, William A. Levinson, PhD, John A. Lewis, PhD, Yvonne E. Lewis, D. Lewis, David Leyshon, William T. Liddle, L. Charles Lightfoot, Robert E. Liljestrand, Wayne B. Lingle, Donna J. Link, Jeff M. Linn, DVM, David E. Lipkin, MD, Jack Lipman, Bryan L. Lipp, Mitchell Litt, PhD, Ed Liwerant, John P. Logan, David M. Lolley, MD, Paul S. Lombardo, DVM, Bruce Long, PhD, Richard K. Lordo, Dale R. Lostetter, Harold Lemuel Lovell, PhD, John Robert Lovett, PhD, Mark Lowell, PhD, Douglas E. Lowenhaupt, Jerald Frank Lowry, Ramon G. Lozano, MD, Louis A. Lucchetti, John J. Luciani, Theodore M. Lucidi, Oliver G. Ludwig, PhD, Dennis E. Ludwig, Gene S. Luff, Frank L. Luisi, James W. Lundy, R Dwayne Lunsford, PhD, Peter J. Lusardi, Arthur P. Luthy, John R. Lydic, W. R. Lyman, John J. Lynch, PhD, Bernard J. Lynch, Roland H. Lynch, Digby D. MacDonald, PhD, Robert A. MacFarlane, Lawrence A. Mack, Ronald B. Madison, PhD, Quirico R. Magbojos, MD, Robert Dixon Mair, PhD, Frank Bryant Mallory, PhD, Frederick J. Managhan, James M. Mandera, Lucia Manea, Samuel John Manganello, Kristeen Maniscalco, John H. Manley, PhD, Frederick J. Mannion, PhD, Mark S. Manzanek, Zhi-Hong Mao, PhD, Bernard J. Maopolski, Arnold Marder, PhD, Anthony B. Marino, Constance F. Marsh, Terrel Marshall Jr., PhD, Harold Gene Marshall, PhD, Edward Shaffer Martin, PhD, Peter M. Martin, William F. Martinek, Albert A. Martucci, John T. Maruschak Jr., Putinas V. Masalaitis, Michael P. Mascaro, Philip X. Masciantonio, PhD, Carmine C. Mascoli, PhD, Carmime C. Mascoli, PhD, Michael John Mash, MD, Robert J. Mathieu, Dilip Mathur, PhD, John Matolyak, PhD, Kenneth D. Matthews, Roger L. Mauchline, Frank D. Mawson Jr., William D. Mayercheck, Eugene A. Mazza, T. Ashley McAfoose, Darrell McAlister, Bruce Ronald McAvoy, Richard J. McCarthy, Earl W. McCleerey Sr., Thomas A. McClelland, Robert McCollum, Robert A. McConnell Jr., John E. McCool, Clifford W. McCoy, PhD, Thomas W. McCreary, Dennis E. McCullough, PhD, Wallace G. McCune, MD, David A. McDevitt, Robert H. McDonald, Ronald W. McDonel Jr., Omer H. McGee, Michael F. McGuire, John Philip McKelvey, PhD, Maribel McKelvy, MD, James Alan McLennan, PhD, James I. McMillen, MD, Clyde S. McMillen, DVM, Kenneth M. McNeil, PhD, Paul V. McQuade, Jack L. McSherry, Paul Meakin, PhD, Rick Meckley, Thrygve Richard Meeker, PhD, John Mehltretter, John T. Melick, A. Meliksetian, PhD, Norman D. Melling, Stephen D. Meriney, PhD, Daniel Merkovsky, Wendle P. Mertz, Robert E. Metzger, William E. Michael, Andrew F. Michanowicz, MD, John J. Michlovic, Raymond D. Mikesell, Robert C. Miller, PhD, Foil A. Miller, PhD, Dale Lloyd Miller CQE, Joseph H. Miller, Lewis E. Miller, George J. Miller, Richard Miller, James R. Miller, Michael R. Millhouse, Howard Minckler, Michael J. Minckler, Tom J. Minock, Richard Edward Mistler, PhD, Charles J. Mode, PhD, Arthur F. Moeller, Elwood R. Mohl, C. John Mole, Gregory C. Moll, Harold Gene Monsimer, PhD, Robert H. Montgomery Jr., Michael R. Moore, PhD, Walter Calvin Moore, George M. Morley, Anthony F. Morrocco, David L. Morton, Thomas E. Morton, Lester R. Moskowitz, PhD, Michael T. Moss, Faith E. Moyer, Walter A. Mroziak, Francis Mulcahy, PhD, Thomas G. Mulcavage, James Alan Mullendore, PhD, Karl F. Muller, PhD, Stanley A. Mumma, PhD, Mark C. Mummert, PhD, William James Murphy, PhD, Michael F. Murphy, MD, Steven R. Musial II, R. Musselman, PhD, Glenn A. Musser, Earl Eugene Myers, PhD, Glenn L. Myers, Donna L. Naples, PhD, Michael Nawrocki, Frank H. Neely, Roy H. Neer, Stuart Edmund Neff, PhD, Myron P.

Nehrebecki, Jeremy A. Nelson, Richard Lloyd Nelson, Bradley G. Neubert, DVM, Frederick C. Newton, MD, Gabriel P. Niedziela, Larry A. Niemond, Thomas George Nilan, PhD, Richard M. Ninesteel, David L. Nirschl, DVM, Edward G. Nisbett, George Niznik, PhD, Edward J. Nolan, PhD, James Noss, James P. Novacek, Timothy K. Nytra, Charles J. Odgers, Orin L. Odonel, Randy Oehling, Sakir S. Oguz, Wm S. Oleyar, David A. Oliver, Andrew M. Ondish, John Allyn Ord, Anthony Ordile, William Orlandi, Robert J. Ormesher, Gus G. Orphanides, PhD, Andrew A. Orr, William D. Orville, PhD, William J. Osborne, Richard H. Osman, Carl W. Ott, Michael J. Otto, PhD, Mark Owens, Gary Page, George A. Paleos, Vincent Palmer, PhD, John A. Pantelis, Stephen A. Pany, Charles A. Papacostas, PhD, Spiro J. Pappas, Robert E. Park, PhD, Donald Parker, PhD, Wanda J. Parker, Frederick L. Parks, Fred L. Parks, A. Paterno Parsi, PhD, Ralph Edward Pasceri, PhD, Robert Patarcity, Edward W. Patchell Jr., Mina G. Patel, MD, Christopher J. Patitsas, MD, Richard G. Patrick, Marcia L. Patrick, MD, Donald Patten, R. Dean Patterson, Anton D. Paul, PhD, Timothy P. Pawlak, Charles W. Pearce, PhD, F. Gardimes Pearson, PhD, James B. Pease, Richard G. Pedersen, Donald F. Pegnataro Jr., Stanley J. Penkala, PhD, John Penn, Charles R. Penquite, James M. Perel, PhD, Victor Perez, Phillip J. Persichini, PhD, Eugene Peters, Raymond W. Peterson, Howard L. Petrie, PhD, Garold W. Petrie, Francis X. Petrus, Herhsel L. Phares, Steven J. Phillips, Edward J. Phillips, Louis Pianetti Jr., George J. Piazza, PhD, Earl F. Pickel, William Schuler Pierce, John E. Pierce, Edwin Thomas Pieski, PhD, Philip A. Pilato, PhD, James W. Pillsbury, Kenneth Elmer Pinnow, PhD, Peter E. Pityk Jr., Michael Pizolato, Lucian B. Platt, PhD, Richard P. Platt, Andrew Walter Plonsky, Tom R. Plowright, James H. Poellot, PhD, Max E. Pohl, Frank C. Polidora, MD, James R. Polski, Vincent J. Pongia, John T. Popp, Thomas J. Porsch, Edward S. Porter, Thomas J. Porterfield, Kenneth A. Potter Jr., Wayne G. Pottmeyer, Daniel B. Pourreau, PhD, Joseph J. Poveromo RMI, PhD, Dwight R. Powell, Derek Powell, Donald L. Pratt, PhD, Frank M. Precopio, PhD, George C. Prendergast, PhD, Richard D. Prescott, Henry L. Price, PhD, Joseph W. Proske, PhD, Leonard J. Pruckner, John Pusatari, Thomas H. Putman, PhD, Albert E. Pye, PhD, Louis L. Pytlewski, PhD, Jose J. Quintero Sr., Sidney C. Rabin, MD, John R. Ragase, James J. Rahn, PhD, William W. Ramage, Robert A. Ramser, Ann Randolph, PhD, Vinod E. Rao, Richard J. Ravas, PhD, Martin A. Rawhouser, Stuart Raynolds, PhD, Nelson Henry Reavey-Cantwell, PhD, Kenneth R. Reber Jr., John G. Redic, Issac R. Reed, O. W. Reen, PhD, Eber O. Rees, PhD, John L. Reese, Floyd K. Reeser, Claude Virgil Reich, PhD, Paul H. Reimer, John B. Reinoehl, Robert G. Reis, Phyllis A. Reis, David Reiser, PhD, M. Paul Reiter, Joseph Francis Remar, PhD, Mack Remlinger, Todd Renney, Robert Kenneth Resnik, PhD, William B. Retallick, PhD, William R. Rex, Douglass C. Reynolds, John C. Reynolds, James D. Rhoads, Gary Rhodes, Kevin Rhodes, James P. Rice, Ralph J. Richardson, PhD, Ed Richman, PhD, Tomas Richter, James V. Ricigliano, Russell Kenneth Rickert, Thomas S. Riddle, Karen A. Riley, PhD, William R. Rininger, William D. Roberts, John Roberts, Charles A. Robinson, PhD, Vincent P. Rocco, Delbert W. Rockwell, Thomas E. Rodwick, John Roede, Charles C. Rogala, Daniel E. Rogers, Robert Romancheck, PhD, John A. Romberger, PhD, Ivor C. Rorquist, Kenneth L. Rose, PhD, Ralph Rose, Cloyd J. Rose, Lawrence W. Rosendalc, Charles Thomas Rosenmayer, PhD, Arthur Leonard Ross, PhD, Lawrence Ross, Arthur B. Ross, John W. Ross, Hansjakob Rothenbacher, PhD, Robert J. Roudabush, Thomas S. Rovnak, Bruce F. Rowell, PhD, Arthur M. Royce, Mae K. Rubin, PhD, Douglas Rudenko, Charles G. Rudershansen, PhD, Charles Gerald Rudershausen, PhD, Thomas W. Ruffner, DVM, Brian Mandel Rushton, PhD, Harold D. Rutenberg, MD, Sigmond S. Rutkowski III, John P. Rutter, Frederick M. Ryan, PhD, Robert P. Rynecki, James A. Salsigiver, Douglas H. Sampson, PhD, James B. Sandford, Vincent J. Sands, Foster C. Sankey, John F. Sarnicola, PhD, Daryl Sas, PhD, Sreela Sasi, PhD, Joshua Sasmor, PhD, Ronald Wayne Satz, PhD, Leonard M. Saunders, PhD, Paul R. Saunders, Theodore B. Sauselein, Gayle E. Sauselein, John J. Sayen, MD, John B. Schaefer, Richard W. Scharf, William J. Scharle, Gary Scheeser, Howard Ansel Scheetz, Frank Schell, Frederick H. Schellenberg, Guy R. Schenker, Robert H. Schiesser, PhD, Lee Charles Schisler, PhD, George J. Schlagnhaufer, DVM, James S. Schlonski, Robert W. Schlosser, David J. Schmidle, Terry W. Schmidt, Frederick R. Schneeman, M. C. Schneider, PhD, Charles F. Schneider Jr., Robert L. Schnupp, Robert J. Schoenberger, PhD, Richard Alan Schofield, MD, Giles M. Schonour, Benjamin A. Schramze, Edward C. Schrom, Steven E. Schroth, Herbert A. Schueltz, Thomas J. Schuetz, Charles H. Schultz, PhD, Earl D. Schultz, August H. Schwab, Carl W. Schweiger, Donna P. Scott, William J. Seaman, PhD, Paul J. Sebastian, James L. Seibert, Jack E. Seitner, Donald M. Self, James Edward Seltzer, PhD, John J. Serdy, Frederick Hamilton Sexsmith, PhD, Charles Lewis Shackelford, Alexander C. Shafer Jr., Brian N. Shaffer, John L. Shambaugh, Brett D. Shamory, Terrry Shannon, Cyrus J. Sharer, PhD, William David Sheasley, PhD, Thomas R. Shenenbarger, Henry A. Shenkin, Anthony M. Sherman, PhD, Malcolm H. Sherwood, Bruce M. Shields, Bruce S. Shipley, Glenn A. Shirey, John G. Shively, MD, Joseph Shott, Scott A. Shoup, David P. Shreiner, Mark E. Shuman, PhD, Michael L. Sidor, MD, Charles Signorino, PhD, Leonard Stanton Silbert, PhD, David L. Simon, Stephen G. Simpson, PhD, Craig Simpson, Samuel J. Sims, PhD, Dom C. Sisti, Lawrence H. Skromme, Gary E. Slagel, Joseph Slusser, Richard Smith, PhD, Susan M. Smith, PhD, Robert Lawrence Smith, PhD, James L. Smith, PhD, Herbert L. Smith, PhD, K. Smith, Ken W. Smith Jr., Emerson W. Smith, Barry R. Smoger, Trent Snider, PhD, Dudley C. Snyder, PhD, Robert K. Soberman, PhD, Donald W. Soderlund, Pierce S. Soffronoff, MD, Joseph C. Sofianek, Walter C. Somski, P. Sonnet, PhD, David E. Sonon, Paul T. Spada, William C. Spangenberg, Richard F. Speaker, Jack M. Speece, Paul K. Sperber, Lawrence G. Spielvogel, Joel S. Spira, W. H. Springer, David T. Springer, MD,

William G. Stahl, Randall K. Stahlman, James J. Stango, Frank X. Stanish, MD, Edward A. Stanley, PhD, Francis J. Stanton, Walter F. Staret, Keith E. Starner, Ronald Staut, PhD, Kathleen P. Steele, PhD, Bruce G. Stegman, Timothy J. Stehle, Thomas H. Stehle, Roger Arthur Steiger, PhD, Bob Stein, Michael A. Steinberg, Kenneth Brian Steinbruegge, Edwin G. Steiner, Herbert E. Steinman, Margery L. Stem, Melinda Stephens, PhD, James W. Sterenberg, Linda T. Stern, DVM, Glenn Alexander Stewart, PhD, Chris G. Stewart, Ronald H. Stigler, Richard X. Stimpfle, Henry Joseph Stinger, Richard Floyd Stinson, PhD, Donna J. Stockton, E. F. Stockwell Jr., Paul A. Stoerker, Sam Stone, William C. Stone, William T. Storey, Edward J. Stoves, Carole Stowell, David H. Strome, PhD, David B. Strong, PhD, Dick Strusz, Kenneth Stuccio, William Lyon Studt, PhD, Jeffrey C. Sturm, Wen Su, PhD, John L. Suhrie, Frederick H. Suydam, PhD, Rens H. Swan, Robert W. Swartley, Robert V. Swegel, Don Sweitzer, Joseph W. Swenn, Robert A. Sylvester Jr., Leonard M. Syverson, Johann F. Szautner, Joseph R. Szurek, Allen C. Taffel, William R. Taft, Jim Tallon, Richard C. Tannahill, Timothy R. Tate, Tom L. Tawoda, Larry R. Taylor, PhD, Joseph George Teplick, Dixon Teter, PhD, Vassilios John Theodorides, Richard B. Thomas, PhD, Ramie Herbert Thompson, Ralph N. Thompson, Richard G. Thornhill, Ruth D. Thornton, PhD, Norman E. Tilden, Walter J. Till, Richard H. Tinsman, John anthony Tirpak, PhD, Ronald M. Tirpak, Peter G. Titlow, Charles H. Titus, Richard H. Toland, PhD, Charles J. Touhill, PhD, Lazar Trachtenberg, PhD, Charles W. Tragesser, Dale B. Traupman, Charles L. Tremel Sr., Karl P. Trout, Richard A. Trudel, Robert C. Tucker, Natalia Turaki, PhD, Michael A. Turco, Richard Turiczek, John C. Tverberg, Somdev Tyagi, PhD, Michael J. Uhren, Alexander Ulmer, Robert Urban, MD, William Andrew Uricchio, PhD, David H. Vahlsing, Jerome W. Valenti, Thomas J. Valiknac, Desiree A. J. Van Arman, PhD, Clarence Gordon Van Arman, PhD, C. G. Van Arman, PhD, Drew R. Van Orden, Richard J. Van Pelt, Samuel W. Vance, Richard A. Vandame Jr., Edward F. Vanderbush, Todd P. Vandyke, DVM, David H. Vanhise, Henricus F. Vankessel, Albert Vannice, PhD, Catherine L. Vanzyl, John Vare, Gabriella Anne Varga, PhD, Jaroslav V. Vaverka, PhD, Paul B. Venuto, PhD, Deepak Kumar Verma, PhD, Glenn E. Vest, Edward J. Vidt, Richard J. Virshup, James F. Vogel, Professor Vohs, PhD, Jason K. Vohs, PhD, Philip B. Vollmer, Norman Vorchheimer, PhD, Emil J. Vyskocil, Stephen C. Wagner, Haney N. Wahba, MD, David Allen Walker, PhD, Rex A. Waller, Jeremy L. Walter, PhD, William T. Walter, James C. Walter PG, W. Timothy Walter, Robert A. Walters, Kevin Ward, John R. Warrington, Stephen Shepard Washburne, PhD, George Wasko, Lin K. Watson, Andrew P. Watson, Elwood G. Watson, Jeff Watson, Donald J. Weaver, James P. Webb, Alfred C. Webber, Gary Weber, PhD, Jan R. Weber, MD, Oliver J. Weber, David Weber, George G. Weddell, Charles P. Weeks, Loraine Hubert Weeks, Dwight Wegman, Robert P. Wei, PhD, T. Craig Weidensaul, PhD, Eugene P. Weisser, Irving Wender, PhD, Michael G. Wendling, Kimberly A. Werner, DVM, Laurence N. Wesson, Thomas E. Weyand, PhD, Joe A. Whalen Jr., Jack Whelan, John P. Whiston, DVM, Malcolm Lunt White, PhD, Chuck White, James R. Whitley, Alan M. Whitman, PhD, Stanley L. Whitman, Joseph C. Wilcox, William A. Wilkinson Jr., Robert A. Wilks, Jack P. Willard, Jack H. Willenbrock, PhD, David G. Willey, Brian Williams, PhD, Bernard J. Williams, Armin Guschel Wilson, PhD, Lowell L. Wilson, PhD*, Thomas L. Wilson, Harry W Alton Wilson Jr., Richard Wiltanger, Gilbert Witschard, PhD, Warren F. Witzig, PhD, David Alan Wohleber, PhD, Kenneth Joseph Wohlpart, Bradley D. Wolf, Robert J. Wolfgang, Mark S. Wolfgang, Tammy L. Wolfram, Thomas Hamil Wood, PhD, William A. Wood, PhD, William T. Wood II, C. L. Woodbridge, PhD, Clifford A. Woodbury 3rd, PhD, Kenneth L. Woodruff, David W. Woodward, PhD, Mark J. Woodward, James H. Workley, Dexter V. Wright, Klaus Wuersig, Professor Wynn, PhD, Richard F. Wyse DI, William C. Yager, Richard Howard Yahner, PhD, Michael M. Yanak, Howard W. Yant, Campbell C. Yates, Thomas Lester Yohe, PhD, Charles L. Yordy, Leland L. Young, Robert Youngblood, Larry M. Younkin, PhD, M. Zagorski, John S. Zavacki, PhD, John Zebrowski, Arthur F. Zeglen, Richard F. Zehner, MD, Bruce Allen Zeitlin, Paul S. Zell, James V. Zello, Michael Alan Zemaitis, PhD, Nicholas A. Zemyan, William N. Zilch, Richard Eugene Zindler, PhD, Donald W. Zipse, William C. Zollars, Richard C. Zolper, Charles W. Zubritsky

Puerto Rico

Jaime Arbona-Fazzi, PhD, Robert Fugrer, Francisco J Martinez, Paul Reiter, PhD

Rhode Island

Roger L. Allard, Carl Baer, PhD, David Bainer, Geoffrey Boothroyd, PhD, Anthony Bruzzese, MD, Bruce Caswell, PhD, Deborah M. Ciombor, PhD, Alan Cutting, Jerry Daniels, PhD, Cynthia J. Desjardins, Peter Dewhurst, PhD, David A. Dimeo, DVM, Harry F. Dizoglio, William Theodore Ellison, PhD, Earl T. Faria Jr., John H. Fernandes, PhD, Walter Frederick Freibeage, PhD, Walter Freiberge, PhD, Daniel S. Freitas, Russell F. Geisser, Peter Glanz, PhD, William H. Greenberg, David Steven Greer, MD, Ram S. Gupta, PhD, William J. Hemmerle, PhD, G. Hradil, PhD, Linda Ann Hufnagel, PhD, William Howard Jaco, PhD, Philip N. Johnson, PhD, Edward Samuel Josephson, PhD, Herbert Katz, Mark B. Keene, Harris J. Kenner, Robert LaMontagne, PhD, Mark Lord, JoAnn D. MacMillan, MD, Carleton A. Maine, Jean M. Marshall, PhD, Robley Knight Matthews, PhD, Kilmer Serjus McCully, James P. McGuire, PhD, John P. Mycroft, PhD, John Tse Tso Ning,

PhD, Stanley J. Olson, Anthony D. Palombo, Jay Pike, PhD, Allan Hubert Reed, PhD, August J. Saccoccio, Saul Bernhard Saila, PhD, John A. Shaw, Theodore Smayda, PhD, Homer P. Smith, PhD, Henry R. Sonderegger, Paul D. Spivey, Eugene F. Spring, Barbara S. Stonestreet, MD, Benjamin Y. Sun, Paul A. Sylvia, Joseph Charle Tracy, PhD, Kenneth M. Walsh, Michael F. Wilbur, Robert Zackroff, PhD

South Carolina

Daniel Otis Adam, PhD, Louis W. Adams, PhD, Gary N. Adkins, Donald R. Amett, Douglas J. Anderson, MD, Albert S. Anderson, MD, Gregory B. Arnold, Luther Aull, PhD, Ricardo O. Bach, PhD, Carl Williams Bailey, PhD, J. Austin Ball, MD, Frederic M. Ball, Tom Bane, Seymour Baron, PhD, Charles William Bauknight Jr., PhD, Norman Paul Baumann, PhD, Richard C. Beckert, Wallace B. Behnke Jr., Warrem C. Bergmann, William H. Berry, Robert G. Best, PhD, Minnerd A. Blegen, William Bleimeister, James A. Bloom, Elton T. Booth, Dwight L. Bowen, DVM, Robert Foster Bradley, PhD, Richard G. Braham, Robert S. Brown, PhD, Robert E. Brown, Jay B. Bruggeman, Carl Brunson, Philip Barnes Burt, PhD, Jake D. Butts, Ed F. Byars, PhD, Vincent J. Byrne, Edward C. Cahaly, Michael J. Cain, Thomas L. Campisi, Howard L. Carlson, Nelson W. Carmichael, George R. Caskey, PhD, Rex L. Cassidy, Curtis A. Castell, Frederick J. Chapman, Ken A. Chatto, Thomas Clement Cheng, PhD, Emil A. Chiarito, J. D. Chism, Frank M. Cholewinski, PhD, Allen D. Clabo, PhD, Hugh Kidder Clark, PhD, Fred R. Clayton, PhD, Daniel Codespoti, PhD, William Weber Coffeen, PhD, Benjamin Theodore Cole, PhD, B. Theodore Cole, PhD, Floyd L. Combs, J. J. Connelly, B. M. Cool, PhD, Bingham Mercur Cool, PhD, Horace Corbett, John J. Corcoran, MD, Leon W. Corley, William H. Courtney 3rd, PhD, Andrew K. Courtney, William G. Cousins, Norman J. Cowen, MD, Garnet Roy Craddock, PhD, Irving M. Craig, Steven P. Crawford, Van T. Cribb, George T. Croft, PhD, Carl J. Croft, Donald C. Cronemeyer, PhD, Peter M. Cumbie, PhD, James L. Current, Bobby L. Curry, William C. Daley, Robert F. Dalpiaz, Colgate W. Darden, PhD, William E. Dauksch, Francis Davis, PhD, Murray Daw, PhD, John D. Deden, Joseph V. Depalma, George T. Deschamps, MD, Jerry B. Dickey, Charles R. Dietz, William R. Dill, Dennis R. Dinger, PhD, Thomas J. Dipressi, Louis Dischler, Barry K. Dodson, Richard M. Dom, PhD, Henry Donato, PhD, Theron W. Downes, PhD, Frank E. Driggers, PhD, William W. Duke, MD, Travis K. Durham, Martin D. Egan, Eric P. Erlanson, Laurie N. Ervin, Henry S. Famy, Pauline Farr, Charles J. Fehlig, Jeff S. Feinstein, Oren S. Fletcher, Peter J. Foley, Dennis Martin Forsythe, PhD, R. S. Frank, David E. Franklin, William R. Frazier, Donley D. Freshwater, Carlos Wayne Frick, Jerry F. Friedner, S. Funkhouser, PhD, Joseph E. Furman, MD, Alfred J. Garrett, PhD, Alan A. Genosi, Eric Gerstenberger, George F. Gibbons, John H. Gilliland, Y. H. Gilmore, John H. Gilmore, Lewis W. Goldstein, Charles Gooding, PhD, Stephen H. Goodwin, Nicholas W. Gothard, Christian M. Graf, Sutton L. Graham, Michael Gray, PhD, Ted W. Gray, John T. Gressette, Edwin N. Griffin, Paul P. Griffin, MD, Fredrick Grizmala, Peter P. Hadfalvi, Gerhard Haimberger, Christian M. Hansen, Henry E. Harling, Eric W. Harris, Don Harris, Jim L. Harrison, Grover C. Haynes, Thomas P. Henry, Walter J. Henson, Don Herriott, Arnold L. Hill, Norman E. Hill, Theodore C. Hilton, Kearn H. Hinchman, John C. Hindersman, MD, Stanley H. Hix, Robert Charles Hochel, PhD, Louis J. Hooffstetter, Jeffrey Hopkins, Alvin J. Hotz Jr., Vince Howel, Monte Lee Hyder, PhD, Robert Hiteshew Insley, Walter F. Ivanjack, Wade Jackson, Doyle J. Jaco, William John Jacober, PhD, Jim J. Jacques, Alfred S. Jennings, PhD, S. Tonebraker Jennings, PhD, Wayne H. Jeus, PhD, Roger E. Jinkins, MD, Edwin R. Jones, PhD, Jay H. Jones, DVM, Henry S. Jordan, MD, John W. Kalinowski, Noel Andrew Patrick Kane-Maguise, PhD, Randy F. Keenan, Douglas E. Kennemore, MD, Jere Donald Knight, PhD, James F. Knight, MD, Charles F. Knobeloch, Harry E. Knox, Jacob John Koch, Lawrence A. Kolze, Norman L. Kotraba, Karl Walter Krantz, PhD, Lois B. Krause, PhD, Thomas A. Krueger, Kenneth F. Krzyzaniak, Donald Gene Kubler, PhD, Jerry Roy Lambert, PhD, Carl Leaton Lane, PhD, Louis Leblanc, Burtrand Insung Lee, PhD, Victoria Mary Leitz, PhD, W. Leonard, Lionel E. Lester, Donald F. Looney, Robert Irving Louttit, PhD, Thomas G. MacDonald, MD, D. E. Maguire, Robert E. Malpass, Robert Arthur Malstrom, PhD, Gregory J. Mancini, PhD, Donald G. Manly, PhD, Ronald Marks, PhD, Leif E. Maseng, George T. Matzko, PhD, James Thomas McCarter, Kevin F. McCrary, F. Joseph McCrosson, PhD, David K. McCurry, James D. McDowall, Roger D. Meadows, Tarian M. Mendes, MD, Paul J. Miklo, John D. Miles, Nawin C. Mishra, PhD, Adrian A. Molinaroli, Al Montgomery, Richard Morrison, PhD, William S. Morrow, PhD, Duane Mummett, Edward A. Munns, Julian M. Murrin, John D. Myers, George D. Neale, Robert Nerbun, PhD, Chester Nichols, PhD, K. Okafor, PhD, Thomas E. O'Mara, Russell O'Neal, PhD, George Franci O'Neill, PhD, Errol Glen Orebaugh, PhD, Terry L. Ortner, Joseph E. Owensby, John Michael Palms, PhD, Chanseok Park, PhD, David W. Peltola, Mark Perry, Edward A. Pires, Branko N. Popov, PhD, William F. Prior, MD, William A. Quarles, Robert C. Ranew, Margene G. Ranieri, PhD, Charles H. Ratterree 3rd, Robert H. Reck, MD, Chester Q. Reeves, William J. Reid III, PhD, Professor Reid, PhD, George M. Rentz, Harry E. Ricker, PhD, John S. Riley, PhD, Elizabeth S. Riley, MD, Samuel E. Roberts, Robert E. Robinson, PhD, R. E. Robinson, PhD, Neil E. Rogen, PhD, Emil Roman, George Moore Rothrock, PhD, Carl Sidney Rudisill, PhD, Harvey R. Ruggles, Raymond J. Rulis, Terry W. Ryan, David J. Salisbury, Hubert D. Sammons, MD, Robert M. Sandifer, Marshall C. Sasser, MD, Frederick Charles Schaefer, PhD, Stephen Schaub, Robert C. Schnabel, James F. Scoggin Jr., PhD, Doug P. Seif, DVM, Joe R. Selig, Taze Leonard Senn,

PhD, Jerry W. Shaw, Thomas A. Sherard, Phillip A. Shipp, John E. Shippey, MD, Jonathan R. Shong, DVM, Jack S. Sigaloff, Michael R. Simac, Edwin K. Simpson, Joseph L. Skibba, PhD, Thomas E. Slusher, Glendon C. Smith, Levi Smith III, DVM, Robert W. Smithem, William H. Spence, PhD, Roland B. Spressart, Nesan Sriskanda, PhD, Robert G. Stabrylla, Paul R. Staley, MD, Edwin H. Stein, PhD, Neil I. Steinberg, PhD, Jeff Stevens, Keith C. Stevenson, William Hogue Stewart, PhD, G. David Stewart, Robert M. Stone, PhD, Roger William Strauss, PhD, Terry A. Strout, PhD, Ronald K. Stupar, John Sulkowski, Arthur B. Swett, William B. Sykes, John L. Tate, Victor Terrana, PhD, Wayne Therrell, Hugh S. Thompson, MD, Jerry R. Tindal, Reuben R. Tipton, Laura L. Tovo, PhD, Dean B. Traxler, James S. Trowbridge, Larry S. Trzupek, PhD, Roy R. Turner, Jerry A. Underwood, Ivan S. Valdes, George C. Varner, PhD, Henry E. Vogel, PhD, Peter John Vogelberger, J. Rex Voorhees, Stanley K. Wagher, Earl K. Wallace, MD, Michael F. Warren, Linda A. Weatherell, DVM, James W. Weeg, Joel D. Welch, William B. Wells, William J. Westerman, PhD, Edward Wheaton, Robert L. Whitehead, Lisa C. Williams, James C. Williamson, Nigel F. Wills, Charles A. Wilson, PhD, David N. Wilson, Rick l. Wilson, John E. Wilson, Robert W. Wise, Walter P. Witherspoon Jr., Herbert S. Wood, MD, Roberta L. Wood, Bruce D. Woods, John J. Woods, James M. Woodward, Walt Worsham, PhD, Stephen L. Wythe, PhD, Franklin Arden Young, PhD, William M. Zobel

South Dakota

Jerrold Abernathy, Dale E. Arrington, PhD, B. Askildsen, Michael J. Barr, Larry G. Bauer, PhD, Jan Berkhout, PhD, Lewis F. Brown, PhD, Jerrold L. Brown, Kelly W. Bruns, Neal Busch, PhD, Bruce W. Card, Harold E. Carda, Robert L. Corey, PhD, Cyrus William Cox, C. H. Cracauer, John T. Deniger, Norm Dewit, Raymond Donald Dillon, PhD, Clifford Dean Dybing, PhD, Jose Flores, PhD, A. Martin Gerdes, PhD, Joseph W. Gillen, Thomas F. Guetzloff, PhD, Robert E. Hayes, Clark E. Hendrickson, Professor Hietpas, PhD, Steve Hietpas, PhD, Samuel D. Hohn, Stanley M. Howard, PhD, Dean A. Hyde, Dennis V. Johnson, L. R. Johnson, Benjamin H. Kantack, PhD, Jon J. Kellar, PhD, Martin J. Kiousis, Clyde A. Kirkbride, DVM, Kenneth F. Klenk, PhD, Paul L. Koepsell, PhD, Robert Kohl, PhD, Dave F. Konechne, Jerrod N. Krancler, Robert J. Lacher, PhD, Richard John Landberg, PhD, Wayne K. Larsen, Jaime Aquiles Lescarboura, PhD, David R. Lingenfelter, Willard John Martin, PhD, Stewart L. Moore, Darrell M. Nielsen, Gary Novak, Ronald R. O'Connell, Thomas K. Oliver, PhD, Gary Wilson Omodt, PhD, Paul M. Orecchia, MD, Recayi Pecen, PhD, Andrey Petukhov, PhD, Terje Preber, PhD, John Prodan, Linda E. Rabe, DVM, Perry H. Rahn, PhD, Dale Leslie Reeves, PhD, Charles P. Remund, PhD, D. Roark, PhD, Thomas M. Robertson, Dale M. Rognlie, PhD, Mark A. Rolfes, Michael Harris Roller, PhD, Rolland R. Rue, PhD, Frank W. Rust, Randall J. Sartorius, Anthony V. Schwan, Jayna L. Shewak, Sung Y. Shin, PhD, Arthur Lowell Slyter, PhD, Thane Smith, PhD, Leo H. Spinar, PhD, David A. Stadheim, Larry D. Stetler, PhD, Glen A. Stone, PhD, Bob Suga, MD, Don Talsma, PhD, Chad Timmer, Merlin J. Tipton, E. Brent Turnipseed, PhD, James H. Unruh, Bruggen Theodore Van, PhD, Theodore Van Bruggen, PhD, L. L. Vigoren, Larry L. Wehrkamp, Carl A. Westby, PhD, Dana Windhorst, MD, Thomas J. Wing

Tennessee

Paul Abbett, Anthony F. Adamo, George F. Adams, Rusty Adcock, MD, Robert A. Ahokas, PhD, Igor Alexeff, PhD, Ernest R. Alley, Sally S. Alston, John Stevens Andrews, PhD, Nick J. Antonas, William Archibald Arnold, PhD, Michael W. Ashberry, Larry P. Atkins, Richard Attig, Drury L. Bacon, A. J. Baker, PhD, Allen J. Baker, PhD, Herbert H. Baker, Ollie H. Ballard IV, Joseph S. Ballassai, Derek M. Balskin, John Paul Barach, PhD, Eric N. Barger, Paul Edward Barnett, PhD, A. V. Barnhill Jr., George H. Barrett, Bruce E. Bates, AZ Baumgartner, W. Z. Baumgartner, Samuel E. Beall Jr., Harold R. Beaver, Rogers H. Beckham, William Clarence Bedoit, PhD, Whitten R. Bell, William D. Bernardi, Thomas A. Beyerl, William Robert Bibb, PhD, Alan P. Biddle, PhD, Jerry N. Biery, Charles Biggers, PhD, Chris M. Bird, Alan R. Bishop, Kurt E. Blum, PhD, Charles Nelson Boehms, PhD, Glenn C. Boerke, Walter D. Bond, PhD, Joseph N. Bosnak, Marion R. Bowman, Randal J. Braker, Charles T. Brannon, MD, George R. Bratton Jr., PhD, David M. Breen, Marcus N. Bressler, W. R. Briley, PhD, Frank Broome, Lloyd L. Brown, Marvin K. Brown, Jim Brown, Charles Bryson, E. Clark Buchi, Edsel Tony Bucovaz, PhD, Larry D. Buess, George Jule Buntley, PhD, Edward Walter Burke, PhD, Calvin C. Burwell, T. Bush, Joel T. Cademartori Sr., George Barret Caflisch, PhD, Edward George Caflisch, PhD, Steven G. Caldwell, PhD, Warren Elwood Campbell, PhD, Susan B. Campbell, MD, Colin Campbell, MD, Jay Caplan, James D. Carrier, James B. Carson, Randy R. Casey, Don S. Cassell, Mural F. Castleberry, Carroll W. Chambliss, PhD, James V. Christian, Warner Howard Christie, PhD, Habte G. Churnet, PhD, Charles D. Cissna, Terry A. Clark, Grady Wayne Clarke, PhD, William L. Cleland, David Matzen Close, PhD, Walter G. Cochran, Frederick L. Cole, MD, Jack A. Coleman, PhD, Jimmie Lee Collins, PhD, George T. Condo, PhD, Gregory J. Condon, MD, Ronald A. Conley, Nelson F. Consumo, David Franklin Cope, PhD, A. D. Copeland, Donald Copinger, Francis Merritt Cordell, PhD, Patrick Core, Eugene Costa, George S. Cowan, MD, Michael A. Crabb, John Craft, Nicholas T. Crafton, Sterling R. Craig, MD, Harvey A. Crouch, James J. Cudahy, John W. Dabbs, PhD, John Irvin Dale III, PhD, J. Marshall Davenport, Wallace Davis Jr., PhD, Montie

G. Davis, PhD, Annita Davis, Philip M. Deatherage, MD, James H. Deaver, PhD, W. Edward Deeds, PhD, Roy L. Dehart, Joe DeLay, PhD, Ordean Silas Den, PhD, Mark F. Dewitt, Albert W. Diddle, MD, John Willard Dix, Mathilda Doorley, Nicholas M. Dorko, DVM, Wesley C. Dorothy, Robert S. Dotson, Thomas C. Dougherty, Michael A. Dudas, Peter L. Duncanson, Linwood B. Dunn, Joseph F. Edwards, Kenneth J. Eger, PhD, Alice Elliott, PhD, J. Michael Epps, Kenneth Eric Estes, David Richard Fagerburg, PhD, Gregory Farmer, Scot N. Field, James Rodney Field, MD, Patrick Carl Fischer, PhD, Gary A. Flandro, PhD, Darryl Fontaine, MD, Bobby Forrester, Edwin P. Foster, PhD, Samuel E. French, PhD, Walter L. Frisbie, Charles S. Fullgraf, PhD, Charles P. Furney Jr., Nelson Fuson, PhD, John F. Fuzek, PhD, Michael L. Gamblin, Floyd Wayne Garber, PhD, Ted D. Garretson, Paul C. Gate, Dale Gedcke, PhD, Larry Gerdom, PhD, Richard L. Giannelli, Edward Hinsdale Gleason Jr., PhD, David L. Gleaves, DVM, Grayce Goertz, PhD, Virginie M. Goffaux, DVM, Clifford M. Gordon, Lee M. Gossick, Nicholas J. Gotten, MD, John L. Grady, MD, Peter Michael Gresshoff, Ben O. Griffith, DVM, William E. Griggs, Ronald Grost, Frederick Peter Guengerich, PhD, Kenneth H. Gum, Donald B. Habersberger, Robert M. Hackett, PhD, Ronald D. Hackett, Werner B. Halbeck, William H. Hall, DVM, Alvin V. Hall, Frank J. Hall Jr., Robert C. Hall, MD, Howard L. Hamilton, DVM, Zhihua Han, PhD, Samuel Leroy Hansard, PhD, William Otto Harms, PhD, Joseph J. Hasper, Stephen G. Hauser, Robert M. Hayes, PhD, James Leslie Heaberlin, Rita W. Heckrotte, Zachary Adolphus Henry, PhD, Gregory W. Henry, Rudolph W. Hensel, Paul E. Hensley, Robert B. Hern, Mark A. Herrmann, Jesse L. Hicks, Willena M. Highsmith, Lloyd L. Hiler, PhD, Milbrey D. Hinrichs, MD, Shean J. Hobbs, DVM, Mary E. Hohs, PhD, Kenneth L. Holberg, MD, Kenneth L. Holbert, MD, David H. Holcomb, Ray Walter Holland, PhD, Richard M. Holland, James N. Holliday, PhD, Kenneth A. Hollowell, Johnny B. Holmes, PhD, Howard F. Holmes, PhD, Moon W. Hong, MD, Fred E. Hossler, PhD, Mark Hostetter, W. Andes Hoyt, Charlie Huddleston, James M. Hudgins, Phillip Montgomery Hudnall, PhD, B. Jerry L. Huff, PhD, B. Jerry L. Huff, PhD, Ericq Huffine, Gene E. Huffine, Ray J. Hufft, Jack A. Hurlbert, Randall L. Hurt, Paul Henry Hutcheson, PhD, James H. Hutchinson, PhD, Bradley J. Huttenhoff, John Anthony Hyatt, PhD, Bradley G. Hyde, Tony Indriolo, John B. Irwin, MD, Donathan M. Ivey, Virgil E. James, PhD, King W. Jamison, PhD, Carol C. Jenkins, Gordon Jonas, Larry S. Jones, Frank E. Jordan, MD, D. Junker, PhD, Karl Philip Kammann Jr., PhD, Jon R. Katze, PhD, Lee Keel, PhD, Robert S. Kehrman, Shane Kelley, PhD, Minton J. Kelly, PhD, Francis T. Kenney, PhD, William Kerrigan, Elbert R. Key, RK Kibbe, Vincent J. Kidd, PhD, Clyde E. Kidd, Earl T. Kilbourne Jr., Anthony W. Kilroy, MD, Keith McCoy Kimbrell, MD, Brice Whitman Kinyon, Bruce W. Kinyon, Ronald Lloyd Klueh, PhD, Terence Edward Creasey Knee, PhD, Roger Lee Kroosma, PhD, Kenneth A. Kuiken, PhD, Nipha Kumar, Robert E. Laine, Paris Lee Lambdin, PhD, Scott Lane, Paul B. Langford, PhD, William D. Lansford, Andrew Lasslo, PhD, Steven Lay, PhD, Paul D. Lee, PhD, Mark P. Lee, Larry H. Lee, MD, Carl F. Leitten Jr., Gary Lynn Lentz, PhD, James P. Lester, MD, Edward Lewis, PhD, Russell J. Lewis, PhD, R. Lewis, Pamela A. Lewis, Alex Lim, Robert Simpson Livingston, PhD, Davie L. Lloyd, Bryan H. Long, Martin Shelling Longmire, PhD, Allen Loy, MD, Martin S. Lubell, C. T. Ludwig, Alvin L. Luttrell, James E. Lyne, PhD, William Southern Lyon, Harold Lyons, PhD, P. MacDougall, PhD, Thomas M. Mahany, PhD, Arthur A. Manthey, PhD, W. Marking, PhD, Daniel E. Martin, Eric Martin, DVM, Mario Martini, PhD, Michael R. Mason, Frank W. McBride, W. E. McBrown, D. A. McCauley, Jack R. McCormick, David L. McCullev, Ted Painter McDonald, PhD, Robert McElroy, Alfred Frank McFee, PhD, Charles Robert McGhee, PhD, Jack W. McGill, Michael B. McGinn, Robert R. McGinnis, Winford R. McGowan, MD, Mark E. McGuire, Carl McHargue, PhD, Sam L. McIllwain, Steve A. McNeely, PhD, David W. McNeil, MD, Fred E. Meadows, Thomas Meek, PhD, Norman L. Meyer, PhD, James L. Miller, PhD, Joseph A. Miller, Truesdell C. Miller, Hugh H. Mills, PhD, Benjamin J. Mills, A. Wallace Mitchell, Standley L. Moore, Robert L. Morgan, PhD, John R. Morgan, MD, Relbue Marvin Morgan, James R. Morris, Stephen Morrow, Gordon Moughon, MD, Vernon B. Muirhead, James Thomas Murrell, PhD, Michael G. Muse, Robert F. Naegele, PhD, Roy A. Nance, Clinton Brooks Nash, PhD, Roland W. Nash, MD, John Neblett, MD, James Warwick Nehls, PhD, John Henry Neiler, PhD, Billy C. Nesbett, MD, Marlyn Newhouse, PhD, John A. Niemeyer, J. Nix, Larry L. Nixon, Thomas J. Nolan, Edward David North, PhD, E. D. North, PhD, Scott H. Northrup, PhD, B. G. Norwood, MD, Clinton B. Nosh, PhD, Lester C. Oakes, James J. Oakes, David Q. Offutt, PhD, Dom W. Oliver, Donald R. Overdorf, Donald F. Owen, Professor Oyelola, PhD, Andreas M. Papas, PhD, William M. Pardue, Robert Paret, MD, Clifford R. Parten, PhD, Arvid Pasto, PhD, James Wynford Pate, MD, James Holton Patric, Billy Patterson, Wayne A. Pavinich, Dewitt Allen Payne, PhD, Earl Pearson, PhD, Jesse T. Perry, Raymond A. Peters, Lawrence Marc Pfeffer, PhD, Brian M. Phillipi, Bob Pinner, Russell Pitzer, David Martin Pond, PhD, M. G. Popik, Glenn W. Prager, Ron Pressnell, Lee Puckett, T. Linn Pugh, Jasmine Pui, John Joseph Quinn, PhD, David R. Raden, Harmon Hobson Ramey, PhD, Ronald D. Reasonover, Ronnie G. Reece, Larry D. Reed, MD, Daniel P. Renfroe, David L. Rex, Joe E. Reynold, Joseph E. Reynolds, Mary Rhyne, Thomas E. Richardson, John R. Rickard CCE, Tewfik E. Rizk, MD, Kelly R. Robbins, PhD, Russel H. Robbins, MD, Dewayne Roberts, PhD, William C. Roberts, DVM, Robert J. Roselli, PhD, Ross F. Russell, PhD, Nicholas Charles Russin, PhD, Edmond P. Ryan, PhD, Michael Salazar, PhD, Jacqueline B. Sales, Norman R. Saliba, MD, L. C. Sammons Jr., MD, Ann G. Samples, John Paul Sanders, PhD, Greg J. Sandlin, Michael Santella, PhD, Royce O. Sayer, PhD, Fred Martin Schell, PhD, Glenn C. Schmidt, Marcel R. Schmorak, PhD, Edward G. Schneider, PhD, John D. Schoolfield, T. a. Schuler,

Theodore A. Schuler, Stephen J. Schultenover, MD, Marc G. Schurger, Todd F. Scott, Paul Bruce Selby, PhD, John R. Sellars, MD, Kirk L. Sessions, PhD, Nelson Severinghaus Jr., Allan Shack, James R. Shackleford III, PhD, Kenneth Shappely, John J. Shea Jr., Gerald L. Shell, Gordon Sherman, PhD, Frederick A. Sherrin, Thomas F. Shultz, Roland G. Siegfried, Suman Priyadarshi Harain Sin, PhD, Priyadarshi Narain Sin, PhD, W. Keith Sloan, Nathan H. Sloane, PhD, Timothy Slone, Glendon William Smalley, PhD, Dan R. Smith, DVM, Rocky W. Smith, Richard Smith, Robert Edwin Smylie, Alan Solomon, MD, Reza E. Soltani, MD, John V. Spencer, William Kenneth Stair, PhD, William P. Stallworth, MD, George N. Starr, Richard Stauffer, William David Stewart, MD, F. D. Sticht, Norton Duane Strommen, PhD, Victor W. Stuyvesant, Skip Swanner, Don E. Syler, Donald W. Tansil, MD, Gordon J. Taras, Douglas E. Tate, Robert C. Taylor, Byron Taylor, Sherle R. Thompson, DVM, Elton R. Thompson, Donald C. Thompson Ph, MD, Ker C. Thomson, Eyvind Thor, PhD, John G. Thweatt, PhD, John L. Tilstra, MD, Norman Henry Tolk, PhD, Harmon L. Towne, Anthony Trabue, MD, Rex Trammell, Jeffrey T. Travis, Nicholas Tsambassis, Ella Victoria Turner, PhD, David Turner, MD, Ed Tyczkowski, PhD, James E. Vath, Robert D. Vick, Richard A. Vognild, Bruce E. Walker, PhD, Samuel J. Walley, PhD, F. John Walter, PhD, W. D. Watkins, William D. Watkins, Marshall Tredway Watson, PhD, David J. Wehrly, MD, Marion R. Wells, PhD, Theodore Allen Welton, PhD, James J. Wert, PhD, Professor Wescott, PhD, Lyle D. Wescott Jr., PhD, John L. White, PhD, Alan Wayne White, PhD, Jerry M. Whiting, PhD, Alan L. Whiton, MD, Phil P. Wilbourn, Alan Wilks, Horace E. Williams, PhD, Doug Williams, Giles W. Willis III, James E. Wilson, Al Wilson, David M. Winkeljohn, Craig Wise, Cyrus Wymer Wiser, PhD, Robert C. Wolfe, John Lewis Wood, PhD, Robert H. Wood, MD, Robert Wood, B. D. Wyse, PhD, Ying C. Yee, PhD, Craig S. Young, Curt Zimmerman

Texas

Wyatt E. Abbitt III, Eugene Abbott, Albert S. Abdullah, DVM, Alan E. Abel, Marshall W. Abernathy, Grady L. Ables, John W. Achee Sr., Gene L. Ackerman, Donald O. Acrey, John Edgar Adams, PhD, Gerald J. Adams, PhD, Wilton T. Adams, PhD, Kent A. Adams, Daniel B. Adams Jr., N. Adams, Steve W. Adams, William D. Adams, Roy B. Adams, Jim D. Adams, William J. Adams Jr., Robert E. Adcock, George Adcock, Marshall B. Addison, PhD, Wilder Adkins, Michael F. Adkins, Perry Lee Adkisson, PhD, Steve E. Aeschbach, Frederick A. Agdern, David Agerton, PhD, Mark Ahlert, Thane Akins, Kenneth O. Albers, Robert M. Albrecht, Robert Alexander, Dennis J. Alexander, Rex Alford, Robert L. Alford, David Allen, PhD, James L. Allen, PhD, Thomas Hunter Allen, PhD, F. J. Allen, Stewart J. Allen, John L. Allen, Randall Allen, Randall W. Allison, Terry G. Allison, George J. Allman, Terry Alltson, Jorge L. Alonso, Ali Yulmaz Alper, John Henry Alsop, PhD, George A. Alther, Vern J. Always, James I. Alyea, Bonnie B. Amos, PhD, James P. Amy, Kenneth L. Ancell, Larry Anderson, PhD, David O. Anderson, PhD, Mark Anderson, Fred G. Anderson, MD, Richard C. Anderson, P. Jennings Anderson, Keith R. Anderson, Greg J. Anderson, Reece B. Anderson, C. M. Anderson Jr., Gilbert M. Andreen, Douglas Andress, T. Angelosaute, Robert H. Angevine, Elizabeth Y. Anthony, PhD, John K. Applegath, Harry D. Arber, Leon M. Arceneaux, William Ard, Christopher Arend, John W. Argue, Robert L. Arms, James E. Armstrong, Lowell Todd Armstrong, Glenn M. Armstrong, Edwin L. Arnold, Herbert K. Arnold, David Arnold, Lester C. Arnwine, Charles H. Asbill, Maynard B. Ashley, Wayne A. Ashley, Monroe Ashworth, Robert S. Ashworth, Curtis L. Atchley, James Athanasion, Arthur C. Atkins, Stanley L. Atnipp, William R. Aufricht, Richard Aurisano, PhD, Joeseph D. Aurizio, Brian E. Ausburn, Harold T. Austin, Ward H. Austin, Jon R. Averhoff, Nathan M. Avery, William P. Aycock, Robert C. Ayers Jr., PhD, Bill E. Babyak, Patrick J. Back, J. Robert Bacon, Tanwir A. Badar, T. Dale Badgwell, Jay K. Baggs, Vincent P. Baglioni, Georgw C. Bagnall, R. A. Baile, C. Bailey, Dane E. Bailey, John A. Bailleu, Robert M. Bailliet, Lee Edward Baker, PhD, Gilbert Baker, Howard T. Baker, Francis J. Balash, Brent P. Balcer, Edgar E. Baldridge, Steven J. Baldwin, Amir Balfas, P. Balis, Craig Balistrire, Jerry C. Ball, Harold N. Ballard, Ashok M. Balsaver, MD, Jerome E. Banasik Sr., John J. Banchetti, Robert D. Bankhead, Attila D. Banki, James Noel Baptist, PhD, Bill Barbee, Anslem H. Barber Jr., Paul Barber, Robert A. Bardo, O'Gene W. Barkemeyer, Theodore S. Barker, Eli F. Barker, Alex Barlowen, Allen L. Barnes, PhD, Mike Barnett, William J. Barnett, Linard T. Baron, Clem A. Barrere, PhD, Damian G. Barrett, Timothy M. Barrett, MD, Christopher M. Barrett, Leland L. Barrington, Oscar N. Barron, Allen C. Barron, Thomas D. Barrow, PhD, Paul W. Barrows, PhD, John Bartel, PhD, B. Bartley, PhD, Hugh B. Barton, Jerry G. Bartos, William P. Bartow, William L. Basham, PhD, George M. Baskin, Andy H. Batey, PhD, Stuart L. Battarbee, Jack L. Battle, Mark S. Bauer, Frederick C. Bauhof, Bernard D. Bauman, PhD, Max Baumeister, John E. Baures, Steve Bayless, Stephen L. Baylock, Melvin A. Bayne, Clifton W. Beach, Charles Beach, Dwight Beach Jr., Bobby Joe Beakley, Paula Thornton Beall, PhD, Terry W. Beall, Bobby D. Beall, MD, James F. Beall, Arthur L. Bear, James B. Beard, PhD, Thomas L. Beard, Reginald H. Bearsley, David C. Beaty, Weldon H. Beauchamp, PhD, Edward G. Beauchamp, Bill Beck, Curt B. Beck, Thomas G. Becnel, Rudolph J. Bednarz, Kenneth E. Beeney, H. Dale Beggs, PhD, Howard Dale Beggs, PhD, Francis Joseph Behal, PhD, Greg P. Behrens, Anthony J. Beilman, Deanna K. Belanger, Richard J. Belanger, Howard F. Bell, Jeffrey Bell, Thomas H. Belter, Randy L. Bena, Gilbert G. Bending, Robert G. Bening, Robert I. Benner, William F. Bennett, PhD, Professor Bennett, Alan Bennett, R. S. Bennett, Faycelo L. Bensaid, Fred

C. Benson, PhD, Harold E. Benson, Robert Lloyd Benson, Kenneth E. Benton, Leonidas A. Berdugo, Brian Berger, MD, T. F. Berger, C. B. Bergin, Mike Bergsmg, Eric N. Berkhimer, Jerry D. Berlin, PhD, David T. Berlin, Franklin Sogandares Bernal, PhD, John R. Berryhill, PhD, James E. Berryman, Robert G. Bertagne, Allen J. Bertagne, Robert K. Bethel, G. W. Bettge, George W. Bettge, Austin Wortham Betts*, Richard O. Beyea, Swapan K. Bhattacharlee, PhD, John M. Biancardi, Peter W. Bickers, Lewis J. Bicking Jr., Edward R. Biehl, PhD, Donald N. Bigbie, Dean Bilden, Charles R. Bills, John R. Birdwell, Gene R. Birdwell, Craig E. Bisceglia, James Merlin Bisett, Amin Bishara, Richard S. Bishop, PhD, Richard H. Bishop, PhD, Joe O. Bishop, Robert Bittle, PhD, Benny Bixenman, Sidney C. Bjorlie, Dean Black, PhD, Victoria V. Black, MD, Dennis Black, Sammy M. Black, William L. Black, Randolph Russell Blackburn, Brian D. Blackburn, James C. Blackmon, Steve Blaglock, Bruce A. Blake, William M. Bland Jr., Linda D. Blankenship, Scott C. Blanton, PhD, George Albert Blay, PhD, G. Blaylock, W. N. Bledsoe, Donald J. Blickwede, PhD, Roger P. Bligh, Stan Blossom, Tedde R. Blunck, Lawrence T. Boatman, Don A. Boatman, Joshua T. Boatwright, Robert S. Bobbitt, Thomas C. Boberg, PhD, Stephen J. Bodnar, PhD, Hollis Boehme, PhD, Jack E. Boers, PhD, David H. Boes, Johnny Boggs, Leslie K. Bogle, Kevin Michael Bohacs, PhD, Mark Bohm, Johhnie J. Bohuslav, Jack C. Bokros, PhD, Regnald A. Boles, Robert B. Boley, PhD, C. Bollfrass, Charles Bollfrass, Frank R. Bollig, Gerald J. Bologna, John Joseph Boltralik, Sam T. Boltz Jr., Patrick L. Bond, Arnold B. Booker, R. J. Boomer, Daniel R. Boone, Paul M. Boonen, PhD, Larry Boos, PhD, Edward J. Booth, James H. Bordelon, Jerry Borges, J. Borin, Annette H. Borkowski, Sebastian R. Borrello, Randal S. Bose, David Boss, Robert Bossung, George M. Boswell, MD, Kathleen B. Bottroff, Harry Elmo Bovay Jr., Roger L. Bowers, Randy Bowie, Gary R. Bowles, Lamar D. Bowles, John T. Boyce, Phillip A. Boyd, PhD, Robert Boyd III, Jimmy W. Boyd REM, Robert Ernst Boyer, PhD, Brad B. Boyer, Sherry L. Brackeen, Brett K. Bracken, James C. Brackmor, Vincent H. Bradley, MD, Samuel Bradshaw, Charles M. Bradshaw, Bruce B. Brand, Richard Brand, Stanley George Brandenberger, PhD, Robert E. Brandt, Thomas Brandt, Raymond Brannan, PhD, Michael S. Brannan, Ross E. Brannian, Glenn S. Brant, William H. Branum, Jeffrey M. Braun, Bruce G. Bray, PhD, Carl W. Bray, James F. Brayton, William Breach, Theodore M. Breaux, Jimmy L. Breazeale, MD, Kenneth J. Breazeale, Bob Breeze, Martin Bregman, PhD, B. M. Breining, Berryman M. Breining, Harry L. Brendgen, John H. Bress, J. R. Brewer, Herbert L. Brewer, James H. Bridges, Claudia Briell, W. Briggs, PhD, Arthur R. Briggs, Robert A. Brimmer, MD, Niz Brissette, Earl Bristow, Ronald A. Britton, Morris L. Britton, MD, Michael W. Britton, Paul R. Brochu, Howard M. Brock, James P. Brock, MD, H. Kent Brock, Russell G. Broecklemann, Phiilip F. Bronowitz, John D. Bronson, Mark A. Bronston, PhD, James Elwood Brooks, PhD, Kent Brooks, PhD, Britt E. Brooks, Royce G. Brooks, John R. Brose, Thomas S. Brough, Jack F. Browder Jr., Rick A. Brower, Leonard F. Brown Jr., PhD, Murray Allison Brown, PhD, Robert G. Brown, PhD, Glenn Lamar Brown, PhD, Byron L. Brown, MD, Steven Brown, Brenda E. Brown, Charles D. Brown, Jim Brown, John T. Brown, Charles R. Brown ll, Jimmy D. Browning, Thomas Broyles, David L. Bruce, MD, George H. Bruce, Paul L. Bruce, Sandra Bruce, Roy S. Brucy, MD, Herman M. Bruechner, DVM, Robert L. Brueck, Larry W. Bruestle, DVM, Tim D. Brumit, MD, Lowell D. Brumley, Harrison T. Brundage, Allen Brune, Scott R. Bryan, Michael David Bryant, PhD, Thomas L. Bryant, John M. Bryant, Charles B. Bucek, Chris R. Buchwald, Charles G. Buckingham, MD, Ellis P. Bucklen, Jack B. Buckley, J. Fred Bucy Jr., PhD, Travis L. Budlong, Kenneth D. Bulin, Paul L. Buller Jr., Rex G. Bullock, Rich Bullock, William H. Bunch Jr., John M. Bunch, Douglas A. Buol, James Burckhard, Brian Burges, Roy A. Burgess, David T. Burke, David S. Burkhalter, James F. Burkholder, Jeffrey C. Burkman, Ralph D. Burks, Ned Burleson, PhD, D. Burleson, PhD, James E. Burnham, Robert B. Burnham, Robert W. Burnop, John D. Burns, Stanley S. Burns, William P. Burpeau Jr., W. F. Burroughs, Arthur B. Busbey, PhD, Donald L. Buscarello, Harry H. Bush Jr., Russel L. Bush, Houston D. Butcher, Arthur P. Buthod, O. Doyle Butler, Don W. Butler, Dennis L. Butler, Bruce L. Butterfield, Charles J. Butterick, Joe W. Button, Byron R. Byars Jr., Nelson Byman, Richard Dowell Byrd, PhD, Edwin Cable, C. Cadenhead, PhD, Stephen A. Cady, James E. Caffey, PhD, Harry J. Cain III, Gregory S. Caine, James B. Caldwell, PhD, Brian S. Calhoun, Ray L. Calkins, PhD, Michael J. Callaghan, PhD, Mike Callahan, Mickey J. Callanan, Lester H. Callaway, Robert Mac Callum, PhD, David D. Calvert, Richardo E. Calvo, PhD, Lee Cambre, Harvey A. Campbell, Lynn D. Campbell, Steve K. Campbell, C. David Campbell, MD, R. L. Campbell, MD, Richard J. Cancemi, MD, Joe A. Cantlon, Hengshu Cao, PhD, Juan J. Capello, MD, Ronald W. Capps, PhD, Philip H. Carlisle, David R. Carlson, Thomas Carlson, Lawrence O. Carlson, Roy F. Carlson, David C. Carlyle, PhD, Walter J. Carmoney, MD, Peyton Carnes, Spencer Carnes, B. Ronadl Carnes, David Carpenter, Leo C. Carr, Brent Carruth, Charles D. Carson, PhD, Joseph O. Carter, J. O. Carter, Steven L. Carter, Greg Carter, E. Forrest Carter, Aubrey Lee Cartwright Jr., PhD, Louis B. Caruana, PhD, Louis M. Caruana, Ralph V. Caruth, Audra B. Cary, Eddie Case, Jeffrey J. Casey, John R. Cassata, Patrick Cassidy, PhD, Ralph J. Castille, Joseph L. Castillo, Ron Castleton, Raphael A. Castro, Xiaolong Cat, PhD, Ken D. Caughron, James C. Causey "MAE, CSP", P. G. Cavazos, Bob C. Cavender, Arthur Vorce Chadwick, PhD, John Chadwick, Barry Chamberlain, Samuel Z. Chamberlin, William S. Chambless, MD, Michael M. Chan, Clarence R. Chandler, Tyne-Hsien Chang, PhD, William Charowhas, Vanieca L. Charvat, Thomas J. Chastant, Ashok K. Chatterjee, Lynn Chcoran, R. S. Cheaney, Curtis A. Cheatham, Paul S. Check, Jimmie L. Cherry, Robert F. Chesnik, Wm. Chewning, William J. Chewning, Russell Chianelli, PhD, Thomas W. Childers, James H. Childres, James N. Childs, Michael J. Chiles,

William M. Chop Jr., Ceasar C. Chopp, Peter S. Chrapliwy, PhD, Ron V. Christensen, Don Christensen, David Christiansen, James P. Chudleigh, MD, C. R. Chung, MD, J. Joseph Ciavarra Jr., Charles J. Cilfone, Charlie J. Cilfone, Atlam M. Citzler Jr., Edwin J. Claassen Jr., PhD, Gary D. Clack, John D. Clader, PhD, Gregory S. Claine, James B. Clark, PhD, Gene W. Clark, J. Donald Clark, Randall D. Clark, Richard T. Clark, Robey H. Clark, Ewell A. Clarke, David B. Clarton, PhD, Calvin Class, PhD, Nick W. Classen, Don Clauson, David Clayton, PhD, William Clayton, Arthur M. Clendenin, W. J. Clift, Fred W. Clinard, J. T. Cline, James T. Cline, Robert E. Cliver, Aaron Close, Mike Clumper, Thomas John Clunie, PhD, William Cobb, Jon F. Cobb, Howard L. Cobb, John H. Cochrane, MD, J. R. Cockerham, Jerry R. Cockerham, William H. Cockerham, Joseph W. Coddou, Charles A. Cody, Curtis Coe, Charles R. Cofer, William R. Coffelt, James D. Coffman, John R. Cogdell, PhD, Clayton Coker, Tom B. Coker, Ralph Coker, Glennq P. Coker, Glenn P. Coker, Joseph F. Colangelo, W. B. Colburn, John F. Cole, PhD, Frank W. Cole, Douglas E. Cole, Forrest Donald Colegrove, PhD, Bobby Coleman, Woodrow W. Coleman, Richard A. Coleman, Don S. Collida, Charles A. Collins, Glynn C. Collins, Ted Collins Jr., Stephen L. Collins, William P. Collins, Bruce G. Collippns Jr., Nicholas E. Combs, John S. Comeaux, William T. Comiskey, Hanson Cone, MD, Carter B. Conlin, Jack D. Connally, MD, H. E. Connell Jr., Ralph L. Conrad, Jesus Constante, Arthur B. Cook, Preston K. Cook, Ann S. Cook, Steven C. Cook, Wendell C. Cook, Douglas H. Cook, Willis R. Cooke, Edward F. Cooke, James M. Cooksey, Denton Arthur Cooley, MD, Daniel F. Cooley, Gordon Cooper, PhD, John C. Cooper, Thomas B. Coopwood, MD, M. Yavuz Corapcioglu, PhD, Jim Corbit, David L. Corder, Eugene Core, Wayland Corgill, Henry E. Corke, PhD, Jimmie A. Corley, Robert L. Cornelius, Holley M. Cornette, Suzanne L. Corrigan, John Corrigan III, Kenneth M. Cory, J. Paul Costa, Mark J. Costello, Steven A. Costello, Richard O. Cottie, William R. Cotton, PhD*, Spencer M. Cotton, Marcus L. Countiss, Gary R. Countryman, Galen L. Coupe, Chris E. Covert, Kenneth W. Covey, Daniel Francis Cowan, Tracy Cowan, Robert S. Cowperthwait, Alice D. Cox, MD, Don C. Cox, Jerry D. Cox, Bruce W. Cox, DVM, Leon W. Cox, Dan M. Cox, David L. Cox, Hiram M. Cox, James A. Cox, Edward Jethro Cragoe Jr., PhD, John A. Craig, Jerry L. Crain, Glenn D. Crain, Richard D. Cramer, John R. Crandall, David C. Crane, PhD, James F. Cravens, Lionel W. Craver, PhD, Doyle Craver, Ken Craver, Russell S. Cravey, Duane Austin Crawford, Carter D. Crawford, James D. Crawford, Don L. Crawford, Ron Creamer, Wendell R. Creech, Prentice G. Creel, T. C. Creese, Sondra L. Creighton, Peter A. Crisi, Harold W. Criswell, J. L. Crittenden, Dan W. Crofts, Thomas J. Crosier, Don W. Cross, George A. Cross, Morgan L. Crow, Carroll M. Crull, Harry A. Crumbling, E. L. Crump, Eligio D. Cruz Jr., Tihamer Zoltan Csaky, MD, Donald Cudmore, Samuel F. Culberson, A. S. Cullick, PhD, Reid M. Cuming, Tom Cundiff, R. Walter Cunningham, PhD, Peter A. Curka, MD, Clarence L. Curl, Gene Curry, Timmy F. Curry, Rankin A. Curtis, Stuart C. Curtis, Charles E. Cusack Jr., Herman C. Custard, PhD, Hugo C. da Silva, PhD, Calvin Daetwyler, PhD, Harry Martin Dahl, PhD, Peter C. Daigle, Joseph W. Dalley, PhD, Jesse Leroy Dally, PhD, John J. Dalnoky, Charles Dalton, PhD, James U. Daly, Jerome Samuel Danburg, PhD, Richard M. Dangelo, Adam S. Daniec, Stephen R. Daniel, Scott Daniel, Ned R. Daniels, William R. Dannels, Ronald Darby, PhD, Frank Darden, David H. Darling, MD, Russ C. Darr, Joseph E. Darsey, Hriday Das, PhD, George F. Davenport, Gregory W. Daves, Cecil W. Davidson, Thomas Davidson, Emlyn B. Davies, PhD, Frances M. Davis, PhD, Wendell Davis, PhD, Joseph R. Davis, PhD, Theodore R. Davis, Donald J. Davis, D. K. Davis, Alfred Davis, James F. Davis, H. R. Dawson, PhD, Wyatt W. Dawson Jr., Mike Dawson, Raul J. De Los Reyes, MD, Frederik Willem De Wette, PhD, William D. Dean, Roy F. Dearmore, MD, Michael L. Deason, DVM, Bobby Charles Deaton, PhD, Charles Deboisblanc, Francis E. Debons, PhD, Howard E. Decker, David G. Deeken, Philip E. Deering, John M. Dees, John A. Deffner, William L. Deginder, Rebecca Dehlinger, John Dehn, PhD, Charles F. Deiterich, Phillip T. DeLassus, PhD, Kirk F. Delaune, Nicholas Delillo, PhD, Mark T. Delinger, Lyman D. Demand, J. Demarest, PhD, David C. DeMartini, PhD, Scott C. Denison Jr., David R. Denley, PhD, Richard G. Denney, Richard S. Dennis, Al M. Denson, James Denton, Newton B. Derby, Edward B. Derry, Peter A. Desantis, Rodney F. Deschamps, John J. Deshazo, John W. Devine, Louis Dewenter, Jim Dews, Lloyd Dhren, Paul J. Dial, John K. Dibitz, Marvin R. Dietel, Ronald L. Diggs, Robert Garling Dillard, Roger McCormick Dille, Howard Dingman, R. W. Dirks, James P. Disiena, Albert K. Dittmer, Charles J. Diver, Howard E. Dixon, Richard C. Doane, Gerard R. Dobson, PhD, Earl S. Doderer, PhD, Charles Fremont Dodge, PhD, Stephen G. Dodwell, Matthew A. Doffer, Harold H. Doiron, PhD, Michael J. Doiron, MD, Ronald U. Dolfi, W. W. Dollison, Calvin W. Donaghey, Bob L. Donald, Allen Donaldson, James E. Donham, George Donnelly, Billie G. Dopstauf, John B. Dorsey, Floyd Doughty, Ralph D. Doughty, Charles E. Douglas, PhD, Arthur Constant Doumas, PhD, Gary L. Douthitt, Calhoun Dove, William Louis Dowdy, James D. Dowell, Fred Downey, PhD, Jack D. Downing, Terrell Downing, Tom D. Downs, PhD, Stanford L. Downs, B. J. Doyle, Charles W. Drake, Rex A. Drake, George L. Drenner Jr., Carl S. Droste, PhD, William C. Drow, DVM, John A. Drozd, A. J. Druce Jr., Del Rose M. Dubbs, PhD, Louis Dubois, Thomas Dudley, Tom Dudley, Roy L. Dudman, Robert J. Duenckel, S. E. Duerr, Taylor Duke, Thomas L. Dumler, Dean D. Duncan, PhD, Raynor Duncombe, PhD, James G. Dunkelberg, Henry Francis Dunlap, PhD, H. F. Dunlap, PhD, Cleo Dunlap, Roy L. Dunlap, Johnny L. Dunlap, R. C. Dunlap Jr., Wade H. Dunn, PhD, Dale E. Dunn, Francis P. Dunn, James F. Dunn, Neil M. Dunn, MD, Nora E. Dunnell, James D. Duppstadt, Dermot J. Durcan, Jack D. Duren, Ray R. Durrett, MD, Allen L. Dutt, Chizuko M. Dutta, PhD, Granville Dutton, Julie A. Duty, PhD, Neil T. DuVernay, Roger L. Duyne, PhD, Isaac Dvoretzky, PhD,

Lawrence D. Dyer, PhD, Bertram E. Eakin, PhD, R. C. Earlougher Jr., PhD, Richard L. Easterwood, John R. Eaton, James H. Eaton, H. Eberspacher, Stanley R. Eckert, MD, Dominic Gardiner Bowlin Edelen, PhD, Richard Carl Eden, PhD, John M. Edgington, Peter J. Edquist, DVM, Leo T. Effenberger, Darryl J. Egbert, James P. Egger, Christine Ehlig-Economides, PhD, Steven M. Ehlinger, C. D. Ehrhardt Jr., Peter B. Eichelberger, Peter M. Eick, Dean L. Eiland, Jack Gordon Elam, PhD, Bill F. Eldridge, Jack G. Elen, PhD, Lloyd E. Elkins Sr., Joseph A. Ellerbrock, David E. Ellermann, DVM, Douglas G. Elliot, PhD, Rodger L. Elliott, Mark H. Elliott, John G. Elliott Jr., Edison M. Ellis, Robert L. Ellis, Walter H. Ellis, James L. Ellis, Grover C. Ellisor, Kevin L. Elm, Sandy Elms, Andy Elms, Howard P. Elton, Gary M. Emanuel, Barry E. Engel, Newton England Jr., Donald D. Engle, Mike S. Engle, Kenneth C. English, Gilbert K. Eppich, Jay M. Eppink, Russ Eppright, PhD, John F. Erdmann, Alvin J. Erickson Jr., Roger Erickstad, Martin J. Erne, James Lorenzo Erskine, PhD, Don R. Erwin, Brenda Eskelson, E. Esparza, Jimmie L. Estill, Claudia T. Evans, PhD, Beverly A. Evans, Kenneth R. Evans, James A. Evans, Charles R. Evans, Harmon Edwin Eveland, PhD, H. E. Eveland, PhD, Thomas M. Even, Keith A. Everett, Robert H. Everett, Richard Eyler, William A. Fader, MD, Dennis E. Fagerstone, K. Marshall Fagin, James R. Fair, PhD, Jack Fairchild, PhD, Ken Paul Fairchild, Leonard S. Falsone, Daniel J. Faltermeier, Billy Don Fanbien, PhD, Robert S. Fant, Timothy Farage, B. L. Farmer, MD, Jim Farr, MD, Charles Farrell, PhD, P. A. Farrell, Elnora A. Farrell, MD, Billie R. Farris, David Faulkinberry, Claude Marie Faust, PhD, C. Featherston, Hank Feldstein, PhD, Thomas Felkai, Steve Fenderson, Edward L. Fennell, Felix West Fenter, PhD, Dave D. Ferguson, Keith Ferguson, Dino J. Ferralli, John M. Ferrell, MD, Robert J. Ferry, PhD, Thomas H. Fett, Mark E. Fey, Carl L. Fick, Bruce Ficken, Kenneth J. Fiedler, Paul L. Figel, Tom Filesi, Marion F. Filippone, R. D. Finch, PhD, Donald F. Fincher, William E. Findley, Jerry Finkelstein, Robert E. Finken, John C. Finneran Jr., Roger W. Fish, James Fisher, John D. Fisk, MD, Glenn D. Fisseler, Travis G. Fitts Jr., Gregory N. Fitzgerald, Mark R. Fitzgerald, MD, Michael J. Flanigan, Adrian Ede Flatt, PhD, C. D. Flatt, William T. Flis, James L. Flocik, John A. Flores, Dagne Lu Florine, PhD, Daniel Fort Flowers, PhD, Joseph Calvin Floyd, PhD, Monroe H. Floyd, Lowell R. Flud, David A. Flusche, George E. Fodor, PhD, Gerald W. Foess, PhD, James L. Folcik, Aileen M. Foley, Charles T. Folsom, MD, Marc F. Fontaine, PhD, R. S. Foote, Jack G. Foote, Robert S. Foote, Phillip Forbes, George E. Ford, PhD, Roger G. Ford, PhD, Donald P. Ford, MD, George H. Ford, Kenneth B. Ford, Edward Forest, PhD, John Wiley Forsyth, PhD, Gerald Foster, PhD, Walter E. Foster, PhD, Donald Myers Foster, PhD, A. Gerald Foster, PhD, C. R. Foster, Randall R. Foster, J. S. Foster, Doyle F. Fouquet, Leon L. Fowler, John Greg Fowler, Mike Fowler, Louis H. Fowler, Donald W. Fox, Michael S. Francisco, Anne Frank, Donald A. Frank, MD, Milton C. Franke, Homer Franklin Jr., Edwin R. Franks, MD, Bruce Frantz, Warren L. Franz, PhD, Frank E. Frawley Jr., Charles W. Frazell, Marshall Everett Frazer, PhD, Don W. Frazier, Richard R. Frazier, Robert S. Frederick, PhD, Chris Frederickson, PhD, Jack C. Freeman, Johnny A. Freeman, Burlin E. Freeze, Emil J. Freireich, Stephen M. Fremgen, Benjamin Dweitt Fremming, Benjamin D. Fremming, Kenneth A. French, PhD, William S. French, PhD, David C. Fresch, Marion T. Friday, Gerald E. Fritts, Charles W. Frobese, Charles W. Fromen, John E. Frost, PhD, Wade J. Frost, David H. Fruhling, William K. Fry, Rodney G. Fuchs, Thomas R. Fuller, Charles L. Fuller, Terry L. Furgiuele, Dionel Fuselier, Morris L. Gabel, William A. Gabig, Leo H. Gabro, Dean E. Gaddy, Robert A. Gahl, Will Gaines, MD, Douglas Gaither, Joseph W. Galate, R. Gale, PhD, Chrisitna A. Galindo, Marcus J. Galvan, Gary L. Galyardt, B. M. Gamble, Harvey M. Gandy, S. Paul Garber, Rafael Garcia, PhD, Hector D. Garcia, PhD, Gerard G. Garcia, Thomas L. Gardner, D. Garett, Fred S. Garia, Norman E. Garner, PhD, R. Dale Garner, Claude H. Garrett, Frederick Garver Jr., Robert J. Gary, R. Gary, Ron Gasser, Carolyn J. Gaston, PhD, Thea B. Gates, DVM, Stephen L. Gates, Anthony Roger Gatti, PhD, John Gatti, James R. Gattis, Herbert Y. Gayle, Al Gaylord, Michael J. Gaynor, Bob J. Gebert, William E. Gee, William F. Geisler, R. Genge, Ronald L. Genter, Joseph C. Gentry, Charles J. George, Robert E. Gerald, MD, Thomas G. Gerding, PhD, George S. Gerlach, Richard J. Geshay, Richard G. Ghiselin, Gordon A. Gibbs, Lee B. Gibson, PhD, Daniel M. Gibson, PhD, George R. Gibson, PhD, Bobby W. Gibson, Byron J. Gierhart, Donald C. Gifford, Hugh W. Gifford, Gerry Gilbert, Joel Gilbert, W. Allen Gilchrist Jr., PhD, William H. Gilchrist, John Giles, Amarjit S. Gill, Jimmy D. Gillard, Robert Gillespie, PhD, Richard C. Gillette, Trauvis H. Gillham, Clarence F. Gilmore, Merrill Stuart Ginsburg, PhD, Walter Glasgow, Bryan Glass, DVM, Robert W. Gleeson, Mark E. Glover, PhD, Robert R. Glovna, Earnest Frederick Gloyna, PhD, John M. Glynn, Barry G. Goar, Forrest Gober, Ferd S. Godbold III, Charles B. Godfrey, Frederick W. Goff, William C. Goins, Larry O. Goldbeck, MD, Michael H. Golden, Charles Goldenzopf, PhD, Fred L. Goldsberry, PhD, R. K. Golemon, Ruth Gonzalez, PhD, Richard L. Good, John Bannister Goodenou, PhD, Loy B. Goodheart, Charles Thomas Goodhue, PhD, Kent Goodloe, Billy J. Goodrich Jr., William A. Goodrich Jr., MD, Philip W. Goodwin Jr., Korwin J. Goodwin, Terry L. Goosey, Stuart Gordon, Scott D. Gordon, Edward F. Gordon, D. Gorham, PhD, Cheryl Goris, Waldemar Gorski, PhD, Paul L. Gorsuch, MD, Gary R. Gosdin, Darrell L. Goss, Nicolas Goutchkoff, Robert D. Grace, Bob Graf, G. Robert Graf, Harold P. Graham, PhD, S. Graham, Jon Graham, Charles Richard Graham, MD, Seldon B. Graham Jr., Marie M. Graham, MD, Bill D. Graham, Irwin Patton Graham, Richard G. Grammens, Curtis E. Granberry, R. R. Grant, Milton J. Grant II, William F. Grauten, Robert J. Graves, Gregory Graves, Leonard M. Graves, William W. Gray, Gordon H. Gray, Joe C. Gray, Gerald T. Greak, Kent A. Grebing, Michael G. Grecco, Bobby L. Green, Hubert G. Green, MD, Tom F. Green, Andrew Green, Taylor

C. Green, Arthur R. Green, John W. Green, Milton Green, Don M. Greene, PhD, Donald M. Greene, PhD, Vance Greene, Donald R. Greenlee, Jack D. Greenwade, Howard E. Greenwell, B. Marcum Greenwood, Ralph D. Greer, Gary C. Greer, Ted M. Gregson, David M. Gresko, Francis J. Greytok, Doreen V. Grieve, Paul G. Griffith, PhD, M. Shan Griffith, Robert W. Griffith, B. W. Griffith Jr., Edward T. Grimes, MD, Jim T. Grinnan, Ricahrd T. Grinstead, Strother Grisham, Norman C. Griswold, PhD, Donald L. Griswold Jr., Fred R. Grote, Barney Groten, PhD, William S. Groves, S. D. Grubb, Frank C. Gruszynski, Harold Julian Gryting, PhD, Johnnie F. Guelker, Gary Guerrieri, Charles G. Guffey, PhD, Eugene P. Gugel, Stephen N. Guillot, David C. Guinn, Professor Guldenzopf, PhD, J. Arvis Gully, PhD, Arnold J. Gully, Mark T. Gully, Alberto F. Gutierrez, Jeng Yih Guu, PhD, Necip Guven, PhD, Frank W. Guy, PhD, Joe M. Haas, Merrill Wilber Haas, Larry G. Hada, Frederick R. Hafner, Robert Hage, Cecil W. Hagen, Ismail B. Haggag, PhD, Gerow Richard Hagstrom, PhD, Wayne A. Hahne, Stephen W. Haines, Anthony Haines, Delilah B. Hainey, Michel Thomas Halbouty, PhD, Gary Dnnis Halepeska, Richard L. Haley, PhD, R. A. Haley, Douglas Lee Hall, PhD, R. W. Hall Jr., PhD, Jared Hall, Rebecca Hall, Billy R. Hall, Gary R. Hall, George Hall, Tommy G. Hall, John Hall, Robert T. Halpin, Robert L. Halvorsen, Barry Halvorsen, R. L. Halvorson, Robert Hamilton, PhD, Robert Hamilton, PhD, Thomas M. Hamilton, PhD, Dixie G. Hamilton, MD, Stephen L. Hamilton, David Hammel, Matthew M. Hammer, Scott Hamon, Andrew W. Hampf, Bernold M. Handon, Eugene Hanegan, Arthur D. Hanna, PhD, Thomas L. Hanna, DVM, Susan K. Hannaman, Robin Hansen, Douglas B. Hansen, MD, Hugh T. Hansen, Judd A. Hansen, Harry R. Hanson, E. W. Hanszen, Richard A. Haralson, Allan Wilson Harbaugh, PhD, Bob C. Harbert, N. J. Hard, PhD, Stephen D. Hard, DVM, Robert Hard, James Edward Hardcastle, PhD, Glenn L. Hardin, William H. Harding, Andrew T. Harding, Henry W. Harding Jr., Robert E. Hardy, Hugh W. Hardy, Jesse W. Hargis Jr., O. W. Hargrove, Mary W. Hargrove, Wendell N. Harkey, Scott I. Harmon, John Harmonson, Ralph K. Haroldson, Jordan Harp, Ronald Harp, Laddie J. Harp, Henry S. Harper, Charles D. Harr, PhD, Ben Gerald Harris, PhD, Dennis Harris, Jimmy D. Harris, L. Harris, William E. Harris, Billy W. Harris, John C. Harris, David C. Harris, Mathew R. Harrison, Maxwell M. Hart, Paul Robert Hart, Louis W. Hartman, Glenn A. Hartsell, Charles M. Hartwell, Dan E. Hartzell, F. Reese Harvey, PhD, Kenneth C. Harvey, PhD, Meldrum J. Harvey, Robert E. Harvey, William H. Harwood, PhD, Syed M. Hasan, Steven R. Haskin, Jill Hasling, Jay Hassell, PhD, Turner Elilah Hasty, PhD, William B. Hataway, Tim Hatch, Coleman E. Hatherly, Charles B. Hauf, Philip R. Haught, S. Mark Haugland, Victor LaVern Hauser, PhD, Rudolph H. Hausler, PhD, Rudolf M. Hausler, PhD, Y. Hawkins, William K. Hawkins, Edward F. Haye, Richard D. Haynes, James O. Haynes, Clay E. Haynes, James T. Hays, PhD, James E. Hays, J. Ross Hays, Stephen M. Hazlewood, Miao-Xiang He, MD, Klyne Headley, James Edward Heath, PhD, Maxine S. Heath, PhD, Forrest Dale Heath, Milton Heath Jr., James E. Heavner, PhD, James B. Hebel, Bobby D. Hebert, Donald Hecker, Bobbie Hediger, John A. Hefti, William Joseph Heilman, PhD, Daniel J. Heilman, William Daniel Heinze, PhD, James R. Heinze, Peter J. Heinze, Mark B. Heironimus, Robert W. Helbing, Stephen C. Helbing Sr., Jerry Helfand, Paul E. Helfer, Ronald A. Hellstern, PhD, Langley Roberts Hellwig, PhD, Donald C. Helm, Stephen A. Helmberger, Robert E. Helmkamp, PhD, Maher L. Helmy, Bill D. Helton, Glenn R. Hemann Jr., Gerald J. Henderson, PhD, Loren L. Henderson, Douglas J. Henderson, Robert J. Henderson, Dennis L. Hendrix, Malcolm Hendry, PhD, Erwin M. Hengst Jr., Ernest J. Henley, PhD, Terry L. Henshaw, Roger P. Herbert, Jonh F. Herbig, John F. Herbig Jr., Stevens Herbst, Milton B. Herndon, Robert K. Heron, Joe S. Herring, Randy B. Herring, Robert P. Herrmann, Charles H. Herty lll, PhD, Henry J. Hervol, Donald E. Herzberg, Allen H. Hess, Barry G. Hexton, Karen Hickman, PhD, Carlos W. Hickman, James L. Hickman, Willie K. Hicks, James M. Hicks, Joseph H. Higginbotham, PhD, Edward D. Higgins, Michael J. Higgins, Margaret A. Hight, William K. Hilarides, Donald L. Hildebrand, Harvey F. Hill, Andrew T. Hill, Lee Hilliard, John V. Hilliard, William D. Hillis, John Hills, Ray Hilton, PhD, Philip M. Hilton, Mark Fletcher Hines, Howard H. Hinson, Tod Hinton, Mark A. Hitchcock, Rankin V. Hitt, MD, Bryan E. Hivnor, Grace K. Hivnor, S. Hixon, PhD, Sumner B. Hixon, PhD, Richard E. Hixon, Wai Ching Ho, PhD, George H. Hobbs, Michael W. Hoblet, Lee N. Hodge, Sidney Edward Hodges, PhD, Albert Bernard Hoefelmeyer, PhD, Gustave Leo Hoehn, PhD, Earl C. Hoffer, MD, Charles L. Chuck Hoffheiser, Paul F. Hoffman, James E. Hoffmann, Gerald P. Hoffmann, Timothy J. Hogan, Laurence H. Hogue, Robert Marion Holcomb, PhD, David L. Holcomb, Howard D. Holden, PhD, Stephen A. Holdith, PhD, Howard Holland, Henry B. Holle, MD, George Hayes Holliday, PhD, Clifford R. Holliday, John C. Holliman, Frank Joseph Holly, PhD, Anchor E. Holm, Eldon Holm, Russell Holman, Hewett E. Holman, Lowell A. Holmes, Ken D. Holt, Robert J. Holt Sr., Bud Holzman, Frank D. Holzmann, Baxter D. Honeycutt, Russell H. Hoopes, Harry A. Hope, George William Hopkins, PhD, Richard B. Hopper, Carlos L. Horler Sr., Frank A. Hormann, Jerrold S. Horne, Michael A. Hornung, John Horrenstine, Randy D. Horsak, Carl W. Horst, Howard T. Horton, Douglas J. Horton, Edward Horton, Roger Horton, Friedrich Horz, PhD, B. Wayne Hoskins, Richard F. Houde, Albin Houdek, Joel S. Hougen, PhD, Jace Houston, James P. Howalt, Ben K. Howard, PhD, William L. Howard Sr., PhD, Wendell E. Howard, Charles H. Howard, Robert L. Howard, Bruce Howard, John Howatson, PhD, Terry Allen Howel, PhD, John C. Howell, Randall L. Howell, John E. Howland, PhD, Donald L. Howlett, Stan J. Hruska, Bartholomew P. Hsi, PhD, Yen T. Huang, PhD, Edgar Hubbard, Russell H. Hubbard, Bradford Hubbard, Terry K. Hubele, Douglas W. Huber, Frank A. Hudson, PhD, Hank M. Hudson, Stephen H. Hudson, Fred B. Hudspeth, Harry J. Huebner, Fred Robert Huege, PhD,

Clark K. Huff, James Douglas Huggard, Michael Hughes, PhD, Dan A. Hughes, Robert G. Hughes, Mark O. Hughston, Robert C. Hulse, David Hulslander, Charles A. Hummel, Ray Eicken Humphrey, PhD, Cathi D. Humphries, PhD, W. Houston Humphries, Dale L. Hunt, Cecill Hunt Jr., William H. Hunten, Hassell E. Hunter, Douglass M. Hurt, Vivian K. Hussey, David Hutcheson, PhD, Carl M. Hutson, James H. Hyatt, Mike Ibarguen, Alex Ignatiev, PhD, Piloo Eruchshaw Ilavia, Cecil M. Inglehart, Robert E. Irelan, James M. Irwin, Jerry K. Irwin, Charles F. Irwin, MD, R. V. Irwin, E. Burke Isbell, Cary Iverson, Turner W. Ivey Sr., Edwin Harry Ivey, Jerry W. Ivie, Cleon L. Ivy, David Ivy, Gerald Jacknow, MD, Charles E. Jackson, Jeral Jackson, William Jackson, Nichole Jackson, James R. Jackson, Scott L. Jackson, George R. Jackson, J. C. Jacobs, PhD, Roy P. Jacobs, Garry H. Jacobs, Donald F. Jacques, PhD, Robert B. Jacques, John E. James, Calvin R. James, Patrick H. Jameson, Harwin B. Jamison, MD, Marilyn R. Janke, MD, Maximo J. Jante Jr., Rupert Jarboe, Richard P. Jares, Kenneth E. Jarosz, Herbert F. Jarrell, PhD, Douglas Jasek, Buford R. Jean, PhD, Thomas T. Jeffries III, Hugh Jeffus, PhD, Michael Jellison, Veronon Kelly Jenkins, PhD, Jack H. Jennings, Stanley M. Jensen, Randall D. Jensen, MD, Walter P. Jensen Jr., Bill E. Jessup, Richard L. Jodry, PhD, Knut A. Johanson Jr., Duane J. Johnson, PhD, Stuart G. Johnson, PhD, Fred Lowery Johnson, PhD, Howard R. Johnson, MD, Raynard J. Johnson, Earl F. Johnson, Thomas P. Johnson, Delmer R. Johnson, Paul D. Johnson, Doug Johnson, Jeffrey L. Johnson, Charles W. Johnson, MD, Marshall C. Johnston, PhD, La Verne Albert Johnston, PhD, Stephen Albert Johnston, PhD, Daniel Johnston, PhD, Marshal C. Johnston, PhD, Bonnie Johnston, William R. Johnston, D. W. Johnston, Stephan E. Johnston, Kevin W. Jonas, Richard A. Jones, PhD, Bill Jones, PhD, Robert E. Jones, PhD, James Ogden Jones, PhD, Granby Jones, Ray P. Jones, James T. Jones, B. C. Jones, Mitchell Jones, George F. Jonke, Duane P. Jordan, PhD, Jonathan D. Jordan, James R. Jorden, Michael J. Joyner, PhD, Paul G. Judas, Cynthia K. Jungman, DVM, Terence B. Jupp, Joseph Jurlina, James Horace Justice, PhD, Richard J. Kabat, Joan D. Kailey, Hugh D. Kaiser, Klem Kalberer, Ronald P. Kaltenbaugh, Medhat H. Kamal, PhD, William W. Kaminer, Mark P. Kaminsky, PhD, Dennis R. Karns, Lester Karotken, PhD, Ross L. Kastor, Ira Katz, PhD, Marvin L. Katz, PhD, Bill Kaufman, Robert R. Kautzman, Don M. Kay, William Kaylor Jr., Marvin D. Kays, PhD, William Kazmann, Lawrence C. Keaton, PhD, Iris Keeling, Joseph Aloysius Keenan, PhD, Ralph O. Kehle, PhD, Byron L. Keil, Kenwood K. Keil, DVM, Morris Keith, John W. Kelcher, Raymond A. Kelinske, Hermon Keller, Paul W. Keller, R. Keller, Michael Keller, Glen E. Kellerhals, PhD, Monica W. Kelley, Bob Kelley, Jim D. Kelley, Dan A. Kellogg, Colin M. Kelly, Sean P. Kelly, Charles H. Kelm, Marc Keltner, Arthur H. Kemp, L. N. Kendrick, Anthony Drew Kennard, Howard V. Kennedy, PhD, William Kennedy, Theodore R. Keprta, Odis D. Kerbow, T. Lamar Kerley, PhD, Linda Kerr, Thomas W. Kershner, James B. Ketchersid, MD, Joe W. Key, Frank Key, Donald Arthur Keyworth, PhD, Daniel E. Kiburz, Harold J. Kidd, PhD, Thornton L. Kidd, MD, Albert Laws Kidwell, PhD, Nat Kieffer, PhD, Robert Mitchell Kiehn, PhD, Rodney Kiel, Marvin E. Kiel, William H. Kielhorn, Charles H. Kilgore, Marion D. Kilgore, John E. Kimberly, Kenneth B. Kimble, Thomas Fredric Kimes, PhD, F. King, Thomas King, Kathryn E. King, Roy L. King, Gerald S. King, Edwin B. King, Karl Kinley, Roy H. Kinslow, PhD, Thyl E. Kint, Ken K. Kirby, Fred Kirchhoff Jr., Earl Kirk Jr., James E. Kirkham, MD, Matthew L. Kirkland, Dennis Kirkpatrick, PhD, Haskell M. Kirkpatrick, Hugh R. Kirkpatrick, Pamela K. Kirschner, Julianne J. Kisselburgh, Mark C. Kittridge, Thomas R. Kitts, Alfred Klaar, Miroslav Ezidor Klecka, PhD, Gordon Leslie Klein, MD, Richard G. Klempnauer, MD, David L. Klenk, Melvin Klotzman, John L. Knapp, Barry Kneeland, Professor Knightes, PhD, William Knighton, Robert S. Knowles, Christian W. Knudsen, PhD, Buford R. Koehler, Wellington W. Koepsel, PhD, Moses M. Koeroghlian, Charles A. Kohlhaas, PhD, Dusan Konrad, PhD, Kenneth K. Konrad, Walter R. Konzen, MD, Kenneth T. Koonce, PhD, Charles B. Koons, PhD, Micah S. Koons, Johnny A. Kopecky, PhD, David E. Kosanda, Charlie Kosarek, Merwyn Mortimer Kothmann, PhD, Christopher Columbus Kraft Jr., PhD, Paul M. Krail, PhD, Stephen G. Kramar, George G. Krapfel, Garry D. Kraus, Dennis A. Krawietz, Robert F. Kraye, M. F. Krch, M. Fred Krch, William F. Krebethe, MD, K. Kreckel, Rodger L. Kret, Robert W. Kretzler, Charles R. Kreuz, Victor Kriechbaum, Daniel R. Krieg, PhD, Magne Kristiansen, PhD, James C. Kromer, Paul H. Kronfield, Tim C. Kropp, Julius Richard Kroschewsky, PhD, Glenn L. Krum, Karen Sidwell Kubena, PhD, Marc S. Kudla, Antonin J. Kudrna, Stanley E. Kuenstler, Janice Oseth Kuhn, PhD, Bernard J. Kuhn, Carl W. Kuhnen Jr., Kenneth K. Kulik, Arun D. Kulkarni, PhD, Edgar V. Kunkel, George William Kunze, PhD, Peter T. Kuo, MD, Joseph M. Kupper, M. Kurz, PhD, Charles R. Kuykendall, Ronnie Labaume, John M. Lagrone, William E. Laing, Dusan J. Lajda, PhD, Jeffrey J. Lamarca Sr., George W. Lamb, W. E. Lamoreaux, S. S. Lan, Malcolm Lancaster, MD, S. Landeur, John R. Landreth, William R. Landrum, Robert Lane, PhD, Alis C. Lane, DVM, Clifford Lane, Newton L. Lang, William R. Lang, Normal L. Langham, Gerald B. Langille, PhD, Carl G. Langner, PhD, Peter H. Langsjoen, Hans A. Langsjoen, MD, Mark Lankford, Richard M. Lannin, Vince L. Lara, William E. LaRoche, Ronald Larson, PhD, Ron Larson, PhD, Donald E. Larson, Don Larson, Lawrence B. Laskoskie, Stanley J. Laster, PhD, Benny L. Latham, Gail Latimer, Pierre Richard Latour, PhD, William H. Laub, Charles E. Lauderdale, Walter A. Laufer, William R. Laughlin, David D. Laughlin, Dallas D. Laumbach, PhD, Bob J. Lavender, Delman Law, James H.L. Lawler, PhD, Harold B. Lawley, Philip Linwood Lawrence, Joseph D. Lawrence, Donald K. Lawrenz, Bill Lawson, Royce E. Lawson Jr., Marsha A. Layton, Robert E. Layton Jr., Lawrence E. Leach, William D. Leachman, Joanne H. Leatherwood, Floyd L. Leavelle, PhD, Jacob M. Lebeaux, PhD, J. M. Lebeaux, PhD, Rebel J. Leboeuf, Thomas K. Ledbetter, Frank F. Ledford, Karl E. Lee,

Larry E. Lee, Steve W. Lee, DVM, Richard F. Lee, Daniel V. Lee, Harry A. Lee, Lindsey D. Lee, Gil L. Legate, Thomas H. Legg, Robert B. Leggett, Ruw W. Lehde, Elroy Paul Lehmann, PhD, William L. Lehmann, PhD, Barbara T. Lehmann, Roger D. Leick, W. L. Lemon, David V. Lemone, PhD, Leonard Leon, Roland D. Leon, Albert O. Leonard, Paul G. Leroy, M. Leutwyler, Donn W. Leva, Stewart A. Levin, PhD, Catherine Lewis, PhD, Robert Lewis, Phillip E. Lewis, Timothy E. Lien, David W. Light, Curt Lightle, Steven C. Limke, Philip V. Lindblade, R. Lindemann, PhD, Gerald S. Lindenmoen, Jay T. Lindholm, Cecil H. Link, Frank Linville Jr., Anthony Pasquale Lioi, PhD, Eugene G. Lipnicky, Merrill I. Lipton, MD, Jim Litchfield, David Litowsky, MD, Jack E. Little, PhD, Larry E. Little, Frank K. Little, Hung-Wen (Ben) Liu, PhD, William H. Livingston, James R. Lloyd, PhD, Sheldon G. Lloyd, David M. Lloyd, Barry H. Lloyd, James R. Lobb, Gene M. Lobrecht, Paul Lockhart Jr., Brent Lockhart, Robert M. Lockhart, William R. Locklear, Travis W. Locklear, MD, Paul L. Lockwood, Alfred R. Loeblich III, PhD, Larry K. Lofton, R. H. Lofton, MD, Robert J. Logan, Thomas L. Logan, Jerry L. Logan, Charles B. Loggie, Nicolas Logvinoff Jr., MD, H. William Lollar, Henry R. Longcrier, Kenneth C. Longley, Guy J. Lookabaugh, Ronald L. Loper, H. C. Lott Jr., L. Richard Louden, PhD, Ralph W. Love, Richard M. Love, Ben A. Lovell, Wayne T. Lovett, Robert F. Loving, Glen R. Lowe, Robert M. Lowe, John D. Lowery, Charles B. Lowrey, PhD, D. Mark Loyd, Dale R. Lucas, Timothy W. Lucas, Michael W. Luck, Gerald S. Ludwig, Wm. P. Ludwig, Donald L. Luffell, Gordon D. Luk, Richard Lumpkin, PhD, J. Lund, Brenda Lunsford, Mark J. Lupo, PhD, W. C. Lust, James R. Lynch, Francis M. Lynch, Michael S. Lynch, James I. Lyons, Robert Leonard Lytton, PhD, Robert L. Maby Jr., Charles B. Macaul, Robert N. MacCallum PE, PhD, Richard E. Macchi, A. MacDonald, Richard Macdougal, Charles E. Mace, Allan Macfarland, Marc Machbitz, Thomas J. Machin, Tommy J. Machin, John B. Mack, Bruce C. Macke, Henry James Mackey, PhD, Patrick E. Mackey, Steve D. Maddox, Randall N. Maddux, Hulon Madeley, PhD, Neil S. Madeley, Jack T. Madeley, James E. Madget II, Kenneth Olaf Madsen, PhD, John M. Maerker, PhD, John J. Magee, Ronald Magel, Robert E. Magers, Kent W. Maggert, Allen H. Magnuson, PhD, John F. Maguire, PhD, William Mahavier, PhD, Salah E. Mahmoud, Charles F. Maitland, Lewis R. Malinak, PhD, James Jo Malley, PhD, Meredith Mallory Jr., MD, William H. Malone, Glenn Maloney, Harold R. Mancusi-Ungaro Jr., MD, Sharad V. Mane, John L. Maneval, J. D. Manley, John D. Manley 4th, T. Mann, A. Bryant Mannin, MD, David T. Manning, MD, Lewis A. Manning, Robert A. Manning, Terry Manning, Stephen M. Manning, Robert A. Marburger, Robert P. Marchant, Karla Wade Marchell, Kirk A. Marchell, Matthew C. Marcontell, Ronald Marcotte, PhD, Roger W. Marcum, Louis F. Marczynski, George Marklin, PhD, Daniel B. Marks, Elbert L. Marks ll, Stuart A. Markussen, Professor Marsh, PhD, William Marshall, Brent H. Martin, John Martin, Benjamin F. Martin Jr., Antonio S. Martin, MD, Monty G. Martin, Rex I. Martin, George M. Martinez, Jack M. Martt, MD, Vernon J. Maruska, Perry S. Mason, PhD, Riaz H. Masrour, Wulf F. Massell, PhD, Lenita C. Massey, John A. Massoth, John R. Masters, DVM, Robert Mastin, MD, T. Mather, John R. Mathias, MD, Francis J. Mathieu, Rickey L. Mathis, Hudson Matlock, Ron J. Matlock, Roy E. Matthews, Charles Matusek, Samuel Adam Matz, PhD, Roger A. Maupin, MD, Margaret N. Maxey, PhD, Arthur R. Maxwell, PhD, John Crawford Maxwell, Jimmy E. May, Henry K. May, MD, Harry L. Mayes, Greg L. Mayes, J. Mayfield, Alfred M. Mayo, Joel T. Mays, C. Gordon McAdams, MD, William N. Mcanulty Jr., PhD, Melinda S. McBee, Carol Don McBiles, William D. McCain, PhD, David McCalla, John R. McCalmont, Michael F. McCardle, A. T. McCarroll, Glenn J. McCarthy, Keith F. McCarthy, Michael J. McCarthy, MD, Bramlette McClelland, James O. McClimans, Jack L. McClure, Lawrence McClure, Jalmer R. McConathy, Stewart McConnell, DVM, Don L. McCord, MD, James W. McCown, Lawrence T. McCoy, R. L. McCoy, Michael L. McCrary, Kem E. McCready, Lynn McCuan, Robert G. McCuistion, David W. McCulloch, Thane H. McCulloh, PhD, Dennis W. McCullough, PhD, Keith D. McCullough, Michael C. McCullough, Martin K. McCune, Dolan McDaniel, William D. McDaniel, Douglas McDaniel, C. McDaniels, Lynn Dale McDonald, PhD, Floyd McDonald, Robert I. McDougall, PhD, Edward McDowell, John C. McDuffie Jr., Paul M. McElfresh, PhD, Raymond E. McFarlane, Michael A. McFerrin, Mickey McGaugh, James M. McGee, Richard Heath McGirk, PhD, Donald Paul McGookey, PhD, Ron McGregor, Brady J. McGuire, Gary McHale, Gary B. McHalle, PhD, Timothy B. McIlwain, Roy L. McKay, Fount E. McKee, Bishop D. McKendree, William R. McKenna, MD, Michael G. McKenna, Samuel McKenney, John McKetta Jr., PhD, Charles W. McKibben, Ron J. McKinley, Samuel J. McKinney, Paul D. McKinney, J. D. McLaughlin, L. A. McLaurin, James C. McLellan, PhD, Jerry D. McMahon, Perry R. McNeil, PhD, Roger J. McNichols, PhD, D. Sean McPherson, Richard C. McPherson, Clara McPherson, P. S. McReynolds, C. L. McSpadden, Kevin D. Mcvey, Samantha S. Meador, Alan J. Mechtenberg, William Louis Medlin, PhD, James M. Medlin, Russel P. Meduna, Donald N. Meehan, PhD, Preston L. Meeks, Paul E. Melancon, James C. Melear, Michael Brendan Melia, PhD, Jim Mellott, James Ray Melton, PhD, B. Melton, Arnold Mendez, William Menger, Samuel H. Mentemeier, Erhard Roland Menzel, PhD, Carl Stephen Menzies, PhD, Sherrel A. Mercer, J. Steven Mercer, James B. Merkel, G. Merkle, John C. Merritt Jr., Mark B. Merritt, Frederick Paul Mertens, PhD, Carl W. Mertz, Charles L. Messler, Ron G. Metcalf, Michael W. Metza, Leslie P. Metzgar, John Wesley Meux, PhD, Thomas R. Mewhinney, Frank E. Meyers, Nicholas Michaels, PhD, C. Michel, PhD, F. Curtis Michel, PhD, W. M. Midgett, MD, C. R. Miertschin, Edward Miesch, PhD, Alton Migl, Nelson F. Mikeska, John A. Mikus, PhD, Otto J. Mileti, Paul B. Milios, Richard T. Miller, PhD, Philip Dixon Miller, PhD, Jeffrey A. Miller, John Miller, Loyle P. Miller, Matt C. Miller, P. H. Miller, Kerry C. Miller, Leslie T. Miller, Gary D. Miller, Clifford A. Miller, Leland

H. Miller, Fay E. Millett, MD, Spencer Rankin Milliken, PhD, John James Mills, PhD, Curtis R. Mills, Thomas H. Milstead, Elmer A. Milz, James F. Minter, A. E. Minyard, MD, Raymond W. Mires, PhD, John P. Mireur, Conarad Mirochna, Gustave A. Mistrot III, Billy F. Mitcham, Edward H. Mitchell, Robert J. Mitchell, Thomas J. Mittler, Perry J. Mixon, Jack Pitts Mize, PhD, Glen Lavell Mizer, MD, Henry A. Mlcak, Richard G. Mocksfield, Jerry L. Modisette, PhD, Fersheed K. Mody, PhD, William R. Moeller, Camilla M. Moga, Traian C. Moga, Mohammad M. Mokri, John Molloy, Thomas D. Molzahn, D. Mommsen, Edward Harry Montgomery, PhD, Gerald Montgomery, Joshua D. Montgomery, MD, Monty Montgomery, Wendell B. Moody, Harley Moody, DVM, Elizabeth A. Mooney, Walter L. Moore, PhD, Jimmie Moore, PhD, Kenneth L. Moore, Craig Moore, B. L. Moore Jr., Daniel C. Moore, William Moorhead, PhD, George A. Moran, Thomas M. Moran, Peter Moreau, Hubert L. Morehead, PhD, Ronald B. Morgan, PhD, Clyde N. Morgan, MD, Jerry I. Moritz, John C. Morrill, PhD, Charles W. Morris, PhD, Larry E. Morris, Ben L. Morris, Brock A. Morris, Robert A. Morris, Robert Morris, Perry B. Morris, William Morrison, Dennis Moseler, Professor Moseley, Ron R. Moser, David A. Mosig, Jerry E. Mount, MD, R. Mowell, Dan L. Mueller, William B. Mueller, Philip M. Muellier, J. Mulcahey, Bertram S. Mullan, MD, James C. Mullen, Stephen K. Muller, Dennis Mulvey, PhD, Michael E. Munoz, Rodney D. Munsell, DVM, Jack G. Munson, Ronald E. Munson, David M. Munson, Henry W. Murdoch, Karl Muriby, Michael M. Murkes, PhD, John R. Murphey Jr., Lawrence Eugene Murr, PhD, Glenn Murray, James W. Murray, Clarence Murray Jr., Daniel M. Musher, MD, Jack Thompson Musick, Harry C. Mussman, PhD, Stuart Creighton Mut, Walter F. Muzacz, George M. Myers, PhD, Glen Myska, Larry D. Nace, Carl M. Naehritz Jr., Harry E. Nagel, Joseph Nagyvary, PhD, B. J. Nailon, Julian Nalley, Jerome Nicholas Namy, PhD, Robert K. Nance, Howard L. Nance, Michael L. Nance, Cynthia Y. Naples, PhD, David Naples, Kenneth P. Naquin, Karen M. Needham, Thomas H. Neel, Joe C. Neeley, Dana Neely, James H. Nelland, James Arly Nelson, PhD, J. Robert Nelson, Mart D. Nelson, Scott R. Nelson, David L. Nelson, Ronald G. Nelson, John J. Nelson, Charles E. Nemir, Jerry E. Nenoon, R. B. Nesbitt, Dan R. Neskora, PhD, Michael E. Nevill, Daniel B. Nevin, D. Bruce Nevin, Roman N. Newald, Jean-Jaques Newey, Robert M. Newman, Sidney B. Nice, C. E. Nichols, Richard E. Nichols, MD, Clifford E. Nichols, James R. Nichols, Robert L. Nickell Jr., Thomas Nickerson, Michael J. Nicol, Billy W. Nievar, James A. Nitsch, James W. Nixon, MD, Paul Robert Nixon, Marion D. Noble, Raymond L. Noel, Theodore N. Noel, Bertram Nolte, PhD, Philip A. Norby, Carl H. Nordstrand, Gregg A. Norman, Hughie C. Norris, Billy N. Norris, Douglas F. North, L. D. Northcott, S. J. Norton, PhD, Michael W. Norton, H. Scott Norville, PhD, Robert J. Noteboom, J. D. Novotny, Shirley E. Nowicki, Gary P. Noyes, PhD, Ronnie L. Nye, DVM, James Eugene Nymann, PhD, Edward L. Oakes, Victor D. Obadiah, Douglas K. Obeck, DVM, Donald Oberleas, PhD, Mark J. O'Brien, George S. Ochsner, John D. Ochsner, J. Oden, PhD, Ron Oden, Charles B. Odom, MD, Vencil E. O'Donnell, Carl O. Oelze, Charles Patrick Ofarrel, PhD, John H. Ognibene, David J. Ogren, D. John Ogren, Robert E. Old, Daniel R. Olds, Enrique A. Olivas, PhD, Arnold W. Oliver, Ray E. Olsen, Christopher E. Olson, MD, Dale C. Olson, Frank I. Ondrovik, DVM, Charles L. Oney, Curtis H. Orear, John A. Oren, J. Dale Ortego, PhD, William F. Ortloff, James Wilbur Osborn, Zofia M. Oshea, MD, Jeffrey Oslund, William T. Osterloh, PhD, David P. Osterlund, Osamudiamen M. Otabor, Leo E. Ott, PhD, Jack M. Otto, Carroll Oubre, PhD, Steve H. Ousley, MD, Susan B. Ouzts, Robert G. Ovellette, Lanny M. Overby, Rufus M. Overlander, F. A. Overly, Scott C. Overton, J. David Overton, Donald E. Owen, PhD, Richard Owen, Prentice R. Owen, William C. Owens, R. M. Ownesby, MD, T. M. Ozymy, Susan Paddock, David R. Paddock, Carey P. Page, John H. Painter, PhD, Lorn C. Painter, Jim R. Palmore, Shambhu A. Pai Panandiker, James M. Pappas, Ronald E. Paque, PhD, Howell W. Pardue, Manuel Paredes, Melissa M. Park, William Park, Sidney G. Parker, PhD, H. William Parker, PhD, Billy Y. Parker, DVM, Raymond G. Parker, Michael D. Parker, Harold R. Parkinson, David B. Parks, Edward M. Parma, Sheldon C. Parmer, W. M. Parr, Charles H. Parr, Clinton Parsons, PhD, Donald A. Parsons, MD, William M. Pate, Margaret D. Patin, Wesley Clare Patrick, PhD, Calvin C. Patterson, PhD, Wayne R. Patterson, PhD, Ben M. Patterson Jr., James C. Patterson, Sharon Patterson, Don R. Patterson, Robert W. Patterson, Jeff D. Patterson, Donald R. Pattie, Robert J. Patton, Cynthia M. Patty, James T. Paul, Ralph L. Pauls, Bernard A. Paulson, Robert C. Paulson, Darrell G. Pausky, Max L. Paustian, F. R. Payne, PhD, Michael A. Payne, PhD, D. Payne, James R. Payne, Barry Payne, Cyril J. Payne, Daniel Bester Pearson III, PhD, Ross E. Pearson, Stephen I. Pearson, DVM, Charles Pearson, Rod W. Pease, Patrick A. Peck, Christopher Peek, Vernon L. Peipelman, Gary Pekarek, John L. Pellet, Richard R. Pemper, PhD, Yarami Pena, Pawel Penczek, PhD, Jim R. Pendergrass, David Pendery, A. Penley, B. F. Pennington, Victor H. Peralta, Luzviminda K. Peredo, James D. Periman, Thomas Perkins, PhD, F. M. Perkins Jr., Frederick M. Perkins, Dean H. Perry, Swan D. Person, Cyril J. Peruskek, David W. Peters, PhD, Joel E. Peterson, D. Peterson, Floyd M. Peterson, Gerald L. Peterson, Christopher K. Peterson, Emmett M. Peterson, Arthur K. Petraske, Greg Petterson, Chester A. Peyton Jr., William D. Pezzulich, Perry Edward Phillips, PhD, Felton Ray Phillips, Kenneth Piel, PhD, Walter H. Pierce, PhD, George Piers, D. Pigott, PhD, Jeffrey A. Pike, Paul E. Pilkington, John H. Pimm, R. E. Pine, Carl O. Pingry, James J. Pirrung, Shane W. Pirtle, Jack Piskura, John Robert Piskura, Richard Pittman, David J. Pitts, Gerald S. Pitts, Gregory S. Pitts, James J. Piwetz Jr., Frank J. Pizzitola, Joe Pizzo, PhD, John E. Plapp, PhD, Carl W. Ploeger, Daniel T. Plume, John F. Podhaisky, Richard D. Poe, PhD, Steve C. Poe, Ronald F. Pohler, Roland F. Pohler, Craig Poindexter, MD, Adrian M. Polit, MD, James K. Polk, William D. Pollard, R. Scott Pollard,

Walter L. Pondrom, PhD, Philip C. Pongetti, Sam L. Pool, Russel Poole, Vernon Ray Porter, PhD, Richard Porter, Mike Posson, Keith M. Potter, Rainer Potthast, PhD, Michael Robert Powell, PhD, Darden Powers, PhD, Don G. Powers, Adam A. Praisnar Jr., Samuel F. Pratt Jr., Scott H. Prengle, Richard S. Prentice, Irving J. Prentice Jr., Tony M. Preslar, Allister L. Presnal, Jackie L. Preston, DVM, Basil A. Preuitt Jr., MD, Charles R. Price, Donald G. Price Jr., R. E. Price, Jerry Priddy, Bill Priebe, J. Prieditis, PhD, Guy T. Priestly, Robert Prince, Vernon Pringle Jr., James W. Pringle, Alan N. Pritchard, Charles A. Proshek, DVM, Jesus Roberto Provencio, PhD, Jay P. Pruitt, Basil Arthur Pruitt, MD, Charles Pruszynski, Stanley E. Ptaszkowski, Richard R. Pugh, Viswanadha Puligandla, PhD, Layne L. Puls, John Pulte, Cary C. Purdy, Paul E. Purser, George T. Pyndus, Jeffrey P. Quaratino, Miller W. Quarles, Richard H. Quinn, PhD, Shirley J. Quinn, John P. Quinn, Perry C. O. Quinn, J. R. Quisenberry, Patrick W. Quist, Don R, Ashley Rabalais, Brian T. Raber, Thomas A. Rabson, PhD, Robert A. Rademaket, Nancy R. Radercic, PhD, Steven R. Radford, Norman D. Radford Jr., Lewis E. Radicke, PhD, Donald E. Radtke, Ralph D. Ragsdale, Joe M. Rainey, Robert N. Rainey, DeJan Rajcic, C. L. Rambo, Frederick H. Rambow, PhD, Rafael G. Ramirez, PhD, Guadalupe Ramirez, Jerry Dwain Ramsey, PhD, Mark Ramsey, Thomas E. Ramsey, Milton H. Ramsey, Jack E. Randorff, PhD, Jesus J. Rangel Jr., C. J. Ransom, PhD, W. R. Ransone, PhD, Marco Rasi, PhD, Mark Rasmussen, Lee Ratcliff, Carroll J. Rawley, Michael B. Ray, PhD, Clifford H. Ray, PhD, Donald R. Ray, Herbert Raymond, Bill E. Raywinkle, Robert C. Reach, W. Rector, Brian Redlin, Cynthia A. Reece, Steven Reeder, MD, Richard W. Rees, Dale O. Reese, W. R. Reeves Jr., M. Loren Regier, Larry M. Rehg, William M. Reid, PhD, Frank E. Reid, Erwin A. Reinhard, PhD, James A. Reinhert, PhD, Samuel Reiser, Russel J. Reiter, PhD, Jimmie J. Renfro, Kevin D. Renfro, Edward G. Rennels, PhD, Kenneth L. Rergman, F. E. Resch, Paul Retter, PhD, Lynn A. Revak, William F. Revelt, Randall H. Reviere, PhD, John E. Rhoads, PhD, James D. Rhodes, R. David Rhodes, John R. Rhodes, Charles N. Rice, Patrick Rice, David A. Rich, Thomas C. Richards, PhD, Otis H. Richards, Russell Richards, Clarence W. Richardson, PhD, George A. Richardson, MD, Albert T. Richardson, J. C. Richardson Jr., Frank Richey, PhD, Louis A. Rickert, Richard L. Ricks, David C. Riddle, PhD, Napoleon B. Riddle, MD, Susan J. Riebe, Edward Richard Ries, PhD, Glen A. Ries, Noel D. Rietman, Charles Riley, PhD, J. W. Rimes, Gregory S. Rinaca, Charles E. Rinehart Jr., PhD, Stephen J. Ringel, MD, David P. Ringhausen, David Rios-Aleman, George R. Ripley, Don L. Risinger, MD, Carolyn J. Ritchie, Steven J. Ritter, PhD, Russell E. Ritz, George A. Rizk, Patrick C. Roark, Norman B. Robbins, Henry E. Roberts, Alvis D. Roberts Jr., Robert H. Roberts, Larry C. Roberts, MD, Arthur R. Roberts, Michael A. Roberts Jr., James W. Roberts, David R. Robertson, Gordon W. Robertstad, PhD, J. Michael Robinson, PhD, M. Robinson, PhD, Elizabeth N. Robinson, DVM, Stephen L. Robinson, Ken Robirds, G. Alan Robison, PhD, Jackie L. Robison, E. Douglas Robison, Mary Drummond Roby, PhD, James C. Rock, PhD, Cary O. Roddy, Jack W. Rode, Rocky R. Roden, Charles Alvard Rodenberger, PhD, Robert B. Rodriguez, MD, Weston A. Roe, Isaac F. Roebuck, Robert C. Roeder, PhD, Tom Rogers, PhD, Marion Alan Rogers, PhD, Dave E. Rogers, MD, Glenn M. Rogers, DVM, Anthony C. Rogers, A. C. Rogers, Howard J. Rohde, Don A. Rohrenbach, Ronald Rolando, Jude R. Rolfes, Albert Rollins, Thomas W. Rollins, Joe T. Romine, Jeff H. Ronk, Charles H. Roos, Paul James Roper, PhD, G. Rorschach, Paul N. Roschke, PhD, Ward F. Rosen, Joshua H. Rosenfeld, PhD, Charles R. Rosenfeld, MD, Randy E. Rosiere, PhD, Hayes E. Ross Jr., PhD, William F. Ross, Norman B. Ross, Nealie E. Ross, MD, Randall R. Ross, Audrey Ross, Audrey Rossi, Charles H. Roth, PhD, Bela P. Roth, PhD, Ronald C. Rothe, Billy J. Rouser, Lee J. Rousselot, Martin D. Rowe Jr., Rex L. Rowell, David A. Rowland, PhD, Lenton O. Rowland, PhD, Stephen Rowley, Richard L. Royal, Tad T. Rozycki, MD, Carter F. Rubane, Jim R. Rucker, Kenneth E. Ruddy, Douglas L. Rue, Walter E. Ruff, T. H. Ruland, Robert E. Rundle, Edward E. Runyan, Andrew Rusiwko, PhD, Charles L. Russell, Carri A. Rustad, Robert Rutherford, Paul J. Rutherford, James D. Rutherford, Durward E. Rutledge, Donald Rux, Lester M. Ryol, PhD, Tom R. Sadler, Harry C. Sager, Winston Martin Sahinen, Nelton O. Salch, Belinda Salinas, Joe G. Saltamachia, Joe G. Saltamacina, Michael T. Sample, Cheryl K. Sampson, MD, Freddy J. Sanches, Isaac C. Sanchez, PhD, Robert M. Sanford, Thomas G. Sarek, Mark Sarlo, Cornel Sarosdy, Robert Sartain, PhD, Ray N. Sauer, Richard L. Sauer, John D. Savage, George P. Saxon, PhD, Hugh A. Scanlon, MD, Paul Scardaville, J. F. Scego, Brett Schaffer, Raymond A. Schakel, Thomas S. Schalk, Laird F. Schaller, MD, Richard Allan Schapery, PhD, Richard M. Scharlach, Marvin W. Schindler, Ray Schindler, Raymond C. Schindler, Brent D. Schkade, Richard D. Schlomach, MD, Lester E. Schmaltz, Paul W. Schmidt, Ralph Schmidt, Brian F. Schmidt, Martin L. Schneider, MD, Allan M. Schneider, William P. Schneider, Lewes B. Schnitz, Arthur Wallace Schnizer, PhD, William R. Schoen, John L. Schoenthaler, Stephen L. Schrader, Martin William Schramm, PhD, Wilburn R. Schrank, PhD, Robert Alvin Schreiber, PhD, Max P. Schreiner, R. J. Schrior, Steve A. Schroeder, William Schrom, Dale R. Schueler, DVM, Frank J. Schuh, Robert E. Schuhmann, PhD, P. Schulle, Michael Schuller, PhD, Norrell D. Schulte, Lowell E. Schultz, Max A. Schumann Jr., John E. Schumann, Gerard Majella Schuppert Jr., Mark J. Schusler, Michael Frank Schuster, PhD, Gilbert C. Schutza, E. J. Schwarz, PhD, Jeffry A. Schwarz, Colman P. Schweikhardt, C. P. Schweikhardt, Thomas R. Schwerdt, Oscar T. Scott IV, PhD, C. J. Scott, Bill H. Scott, Linda Scott, Wayne S. Scott, R. W. Scott, Michael E. Scribner, PhD, Richard Burkhart Sculz, Harry G. Scurlock, Daniel R. Seal, Ryan B. Seals, Brian E. Sealy, Michael T. Searfass, William Sears, PhD, Mary Ann Sechrest, Paul R. Seelye, Philip A. Seibert, James A. Seibt, William Edgard Seifert, PhD, Jerold Alan Seitchik, PhD, Joseph J. Sekerka, Joe Selle, John S. Sellmeyer, Scott

H. Semlinger, S. Semlinger, Edwin T. Sewall, James W. Sewell, Franklin W. Shadwell, W. A. Shaeffer III*, William L. Shaffer, William L. Shaffes, James L. Shanks Jr., Al M. Shannon, Edward M. Shapiro, James W. Sharp, Stephen L. Shaw, David R. Sheahan, Robert E. Sheffield, Joseph Sheldon, Robert C. Shellberg, William T. Sheman, Mark B. Shepherd Jr., Kalapi D. Sheth, Scott Shifflett, Don I. Shimmon, Ross L. Shipman, Richard R. Shirley, Gene M. Shirley, Louis I. Shneider Jr., William C. Shockley, Dale M. Short, Allen Shotts, Michael Shouret, Loy William Shreve, PhD, Willis P. Sibley, David E. Sibley Jr., Harold L. Siegele, Wayne L. Sievers, PhD, Curtis J. Sievert, James Sigmon, Henno Siismets, John William Sij, PhD, I. J. Silberberg, PhD, Jerome L. Silverman, MD, John Simion, Larry B. Simmers, Kelly V. Simmons, Charles Simmons, Rau E. Simpson, Lynn A. Simpson, David C. Sims, John C. Sinclair, Robet B. Singer, Raj N. Singh, Joseph R. Sinner, Melvin M. Sinquefield, Lou Di Sioudi, J. L. Sipes Jr., William Allen Sistrunk, PhD, Richard L. Sitton, Michael Sivertsen, Phillip S. Sizer, Mertonm Skaggs, Damir S. Skerl, Allen C. Skiles, Marvin R. Skinner, Leslie D. Skinner, Nicholas R. Skinner, Bill E. Slade, Clifford V. Slagle, Ronald N. Sleufca, Jim H. Slim, William M. Sliva, PhD, Harold S. Slusher, PhD, Jeffrey S. Small, Samuel W. Small, G. A. Smalley Jr., T. Smiley Jr., Derek L. Smith, PhD, Louis C. Smith, PhD, Alan Lyle Smith, PhD, Milton Louis Smith, PhD, Raymond H. Smith, Tommy L. Smith, Oziel L. Smith Jr., Ead C. Smith, MD, Todd G. Smith, David L. Smith Jr., Al Smith, Louis J. Smith, Floyd A. Smith, Tina Smith, Thomas L. Smith, O. Lewis Smith, Eugene A. Smitherman, Dennis R. Sneed, MD, Billy J. Sneed, Glenn C. Snell, Jon S. Snell, Gilbert W. Snell, R. Larry Snider, Paul R. Snow, David A. Snyder, PhD, Blaine Snyder, Nicholas Snyder, Fred F. C. Snyder, Robert B. Snyder, Charles F. Snyder, E. H. Soderberg, Dean E. Soderstrom, Harold K. Sohner, Robert E. Sokoll, Dale M. Solaas, Turner Solari, Albert K. Solcher, Eugene A. Soltero, Siva Somasundaram, PhD, Xiaohui M. Song, PhD, Philip M. Sonleitner, Gordon Guthrey Sorrells, PhD, Danny C. Sorrells, Armand Max Souby, Robert G. Spangler, PhD, Tom Sparks, Aubrey A. Spear, Gerald E. Speck, Tim R. Speer, Frederick Speigelberg, William A. Spencer, MD, George V. Spires, Marion E. Spitler, Maurice L. Sproul, Eve S. Sprunt, PhD, Hugh H. Sprunt, Charles F. Squire, PhD, Douglas E. Stafford, Frank B. Stahl, Fred Stalder, Dennis D. Stalmach, Michael R. Stamatedes, Albert L. Stanford, Drago Stankovic, John L. Stanley, Steven Stanley, Robin L. Stansell, Jerry Staples, John Starck, Kelly L. Stark, Richard R. Statton, Eric A. Stauch, Frederick L. Stead, Werner W. Stebner, Jame Harlan Steel, DVM, George M. Steele, Donald N. Steer, Mark C. Stefanov, Tom J. Steffens, Neil A. Stegent, William H. Steiner, Ray L. Steinmetz, Michael F. Stell, William K. Stenzel, Pamela Stephens, PhD, P. Stephens, William C. Stephens, Michael Steppe, Charles A. Sternbach, James Stevens, William L. Stewart, W. L. Stewart Jr., David W. Stilson, Louis Stipp, Dan Stoelzel, Kim R. Stoker, Dana D. Stokes, Michael F. Stolle, Jay D. Stone, PhD, Michael E. Stones, MD, Gregory J. Story, Charles L. Strain, David A. Strand, Kurt A. Stratmann, William Straub, Robert Lewis Street, PhD, John C. Strickland, Sarah Taylor Strinden, PhD, John J. Strojek, James E. Strozier, Glenn A. Strube, Malcolm K. Strubhar, M. Howard Strunk, John B. Stuart, Roger G. Stuart Jr., MD, Telton Stubblefield, PhD, Harry T. Stucker, Donald P. Stuckey, David Owen Stuebner, Robert J. Stupp, Jerry D. Sturdivant, G. Sturges, K. Stutler, Ralph E. Styring, H. Su, PhD, Felipe J. Suarez, Daniel Subach, PhD, Daniel J. Subaen, PhD, Jonathan D. Such, John Suggs, Bruce M. Sullivan, Carl Summers, Charles Summers, Norman A. Sunderlin, A. J. Sustek Jr., PhD, Charles Suter, William R. Suter, James A. Sutphen, Thomas C. Sutton, PhD, Paul A. Svejkovsky, Robert S. Svoboda, William C. Swart Jr., John H. Swendig, James E. Swenke, Ronald F. Swenson, Gary S. Swindell, Rita D. Swinford, MD, Charles J. Swize, Paul M. Swoboda, James R. Sydow, Robert E. Sylvanus, Elwood Sylvanus, Ronald E. Symecko, Edward J. Szymczak, Ed Szymczak, Jerrry L. Tabb, Kelley A. Tafel, PhD, Gerald W. Tait, Emil R. Talamo, Alvin W. Talash, PhD, J. S. Talbot, Larry D. Talley, PhD, Russell Talley, James L. Tally, Edward A. Talmage, MD, Joann H. Tannich, John Tarpley, Jeffrey J. Tarrand, MD, Alan R. Tarrant, Michael J. Tarrillion, Nahum A. Tate, Gordon E. Tate, Lyndon Taylor, PhD, Richard Melvin Taylor, PhD, Steve D. Taylor, Gordon E. Taylor, Ben E. Taylor, William Charles Taylor-Chevron, Neal Teague, Edward Teasdale, Todd X. Teitell, Robert W. Temple, Robert J. Templin, Peter W. Ten Eyck, Richard N. Tennille, Jamie B. Terrell, Robert E. Terrill, Earl Tessem, Norman Jay Tetlow, PhD, W. G. Teubner, Raynold J. Thibodeaux, Kenneth A. Thoma, Charles Thomas, PhD, J. Todd Thomas, A. D. Thomas, James R. Thompson, PhD, Richard J. Thompson, PhD, David B. Thompson, PhD, Blair D. Thompson, MD, Jack Thompson, Evan C. Thompson, Tommy L. Thompson, Ronald E. Thompson, J. Christy Thompson, Richard W. Thompson Jr., Guy Thompson, Greg Thompson, MD, William S. Thompson III, Walter Thomsen, Professor Thorleifson, Robert L. Thornton, Robert F. Thrash, Purvis J. Thrash Jr., Billy H. Thrasher, PhD, Ben H. Thurman, MD, Kenneth Shane Tierling, Richard B. Timmons, PhD, Clarence N. Tinker, David R. Tinney, William R. Tioton, George R. Tippett, Craig A. Tips, William R. Tipton, Herbert G. Tiras, B. H. Tjrasjer, PhD, Robert M. Todor, Travi Toland, James L. Tomberlin, Jocelyn Tomkin, PhD, J. Tomkin, PhD, William Harry Tonking, PhD, George Tope, Mary E. Totard, Mills Tourtellotte, Lawrence E. Townley, Phinn W. Townsend, Charles D. Towry, Laurence Munro Trafton, PhD, George Thomas Trammell, PhD, O. E. Trechter, J. Trevino, David C. Triana, Leland Floyd Tribble, PhD, R. G. Tribble, Jay H. Troell, John S. Troschinetz, J. Michael Trotter, Leonard L. Trout, C. E. Trowbridge, John Parks Trowbridge, MD, G. I. Troyer, Robert E. Truly, Thomas H. Tsai, Julio C. Tuberquia, MD, W. Tucker, Jasper M. Tucker, Bill C. Tucker, B. C. Tucker, W. David Tucker, Daniel Tudor, PhD, John O. Tugwell, Frank Tull, MD, Alton L. Tupa, Peter L. Turbett, D. Turbeville, Charles Paul Turco, PhD, James H. Turk, MD, Albert J. Turk, Morris Turman, Rick Turner, Michael D. Turner, Dwight J. Turner, M. O. Turner, M.O. Turner, E. W. Tuthill,

Ronnald P. Tyler, James O. Tyler, William S. Ullom, MD, L. T. Umfleet, Adelbert C. Underwood, Paul Walter Unger, PhD, Simon Upfill-Brown, Chester R. Upham Jr., James Upton, J. E. Upton, Randal W. Utech, Alfred L. Utesch, Raymond E. Vache, Ashokkumar N. Vachhani, MD, C. Valenzuel, William Pennington Van, PhD, Jack C. Van Horn, Earl D. Van Reenan, Rick Van Surksum, William E. Vanarsdale, PhD, John L. Vandeberg, PhD, Jerry L. Vanden Boom, PhD, Rainer A. Vanoni, William D. VanScoy, George G. Vanslyke, Kenneth L. Vantine, James E. Varnon, PhD, Mihal A. Vasilache, Joe E. Vaughan, PhD, David D. Vause, MD, William Austin Veech, PhD, Felix J. Vega, Steve Venner, Bruce L. Veralli, G. Verbeck, PhD, John D. Vermaelen, Lonnie W. Vernon, PhD, Billy E. Vernon, Richard R. Vernotzy Sr., Ralph W. Vertrees, Harry A. Vest, Dan E. Vickers, Keith V. Vickers, Fredrick L. Vieck, Rodolfo L. Villarreal, MD, Mikhail M. Vishik, PhD, Paul W. Visser, Russel C. Vlack, Jason P. Volk, Walter W. von Nimitz, PhD, Max R. Vordenbaum, Steve C. Voss, Bill S. Vowell, MD, Daniel P. Vrudny, Don C. Vu, James W. Wade, PhD, John C. Wade, William Wadsworth, Don B. Wafer, Ray F. Wagner, David P. Wagner, Alfred Wagner Jr., Marvin L. Wagoner, Richard B. Waina, PhD, Charles Wakefield, PhD, Brian E. Waldecker, PhD, Harry M. Walker, PhD, William F. Walker, John A. Walker, P. David Walker, Rodger L. Walker, Mark A. Wallace, Lynn H. Wallace, James P. Wallace, Anthony Waller, William Walls, William N. Wally, Bruce W. Walter, James C. Walter, D. Wambargh, Donald C. Wambaugh, David Y. Wang, PhD, Gordon P. Ward, T. G. Ward Jr., John B. Wardell, Ray W. Ware, MD, Robert A. Warner, Darrell G. Warner, Donald R. Warr, Bruce A. Warren, Cedric D. Warren, Joseph F. Warren, MD, Robert L. Warters, Richard Wasserman, MD, G. S. Wassum, Damon L. Watkins, Michael J. Watkins, Richard L. Watson, PhD, Mildred E. Watson, MD, Randy K. Watson, George Watters, Jack T. Watzke, Darel A. Wayhan, William Dewey Weatherford Jr., PhD, Mark Weatherston, Samuel R. Weaver, John M. Weaver, Ronald R. Weaver, George L. Weaver, Theodore Stratton Webb, PhD, David J. Weber, Monty Weddell, Timothy R. Weddle, Curtis E. Weddle, Olan B. Weeks, Scott C. Wehner, Bernard William Wehring, PhD, Jorge S. Weibel, Felicia K. Weidman, Donald G. Weilbaecher, MD, Richard D. Weilburg, MD, Lawrence Weinman, R. Stephen Weis, PhD, Lee Weis, Kent M. Weissling, M. E. Welbourn, Thomas L. Welch, Joe H. Wellborn, Lewis W. Wells, Howard T. Wells, MD, Roger Murray Wells, Bruce Welsh, Clayton H. Wene, Richard A. Werner, Kenneth G. Wernicke, Sidney E. West, MD, David E. West, J. C. West, Glen R. Westall, Gerald T. Westbrook, Mark E. Westcott, Jim P. Westerheid, William M. Westhoff, Thomas D. Westmoreland Jr., PhD, Harry Westmoreland, Gerhard Westra, Scott A. Westveer, Mitchell R. Whatley, Douglas H. Wheeler, William L. Wheeler, Clyde C. Wheeler, C. Wheeler, Thomas J. Wheeler, Lloyd Leon Whetzel, Richard M. Whiddon, Christian L. Whigham, Jerry L. White, D. J. White, B. Lee White Jr., MD, Charles Hugh Whiteside, PhD, C. H. Whiteside, PhD, Jack Whiteside, Montague Whiting, PhD, Raymond B. Whitley, Richard E. Whitmire, DVM, Philip Whitsitt, Christopher Whitten, James C. Whitten, Lester B. Whitton, Charles D. Whitwill, Paul A. Wichmann, S. A. Wickstrom*, Steven G. Widen, PhD, Vernon R. Widerquist, Robert Widmer, J. A. Wiebelt, PhD, G. Wieland, John Herbert Wiese, PhD, Alan Wiggins, Larry Wiginton, Kenneth A. Wigner, Herman S. Wigodsky, PhD, Bill O. Wilbanks, Hugh M. Wilbanks 3rd, Joe A. Wilbanks, Kenneth Alfred Wilde, PhD, Charles Wiley, Richard B. Wilkens, James Wilkes, Lambert H. Wilkes, Monte G. Wilkes, Stella H. Wilkes, Eugene M. Wilkins, PhD, Kevin L. Wilkins, Hector M. Willars, Richard D. Williams, PhD, C. H. Williams, PhD, Danny E. Williams, Reginald D. Williams, MD, Al V. Williams, MD, Roy D. Williams, Gary L. Williams, DVM, Talmage T. Williams, H. Hr. Williams, Jim Williams, Douglas B. Williams, Robert A. Williamson, Joe W. Williamson, Glen R. Willie, Allen H. Williford, H. Earl Willis, Gary L. Willmann, DVM, Charles L. Willshire, Bobby Wilson, PhD, William R. Wilson, Willie J. Wilson, David A. Wilson, Rick Wilson, MD, Owen D. Wilson, D. Winans, Lars I. Wind, Edgar C. Winegartner, Christopher L. Wingert, Herald Winkler, PhD, Weldon E. Winsauer, Donald K. Winsor, J. E. Wirsching, Joe E. Wirsching, Michael B. Wisebaker, Del N. Wisler, Eugene Harley Wissler, PhD, Wojciech S. Witkowski, MD, Donald A. Witt, A. J. Wittenbach, Thomas R. Woehler, H. B. Wofford, Craig A. Wohlers, Earl G. Wolf, John C. Wolfe, PhD, Robert Womack, Gary L. Womack, Bob G. Wonish, Scott Emerson Wood, PhD, David R. Wood, Steve Wood, Charles R. Woodbury, Edward G. Woods, PhD, John P. Woods, PhD, Robert F. Woods, Herbert H. Woodson, Gary R. Wooley, PhD, Stphen T. Woolley, Bobby D. Woosley, Rodney L. Wooster, Joe Max Word, DVM, J. Max Word, Roy A. Worrell, Jonathan H. Worstell, PhD, Conrad H. Wright, Harold E. Wright, Thomas R. Wright Jr., Keith H. Wrolstad, PhD, Gang M. Wu, PhD, Peter T. Wu, PhD, W. H. Wurth, Reece E. Wyant, Philip R. Wyde, PhD, James M. Wylie, E. Staten Wynne, PhD, Elmer Staten Wynne, PhD, Will Yanke, Harold L. Yarger, PhD, Tommie E. Yates, M. Yavuz Corp., PhD, Curtis Yawn, J. C. Yeager, Wilbur A. Yeager Jr., Jim P. Yocham, B. Biff Yochum, John G. Yonkers, Farrile S. Young, PhD, Joe A. Young, Clifton L. Young, Ruby D. Young, Susan W. Young, James L. Youngblood, PhD, James D. Younger, William M. Zahn Jr., Joseph E. Zanoni, Hua-Wei Zhou, PhD, Lois A. Ziler, John Zimmerman, PhD, James S. Zimmerman, Ralph Anthony Zingaro, PhD, Clarence R. Zink, Richard J. Zinno, Darryl E. Zoch, Jerome Zorinksy, PhD, Alfonso J. Zuniga, Philip L. Zuvanich

Utah

Jason Abel, Terry Ahlquist, Marvin E. Allen, Merrill P. Allen, Raul C. Alva, D. Andersen, Wilbert C. Anderson, John O. Anderson, Russell Anderson, M. B. Andrus, PhD, Robert Apple, Melvin B. Armstrong, Kenny Ashby,

John R. Atkinson, J. R. Atkinson, D. Austin, PhD, Lloyd H. Austin, Robert J. Baczuk, Jay M. Bagley, PhD, R. E. Bailey, Ramon Condie Baird, PhD, Roger E. Banner, PhD, Mark Owens Barlow, M. D. Barnes, PhD, Howard F. Bartlett, T. David Bastian, Joseph Clair Batty, PhD, Peggy Beatty, Ken L. Beatty, Albert I. Beazer, Boyd R. Beck, PhD, Merrill W. Beckstead, PhD, Blake D. Beckstrom, Gregory J. Bell, Alvin Benson, PhD, Wesley George Bentrude, PhD, David Alan Berges, PhD, John A. Bianucci, Kip A. Billings, Robert F. Bitner, MD, George R. Blake, Clyde Blauer, Douglas Bledsoe, Jerry C. Bommer, PhD, Blair E. Bona, PhD, Jay Frank Bonell, P. R. Borgmeier, PhD, David Borronam, John F. Boyle, MD, Bruce Bradley, Ernest T. Bramwell, William W. Brant, Kennethe Martin Brauner, PhD, Thomas O. Breitling, Lynn H. Bringhurst, H. Smith Broadbent, PhD, H. Smith Broadbent, PhD, Hyrum Smith Broadbent, PhD, Boyd C. Bronson, Billings Brown, PhD, John N. Brown, Arthur D. Bruno, Shawn P. Buchanan, Wallace Don Budge, PhD, Mark D. Bunnell, David D. Busath, MD, Clinton Bybee, Charles H. Cameron, Earl E. Castner, Norman L. Challburg, MD, Kenneth W. Chase, PhD, Norman Jerry Chatterton, PhD, Joseph A. Chenworth, Allen D. Child, Joseph G. Christensen, Jay P. Christofferson, PhD, John C. Clegg, PhD, Calvin Geary Clyde, PhD, Ralph L. Coates, PhD, Richard M. Cohen, PhD, Don J. Colton, Jack Comeford, PhD, Melvin Alonzo Cook, PhD, Vernon O. Cook, Michael L. Cosgrave, MD, Robert E. Covington, Mac Crosby, Larry D. Culberson, PhD, Gary Monroe Cupp, Lowell C. Dahl, Donald Albert Dahlstrom, PhD, Jonathan H. Daines, MD, Robert Elliott Davis, PhD, Leland P. Davis, Tom Dawson, Karl Devenport, C. Nelson Dorny, PhD, Andrew Drake, John J. Drammis, MD, Gary L. Draper, Bryan B. Drennan, William S. Dunford, MD, William R. Edgel, PhD, Allan C. Edson, George Eisenman, George L. Eitel, David A. Eldredge Jr., Robert W. English, Norman T. Erekson, PhD, Jerry A. Erickson, PhD, Creed M. Evans, Jeff Farrer, PhD, David Feller, PhD, D. Feller, PhD, David Allan Firmage, D. Allan Firmage, Thomas H. Fletcher, PhD, Paul V. Fonnesbeck, PhD, Grant Robert Fowles, PhD, Richard L. Frost, PhD, Norihiko Fukuta, PhD, Ron Fuller, Blair O. Furner, Charles O. Gale, Lynn E. Garner, PhD, S. Parkes Gay Jr., Mark G. Gessel, Thon T. Gin, PhD, George R. Glance, Fred L. Greer, MD, K. Greer, Glen Griffin, MD, Richard W. Grow, PhD, Pamela Grubaugh-Littig, Michel B. Guinn, Robert L. Haffner, Edward H. Hahne, Bill A. Hancock, Dallas Hanks, Darrell G. Hansen, Wayne R. Hansen, Larry R. Hardy, Franklin S. Harris Jr., PhD, Ellis D. Harris, Ronald L. Harris, William Joshua Haslem, Scott E. Hassett, Stuart Havenstrite, Ralph Hayes, Creed Haymond, Dale G. Heaton, Lavell Merl Henderson, PhD, Deloy G. Hendricks, PhD, R. Dahl Hendrickson, James O. Henrie, Lyle G. Hereth, Charles Selby Herrin, PhD, John C. Higgins, PhD, Archie Clyde Hill, PhD, Allen E. Hilton II, Clifford M. Hinckley, PhD, Robert L. Hobson, PhD, Grant Holdaway, David E. Holt, Ralph M. Horton, PhD, M. I. Horton, PhD, Frederick A. Hottes, Clayton Shirl Huber, PhD, J. Poulson Hunter, MD, Harvey L. Hutchinson, Kyle Jackson, Daniel J. Janney, Dan Janney, August Wilhelm Jaussi, PhD, Marcus Martin Jensen, PhD, Leland V. Jensen, Layne D. Jensen, Brian Jensen, L. Carl Jensen, Kendall B. Johnson, PhD, Arlo F. Johnson, PhD, Todd Johnson, PhD, Owen W. Johnson, PhD, Von D. Jolley, PhD, Percy C. Jonat, MD, Merrell Robert Jones, PhD, Walter V. Jones, John Jonkman, Royce A. Jorgensen, Mark Kaschmitter, Stephen Jorgensen Kelsey, PhD, Boyd M. Kitchen, PhD, Kenneth T. Klebba, Frederick Charles Kohout, PhD, David L. Kooyman, PhD, Steven K. Koski, William B. Laker, Burt Lamborn, Burton B. Lamborn, Lloyd Larsen, PhD, Robert Paul Larsen, PhD, Dale G. Larsen, Robert W. Leake, Charles Lear, Gregory L. LeClaire, James Norman Lee, PhD, David J. Lee, Lawrence Guy Lewis, PhD, Stephen Liddle, PhD, Thomas W. Lloyd, Wilburn L. Luna, Mark Wylie Lund, PhD, Charles P. Lush, Joseph L. Lyon, William E. Maddex, Robert K. Maddock, Jules J. Magda, PhD, Kenneth A. Mangelson, PhD, Brent P. Marchant, Eugene Marshall, Vern T. May, John May, D. Maynes, PhD, Robert Eli McAdams, PhD, John McDonald, PhD, Susan O. McDonald, Timothy W. McGuire, Jeffrey D. Mckay, Cyrus Milo McKell, PhD, Jefferson D. McKenzie, Hugh A. McLean, Dick N. Mechem, John Mercier, Daniel W. Miles, PhD, John G. Miles, Wade Elliott Miller II, PhD, Gene W. Miller, PhD, Paul Mills, Bryant A. Miner, PhD, Robert Alan Mole, J. Ward Moody, PhD, M. Lyman Moody, MD, Karl G. Morey, John G. Morrison, Kay S. Mortensen, PhD, William R. Mosby, Thomas C. Moseley, Loren Cameron Mosher, PhD, Alfred R. Motzkus, Glenn L. Mower, Harold W. Mulvany, Grant R. Murdoch, Donald L. Myrup, Dave Neale, Michael G. Nelson, PhD, Manfred R. Nelson, MD, Pamela Nelson, Kenneth W. Nelson, Gregg Nickel, Donald R. Nielsen, PhD, Barry C. Nielsen, Dennis M. Nielsen, Edwin Clyde Nordquist, Robert Quincy Oaks Jr., PhD, Hayward B. Oblad, PhD, David Oehler, Leonard Olds, Larry S. Olsen, Merrill H. Olson, Ted Olson, Robert E. O'Neill, Alfred M. Osborne, Robert Pack, PhD, Lowell L. Palm, Tom T. Paluso, Joseph M. Papenfuss, PhD, Robert Lynn Park, PhD, Gerald M. Park, Robert Walter Parry, PhD, Forest Parry, Ernest B. Paxson, PhD, Clifford C. Payton, Justin B. Peatross, PhD, Leslie H. Pennington, Danial L. Perry, Jay D. Peterson, Randall D. Peterson, Jay W. Phippen, PhD, Paul E. Pilgram, MD, Michael L. Pinnell, William G. Pitt, PhD, Charles H. Pitt, PhD, Steven J. Postma, Bradley M. Powell, John D. Prater, Jim S. Priskos, Frederick Dan Provenza, PhD, Ronald J. Pugmire, PhD, Samuel C. Quigley, Francis Rakow, Carole A. Ray, Jory Ty Redd, PhD, Donal J. Reed, PhD, Alvin C. Rencher, PhD, Alvin C. Reniher, PhD, Brian W. Rex, Max J. Reynolds, Michael D. Rice, PhD, Lynn S. Richards, PhD, Gary Haight Richardson, PhD, Harold W. Ritchey, PhD, Samuel P. Roberts, T. F. Robinson, PhD, Clay W. Robinson, DVM, Alden C. Robinson, Lee E. Rogers, William C. Romney, Simpson Roper, Harold L. Rosenhan, George W. Sandberg, LeRoy J. Sauter, Keith Jerome Schaiger, PhD, Ernest F. Scharkan, Edward B. Schoppe, Spencer L. Seager, PhD, W. Kenneth Sherk, Jay G. Shields, Charles W. Shoun, Richard Phil Shumway, PhD, Val E. Simmons, PhD, David Michael Sipe, PhD, Duane Sjoberg, Ross A. Smart, Hyrum M. Smith, Tracy

W. Smith, Leonard W. Snellman, PhD, Richard L. Snow, PhD, Phillip T. Solomon, Carl D. Sorensen, PhD, Wesley K. Sorensen, Brent A. Sorenson, Forrest L. Staffanson, PhD, Norman E. Stauffer, PhD, K. S. Stevens, PhD, Leo M. Stevenson, MD, Kenneth J. Stracke, Glen Evan Stringham, PhD, William J. Strong, PhD, Calvin K. Sudweeks, Robert Summers, PhD, Richard Swenson, B. A. Tait, PhD, Carlos Tavares, James S. Taylor, PhD, Randall L. Taylor, Doug Taylor, Lester Taylor, Richard Tebbs, Abraham Teng, PhD, Lawrence E. Thatcher, John D. Thirkill, Don Wylie Thomas, PhD, James H. Thomas, PhD, Grant Thompson, PhD, Philip Thompson, Richard M. Thorup, PhD, Richard N. Thwaitis, PhD, Rudy W. Tietze, Kerry Tobin, David O. Topham, Anthony R. Torres, MD, Del Traveller, J. Paul Tullis, PhD, George Uhlig, PhD, Richard M. Vennett, PhD, John M. Viehweg, Charles T. Vono, John W. Vosskuhler, MD, Kathleen L. Wegener, Lewis F. Wells, Joseph C. Wells Jr., Eleroy H. West, D. R. Westenskow, PhD, Edward B. Whicker, Lowell D. White CIH, PhD, Brent L. White, Thomas G. White, Leslie Whitton, PhD, Harry E. Wickes, PhD, Clifford Lavar Wilcox, PhD, W. Vincent Wilding, PhD, David P. Wilding, Bill Beauford Wiley, PhD, Charles Ronald Willden, PhD, Arnold Wilson, PhD, Byron J. Wilson, PhD, Stephen E. Wilson, Robert J. Wise, John K. Wood, PhD, Jack L. Woods, Richard E. Wyman, Thomas B. Yeager, Gordon Young, Glen A. Zumwalt

Vermont

Paul A. Bailly, PhD, Paul A. Bailly, PhD, Robert A. Baum, Eric Bellows, Bruce Irving Bertelsen, Lawrence Bilodeau, Larry Bilodeau, James H. Burbo, Bernard Byrne, PhD, Robert E. Chiabrandy, Donald Lyndon Clark, PhD, William Wesley Currier, PhD, Barry S. Deliduka, Blair J. Enman, Nils C. Ericksen, James Evans, MD, Paul D. Fear, Daniel P. Foty, PhD, Daniel Foty, Paul D. Gardner, William Halpern, PhD, Ray A. Hango, Grant Hopkins Harnest, PhD, David Japikse, PhD, Thomas J. Laplaca, PhD, Anthony Lauck, Peter P. Lawlor, MD, George Butterick Maccollom, PhD, Kenneth Gerard Mann, PhD, William W. Martinez, John McClaughry, Jack Noll, Duncan G. Ogden, Donald C. Oliveau, MD, Frank R. Paolini, PhD, Henry B. Patterson, Malcolm J. Paulsen, MD, Hans J. Pfister, Kerri L. Polli, Olin E. Potter, F. H. Raab, PhD, Frederick H. Raab, PhD, Benjamin F. Richards Jr., PhD, Alvert L. Robitaille, Albert L. Robitaille, Thomas Dudley Sachs, PhD, Phillip J. Savoy, Christian T. Scheindel, Josh Schultz, Byron G. Sherman, MD, Thomas Smith, PhD, Frank J. Thornton, Waclaw Timoszyk, PhD, Ralph Wallace, PhD

Virginia

Allwyn Albuquerque, Ernest Charles Alcaraz, PhD, James F. Alexander Jr., David M. Allen, Kristin L. Allen, Frank Murray Almeter, PhD, Gerald L. Anderson, John Andrako, PhD, Scott Andrews, PhD, Steven T. Angely, Lee Saunders Anthony, PhD, Richard J. Ardine Arthur, William E. Armour, Randolph Ashby, PhD, Michael J. Atherton, PhD, James C. Auckland, Brian Augustine, PhD, Alex Avery, Vernon H. Baker, PhD, Mark A. Ball, Greg Ballengee, George R. Barber Jr., Theodore K. Barna, PhD, Scott A. Barnhill, Maria V. Bartha, John Wesley Bartlett, PhD, Thomas A. Bartlett, Mark D. Basile, James Bateman, Alan P. Batson, PhD, Kirk Battleson, PhD, Bradley M. Bauer, Peyton B. Baughan, Lester F. Baum, Mike B. Bealey, George A. Beasley, Kenneth L. Bedford, PhD, Paul J. Berenson, PhD, James R. Berger, Marion Joseph Bergin, Peter F. Bermel, Simon S. Bernstein, PhD, Robert W. Berry, Peter J. Bethell, Eguene R. Biagi, Rudolf Bickel, MD, Charles F. Bieber, Billy Elias Bingham, PhD, Rebecca B. Bittner, Thomas E. Bjerke, Albert W. Blackburn, Paul M. Blaiklock, PhD, Robert V. Blanke, PhD, George K. Bliss, John C. Bloxham, DVM, Randy L. Boice, Arthur F. Boland, Robert G. Boldue, W. Kline Bolton, MD, Robert A. Book, PhD, John W. Boring, PhD, Robert Clare Bornmann, MD, Benjamin A. Bosher*, Truman Arthur Botts, PhD, Charles Bowman, Donald C. Bowman, Ricky L. Bowman, Joseph V. Braddock, PhD, William L. Brandt, Townsend D. Breeden, William B. Brent, PhD, Philip W. Brewer, Frank Brimelow, Robert Britton, John A. Brockwell Sr., Kevin J. Brogan, PhD, Steven D. Brooks, Paul Wallace Broome, PhD, Jerry W. Brown, PhD, Jeffrey P. Brown, James A. Brown, Henry B. R. Brown, Doug L. Brown, J. Paul Brown, Christopher J. Brown, Robert D. Buchy, Joseph A. Buder, MD, Merton W. Bunker Jr., Kenneth Burbank, PhD, Thomas J. Burbey, PhD, Robert Burger, John P. Burkett, Harold Eugene Burkhart, PhD, Rhendal Butler, Robert Campbell, Homer Walter Carhart, PhD, David R. Carlson, MD, Aubrey M. Cary Jr., Douglas R. Case, Davis S. Caskey, Armand Ralph Casola, PhD, Neal Castagnoli, PhD, Derek Cate, James R. Cavalet, Steven L. Cazad, Charles Mackay Chambers, PhD, Sanjay Chandra, Fred R. Chapman, Rees C. Chapman, MD, Telesphore L. Charland, John T. Chehaske, John Chehuske, PhD, Wayne P. Chepren, PhD, Nancy A. Chiafulio, Melvin C. Ching, PhD, Alfred N. Christiansen, John A. Cifala, MD, Randall A. Clark, Donald T. Clark, R. Clay, Dennis Cline, Daniel G. Coake, Walter Cobbs, PhD, James F. Coble, PhD, Benjamin R. Cofer, Murry J. Cohen, MD, Albert R. Colan, William F. Collins, PhD, James E. Collins, Timothy B. Compton, Bryan Keith Condrey, David A. Conley, John Irving Connolly Jr., PhD, Frederick E. Conrad, MD, Richard H. Coppo, William P. Corish, Roscoe Roy Cosby Jr., MD, David G. Cotts, Edwin Cox, Forrest E. Coyle, Barry D. Crane, PhD, Stephen J. Creane, A. Scott Crossfield, Lloyd R. Crowther, Daniel J. Cunningham III, Thomas Fortsen Curry, PhD, James M. Cutts, James Frederick Dalby, PhD, Harry P. Dalton, PhD, Thomas J. Dalzell, Joe E. Darby, Ralph E. Darling, DVM, Bradley Darr, Philip E. Davis, John Siv

Davis, MD, Barry G. Dawkins, DVM, James Carroll Deddens, Gary Constantine Defoti, PhD, Gary C. Defotis, PhD, Rosalie F. Degiovanni-Donnelly, PhD, Stephen Degray, Michael P. Deisenroth, PhD, Joseph F. Delahanty, Barbu J. Demian, PhD, Edmund G. Dennis, Alan M. Dennis, Raymond Edwin Dessy, PhD, Raymond A. DeStephen, G. W. Detty, John F. Devaney, James A. Deye, PhD, John Dickmann, Robert B. Dillaway, PhD, John K. Dixon, PhD, Wayne A. Dixon, Robert Dobessette, D. C. Doe, Robert C. Dolecki, Jocelyn Fielding Douglas, PhD, Rose T. Douglas, Basil C. Doumas, PhD, Frederick Joseph Doyle, PhD, David J. Drahos, PhD, Bill Drennan, P. Du, Michael Serge Duesbery, PhD, Samuel M. Dunaway Jr., Charles F. Dunkl, PhD, Kevin M. Dunn, PhD, James H. Durham, Thomas Earles, W. S. Easterling, PhD, Charles J. Eby, PhD, Michael T. Eckert, Arthur L. Eller, PhD, Stanley M. Elmore, MD, R. Elswick, PhD, Thomas C. Elwell, Thomas H. Emsley, John J. Engel, MD, John R. English, Gerard J. Enigk, James W. Enochs Jr., Jeffrey F. Eppink, James L. Erb, John R. Esser, Edward R. Estes Jr., Juliette A. Estevez, Pamel F. Faggert, Dennis A. Falgout, PhD, Michael A. Farge, Anthony L. Farinola, W. Michael Farmer, PhD, Ollie J. Farnam, Frank Hunter Featherston, PhD, James Love Fedrick, PhD, Michael B. Feil, Harvey L. Fein, PhD, Michael D. Fenton, PhD, Joseph L. Ferguson, William P. Fertall, David C. Finch, Alvin W. Finestone, MD, Martin C. Fisher, Richard Harding Fisher, MD, Donald E. Fleming, G. Flowers, PhD, Michael Shepard Forbes, PhD, R. C. Forrester 3rd, PhD, Mark A. Forte, Russell Elwell Fox, PhD, Eugene K. Fox, Roger Frampton, PhD, Rogert D. Frampton, PhD, Bill Franklin, Daniel Frederick, Herbert Friedman, PhD, Keith Frye, PhD, Charles S. Frye, C. Sherman Frye, Michael L. Fudge, Harold Walter Gale, PhD, Mario R. Gamboa, A. K. Ganguly, PhD, Hessle Filmore Garner, PhD, Jerry H. Gass, Stephen Jerome Gawarecki, PhD, Henry T. Gawrylowicz, James J. Gehrig, Richard B. Geiger, Daniel F. Geldermann, Jerauld Gentry, George C. Gerber, Edward T. Gerry, PhD, David P. Gianettino, Jonathan Gifford, PhD, George Thomas Gillies, PhD, Mark S. Goff, Arthur A. Goodier, Hubert C. Goodman Jr., Louie Aubrey Goodson, Heinz August Gorges, PhD, Paul Gorman, Steven D. Goughnor, R. Robert Goughnour, PhD, S. William Gouse, PhD, Martha S. Granger, MD, George A. Gray, PhD, Michael N. Greeley, Steve R. Green, John P. Greenaway, Everette D. Greinke, Norman J. Griest, Ernest E. Grisdale, Bernardo F. Grossling, PhD, Daniel G. Hadacek, DVM, Henry A. Haefele, Gary J. Hagan, Harold B. Haley, MD, Brian J. Hall, Brian Hall, Christian L. Haller, Gordon S. Hamilton, Edward Hanrahan, PhD, Robert H. Hansen, Richard C. Hard, MD, Mary K. Harding, P. L. Hardy Jr., Robin C. Hardy, Thomas J. Harkins, David W. Harned, Russell S. Harris Jr., Hetzal Hartley, Ken Haught, PhD, Dexter Stearns Haven, Harold E. Headlee, Sean M. Headrick, David R. Heebner, Glenn R. Heidbreder, PhD, Robert Virgil Hemm, PhD, Frank D. Henderson, Ronald J. Hendrickson, George Burns Hess, PhD, William R. Hestand, Dennis W. Heuer, James Veith Hewett, PhD, Richard M. Hicks, Ronald Earl Highsmith, PhD, Peter J. Hill, Edward W. Hiltebeitel, Barton Leslie Hinkle, PhD, Jeffery G. Hinson, Donald A. Hirst, PhD, Charles C. Hogge, MD, Richard Holcombe, Michael D. Holder, W. J. Hooker, PhD, Carroll B. Hooper, Philip E. Hoover, T. E. Hopkins, William J. Horvath, Eric W. Howard, James Secord Howland, PhD, Tsuying Hsieh, PhD, Juergen Hubert, PhD, William L. Hudgins, Greg R. Hughey, David M. Human, Jeffrey E. Humphrey, PhD, Joe Hundley, Joseph W. Hundley Jr., Lee McCaa Hunt, Thomas C. Hunter, Samir Hussamy, PhD, James B. Hutt Jr., Michael B. Hydorn, PhD, Robert Mitsuru Ikeda, PhD, Anton Louis Inderbitzen, PhD, Jeffrey Ingram, Carl T. Jackson, George A. Jahnigen, John A. Jane Sr., PhD, Dale R. Jensen, Mark Jerussi, William A. Jesser, PhD, Tedd H. Jett, Charles Minor Johnson, PhD, Robert S. Johnson, PhD, Wellington H. Jones, Gerald L. Jones, Richard D. Jones, Oliver Jones, C. R. Judy, H. Julich, Mario George Karfakis, PhD, Jeffrey M. Kauffman, Peter W. Kauffman, Saul Kay, MD, John Kckert, Ray N. Keffer, Seth R. Kegan, Karl S. Keim, Bernhard Edward Keiser, PhD, Claud Marvin Kellett, Jack Martin Kerr, John C. Kershenstein, PhD, Donald J. Kienast, Theo Daniel Kimbrough, PhD, Bessie H. Kirkwood, PhD, Ahto N. Kivi, George J. Klett, Denny L. Kline, S. J. Kloda, John M. Knew, Maurice Kniceley Jr., C. P. Koelling, PhD, Gary L. Koerner, Fred Koester Jr., Joshua O. Kolawole, PhD, Andrew Kolonay, Brent D. Kornman, Theresa M. Koschny, Geoffrey A. Krafft, PhD, E. H. Krafft, David E. Kranbuehl, PhD, Robert K. Krout, Peter George Krueger, PhD, Eric M. Krupacs, John M. Lafferty Jr., William A. Laing, Stephen A. Lamanna, Roland J. Land, Richard A. Lander, Calvert T. Larsen, PhD, Jeffrey G. Larson, Thomas J. Lauterio, PhD, William F. Lavecchia, Armistead M. Leggett, Daniel D. Lelong, Stanley H. Levinson, PhD, Michael D. Lewes, Scott B. Lewis, PhD, David W. Lewis, PhD, Verna M. Lewis, Peter E. Lewis, Gabriel Lifschitz, Philip D. Lindahl, Robert B. Lindemann, Charles J. Lindemann II, Hal Lion, Lenny W. Lipscomb, Clement M. Llewellyn Jr., Krystyna Kopaczyk Locke, PhD, Raymond Kenneth Locke, David Loduca, Edward R. Long, PhD, Jean E. Loonam, PhD, William Farrand Loranger, PhD, Thomas A. Loredo, James L. Loveland, James A. Lovett, David N. Lucas, Daniel D. Ludwig, PhD, John Henry Lupinski, PhD, J. W. Luquire, PhD, Travis O. Lyday, William G. Maclaren Jr., PhD, Michael T. Madden, Dave N. Mahony, Thomas H. Maichak, Albert C. Malacarne, Robert R. Mantz, George E. Marak, MD, Glenn R. Marchione, Thomas Ewing Margrave, PhD, Michael Markels Jr., PhD, John L. Marocchi, Robert L. Marovelli, Patrick D. Marsden, Sewell R. Marsh, James A. Marshall, PhD, Robert D. Matulka, PhD, Steven E. Mays, John Hart McAdoo, PhD, William C. McCarthy, MD, Robert F. McCarty, James K. McClanahan, Tracy McCombs, Fred Campbell McCormick, PhD, Irwin H. McCumber, Daniel F. McDonald, PhD, Diane McDonaugh, Tomas T. McFie, PhD, Charles Wesley McGary Jr., PhD, Thomas J. McGean, Henry Alexander McGee Jr., PhD, James G. McGee, Thomas H. McGorry, MD, Lea B. McGovern, DVM, James E. McGrath, PhD, Robert J. McKay, Thomas E.

McKiernan, George McKinney, Robert L. McMasters, PhD, John W. McNair, Harry W. Meador, Walter S. Medding, Barbara Mella, MD, Arthur Mendonsa, T. Metzgar, PhD, William F. Meyer, DVM, Earl Lawrence Meyers, PhD, Patrick J. Michael, PhD, David John Michel, PhD, Robert Michel, Brooks A. Mick, MD, Ronald J. Mickiewicz, Marshall Miller, Charles R. Miller III, Dan Millison, Larry L. Misenheimer, Alfred F. Mistr Jr., John E. Mock, PhD, Jacob T. Moll, PhD, Thomas W. Moodie, Thomas K. Moore, PhD, Matthew Moriarty, Cecil Arthur Morris, PhD, Professor Morrow, PhD, Melody A. Morrow, MD, Vivekanand Mukhopadhyay, PhD, V. Mukhopadhyay, PhD, Ragnwald Muller, Robert Murdock, MD, Roy K. Murdock, Robert Stafford Murphey, PhD, Wayne K. Murphy, PhD, Clifford A. Myers, Larry K. Myrick, Fred W. Nagle Jr., Brett Newman, PhD, Nancy Newman, DVM, K. D. Ngo, PhD, Lee Lockhead Nichols, PhD, Alvin E. Nieder, Mark J. Norden, Pamela Norris, PhD, Thomas Nyman, E. J. O'Brien, Walter Clayton Ormsby, PhD, Peter P. Ostrowski, PhD, Wesley Emory Pace, Jack Paden, Robert R. Palik, Nina Parker, PhD, K. W. Parrish, H. D. Parry, Joseph A. Paschall, Thomas Joseph Pasko, Marvin P. Pastel, PhD, Wilbur I. Patterson, PhD, Kerry B. Patterson, Harold J. Peake, Edward F. Pearsall, PhD, Eugene Lincoln Peck, PhD, Thomas R. Pepitone, PhD, Paul E. Perrone, John Edward Perry, Rafayel A. Petrossian, David Van Petten, Gerard David Pfeifer, PhD, Arun G. Phadk3, PhD, Roland W. Phillips Jr., John J. Phillips Jr., Timothy Pickenheim, Rhonda L. Pierce, DVM, O. Pierrakos, PhD, Vincent A. Pierro, John B. Pietron, H. Alan Pike, PhD, Herman H. Pinkerton, PhD, Ricker R. Polsdorfer, MD, Benjamin W. Pope, MD, William W. Porterfield, PhD, H. W. Porterfield, John T. Postak, Donald H. Potter, Edward T. Powell, PhD, Arel W. Powers, Mary K. Prettyman, Steven Price, PhD, Fred H. Proctor, PhD, Anthony J. Provenzano, PhD, Charles S. Pugh, Joan L. Purdy, Walter V. Purnell Jr., Robert H. Pusey, PhD, Richard Lee Puster, William P. Raney, PhD, Richard Travis Rauch, PhD, Tomas Reamsnyder, Kay P. Reasor, DVM, John G. Reed, Barry G. Reid, Keith W. Reiss, PhD, David E. Reubush, James M. Reynolds, Fred R. Riddell, PhD, Harold E. Ritter, Joseph Peter Riva, Joseph A. Robinson, Samuel A. Rodgers, Henry M. Rogers, MD, David Rogers, Thomas M. Rohrbaugh, Oscar A. Rondon-Aramayo, PhD, Thomas J. Rosener, PhD, Fred Rosi, PhD, Tom L. Rourk, John Rowland, PhD, Charlotte E. Roydhouse, DVM, John Rudolf, John R. Ruff, Larry E. Ruggiero, Clifford D. Russell, Todd M. Rutherford, John Ruvalds, PhD, Fredrick J. Ryan, Robert R. Ryland, Aubrey E. Sadler, Donald L. Sage, Gerald O. Sakats, Donald R. Salyer, W. J. Samford, Vernon C. Sanders, G. S. Santi, David P. Sargent, James M. Sawhill Jr., PhD, Francis T. Schaeffer, Joseph T. Schatzman, Frank R. Scheid Jr., Karl A. Schellenberg, PhD, Joseph A. Schetz, PhD, Robert J. Scheuplein, PhD, Raymond Schneider, PhD, R. Wane Schneiter, PhD, Robert W. Schneiter, PhD, Matthew J. Schor, Dunell V. Schull Ret, Eugene H. Scott, PhD, James Byrd Seaborn, PhD, John H. Seipel, PhD, J. Michael Selnick, Karl A. Sense, John L. Sewall, James Shaeffer, PhD, Donald G. Shaheen, Paul Shahinian, PhD, Donald E. Shaneberger, John A. Shannon, Anthony R. Sharkey, Steven Shaw, James J. Shea, Gary A. Sheehan, Jennifer P. Sheets, Scott T. Shipley, PhD, Gilbert R. Shockley, PhD, Stephen A. Shoop, MD, George M. Shrieves, George John Simeon, PhD, Gordon B. Sims Jr., S. Fred Singer, PhD, Herbert James Sipe Jr., PhD, Jerome P. Skelly FCP, PhD, Alfred Skolnick, PhD, J. L. Slaughter, Daniel F. Sloan, Gregory E. Slominski, Anthony R. Slotwinksi, Dale Smith, PhD, Ray M. Smith, MD, Emerson W. Smith, Bryan W. Smith, Blanchard D. Smith, Lyle C. Snidow III, Glenn J. Snyder, Jardslaw Sobieski, PhD, Jaroslaw Sobieski, PhD, Joseph E. Sohoski, Andrew Paul Somlyo, MD, Donald E. Sours Sr., Samuel V. Spagnolo, David W. Speer, Gilbert Neil Spokes, PhD, Lucian Matthew Sprague, PhD, Edward James Spyhalski, PhD, William S. Stambaugh, PhD, Raymond M. Standahar, Richard G. Starck II, Lendell Eugene Steele, Bland A. Stein, Kenneth Stepka, Scott M. Stevens, Robert R. Stimpson, Jan Stofberg, PhD, Evangelos P. Stoyas, Sharon R. Streight, PhD, Walter Strohecker, Harry M. Strong, Erick Stusnick, PhD, Jack A. Suddreth, Ronald M. Sundelin, PhD, William G. Sutton, PhD, Waller C. Tabb, MD, Keith A. Taggart, PhD, Sandra R. Tall, DVM, Lukas Tamm, PhD, Suren A. Tatulian, PhD, Gilbert A. Tellefsen, Wilton R. Tenney, PhD, Milton D. Tetterton Jr., Matthew A. Thexton, Thomas Thorpe, Albert William Tiedemann, PhD, Samuel C. Tignor, PhD, Calvin Omah Tiller, James F. Tobey Jr., Joseph J. Tobias, Gregory A. Topasna, PhD, Edward Thomas Toton, PhD, Priestley Toulmin, PhD, Richmond S. Trotter, Walter L. Turnage, John Charles Turner, PhD, Ian Charles Twilley, PhD, Russell K. Tyson, George J. Vames, Jim VanEaton, PhD, Dirk G. Vanvort, Frederick Vastine, PhD, Sidney Edwin Veazey, PhD, Karl F. Veith, PhD, Richard W. Vogel, Edward J. Vollrath, Willard A. Wade II, Jon A. Wadley, Sharyl E. Walker, PhD, Richard D. Walker, PhD, Ann S. Walker, DVM, Raymond Howard Wallace, J. L. Wallace, Richard C. Walsh, DVM, Theodore Ross Walton, PhD, John W. Ward, PhD, Holland Douglas Warren, PhD, David T. Warriner, William A. Watson III, PhD, Harry Weaver, Randy L. Weingart, Brian L. Weinstein, Martin Weiss, PhD, Elizabeth Fortson Wells, PhD, John L. Welsh, DVM, Lewis Wertz, Roger L. Wesley, MD, Alfred L. West II, Warwick R. West, Burt O. Westerman, Kurt O. Westerman, David E. Wheeler, Oliver B. White, Richard P. White, Dale Whitman, Robert R. Wiederkehr, PhD, King W. Wieman, Donald Richard Wiesnet, Stafford H. Williams, Gaylord S. Williams, MD, Sheldon P. Wimpfen, Russell Lowell Wine, PhD, Billy K. Wingfield, DVM, Reed H. Winslow, Eleanor Stiegler Wintercorn, PhD, Dermor M. Winters, Dermot M. Winters, James C. Wirt, Lawrence Arndt Wishner, PhD, Abund O. Wist, PhD, Norman C. Witbeck, PhD, James M. Witting, PhD, Marcus M. Wolf, Eligius A. Wolicki, PhD, Walter Ralph Woods, PhD, Eugene G. Wrieden, Ed Wright, M. R. J. Wyllie, PhD, M. R. Wyllie, PhD, Yijing Xu, PhD, Edward Carson Yates Jr., PhD, Philip R. Young, PhD, Joseph A. Zak, PhD, Todd Zischke, Laura Zischke, Warren Zitzmann, Ernst G. Zurflueh, PhD

Washington

William M. Adams, PhD, Grant Alberich, Marcus Albro, Garrett D. Alcorn, Joel W. Alldredge, William Allen Jr., Sidney J. Altschuler, Dayton L. Alverson, PhD, Larry C. Amans, Donald Heruin Anderson, PhD, Theodore D. Anderson, Tom P. Anderson, Mark A. Anderson, Norman Apperson, William S. Arnett, Alvin G. Ash, Eugene Roy Astley, William Dudson Bacon, PhD, Quincey Lamar Baird, PhD, George M. Barrington, PhD, William G. Bartel, Z. E. Bartusch, Edward J. Barvick, Dale E. Bean, John A. Bell, PhD, James C. Bellamy, MD, Randy Belstad, Dean A. Bender, John A. Bennett, John C. Berg, PhD, Andrew W. Berg, Richard A. Bergquist, Bertram Rodney Bertramson, PhD, Nedavia Bethlahmy, PhD, Jack S. Bevan, Joseph John Bevelacqua, PhD, Hans Bichsel, PhD, Darrel Rudolph Bienz, PhD, Theo Karl Bierlein, PhD, J. Bierman, George A. Block, Leo R. Bohanick, Michael A. Bohls, Mary Ann Bolte, MD, Glenn G. Bonacum, MD, L. P. Bonifaci, John Franklin Bonner, PhD, Peter B. Bosserman, Kaydell C. Bowles, James Boyd, Kim R. Boyer, James A. Boyes, James A. Bradbury, Douglas G. Braid, Grigore Braileanu, PhD, William C. Breneman, Henry W. Brenniman Jr., Larry K. Brinkman, MD, Larry Brinkman, Richard K. Brinton, Chirs Brioli, Alfred Carter Broad, PhD, Edwin C. Brockenbrough, MD, Casey Brooks, Gordon W. Bruchner, Hayes R. Bryan, PhD, Ben S. Bryant, PhD, John P. Buchanan, PhD, Fred C. Budinger, Robert Joseph Buker, PhD, Wilbur Lyle Bunch, Sherman K. Burd, Robert S. Burdick, Everett C. Burts, PhD, Robert C. Buto, Jerry R. Cahan, Dennis J. Cairo ACF, John M. Calhoun, Brian K. Callagan, Martin J. Campbell, MD, Milton Hugh Campbell, Carl M. Canfield, Frank Caplan, Frederick Paul Carlson, PhD, William D. Carson, Joseph W. Cartwright, Paul H. Casey, Robert L. Cashion, Stan J. Casswell, Dominic Anthony Cataloo, PhD, Howard E. Ceion, Kyle W. Chapman, Douglas E. Chappelle, William R. Chastain, Thomas David Chikalla, PhD, John G. Chittick, Darrel L. Choate, Mahlon F. Christensen, Robert N. Christenson, Wiley Christie Jr., Robert J. Cihak, MD, Marc Cimolino, PhD, Arlen B. Clark, Kenneth Clark, Gerhardt C. Clementson80120, William A. Clevenger, Gary S. Collins, PhD, Ralph J. Comstock, Michael W. Conaboy, John P. Conway, Mary W. Conway, Peter Cooper, Charles J. Cordalis, Jeffrey A. Corkill, PhD, Neil Cornia, Matthew Corulli, Kirk D. Cowan, Dan Crackel, Elmer M. Cranton, MD, Richard A. Craven, William S. Croft, Harvey D. Curet, Walter E. Currah, Roy E. Dahl, PhD, Robert Arthur Damon, PhD, Jess Donald Daniels, PhD, Edwin M. Danks, William C. Davis, D. M. Day, Gary M. De Winkle, Douglas A. Dean, Samuel J. Dechter, Hans G. Dehmelt, Douglas C. Dennison, Herman A. Dethman, Roy J. Dewey, Ian Andrew Dick, Ronald John Dinus, PhD, Arnold D. Ditmar, Carroll Dobratz, PhD, Richard Dumont Doepker, PhD, Ralph J. Domsife, Bruce R. Donaldson, Roark Doubt, Philip Gordon Dunbar, PhD, Michael J. Dunn, Kenneth Laverne Dunning, PhD, Mark W. Durrell, Frank Arthur Dvorak, PhD, David L. Dye, PhD, Fred Edelman, Maurice R. Egan, PhD, Everett L. Ellis, PhD, Mark S. Erdman, Dale L. Erickson, DVM, Roger Eriekson, Peggy R. Erskine, Bruce V. Ettling, PhD, William Henry Eustis, PhD, Thomas Walter Evans, F. R. Fahland, Robert E. Fankhauser, Marc W. Fariss, PhD, David Farrell, William D. Farrington, George W. Farwell, PhD, Felix Favorite, PhD, W. Dale Felix, PhD, V. Robert Feltin, David L. Feray, Robert B. Ferguson, Kenneth A. Feucht, PhD, Tim Figgie, Roy H. Filby, PhD, M. Firpo, Trevor Fitzgerald, Jane A. Fore, Harold K. Forsen, PhD, Mark B. Fosberg, DVM, Norman Charles Foster, PhD, Michael R. Fox, PhD, Earl Fox, E. L. Freddolino, James Harold Freisheim, PhD, George M. Frese, Roman D. Fresnedo, PhD, Gary S. Friehauf, Robert O. Frink, Paul F. Fuglevand, Charles V. Fulmer, PhD, Alan D. Fure, Charles Gades, Paul Galli Jr., Roger W. Gallington, PhD, Scott Garbarino, Todd Garvin, Michael Gelotte, William W. Gill, PhD, George A. Gillies, PhD, William A. Glass, John Glissmeyer, Patrick Goldsworthy, PhD, Guillerme Gonzalez, PhD, Howard Gorsuch, John C. Graham, Arvid P. Grant, PhD, J. T. Gregor, Lawrence E. Gulberg, PhD, Alankar Gupta, Stephen A. Habener, Nathan Albert Hall, PhD, John Emil Halver, PhD, John K. Hampton, PhD, William Hankins, Barry Hankins, Jeff Hanna, Bill H. Hanson, Mervyn Gilbert Hardinge, PhD, Stanley Harris, MD, Francis L. Harrison, Douglas R. Hartsock, Reese P. Hastings, Gerald D. Hauxwell, PhD, Gordon W. Hayslip Jr., Louis W. Heaton, E. Helrogt, E. Helvoqt, Charles H. Henager, Gary W. Henderson, Wayne A. Hendricksen, John P. Hendrickson, Malcolm Hepworth, PhD, Nicholas A. Hertelendy, Donald E. Hetzel, PhD, Donald E. Hetzel, PhD, Harry V. Hider, William Higham, Eugene R. Hill, Dell E. Hillger, Richard M. Hilliard, John E. Hiner, Jack W. Hitchman, DVM, John B. Hite, Dean Hobson, Lawrence D. Hokanson, PhD, Eric H. Holmes, PhD, David B. Holsington, Stanley P. Horack, Terry Horn, J. R. Hoskins, PhD, Ric Howard, Gerald R. Howe, Warren B. Howe, MD, William P. Hoychuk, Pavel Hrma, PhD, Jeff T. Hubbell, John R. Huberty, PhD, Glen W. Hufschmidt, Rodney William Hunziker, PhD, Charles W. Hurter, David Hylton, Roar L. Irgens, James Ivers, Rick L. Jackson, Glen O. Jacobson, Neal M. Jacques, Jiri Janata, PhD, Cole Janick, James J. Jarvis, Keith Bartlett Jefferts, PhD, K. B. Jefferts, PhD, Creighton Randall Jensen, PhD, Anchor D. Jensen, Daryl T. Johns, Donald Curtis Johnson, PhD, William Everett Johnson, PhD, Ronald M. Johnson, Sheridan Johnston, PhD, Wright H. Jonathan, DVM, Kay H. Jones, PhD, Robert F. Jones, MD, Gary Jordan, John D. Kaser, PhD, Yale H. Katz, Armen Roupen Kazanjian, PhD, Bruce J. Kell, Bruce J. Kelman, PhD, John R. Kennedy, Kenneth H. Kinard, MD, Charles J. Kippenhan, PhD, Roderick R. Kirkwood, James D. Klein, John G. Kleyn, PhD, Max E. Kliewer, Gary L. Kloster, Barry S. Knight, George F. Koehler, Milan Rastislav Kokta, PhD, Lee R. Koller, PhD, Roger W. Kolvoord, PhD, David V. Konsa, Edward F. Krohn,

James W. Kross, James D. Krueger, MD, Jerry Krumlik, MD, Peter M. Kruse, Mathew H. Kulawiec, Robert W. Kunkle, PhD, Lydiane Kyte, Michael M. Landon, Charles J. Lang, John Clifford Lasnetske, Albert Giles Law, PhD, Girvis E. Ledbetter, John Leicester, Jennifer B. Leinart, Robert W. Lemon, Stan Lennard, MD, Gary R. Letsinger, Richard H. Levy, PhD, Milton Lewis, PhD, Donald H. Lindeman, Wesley Earl Lingren, PhD, Winston Woodard Little Jr., PhD, Thomas J. Lockhart, Robert L. Loofbourow, John V. Loscheider, Harry Michael Macksey, PhD, Elwin A. Magill, Michael F. Maikowski, Stephen C. Maloney, Lawrence Frank Maranville, PhD, L. Frank Maranville, PhD, John D. Marioni, Michael Markels Jr., PhD, Franz J. Markowski, Todd H. Massidda, Charles E. Mathieu, Donald W. Matter, C. J. Mayer, Roy T. Mayfield, Sam Mc Ilvanie, DVM, William Bruce McAlister, PhD, Donald R. McAlister, PhD, Donald Lee McCabe, MD, Donald Lee McCahe, MD, Andrew McComas, Richard P. McCullough, Leslie Marvin McDonough, PhD, Les McDonough, PhD, William McElroy, PhD, Dean Earl McFeron, PhD, Dwaine McIntosh, DVM, Ernest J. McKeever, Doug McKeever, Stephen M. McKinney, John C. McMillan, MD, Natalie C. Meckle, David H. Meents, William K. Mellor, James A. Mercer, PhD, Robert Mermelstein, PhD, Norbert E. Methven, Leroy R. Middleton, M. Howard Miles, PhD, James A. Miller, Howard Miller, Claude P. Miller, Ralph Hugh Minor, MD, Paul M. Mockett, PhD, Mahmoud Mohamed Abdel Monem, PhD, Jon F. Monsen, PhD, Fred Moore, PhD, Kou-Ying Y. Moravan, PhD, John Rolph Morrey, PhD, David J. Morris, Arne Mortensen, PhD, Charles S. Mortimer, Lonnie E. Moss, Karl W. Mote, George E. Mueller, PhD, Mark P. Mullen, Peter J. Murray, PhD, Harold E. Musgrove, Robert J. Musgrove, Gerald B. Myers, Cliff R. Naser, Carolyn R. Nelson, MD, Bud D. Nelson, Charles L. Nelson, Errol Nelson, Jay C. Nelson, Arthur Hobart Nethercot, PhD, Edward F. Neuzil, PhD, R. Newhouse, Darrell Francis Newman, Walter F. Nicaise, PhD, Davis Betz Nichols, PhD, Robert Fletcher Nickerson, PhD, Ronald D. Nielson, MD, Kerry M. Noble, Sherman Berdeen Nornes, PhD, Bruce W. Novark, MD, Jack H. Nuszbaum, Hugh Nutley, PhD, M. G. Oliver, Edwin A. Olson, PhD, Bertel O. Olson, Joe R. O'Neal, W. E. Osborne, Prosper Ostrowski, John D. Palmer, PhD, Steven P. Pappajohn, James Lemuel Park, PhD, James Floyd Parr, PhD, Jerry A. Partridge, PhD, Ian J. Patterson, Ronald Stanley Paul, PhD, Craig L. Paulsen, Russell D. Paxson, Edson Ruther Peck, PhD, John L. Perreault, David L. Perry, Donald Peter, Rich Phillips, Kenneth M. Phillips, Professor Polinger, PhD, Karl Hallman Pool, PhD, Gary R. Porter, Gerald J. Posakony, Dale E. Potter, PhD, David T. Powell Jr., R. C. Powell, John D. Power, Ekkehard Preikschat, PhD, James Price, Robert L. Pritchett, Dean C. Ralphs, David C. Ransower, Lowell W. Rasmussen, PhD, Jack G. Raub, William R. Rauch, Glen Reid, Ronald J. Reiland, Susan Rempe, PhD, Jeffrey M. Reynolds, PhD, Nick Rezek, Brian Rhodes, Hollis E. Rice, Gerald L. Richardson, William T. Riley, Gary A. Ritchie, PhD, Jonathan Ritson, PhD, John Rivers, Lamont G. Robbins, Gregory F. Robel, PhD, Joseph L. Roberge, Norman Hailstone Roberts, PhD, Gary Robertson, Daniel B. Robertson, Roger Robinett, MD, Steven P. Roblyer, Gordon W. Rogers, G. J. Rogers, Duane I. Roodzant, Erik J. Rorem, John J. Rosene, Thomas M. Rothacker, Sue Ruff, Susan E. Rutherford, MD, Thomas B. Salzano, William Henry Sandmann, PhD, Wayne Mark Sandstrom, PhD, Larry A. Sargent, Lynn Redmon Sarles, PhD, Lester Rosaire Sauvage, MD, Eric A. Schadler, Ed R. Schild, Lucien A. Schmit Jr., D. J. Schoenberg, Michael J. Scholtens, Roderic Schreiner, Paul M. Schumacher, Kevin N. Schwinkendorf, PhD, Marvin L. Scotvolt, MD, Joel K. Sears, MD, Timothy A. Sestak, James M. Severance, MD, William L. Shackleford, PhD, Richard U. Shafer, Grant William Sharpe, PhD, Robert G. Sheehan, Matthew M. Sherman, Frank Connard Shirley, PhD, Harry C. Simonton, John C. Sindorf, MD, Thomas H. Skrinar, MD, Rolf T. Skrinde, PhD, John R. Sladek, Robert E. Slalen, Frederick Watford Slee, PhD, Sam Corry Smith, PhD, S. T. Smith, Brenton N. Smith, Maurice Smith, Francis Marion Smith, Norman D. Sossone, PhD, Norman D. Sossong, PhD, Darrel H. Spackman, PhD, Walter Spangenberg, Kemet Dean Spence, PhD, Mike Stansbury, George J. Stead, MD, Robert B. Stewart, Arthur L. Storbo, Conrad Suckow, J. Michael Summa, PhD, Earl C. Sutherland, PhD, Jordan L. Sutton, Thomas B. Swearingen, PhD, Raymond T. Swenson, R. Paul Swift, PhD, David M. Sypher, Ronald Lee Terrel, PhD, L. T. Thomasson, Lael J. Thompson, Joseph J. Thompson, Robert Kim Thornton, PhD, A. E. Thornton, Richard L. Threet, PhD, Patricia Tigges, Darrol Holt Timmons, PhD, Frederic E. Titus, Michael L. Tjoelker, Victor E. Tjulander, Harvey C. Trengove, James Ray Tretter, PhD, D. H. Treusdell, Willard Tribble, Gerald P. Trygstad, William L. Ullom, Juris Vagners, PhD, Richard Van Blaricom, PhD, Gregory Van Doren, Donald Vandervelde, Patrick R. Vasicek, John R. Vasko Jr., MD, Thomas E. Vaught, Gerard Verkaik, Joe Vierra, M. Douglas Vliet, Doug Vliet, Kenneth R. Wahlhutor Sr., Mark R. Waldron, C. B. Ward, Vernon D. Warmbo, Bruce P. Warren, Maurice Wassmann, Bill Webb, Thomas L. Webber, Alfred Peter Wehmer, Alfred P. Wehner, MD, Ben Weigandt, Selfton R. Wellings, PhD, Howard E. Wellsfry, John A. Westland, PhD, John R. Wheatley, Kerry M. Whitaker, W. E. Whitney Jr., Gary W. Wilcox, PhD, Larry Wilhelmsen, Richard S. Wilkinson, MD, William H. Will, Max W. Williams, PhD, Bradley R. Williams, Jerry Williams, C. Ray Windmueller, Sam R. Windsor, Philip C. Wingrove, Holden W. Withington, Casey W. Witt, Charles Edward Woelke, PhD, Jerry Wolfkill, R. P. Wollenberg, Frank William Woodfield, David Dilley Wooldridge, PhD, Mark D. Workman, Jonathan V. Wright, MD, Robert C. Wright, Milo Wright, Peter Wyzinski, Edwin York, William B. youmans, PhD, Tim A. Younker, Ralph Yount, PhD, Ivan Zamora, MD, Waldo S. Zaugg, PhD, Tianchi Zhao, Gerald A. Zieg, Bernard M. Ziemianek, Douglas Jerome Zimmer, Edward E. Zinser, Steven C. Zylkowski

West Virginia

M. H. Akram, PhD, Charles Alt, Stephen Edward Always, PhD, Guvenc Argon, Jerome C. Arnett Jr., Jay K. Badenhoop, PhD, Carlos T. Bailey, Ed Bailey, Barton Scofield Baker, PhD, Ever Barbero, PhD, Kevin P. Batt, Thomas P. Baumgarth, Franklin L. Binder, PhD, Samuel Oscar Bird II, PhD, Samuel G. Bonasso, Stephon Thomas Bond, Anthony John Bowdler, PhD, S. D. Brady III, Donald M. Brafford, W. E. Broshears, Robert William Bryant, Warren Burch, Michael J. Burrell, Darrell K. Carr, Richard H. Clapp, Alan R. Collins, PhD, Sabin W. Colton VI, PhD, Roddy Conrad, PhD, Ronald E. Cordell, MD, Richard L. Coty, Rex R. Craft, Edward Hibbert Crum, PhD, Ricky E. Curry, H. Douglas Dahl, PhD, Warren Edgell Dean, PhD, Ronnie L. Delph, Edmond Joseph Derderian, PhD, Albert John Driesch, Norwood F. Dulin, Herbert Louis Eiselstein, Richard W. Eller, MD, Nick Endrizzi, DVM, Alvin L. Engelke, Philip L. Evans, Gary D. Facemyer, Joseph A. Farinelli, David F. Finch, Gunter Norbert Franz, PhD, Arthur L. Fricke, PhD, Frank L. Gaddy, Joyce A. Gentry, Mark W. Getscher, Lawrence J. Gilbert, William Harry Gillespie, Donald Wood Gillmore, PhD, Eugene Gladfelter, PhD, John Gottschling, Joseph W. Grahame, Teddy Hodge Grindstaff, PhD, James Hansen, PhD, R. Thomas Hansen, PhD, William W. Hartman, Timothy M. Hawkes, H. G. Henderson, PhD, Roger L. Henderson, Gregory E. Hinshaw, Jay W. Honse, Charles G. Howard, J. David Hurt, Wilber C. Jones, PhD, George S. Jones, Mitchell M. Kalos, Everett Lee Keener, Lynette Kell, Richard S. Kerr, MD, A. Wahab Khair, PhD, Gregory A. Kozera, Scott Kuhn, Andrew G. Kulchar, William C. Kuryla, PhD, Richard A. Lambey, Thomas Lee Lantz, Howland Aikens Larsen, PhD, Dickey L. Laughlin, Layle Lawrence, PhD, Gerald Roger Leather, PhD, Paul Lee, PhD, D. M. Lee, H. William Leech, PhD, Arnold David Levine, PhD, Antonio S. Licata, MD, Andrew J. Lino, Ashby B. Lynch Jr., Louise Tull Mashburn, PhD, Thompson Arthur Mashburn, PhD, Marvin Richard McClung, PhD*, Douglas E. McKinney, MD, Scott D. Melville, Andrew J. Mesaros, Edwin Daryl Michael, PhD, Michael H. Mills, Robert E. Mitch, Raymond F. Mize, Professor Morrison, PhD, Kenneth L. Murphy, PhD, Larry T. Murray, Hannah Murrell, Bruce V. Mutter, PhD, Charles H. Myslinsky, Jeffrey O. Nelson, Roy Sterling Nutter, PhD, Richard Oldack, Michele O'Neil, Brian M. Osborn, Joseph R. Overbay Jr., Gary A. Patterson, Arthur Stephen Pavlovic, PhD, Henry E. Payne III, PhD, Salvatore Pecoraro, MD, G. Albert Popson, PhD, John M. Praskwiecz, Charles D. Preston, Jacky Prucz, PhD, Robert L. Raines, Herman Henry Rieki, PhD, Robert L. Ritchey, James Ritscher, PhD, Lee A. Robinson, Satya P. Rochlani, MD, Robert M. Rohaly Jr., Norman H. Roush, Daniel Rubinstein, PhD, John W. Rudman, Tim A. Salvati, Robert Lee Sandridge, PhD, Dalip K. Sarin, Todd V. Sauble, DVM, John L. Schroder, Gregory L. Schumacher, Edward L. Scram, Robert G. Shirey, MD, H. Drexel Short, Paul E. Smalley, Percy Leighton Smith, Daniel D. Smith, Gregory C. Smith, Nicholas M. Spands, Don S. Starcher, William K. Stees, Walter M. Stewart, Dan L. Stickel, Calvin L. Strader, Thomas B. Styer, Francis Suarez, Elizabeth Davis Swiger, PhD, Thomas E. Tabor, Jasmin A. Tamboli, Richard L. Terry, Lester A. Tinkham, Michael W. Tobrey, Kathleen Umstead, Thomas E. Urquhart, Jess H. Wadhams, Charles R. Waine, Kim A. Walbe, Haven N. Wall Jr., Glen C. Warden, Royal J. Watts, Ronald Kevin Whipkey, Harry V. Wiant Jr., PhD, W. Randy Williams, PhD, Steve Williams, Walter E. Williamson, MD, Dayne A. Willis, Henry N. Wood, PhD, Gregory Wooten, Charles S. Workman, Paul Zinner

Wisconsin

Albert H. Adams, MD, James William Adams, Rafique Ahmed, PhD, John F. Alleman, Jason D. Allen, Roger O. Anderson, Mary J. Anzia, PhD, Eric C. Araneta, T. Philip Arnhol, PhD, Philip John Arnholt, PhD, Jacob F. Asti, Carlton L. Austin, Edward T. Auth, Bruce D. Ayres, PhD, Edward A. Baetke, A. D. Baggerley, DVM, A. D. Baggerly, DVM, Robert R. Baker R. Baker, PhD, Robert W. Baker, PhD, Jeffrey M. Baker, DVM, Gilbert B. Bakke, James R. Bakken, Cathy Bandyk, PhD, Robert F. Barnes, PhD, Jack Bartholmai, MD, Rose Ann Bast, PhD, Joseph H. Battocletti, PhD, Roy M. Bednarski, Ralph J. Beiermeister, Robert W. Bellin, J. C. Belling, Thomas E. Bellissimo, John P. Benecke, Ralph E. Benz, Laurence C. Berg, Joseph S. Bernstein, MD, Floyd Hilbert Beyerlein, PhD, Katherine Bichler, PhD, John A. Bieberitz, Harvey A. Biesel, John Merlyn Bilhorn, Russell A. Billings, William P. Birkemeier, PhD, Gerald E. Bisgard, PhD, Martin T. Bishop, Clarence L. Blahnik, MD, Brooks K. Blanchard, Philip J. Blank, PhD, Gilbert K. Bleck, Fred M. Blum, Gregory E. Bolin, Jack M. Bostrack, PhD, R. K. Boutwell, PhD, Francis J. Bradford, DVM, Daniel C. Bradish, Michael L. Bradley, William M. Breene, PhD, Charles F. Bremigan, Gunnars J. Briedis, Robert P. Bringer, PhD, Dean A. Brink, Timothy C. Bronn, Charles E. Brown, DVM, Carl W. Bruch, PhD, Eugene S. Brusky, MD, Reid Allen Bryson, PhD, Ellen F. Buck, Robert O. Buss, MD, Bruce J. Calkins, Hugh W. Carver, Russell J. Cascio, Michael R. Cesarz, David T. Champion, Peter D. Chapman, Lyle E. Cherney, Julie L. Chichlowski, Paul I. Chichlowski, Edward F. Choulnard, PhD, Richard W. Christensen, PhD, Joyce R. Christensen, Dennis Christopherson, Patrick E. Ciriacks, James L. Clapp, PhD, William B. Clayton, W. Wallace Cleland, PhD, Mark A. Clemons, John E. Clemons, MD, Peter G. Cleveland, PhD, Donald T. Clickner, Edward D. Coen, Robert E. Coffey, Mark V. Connelly, MD, Mark Eric Cook, PhD, Kenneth Cook, Tanya M. C. Cook, Fred A. Copes, PhD, Frederick Albert Copes, PhD, Dennis M. Corrigan, Grant Cottam, Robert P. Cox, James E. Craft, David R. Cress, Chris

Cruz, Ronald E. Cunzenheim, Frederick D. Curkeet, M. L. Curtis, John W. Curtis, Shannon Czysz, Frank J. Dadam, Kenneth R. Dahlstrom, Ruth M. Dalton, MD, Heather M. Daniels, Eugene F. Dannecker, Paul R. Danyluk, Anthony C. De Vuono, PhD, Roger J. Debaker, Mark E. DeCheck, Randall L. Degier, Raymond A. Delponte, Gerald L. Demers, Edward P. DePreter, Jerry J. Dewulf, Charlesworth Lee Dickerson, PhD, John M. Dierberger, Daniel M. Dillon, Michael P. Doble, William V. Dohr, Joseph Domblesky, PhD, Edwin Dommisse, John J. Donnell, Lloyd H. Dreger, PhD, Jack C. Dudley, Thomas D. Durand, Ernest John Duwell, PhD, Dwight Buchanan Easty, PhD, Dean W. Einspahr, PhD, David A. Ellis, Mark Engebretson, Ron J. Engel, Leon R. Engler, Richard C. Entwistle, William A. Erby, PhD, Karl L. Erickson, PhD, Robert H. Erskine, Thomas Alan Fadner Sr., PhD, Gary A. Fahl, Donald Fancher, PhD, Dennis C. Fater, PhD, Jeanene L. Feder, Robert J. Felbinger, William M. Fesenmaier, Brandon M. Fetterly, PhD, Peter A. Fitzgerald, Stephen Wayne Flax, PhD, Eugene J. Fohr, Brandon A. Foss, Raymond A. Fournelle, PhD, James Foy, PhD, Lowell Frank, Margaret Shirley Fraser, PhD, Robert Watt Fulton, PhD, Lloyd C. Furer, PhD, Richard A. Gaggioli, PhD, Richard A. Gagglioli, PhD, Tom A. Gardner, Cheryl L. Gardner, Jerry Gargulak, PhD, Ronald L. Garrison, James C. Gaskell, Robert C. Gassert, Dave Gaylord, Jolene K. Geary, R. Geerey, PhD, Richard L. Geesey, PhD, Charles E. Geisel, Barbara Geldner, MD, Robert R. Gerger, Kenneth H. Gersege, Frederic Arthur Giere, PhD, Rodney L. Goldhahn, Russell S. Gonnering, MD, Tom O. Goodney, G. Robert Goss, PhD, Zech Gotham, Larry F. Gotham, Charles Thomas Govin Jr., Kin A. Gowey, Alice L. Grace, John Graf, Ray H. Griesbach, Lynn M. Griffin, Edward Griggs, Karl P. Grill, MD, Paul J. Grosskreuz, Leonard Charles Grotz, PhD, James A. Gundry, Paul B. Gutting, Earl Hacking, James E. Hagley, Albert C. Hajny, Donal W. Halloran, Gary C. Hamm, Perry T. Handziak, Robert B. Hanna, Jerome Scott Harms, PhD, Lynn Harper, David Harpster, PhD, Heather Harrington, Leon Harris, James P. Harsh, John Michael Hassler, Gregory Dexter Hedden, PhD, Donald J. Helfrecht, Roger W. Helm, Michael R. Henderson, Phillip S. Henkel, MD, Philip S. Henkel, David Henzig, Mike S. Hess, William R. Hiatt, MD, Robert C. Hikade, Duane F. Hinz, Lawrence H. Hodges, Gary L. Hoerth, Gregory J. Hofmeister, Samuel E. Hoke, MD, David Henry Hollenberg, PhD, Donald E. Honaker, Earl W. Horntvedt, Ealr W. Horntvedt, David R. Horsefield, Steve Horton, Mark Hostetter, Lowell A. Howard, Calvin Huber, PhD, John L. Hussey, MD, George Keating Hutchinson, PhD, Reinhold J. Hutz, PhD, Erik J. Hyland, Steven J. Hynek, Donald V. Hyzer, Charles Albert Ihrke, PhD, D. Ingalls, Donald D. Ingalls, Raymond W. Ingold, Jerome M. Iverson, Thomas J. Jacobi, George Thomas Jacobi, Lois Jean Jacobs, PhD, Robert L. Jeanmaire, Al J. Jenquin, Roy J. Jensen, Mary A. Johanning, PhD, Eric W. Johnson, S. Johnston, PhD, David Jowett, PhD, Joe Kahm, Dean M. Kaja, Robert J. Kalscheur, Gabor Karadi, PhD, Vernon D. Karman, Mack A. Karnes, MD, E. A. Kasel, Charles B. Kasper, PhD, Michael J. Kasten, Richard Keller, Andrew Augustine Kenny, Chris E. Kensel, Patrick J. Keyser, Todd D. Kile, Bruce F. Kimball, Peter O. Kirchhoff, Arthur S. Klein, Richard G. Knight, PhD, Henry Koch Jr., Eldo Clyde Koenig, PhD, Robert L. Kogan, PhD, Lewis E. Kohn, Van E. Komurka, Kirk A. Konkel, Jeffrey A. Konop, Mary K. Kopmeier, Joseph Edward Kovacic, Joseph D. Kovacich, Jeffrey G. Kramer, Melvin W. Kraschnewski, Kenneth W. Kriesel, Larry A. Kroger, PhD, Gary Krogstad, Gary S. Krol, Oliver M. Kruse, Paul Kubicek, Peter Mouat Kuhn, PhD, Bernard P. Lakus, C. M. Lang, PhD, Ivan M. Lang, PhD, Conrad Marvin Lang, PhD, Richard C. Lange, Albert U. Langenegger, Elma Lanterman, PhD, Philip Rodney Larson, PhD, David L. Larson, MD, Clifton E. Lawson, Bruce W. Leberecht, Davin R. Lee, Kenneth B. Lehner, John P. Leifer, John Lein, Paul B. Lemens, Ron Lenaker, Thomas J. Leonard, MD, Richard J. Leonard, Bohumir Lepeska, PhD, Larry A. Lesch, Robert J. Lex, John Lien, Mark D. Lillegard, Keith R. Lindsley, Emil Patrick Lira, PhD, Gregory R. Lochen, Donald M. Lochner, PhD, A. Locke, Leo J. Lofland, MD, Robert S. Logan, Julian H. Lombard, PhD, Steven Paul Lorton, PhD, Edward Thomas Losin, PhD, Scott T. Luckiesh, Rita M. Luedke, Steven H. Lunde, Glenn R. Lussky, Michael J. MacDonald, Paul Machmeier, PhD, Frederick Mackie, Greg J. Magyera, Gregory H. Mahairas, MD, Ingo G. Mahn, PhD, Guenther H. Mahn, Frank Mahuta Jr., PhD, James D. Maki, Randall L. Maller, Steven J. Mamerow, MD, Swarnambal Mani, Richard F. Manthe, Marian Manyo, Anthony Maresca, Jeffery P. Martell, David K. Mathews, Johan A. Mathison, MD, Timothy V. Mattson, Stephen A. Maus, Deanna J. May, MD, Jerome S. Mayersak, MD, Percy M> Mayersak, MD, Roger D. Mayhew, Don A. McAllister, Greg W. McCormack, George W. Mead, Edward C. Mealy, PhD, Lynn A. Mellenthin, Michael D. Mentzel, Steven L. Merry, MD, Lynn D. Meyer, Steven L. Meyer, DVM, Cynthia Meyer, Victor L. Michels, PhD, J. R. Miller, Roger G. Miller, Lee Miller, Bruce Mills, Mark J. Mobley, Kennth G. Molly, Randy Montgomery, John Duain Moore, PhD, Marion Clyde Morris, PhD, David L. Morris, MD, Michael C. Mortl, Carl Mueller, Lee J. Murray, Mark L. Nagurka, PhD, Gangadharan V. M. Nair, PhD, Phil Naunann, Daniel J. Naze, Percy L. Neel, PhD, Amy L. Nehls, Kenneth R. Neil, Elwyn F. Nelson, David M. Nelson, Sherry L. Nesswenum, MD, Arthur Nethery, PhD, Joachim Peter Neumann, PhD, Manfred E. Neumann, Paul Nevins, Carroll Raymond Norden, PhD, Dexter B. Northrop, PhD, Gerald Novotny, Lynn E. Nowak, Richard O'Connor, T. A. O'Connor SC, MD, David P. Ohrmundt, Andre Olivas, Randy Olson, PhD, Marshall F. Onellion, PhD, Edward Scott Oplinger, PhD, Apolonio M. Ortiguera, Joseph C. Ostrander, David Ozsvath, PhD, Dale R. Paczkowski, Edward H. Pahl, John Charles Palmquist, PhD, William C. Pappathopoulos, Andrew M. Paretti, Hyunjaz Park, PhD, Robert O. Parmley, J. Parrish, Marshall E. Parry, Scott A. Patulski, Kermit E. Paulson, David M. Paulus ., PhD, Paul E. Pawlisch, PhD, Thomas E. Pelt, Roy L. Peterson, Lynn A. Peterson, Terrance A. Peterson,

John Phillips, Keith M. Picker, Adam J. Pientka, William G. Piper, Jeff Plass, Huberto R. Platz, Robert J. Plucker, William A. Polley, Harvey Walter Posvic, PhD, Rial S. Potter, Richard H. Preu, Timothy B. Pryor, Mary J. Purvis, Arnold J. Quakkelaar, Daryl Raabe, Dennis S. Rackers, Richard E. Radak, MD, Hershel Raff, PhD, Tom Rank, PhD, Mike Ratcliff, Hukum Singh Rathor, PhD, Michael P. Rau, Gerald W. Rausch, PhD, Paul Reesman, David A. Reid, DVM, William Stanley Rhode, PhD, Karl W. Richter, Michael Riley, William Robisch, Michael J. Robrecht, William H. Roche, Randall J. Roeder, Martin A. Rognlien, Ellen A. Roles, Carl B. Rowe, Paul Allen Roys, PhD, Charles A. Rucks, DVM, John A. Rybicki, Stephen L. Saeger, Eric M. Sanden, PhD, Robert A. Sanders, Louis W. Sandow, Donald C. Sassor, Professor Sawyer, Umesh K. Saxena, PhD, Fred W. Schaejbe, William J. Schapfel, DVM, Leo J. Scherer, Michael R. Schindhelm, Jeffrey D. Schleif, Donald A. Schlernitzauer, Charles A. Schmitt, David L. Schmutzler, Carl P. Schoen, PhD, Randall R. Schoenwetter, John L. Schrag, PhD, Hans Schroeder, Arthur R. Schuh, F. H. C. Schultz, PhD, Frederick H. C. Schultz, PhD, Lynn V. Schultz, DVM, Steve A. Schultz, Clemens J. Schultz, Michael Schulz, Glen R. Schwalbach, James Schweider, Carol D. Seaborn, PhD, Ralph Walter Seelke, PhD, Steven Seer, Daniel F. Senf, Liza Servais, Paul E. Seul, Keith R. Seward, Richard A. Shellmer, Alan D. Shroeder, Larry R. Shultis, Barteld Richard Siebring, PhD, Terry V. Sieker, DVM, Jeff P. Simkowski, John C. Simms, PhD, Doug Sitko, Thomas G. Sladek, Lisa A. Soderberg, Dave Allen Soerens, PhD, James Alfred Sorenson, PhD, Alan R. Sorenson, William E. Southern, PhD, Dale A. Spires, Gary A. Splitter, PhD, Julien C. Sprott, PhD, Joseph Staley, Glenn Stanwick, Gary M. Stanwood, Richard Steiner, Shawn D. Steinhoff, William John Stekiel, PhD, Richard A. Steliga, MD, Michael Fred Stevens, PhD, Patrick J. Stiennon, James R. Stieve, E. N. Stillings, John Stoffel, Lawrence W. Strelow, DVM, D. H. Strobel, John R. Stubbles, PhD, Warren Robert Stumpe, Harry W. Stumpf, Glenn Richard Svoboda, PhD, Stacy L. Swantz, DVM, Neal L. Sykora, Steve Stanley Szabo, PhD, Ronald J. Szaider, Al P. Szews, PhD, Lars J.S. Taavola, Kuni Takayama, PhD, Louis J. Tarantino, Paul J. Taylor, PhD, Kenneth J. Terbeek, PhD, Roger Thiel, Julian C. Thomson, PhD, Theodore William Tibbitts, PhD, Jon Tiger, Arthur T. Tiller, Brian P. Tonner, PhD, John W. Troglia, Vladimir M. Uhri, MD, George Uriniuk, Mary P. Utzerath, David A. Vancalster, S. Verrall, PhD, Thomas E. Vik, James F. Voborsky, Randall Vodnik, Bill Vogel, Joseph P. Vosters, Allan G. Waelchli, Richard F. Wagner, James E. Waldenberger, John L. Walkowicz, Gordon David Waller, PhD, Robert R. Wallis, Roger C. Wargin, MD, Frank E. Weber, PhD, Mary Weber, Randall James Weege, Mark J. Wegner, Eugene Allen Weipert, PhD, Allen C. Wendorf, John W. Westfall, Richard L. Westmore, Donald Edward Whyte, PhD, Robert C. Wiczynski, Matthew Wielgosz, Everette C. Wilson, Richard D. Winter, Ronald Wolf, Carl E. Wulff, Clyde W. Yellick, MD, Sharon H. Young, Nathaniel K. Zelazo, Brad W. Zenko, Carl Zietlow, Bob Ziller, Robert Ziller, Myron E. Zoborowski, Edward John Zuperku, PhD

Wyoming

Charles K. Adams, John W. Ake, William W. Allen, Percy G. Anderson Jr., Lowell Ray Anderson, Marion L. Andrews, Lance L. Arnold, Joseph P. Bacho, Donald T. Bailey, Robert C. Balsam Jr., Charles J. Barto Jr., Curtis M. Belden, John C. Bellamy, PhD, Joseph C. Bennett, Donald W. Bennett, Floyd A. Bishop, David Bishop, Lloyd P. Blackburn, Richard G. Boyd, Dennis Brabec, Lee Brecher, PhD, Francis M. Brislawn, Paul Brutsman, J. B. Bummer, Roger T. Bush, John D. Campanella, Scott P. Carlisle, Carl D. Carmichael, Keith T. Carron, PhD, Paul C. Casperson, MD, Marci M. Chase, Robert H. Chase, Robert G. Church, E. James Comer, Daniel P. Coolidge, Robert F. Cross, PhD, John J. Culhane, Ray Culver, William Hirst Curry, PhD, Jan Curtis, Steve L. Dacus, Mark A. Davidson, Dick Davis, PhD, Robert Joseph Dellenback, PhD, Hugh D. Depaolo, Martin L. Dobson, Scott N. Durgin, John C. Elkin, Fred M. Emerich, DVM, Paul M. Fahlsing, Susan J. Fahlsing, Kenneth K. Farmer, S. R. Faust Jr., Ray A. Field, PhD, Stuart C. Fischbeck, J. Goolsby, PhD, James E. Greer, Richard C. Greig, Durward R. Griffith, Falinda F. Hall, Daniel J. Haman, Homer R. Hamilton, PhD, C. J. Hanan, W. Dan Hansel, Paul Michael Harnsberger, Robert A. Harrower, William D. Hausel, W. Dan Hausel, Mike C. Hawks, Henry William Haynes Jr., PhD, Scott J. Hecht, Bill K. Heinbaugh, John H. Hibsman Jr., Paul R. Hildenbrand, Mark Hladik, Michael S. Holland, Kenneth O. Huff, G. William Hurley, Irven Allan Jacobson, Eldred D. Johnson, Archie C. Johnson, Terrell K. Johnson, Jack B. Joyce, Victor R. Judd, William T. Kane, PhD, J. Kauchich, William Keil, Kevin Kilty, PhD, Leroy Kingery, Robert W. Kirkwood, Duane D. Klamm, Paul Koch, PhD, Robert A. Koenig, Bernard J. Kolp, PhD, Joe E. Kub Jr., Harry C. La Bonde Jr., Richard Laidlaw, PhD, Jerry T. Laman, Donald Roy Lamb, PhD, John R. Landreth, Robert B. Lane, William Anthony Laycock, PhD, Lewis A. Leake, Howard R. Leeper, Dayton A. Lewis Jr., Don J. Likwartz, Michael C. Lock, Thomas L. Lyle, Richard E. Mabie, Don Madden, Rick D. Magstadt, L. C. Marchant, Leland Condo Marchant, Robinson McCune, John F. McKay, PhD, Robert "E. ""Bob""" McKee, Edmund Gerald Meyer, PhD, John W. Miller, Reid J. Miller, Kenneth R. Miller, Terry S. Miller, Tom D. Moore, Howard B. Moreland, Harold Mosher, Roger B. Mourich, Lance T. Moxey, DVM, Evart E. Mulholland, Ralph W. Myers, Lance Neiberger, Judith E. Nelson, Daniel Anthony Netzel, PhD, Keith A. Neustel, Mark A. Newman, Despina I. Nikolova, Lee Nugent, Edmond L. Nugent, Robt D. Odell, R. D. Odell, Robert D. O'Dell, Paul O. Padgett, Thomas Parker, Bruce H. Perryman, Paul T. Peterson, Donald Polson, Larry C. Raymond, Wallace K. Reaves, Paul Albert Rechard, Kenneth F. Reighard, Steven Y. Rennell, Timothy C. Richmond, Robert W. Riedel, Terry P. Roark, PhD, W.

F. Robertson, Ted Roes lll, A. R. Rogers, Arthur R. Rogers, Robert G. Rohwer, Larry J. Roop, Richard D. Rosencrans, David H. Scriven, Leslie E. Shader, PhD, Riley Skeen, Terry K. Skinner, Ralph Smalley Jr., Ray C. Smith, DVM, Thomas B. Smith, Stan Smith, James P. Spurrier, Robert J. Starkey Jr., PhD, Richard Steenberg, Larry R. Stewart, Donald Leo Stinson, PhD, Tony C. Stone, Eldon D. Strid, K. Sundell, PhD, Archer D. Swank, Tim L. Thamm, S. Thompson, Keith A. Trimels, John F. Trotter, Ron M. Tucker, Kenneth F. Tyler, Ronald D. Wagner, Jon H. Warner, B. Watne, PhD, Larry Weatherford, PhD, Michael Wendorf, Frank D. Werner, PhD, Robert J. Whisonant, Douglas C. White, Donna L. Wichers, James Williams, Larry Dean Hayden Wing, PhD, Robert D. Winland, Bruce M. Winn, Charles K. Wolz, Bret H. Wolz, Marcelyn E. Wood